The Trident Series Volume 3
The Trident and the Resurrection

Vic Broquard

Published by: Broquard eBooks
http://Broquard-eBooks.com
103 Timber Ln, East Peoria, IL 61611
Contact: author@Broquard-eBooks.com

Art work by Crooked Willows Studio

For Morgan and L. Ron Hubbard

Table of Contents

Chapter 1 The Winter

It was the dead of winter in the lands of Verbenloc. Yet few of the many peoples here were hibernating in their homes as one might expect. On the contrary, happiness borne of great hope, along with much industry, filled the hearts and bodies of everyone here in the central grasslands section. Just a few months ago, in the late summer, Saint Jon Brown, the Redeemer, as he was proclaimed by Father Ukko, the supreme God of the land, had helped his fiancé, Alison d'Ambrose, find and rescue two of her brothers and a sister, whom she had not seen for over the last twenty years.

When she was three years old, Alison lived in Castle d'Ambrose before it became ruins. Her father, thirty-five year old Basil, was a powerful priest of the Church of Ukko and had built this castle for his ever growing family. Anna, his wife who was thirty-three, bore them eight children, of which Alison was the youngest at three. Lennard, who was called Lenny for he disliked the more formal sounding name, was five. Next came the twins, May and Mat who were seven and who constantly teased their little sister, Alison. Ruben was a young lad of eight who insisted on following his father about, whenever the cleric was actually here at the castle that is. Ruben also loved gold and gems and could always be counted upon to help his dad tally their funds. Christina was ten with lovely, long brown hair. She always had time to play and help take care of Alison. Heinrich, who was eleven, loved dogs and was normally outside in the nearby fields playing with them. Finally, the eldest child, Stephen, who was twelve and nearly a man and trying to act the part, attempted to perform his father's chores when their dad was off on one his many adventures. It was a large, happy family until that fateful day.

Basil went on a mission to rescue the Royal Scepter of Ukko given to d'Argo the Holy, for the Holy Retribution Wars in the Abyss some two hundred years ago. During that campaign, d'Argo was slain by the demons. One particular Demon Lord, Metrarch, found Royal Scepter on the battlefield and kept it. However, when this evil demon picked up the scepter, it burned his hands severely, giving him wounds which never healed. Another property of this holy relic was that no one could tell a lie in its presence. Discovering this aspect, Metrarch had the scepter embedded in a block of glass and placed centrally in his throne room, deep in the 66th layer of the Abyss. It was here that Basil and his friends came that fateful day. They stole the scepter from Metrarch's throne room and brought it back to Verbenloc.

It was nighttime when Basil returned home with the Holy Scepter to Castle d'Ambrose. That evening, Alison got to see and touch it with her hands. However, shortly after she went to bed, the castle was attacked by unknown assailants. (To this day, no one knows who the assailants were that fateful night, but whoever they were, they were very powerful indeed.) The attackers turned much of the stone of the castle into mud and brought the entire castle crashing down, killing most of the defenders outright. As the ceiling began to fall, Alison's nanny rescued her, taking her to the safety of the underground dungeons. The next day, all of her other relatives were nowhere to be seen, presumed dead or lost, as were all of the castle servants and guards.

Now earlier, Basil commissioned the famous Bard Wendell Theodore Zandras to create eight identical magical picture books, one for each of his children. Each contained around fifty pages, each page containing a painting of some scene. Some were paintings of castles, some towers, some lakes, some villages, and so on. So great were the paintings of Wendell, that both Dispater, the Arch-devil, and Jous, the Uncaring, god of magic, took an active interest in his work. In fact, both deities combined forces to cast a special spell over all Wendell's works. If he painted a small trident somewhere in the painting, then, if one concentrated upon the painting, he would find himself magically transported to that location to be able to observe it first-hand, or so it was assumed. Each of the fifty or so paintings in the eight identical picture books contained a trident.

How Jon Brown, a music student at the University of Illinois, acquired one of these picture books some twenty years later is by the strangest chance. His grandfather once met a man who looked badly wounded and who was carrying only this book with him. He mumbled something about being chased by Hell Hounds and gave him the book for safekeeping. The young man never did return to get back the book, and, in time, his grandfather discovered its magical properties and began visiting these places. Of course, he made friends with people in these lands and aided them. When his grandpa passed away, Jon inherited the book.

Of course, Jon also discovered its properties. About a year ago, he began visiting these lands and met his three companions, Alison d'Ambrose, Mandy Blackthorn, and Darless Thornapple. All three were very beautiful women and great adventurers themselves.

The long, brown haired Alison d'Ambrose is now a powerful mage. She began her adventuring career with a band of men led by Sir Thomas le Bonnaire, a Holy Paladin of Ukko. She was the party's wizard. Now having at last become a power in her own right, she set forth on her life's goals: to find what had happened to all of her family members that fateful evening and to rebuild Castle d'Ambrose once again. Magic-use is the central focus of her life. Alison is totally lawful in nature; she always goes by the book, so to speak. Jon felt that she could never even contemplate an evil action. Alison is now twenty-three and stands five feet-eight with blue eyes, dark-brown hair that reaches her slim waist. She has a mellow alto voice that enthralled Jon. Beneath her white nondescript robe, she always wears very expensive clothes, always in excellent taste. She prefers brown pants with an ermine belt and white silk blouse. Jon has fallen totally in love with her and now they plan to be married soon.

Mandy Blackthorn is a Ranger of Reylona, the goddess of the forest, woodlands, meadows, animals, flowers, and fertility. Of the three, Mandy is the most stunning. She is five feet nine with mischievous, dark brown eyes. She has long, light brown hair with bangs trimmed at her eyebrows. Often, she wears a leather headband with eagle feathers accentuating her high cheeks and pointed chin. Jon swears that she has the most perfect lips imaginable. Her high leather boots with feathers matches both her hair and tunic, as does the pair of leather arm bands that doubles as bow string guard. In a word, Jon finds her stunning. Yet, she is a superb swordsman, highly trained and skilled — an outdoors, nature loving, nature-protecting woman. She also has some limited mental powers, including the ability to read Jon's thoughts, and she even has mastery of simpler magical spells and many druidic spells. Mandy is both powerful and dynamic — a rugged individual with her own ideals which she holds as the absolute truth. What Mandy wants to do, she does. Chaotic and unpredictable? Yes, but her actions are always good in nature, never evil. She owns Blackthorn Castle, which she inherited from her father, located in the Gnarled Oak Woods, so named from all the twisted oak trees that grow there.

Darless is a very sexy alu-demon. Her father was the late Hugo Thornapple, a human mage. He was married to the Lady Ursla, the Great Druid of Hollybine Woods, who was unable to have children. So desperate was he for a child that he mated with Myleen Dogoroth, a succubus demon of the Abyss, who was both chaotic and evil in nature. When she was born, her father raised her by himself, and she had a wonderful childhood. However, when her jealous mother, the demon, wantonly killed her father, Darless, in turn, killed her mother. She is half-demon and half-human, a form cursed by all. To disguise her true semi-demon body, she normally creates the illusion of a beautiful woman. Only Jon has been able to penetrate her magic alteration. To Darless, her true self, until recently, is degrading, for she wants more than anything else to be just a normal woman and raise children. But finding a man she can love and be loved by has been almost an insurmountable barrier.

Darless is twenty-four years old now, but appears to look somewhat older because of the unnatural aging caused by her forced use of magical wish spells. She has long curly black hair and coal-black eyes that pierces one to their soul. Until recently, she always wore the thinnest gauzes of clothing leaving nearly nothing for the imagination. Though most people see her illusion of an extremely beautiful woman, Jon can also see the tiny horns that protrude from her head and the tiny bat-like wings on her back. In her true form, she is still remarkably beautiful; her illusion that she creates for others to see is merely minus the horns and wings and a lift here and there.

Until Jon came into her life, everyone merely exploited her demon nature for their own purposes. Jon had given her the greatest gift possible — her freedom from such exploitations. Any demon can be summoned into servitude if the true name of that demon is known. Jon and his friends rescued her from the clutches of an evil mage and Morrigan, the goddess of war. By discovering her true last name, Thornapple, which even Darless had not known before, Jon has given her the best possible present in the universe. From that point in time onward, no one can now summon her against her will, for the summoner must know her true name, which few now know.

Darless is a powerful magic user, in-tune with the Abyss and has mental powers similar to Jon and Mandy. She can read his thoughts with great ease. And she does so. Darless, like Jon, is fundamentally neutral between the forces of law and chaos, looking out for oneself is crucial — in her case, certainly no one else will do so. But unlike Jon, she is also neutral between the forces of good and evil, raised this way by her father and later on by her friendship with the Lady Ursla Thornapple, the Great Druid of Hollybine Woods. Darless uses actions to aid her survival, no matter if evil or not, while Jon always tries to do only things that were fundamentally good in nature.

This past summer, these four performed great deeds which including preventing a war. Ultimately, they had to face the wrath of Morrigan herself because she was the instigator of that conflict. When Morrigan threw her Spear of Death in retaliation, intending to slay Jon, Alison realized that she loved this man and, in a heroic effort, jumped between them, taking the spear meant for Jon. Father Ukko then intervened, primarily because Morrigan had broken the rules of god/goddess conduct in the slaying of Alison. He brought her back to life and proclaimed that Jon was to be hereafter called Saint Jon Brown, in honor of all his efforts.

While Alison is a powerful magic user, Mandy, a strong ranger, Darless, a nearly indestructible magic user, Jon is only a musician. However, Jon discovered the powers of his mind or rather his spiritual nature. It began as a gradual thing, a bit of desperate healing of wounds here and there. Over time, and out of dire necessity, the effects he creates grow more and more powerful. In this world, Mandy and Darless refer to these effects as the psi power, something you are born with or not and can never change, at least they, nor anyone they knew, ever could. But untrained, Jon is a wildcard, breaking all known barriers for such feats. Yet, all he wants to do is make music.

Things took a turn for the worst late last summer when a flock of Chasme bugs, vile evil creatures from the Abyss, attacked and nearly killed Alison, who was in her underground dungeon home, all that remains from that terrible night of destruction twenty years ago. Though Jon was in his home in Urbana at the time of the attack, he heard her call for help across the vastness of space and went to her. Shocked beyond belief at her seeming bloody death, he immediately sought the help of Darless and the Great Druid, Lady Ursla. Mandy, also attuned to her friends, arrived and between them, they managed to restore life to Alison. Darless then realized that she cared more for these three friends than anything else in the world.

Sir Thomas, a powerful Holy Paladin of Ukko, also came to Alison's aid, mostly because he was tracking the path of these demon bugs. Darless met this tall, handsome man and had a lengthy discussion with him one night. She and Sir Thomas were at least civil to each other, for the holy paladin was pledged to slay demons. In his mind Darless fit that category. Yes, he was at that time highly prejudiced toward demons. Unfortunately, the paladin often arrived at wrong conclusions, which is one reason Alison had been one of the most valuable members of his party. She was almost never wrong in her observations. Though Sir Thomas had long been vying for Alison's hand and heart, she was not interested in him.

When Alison recovered from her near-death encounter with the Chasme, she and her friends arrived at a very different conclusion about the path that the Chasme were following than the conclusion reached hastily by Sir Thomas. They set out on horseback to catch up with these evil creatures and destroy them. The chase led them hundreds of miles from Verbenloc to the ruins of Leeds which, long ago, had been a tower or castle of some sort. Along their way to Leeds, necessity forced Jon to discover an interesting aspect of the human mind and spirit.

The attack on Alison occurred at eleven in the morning. Each day, as that hour approached, Alison basically went insane, reliving the attack, oblivious to her surroundings. Jon discovered that she had mental pictures that recorded every detail of the attack. In desperation, he had her go over and over these pictures, each time telling him what had happened. He discovered that after enough recountings, the effects of these mental images lessened, but they did not go wholly away. He soon found out that Alison experienced a similar trauma when her castle was being destroyed when she was three. After running through these earlier memories, the entire insanity evaporated when she spotted a basic consideration that she had made at that time. More importantly, the nightmares never came back after that.

Later on, Jon had another opportunity to experiment with this phenomenon. On their journey to Leeds, a fledgling young paladin just beginning his career, Lonnie Smith, accompanied them. During a fight with some bandits, his shield arm was broken. Jon applied these same techniques to him and discovered the trauma of the injury was erasable and, when gone, resulted in a much more rapid healing process.

When they got to Leeds, Jon located by accident an imprisoned Air Maiden of Ukko, Fruella. She had been magically entombed far underground by a foul demon from the Abyss some two hundred years earlier. With his friends' aid, she was released. To show her gratitude at her rescue, she gave them all a gift. By assisting them as spiritual beings to move out of their bodies, all four realized that they were beings and not merely bodies or minds. The experience fundamentally changed all four of them. It is hard to say who was the more affected.

For Jon, his supposed psi powers were a misnomer. He discovered that he was just fundamentally exercising his native powers as a free being, the depths of which had not been fully explored or determined. For Alison, discovery that she was a being and who also had personal power led to a two-fold change. First, she slowly became able to telepathically communicate to the other three and no longer felt "brain-dead" or rather left out. Second, she observed that, for her, the boundaries of magical spells and spiritual powers blurred. Over time, the boundaries began slowly dissolving. Father Ukko encouraged her further exploration in these matters when they met the second time, but that is getting ahead of the events.

For Mandy, well, she just basked in the after-glow of serenity; she truly enjoyed just being. Her outlook on life mellowed somewhat, perhaps allowing for love to enter her life for the first time. For Darless, the dual combination of learning how Jon was able to really help people with his newly discovered assist methods and that she was a spiritual being and not an "alu-demon" totally altered her outlook on life. She cast aside the gauze, see-through dress, favoring now traditional, but elegant clothing. She stopped "mate hunting" altogether, and she dedicated her life to pursuing the teaching of Jon's methods to others; that is, she decided to build a college in which the techniques could be taught to others who cared to learn.

Next, the foursome found those evil people who were controlling the Chasme demons and a huge battle ensued. Just as they were gaining the edge in the combat, huge vulture like demons began to arrive into the fray, gated here to Leeds from the Abyss. Eventually, with all but Darless at death's door, the same gate to the Abyss opened, sucking Jon, Alison, and Mandy down into the Abyss. Darless refused to abandon her friends to this evil fate and swan-dived into the gate to join them and help them. Of note, Sir Thomas arrived too late for the battle, but just in time to see Darless swan-dive into the gate to save her friends. Seeing that action occur had a life changing impact on Sir Thomas.

Now ever since the party began their journey in search of those who were controlling the Chasme demons, Jon had picked up and was carrying what appeared to be an ordinary walking stick previously owned by Basil himself. Her father was fond of walking sticks and Alison had now recovered nearly two dozen of them. This one was, in actual fact, the Holy Scepter of Ukko in a disguised form, for this scepter had a life force of its own and was seeking to survive as well. Although neither Jon nor any others in the party knew that it was the Holy Scepter, they missed many clues that it was assisting them in their quest. While they were in the process of being gated to the Abyss and near death's door, the scepter took control and performed one of its many functions, that of fully healing the wounded. Thus, the party arrived in the Abyss alive and well, quite the contrary of what their summoner had expected.

Indeed their summoner was none other than Metrarch himself, the very Demon Lord who previously held on to the holy relic Jon was carrying. The Demon Lord wanted to obtain the services of these four. In his convoluted thinking, sending the Chasme to in effect "fetch them hither" in a grievous state of health would make them more readily agree to assist him. It failed utterly. More surprising still, Dispater, Lord of Hell, arrived and appeared to be personally assisting Metrarch! And it was the Arch-devil's order that was finally obeyed by all: "Take them back to their world, let them sleep and eat, and then discuss your request." So within five minutes of arriving at the most abysmal location that any had ever seen, save Darless who grew up in the Abyss, the party found themselves in Ravenwash Castle, located in an unknown land, but in their world at least.

Metrarch desired their services. He presented Alison with her long lost brother, Lenny and his picture book. Unfortunately, Lenny had been imprisoned all these years somewhere in the Abyss and his body was leprous and diseased, just barely alive. His mind was totally gone. In short, he was insane. Later Alison took Lenny to Lady Ursla of Hollybine Woods, who agreed to see if she could heal his body. The Great Druid was able to heal Lenny's body but she was unable to do anything for his insanity.

In return, the foursome agreed to be Metrarch's bodyguards for twenty-four hours during the Council of Seven which met in Freetown, about seventy miles south of Ravenwash, to elect the next Supreme Lord of the Demester (twenty years). Every twenty years, a new ruler was elected by the Seven Ruling Houses of Ashina of the 66th Level of Abyss. Once the meeting in Freetown was done, then the seven lords and their follower's armies held a vicious war game, the winner and new ruler was he who held the central well in Freetown for a twenty-four hour period.

Why did Metrarch desire their protection? He had, via Dispater, learned of a plot by persons unknown, but likely another Demon Lord, to have him assassinated during his short visit in Freetown before the Games began. Now just why Metrarch should choose these four people of all the others in the universe to protect him was not clear to anyone other than Metrarch, though Darless suspects Dispater may have been behind that decision. The assassination was a very real threat; south of these lands lived a highly prominent band of powerful assassins, the Assassi. El Hadid, a most wicked and clever and powerful assassin led the group. They were widely feared, even by the Demon Lords.

Now it happened that Jon, with all of the commotion surrounding Metrarch, realized just why, for two hundred years, Metrarch's hands had never healed.

And he secretly whispered to him that if he, Metrarch, were game, he, Jon, would try to cure him. So it was that Metrarch arrived in Freetown a night earlier than expected to give Jon the opportunity to try. Jon used the same method that he used with Alison and Lonnie. Indeed, Metrarch had a great many incidents to view and confront, and the process took many hours. In the end, it worked; Metrarch finally realized that because he merely stole the Holy Scepter from the battlefield and then subsequently claimed he had won it in mortal combat with d'Argo, that lie had kept the burns from ever healing.

Now when the actual assassination attempt occurred the next day during the council meeting proper, Metrarch faked his own death. While the four managed to defeat and kill the assassin, to everyone else, it appeared that it was all in vain; Metrarch lay dead. His assistant, Zugblat, the Unholy, then assumed Metrarch's vacated throne for himself, something he had coveted and sought for a long time. Unbeknownst to anyone, Metrarch had decided this was his chance for a new life, a way out of being a vile Demon Lord of the Abyss. He felt an obligation to make amends for some of the killing and injuries he had recently committed. Thus, he instructed Darless to perform a magical chant upon his death. When she did it according to his orders, to her utter amazement, a portion of Metrarch's treasury appeared and deposited itself in her room. He had given her a vast treasury from which she could dole out some small measure of recompense for the recent victims of the Chasme attacks. Noteworthy also is that the assassin carried a paper stating the terms for this assassination, papers signed by Lord Jarred, a rival Demon Lord.

Where Metrarch went and what he is now doing, none can say. Perhaps, Dispater was in on the plan. And then again, maybe the plan only came into being after

Jon helped him heal his eternal burns. Only Metrarch knows for sure.

However, Freetown was now in danger, as it was every twenty years. Once the official battle had been won, remnants of the seven armies looted, pillaged, and raped those in Freetown. The cycle had been repeated endlessly for two hundred years. However, within the last twenty years, a new force for law and order had appeared in this town, the Twins. Dressed from head to foot solely in black, they would bring justice to townsfolk in the dead of night. So legendary were their exploits, that many now called the town Twins Town, in their honor. Jon and the three women just had to meet these town protectors to see how they could help defend the town from the invading seven armies.

During that first meeting, Jon discovered that the Twins were, in fact, May and Mat d'Ambrose, Alison's slightly older brother and sister! A joyful reunion followed. The twins' story was a simple one. That horrid night when their castle was destroyed, they were trapped in their bedroom as the ceiling began collapsing. The only way out was to use their picture book and move to another location. Mat left his book open so they could step into the picture, while May brought hers with them. They arrived here in Freetown. Because they were only five years old and had no money or acquaintances in the town, life was hard for them. They spent many years living in the city sewers and made a living by thievery. Yes, Freetown was really a thieves den at this time in its history. May's picture book was sold for money for their survival. When they became older, May took up the illusionist discipline, that is, a magic user who specializes in the creation of illusions. Mat took up the martial arts becoming a monk.

Together, dressed in black, they began to bring law and order to this lawless frontier town. After nearly fifteen years, they had made great strides towards making

Freetown a decent place to live. Yet now it was about to be destroyed once again. All four pitched in to help May and Mat defend the town. They went about the task methodically and intelligently. After careful research, they discovered that the town was founded by priests of Ukko. More importantly, a great protective device was built to shield the town in the early days from the attacking demon armies. When the device was activated, no evil could pass through its shield around the town.

However, in modern times, the city had grown far beyond the area protected by the device. Some eighty percent of the town was unprotected. Further, over two hundred years ago, the Demon Lords had raided the Church of Ukko and killed all of the priests. As a result, the very location and means of the machine's operation were lost; the protection of Ukko fell into abandonment. Now, only a single Church of Ukko remains, badly in need of repairs. Needless to say, Jon discovered the location of the device and got it back in service to protect one fifth of the town.

To protect the remainder, Alison and Darless, together with six other powerful mages of Freetown, used a huge number of magical spells to defeat the legions of the attacking armies. May and Mat as well as Jon and Mandy assisted with those that eluded the wizards. Slowly, they were aided by more and more of the local townsfolk. Until at last, it appeared that they would win the day. The ringleader of the attacking demon armies was the very same Lord Jarred, who was determined to claim the throne of Supreme Lord. His outrage at his defeat was monumental. It didn't help his anger either when Jon, aided by Mandy, hit him in the face with the Holy Scepter of Ukko. Actually, it was all the doing of the scepter, for it controlled Jon and Mandy. Lord Jarred now had a facial burn, which, like Metrarch's, would never heal!

Refusing to admit defeat, Lord Jarred opened a gate to the Abyss and brought forth an army of the huge vulture demons to crush all opponents. At this point, Father Ukko intervened, sending a host of his Air Maidens to stop this Demon Lord. Lord Jarred was forced to abandon the town in a very hasty retreat. The Air Maidens took all six of the party plus the Holy Paladin, Sir Henry, who had been the sole defender of the last Church of Ukko in Freetown all these many years, up to Ukko's realm. Jon gave Ukko back his Holy Scepter and Ukko bestowed upon him the title Saint Jon, the Redeemer. Ukko gave Jon a magical walking stick more suited to Jon's needs, one that did a fair amount of healing and such.

Ukko awarded the twins several fold. From now on, they were to be known as the Holy Children of Ukko, though Jon still does not know its significance. However, the twins can now perform healing by the laying on of their hands, much like Sir Thomas, the paladin. He also told them that they would finally find the love of another set of twins. Neither of the twins was married at this point in time.

Ukko rewarded Darless by making her a Holy Paladin of Ukko. Normally, paladinhood is reserved for stalwart fighters, not alu-demons nor mages. Later on, Darless suspected there were other reasons for so giving her this unheard of status. Finally, to Alison, Father Ukko declared her to be the Holy Mage of Ukko, gave her some magic theory books containing many very high level spells, told her the name of the spell that had been used to destroy her castle, and told her that she would discover the means to have her castle rebuilt on her trip home.

Ah, the trip home. It would have taken them no time at all had it not been for the actions of others in Freetown. When news of the impending demon attack came, well over six hundred folks decided it was time to leave Freetown permanently — time to seek their fortunes elsewhere. They formed a caravan of some two hundred wagons, carts, and buggies and left, heading west, the day before the attack was to take place. It was suicide. Not only were they close to two of the Demon Lord's armies, but just beyond lay an immense land controlled by followers of Morrigan, goddess of war.

Unbeknownst to any here, Mandy's goddess, Reylona, called upon the services of another of her followers, one William Conners, a simple baker in Mandy's village, Blackthorn. She had seen him occasionally in her village (she was often off on adventures), but she never suspected that he was also a servant of Reylona. Nor did she ever suspect that he had any special powers. He was born with a power or gift of making angry people put down their weapons and go home quietly. Indeed, it had never before occurred to Mandy why she never, ever had to settle any squabbles in Blackthorn; there never seemed to be any arguments, compliments of William.

So into Freetown came William whose task, set by Reylona, was to protect this very caravan from the evil that would have befallen it. The chance meeting of William opened Mandy's eyes to this mild-mannered man. She fell in love with him; all these years, she had never met a man she could love. Yet here he was in her own backyard and she had never seen it! Yes, William saved the caravan from destruction, while the others were fending off Lord Jarred's onslaught of Freetown.

Once the battle for Freetown was done, the four, plus May and Mat, galloped to the rescue of the embattled caravan, arriving just in time. However, now they had to get this caravan across the Lost Steppes, over the Desolation Mountains, and safely to better lands. They had no maps and no idea where they were going. It took a combined effort of all six plus William to accomplish this enormous task.

The key reason for the magnitude of the task, though this was only discovered by the party near the very end of the journey, lay in Morrigan herself. She had ordered her followers, the cavalry of Vyndoc to attack and slay Saint Jon and his party. First, a small ambush was tried. When that failed, an entire regiment of cavalry attacked them. When that failed, they let loose an entire division of heavy cavalry, fully six hundred strong. Yet, even that attempt failed with the loss of every man, save twenty-six. By now the caravan was very close to the tall mountain range, Desolation. One last attempt had to be made.

But since a major mountain dwarf settlement lay just north of the caravan's route, one division was sent to cut off any possibility of their seeking aid from the dwarves, while a second division moved up from the south. The idea was to hit the caravan simultaneously from both sides at once and put an end to them once and for all. It would have succeeded except for a chance encounter with a stone giant named Rolf.

These Vyndocians were making enemies right and left. Many stone giant clans lived in the Desolation Range in large caves or cavern complexes. Many clans had been attacked and prisoners taken. In fact, Rolf's wife and son had recently been captured while he was away. He was now on his way to try to organize a party of giants to go to their rescue. Instead, he ran into Mandy and Jon and the others. They quickly became friends and the party agreed to rescue his family. All traces of the caravan quietly disappeared from the land. Secretly and at night, the caravan wagons were moved inside Rolf's caverns to rest out of harm's way.

Yes, Jon and the others did rescue his wife and son and another ten stone giants as well, earning the eternal gratitude of Rolf. Now it just so happened that for the Vyndocians to conquer the defenses of the giants, they cast a powerful spell that converted portions of their rock barrier walls into mud slides that slid down the steep mountain side. Alison noted that the grey granite stones of Rolf's wall had been so transmuted. However, Rolf had also used some stone blocks he called "blackys." These, the spell had not harmed. Further, there were traces of a silver metal of some kind embedded in this black basalt rock. Inside his cavern, Rolf used this special stone to make his furniture, giving it a highly polished surface. When so polished, the effect was dazzling and magnificent indeed. Alison now knew that her castle was going to be built from this type of stone, whatever it actually was. Rolf was only too glad to mine it in return for gold. He loved gold, but had little of it.

While the party was recovering at Rolf's cavern home, several dwarves came with an urgent message for Rolf. The Vyndocian cavalry, having lost track of the caravan, was actually attacking the mountain dwarves! A young dwarf, Draken, son of the Lord of the City, Dathor, came asking for Rolf's immediate aid. Dathor, it turns out was the son of Nain Anzulbizar whom the party had met on their way into Freetown more than a month ago. Although they did not know it at the time, Nain is a very powerful priest and fighter of great renown among the dwarves and perhaps one of the most highly skilled weapons and armor maker in all the lands.

Alison and Jon felt that the dwarves were likely being assaulted in part because of them — that they were in some way responsible. Once again, with the caravan under William's protection slowly ambling its way up the Deadman's Pass high into the mountains and far from these cavalry divisions, the six headed to the dwarven city to help as they could. Their help was most definitely needed. The dwarven city was actually an underground city. They found themselves protecting the entrance way where outsiders came to trade with them. Two divisions of Vyndocian cavalry were planning to attack the dwarves.

The first charge of the Vyndocian cavalry was completely stopped by Mandy alone. The weather was threatening a storm; so she used her new prayer to Reylona to summon a storm. She rather overdid it, as it was just her first attempt at controlling weather. Torrential rains with heavy hail and much lightning completely ended the cavalry's first assault on the dwarves. However, Dispater, the Arch-devil, showed up in time to watch the battle, or so he claimed. The high priest of the Vyndocians arrived and completely dispelled Mandy's storm in just a few minutes time. However, the damage was done; the division was in shambles and routed.

The next day, they attacked once more. This time, re-enforced by the second cavalry division, they left the horses behind and closed to battle on foot. Their entire front line hid behind a makeshift horsehide shield wall. However, boulders thrown by the stone giants and volleys of arrows from the dwarves and Mandy cut down their numbers before the battle joined. The high priest accompanied by four powerful wizards simultaneously attacked Alison, Darless, May and Jon. Although outnumbered and "out-spelled," they still managed victory by working together as a team. During this battle, Jon learned a new skill. May used an illusion of fear to keep all enemies from getting any closer than twenty feet from her. Jon watched how she did it, and then he added to it and expanded it. He got so into the spell he was weaving that it nearly took control of him. In the end, Jon had routed the entire army as well as the remaining wizards. Only the high priest remained on the battlefield and he offered his surrender, for Jon must be a god; he had no other explanation for what had just occurred.

Jon realized something vitally important in the few words he had had with Dispater the previous day. Jon asked Dathor to list all of the grievances he had with the Vyndocians. For each of these, he asked how he knew that, who told him, who had said it. Very often, the trader, Red Jordral's name came up. Next, he asked the surrendering high priest of Vyndoc these same questions. Lo and behold, the name of the trader, Red Jordral, kept coming up on his list too. Darless cleverly pointed out that Red Jordral was an anagram for Lord Jarred! And so the real source of who had been inciting the two sides to war became exposed to the light of day. It is said that truth shall set you free; it did so. Within minutes, the two warring factions made peace and the dwarves even cared for many of the wounded cavalrymen within their underground halls!

Yet, the action was not done just yet, for Morrigan arrived to personally slay Saint Jon. This time, Jon got everyone else out of the way; he did not want someone else dying while trying to save him. He went forth to talk directly to this evil goddess. Immediately, Jon observed that she had him confused with some other person, one Vainamoinen, of whom Jon did not know. She did try to kill him with her Spears of Death, but Jon just appeared in the space before them, after they had passed through that space. The spears clanked harmlessly on the rock behind him, infuriating her further. Again, since she obviously had Jon confused with someone else, he took control and had her move through her mental pictures and got her to erase one of them, at which point she realized that Jon was not this other fellow. Jon found out later that Vainamoinen was a hero of note and was the person who had actually damaged her face, which looked like blackened skin stretched tightly over bone, in a word, hideous. To save grace and face, both declared that a mistake had been made and that Jon was free to go. Thus, Jon and Darless had further confirmation that their newly discovered mental techniques would work even on gods and goddesses!

Nain Anzulbizar arrived with a host of dwarves and priests to help the healing, but he arrived after the battle, while Jon was sleeping and recovering. Now the dwarves had to reward them all for their services. Nain asked Jon what he wanted, fully prepared to pay a king's ransom for the services he had done. Both his son and grandson would otherwise have perished before he arrived, if it had not been for Jon and his friends. Jon asked if he could return one day and learn the art of dwarven music! For Mandy, Nain agreed to craft a special bastard sword of speed more suited to Mandy's strength and agility. For Alison, Nain agreed to have the dwarves build her castle and town, with the assistance of Rolf and the stone giants, who were to provide the rough-hewn "blacky" stone from which it was to be built. Further, he agreed to her terms of using a triple work shift, of course, for triple pay. It was a high honor to have the dwarves build your castle. She would still have to pay for their services.

Their recovery time with the dwarves was cut short because the first winter storm of the season stuck. The high country through which the caravan was traveling was hit with three feet of snow. These were desert dwellers; none were equipped to withstand the cold or to travel through this depth of snow! Hastily, the six headed back to catch up with the caravan which was indeed in dire trouble. Most were slowly freezing to death.

The first night, utilizing all of their resources, the mages managed to create four magical mansions and get all of the folks inside and into warmth. However, this was only a temporary solution. The dwarves had told them that they might find aid at the Lost Ruins and so the next day, they made for the ruins. The sole inhabitants were the Newcastle twins, Jake and Jennifer. The twins had discovered the ruins in this narrow side valley and made it their home for the last ten or so years. They made their living by making dried trail rations and heavy winter clothing from various furs which they traded for supplies each fall. As luck would have it, the buyers had not yet arrived to purchase this year's products. Thus, the Newcastle's were able to provide a huge amount of food and much needed winter gear to all of the caravan folks.

The ruins were actually an underground city carved from the bedrock by a people long gone. Mandy later discovered, by visualizing the psychic residue left by the prior inhabitants, that these strange people were killed by a red dragon. The warm cavern rooms easily housed the entire caravan, horses and all. It was most welcome indeed.

During their respite here with the Newcastles, four things occurred. First, Mandy discovered their secret. They both had lycanthropy; that is, both were were-bears during the times of nearly a full moon. This is why they were living here isolated in the high country nearly a mile high. Of course, they were cured, but not in the expected manner. Jon was the first to realize that since they had lived with this shape-changing for so long, changing into bears had become a part of their beingness. So instead of curing the disease, Alison, May and Darless did a triple remove curse spell on them driving the evil life force from their bodies. Mandy, who could shape-change at will since birth, helped them learn how to do it on their own and under their own control.

Second, the twins, May and Mat, fell hopelessly in love with Jake and Jennifer, who also fell in love with the twins. It was a match made in heaven, so to speak. When it was time for the caravan to leave, the Newcastles went with them.

Third, while examining the trail ahead of them to see if there was any let up in the huge snow cover, Jon was nearly assassinated himself. He would have died had Mandy not cast her neutralize poison spell. Darless slew the assassin with a disintegrate beam, blowing a one inch hole through his head. The assassin carried a paper with the terms of his contract, again signed by Lord Jarred.

Fourth, a friend of the Newcastles, Rufus, a gnome illusionist and inventor of gadgets, hastily returned from his trip to sell his wares in Tannersville, just beyond the mountains. He returned because he found the normally empty plains full of hobgoblins, thousands of them. They were lying in wait at the end of Deadman's Pass and had killed the entire group of traders who were heading for the Newcastles.

It took only a little thought to figure out who was behind the hobgoblins. Lord Jarred's stronghold in these lands was adjacent to the cold northern lands in which these foul creatures ordinarily lived. It had to be Lord Jarred once again. The situation was hopeless. The caravan could not go any further along the pass because of the depth of the snow fall; any day more snow would surely come. If they stayed here, sooner or later they would be assaulted by thousands of hobgoblins, far more than they could handle. Help this time came from an unlikely source, Rufus the gnome.

He lived in another of these ancient ruins about ten miles from the Newcastles. In the back of his cavern, there was a natural set of caverns that went on for miles. Indeed, the ancient peoples, who built these cities, had enlarged it and extended it. His cavern ran all the way down to the plains far below, exiting some twenty miles south of the location where Deadman's Pass met the plains. Thus, Rufus led the caravan to safety down to the plains.

Now all that remained was to lead the caravan across the plains, bypassing the hobgoblins, which lay in wait for them. They very nearly succeeded, except for the single fact that Lord Jarred himself, disguised as a hobgoblin, was present. So great was his rage against Jon, that he intended to personally see to his destruction. Just as they were about to completely bypass the horde, Lord Jarred transported over a thousand of these fell creatures directly into their path. They had no choice but to fight it out.

The battle went well for a time, but eventually the overwhelming numbers of the enemy crushed the defenders. Jon was kept busy using his walking stick to heal those that neared death. Only when all was about lost, did Darless finally recognize Lord Jarred. She realized her dear friends were likely doomed to death. So she flew high across the battlefield to directly attack the demon herself. Normally, an alu-demon is no match for a Demon Lord, but Lord Jarred had already cast all of his damage causing spells and was weary from his exertions. She somehow found the inner strength to tackle him. They resorted to physically bashing and thrashing each other. In the process she sustained two broken legs and several crushed ribs, but so intent was she on destroying Jarred, she did not notice the pain until afterwards. At long last she just grabbed on to his arms and attempted to do what Jon did, to be elsewhere, three feet behind where she was. And so she was, arms and all. The effect was that the Jarred's arms were pulled from their sockets. But he still refused to quit and kicked at her relentlessly. She then ripped his head from his body, at which point his body in its entirety ceased to exist on this plane. He was forced back into the Abyss and could not return to this plane for fifty years! She then collapsed in grave pain.

As she was fighting her final battle with Lord Jarred, Sir Thomas, the Holy Paladin of Ukko, was charging to their rescue. Back at Leeds, the Air Maiden Fruella had told him to raise an army and head here to rescue Alison and friends. He had done so and came charging into battle with five hundred cavalrymen. He bore witness to Darless's fight and defeat of the Demon Lord. All of his life, his goal had been to do just what Darless had done, to defeat a Demon Lord. He was the first to reach her side, turning away from his duties to rescue the others, leaving that to the rest of his men. He personally healed her as best he could and carried her to Father Johnas, his high priest, who finished the healing process.

Later that day, Sir Thomas found out that Darless was indeed now a Holy Paladin of Ukko, just as he was. That was the final turning point for him, for he was in love with Darless, an alu-demon. He finally learned that a person is a being, not a body. He saw it as a personal message from Father Ukko to himself, a message saying, look she is just as worthy as you! He begged her to let him court her, and she was only too willing, as she had long before fallen for him. Darless had at long last found a person who would love her as her, accept her as she was.

Thus, when the caravan finally arrived back home in Verbenloc in late November, the five couples had decided on a joint wedding on the first of May. Alison and Jon, Mandy and William, May and Jake, Mat and Jennifer, and Darless and Sir Thomas. When they arrived, the dwarves were already here; work on the town and castle construction was well underway.

Nain arrived shortly after they did. First, he presented Mandy with her new highly enchanted bastard sword of speed, a prize fit for a king. Second, to speed the construction project, Nain cast a gate spell connecting Rolf's secret stone quarry, where the "blacky" stones were mined, with the construction site here, cutting at least six months off of the total construction time. Third, he wanted to take possession of the million gold pieces Alison had promised for their work.

When Alison next visited the Great Druid, her prayers were answered, for Lady Ursla had successfully healed Lenny's body of the Abyss sickness, though he still was quite weak from lack of exercise for twenty years. He was still insane. She explained to Alison that he behaved obligingly as long as you were nice to him.

So it was that Darless began to use the techniques, which she and Jon had pioneered, to slowly erase the twenty years of trauma that Lenny's captivity in the Abyss had wrought. Daily, she had Lenny confront and eventually erase these nasty incidents in his mind. Jon monitored every session, gradually building up his own confront of the horrors of Abyss life. Yes, progress was slow; at first he could only confront and face times that he had had fun as a child playing in these very dungeon passages. Yet after a time, Lenny recognized his brother and sisters, calling them by name, bringing tears of joy to their eyes.

Thus, throughout the early winter, Darless and Jon had to be with Lenny for many hours each day to continue with his recovery. In the remaining hours, Darless also had to help the dwarven engineers plan the basic layout of her new college building.

Alison's plans called for a walled village with her castle complex integrated within the village. After much discussion, she decided to name them, in her father's native tongue, Chateau d'Ambrose et Ville Bon Liberte, Castle d'Ambrose and the Good Free Village. Of course, that was a mouthful and so in time the complex became known as Ville d'Ambrose.

The village was laid out as a square, one mile on a side, with the Chateau proper occupying the northwestern corner. The Great Wall surrounded the village, fully ten feet above the ground and four feet thick, with its roots resting securely on bedrock far underground. The walls were made of the highly polished "blacky" stone of Rolf, the stone giant. That is, it was hard black basalt stone with myriad swirls of silver mithril intertwined. With the stone giant's careful polishing, the combination of shiny black with blinding silver was incredible to behold.

Precisely in the middle of each side, four gate houses stood, each with heavy iron doors that could be shut to withstand a siege if need be. Thus, entrance to the Ville could be carefully monitored, providing greater safety to the inhabitants of the town. The Chateau proper was even more imposing in the northwest corner. Here the outer walls rose thirty feet and were fifteen feet thick at the base, again anchored securely to bedrock. Plus, Alison added a little extra. Precisely in the middle of the width of all the walls, she cast a thin vertical wall of force also anchored to bedrock. Each of these force walls she made permanent. Thus, should the outer five feet be breeched by some means, an impregnable barrier still protected the inner five foot wide section. Needless to say, what with three shifts of dwarves working night and day, she was kept constantly busy preparing and casting her spells.

The huge outer walls of the castle proper were five hundred feet long, forming another square. (Alison loved order.) Like dragon's teeth, barbicans were spaced uniformly along the top. But at each of the four corners, forty foot square guard towers continued rising upwards another ten feet. Each had many windows for the defenders to launch arrows and the like down upon their attackers. Boasting four floors above ground and one below ground, the identical four guard towers' underground floors provided storage for defensive supplies, while the middle floors provided bedrooms for the castle guards. Additionally, the nearly flat stone roofs could be used as well; the view from these heights was superb in all directions.

These tall chateau walls had only three exits. In the middle of the south and east walls, which opened into the middle of the village, two small gate houses stood each with heavy iron doors. However, in the middle of the north wall stood a large gate house — this was the main outside entrance to the Chateau. This gatehouse was double the dimensions of the other two. Precisely in the middle of the five hundred foot square stood the

Chateau's main tower, rising sixty feet above the ground. This was their home and was two hundred feet on a side — a commanding building, done in the highly polished "blacky" stone. The very top also had barbicans but with an iron fence between each section to prevent accidental falls.

To really appreciate the magnificence — the awe inspiring splendor — of this castle-village, one only needs to view it from a mile away when the sun is shining on it. Sunrise or sunset is particularly breathtaking — highly polished black stone with blinding swirls of silver.

The walls of the main house also were planted on bedrock and were very wide at its base, slendering as it rose, floor by floor. Each of the six stories had nearly ten-foot ceilings with polished oak floors. Two more floors were below ground and still a third secret floor had been carved inside the bedrock itself, for here was her ultimate retreat or treasury rooms, depending upon circumstances. Alison left nothing to chance; it also had a secret underground exit. Alison had made no provision for dungeons.

While the Chateau is the dominate feature that first catches the eye, two smaller structures are most noteworthy. Located in the southeast corner near the corner guard tower is Darless' school — the College of Free Beings, where she intends to teach others how to handle the traumas of the mind, using Jon's methods. Likewise built from polished "blacky" stone, this two hundred by forty foot, three-story building is architecturally quite different. It sports a gabled roof with red tile shingles. The entrance way has a twenty foot tall archway supported with giant columns in the Roman style. Periodically along the outer front wall, ten great statues protrude, each a likeness of famous ancient Holy Paladins of Ukko. (Sir Thomas provided the descriptions.) The interior is just as spectacular, done entirely of mahogany, polished to a high sheen. Darless spared no expense to make her college worthy of such high endeavors. Finally, a small five foot tall wall of grey granite stone entirely surrounds the grounds of the college, which provides needed privacy for those in need of therapy.

The second structure is the Church of Ukko, located just south of the eastern gatehouse and some three hundred feet north of the college. Here, Alison followed Jon's suggestion, building a small replica of the imposing Church of Ukko in Zaire that they both loved. Indeed, the grounds of the church boast numerous iris beds, small ponds and three fountains. It is noted here that Alison, Jon and the legendary dwarven engineer, Thraxton, made several trips to Zaire to carefully study the church and make scaled-down drawings. Jon so hoped that the acoustics of the holy chapel would be to his liking; he had found none better than the one that they were modeling.

On their first visit to the Church of Ukko, Zaire, Jon took along Zender, the dwarf musician, who was forced into being the cook for the working dwarven party. They had become fast friends and Jon wanted him to hear firsthand the best acoustics ever. Jon's party received a royal welcome from His Holiness, Prince Reginald Noxwood, Archdeacon of Zaire. Of course, he insisted on hearing a full account of their latest adventure, pressing them for exact details with their second encounter with Father Ukko. In fact, the Archdeacon had scribes take down the entire encounter as well as the freeing of the Air Maiden, Fruella. He implored them to stay the night so that a proper celebration in their honor could be arraigned. While neither Jon nor Alison wanted such, the pleadings of the Archdeacon could not be ignored. Besides, Jon wanted to play in his chapel once again. Thus, Alison and Zender got a chance to hear Jon's mellow flute playing during a special service in their honor. Among the several pieces he played was his rendition of a "Fantasy on a Theme by Thomas Tallis" and "Kannon in D." Both of these two brought tears of joy and holiness to even Zender's eyes. Never had human music so affected a dwarf! Both Zender and Alison now fully understood why Jon had been so insistent on the design of Alison's new church — if only it sounded nearly this good.

Alison's Church of Ukko would be a one-fifth reduction in overall scale, complete with flying buttresses, though Thraxton insisted that these were not needed on a building this size. Jon insisted because they looked great! His view won the day.

Now all of the other houses within the Ville are made of either orange or grey granite, some of it reworked from the rubble of the original castle. Slowly, the dwarves removed the rubble and made use of what stone was still salvageable. It was cheaper than hauling in new stone and faster too. The villager's homes did not need to provide defense, just the functionality of a one or two story home or business. The northeast quadrant held three hundred stone houses laid out in city blocks some five hundred feet square with ten foot wide roads between. She attempted to leave some yard space for each home.

The remaining three quadrants boast numerous shops with the granaries and stables located in the southwest quadrant. Precisely in the center of the Ville, is an octagonal central well and park. Alison was thinking of the children and wanted them to have a huge space in which to run and play, as well as a park for evening, romantic strolls. Still with all this construction, fully a quarter of the space was left for future growth. Jon marveled at just how fast this large construction project, from his point of view, was being completed. Dwarves are industrious, and with three shifts, night and day, progress was rapid. Alison insisted that a fair number of homes be finished as rapidly as possible so that her caravan tradespeople could move in and start creating the village operations.

Other than the church, with one exception, Jon had no real input on the designs. One thing he noticed was absent: running water with proper toilet facilities. From history lectures he'd heard that in mediaeval times, disease was often spread by unhygienic living conditions, and he was determined to avoid that here. How best to achieve running water and a sewer system in this environment was a challenge. In the end and after much input from Thraxton, a large barrel was built some fifty feet above ground. Pipes were run from its base to all of the houses. Although the pressure was not great, it sufficed, if everyone did not use it at the same time. A simple toilet facility complimented the running water, flushing refuse by dumping a bucket of water to force it all down and into the sewer drains and on out of the village.

The real trick was pumping the water from the well into the water tower. This was solved by a mule power. The mules walked on a treadmill, rather like grinding wheat in pioneer days Jon assumed; he recalled having seen something similar at New Salem on a class field trip in eighth grade. A set of gears then relayed the power to a crude mechanical pump that raised water up into the barrel.

However, obtaining hot water was another matter. Jon went to visit Rufus, the gnome illusionist and inventor and convinced him to come and see what he could invent. Needless to say, the gnome suggested many changes to the cold water system that improved it substantially. He then designed a boiler oven that heated water before pumping it out into all of the pipes. It worked properly on the first attempt. Excited about having unlimited hot water, Alison then added a communal bath house to the buildings under construction. "This town will have the luxury of a hot bath!" she exclaimed.

And so the construction progressed. Not until next winter would all of the stonework be completed and the dwarves depart. Of necessity, the castle or chateau would be the last to be fully completed. Once all of the stonework was finished, furnishing the castle, church and other buildings would get underway. However, Alison also had the pressing matter of finding castle staff and stewards as well as strong a guard force. She had no intention of spending the rest of her days here on guard duty. However, since she needed to cast many spells each day as the outer walls grew, she could not go off in search of such help just yet.

With the three hundred medium war horses they had acquired on the trip home along with the hundreds of suits of chain mail and multitudes of weaponry, just as soon as they found the men, they could be fully equipped. Sir Thomas advised that she keep a three hundred strong cavalry at her command. He also suggested that an additional fifty castle guards be hired. When the cavalry was not off on patrols and such, they could also pull guard duty. Raul d'Freeze, the retired fighter who had led the caravan, agreed to be the captain of the castle guards, while his twenty-five fighters preferred to be in the cavalry, for they were young and restless; pacing along a wall was not what they had in mind just yet. Alison did have a start in building up her force.

May also added her touch. Once she saw just how beautiful the polished "blacky" stone walls really looked, inspiration struck. She went on a shopping spree in Jascar Mines and returned with many bolts of a black cloth and a silver dye. She dyed the black cotton with streaks of silver, which then looked rather similar to the polished walls. Throughout the winter months, she sewed three hundred and fifty sets of outer tunics for all of the guard and cavalry men. Thus, the livery of Chateau d'Ambrose et Ville Bon Liberte matched the outer walls! So pleased with the final product was Alison that she had May also make numerous flags and banners to fly about the town and to be carried by the cavalry.

By spring, the first of the grey and orange granite stone homes were ready for occupation and the caravan families began moving in and building new lives. Now the running of the town was handled very differently than other areas of Verbenloc. Alison did not want the townsfolk paying her tithes or fees or taxes. However, Jon also pointed out that for the integrity of the folks coming here to live, an exchange was necessary. "Look Alison, if a man is not allowed to contribute as he can, he becomes criminal. I hate taxes just as much as you do. So let's find a better way. It is obviously going to require a great deal of food and such to support your cavalry and chateau. We are going to need all kinds of supplies, blacksmith work, charcoal, firewood, stable hands; the list is endless. Why not let each person contribute to the cause in a manner best suited to them?"

"Oh I get it," she saw his point, "All I need to do is establish some minimum amount of contribution, say twenty gold pieces a year, and then let each supply what they will of like value. A banker may well choose to donate coin, while a seamstress, like May, may donate clothing. Brilliant, unless we end up with everyone donating the same thing! That's where a steward will be most useful." She paused a moment thinking along a similar line, "There's another detail; I am building the homes for everyone. Now I can either own the homes ,and say, rent them out, or I can sell them to the families." She threw her head back, "Yes, they should buy their own homes for their own sense of integrity! Thanks, Jon, I've been wrestling with that decision ever since I decided to build the town. All I have to do is figure out the base price of a home and let them buy it from me over time. Boy do I ever need a steward! This is going to be a full-time job and I sure don't want it!" Both laughed, neither wanted to deal with those kinds of problems.

It was late December when the dwarves began to excavate the old castle ruins in earnest, reusing what good stone remained. When the dwarves first arrived, they used some of the stone to build themselves winter shelters. In removing the stone, they had uncovered over a dozen skeletal remains. Mandy used her new-found mental powers to view any physic residue and found that these were the remains of castle guards that died in the collapse that fateful night. When the dwarves began to remove vast quantity of the rubble in late December, many more remains were uncovered.

Again, Alison had Mandy come over to attempt the identification of the remains. As always, the mage held her breath as Mandy made her observations, for any moment, she expected to hear the ranger announce, here is your father or mother or a brother or a sister. But each time, Mandy, if she were doing this observation properly, declared they were more guards or castle staff. By the time the excavation had finally reached the uppermost portion of the dungeon area in which Alison and the others were now living, one hundred and eleven bodies had been recovered and partially identified. To everyone's amazement, none were Alison's family! Mandy had seen ghostly images that she found disturbing and confusing. She thought she saw a hint of something really powerful, but was as yet unwilling to reveal to the others for she, herself, was not certain of its authenticity.

It might also be noted here that many crushed possessions of the d'Ambrose family were also found and recovered. Most were unsalvageable. However, Basil's journal of the history of the d'Ambrose family was still intact after all these years. The three d'Ambrose children spent long nights reading it aloud to each other; it was as if their dad were speaking to them from the dead telling them of their heritage.

Now after dinner on the thirty-first of December, while Mandy and the others sat around the table drinking tea and discussing what could have possibly become of the other d'Ambrose family members, a rather unexpected event occurred. Lenny came wandering in to join them, standing quietly and shyly at the back of the room, both listening to their conversation and looking at one of the magical picture books Alison had given him so he would have something to do. Alison was explaining, "This is most confusing indeed. Yet, the signs all seem to point to the simple fact that none were killed here in the collapse. What could have become of them? Take Christina, she was only ten then."

A small quiet voice, not unlike a shy five year old making a small, insignificant observation, startled everyone. None had seen or heard Lennard enter. He said, "Tina loves Horgath."

Everyone turned around to see Lenny, book open, pointing to one of the pages. May was the first to reply, "What was that about Tina, Lenny? What's Horgath?"

He repeated himself but pointed to the page he at which was looking, "Tina loves Horgath." He added, "Here." May went to see what he was looking at.

"By golly, I do believe he's right!" May exclaimed. "Can I show them the picture, Lenny?" He nodded and smiled; he felt happy that he did something important. May held up the page so all could see. The painting showed a rural, rustic village or hamlet, whose name was Horgath.

Mat added, "I seem to recall that that was Christina's favorite picture, if my memory is right. I was only seven then." The germ of an idea began forming in Jon's mind. While the others chatted about Lenny's recollection and complimented him for telling them, Jon's mind was racing down various tracks, exploring possibilities.

At last he spoke, "You know, that gives me an idea. May, when your ceiling began crumbling, you had to get to safety really fast. You and Mat used your picture book to get away to Freetown. Why did you pick that picture as opposed to the one I really like, the lake and swans, Stilmar Pond?"

May answered, "It was our favorite picture; little did we know what kind of place it really was! If we had, we might have picked a better spot."

"Oh, I see!" exclaimed Mat. "You think that Tina did the same thing — that she went to Horgath!"

"Brilliant, Jon," exclaimed Alison. "Tomorrow, it's off to Horgath in search of Christina!" Then, her current circumstances came back to mind, "Rats, I best not go; I've got all these wall of force spells to do, but maybe I can squeeze in some time somehow."

"We want to go too," put in the twins in unison.

The next day, Mandy returned to Blackthorn Castle; they would not need her services; they were just visiting a town. Besides she had lots of her own work to do; she was in the middle of making major renovations to her castle and village. Besides, she was still puzzled by some of the ghostly images she had viewed from the hundred plus people that had died here that night and wanted time to try to sort them out. Sometimes, she secretly wished that she was as smart as Alison or Darless. In the end, she decided that all she needed was time, time to study and reflect. It would, in time, become clear to her, she hoped.

Chapter 2 The Village of Horgath

Around noon on the first of January, when Alison finished the last of her needed spells that day and when Jon and Darless's therapy session with Lenny was completed, the five of them prepared to go and visit the small village labeled Horgath in their picture books. May, Mat, Jon, Darless, and Alison put on their warm fur clothing and made final preparations. From the picture, the village seemed harmless enough, peaceful and rustic, but at Alison's insistence, they all prepared for the worst. She explained, "The hallmark of a good, successful adventurer is always go prepared for any eventuality." Jon took his walking stick and a large supply of rations and water. The latter were stowed in the third portable hole that they had gained from the assassin, who attempted to kill Metrarch last summer. Jon assumed that Alison had all kinds of magical devices and such in hers. The twins strapped on their short swords, grumbling all the while that this was only a friendly visit, or so they hoped. Darless ended the grumbling by totally agreeing with Alison.

"Now then, everyone ready?" Alison asked. The others nodded that they were. "Okay, now how best to get there?"

"Well," Darless began in her methodical tone of voice, "we had best not just arrive right there in front of that blacksmith shop. We might just frighten everyone or give them a scare. Plus we don't know what we are getting into, so caution is the best way. I vote we arrive some distance away and walk in on foot to the blacksmith shop."

"Good idea, Darless," Alison agreed, "I'm counting on you all to get us there this time. I'm afraid I've used up most all of my more powerful spells on the castle construction this morning."

"No problem," Jon replied, "I'll just step us all there. That way, you all can keep your magic in reserve, in case we need it." The spell casters thought this was a good move; Jon had them all hold hands as he took a hold of Alison and Darless. "Okay, now all together, let's just take one step forward," and he stepped forward, getting the idea firmly in his mind of having already arrived there and pulling on the other's hands, then he added, "and here we are." May and Mat, still unused to this sudden shift of viewpoint, stumbled and fell into the snow that covered the ground. They grumbled a bit as they got up and dusted themselves off.

Darless commented, "It is about three in the afternoon here. Be dark in about two hours or less. Okay everyone, look around and let's get our bearings."

They were on the side of a hill in the middle of a thinly forested area. Low hills dotted with leafless trees lay in all directions. Below them in a valley lay the small village of Horgath. "I was here once looking for any of my family," Alison said breaking the silence. "It seemed harmless enough then. Looks like it still is. I didn't find anything though. I hope we have better luck this time. Well, I guess it's off to the village down there."

As they walked the half mile down the hill toward the village, Jon marveled at the black smoke clouds rising from the scattered buildings and homes. He estimated that there were at least a hundred smoke clouds spiraling skyward. "Where to first?" he asked as they neared the village and could see a few people bundled up against the cold, much as they were.

"The blacksmith shop," Darless replied, "because that is the most prominent feature in the painting. Surely that played a part in Christina's fondness for that painting. Further, in a small village, the local blacksmith knows everyone, for who doesn't need his services at one time or another?"

"Good point," Alison acknowledged, "I had not thought of that the last time I were here, but that was at least five years ago. I did not visit the blacksmith."

The blacksmith shop was one of the larger buildings in Horgath. The front portion was open on three sides so that wagons, horses and the like could easily be brought up to the blazing hearth for work. The rear of the shop was actually the front wall of the residential portion, Jon concluded. The hearth was roaring and a tall man was busy pounding on an anvil, the sharp clanking sounds echoing in the otherwise relative stillness of the late afternoon. Slowly they made their way there. An enormous amount of tools, harnesses and supplies hung from the only wall or lay upon boxes stacked just in front of the wall, all safely out of direct contact with the elements.

As they approached, the man looked up and noticed them. "Hail, strangers. It's not such good weather for a walk. Come close and warm yourselves by the fire. Helmut Watson, blacksmith. What can I do for you?" His deep bass voice echoed his warm sentiments. Jon sensed that he was genuinely glad to see new people in town. This looked very promising indeed.

Alison asked, before anyone else got the chance, "Hello Helmut. We are looking for Christina d'Ambrose; she would have arrived here as a young child some twenty years ago. Of course, she would now be about thirty."

Jon watched the name register on the smiling, burly man. He reacted strongly, but tried not to show it. Jon saw all of the man's muscles suddenly tense. In a flash, a stern, almost angry countenance, replaced his good-natured smile. "What's it to you? Who are you anyway? What are you doing around here? You best leave soon."

His dramatic mood change took Alison by surprise. Jon hastily interceded, "I am Saint Jon Brown, the Redeemer. Perhaps you have heard of me? We mean you no harm. These are all three d'Ambrose children, who are looking for their long lost sister."

The big man attempted to look mean. "There's no one here by that name. We don't need no saints. I don't believe in no saints. How do I know you are a saint? Just cause you say so?" He paused briefly, hatching a plan. Before anyone could react, he swung the red hot iron that he had been forging and touched Jon's hand with it.

"Ouch, cripes that hurts! You burned me," exclaimed Jon, swinging his arm wildly to cool it off, as if somehow that would lessen the intense burning pain shooting up his arm.

"Don't look like no saint to me," he growled. Instantly, May and Mat whipped out their short swords, while Alison contemplated which spell she should use.

Jon was annoyed and his hand hurt like fire; he glared at the man. "Oh, alright then. Watch!" Jon began the healing process on his burn, concentrating on first dissipating the heat and then repairing the cells. He did not see several curious children coming out the front door followed by a woman, who was in the process fastening her winter coat.

Helmut's eyes nearly popped out of his head or so May later described his reaction to Jon. Indeed the blistering wound slowly regained normal flesh color and shrank in size and finally disappeared. Jon heard a woman's voice inquiring, "What's going on, Helmut?"

"It's — it's what you always feared! Grab the children and run!" exclaimed Helmut, unsure what to do next, for he was convinced he was confronting gods or witchcraft or devilry.

With his awareness coming back to the world, Jon commanded sternly, "I said that I am Saint Jon Brown and we intend you no harm." Seeing the children and woman backing hurriedly toward the front door and sensing their panic rising, Jon sent out a flow of calm and tranquility over the whole area, imagining a beautiful waterfall in the summertime with light beams sparkling off the falling spray. He smiled; it was working. Their panic ebbed and the woman and children paused.

"Mommy, what's he doing? I see a waterfall?" the older girl who was about ten asked.

Smiling and duly noting that this young girl was very observant indeed, Jon said very quietly, "These are three of the d'Ambrose children of Basil. We are looking for information on their long lost sister, Christina. Honestly, that is all we want, just any information, any clues that we might use to find her."

To Jon, the woman's eyes betrayed her. For an instant, he saw some dim, long-forgotten hope suddenly rekindled in a flash. But in the very next moment, he watched doubt replace the hope. "It's okay, Helmut," she said, the tone in her voice demonstrating that she was in control here and calming his fears. "Christina's dead — been dead a long, long time. How do we know you three are who you say you are? Careful what you say for I am the village cleric and soothsayer — I will know if you speak truth."

Alison's face echoed her deep disappointment — dead for so long. If only she could have come sooner. Regrets of her past ineffective searching began haunting her mind. Jon felt her thoughts. To Jon's surprise, Mat began to speak. "I am Mat d'Ambrose and this is my twin sister, May; we are now the Holy Children of Ukko. This is our baby sister, Alison, the Holy Mage of Ukko. We would not lie to you on such a grave matter. Christina was ten when our castle home was destroyed. May and I used our magical picture books to escape being crushed to death. We had hoped that Christina may have done the same and perhaps come here to this village. We have only just discovered that the picture of this village was her favorite picture in the book."

He continued, "How to prove ourselves to her? Well, Tina, that's what we called her, was a lot like mom; she cared for the needs of us three little ones. I remember she used to say to Ali here, when she was changing her diapers, 'Well, from the size of this one, I'd say you are going to be a really big girl!' jesting with her. That's why May and I always called her Runtling or Runtkin — just the opposite."

Jon watched the color drain from the woman's face; she staggered. Helmut dove for her and grabbed her just as she was about to hit the ground. The three children began to cry and scream "Mommy!" Jon expected Helmut to glare at them and say 'Now look what you have gone and done!' But he didn't; instead, his strong arms lifted her up gently and softly he told his children, "Open the door for daddy, now, quickly. Mommy's okay. She just had a bad shock. She'll be alright. We just need to lay her on the couch. Now hurry up." He turned sideways to the four and said, "You'd best come in too." Timidly, they entered the blacksmith's home; each looking at the other, speculation running rampant.

He blacksmith laid his wife carefully on the couch in the large front room; the children's toys were scattered about this homey, rustic room. Various bits of clothing lay here and there. The companions moved a toy here and a sock there so they could sit down. The three children hovered over their mother, but she was coming out of the faint. "Ellie, Billie, see to their coats. Annie, go fetch a glass of water for your mom," Helmut requested of his children. They scampered to their tasks.

"May I take your coat, ma'am?" the eldest child, Ellen asked politely of Alison. Although her look of concern for her mother was not totally gone, she managed a brave front, for a girl of ten. She had long blond hair and deep blue eyes, just like her mother; she wore a plain cotton brown dress, very earthy in texture.

Alison smiled, handing the girl her ermine fur coat, "Thanks. I'm truly sorry that we scared your mother so badly. You certainly have very nice manners," she complimented. That brought a smile to Ellen's lips. All of her practicing had not been in vain. She made a note to tell her mom about it, if only she would be all right.

Billie, a bit on the shy side, very quietly asked May the same thing. He was eight years old, wearing soft leather pants similar to his father, and had dark black hair, quite the opposite of his parents. Helmut had rather long blonde hair but with a hint of brown; his eyes were grey. Billie had blue eyes. Both children scampered over to a series of pegs near the door and carefully hung the winter coats. Then, they returned for Mat's and Jon's.

By now, Annette, who was just six, came back holding a large glass brimming with water, moving carefully so avoid spilling it. She had that grin on her face that cried out "Boy, am I doing something important!" Her mom had recovered enough to sit up and welcomed the glass. "Thanks honey. Mommy just had a bit of a surprise is all. Don't fret; I'm just fine now that I have a drink." She patted Annette on the head.

She looked long at the twins and Alison, fighting her emotions. Tears formed and trickled down her cheeks. She took a deep breath and said, "I'm Christina." In the releasing of that simple statement, twenty years of fear, worry, and tension released its grip on her and Helmut, who visibly relaxed and sank deep into the couch. He put his arm around her for support.

"Oh my. . ." Alison cried. Words failed her as her eyes watered so heavily she could not keep them open.

"Tina, oh Tina! God have we ever missed you!" exclaimed the twins in unison. All three got up and hugged onto Christina for dear life.

Amid the sobbing, Jon heard Tina say softly, "You don't know how much we've missed you too!"

Jon looked at Helmut and Helmut, at him. The big man was also overcome with emotion. "I'm — I'm sorry that I burned you outside. Please forgive me. I was only trying to protect Tina here. We have worried about someone coming for so long, I think we just got paranoid or something. Are you sure you are not still hurt from that burn?"

Jon smiled, "I'm just glad you didn't try to hit me. You look like one very strong man. No, I am fine. I heal very fast, as you saw. Why don't we make us all some tea or something? I could use a cup. I assume you have tea here." He nodded and without disturbing the others he and Jon went into his kitchen to fix something for everyone. The children, a bit taken aback by all the emotion, followed their dad.

"Why's mommy crying?" Ellen asked the burning question in her mind and well as the other two.

"Those are mommy's long lost bother and sisters," he explained as he set about the task of fixing up the tea pot. Water was simmering on the stove already.

"You mean like Uncle Stephen?" inquired Billie.

"Yes, just like Uncle Stephen," he replied. "Now you three carry these cups in for the others, and you can have a cup of cocoa tonight. It is a very special time!" That produced the desired effect. They gaily scampered into the living room with the cups; this treat was usually reserved for very special occasions in this household.

"Oh my god!" exclaimed Jon. "You mean their brother Stephen d'Ambrose is also in these parts?"

"Sure, didn't you know? No, I see that you didn't," he answered his own question after seeing the surprised look on Jon's face. "We'd better go tell the others about Stephen, too!"

Shortly, they brought the steaming teapot and a tray of cookies and three mugs of cocoa into the living room. The others were finally wiping their faces and blowing their noses, having finally gotten their joy under better control. "Here you go," said Helmut, sitting the tray down. The children grabbed their mugs and hurried off to one side of the room to sit down and drink it and listen to the adults talk. "Ah, there is another thing you should know, Stephen d'Ambrose is also here in this village." After gasps, the emotions flowed yet again out of control.

Helmut looked at Christina, who had mostly recovered the shock of seeing her family, and asked, "Should I send Billie to fetch Stephen? I think he is still here."

"Oh, yes, yes!" she exclaimed. "Billie, I want you to go to Uncle Stephen's house. Tell him that three of his younger sisters and brother are here. Tell him I said for him to bring his whole family. Can you remember all that?"

The shy look on his face told her no, and Ellen volunteered to go with him, "Mom, I'll go with him and see that he doesn't forget any part." Both nodded to each other. Ellen was acting more and more like a grownup this last year. She was politely looking out for her younger brother and sister, which took quite a load off of Christina.

"Look at you," Tina said to Alison and the twins. "You are all grown up. You both have mom's eyes!"

"Yes, but you have mom's hair," Alison countered with a big grin. "And we all have dad's hair." Jon surmised that their mother had blonde hair, while Basil had brown. By mutual agreement, they did not discuss anything of importance until Stephen could be here. No sense in telling everything twice.

Alison told her that they were all getting married in May. Jon blushed when she introduced him as her fiancé. "The twins are getting married?" Tina gasped, "Now that is impressive. I've often wondered how they would ever manage that. You two are still really close, aren't you? Still knowing what the other is thinking?" The twins nodded. "You know I was **so** jealous of you two because you could do that and I couldn't. The silly things we get so vexed about!"

Jon added with a broad, teasing grin, "And you would not believe who they are getting married to — another set of twins, who are just as close, if not closer, than they! Like four peas in a pod." Everyone roared with laughter and Tina quickly gave Helmut an explanation of life around the twins when they were growing up. No matter what you did or said to one of them, the other always knew about it without being told. It was maddening to Tina.

Then, Christina realized that shortly four more would be arriving. "Helmut, we had better quickly clean up this mess around here pronto and get the spare chairs out." His "Oh my, yes indeed!" told all. Everyone lent a hand and in short order had the room straightened up and more chairs arraigned, and just in time too. Ellen and Billie came bursting in the door followed by a breathless man wearing leather armor covered with a fancy tunic followed by a dark haired woman and two more children. Evidently, they had run all the way.

Stephen paused just inside the door, gazing at the four strangers. "Stephen," cried Alison, May and Mat, and they rushed to hug him. Even this stalwart fighter lost control of his emotions and began crying tears of wonderment. Meanwhile, Christina, her cheeks flushed, said, "Mary Ellen, Fred, Basil, come on in and take off your coats and have some tea and cookies. Ellen, bring the entire cocoa can in here please. Yes, you can all have another with Fred and Basil." The five kids let out a whoopee and rushed to the kitchen to fetch spoons and the large can.

Stephen was thirty-two and the eldest of the d'Ambrose children. He was tall like his father, with the same dark hair and blue eyes. He was a strong man as well. Jon could tell that he was likely a fighter type, similar to Mandy.

Once the hugging died down, Christina said, "Okay, let's proceed in an orderly manner. We need some introductions all around, especially for the children. As you kids all know, Stephen is my brother, your Uncle. Today, you get to meet more of my brothers and sisters! We have not seen each other for over twenty years! Now this here is your Aunt Alison and this is your Aunt May. And this is your Uncle Mat. Alison is soon to marry Jon here, so when that happens, he will be your Uncle Jon. Got it?" The children looked at all these new, strange faces, and bewilderment was obvious.

Annette piped up, "Will you play with us, Aunt Alison?"

"You betcha!" she replied.

"And can we get some copper pieces from you Uncle Mat, that is when we really need some?" asked Fred, not the bit bashful, seeing a chance to get more spending money.

Mat laughed, "Nephew, it's not coppers that I give out, but gold pieces. I got lots of them any time you need them!" Needless to say, five sets of eyes opened very wide indeed!

Mat went on, "But first, Tina or Stephen, can you tell us about your escape and all that. Ours is a very long tale indeed!"

She looked at him, and he, her. "Okay, I'll do it," Tina agreed. "Well that night when our castle was attacked, Stephen and I were reading our bedtime stories together, like we always did. A chunk of the ceiling fell down and blocked my doorway. We could not get out. We heard more crumbling sounds and tried everything we could think of to get out. Finally, I thought of the picture books. You know, kids, the special one I show you on very special days?" They nodded excitedly. "Stephen saved my life that night. He got out his book and opened it to my favorite page, not his. Well, I hung on to my book and we both ended up here, just outside Horgath. We had the sense enough to bring along our meager coin pouches so we were able to afford a room in the only inn here in the village. When the money ran out, Stephen sold his book and used some of it to buy a sword. It was all for the best. Sometimes, it is amazing how things work out."

"Helmut's dad and mom eventually took us in — rather adopting us. His father ran this very blacksmith shop back then. They passed away before the children were born, though. So we grew up being loved in a family. That really helped a lot. I decided that I wanted to be a healer. Way out here near the edge of Rhineland, there is not much help if you get sick or hurt, you see. So I studied and became a fairly good healer, if I do say so myself. Of course, I had to quit studying and learning when I got married, though." She grinned at Helmut; it was obvious that they were still very much in love with each other. "When anyone is hurt, they come to me," she added.

"Stephen always wanted to be a fighter. He got his chance one day when King George and his band came here to inspect how the village was doing. Thanks goodness he only comes around once a year at most. Perhaps, Stephen, you should tell them about your situation," she deferred to him.

"Well, King George said I had potential and awarded me a squire's status at his Veders Castle, in the largest city in Rhineland. I did well and am a fair fighter, advancing to a lieutenant. But you know I was always good with figures and planning, and I ended up being one of King George's many castle stewards," he explained.

"You are being modest again," Tina teased. "He's the best! The others there would be lost without him!"

"Oh yes, we both married. Here's my lovely wife, Mary Ellen and my two kids, Fred and Basil. Fred's twelve and wants to be a fighter like his dad. Basil, who's turned ten last week, takes more after his Aunt Tina, he wants to enter the priesthood and become as famous as his grandfather, his namesake." Basil grinned affirmative.

"And you've already met my children. Ellen is the oldest, she's ten. Billie's eight and Annette is six. Stephen is often away for weeks at the castle, which is about a hundred miles to the north of here. I've only been there once. I thought it rather a dreary castle," she said.

"Ah, but the pay's great," Stephen added. "We really have all the basic necessities. I've always been looking out for big sis here, and she, me. And really that is all there is to tell. We long ago gave up all hope of ever seeing our family again. When we saw the total destruction of the castle in the picture book, we assumed, obviously incorrectly, that no one could have lived through that."

"Oh yes, and ever after, we lived in terror that whoever attacked us would one day try to come find us. We were terrified we'd be found out, you know, captured or killed," Christina explained. "So we worked out all sorts of signals just in case someone should come looking for us."

"Yes, and that's why I treated you so badly," Helmut added looking a bit downcast. "I had long forgotten about it. Your arrival saying you were looking for her rather shook me up, if you follow me."

"Rightly so!" declared Alison. "Now it's our turn. Prepare yourselves; you too, nieces and nephews. Let me begin by giving you our full titles. That may help put all this into perspective. My fiancé here is Saint Jon Brown, the Redeemer, a title bestowed upon him by Father Ukko himself, personally." Everyone gasped as the significance of that pronouncement struck home.

"Not our god himself? Oh my goodness!" exclaimed Christina. Suddenly everyone in the room looked at Jon with awe and wonderment in their eyes and faces.

"Yes, Jon and I have been in Father Ukko's realm twice now. He has bestowed upon me the title of the Holy Mage of Ukko. May and Mat here were given the title of the Holy Children of Ukko." This news hit them hard. It was difficult to imagine their god personally visiting with one person, but all four was nearly incomprehensible. Alison had to answer many questions before she could continue with their tale.

Then, she began to outline her life and that of May and Mat. A hush filled the room; you could have heard a pin drop. Spellbound, the five children and their parents sat and listened trying to grasp the significance of everything. Four hours passed before she finished up, telling them in detail about how the new Chateau d'Ambrose et Ville Bon Liberte was being constructed this very minute.

When she finished, no one said a word for a time, until Fred gulped and said, "Dad, Uncle Mat was not joking when he said I could get gold pieces from him!" Stephen nodded.

Tina began slowly, "This must mean, Alison, that you are nearly to an archmage status, do I near the mark, little sis?" Alison blushed; she did not like to think of herself as a stuffy old book worm, which is how the few archmages she knew appeared to her, but nodded yes. "And you twins, you two are powerful and straightened out a whole city single-handedly?"

"We had each other," May acknowledged.

"And she is more than enough help," finished Mat.

"And now you can heal just by touching the injured? I am truly amazed! I have to pray and hopefully, Father Ukko will grant my wishes and heal through me. What a family I have!" Then, she looked sternly at Jon, "Do you really think you will be able to cure Lennard's insanity? Really? I don't even know if the most powerful and faithful priests can even do that? But you are not a priest, correct?"

"Yes and no," Jon replied. "Yes, I believe Darless, who's doing most of the real work, and I will be able to do it. Remember, it was Lennard that gave us the real clue to find you two! And no I am not a priest. Ukko told me that I do not need to worship him, in spite of what all I have done to help him and his followers. But say, I am starving. How about some dinner? It is totally dark outside!"

They broke for the evening meal. The ladies went to work in the kitchen while Stephen and Helmut examined May and Mat's weaponry, for their blades were enchanted and neither had ever held a magical blade. Meanwhile, Basil wanted to touch Jon's walking stick and plied him with questions about Father Ukko. Jon let him hold it and the lad grasped it as if it were a holy relic. Stephen saw his son holding it and chided him, "You should not be holding Saint Jon's healing staff. What if you should drop it or break it?"

"Jon, please, just Jon. He cannot damage it in any way. Besides, it comes to me on command any time I need it. See, I'll show you." He spoke a single word and instantly the walking stick disappeared from a very startled Basil's hands and appeared in Jon's right hand. He promptly handed it back to Basil. The children were very impressed indeed.

Christina gave little thought to sparing expenses for this meal and used the best that they had to offer. This was perhaps the most important night in her life. She was so happy. She could not remember ever being this excited or happy, except for that night when Helmut proposed to her. Gaiety filled the house that evening.

Over dinner, Alison at long last asked the question that she really wanted to ask, but had been a bit uncertain about how to best say it. "You know, I would really, really, really love it if you all would consider moving back to our newly built town and castle. It really is partly yours, you know. But I can understand if you would rather stay here. I know you have all your friends and spouses' families to consider."

Of course, all five children immediately began to beg and plead to move to the Ville! Alison added above the din, "And Stephen, I am really, really desperate for someone to actually run the castle. I'm afraid I know almost nothing about it! Please consider it, please. And we really need blacksmiths and a healer that would really help out! I still have to try to find Henry and Rubin and mom and dad. I cannot devote time to that if I have to run everything else."

Getting in on the action, Mat added, "And with the Twins in town, you can count on the fact that there will be law and order. It will be an extremely safe environment to raise families. I personally guarantee it; I'm going to start mine with Jennifer just as soon as we get married! Please say yes, big brother! Littlest brother is begging you."

Not to be left out, May added, "And with all of the picture books that we have, Mary Ellen and Helmut and everyone can come back here for visits any time they want too. Unless, of course, we can figure out where Rhineland is from Verbenloc and can ride here."

Christina looked at Helmut; Stephen looked at Mary Ellen. Helmut spoke softly, "We don't want any handouts. We must earn our keep."

Jon answered him before Alison could get a word in, "Helmut, on that you can count. If we ever give you a free-ride, you have my permission to hit me over the head with your anvil!" He roared, grasping the image Jon just placed into his mind.

"Then, it is fine by me," Helmut said, "I have very few relatives left anymore. I welcome an opportunity for my children to grow and to learn in safety."

"I'm all for it," Mary Ellen agreed, "but for a different reason. It gets awfully lonely out here when Stephen is away at the castle for so long. He only gets to come home here perhaps once a month. It will be heaven to have him around all the time. He can help raise the children!" Everyone laughed with her, but Stephen blushed. He knew that it had been taking quite a toll on his wife; he just had not realized just how much.

Christina, ever the practical one, asked, "I've only one question. Just how do we move all this stuff?" she pointed in a wide arc around the house.

Alison, overjoyed, declared, "Well, you do have a pair of powerful wizards in your family and Darless will also help. You just pack it all up and leave the rest to Darless, May, Jon and myself. We'll let Jon move the really heavy stuff, like his anvil." Everyone roared with laughter, including Jon. He knew he was going to be stuck moving that heavy piece of iron.

Finally, it was time to go. Alison said, "We'd really like to stay the night, sis, but we cannot. I've got more spells to cast tomorrow morning and Jon has to assist Darless with Lenny. But here, Stephen, here is one of the picture books. Now both of you can pop in any time you want. Just let us know when you are all ready to move. Give us at least a couple of months to get temporary housing finished. I believe Thraxton said that folks can move in around the first of March, so that gives you plenty of time to pack and all that. I will pop in for visits just as often as I can get away."

"I understand, baby sister," Tina acknowledged. "It will give me time to fully train someone to take over the village healer position as well as pack."

They all said their farewells for a just a brief while. Hope and joy filled everyone's hearts. Jon had the five kids come outside to watch them go. "Watch closely," Jon explained. "See I have all of their hands in mine; everyone is holding hands. Now we will just take one step forward and we will be back in Verbenloc. Now watch, here we go. Okay, step forward," he said dramatically. He knew that the children would be most impressed with their sudden disappearance, and he was right.

The day had been one terrific day indeed.

Chapter 3 Steinfold, Rhineland

"Ruben loves money." That was the next clue Lenny provided some two weeks later, again while they were all gathered around chatting after supper one evening. Two weeks had passed since Alison had been reunited with Christina and Stephen, her oldest brother and sister. Indeed, she had gone back to visit them twice, and they and their families had visited her here, inspecting the construction site. They were very impressed, particularly with just how magnificent the "blacky" polished stone actually was. Of course, the children wanted to move in at once; something wonderful and exciting was going on. Dwarves were everywhere; there was so much to see!

Thraxton had helped out a bit, proclaiming that two stone homes could be ready in just two weeks, if they wanted to come that soon. Yes, both families were eager to move the timetable up a month. The planned moving day was set for the first of February.

But now, Lenny had just provided yet another clue — information to where Ruben might have escaped. Excitedly, Alison, Jon, May, May, and Darless flipped through the pages of the picture books, trying to figure out how money could influence a destination choice. If only they had been older when the disaster had come or had known more about the likes and dislikes of their slightly older brother. . . But they were only three and seven at the time and could be forgiven not knowing such.

The hours went by, but they found themselves no closer to knowing what picture Ruben, with money in mind, may have chosen. In the end, Jon's idea won out, "Let's go ask Christina and Stephen — see if they have any ideas."

The next day, just after lunch, after the day's spells were cast, and after Lenny's therapy session was done, Alison and Jon went to visit them. They found Helmut outside as usual, but this time, he was showing another man, obviously an apprentice blacksmith, just how to set up a shop. "Hi there, just showing Tom here how to setup a shop the right way. I'm giving him my shop and house here. Tina's inside, I expect you'll want her. Just go on in." They did, but knocked first.

Alison excitedly explained to her oldest sister the latest clue that Lenny had told them. Christina looked carefully through all the pages, but like the others, could not see any connections. So she sent Ellen off to find Stephen, on the off-chance he might know. Five minutes later, he arrived.

"Well, I've given them my notice and am home packing. What's this about news?" he asked. "Ellen said it was very important." Alison explained what Lenny had said — Ruben loves money.

"We've been over and over these pictures," Alison continued. "But none of these seems to have anything to do with money. Do you have any ideas? I'm fresh out."

Stephen commented, "Well, sounds like you are indeed making progress with Lennard. He's right; Ruben was always helping dad count money. I would be playing soldier, but Ruben never wanted to play. He kept wanting me to play banker. Yuck. Well, let's see." He too paged through the book. At first, he was just as baffled as they were. Still, he looked through all the pages a third time. Suddenly he had an idea.

"This one, here, Steinfold, Rhineland. I recognize it now. It is the second largest town in this country — has something like five thousand people in it. Look closely at this picture. There, see that building. I can make out the word, 'Bank.' Perhaps, Ruben saw that too. That's the best I can do."

"Boy, you've got good eyes," said Alison, "I've been over and over these pictures a thousand times and never saw that one! Okay, then we are off to look for Rubin in Steinfold. Come on, Jon; let's go tell the twins where we are going. Thanks, you two. We'll let you know how it turns out."

"Bye," said Jon, and he took Alison's hand and stepped back into her underground dungeon dining room.

"Well?" said May eagerly as they suddenly appeared. Both had been anxiously awaiting their return.

Alison showed them the picture and pointed out the bank.

"This should be very easy," declared Mat. "We only need to walk into the bank and ask for Rubin, er, that is if there is only one bank."

May added, "But since it is a rather large town, be on the alert for pickpockets and the likes. Freetown is full of them. This time you really need the Twins on the search," she and Mat insisted. The four made their preparations.

Jon looked at the open picture book, concentrating on the image of the town of Steinfold. With no fanfare, he pulled the other three with him, as he stepped onto the road leading into the town. No one stumbled this time and they continued walking down the road, which was rather muddy from melting snow crushed by horses and carts. Indeed several times they had to step off the road to avoid wagons heading into and out of the main gates ahead of them. The land about them was rolling hills with patches of dormant trees poking up like match sticks. Sunlight gleaming off of the white lands tended to blind them somewhat; Jon found himself wishing for his sun glasses. By the time the four reached the gatehouse, their boots were covered in mud.

At the gatehouse, a tall, thin man, very bored, said, "Three coppers per person, please." Evidently, people had to pay to enter the town, Jon surmised. May expected this and handed him three silver pieces telling him to pocket the change. For a brief instant, his boredom was replaced by curiosity and mild interest, "Thank you, ma'am! And a fine day to you. You can wipe your boots in the trench just inside."

The four were following another trader into the town and they watched how he handled his boots. A trench with water, now rather muddy, was off to the right out of the main pathway. He stepped into the trench and used a straw brush to clean off the mud. The four followed suit. "At least we don't look too grungy," Jon apologized. "Now what?"

"Ah, leave that to us," Mat smiled. "You two stay over here out of the way while we get some directions. Back shortly." They left before either Alison or Jon could protest.

"I don't like all this splitting up," Alison grumbled. "It is not a wise action, but then I guess they are better able to handle rowdy towns than we are," she rationalized. Instead, they looked around at what they could see of the town. It was perhaps a couple miles in diameter; the center of it was on a hilltop and then it grew haphazardly down the slopes into the valleys and partway up the nearby hills. The streets were all cobblestones and Jon enjoyed hearing the distinctive clip-clop sounds that the horses and wagons made as they rolled by the two. It was new and novel to him. The buildings that they could see reminded him of Freetown. Some were made of stone or brick or perhaps adobe, he could not tell at this distance, and some were wooden, akin to log cabins in Jon's mind. They did not have long to wait.

The twins strolled up to the waiting pair. "Okay," Mat informed them, "there are four banks, roughly scattered about the town."

"To narrow the search, I asked if any one of the four were larger than the others," May continued. "The First Steinfold Bank is the oldest and largest. We suggest we try there first." She had a satisfied look on her face. This seemed reasonable to Alison, and she and Jon fell in behind the twins, who led the way, pausing occasionally to ask for updated directions. After about a mile and deep into the town, the buildings all were of significantly better construction. This was a wealthier portion of town. At last, they paused in front of an imposing three story red brick building which had a large sign saying First Steinfold Bank. Jon noticed that the scant windows all had iron bars on them and iron shutters on the inside. A bank is a bank no matter where you go, he thought to himself.

Quite a few people were entering and leaving and they had to get into a line just to get inside the doors. Once inside, they found themselves in a huge, spacious room, nearly empty of furniture, save for small tables centrally located. Against the far wall was a long row of teller windows. "It's just like banks where I come from," Jon said rather quietly to Alison. May was already looking about, getting her bearings. Satisfied she knew where she wanted to go, she moved on ahead, leading them to a window which had a sign reading "Information."

A young woman in her late twenties smiled at May and asked, "May I help you?"

"Well, I do hope so," May began using as propitiative a voice as she could muster. "We are from out of town and are looking for Ruben d'Ambrose. We believe he works at a bank here in town. By chance, is this the right place?"

She smiled, "Well, welcome to Steinfold; I hope you have a nice stay. Yes, you have found the place. One minute, I'll tell him you are here. What name should I say?"

"Oh thank you so very much! Please tell him that May, Mat, and Alison d'Ambrose are here to visit him. We have not seen him in a very long time."

The woman nodded and headed into a back room. "Boy this is sure easy!" May exclaimed. The others agreed, hardly able to contain their excitement. Shortly, six armed guards came marching into the room accompanied by the information teller.

She motioned for them to come to her, "This way please. The guards will take you to his office on the third floor." May thanked her and the four fell in line with the guards, who were obviously strong fighters in chain mail with imposing long swords at their waists. They marched down a long hallway and up two flights of stairs, but said not a word. Jon noticed the strong odor of polished wood, the intricately carved banisters and the enormous wood frescoes that adorned the walls of the stairway. This was obviously a well-established, wealthy bank.

They halted before a large walnut door with a large placard proclaiming Ruben d'Ambrose, Vice-president. A guard knocked once and a voice said "enter," and the guards opened the door and led them in. This was indeed a wealthy banker's office, plush in all aspects, from the royal blue carpeting, to the magnificent tapestries and paintings on the walls, to the mahogany, enormous desk. Even the chairs for the guests were exceptionally well-made and quite expensive. The guards did not leave, but instead formed into a line against the back wall by the door. The four walked up to the desk as the rotund figure rose to greet them.

Ruben was now twenty-eight and about Alison's height, but weighed two hundred pounds, most of it in a rather large pot-belly. He spouted a magnificent mustache and had well-oiled hair, neatly trimmed. He wore a silk business style suit and looked much like a grand dandy, a ladies man. "Ah welcome, please have a seat," he said most business-like. There was not the slightest hint of excitement in his voice or mannerism, no trace of an emotional reunion. The teller said that you wanted to see me? Something about arriving from out of town and having the same last name as I? How may I be of service?"

Alison could contain her excitement and enthusiasm no longer. "Ruben, it's us — your youngest brother and sisters! We have found you at last! I'm Alison and this is May and Mat, the twins." Jon noted that he had no reaction at all, unless that of boredom could count. "I have been looking for you for years!" Seeing no response from him, she added, "Aren't you glad to see us?"

He commented dryly and disinterested, "Well, how should I know if you are indeed who you say you are? Why, anyone could walk in here and claim they were my long dead sister, Alison. I have not seen any of them for over twenty years. They were all killed when my father's castle was destroyed. I saw it with my own eyes."

"But we escaped! Nanny took me to the dungeons and out to safety. May and Mat used their picture books to go to another place. We just found Christina and Stephen, and they did the same thing, used the books to escape. It's us!" cried Alison nearly in tears trying to get him to believe her. She had never expected that her family members would not welcome or believe her. She was getting more and more emotional. "I am now rebuilding the castle and making a town for us all. Only now are we finally getting clues to where everyone scattered to — that's how we found you, Lenny remembered you liked money and Stephen recognized the bank in this town, so we hoped you may have escaped here."

"Yes, yes, yes, my dear," he said matter-of-factly, "I did come here to this town to escape, but then that fact is widely known by all that know me in this town. And I might add," he said rather pompously, "that is likely to be nearly half of the population of Steinfold! But come, come, you are indeed a very pretty young woman. You have all obviously traveled a good distance to come here. It is nearly quitting time anyway. How about you all joining me for an early dinner and you can tell me all about it. My treat, mind you," he added, "for I would, at least, like to hear your story in full detail." He rose without waiting for an answer or acceptance; he just fully expected his requests to be obeyed, especially by pretty young women. "Follow me and my body guards. I always dine at the Rose Garden, perhaps the finest eating establishment in all of Steinfold." They could do nothing but follow him out the door.

As they walked along, Alison fairly screamed into Jon's mind, *I don't get it! What's the matter with him? How can we convince him?* Obviously, she was very upset over his welcome.

Jon tried to console her, placing in her mind, *Relax, he does have a point. Apparently, his life story is well known here. As he says, anyone could try to pretend they were his long lost sister. At least he is willing to hear your story. Perhaps when he has heard it all, he will change his mind.* Jon then sent a similar message mentally to May and Mat. He sensed all three relaxing somewhat, though not completely.

As they walked along the streets heading for the Rose Garden, Jon could not help noticing how many passers-by greeted Ruben by name. To each, he nodded and said "Good Afternoon." Ruben was definitely a very well-known figure about the wealthier part of town, no doubt about that. Jon also observed that Ruben exhibited an overly large self-pride.

They entered the inn; it was all Ruben had indicated. This was the fanciest establishment Jon had yet seen in all these lands. Posh, did not cover this inn; that was an understatement. Everything from the deep, soft carpet on which they walked, to the elegantly carved tables and chairs, to the wall hangings and paintings, to the service staff — everything was of the highest quality and perfection. They even had four musicians playing soft background music. Alison sent Jon, *Now don't get so wrapped up in the music that you forget what we are here for!* She was very worried indeed.

"Your usual table, Master d'Ambrose," said their waiter, who was himself the epitome of elegance, richly dressed. Ruben nodded and the waiter led the way to a large table, off to the side from where one could observe everyone else who was here. It was also raised about one foot above the floor, obviously a very special table. Quickly, the waiter adjusted the table settings for five, and helped each of the women into their chairs, placing their coats across the back of the chairs for them. The six guards positioned themselves in a hexagon formation at tables nearby on all sides, except the rear, for this reserved table was against the wall. When they were all seated, the waiter produced five menus and asked, "Drinks as usual, Master d'Ambrose?"

"Ah yes, Perkins. I'll have the usual." Then to the others, he added, "Will you care to join me in a decanter of Chateau Blanc? It is the finest white wine I have ever tasted." Somewhat taken aback by all of this service and elegance, the three d'Ambrose siblings nodded affirmative.

Jon exclaimed, "No thanks. I just noticed that they have a special Earl Grey tea. I have got to try it!" Ruben smiled and began to study the menu.

Alison sent to Jon, *This is unreal; the typical meal is about three gold pieces!* There were twelve main courses; all expensive, but likely very good.

"May I suggest the Roast Pheasant Under Glass? It is exceptionally delicious," Ruben volunteered and so indicated that that would be his choice to the waiter. The others went along with his suggestion; all were intimidated by this inn. Soon the waiter arrived with the bottle of wine and the pot of tea. Once Ruben had sniffed it and tasted it and agreed it was acceptable, the waiter poured four hand-blown crystal goblets for them and departed.

"Now this is a super tea!" Jon exclaimed. "You are right; this is perhaps the best Earl Grey I have ever had!"

"Yes," smiled Ruben self-satisfied that they appreciated this meal. "Now pray, Alison, for that is whom you claim to be, please tell me your full tale. You have my undivided attention." And he did pay attention to Alison's lengthy summary of her life. May and Mat added theirs to the tale as they went along. Jon, in spite of Alison's warning, found his attention constantly drifting to the music and the musicians and their instruments. The meal passed slowly as time went by. Evidently, Ruben was in no hurry either. He was wont to spending long hours in this inn. Jon noticed that Ruben did indeed seem to enjoy their story, much as a child would enjoy listening to an exciting bedtime story. Jon guessed that Ruben did not believe a word of it, though.

When they finished about two hours later, Ruben complimented them, "My, that was the most interesting tale that I have heard in many long years. Indeed it most definitely was worth the price of the meal! Many thanks, I say." Immediately, he saw all three begin to protest, and quickly added, "You must realize that I have no way of knowing if any of what you have told me is the truth."

"But couldn't we get a local priest to detect if we were lying?" protested Alison.

"My lovely, it still would make no difference. Look. Even if you are my baby sister, I know you not. It has been twenty years after all. We were just children then. Besides, I don't want to be associated with 'adventurers;' it is bad for business, to say nothing of one's health. Look what befell by father? Dead before his time. No, I am well-respected here, I am wealthy, I have my pick of the finest women. What more could I desire?" He saw they were getting more upset, not less, so he got more serious. "Look, money is everything. There is really no profit to be gained here. When you first walked in, I figured you were going to ask me for a loan to rebuild your castle or some such venture. It would not be the first time I have been so asked. But I can see by your dress that you are not lacking in funds, those are ermine coats you four are wearing, if my eyes do not deceive me. But one must be cautions of illusions, you know. There are any number of illusionists about who can make one appear in any form or style. For all I know, you are really trolls disguised as people. Who knows for sure? Certainly not I. You must understand my position. I am a very wealthy banker. I make my living, such as it is, by handling the financial affairs of others. Trust, it is all in trust. They trust me. For without trust, I'd just be another pauper on the streets. I must therefore uphold my trusted image. Besides, what did dad ever do for me, except try to kill me?"

His last sentence brought Jon totally out of his reverie with the music. He knew what lay behind those words. Before anyone could react to his lengthy speech, Jon gave Ruben a command, utterly certain that this man would follow it. "Ruben, look at those mental pictures you are seeing of that night, twenty years ago. Go through them moment by moment and tell me what you are seeing as you go along." Jon gave him his complete attention.

Alison's protest fell into the silence. She suddenly realized what Jon was attempting right here in the middle of the inn. She sent a mental message to the twins trying to explain what she thought Jon was doing. All three listened to Ruben. "Well, I was counting out the receipts for the day, and there came sounds of a fight, yes, clanking noises. I supposed it was the guards toying with their swords, as fighters are wont to do. Therefore, I went back to counting the funds. Next thing I knew, the ceiling over the left doorway came crashing down, blocking that exit. I got up to head out the right door to find out what the blazes was going on with the darn run-down castle, when that doorframe crashed too, pinning me inside. I got my book out and left, came here. That's all."

"Thank you very much, Ruben. Now, go back to the very beginning of it and move through it once more and tell me all about it," Jon commanded. He obeyed, though he knew not why, he began to relive it once more. This time, he became rather frightened as he recounted it. The next time through, he got angry. The fourth time, he became rather antagonistic towards his father who had the audacity to let this catastrophe happen. Then on the fifth recounting, he said, "I grabbed dad's large sack of gems that I was counting and then used my picture book to come here, expecting to find a bank. Oh, I guess you could say that I stole dad's gems!" Suddenly, for no apparent reason he began laughing. Actually, a chuckle came first, which progressed into a full belly laugh and his whole robust frame fairly jiggled. He'd occasionally mutter, "Stole it." Jon knew precisely what he meant.

Smiling, Jon said, "Well done Ruben. If you ever want more of this, please come to Darless's College of Free Beings where the old Castle d'Ambrose once stood. Alison, will you give Ruben one of the picture books so he can come and visit when he chooses?" She did so. While she was retrieving it from her portable hole, Jon added, "Ruben, in time, the picture of the castle ruins will change to reflect the new Chateau d'Ambrose et Ville Bon Liberte. If you choose to come just before the first of May, you can meet many of your siblings and join us for their weddings. And now, we have taken up far too much of your time. Thank you for a most excellent meal." He got up and shook the banker's hand firmly. The three others followed his lead. They left leaving him still chuckling to himself and ordering another bottle of the most excellent wine.

When they were outside the inn, Jon took hold of their hands and stepped them back into Alison's dining room, where Darless was patiently awaiting their return. All of this happened so quickly, that none of the three d'Ambrose children had a chance to even comment.

From the looks on all of their faces, Darless knew that it had not gone as planned. She was a good listener and let them do the explaining. Alison began at once. "Well done, there Jon. I cannot believe you did that right there in the inn! And it seemed to work. But what is *wrong* with Ruben? Yes, Darless we found him. But no matter what we say, he just will not believe we are who we say we are!" Tears began to flow; she'd held them in check now for hours. May did likewise. Mat just sat in one corner looking forlorn. Jon did the explaining for Darless.

After he summarized their meeting with Ruben, Jon added, "You see, I think he really still believes that his father is to blame for deserting him or allowing it to happen. He managed to work his way up to that of a very wealthy banker. I suspect he only looks at the profits to be gained. I don't think he really trusts anyone, assuming that women are just after his money and that men are trying to get a loan. I think that he really is a very lonely man, in spite of appearances. He is just plain in love with money."

"Yes, Ruben loves money," said Lenny, who hearing the voices of his family had meekly entered the room.

Wiping her tears, Alison said to him, "Yes, Lenny, you are very right about Ruben; Ruben loves money. It's pretty sad, though. Jon, do you think he will ever come around and visit us here? You know, come to his senses?"

"Well, my love, that is what I tried to make happen. That's why I tried a bit of therapy there on him at the inn. I knew I'd never get another chance to try. It worked, so maybe there is yet some hope. Maybe once the castle is rebuilt and appears as such in the picture books, you know it is going to look fabulous, he might get curious enough to come. I just don't know."

They discussed Ruben's fate for several more hours, but it was always a sad ending at which they arrived. Darless was still optimistic; she commented, "Look that leaves only Heinrich and your parents unaccounted for now. We should concentrate on finding them now. We still have no clues as yet that I know of, correct?"

Her subtle shift of focus did the trick. Alison, May, and Mat began chatting about their remaining brother and parents. Darless pointed out, "Number 1, their bodies have not been found in the rubble. Number 2, we can therefore conclude they did not perish inside the castle. Number 3, they most certainly were inside when the attack came. Number 4, it is highly likely that one or more of them went to the roof or some such place from which to assess the attack. Number 5, realizing this, today, I had a number of dwarves systematically scour the surrounding land for traces of bones and such. They built me a really big sieve and I used a dig spell and together we sifted through the top couple inches of dirt around the more well-traveled areas of the ruins, looking for trace evidence. Number 6, we found only this." Darless laid a jeweled broach that had been somewhat crushed on the table. A green emerald was the main stone surrounded by a rather bent, but elegantly crafted golden frame. The chain was broken. "Number 7, the broach was not unfastened and dropped, but was torn off in some manner."

"Hold on! You are going too fast!" exclaimed Alison trying to grasp all this sudden news. "You did all this while we were gone? That was a brilliant idea. I searched and searched the grounds, but never found much of anything, save a few walking sticks. So it was buried in the dirt?"

"Yes, I scooped up about an inch or two. It was not on the surface, that's for sure. Of course, the real question is to whom did it belong and when was it lost? It may have nothing to do with this mystery at all," cautioned Darless. "By any chance, do you recognize it?"

"No, I was too little," Alison's hopes sank.

"Me too," May dolefully added. "I've only the vaguest of recollections of what mom wore. I'm no help."

"Don't look at me," put in Mat. "Maybe Christina? She was ten then. Girls that age take note of jewelry and such. Let's pay her a quick visit and see."

"I'll go," Alison said, "No need for all of us to go traipsing into her house. I'll be right back." Alison put her warm coat back on, grabbed her staff, tucked the broach safely into a pouch and chanted her command word. While she was gone, the others complimented Darless on a job well done, as well as wondering how she ever thought of doing the excavation. She just smiled, claiming it was most logical to do so.

Alison was back in less than five minutes. From the look on her face, everyone knew the answer even before she so hastily spoke. "Yes, it *is* mom's! Christina remembers trying it on. She said dad gave it to her as a wedding present and she hardly ever took it off! We are on to something!" Of course, they had no idea of its significance just yet. Speculation ran the gambit from as simple an explanation as she lost it one day all the way to she lost it in her final struggle that fateful night. None would prove correct.

After a half hour of brainstorming the possibilities, Jon realized something, "Hey, wait a minute. We are forgetting about Mandy. Perhaps she can sense what last happened with the broach."

Darless's comment reflected the others, "Duh, why didn't I think of that!"

"Well, should we take it to her or have her come here?" Jon asked.

"Perhaps, the less handling the broach has, the easier time she will have sensing anything about it," observed Alison. "Besides, I'd love to see here again. But perhaps you, Jon, should let her know I want to come get her, when it is convenient for her to come, that is."

Thus, Jon sat back in his chair, calmed his mind and expanded his awareness outward. It was easy to detect the presence of Alison, Darless, and the twins. Slowly he reached across space to Blackthorn Castle and then felt Mandy. He established mental communication and quickly relayed what was wanted. In less than five minutes, Jon brought his attention back to those in the room.

"Okay, Alison, she said give her a half hour to get ready. She and William were out for an evening stroll, enjoying the recent snowfall there. You are to arrive just outside the castle gatehouse, she doesn't want to alarm the guards," Jon announced. So Alison got her coat and wizard staff ready, but the half hour seemed more like six hours to her and the others.

Finally, Alison proclaimed, "Okay everyone, back in a flash with Mandy." She chanted her teleport spell, the version that had no chance for error in arrival location. Two minutes later, she reappeared with Mandy beside her.

"I see you all missed me," teased the ranger, removing her fur coat that she had bought from May, revealing a dress instead of her usual ranger attire. Jon whistled at her. "Glad you noticed, big boy," she teased him back. "Really it is good to see you all. I do miss you, but the renovations are taking some time. It has to be ready by May Day. So what's all this about a missing broach?"

Alison brought her fully up-to-date. "Way to go, Darless! That was good thinking," the ranger complimented. "I doubt that I would ever have thought to sift through the dirt of the roadways looking for clues.

Well, okay, let's see it." May handed it to her. Mandy held it in her hand and closed her eyes and became as receptive as possible to any residual physic energy that may yet be on the broach. Involuntarily, she closed her hand on the broach, clutching it tightly. Then the images came into her mind.

Mandy began whispering softly, "We are captured. Not killed. Rescue us. Hurry." Then the images faded. She opened her eyes and blinked. It was always so disorienting for her to see these images of the past. Is now then or now, is here there or here, that kind of thing.

"Zagroot zounds! And double zagroot zounds!" she cried out very annoyed with herself. "Mandy you dumb fool!"

"What?" implored the others nearly in unison.

"This is not just a broach! It is a magical broach, priestly magic, if I am not mistaken. When one is in dire circumstances, one speaks a message to it and the message remains until it is played back. Your mother was not dead when she purposely dropped this broach. In fact she was trying to send a message to someone. Her words were 'We are captured. Not killed. Rescue us. Hurry.'" Before Mandy could say more, everyone began talking at once. Waving her hand in protest, Mandy exclaimed above the others, "Wait, hold your horses, gang, there is more!" Instant quiet appeared.

"I was able to pick up some faint images of that recording. It was night. She and another man, perhaps your dad, were tied up and riding atop a very large winged creature. It had just taken flight when she whispered her message and dropped the broach into the road below. Shortly after that, a cavalry horse stepped on it, mashing it deep into the relatively soft earth. There it has sat for twenty or so years," Mandy paused for breath.

"But I already knew this information a month ago, only I didn't realize it! You remember all those guard's remains you had me examine?" Alison nodded. "Well, at least four times, I saw the dim outline of a huge flying creature with what appeared to be two small bundles on its back flying off. It was very dark and, at the time, I just thought it was the imagination of the deceased playing tricks on them. Now it makes sense. What kind of flying creature, I cannot tell. I can draw you its basic shape, but I am a lousy artist. Why don't I just place those images in your minds?" The other five watched the dark images appear in their minds. The creature was indeed huge. If the two tiny forms on its back were indeed Alison's parents, then it was perhaps one hundred feet long. It had a very narrow body but an enormous wingspan.

"Oh my gosh!" exclaimed Darless. "I've seen those images a couple times. Lenny has run across them several times, though he still does not know what it is. We both thought it was just a hallucination. Make that a triple zagroot zounds, Mandy!" Both women laughed.

"Don't blame yourselves," Alison pleaded, "it was nearly pitch black and you can only barely tell what it is. But this throws an entirely different complexion on the entire affair. They were kidnaped, taken away by unknown means by person or persons unknown. They were not killed as we all thought. You don't suppose they are still alive? I wonder where they were taken. Where they are at now?"

Everyone began presenting various theories. The most likely one was a dragon had borne them away. But if so, what kind? Mandy, Alison and Jon had encountered white dragons before, when they went in search of the healing tree for Lady Ursla last summer. That was Jon's only experience with dragons, one that he did not like. In spite of all of her travels, Darless had never seen one and had little knowledge of them. Mandy had seen several others, a red, a green and a black dragon. None of these looked anything like what she had just seen. Alison knew a bit about dragons, having fought a green one once on an adventure with Sir Thomas. Again, this one did not look like any kind about which she had read. "Too bad it was so dark that we cannot see its color, that would give us a really good clue as to the type of dragon," she said glumly.

"Are there many dragons around here?" asked Jon, more than a little unsettled about all this talk of dragons.

"Not really, Jon," Alison explained. "They are a rare species, though some sages say a dying species because men and dragons do not abode well together. They eat our herds and steal our valuables or even eat us. If one appears, men band together to hunt it down and kill it. The one I helped kill was a very long way from here."

"How's this likeness" inquired May. While they were all talking, she had been trying to make a charcoal sketch of the dragon from the images Mandy had placed into her mind. Actually, it was quite good and she received compliments from everyone. They stared at her drawing wondering what it was.

While they were engrossed in studying the sketch, the tell-tale sound of metal on stone echoed down the long tunnel entrance to these underground dungeons: clank, clank, clank, rhythmic footsteps. Darless recognized the pattern at once and her eyes began to glow. Shortly Sir Thomas walked into the room, dressed as usual in his full plate armor. He had been off far to the south running that errand for Darless, recompensing victims of the Chasme demon bugs. He did have his helm in his hand, though.

Darless rushed to him and they embraced warmly, for she had not seen him now for several weeks. "All went according to plan, My Lady," he said formally, more for the benefit of the others than for hers. "If I was famous in these lands before, I am triply so now. It should have been you, My Lady, that received all the credit for this deed, but alas, the simple villagers only saw me. But I did try," he sounded apologetically, though Jon saw that he really did enjoy the high esteem which he encountered wherever he went. It was part of being a Holy Paladin, Jon figured, and he was only too glad people did not recognize him as they did Sir Thomas.

Then, surprising everyone, he asked, "Why are you all looking at a sketch of a dragon?" Quickly, Sir Thomas was brought up-to-date on all of the recent events, from the finding of Christina and Stephen, to the sad tale of Ruben, and finally to the broach and Mandy's visions of the dragon. "Well, I'll be," he said over and over, a dozen times during their discussion.

"Perhaps none of your family was actually killed. Congratulations, seven out of eight children found. That is indeed miraculous! Very well done to all of you!" He sincerely meant it. "Not to change the topic, but I have been riding hard since before dawn to get back here today. I know it is only about eight, but can I be excused to take a much needed bath and then perhaps one of you will supply me with some supper. I have only been snacking most of the day. I will ponder this dragon meanwhile. Something about it seems vaguely familiar, like I should recognize it, but I don't. It is a very unusual dragon, if the scale is correct. Too bad we cannot see its color."

Alison pointed him to her bathroom and got him clean towels. Darless helped unfasten the plate armor and then warmed up some leftovers from their dinner for her lover. Meanwhile the others continued their speculations. Just why would a dragon be involved in this sinister plot, none had a justifiable defense. A half hour later, Sir Thomas sat at the table eating and examining the sketch once more. Only now, he looked like a man, not a robot, Jon thought. He had on brown cotton pants and a light blue cotton shirt, a remarkably earthy blend. Jon finally saw what Darless saw in him, he was indeed a striking figure, quite handsome when he was not encased in his armor.

Mandy asked trying to be useful, "Would it help to see the actual images, first hand, like I saw them?"

"Most certainly, but I'm afraid that I do not know anything about viewing these mental images that many of you have. I've no training in such," he replied quite honestly.

"Nothing to it," Mandy replied with just a bit of cockiness in her voice, "Close your eyes and look at this." She replayed the short series of images she picked up from the broach. "And here are the others I picked up from some of the remains of the guards that died here." She recalled in her mind several more images as best she could remember them.

"Now that *is* fascinating indeed! Well done, Mandy," Sir Thomas complimented her. Mandy noted that for the first time, he really paid her an honest, sincere compliment. He *has* changed since I last met him here last August when we were all healing Alison from the Chasme bugs, she thought to herself.

Just then, a small, almost childish voice, spoke up, "Don't like brown dragons." Lenny had walked into the dining room and had been watching, peeking at the drawing of the dragon. All eyes turned to Lenny, staring at him in disbelief. He repeated his speech, "Don't like brown dragons."

"I don't like dragons, period, Lenny," Jon stated flatly, of that he was certain. "Not brown, not white, not green, not any of them. They are dangerous indeed!"

"All dragons are not evil, Jon," corrected Sir Thomas. "Now you take the gold dragons. They are very good creatures; silver, likewise. But yes, red, green, white, black — these kinds are bad. You see, the race of dragons is very much like the race of men. There are both good men and evil men. So it is with dragon-kind. Some are good and very worth knowing and others you want to avoid. Wait a minute! Brown? Lenny, did you really mean that the dragon you saw was a brown one — not copper colored, or brassy or bronze?"

A tear formed in his left eye and slowly dripped down his cheek. He mumbled only, "Yes, not those colors."

"Enough, Sir Thomas," Darless quickly interceded, "we have not yet handled those harmful images. Please, for his mental sake, ask him no more about it." Turning to her patient, she said, "Enough of dragons, Lenny, let's go play a quick game of ball." His eyes brightened up and he rushed to fetch his ball. "You'll excuse me for a couple minutes; I want to make sure he is doing okay." They all agreed and thanked her. Darless took her job very seriously.

"Do my eyes deceive me or is he mostly like a little boy, though his body is twenty-five?" asked Sir Thomas, rather startled by his own observation.

"I'm afraid so," Jon explained. "You see, he was taken prisoner at age five. For twenty years, he has known nothing of life but the most abysmal Abyss prison conditions. He has not matured beyond that point yet. When you look at him, if you can imagine you are talking to a five year old person, you will hit the mark."

"How very sad indeed," Sir Thomas replied. "Will he recover? I mean sort of grow up?"

"We hope so, given lots of time," Jon answered. "If anyone can salvage him, it's Darless. She is just fantastic at it, a natural."

"I am the luckiest man in the entire world," Sir Thomas acknowledged, "that Darless would pick me to wed!" Everyone else grinned in agreement with him.

"You know, Sir Thomas," Mandy spoke up, "when we first met, I thought to myself, 'That man needs an attitude adjustment!' but now I must admit that is not true. Yes, Darless is a treasure of a woman."

With a bit of fire in his cheeks, Sir Thomas hastily re-examined the dragon sketch in an effort to hide his slight embarrassment, muttering over and over "brown, brown, brown."

"There are no brown dragons," he proclaimed loudly. "No, I speak hastily. I have never, ever heard of a brown dragon. There is a difference. Pray, permit me to consult with some of my acquaintances who are more knowledgeable in dragon lore than am I. I will see to it tomorrow, if that meets with your approval."

"Sure, that would be most helpful," Alison replied, "but you do need to spend at least one night here with Darless. I know she has missed you terribly." He blushed once again. "I know you like to ride Acheron everywhere you go, but it does take a lot of time traveling by horse. If we could just teleport where you desire to go, then I could come with you and it would take a lot less time."

"Yes, what is a paladin without his trusty steed?" he chuckled and then answered his own question, "but a mage without her staff." Everyone laughed. "If this had occurred recently, I would beg you to use all spells with the greatest of haste so that we may yet be in time to rescue Basil and Anna. This message comes after twenty years, so haste is not needed. Nevertheless, I am willing to let you use your magic to transport us, Alison. Just don't land us underground." Everyone chuckled; here was a man who really did not like magical means of transportation. He preferred to get there by his own means, on horseback. He added, "Also I would like to show Darless my castle at le Bonnaire; she's never seen it."

"What castle?" Darless returned in time to hear his last words.

"My Lady, I keep forgetting to tell you I own a castle at le Bonnaire, a small village on the western edge of Lockwood Forest. It's about a week's riding if you go by the roads, or only two long days if you cut across country, as I usually do. It's a modest castle, for my meager needs. I am seldom there, though. I would love to show it to you, when you have time." Ordinarily, Darless would have jumped at the chance to spend time with him and see his castle, but just now, she was torn between her desires and those of her patient, Lenny, whom she was giving daily therapy sessions.

"Darless, please take a few days off from Lenny," implored Alison. "Jon can probably fill in for you for a little while. You deserve some time for yourself! You've been at it daily for months now.

"I insist, too," Jon agreed. "I can continue with Lenny for a couple days. Go have some fun with Sir Thomas. When he gets back, we can try to figure out this dragon business."

Darless started to protest, but both Alison and Jon were insistent. She agreed. Hugging Sir Thomas, they went for a private stroll around the confining dungeon areas.

"Well, I'm off," Mandy announced. "William's expecting me back soon. Can anyone give me a lift?"

"I'll take you," Jon said. "I need some air. Back in a jiffy, love." Jon stepped Mandy back to her castle, arriving just outside the gatehouse.

"Thanks, Jon," she said and gave him a bye kiss. As she walked slowly toward her gatehouse, Jon heard her muttering to herself, "There is no such thing as a brown dragon or my name isn't Mandy Blackthorn!" He stepped back into Alison's dining room, thinking of dragons.

Chapter 4 Of Threngold, the Brown Dragon

The red glow of Friday's dawn streaked streams of fire across the whitened lands about Castle d'Ambrose. Sir Thomas, always up at the crack of dawn, watched the splendor of the new day grow. It was quite cold and his fingers were getting numb as he finished saddling his large heavy warhorse, Acheron. He'd already tacked Darless's light riding horse. "I'm going to have to teach her about horses," he mused. "She should be riding at least a medium warhorse, if only for her own protection. Yes, she did ask for sword lessons; I really wonder which type of sword she will pick."

"Why, dearest, is there any difference?" Darless asked curiously. She had finished dressing up in her warmest clothes and had come outside, overhearing his question. "It sure is a pretty winter morning. Bit cold though."

"Ah, the morning pales when you appear, My Lady," and he meant it. She smiled and they shared a brief kiss. "Well, yes, the type of sword does matter," Sir Thomas remembered her original question. "But we can discuss it when you are ready for sword lessons. Are you all set to go?"

"Yes, everything is taken care of and I've packed a few things we may need in my portable hole. I guess we are off. I am glad you are not wearing your plate armor this trip, I get to see more of you," she teased. The paladin had stowed his armor in a large bag now hooked to his saddle. He wore his heavy winter deerskin coat lined with wool. Still, he wore his white tunic with a blue cross over his outer coat, so that the symbol of his paladin-hood was always unmistakably clear. "Let me help you mount." He graciously helped her climb into the saddle, though she really did not need such. She realized that she could safely act the part of a "fine lady" when she was around him, for he treated her as such. She found it both surprisingly comfortable and enjoyable. For most all of her life to date, she had to look out for herself, no one else would.

He put on his gloves and sprung into the saddle. *What grace in his well-practiced movements*, she thought. "Which way?"

"Due northwest. My place is virtually northwest of here about seventy miles. We can ride side by side cross-country. Look, we now are making our own path in the virgin snow field," he replied. She looked up at him, perched about two feet higher then she was; Acheron was quite tall. He looked down at her. "My stallion here is called Acheron, the Fearless. He has seen many battles and has never flinched from combat. He's a fine companion on a long journey. What do you call your mare? She has good conformation."

"Why, do they have names? Mandy neglected to tell me that. I don't know. I've been calling it just 'horse.' One minute and I'll ask her. Fleetfoot, she likes to be called Fleetfoot. I think she likes to gallop swiftly," she chuckled. "She sure is smaller than Acheron. I guess there are a lot of different types of horses."

"Oh, there most certainly are! I am a fine judge of horseflesh," he commented. "Due to my training as a paladin," he added quickly so as to not seem overly boastful. "I've been meaning to discuss the possibility of training you to ride a medium warhorse. It can carry more weight, can actually fight in your defense, looks after you if you are down, and can bear up to those unexpected surprises one occasionally meets while on the road. That is to say, a trained war horse does not spook easily, if at all, whereas your riding horse probably already has. Besides, when we ride together, we'd be more nearly at the same level," he grinned.

"My Love, I've been meaning to ask you something rather personal," Darless changed the subject to one that she had been debating for weeks. "Perhaps you know that many of my friends and I use what might be called mental telepathy to communicate with each other and so on. Jon, Alison, who has only recently gained the ability in part from Ukko's touch I believe, Mandy and I, we all use it to our advantage. But there are ethics involved with its use. While I can easily read another's mind, their current thoughts, I do not do so unless the other first gives me permission to do so."

"I can see why. One's thoughts are private! Sometimes, what one thinks at one moment can change utterly at another. Had you read my thoughts when I first met you, why you would think I was plotting your death. Yet, if you read them now," he grinned teasingly, "I might be very embarrassed. But what is your question, My Lady?"

She hesitated, "When I have need to communicate with you and speech is not optimum, may I have your permission to plant my thought into your mind? I promise to read only your reply, if it is a question."

"Sure, you so have it. But does it hurt? I have never had such an experience. How will I know it is your thought and not some stray idea that has chosen this moment to pop into my mind? They do, you know, stray thoughts, pop into my mind, unbidden."

It's me. I love you. Darless reached out and pervaded his being and placed those thoughts in his mind.

His reaction was just as she expected. "Oh my! There cannot ever be any doubts of its origin! But, but," he faltered for words, unsure of how to explain what he felt. He said rather hesitatingly, "Why, this is *so* intimate, like a gentle wisp of air blowing against your face, if that's an accurate description. I really am at a loss for words to describe it."

"Yes, intimate is the closest word for it. To do it, I must form a bond with you and momentarily rather be you. I share your space. Jon can even take over total control of your body. He's done that to help save the day on a number of occasions, though I have no idea how he does that."

"Can I learn how to do that, to communicate with you without words?" he asked.

"I don't know. If you had asked me a year ago, I would have answered, no, you are either born with the ability or not. Yet, so much has changed in the last year. Jon certainly has been the catalyst. I now see Alison blending magical power with spiritual power; she says the lines between them are thin. And the two sets of twins, why they always know what the other is thinking. So now, my best guess is that as we come to know each other really well, perhaps you will be able to reach out to me and touch me mentally. I just don't know. It must be really hard for people not to be able to do this. I just cannot imagine life without it."

"Until a moment ago, I did not know I was missing anything!" and he roared with mirth; she likewise.

"Say is that a house I see up ahead?" Darless inquired. In the distance, about a mile off yet, a single adobe home took shape, smoke curling from its chimney.

"You have good eyes," he replied. "Yes, that'll be the Walpole's place. All these lands about us are deeded to the d'Ambrose family. She really has about six hundred and forty square miles of fertile grasslands to her name. Her family's land grant goes from the edge of the Verbenloc Mountains about forty miles to the east all across the grasslands to the Rolling Hills about forty miles to the west and from the edge of the Lockwood Forest up north to the edge of the Druse Woods to the south. Stonefist Castle guards all of the Rolling Hills. My meager castle is at the western edge of the Lockwood

Forest and commands many miles of range lands further west."

"Ah yes, now it is starting to make more sense. Alison found some of Basil's journals and we were reading them. One section dealt with the land grant. I really know nothing about such matters. Never had the need to know," she explained.

"Care for a bit of history as we ride along?" he asked as he waved to one of the Walpole children, who was doing some chores outside the cabin. She nodded eagerly.

"About seventy-five years ago, all these northern lands were wild and untamed. Many fell creatures roamed at will. Now far to the south, several hundred leagues, I'm not quite sure of the distance, no maps, lies the great kingdom of Greylands and the huge city of la Grande Ville Grise, the Great Grey City, where all of our ancestors came from originally. Now occasionally the evil creatures that inhabited these lands would foray down into the more remote northern parts of the kingdom, wreaking havoc. So King d'Ville offered land grants to those hardy adventurers who would come up north here and drive the evil, wild men out. My grandfather, Sir Herman le Bonnaire — also a paladin, he influenced me into taking up this profession, actually — and Raven d'Ambrose — who was Basil's father — Louis la Fontaine, Herman Fitzgerald, Edward Fist, Helmut Sharpedge, Melvin Jascar, Lalos Duncan, and Friar le George, all took up the challenge. They formed one large party and drove the evil from these lands far into the northern wastes. That is why they each received land grants about seventy-five years ago."

"Ah, suddenly all these towns make more sense," said Darless. "Melvin Jascar settled in Jascar Mines, Louis la Fontaine founded la Fontaine, Raven d'Ambrose started to build Castle d'Ambrose and probably finished by Basil, Herman Fitzgerald, Fitzgerald Castle, but I am not so sure where the others fit in."

"Helmut Sharpedge, was half-elf and he founded Edgeway. Edward Fist, Stonefist Castle, Lalos Duncan, Duncanville, Friar le George, who had a mostly bald head with tufts around his ears I'm told, founded Fountain Head, mostly as a joke, I assume," he explained.

"I guess he had a sense of humor. Is your grandfather still alive? Say, what about the rest of your family? Of them, I know nothing!" she suddenly realized how little she knew of her man.

"No, my grandparents are all long deceased. My father, Henry, a retired fighter, and mother, Louisa, are in their late fifties and still live in the castle. You will get to meet them, if you choose. I know they are dying to meet the woman who at long last captured their eldest son's heart! I think that they had pretty much given up on me," he jested. "I have an older sister, Jenny, who is married to a hunter and they have three children and live just within the boundaries of Lockwood Forest. I have a younger brother, Samuel, who is away down south in a monastery learning to be a priest. At the castle proper, are just my parents and our staff, some fifty guards, my five squires, and my personal cavalry, some fifty strong. Actually, the main house of the castle is quite deserted. We can have an entire floor to ourselves, if we like. I just use it as a home base of operations, for I am on the go, so to speak, so very much of the time." He paused and added rather quietly, "You know, it is rather dull and boring around there. You were very wise to build your college in Alison's new town. I really think it will be a better place to raise a family, too."

They rode in silence for some minutes. Sir Thomas had a strange thought, "My Love, when I am off far away from here, will you still be able to reach me with your thoughts? To touch me as you did a while back?" He turned in the saddle to look her full in the face.

She turned to face him, eyes glowing, "My Love, my thoughts span all distance, for it knows no distance. Yes, you can be hundreds of miles from me, and I can still place my thoughts in you just as I did earlier. You would notice no difference. Jon and I have done so across a huge distance." He grinned shyly; she could tell that he was more than pleased to hear that conclusion.

"Pray, talk to me often when I am away! You cannot know how lonely I felt these last three weeks while I was off recompensing the Chasme demons' victims. My heart longed for thee."

"Yes, I do, for I longed for thee as well!" she replied. "But since I had neglected to ask you before you left, I hesitated doing so. I will hesitate no longer! Oh yes, if I am contacting you at an inconvenient time, say while you are fighting a battle or using the latrine, why think it so to me. Jon always gets so embarrassed when he contacts me and I am using the restroom." Both chuckled.

"Say, what do you make of this brown dragon thing?" she asked. "Do you suppose that Lenny got his colors confused? The images Mandy saw were so dark, color was impossible to tell. May be Lenny also could not see well."

Sir Thomas rattled off the litany list of dragons, known by their skin colors. Whites were often found in regions of perpetual winter, for they loved the cold and their breath blew a chill wind, as Darless already had knew from Jon and Alison. Reds breathed a hot fire and flames. Greens, a noxious gas. And so went the litany, but no browns. "Where did dragons originate?" she asked.

"Well, sages suggest that in the depths of Hell lives the maker of dragon-kind, Tiamat, the multi-colored dragon, mother of all dragons. From her, it is said, all the other dragons were begat. But I cannot vouch for the veracity of that statement, for it seems too unlikely in my mind. Tiamat is the epitome of evil. It is said she retains a compliment of special male breeding dragons that she mates with from time to time," he answered, recalling his earlier training from when he was in his early teens. "I was awfully young when I was studying about dragons, not much call for dragon lore in these parts. I did not pay as close attention as I should have, regrettably."

"Hum, I assume then that her breeding males were of these various different colors? So if she wanted to create more red dragons, she'd breed with her special red male?" she presumed.

"Ah, now, well, no. Oh my gosh! How stupid of me to have forgotten! Browns! The breeding males were all browns! We've identified it! Darless, you have done it!" He got very excited indeed.

"No, you did it, I was just asking," she replied. "We just pulled up a long forgotten, and probably quite useless, fact you crammed into your head more than a dozen years ago, that's all. I'm glad you remembered it. Now that we have identified them, what can you tell me about brown dragons?"

He scratched his head and thought for a minute. Sheepishly, he answered, "That is about all, I fell asleep shortly after the sage began talking about them. I do recall that they were all usually located somewhere in Hell. So that doesn't do us much good, now does it?"

"Hum," Darless bit her lip, "Jon is not going to like this one bit. Dispater, the Arch-devil of Hell, has been in and around us on numerous occasions now. Why does that strike me as very significant? Or am I just being paranoid?"

"I don't see how Dispater and Tiamat, either one, could have been behind the castle's destruction twenty years ago. What would be their gain? No, it seems more connected to the Holy Scepter of Ukko and the Demon Lords than it does to the denizens of the planes of Hell," he answered.

"Okay. But I'll let Jon know about the brown dragons." She concentrated a moment. "There, he knows and will let the others know."

"What, you already communicated with Saint Jon?" he asked a bit bewildered by the nearly non-existent passage of time.

"Yes, mental telepathy, you may call it. Fast and efficient, don't you think?"

"Wow! Yes, yes indeed! The speed, this is something for me to marvel over! I see now that this ability or gift can be incredible useful, My Dearest Lady!" He was genuinely sincere.

I know appeared in his mind; Darless smiled at him. They rode on across the white lands.

When Jon relayed Darless's message about the brown dragons, Alison got very excited. She insisted on learning more about the browns right away. No one could restrain her enthusiasm to get started on this new project. After her spells were cast for the day, around one o'clock, she bid Jon a brief farewell. She was off to try to get a visit with the Archmage Coventry Banner, in Banner Towers.

Jon had just finished washing up all the dishes around the place when she reappeared, looking quite dejected. "Hi honey, you're back awfully soon. Did you meet with your Archmage?"

"No, he would not see me. His savant said that he was too old and worn out to see people any more. But at least he did give me one suggestion. I was told to seek out Artimus, the Wise, whoever he is. But it is more like 'where he is' — that's the problem — no one knows exactly where he is at the moment. So I got nowhere. Darn, I was so hopeful."

"I know, I know. Maybe in time we can find this Artimus fellow. We can check around, perhaps someone will know," he tried to sound a bit optimistic. But there was no changing her dour mood that afternoon.

Eventually, Jon went down to the construction zone to see Zender, his dwarven musician friend, coerced into being the main chef for the working crews.

He found him stirring several large vats of stew for the next meal. "If only dwarves did not eat so much," complained Zender. "What brings you here, Jon, a desire to stir perhaps?" he said jokingly.

"Nah, Alison's moody. She tried to see an archmage who was too old and feeble to see anyone any more. She was told to seek out Artimus, the Wise, but no one seems to know where the fellow is at right now," Jon explained.

"Ah, mages can be fickled, yes indeed." After giving it another stir, he inquired, "And what would a powerful mage like Alison want to go see an archmage for, if you don't mind my asking?"

"Dragons. We suspect a brown dragon may have had something to do with the castle's destruction here, some twenty years ago. She wanted to find out information about brown dragons. That's all," Jon replied, nibbling on one of Zender's apples.

"Ah dragons, brown even," his eyes twinkled. He quickly grabbed his stringed instrument, something of a cross between a lute and a guitar and began to play. The woeful sounds of a major lament echoed through the room. Jon noted that it was likely in a minor key, if indeed dwarven music even had key signatures. Then, Zender added the beginning words to the lament.

"Far across the distant times
Came the giant, Tiamat,
Fell dragon dark and bold,
Mother of the dragon folds.
Through Browns she does but blend
All colors strong and proud.
From Brown, she does extract
The Reds she then begat.
From Brown, she does extract

The Whites she did begat.
From Brown, she does extract
The Greens she doth begat.
And Silvers, Golds, and Bronzes too,
And Coppers, Brass and Black were made,
All these she did begat,
Far deep in torment lands.
Oh, Tiamat, why did'st thou thus?
To maim and kill us all?"

He paused and said, "Lament of Tiamat, tis called; it goes on for about a half hour."

Jon cried, "Zender! That was a fantastic sound, great song. I didn't know you knew all about dragons!"

"Dwarves know much about dragon-lore. We have to because we lay claim to great wealth, great piles of gold and jewels. Dragons love and greatly desire such treasure. So we are the prime targets of a dragon's ire," he explained.

"So you know about the brown dragons?" Jon asked incredulously.

"Certainly, what is it you wish to know about the browns?" replied the dwarf, only too anxious to get out of his chef duties for a time.

"Hold on, let me go get Alison so she can hear this too first hand! Thank you, Zender!" Jon ran as fast as he could go to get Alison.

She was absentmindedly straightening up the kitchen as Jon ran into the room. "Come on — right now," he cried excitedly. "You'll never guess who knows about brown dragons!"

Those two magic words instantly brought the sullen magic user out of her doldrums the very moment they were uttered. She grabbed her coat and followed him down the tunnel, "Who, for heaven's sake, who?" He teased her by not answering until they reached Zender's place.

"Zender!" Jon exclaimed. "They, the dwarves, need to know all about dragons just to protect all that wealth they accumulate. He's about to tell me all about the browns. But you gotta hear the start of his song, Lament of Tiamat; it's great! Zender, we're here." So Alison, too, heard the start of this sad lament. However, she was more anxious for him to finish and to begin telling her about the browns.

"Patience dear mage," Zender cautioned, "the fates of browns are tied inextricably to that of Tiamat, Queen of Darkness, Lady of the Fires of Hell, herself. This vile, evil incarnate creature has birthed all the races of dragons, it is said. Fortunate are we, that she desires to mate so infrequently, for it is written each mating produces a new race of dragons to defy us all. Now it is said that she spawned the race of browns for the sole purpose of her breeding, satisfying her despicable lust. She forbids any browns to mate with any other dragons but her. Nay, they are wholly unable to do so, unless they desire to risk her wonton ire."

"Browns number twenty at last report, since Singahl met his doom at the hands of the elfin princes some fifty years ago. Each brown is highly jealous of the others; each desires to be the one next chosen by Tiamat, when her mood is wont. Thus, of necessity, browns live a very isolated life, far from each other. They are scattered far and wide across the planes of the universe. Each amasses vast wealth, particularly gold and jewels, by which to impress Tiamat of their worthiness to breed. They are cunning, vicious, without remorse, ever seeking more wealth by any means possible."

"Physically they are between one hundred and one hundred-eighty feet long, with narrow, slender bodies and great wings of power, each with claws of iron and hooks of steel that can shred flesh as though parchment. Powerful legs, capable of tireless running, propel them overland, though not as swiftly as a horse bears a man.

Yet, each leg can rend a man or dwarf in half, crushing it to tiny particles. It is said that a flip of its tail crushes boulders into pebbles. Its skin is like steel, though flexible as leather. No sword's edge can penetrate its hide, save those that are highly enchanted."

"And their breath is so foul, so toxic, that, should a brown breathe on you, you'll swoon and fall unconscious to your doom. Tales tell of a dwarf's flesh rotting off his bones from this vile dragon breath." Zender now was highly animated, "And if this is not enough, each brown is an accomplished magic user with many powerful spells in his arsenal. Indeed, they have some form of built-in immunity to many magical spells, such as fire and cold ones. They are devious and treacherous, for they often assume the form of a man or dwarf to spy out their next victims. Woe be to any man or woman who stands in the way of a brown!"

He calmed down a bit, "We dwarves have a saying, 'See a brown, run like hell' and we do. So I say to you, if a brown dragon is connected to your plot, leave it alone, go away, forget about it."

"Gosh, don't they have *any* weakness?" implored Alison who was getting a very bad feeling about this brown dragon situation.

"None," Zender paused. "Well, they do love to talk and bargain, if you call that a weakness."

"Are any browns supposed to be around here? How do we go about finding out where browns are likely to be? Where do they live?" she asked one after the other. "They must, of necessity, be extremely rare creatures."

"As for your first query, probably not, or we would have been given strict orders to be on the look-out for them. But I will send along a message to Nain asking him about it, if you like."

"Oh yes, please do. Thanks," she replied.

"To your second, dunno. I have no idea. We are told they live in remote, desolate areas, usually in some kind of underground chamber, which they fill with many spells and webs of protection designed to ward off intruders and to protect their vast wealth, when they are away accumulating more."

"Zender? Where's our meal?" A red-nosed dwarf stood in the doorway, complaining about the delay.

"Coming right up," Zender hastily proclaimed in order to shut him up. "I've got to get going and feed this crew."

"Thanks, you've been exceedingly helpful," Alison graciously acknowledged him and she and Jon left, walking slowly back to her underground dungeon, home for only a little longer. Neither said much until they sat down at the kitchen table.

There, May and Mat, of course, wanted to know all about what she had learned. The mage repeated what she had learned from Zender. Then she asked, "Oh, Jon, can you let Darless and Mandy know what we've found out, please dear?"

Jon spent the next half hour communicating this new information to the alu-demon and to the ranger. Neither was particularly pleased to hear the details, especially the nearly impervious to attacks part. He had finished and Alison had just made everyone a pot of tea, mostly to have something familiar to do while she pondered all of this rather ill news, when suddenly a bird flew into the room. It had entered at the tunnel's entrance and came straight into the kitchen, perching on the top of an empty chair.

"It's a snowy owl," exclaimed Alison is complete surprise.

"How'd it get in here?" wondered Jon.

The white bird ruffled its feathers and straightened itself up and spoke, shocking everyone! "Archmage Coventry Banner has sent me with the following message for Alison d'Ambrose. The message is:

'My apologies for being physically unable to see you. I'm afraid my body has grown far too old for me. Ahem. You are to tell her this: nearly twenty-one years ago, in the early evening I saw a dragon fly just to the south of my towers heading in a sweeping curve in your general direction. Then, late the next night, I saw it retracing its route, heading off nearly eastward from here but slightly to the south. On the return flight, I glimpsed its color, brown, if I am not mistaken. The only brown on this plane in the last two hundred years goes by the name of Threngold, a consort of Tiamat. Location: unknown. Estimated flying time from here to your castle is twenty-four hours.'

End of message. Do I need to repeat it?" The bird sat patiently awaiting her reply.

"Er, no. Tell the Archmage, thank you very, very much!" Alison could not believe her good fortune in hearing from the most skilled magic user that she ever had heard about. With that, the bird took flight, departing just as suddenly as it had come.

"Remarkable indeed!" exclaimed Jon, "A talking bird. I never knew that they could talk, aloud, that is."

"It probably is Coventry's familiar and has been endowed with much magic," explained Alison, absentmindedly, for her mind was racing over the import of his message.

"Wow! He sent you a personal message," exclaimed May. "Boy do you ever rate! What an honor indeed! Things are now making a bit more sense. A brown dragon was aiding or helping attack the castle here that night. That explains how so much damage was done to the walls so quickly. And it ties in with the images of mom and dad being carried off on the back of the dragon."

"But why?" interjected Mat. "If the browns only do things to gain them wealth, why would he attack this castle and run off with our parents? There was certainly no wealth to be gained. Admittedly, I was pretty young, but I cannot remember our folks having any great treasures here, save the Holy Scepter. No, it does not make sense yet. We must be missing something."

"Yes, it both fits and it doesn't fit," Alison continued their train of thought. "It fits from the point of all the sudden destruction and matches the physic trauma images Mandy observed. But you are right; it doesn't fit from all that we just learned from Zender. Either Zender is loose with his facts or this Threngold was perhaps only following orders."

Jon spoke up, "Darless wants me to tell you another theory. Suppose Lord Jarred was behind the whole affair in an attempt to obtain the Holy Scepter. Maybe he hired Threngold to help him carry out the affair. That would make it make more sense and also answer why the dragon could be seen flying off with your parents. He was following orders. Oh, yes, I relayed the owl's visit to Mandy and Darless," he added. Alison nodded her thanks.

"Well, where could he have taken them?" wondered May. "We all just came from that direction. We saw no signs of dragons anywhere along the way."

"I'm afraid I need to see the maps," Jon added, "I'm just not very familiar with these lands yet." Alison got out all of her maps. There was no single map that covered everything. But she laid out her local map that included Verbenloc and the Greenway. Beside it, up north, she overlayed another that showed the trail all the way to Banner's Tower. Next to it, she laid out the more recently acquired map that showed Tannersville and the Desolation Range which they had crossed with the caravan a few months ago. Finally, she laid out yet another map showing the southern Plains of Gorsagatha all the way to Leeds Tower. There was, of course, a huge gap — there was nothing shown below Banner's Tower down to Leeds, and nothing at all west of Leeds to where it might connect to the southern portion of the Desolation Range. Jon's comment summed it up. "Well that part fits, the general area the dragon was heading toward appears to be about as deserted and desolate as possible!"

May commented, "Well, if Darless were here she'd probably say something like, Number 1, we know that the dragon took your parents away alive. Number 2, he went eastward toward the Desolation Range. Number 3, it does indeed appear desolate on these maps. Number 4, that is in keeping with what we assume to be the traits of a brown dragon." Everyone chuckled at her observations, but she added seriously, "Now what do we do? Try to search every inch of that area? That could take a long time and who knows what all we may encounter besides that dragon?"

Mat appended, "We are city dwellers and have no experience with these kinds of situations, Runtkin. It would seem a rather difficult task to launch an expedition here in the late winter."

Alison smiled hearing the name the twins used to call her when she was three. "I would agree. Winter is not the best time to go searching unknown territory. Besides, what are we going to do if we should find his lair? Walk right in and ask: 'What did you do to our parents twenty years ago?' I think we would all be toasted on the spot. I'm afraid I have to think on this a good deal. If this was the day after the attack, why I'd drop everything and charge forward. But it's been nearly twenty-one years now. As much as I hate it, I need more time to devise something workable. The first thing must be to find a way to narrow the search. For all we know, his lair is beyond

Desolation. It could be in the range beyond Freetown or even farther." Dejection covered everyone's face.

"Well, how far is Banner's Tower from here, as the dragon flies, so to speak?" Jon asked, reflecting upon the snowy owl's message. "The bird said that the flying time is twenty-four hours from here to there. Maybe that gives us some ideas." Alison measured the maps and estimated perhaps two hundred miles. "Then, that would mean another twenty-four hours from Banner's Tower to the Desolation Range. Certainly the dragon cannot fly non-stop for two days here and another two days back. Surely, he must have rested somewhere. If it went to the mountains beyond Freetown, that is at least another four days travel time, ignoring resting."

"Why would a dragon who has magic spells be flying them instead of just teleporting them?" asked May. "If he did not know the teleport spell, then I'd say he were not a very powerful magician." May was alluding to her own lack of skill in not knowing that spell while in Freetown. Only recently had she learned it after gaining so much experience on the long caravan trip. Secretly, this was her standard for measuring the worthiness of a mage. Until they could use the teleport spell, as far as she was concerned, they were just beginning wizards.

"Perhaps not all wizards know that spell," offered Jon.

"No, she's right. Learning to teleport is fundamental to all higher level mages. It is inconceivable that this brown dragon cannot use that spell," Alison defended her older sister. "It might be that he used up all his higher level spells and had to resort to flying away. But then what would keep him from teleporting the next day? If so, he could be anywhere at all." Again, dejection filled all faces.

"I've an idea," Jon said breaking the gloomy silence. "If Coventry saw the dragon flying at night, why could not someone else have seen him as well?"

"You mean that we should go around asking folks if they saw a dragon flying high in the sky twenty-one years ago?" asked Alison in disbelief.

"Well, it might work if there were any towns or villages out there in this vast emptiness between Banner's Tower and the southern part of Desolation," Jon sighed, realizing the futility of that idea. "I guess it just boils down to the simple fact we have no idea what or who is out there — no maps."

May offered an idea, "I could take Jake and go to Tannersville and visit all the map shops and gather what I can find. Perhaps we can get some idea what lies to the south of Tannersville."

"Now you're talking sis," exclaimed Alison. "And I can take Jon and search the map stores down around Duncanville for anything north and east of there. Maybe we can fill in some holes in our maps." Thus, the discussion ended for the time being.

The next day, May teleported Jake and herself back to Tannersville in search of maps. In the afternoon, Alison did likewise, taking Jon and herself down to Duncansville.

That evening, everyone poured over the new maps, discussing what they now knew. Alison began with a description of the southerly Plains of Gorsagatha. This region consisted of arid, low rolling, reddish hills. Vegetation was sparse; little rain fell here. The desert-like conditions got worse and worse as one approached Last Town and the Sea of Salt. Just beyond Last Town, the land became too salty for anything to grow. This area, the Saline Flats, was a band about twenty miles wide around the Sea of Salt.

But the further reaches of the plains, though desert-like, were inhabited by nomadic bandits and a few metal workers. Ore and coal veins occasionally surfaced on a hillside, convenient for those hardy enough to take advantage. Alison explained that a hundred years ago, priests of Ukko united and cast all brigands out of the fertile valleys of the north and the forest of the east. They were driven onto these arid plains as the priests of Ukko brought law and order to one and all. Not much was known of the lands beyond the Sea of Salt, though. Alison had found one rough map which showed the Red Hills as a circular band of rolling, semi-arid hills some hundred-twenty miles in diameter. They began just east of the Sea of Salt and stretched north and eastward, ending at large river called the Gorge of Diego, presumably a mostly dry river. It was rumored that the hills were inhabited by metal workers and bandits.

Now this coincided with the maps May and Jake had discovered. Their newly acquired map showed a name for the huge arid plains that the caravan had crossed and where they had defeated the Hobgoblin hordes and Lord Jarred; it was called the Arid Plains. No towns or villages were marked on its vast open space. However, just south of there, their maps illustrated a region named the Canyon Lands, bordered on the west by the Gorge of Diego and ending some forty miles from the foothills of the southern portion of the Desolation Range. Rumors were rampant on this area. Yet, all agreed upon two points: the canyons were indeed spectacular to behold and the inhabitants were nomadic tribes who were brown-skinned.

"You know, if I just had an airplane, we could fly over the region and see for ourselves," Jon declared a bit frustrated. Of course, he then found himself trying to explain that it was a flying machine. He regretted his outburst.

"Well one thing is clear," Jake added, "if you go there, you need to take a rather large amount of supplies with you. It sure doesn't look like you could resupply anywhere once you leave Banner's Tower or perhaps Tannersville."

Thus, the acquisition of some crude maps did aid in their understanding of their situation, but offered no new ideas on how best to proceed, rather that information arrived nearly a week later via Zender.

In the middle of the afternoon, Zender came stumping down the underground tunnel entrance, calling out Jon's name in a rather excited tone of voice. "Hi, Zender. Come on in. What's got you so chipper?" Jon said. He and Alison were once more looking at the maps, searching for ideas.

Proudly, the dwarf exclaimed, "I've heard back from Nain himself!" He considered it a high honor to have this legendary dwarf actually personally ask him to relay a message to Alison. "Nain did some searching concerning your brown dragon, Threngold. He got word to the stone giants that we were looking for any traces of Threngold. And you will never guess what he found out."

"I'm all ears," teased Alison, rather impatient to hear this latest news.

The dwarf continued, eyes shining with delight, "Threngold has been seen frequently by the stone giants of South Wash! Here, I'll show you where their clan is located on your maps." He pointed to a spot within the southern extremities of Desolation just opposite of the Canyon Lands to the west. "Nain says the giants report that he has been sighted flying from south of South Wash out over the plains into the Canyon Lands and flying from the Canyon Lands back over Desolation. He's been sighted a dozen times doing this in the last month! Nain also says you should stay far, far, far, far away from brown dragons."

"Wow! Now that is the very news we have been desperately wanting!" exclaimed Alison, who felt a huge burden lifted from her shoulders. "Thank you, thank you, thank you. Tell Nain that I really needed that information. It is very timely indeed! Now we can make plans at long last."

"You, you are really not going after this dragon, are you?" he asked sheepishly. From her eyes, he got all the answer he needed. "Oh no! Don't do this. It will be your doom!"

"I certainly hope not or all this castle building will be for naught!" she replied. "Don't worry, we will be extra careful. I want to live to a ripe old age in my new castle, Zender."

"Hi all. Did you miss us?" the voice of Darless broke in on them. She and Sir Thomas had just returned from a vacation visit to his castle up north. From the rosy color in her cheeks, Jon knew that she had had a very enjoyable time with her paladin fiancé.

"Oh please, dear lady, please talk her out of tangling with this brown dragon!" Zender animatedly cried out. "Tis folly. Only death and worse awaits you. Run from the dragon; that's the dwarven way." He left to resume his chef duties, shaking his head all the way out of the tunnel.

"Hi Darless, looks like you and Sir Thomas had a wonderful time. Glad you are back though. I give you back your patient, Lenny," Jon teased. Darless and Sir Thomas were welcomed back and plied with many questions. It was obvious to all that the private time the two shared had been most welcomed by the two lovers. Then, both were briefed on the latest news of the sightings of Threngold and the presumed locations on the patch-work maps.

"Probably a journey of four hundred miles to the edge of the Canyon Lands," commented Sir Thomas, "assuming we go by way of Banner's Tower before we cut southeast. Also, assuming we do not push either the horses or ourselves, it's around twenty days of travel. Though, in the wintertime, only a hardy soul would camp out at night."

"That's for the best," Alison sighed, "for with this construction, I cannot leave for at least another month.

But who should go with me? This is likely the most perilous adventure I've heard about. I cannot ask any of you to go with me. Frankly, with the coming of spring, I am desperate for someone to organize the townsfolk and oversee the construction while I am away. We all cannot go."

"Mat and I volunteer to see to the Ville and, with the help of Stephen, we should be able to handle everything in that department. I really do not relish another long trip," May declared.

"Well, that takes a load off of my mind," Alison agreed. "Thanks. If we should need you, one of us can come and get you in a blink."

"I am for sure going," said Jon.

"Me too," pronounced Darless. "By then, Lenny ought to be in good shape."

"And don't forget me," said Mandy, who just appeared, picture book in hand. Jon had just summoned her. He knew she would feel very offended if she were left out. "You will most definitely need the services of a ranger on this trip."

"Where'd you come from? Or rather," Alison exclaimed, startled by her sudden appearance, but she didn't finish her sentence. One glance at Jon's sheepish smile, told her it was his doing. "Hi Mandy. No, I would not think of not giving you the chance, but really it is very dangerous this time. We may all die in the attempt."

"Verily, you shall not perish as long as Sir Thomas yet breathes!" he declared. "So do I bring my cavalry or just my squires or perhaps my other fellow adventurers?"

Alison tried to be diplomatic, "If we travel with the whole cavalry, certainly we will be safe from bandits along the way. But should we encounter the dragon, they would most certainly be doomed. No, I think no cavalry this trip, don't you think?"

"You speak truly, great mage. I shall settle for my squires, then," the large man replied.

"But they would be in the same situation," she protested.

"Well, I do need someone to help me put on my plate armor and to fix it and such," Sir Thomas protested.

"I have just the solution," the familiar voice of Lonnie called out from the back of the room. He and Thea had quietly stolen in — neither wanting to be left out of the coming adventure.

"What?" cried Alison. "Does everyone know of my plans?"

"Forsooth, tis hard to hide the fact that you are shortly to be off in search of your parents and their fate. I am a paladin and, though not even vaguely as skilled and knowledgeable as Sir Thomas, I can serve as his squire as need be. I am familiar with armor and weapons and horses. I can stay behind and protect them, when you close with the dragon. I would be most useful."

"And where Lonnie goes, I am going too," called out Thea defiantly. "I know I am just a beginner, but I want to go and learn all I can. Besides you will need a cook and mender of clothes on so long a journey. I promise to stay out of the way. Besides, I do know some magic and can help Lonnie protect the horses and stuff. Please, Mage Alison, please don't leave me behind." Her pleading could not help touch Alison's heart. She saw at once that these two were falling in love with each other; she knew the pain of being parted.

"But Thea, this promises to be a very, very dangerous mission we are embarking upon. Are you really sure about this?"

"I promise to protect her with my life," interjected Lonnie.

"Yes, ma'am, I am very certain. I want to go too," she said, still pleading desperately with her voice and emotions.

At last Alison consented, but only if her parents approved of it. Thea promised she would get their permission the next day.

"Now then, we have Mandy leading the way," Sir Thomas summarized, primarily to get it straight in his mind. "With me as my squire comes Lonnie and Thea, as cook. Then, comes My Lady Darless, and Jon and yourself. Correct?" She nodded. "Okay, that makes us a party of seven. Now because of the nature of this long journey and its inherent dangers, I insist that each of us ride and be fully capable of handling a medium warhorse. For these are hardy steeds, capable of much toil, and they can assist in defending their riders from attacks. That means several of you are going to need some training."

"I sure do," said Jon.

Not only Jon, but also Darless, Alison, and Thea needed to learn to ride and handle a medium warhorse. Sir Thomas pronounced, "I estimate that a good two weeks with you four and I will have you in good shape to handle one. There is yet another matter, and that is sword training. My Lady wishes to learn the skills of a sword before we go. Do any of the rest of you want to learn as well?"

"Count me out on this one," Jon proclaimed, "I'm sure all I'll do is cut my foot!" Everyone chuckled at him. No one could see this musician wielding a sword. Alison had no time for it really, nor interest.

"I'm not really interested in sword fighting," Thea said timidly. "But if you think I ought to have some skill in it, then I will try my best."

"Well, I would rest better if I knew that you had some backup for protection when you have used up all of your spells," explained Sir Thomas. "However, I believe it is your master's decision, Thea. What say you, Mage Alison?"

She thought long on this point. "Magic users seldom use swords, though I do know of a very few who do. We just do not have the time to spend on it. However, on the battlefield with the hobgoblins, Thea demonstrated the most remarkable courage I've ever heard tell of in apprentice wizards. She kept her head and performed brilliantly where most others would have faltered. There is also the example set by my own sister, May. So yes, I give my permission. However, please make it just a short sword." Then, she added, "Oh yes, she does need training in the use of a long bladed knife. I have just not had the time to teach her anything about knives."

"Agreed. With her small size, a short sword will be a perfect match, sword and dagger, a lethal combination," the paladin spoke reassuringly. Thea giggled a girlish laugh. She was very pleased indeed.

"Well, can I add my thoughts?" Mandy inquired. All looked at her so she continued. "From all descriptions of this brown dragon, only highly enchanted weapons can pierce its hide. Now I have several bastard swords that would suffice; however, I shall put Zond to the test. It may prove to be the best weapon I own. Now how about the rest of you? We must go armed with very magically enchanted weapons." This comment by Mandy would save their lives, but this is getting ahead of the story.

"Verily, Pentegrast, the Demon Slayer, my holy two-handed sword, is highly enchanted. I fear that we shall have to find suitable blades for the others, Mandy. We will need a good short sword and dagger for Thea, a long sword for Lonnie, and," he could not resist teasing Mandy, "guess what type of blade My Lady has chosen to learn to wield?"

Mandy raised her eyebrows in a teasing challenge to him, "Okay, let me predict. Short sword? No way, she wants to do major damage to the evil ones. Long sword? No, she has no desire for finesse during mortal combat, when she must resort to a sword. Bastard sword or two-handed sword? No, she has not the build for those huge blades, though I would predict she would try them out first. No, in the true spirit of a Holy Paladin, I predict she would choose a broadsword. Am I right?" She, of course, knew that she was precisely correct, for she was a good judge in these matters. From the surprised look on his face, she knew she was.

"Ah, right you are, ranger," he confirmed. "Astute observer!" He nodded and made a mental note not to bandy with Mandy again! "Yes, she chose to learn the broadsword. Let's put our heads together and see what we can do to give them the best possible weapons to match our deadly foe!" The two began comparing the blades that they had in reserve.

In the end, Mandy produced an excellent short sword for Thea, which Sir Thomas complimented with a quality magical dagger. The paladin also had a fine magical long sword for Lonnie. Mandy had a fairly good, though not super powerful broadsword for Darless, which was better than the one that Sir Thomas had. Alison insisted on paying them both for their weapons, for she knew only too well how difficult magical weapons were to be found. It was a small compensation for what these two friends were giving away.

Next, Sir Thomas insisted on a formal presentation of the weapons to their new owners. He was always big on ceremony. It went with his style of life, honor, chivalry, bravery above all things. Lonnie, also a paladin, took the matter of the gift of a magical blade very seriously. It is noted here that he had already returned the magical blade they had found in Leeds to its rightful family heirs. He got down on one knee and formally accepted the blade from Sir Thomas, carefully saying just the correct words he had long ago memorized by heart for just such a day as this.

Thea, unused to their weight, nearly dropped the short sword and dagger when Sir Thomas presented them to her. She thanked him repeatedly. This was a day she would long remember!

Lastly, Mandy presented her magical broadsword to Darless, though with far less ceremony. "Thanks, Mandy," Darless spoke. "One day soon, in the heat of battle, I and this broadsword will have a pleasant surprise for you all," she taunted, but would give no further hint of her meaning. Her eyes shown bright and sparkled. Mandy knew something significant would come of this, though she knew not what. Even Sir Thomas did not know what she meant, but he too would one day see for himself. Of that, Darless was certain.

"All that remains," continued Sir Thomas, "is to pick the day of our departure. I suggest the twenty-first of March, the first day of spring."

"I like that touch, Love," Darless commented smiling, "it's the first day of spring, a new beginning of life. Very symbolic of what we embark upon. What say you, Alison?"

"I agree, I think all can be ready by then. I hope you all don't mind Sir Thomas. He tends to be a bit on the take charge now side," she was trying to be polite about his seeming control over events.

He roared with mirth, "Verily, on these mundane matters, I am highly trained. But I so swear that once we hit the trail, I bow totally to our ranger here in all traveling matters." To Lonnie, he said mostly for his benefit, "On the trail, there is no one more suited to lead than a ranger. Remember that, Lonnie, a ranger never lets you down. Trust in your ranger as you would your blade in a combat." Mandy blushed at this unexpected, yet correct, compliment.

"Finally, it is Alison's mission, and I swear to abide by her decisions on all such matters," he said formally, trying to put her mind at ease. "Though I might make a suggestion from time to time." That brought a smile to her face, as she recalled dozens of times he had done just that in the past, but he had the wisdom to always follow her decisions. She had never let him down either.

Darless then said, "Number 1, we train; number 2, we get prepared for the journey; number 3, we go in search of the brown dragon; number 4, we deal with the dragon. Say, how *do* we deal with a dragon anyway?" That brought another round of mirth. None had the slightest idea. The alu-demon then said ceremoniously, "Threngold, we are coming for you!" The others cheered. Five hundred miles away, deep inside his cavernous home, the sleeping brown dragon had a terrible dream that he was being besieged by fiery warriors. He awoke in a foul mood.

Chapter 5 The Journey to Canyon Lands

Jon found learning to ride the significantly larger medium warhorse a bit daunting, the beast was substantially taller than his light riding horse. That meant, of course, the ground was farther away should he fall. He found confusing all of the subtle clues he should be giving the horse as directions. It did indeed take a full month for Jon to get sufficiently skilled in controlling his new medium horse, especially if he needed the horse to attack his opponent. It had all been so much easier when he had just talked with the horse and asked it what to do or asked it to do something. He struggled all the way.

Darless, likewise, had a difficult beginning with her new medium warhorse, but mostly because she had never really been around horses. She was a fast learner and, in less than a week, became rather skilled at controlling hers. Thea had very little trouble picking up the skill of commanding hers for she had been around horses all of her life. Alison, though very busy, managed to meet Sir Thomas's skill level fairly quickly. Hence, Jon felt very alone and silly, but persevered, determined to somehow get the hang of it. He was thankful that he did not have to also spend hours learning sword fighting skills!

It is noted here that Sir Thomas examined each of the three hundred medium warhorses that they had brought back with them from their caravan journey. He chose the best twenty from these and then matched each horse with its rider's personality, temperament, and potential skill level. Then, for insurance, and at Mandy's insistence, he chose another two that would go on the journey as spares in case one of the others became injured.

During this same time period, the sword fight training progressed even better than Sir Thomas had hoped. Darless, as usual, was a very bright student and picked up the finer points quite rapidly. It was not until the third week of training that Sir Thomas finally realized how Darless could pick this new skill up so quickly. She had been observing his thoughts and attempting to duplicate them in her actions. He found another thing over which to marvel about his beloved.

Meanwhile, Mat saw to the training of Thea. He felt that this was something he could contribute to the overall cause. Yet, he volunteered for two other reasons. First, short sword and dagger was his main method of combat in the days when he had been just a thief, albeit a "good" thief. Second, he and May shared a similar mind set to that of Thea. For the twins, sword play was not their major interest or activity, just as with Thea, for she was a beginning wizard. Skill with swords was simply a secondary aspect. He felt a kinship of sorts with her and could relate to her situation and difficulties, more so than a fighter whose profession was the sword. Besides Thea was similar to May in that she had not a fighter's physic. Like May, Thea found even the short sword growing very heavy after only a few minutes practice. Mat therefore knew just how to train her. Thea progressed very well indeed under his tutelage. By the time they were ready to set out on the adventure, Thea could hold her own position very well. She was a defensive swords woman.

Jon welcomed the respite that came on moving day, the first of February, the day that Christina and Stephen were to move their families here to Ville. True to their word, the dwarves had two of the new stone homes ready for occupancy. Jon suspected all along that his capacity to move objects would be heavily relied upon, for the mages had only a limited number of teleport spells. However, he forgot that they could also make use of their staves for additional uses of the spell.

First, the three mages, Darless, May and Alison, teleported both families to their new homes here in Ville. Of course the five children were very excited and wanted to see everything at the same time. Mat, Jennifer, and Jake took them on a grand tour, keeping them out of the way, while the other adults moved all of their possessions. To conserve spells, the mages and the men returned to Horgath via the picture book. The two wives stayed behind to begin bringing order from the piles and boxes that shortly began arriving.

On each trip, the three portable holes were filled to capacity with as much stuff as would fit. Jon took care of the larger objects, stepping them from the blacksmith's home in Horgath to just outside their new homes. Yes, he did manage to bring the heavy anvil for Helmut. In fact, all of the boxes and packages and sacks were moved far faster than they could be sorted out between the two homes. In less than two hours, all their possessions were safely in their new homes. Now the real work began, trying to sort it all out and figure out where it all went in their new lodgings. It is noted here, that Alison's designs for dwellings allowed for spacious rooms and plenty of bedrooms for larger families. In fact, both families discovered that they now had approximately twice as large a home as before.

What impressed all seven of them, including the children, was the hot and cold running water and indoor toilet facilities. These, they had never seen before and were considered a magical marvel. All now believed that they were embarking on a life of utter luxury! The children cheered for now they no longer had the chore of fetching water from the village well, a drudgery task none enjoyed.

During the next two weeks, Alison and Jon spent several hours each day playing with and getting to know their nieces and nephews. This also helped their parents out, giving them more time to settle in properly. Helmut adapted to having his blacksmith shop located across the village in the southwestern section and not in front of his front door. After a week, he discovered that he enjoyed being able to leave his work behind him when he came home to his family.

Stephen very quickly adjusted to his new post as chief steward. Once Alison had briefed him fully on her plans and had a chance to interview the twins about the skills that the caravan folks would be bringing with them as they moved in later in the spring, he immediately saw where things were lacking. He set about making plans to rectify them. He too wanted this to be the most thriving village in the entire area.

Though it was Christina who pointed out the one significant flaw in the operation, "Look, you are going to have one magnificent Church of Ukko. But you forgot one very vital thing," she pointed out to Alison and Jon over tea one morning. Both had blank looks on their faces. "The priest! You haven't gotten a holy priest to run your church or services!" The blank look changed to that of "How stupid of us!"

Sheepishly, Alison said, "I had not thought about that. Now what do we do? When the folks move in later this spring, many of them will want to worship there, as many are followers of Ukko, I believe. I have no idea at all how you go about getting a priest. Help!"

"Well, I am a priestess of Ukko, though not a very powerful one. I guess I can manage to run services for a time. I am a healer and not a tenderer of souls. My training lies in the healing of the sick and injured. However, I will send out word that we are looking for a full-time priest, if that is all right with you?"

"Terrific, Tina," Alison exclaimed, greatly relieved. "I leave the running of the Church of Ukko completely in your hands! Say, I just thought of another thing. I've been playing with the children. Until now, I have not been around them much at all. Now where Jon comes from, there are public schools where all children can go and get a basic education. What do you think of the idea of having a common school where all of the village's children can go and learn basic skills, such as reading and writing? Then, you and all of the other parents would have more time freed up since you won't have that chore to do?"

"Now that is a good idea. We'd need a building probably dedicated to their schooling and we would need one or more teachers — teachers that we know will do as good a job as we do or even better," Christina replied. "Someone who loves children and respects them and is good with them," she added.

"Great. I'll provide the school building. I'm sure that the dwarves won't mind making a slight alteration to one of the as yet unfinished homes around here. I know, I'll provide the facilities and you see what you can do to find us a teacher or two," Alison said hopeful that her sister would agree.

She did. "Look, Alison, after all you are doing for us and our families, this is the very least I can contribute. I'm no adventurer, but these things I can and will do. We are going to have the very best village ever!" Then she looked quizzically at her little sister, "I don't know if this is the proper time to mention this or even if I should, but it has been in the back of my mind now, ever since you found us and I heard that you were getting married." Alison had no idea what she was alluding to, so just nodded encouragingly. "Well, I will look after any and all children you and Jon have, when you are away on your adventures. I'll be your nanny. I don't know if you have thought that far ahead, but I'm sure you will want children, right?"

"Tina! That is a fabulous offer! Truly, I accept!" she exclaimed. "Yes, I have thought long about it. Jon and I both want children, I'm afraid he may want many more than I do, actually. I have been most worried about what to do with them when I am needed elsewhere. Jon and I just assumed that we would somehow find a nanny, like mom did with me, when that time came. But this is a godsend! Thank you!"

Christina smiled, "Hey, isn't that what sisters are for?" Both chuckled at that oblique comment. They had not had this experience for nearly twenty-one years.

By early March, Darless completed her therapy with Lenny. His insanity was gone. No nightmares, no lingering after-effects. She got rave compliments from everyone, and well-deserved ones at that. For using Jon's techniques, she had performed a miracle. Still, Lenny presented a major problem. His education and outlook on life was still that of a five year old boy. A surprise to everyone, it was Helmut who remedied this. Indeed, there was little for him to do just yet, once he had his smithy setup. He had time to spare.

One day, he took Lenny for a walk and discovered the young man had an intense interested in bees. With Alison's permission, he and Darless took him to Horgath to visit the village's beekeeper. That one trip was all that it took. Lenny wanted to become a beekeeper and make honey. For the next six months, Lenny apprenticed as a beekeeper and then started his own operation in the meadows around the Ville. Under Helmut's careful eye and great patience, Lenny gained his self-respect and developed rapidly mentally toward manhood. It is noted here, that in one year's time, he was supplying the entire village's needs for honey. In three years, he had a hugely successful honey business in full operation.

As the days passed, the last lingering snow melted and early spring wild flowers sprouted. Daily the rich green grasses of the Verbenloc valley grew anew, bursting forth in splendor once more. Alison loved the spring time, the renewed life growing everywhere, the massive fields of wild flowers that grew everywhere, the freshness of the air. Inwardly she hated to have to leave so soon, but she told herself there would be plenty of springs to come.

Instead, she spent at least a third of each day attempting to work out a plan for dealing with the brown dragon, Threngold. The finding of him, though difficult and uncertain, was a problem with which they could easily deal, consisting of just searching until one found him, perhaps even seeing him flying on one of his trips to or from the Canyon Lands. No, it was how to actually confront and deal with him after they found him that deeply concerned the mage. It was just as Sir Thomas had said; it was her call, her decision, on how to handle Threngold. The twenty-first was getting closer, and she still had no real plan.

Jon sensed her tenseness and worry over the matter each evening as they lay beside one another. He never failed to give her a back rub until the involuntary taught muscles relaxed. His optimistic words were always, "Don't worry, we'll think of something when the time is right." She wished she could share his eternal optimism. *Maybe all this worry is just part of being the leader*, she thought to herself. *He isn't doing the leading.* She made a mental note to ask Sir Thomas about this effect.

When the twenty-first of March came, the seven were trained, equipped and ready for the journey. On a lengthy journey such as this, the paladin was used to bringing along a string of pack horses to carry all of their supplies. He found it unsettling that this party carried everything in their portable holes and thus had no need of any pack animals. He continually found himself attempting to stow a sack of needed items onto a non-existent pack horse, after which he begrudgingly had Jon stow it in his portable hole. As much as he would have liked to get an early start on the trail, too many last minute details arose and the many farewells took time. At long last, around midmorning, Mandy, Darless, Sir

Thomas, Lennie, Thea, Alison and Jon finally set out on their quest to find the brown dragon, Threngold, and hopefully find some answers to the long standing riddle of just what had happened here that night twenty-one years ago.

Their initial route was clear, follow the dirt road north to Edgeway, continue their northerly travel through Lockwood Forest to La Fontaine, then veer eastward toward Fitzgerald Castle and still further east to Banner's Tower. From there, they would turn southeastward into the uncharted lands. The first two hundred forty miles to Banner's Tower were routine and through friendly lands. Traveling as light as they were (all of the heavy gear was stowed in the portable holes), their horses could travel swiftly, though Jon discovered that a medium warhorse was nowhere near as fast as his light riding horse, but it had a much greater endurance. Sir Thomas urged them to spend ten hours a day on the trail, so that they could cover forty miles each day, making Banner's Tower only a six day journey. When on the trail, the paladin always tended to be in a hurry, Alison explained to the others, who then chuckled and agreed.

Because the chances of any mishap occurring in these friendly lands was very low, their riding order was thus: Mandy, Sir Thomas, and Darless led the way with Darless in the middle of the two; Jon and Alison rode together in the middle; Thea and Lonnie, who led the two spare horses, brought up the rear. This way, the lovers could chat with each other as they rode along. Indeed, the days were mild and relatively sunny for early spring. Everyone's spirits were high. At dusk, either Alison or Darless would cast their magical mansion spell so that each night was spent in total safety and warmth, with no concerns whatsoever. That also meant a good night's sleep for everyone.

By the time they reached Banner's Tower, Jon, Darless, and Thea finally had their horse legs, that is, their legs no longer ached mercilessly at the end of the day's riding. This sixth night, after dinner was finished, they sat on the plush pillows of the mansion's main hall and chatted. Sir Thomas proclaimed, "This is the first expedition I've been on in which every night was spent in the comfort of these magical mansions. Such comfort, such ease, no guard duty, no worries. You know, I could really get used to this!" Everyone roared for they all had the very same opinion.

Alison teased, "You know Sir Thomas that I always travel in style and excellence!" She added, "And if Darless and I are forced to use up all of our spells in some combat, I have already given Thea several scrolls containing the mansion spell which she can cast for us. So theoretically, we travel this way the whole time." That brought numerous cheers. Thea smiled and felt important too; she was their backup. Secretly, she vowed to herself not to let them down.

"Well, tomorrow, we go southeast out onto the empty Arid Plains," Mandy got them back on the advance planning. "From this point onward, the maps are vague and only tell us the general possible location of things. Am I correct in assuming that we wish to find the Canyon Lands first and then make our way toward the Desolation Range?"

"I think that is the best idea. Supposedly the canyons are something like a hundred miles across. If we head southeast, we should be able to find them and then attempt to get our bearings and locate roughly where the stone giant clan is at — from where they spotted the dragon," Alison outlined.

"Agreed, the maps would have to be horribly wrong for us to miss the canyon area completely, if we stay this southeastwardly course," Mandy said. "Sir Thomas and I will keep an accurate estimate of the total distance traveled from Banner's Tower. That way, when we think we are near them, I can shape change into an eagle and spy out the land for miles from high. I'm confident we can find the canyons. Sir Thomas, what kinds of perils do you suspect we might encounter out here on these Arid Plains? I am really unfamiliar with these lands and we all should have some idea what to be alert for, you know, bandits and the like."

"Right here where we are now, Banner's Tower, is defined to be a neutral zone. Our ancestors drove the evil creatures out of the general Verbenloc area out here to these plains and also to the Plains of Gorsagatha and the Red Hills, both far to the south of here. These days, this immediate area is just neutral, a meeting ground for both sides. Merchants and peddlers come and go between the various lands. For another day or two, we should be safe enough. But the further south we go, the less such will be. I've not been more than about forty miles south of Banner's Tower. All I have is rumor to go on from there. If I were to hazard a guess, I'd say we might run into an occasional band of highway men, bandits, if you please. There could be goblins and orcs and similar fell creatures. We will not have to worry much about poisonous snakes and scorpions since we stay in style and comfort in here, not camping on the ground. Wolves, wild boars and hyenas would be a concern, if we camped out, though. Oh yes, I suspect we may come across ogres and trolls out here in these wastelands. There is always an outside chance that we might meet up with a gorgon or a cockatrice."

"What is a gorgon and what's a cockatrice?" Jon asked. Thea nodded too, she'd never heard of them either.

"Well, they are very nasty critters. The gorgon is rather like a large bull, but it breathes out a noxious gas which, if you get a good whiff of it, can turn your body into stone! A cockatrice is a bird-like creature, I've heard tell, and the touch of whose feathers can also turn you into stone. If we run into a gorgon, stay well back from it and stay away from its front, its mouth. Mandy and I and Lonnie can dispense with it rapidly, I'm sure. However, we are highly unlikely to run into these. No, what has me a bit more worried is the off chance that we may run into some lesser demons from the Abyss. Before we left, I looked over my grandfather's journal and he spoke also of driving demons out of Verbenloc as well. So they may have taken up residence way out here."

"One thing we should try to do is avoid the watering holes," Mandy pointed out. "Out here in this semi-arid land, water is precious to all creatures and those places are a natural focal point for life. Therefore, if we always encamp far from water holes, we may stay well out of harm's way."

"Ah, that's a good idea," Sir Thomas concurred, realizing once more that this party did not have to find watering holes each day. This was certainly being a very different kind journey for him. "I have always said, it's wise to have a ranger in the lead when in the wild!"

On the seventh day of their journey, the party turned southeastward, leaving the tall towers behind them. The land, though generally arid, was also experiencing its spring. Wild flowers sprouted here and there; tufts of hardy grass grew green from the early spring moisture. The land was rather flat; here and there, stunted trees, perhaps eight feet high, showed the first traces of budding leaves. Some of the low lying bushes already had their dark green leaves half-grown. But there was no road to follow. A vast emptiness lay before them as they rode onward.

As they rode along, Mandy pointed out some signs to the others. Here a boar had passed before them. There a pack of wolves had taken a deer; the bleached bones bore silent witness. They even saw an occasional herd of sheep. For two days, nothing of any real interest appeared, but midmorning the next day, the hairs on Mandy's neck bristled. "Okay everyone, alert time. About a mile or so to our right — two men on horseback are watching us. Stay alert."

Jon strained to see, but could not see them until they moved a bit. "This brush and low trees make it hard to see them. Could we get ambushed in this type of country?"

Truly, tis always a possibility," Sir Thomas replied, turning around in his saddle to face Jon. "But with a ranger, not too likely. She saw them even before I did!" Turning back to Mandy, he added, "Well done." She smiled; this was her job; this was what she loved to do. She thoroughly enjoyed it." The two men trailed them for about an hour before they disappeared from view entirely.

An hour later, Mandy called out, "Hey, well look at this!" She called a halt. Up ahead perhaps a mile distant, smoke clouds drifted aimlessly up into the sky, zigging this way and that as they caught the heat waves from the lands. "Village ahead. Not on the map. Suggestions?"

Alison called out, "Can we bypass it? Maybe go around it? I'd rather not take any unnecessary risks."

Dutifully, Mandy changed course to due east for a couple miles before resuming her southeastward path. Darless asked, "Say I've been wondering something, Mandy. How do you always know what direction we are going? Out here, I only have the vaguest notion."

"Well, I will admit that this time I am cheating a bit. Here, see this?" She showed her a small compass attached to a gold necklace around her neck. "Jon gave me this as a present some time ago. It's from his world, a magical direction finder. The black needle always points due north. But I really don't need it. See the sun? See our shadows? It points the way as well. Only one does have to continually make allowances for the time of day. It is really hard to get me lost, direction wise. About the only time I get confused at all is in a very dense, dark forest where there is almost no light. Or in a dungeon underground," she added recalling how often she had gotten lost in some of her earlier adventures before meeting these dear friends.

"Wagon ahead," Mandy called out. Sure enough a man driving a two horse wagon was coming from their right. From its slow speed, Mandy guessed it was loaded down. "Hello, top of the day," she called out to its driver when the wagon drew close enough. The man was middle aged and wore tattered clothes that had seen better days. He had relatively long, unkempt hair and a weather-beaten hat to keep the sun out of his tanned face. The back of the wagon was covered with a tarp and bulged here and there with unseen bundles. Mandy also caught a glimpse of another person hiding under the tarp and she distinctly saw the tip of a crossbow pointing their way.

Man with a crossbow pointed at us is hiding under the tarp, she sent mentally to everyone, startling Thea and Lonnie, who were very unused to having another's thoughts suddenly appear in their heads.

"G'day to you ladies," he answered dryly, but with a slight hint of sexual arousal. "Rather missed Flaton, back there, miss," he pointed to the direction he had come.

"Nah, on purpose, we have no business there. Heading south as you can see. Enjoy the day," Mandy said cheerily and nudged her horse onwards. The others nodded at the man and followed her lead. Soon the wagon was left behind. "Well, someone remember to put Flaton on the maps when we stop tonight," she airily exclaimed.

"Verily, keen are the eyes of a ranger," Sir Thomas spoke warmly. "I can see how valuable it is to have your warning just appear in my mind! I do believe that I understand My Lady better now, when she described just how you all worked as a team to defeat all of those wizards attacking you at the dwarven city. It is pretty darn amazing!" Both women grinned at him. Meanwhile,

Lonnie and Thea kept a sharp eye on the receding wagon, but it continued its eastward travel.

At the end of the third day as the sun set red in the west, they could see red glowing hills rising far off in the distance ahead and to their right, the northern start of the Red Hills. Again, they made camp settling down for the night inside of another magical mansion. As they led the horses inside, the howling of wolves and jackals echoed about the desolate land. All were glad for the homey comforts of the mansion.

By noon of the fourth day, their path intersected a shallow, dry riverbed some twenty-five feet across. Here they halted and examined their sketchy maps. Their conclusion was this was the beginnings of the Gorge of Diego. They were now certain that they were on the right path. The river bed snaked its way this way and that, but always heading mostly southeasterly. They decided to follow it for a while.

They had not gone very far when Mandy again called out a warning, "Man ahead. On foot. Sword on back." Slowly they rode up to him as he walked toward them. When they drew close, they saw a very bizarre man indeed. He wore no clothes, save a leather loin cloth. His feet were bare and his feet left tell-tale patterns in the dry, sandy soil of the river bed. He carried a broadsword in a cheap, nearly worn-out leather scabbard slung over his back. In sharp contrast, the sword's pummel contained a large ruby, denoting a sword which was very valuable, perhaps even magically enchanted. His skin was dark and tanned. A roll of skins was also tied across his back, evidently a sleeping blanket. His hair and beard were unkempt and fluffy and very long. About his waist hung a knife, some various odd bones and twigs tied on with rawhide strips, and even what appeared to be a gourd rattle of some kind. However, it was his coal black eyes that commanded their attention. Piercing, his eyes radiated a sort of crazed insanity. "Greetings stranger.

Beautiful day," Mandy greeted him. "I am Mandy Blackthorn, Ranger of Reylona."

When he spoke, he had the weirdest mannerisms. He rotated his head from shoulder to shoulder randomly. In a crackle voice and very, very slowly, emphasizing each syllable, "I am Jackal, the Accursed!" Indeed, he looked the part, Jon thought. Swiveling his head about, he stared at Mandy, "Ranger of Reylona, you are far from your forests! Beware your doom, a dozen winged beasts want your blood; strike swiftly!"

Taken completely off guard by his words and tone, Mandy had no idea what to reply. "I want my own blood, thank you," but he had move on to another person. "Ah, alu-demon even. Paladin-paladin's mate, it's true! I say unto you, do not separate your fates; demon slayers!"

Darless, at first shocked that he saw through her illusion and correctly identified her true form, was startled by his instantaneous recognition of her paladinhood and her fiancé. She couldn't think of a single word to say and so said nothing, which was just as well, for Jackal had turned his crazed stare on to Alison. "To you I say, there is life underground, though it seems not. But beware a man bringing gifts, for he is not what he seems." This, of course, made no sense whatsoever and she couldn't think of anything to ask, so taken aback by his strange pronouncement.

Moving along, to Jon, he said, "Ah, a musician and savior, if only you could save me, for I am Jackal, the Accursed. But I say unto you, save the old man." This so startled Jon, that he could not think of anything to say either. Which was just as well, for the crazy man immediately turned his gaze upon Thea.

"Now here's a pretty lass. Leave not his side, for you will marry him. Yet, leave his side, and he will die!" Thea, having heard all of the previous pronouncements, had the wits to reply quickly, "Leave who's side? And do you need anything? We have lots of provisions, though it may not appear thus."

Jackal, nodded towards Lonnie and then back to Thea and spoke, "Water, could you spare water for Jackal, the Accursed?"

"Surely," Thea blushed as she looked at Lonnie, who also blushed. Quickly, she dismounted, grabbed her canteen from a saddle bag and handed it to him.

"Ah most kind of you, yes." He pulled out a seed which he had wedged in his leather loincloth belt. Using a finger, he poked a hole in the soft sand, dropped the seed into it and covered it up. He poured a bit of the water over the pile and took a drink himself. Then, he handed the canteen back to her, untied his rattle and began a chant, stomping his feet in the soft riverbed sand, shaking his rattle all the while. After a minute, he stopped and tied the rattle back onto his waistband. Raising both arms skyward, he proclaimed, "From here shall sprout a lowly date tree, which then blossoms into a grove. In twenty years' time, a village shall rise here and it shall be called Theaton. So speaks Jackal, the Accursed! Adieu." Shaking his head negatively, he added, "If only Jackal could see his own path." Then, looking about, he cheered up, "Ah, perhaps it lies in this direction." Without another word, the strange man wandered off due north and was soon lost among the scant vegetation.

Mandy was the first to speak breaking the confused silence, "Who or what was that?"

"He called himself Jackal," Thea repeated, "I think he looked a little like a crazy man, though. Do you think we should go after him and see if he wants any supplies? I should think he would need some clothes, food, and supplies. He didn't even have a canteen, no water, and him being out here and all. How can he survive?"

"Crazy is right! He looked healthy enough to me, physically," Mandy answered. "Normally, I'd just say he was a bit off his rocker, but he soothsaid or prophesied or fortune told or whatever to all of us. Strange man."

"Number 1, he saw immediately that my body is that of an alu-demon," Darless began finally able to speak. Jon noticed the subtle change in the way she referred to her body and raised his eyebrows in surprise. "Number 2, he saw that both Sir Thomas and I were paladins, though our tunics announce that fact pretty plainly. Number 3, he saw that we were betrothed. Number 4, was the rest of his message a warning or also just stating facts, the demon slayers part and not separating ourselves? Number 5, is he just a keen observer of details or is he some kind of soothsayer? Number 6, it would seem his messages to Mandy, Alison and Jon were warnings about the future."

"Well, I don't place much stock in a man who runs around the country side half naked!" declared Sir Thomas. "I say let's leave the crazy man alone and get moving; we still have half a day to travel." Mandy nudged her horse forward and the pace began once more. The somber, strange mood that had come over all of them was hard to dispel, except for Thea, who was only fifteen.

Within a few miles, steep dirt banks rose on either side of the fifty-foot wide river bed. Already they were approaching three feet. "I think it best if we cut up the bank and ride topside. It the walls get higher, we'd be sitting ducks for an ambush," consoled Mandy. They climbed up out of the sandy bed onto the harder plains.

An hour later, the plains gave way to low undulating hills and valleys. Presently, Mandy spied a dark thicket of stunted trees ahead, perhaps several hundred feet wide. As they moved slowly in its direction, Mandy sensed trouble and ordered the others to make ready. "Curses! I've wholly forgotten to put my plate armor on today. Of all the luck, a Holy Paladin without his armor," cried Sir Thomas in alarm.

"Make do," Mandy tensely suggested, concentrating her full attention on the dark grove. In her mind, this thicket could conceal many horsemen who might leap upon their right flank as they passed by.

"Bypass it," Alison relayed to Mandy, but it was too late for that tactic. A quarrel whizzed past Mandy's arm thunking into her saddle.

"Ambush!" yelled Mandy, whipping out her special bastard sword, Zond. She kicked her steed into a full gallop, charging forward to meet the as yet unseen attackers. Sir Thomas was only a fraction of a second behind her, his two-handed sword pointed forward, lance-like. Several quarrels flew past the flying pair, but due to their speed, all missed. Now from out of the dark patch of trees, twenty-five mounted riders came, kicking their horse's sides into a full gallop. They wore leather armor and carried a small round hide covered shield. Each had a cutlass poised high in the air ready to strike. They charged toward the two.

The gap narrowed, three hundred feet, two hundred fifty. Three blazing balls of fire suddenly exploded in the rear of the charging bandits, cutting their numbers by two-thirds in that split second. None of those that fell survived the blasts. One hundred feet, and then came the crush of opposing wills, horses, and men. Mandy swung Zond in a wide sweeping arc using both hands, controlling her mount with her knees, while ducking the chopping swing of a rider passing her on her left. She was not quite prepared for the speed and cutting edge of Zond. Severed body parts flew in all directions as Zond cut through armor, steel and bone as though butter. "Zagroot zounds!" she cried as she wheeled her horse around to come back for a second charge, for now she could see the damage done. Three of the four men who charged into her were down, the fourth now galloped eastward away from the carnage as fast as he could kick his poor mount.

Sir Thomas also wheeled his large warhorse, preparing to charge again. Two of the four who challenged him lay bleeding profusely upon the ground, while the remaining two galloped after the lone rider who abandoned the attack on Mandy. Together they trotted back toward the others. Both wizards still held their staffs high, eyes searching the trees for any others that might be lurking. Thea was chatting with Lonnie about how effective her fireball had been; she was quite excited.

Jon, on the other hand, was watching six horses running wildly past him, riderless, and another six who had survived the fire explosions frantically galloping in all directions. He felt pity for them and sent out waves of calm and tranquility to their animal minds. Five minutes later, thirteen horses came wandering back to the party halting near Jon and his much larger horse.

Meanwhile, Sir Thomas and Mandy, neither of whom had so much as a scratch on them, dismounted and began examining the fallen. "This one is still alive," Sir Thomas spoke coldly, "I'll bind his wounds." Mandy fashioned a tourniquet for one of those whom Zond had only severed an arm. The others were dead.

She looked up and watched the parade of light warhorses coming to Jon. "Well done indeed!" she called out to him.

When Sir Thomas looked to watch the sight as well, a broad smile creased his lips. He muttered, "The man can barely ride, yet horses come to his beckoning. That is a paradox!" Mandy chuckled. They helped the two injured men onto a pair of horses and let them go.

Alison still was not satisfied that others might be lingering in the thicket of trees and so stood vigil. Meantime, Darless quickly searched the fallen men. When she finished, she had made a small pile of valuables including a couple cutlasses that she thought could use a closer inspection. Then, she cast a dig spell and quickly dug a burial pit. She watched as the two bandaged bandits rode off eastward.

"Excellent, My Lady," Sir Thomas complimented when he saw the pit. "Permit me to fill it." He piled the fallen bandits into the hole." Without ceremony, Darless commanded her magical shovel replace the earth. Only a low mound would mark this spot. "Okay, are we ready to continue our journey?" asked the paladin.

"No, I think we should explore that grove of trees from which they came," Alison requested. "I just have a feeling about this. Can we check it out? It should only take a few minutes. I don't relish taking a quarrel in my back as we ride out."

So they mounted up and rode into the trees, leaving Lonnie, Jon and Thea to deal with Jon's new acquisitions. Lonnie found some rope and tied the remaining eleven horses into a string that he could lead, giving Thea the rope for their two spare medium warhorses. While he was thus engaged, three men carrying heavy crossbows came rushing out of the dense trees. Momentarily, they halted seeing the three. Thea saw them and sounded the alarm and began making exaggerated arm motions, as if she were about to cast another spell. They took one look at her and bolted, running as fast as they could eastward.

"Way to go Thea!" Jon grinned. "They fled from you and you were only threatening them. That's pretty darn good."

"Well, I really don't like hurting people, if I can avoid it," she replied. "I think wizards are supposed to do really helpful things, like Darless did by digging the burial pit. It would have taken the rest of us hours and hours to dig that deep a hole." She would have continued, but just then the others rode out of the trees.

When they were closer, Jon called out, "Alison, you were right. Three men with crossbows came running out over there after you went into the trees. Thea threatened them with a spell and they bolted that way, running for dear life."

"Ah ha. Very well done, Thea," Alison complimented her. Then, she threw down a large, heavy sack and dismounted. "We found their stash of gold and gems. You can count it tonight, Jon. Just tie it onto one of the horses for now. It looks like we are collecting horses once more!"

"Ah, the man collects horses," teased Sir Thomas, "yet cannot ride them properly."

"Nah, it's all those funny knee pressure kind of things," Jon retorted playfully, "it is far simpler just to tell them what you would like them to do for you." Everyone laughed at his jest. Mounting up once more, they continued their southeasterly course. This band of bandits had delayed them only about a half hour.

By evening, the country side became breathtaking; they had entered the Canyon Lands proper, which began to the left or east of the Gorge of Diego whose sides were now some twenty-five feet above the mostly dry river bed. To their right, the Red Hills, so named from the red iron oxides that formed the soil, undulated like a sea of red waves. Yet, it was the view into the Canyon Lands that held their attention. Here was one of the great wonders of the world. In times past, great rivers had carved deep valleys in the softer stone, much like our Grand Canyon, exposing layers of red, orange, yellow, beige, brown and black soft stone. At their feet, small gorges began slicing ever deeper down toward the east. Occasionally, isolated mesa tops could be seen, small remnants of this very layer of ground upon which they were riding. In places, some of these mesas could be reached by following the narrow tracts from where they were out to the very end when the sides fell at a steep angle downward. The depth of canyons grew deeper the farther south and east one went from their current viewpoint on the north edge.

Great eagles soared above the canyon floors. Mandy counted six of these majestic birds in the time they spent gazing, admiring the incredible view. No one had any desire to travel further, so camp was made here an hour earlier than usual so they could gaze at their leisure. Mandy got out her "Eyes of the Eagle," the binoculars Jon had given her last year, and scanned the canyon floor. "Looks like there is a small stream away south." She passed the binoculars around to the others who wanted try them out as well. Many "wow's" and "oh's" resulted. Other than the wildlife, no signs of human habitation could be seen from this vantage point.

"With all the twisting and turnings of the canyons, it is rather like a giant maze," commented Jon. "Wonder how we get down there? Right here, it looks way too steep to even try."

"Perhaps further on south there will be a passage into these lands," Mandy sounded hopeful. "Either that or we must skirt around its entire western side and find the mouth of those rivers way down there."

"From these sketch maps, there appear to be a couple of rivers that join up with the Gorge of Diego," Alison suggested. "We may reach one of them tomorrow. Our way lies through the canyons, perhaps a hundred miles or more." Still everyone just stared at the grandeur before them until at last the setting sun brought down the veil of darkness upon the canyons. Only then, did the mage stir and cast her mansion spell at which time they entered for the night.

While the others were leading the horses and themselves into the mansion, Jon lingered still. The depths of the canyon were now black and unseen; he could not tear his gaze away. Then he saw something, "Mandy, what do you make of that?" She, along with Jon, were bringing up the rear, making sure that all the horses got safely inside. She turned to look where he was pointing.

Far off on the distant horizon south and east of them a reddish glow seemed to flicker and rise above the canyon floor hidden behind many buttes and mesas. It ebbed for a bit and then grew stronger only to fade once more. The cycle repeated itself though randomly, it seemed to their eyes. "Dunno," she finally replied. "I've never seen anything like it. It cannot be the fires of a town. If it was a bonfire, it would have to be an immense one to cause that glow. But the glow is akin to that of a bonfire. I don't know how to read this one. Perhaps we should get the others?" Just then the strange light faded altogether. Expectantly, both waited for a brief time but it did not return, so they finally went into the mansion for the night. They did not see the glow reappear two hours later. Amid the cooking of supper and handling of horses, both forgot about the red glow.

The next morning even Jon was up at the crack of dawn eager to get underway. The magnificent canyon scenery beckoned to one and all. This was something not to be missed! Breakfast flew by them and they hit the trail an hour earlier than normal, which more suited the paladin, for Sir Thomas was anxious to find the dragon and get on with things. The sun was low in the east to their left, casting long unusual looking shadows from the myriads of peaks and crests and layered ledges hampering their view. A lone white cloud floated aimlessly above the center of the Canyon Lands far off to the southeast, adding to the early morning beauty. Only two hours later when the cloud finally disappeared did Mandy finally realize something had been unusual about that cloud. "Strange, I've only just now realized that that cloud should have been moving westwards," she muttered to Darless beside her. "See the prevailing winds, light though they be, are out of the east. While it lasted, the cloud did not move. Strange."

Darless reflected in thought a minute before answering, "I didn't notice it moving either. Maybe there was no wind where it was at." Her explanation satisfied both of them. They rode on. Still their route held true. The party was riding along a narrow stretch of land that separated the ever deepening Gorge of Diego from the deeply carved Canyon Lands. At times this narrow strip shrunk to perhaps five hundred feet; at others, it broadened to nearly a mile. However, on both sides the drop off steadily increased. As Jon had pointed out yesterday, the drop would have been perilous for man or beast had they chosen to ride on down into the canyons. By noon, it would have been utter folly to even try, for the drop into the canyons to their left was well over a thousand feet and nearly vertical, while the drop to the gorge had increased to a hundred feet. Vegetation dwindled to low sage brush and similar low-lying bushes. No trees were to be seen except for those on the far side of the gorge, in the Red Hills.

During their noon break, Jon made a startling discovery. He had been staring at the panoramic view for most of the morning's ride and still while he ate he looked. "Say, look there. This place is inhabited! Or was inhabited, I should say." They were stopped near the edge of another starting point of a canyon. Out beyond them about a thousand feet and cradled into the sides of the canyon were the unmistakable signs of cliff dwellings, whose outer walls were adobe blocks. Three such homes were perched in close proximity; a narrow ledge connected them. The houses were at least a thousand feet above the canyon floor and about a hundred from the top. No ladders could be seen nor ropes. No people either. It appeared abandoned. "I wonder how they got up there."

"Why, might be a better question," exclaimed Alison. "Golly that looks like an awfully dangerous place to get to! How would you get your food up there?

Mandy got out her "Eyes of the Eagle" once more and took a closer look. "Look there are tiny windows and doorways, even." Quickly she passed the binoculars around.

"Wait a minute," called out Darless, when she finally got to take a close look at the three cliff dwellings. "Look just below the windows. I'd swear they are damaged. It's like some immense claws of the gods tried to scratch their way into the homes!" Quickly the others took another look through the binoculars. All verified her observation.

"What could cause such huge scratch marks?" wondered Mandy. "You don't suppose that is the work of our Threngold, the brown dragon do you?"

"Nay, I do not think so," Darless commented.

"Why do you say that, My Love? It would sure seem to my eyes that is a most reasonable explanation," asked Sir Thomas. "He tried to claw his way into the homes presumable to eat the occupants."

"From all descriptions of this Threngold, he is so big and powerful that if he wanted entrance to these adobe homes, he could have easily destroyed the entire wall structure, not merely make claw marks," she explained her hunch.

"Ah, that makes sense. Yes, Threngold is supposed to have helped smash the stones of Castle d'Ambrose. What is a little adobe to him? I see, I should have figured that one out myself." He added, "Perhaps I should now don my plate armor. We may run into a fight sooner than we expect. Hence, the lunch break was extended another half hour while Lonnie assisted him in putting on the heavy full plate armor and then helped him into his saddle. The others now saw just how heavy the armor was and how difficult it was to use. From now on, they all more fully appreciated their "tin man."

They rode on. Jon continually looked for more of the cliff dwellings as they passed by each new canyon. He spied another three that appeared much as the first: abandoned. Around mid-afternoon, Mandy pointed out circling vultures several miles ahead. Instinctively, she quickened their pace. As they neared the carrion hunters, they found that here the flat land on which they were riding widened and far off to their left out near the edge or rather the beginning of another canyon lay a form on the ground. Without really thinking about it, she changed course to go see what was there. The track of land became perilously narrow. Finally, she stopped. "Let's leave the horses here and go on foot. It's too dangerous for the horses. One misstep and it's a thousand foot fall! Also, Sir Thomas, you are now so heavy and this ground so soft, that I think it wisest if you stay back here with the horses. I don't want you falling." Begrudgingly he concurred with her observations, for, when he dismounted, his feet sank noticeably in the soft earth. Jon, Alison, Mandy and Darless strode single file out toward the form which lay dangerously near the edge. The view, on the other hand, was positively spectacular for the entire canyon lands opened before their eyes!

When they got closer, they saw that an old man sat facing the canyons, a clay pot was on his right and another on his left. Mandy observed that there were three sets of human footprints, barefoot, both leading to this man and coming from him. When they were sufficiently close, she hailed him, "Hello there. Are you in trouble? The vultures are circling." He made no movement or sound. She got as close as she dared, only one foot of ground remained on three sides of the man. She could see his left leg was badly injured. Plain to her eyes was the man's plight. A compound fracture to his lower leg showed many ill-fated attempts at healing. It was festering and gave off the distinct odor of rotting flesh. Gangrene had set in. He was dying. Because of the very narrow space, they had to back up a bit to confer. She told them what she had seen.

"Well, then there is only one real answer," Jon said, "My stick. Let me cure him. But can we maybe pull him back a bit? I'm leery of being so darn close to the edge." Mandy gently put her arms under the old man's shoulders and pulled him back about ten feet. Then, she went and got his two bowls, one had a tiny bit of water in it, the other held various bric-a-brac, some eagle feathers, some white power, some tiny bird bones, snake fangs, and so on. She sat them beside the man as Jon spoke his command word to his walking stick.

The man was old with long white hair, though very thin. His skin was tough as leather, though lined heavily with age and very brown in color. His feet were bare and he wore a loin cloth and a light woolen shawl to ward off the evening chill. His muscles were flabby and he guessed the man was in his early seventies. He touched the man with his stick and the tell-tale flash of yellow healing energies of Ukko briefly outlined the sitting form of the semi-unconscious man. Jon watched fascinated as the rotting limb slowly reformed and healed. In a few minutes, the man opened his eyes and uttered ever so softly, "Are you the Great Spirit God? Time to take me to the Happy Hunting Grounds? I am ready now."

"No, I am Saint Jon Brown. With the help of Ukko, I have healed your broken leg. How do you feel?" he replied, having no idea who this Great Spirit God was.

Slowly, reality came back to this man. He reached for his drinking pot and finished off what little water was left. Mandy got her canteen and handed it to him. He drank much for he was quite dehydrated from his ordeal. Finally, he spoke, "I am called Running Bear. My leg is better — a miracle." He was very confused, "If you are not the Great Spirit, then are you Meglin, the Healing Maiden? But no, you have the form of a man — outsider — a pale-face."

"Er, can you help me out here?" Jon begged in the direction of the three women.

Mandy spoke up, "He is considered a great healer in our lands. We are indeed outsiders here. I am Mandy

Blackthorn, a Ranger of Reylona." He looked even more confused than ever. In a spurt of intuition, she added, "I am a warrior maiden and tracker. I do great deeds for the goddess of the woodlands and forests and nature. This is Alison, a great spell caster, also in the service of the Great Spirit, and Darless, an equally great spell caster. With us is a great holy fighter clad in metal and two younger ones, a fighter and fledgling spell caster."

"Ah," his eyes light up in excitement for he was slowly beginning to understand her, "messengers of the Great Spirit then come to help us at long last?"

"Sure," said Jon, mistaking his meaning. "I saw your plight and could not let you just die here and be food for the carrion birds."

"I was at peace. My people brought me here so I could leave this body and go to the final resting place; my time here is at an end. I was floating over the canyon when you came. I saw you approach, but not with my eyes. Great white and yellow glows you be; I thought servants of the Great Spirit have come for me at last. But no, it be not." He paused a moment and added, "It must be then that the Great Spirit has something more for me to do before I depart. Though I do not yet know what it may be, I, Running Bear, will do it somehow," he added with determination.

Ever practical, Mandy asked, "Can we move you back away from the edge, back to where the others are at? We are a bit fearful of falling over the side." He nodded and Jon helped him to stand. He was weak with lack of food and staggered step by step, marveling at the man in shining silver. They laid him down on the soft earth and Alison quickly brought out some food. He ate slowly and drank even more water. As they watched, some of his strength slowly returned.

After he had eaten, Mandy asked him, "Running Bear, since we are outsiders, we do not know of your plight. How came you to be so badly injured? Could your people not heal your broken leg? It looks like someone tried several times."

"I am called Running Bear and have seen seventy beautiful springs here in Wavapata, the Canyons of the Great Spirit, in your tongue. As a child, I ran with the brown bears and so found my name. I became a great spirit among my people in my youth and wed Morning Breeze. She has been by my side for fifty-one springs. She is the leader of my tribe, the Morning Wavas, for we all love the morning hours. My eldest daughter, Many Braids, does not listen to council of her mother any more, and alas breeds discontent among my people. Many now follow Many Braids. I tried to capture another eagle feather from the Eyrie of Thong, the Great, hoping to regain back the support of my daughter. Alas, though I am ever willing, my body has gone frail. I fell and broke my leg. Morning Breeze tried to heal it twice but it was not to be. Many Braids declared that it was my time to go back to the Great Spirit. She had three braves bring me hither, positioning me at the edge that I might float out of this frail shell and rejoin the Great Spirit. No greater kindness could she have shown me. For two days did I gaze out upon my beloved Wavapata, reflecting upon all the deeds of my long life, preparing the way, my path to the heavens. I was ready for the Great Spirit to take me, when I saw your approach and mistook you for his servants."

"Well, perhaps we are his servants, only that we come from a far distant place," Jon offered, trying to set his mind at ease. Alison gave him a look to say "what are you saying," but he continued, "I say this because we four here know we are spiritual beings, while the vast majority of the others in our lands have lost touch with what they really are and think of themselves as bodies. Darless and I are on a sort of life's quest to open their eyes to their real nature. Here, I find that you are fully aware of your true nature. I am amazed indeed. Are all of your people aware of their true spiritual being?"

A look of shock and surprise filled his face, "You mean your people only see themselves as bodies? How lonely that must be! To be ignorant of, to be denied of your own abilities and senses, to be unable to see without eyes? How horrible! How could that happen? Yes, to be a Hatchawa Wavapata, or Children of Wavapata in your tongue, is to be a spiritual being, to know and to perceive as one. You mean that your people cannot face the west and still see the Wavapata? How dismal their lives must be!"

Secretly, Sir Thomas faced the western Red Hills and tried his best to see the canyons but could not. Lonnie, spying what his liege was doing, also tried it and failed. Thea spying them both making the attempt, followed suit. "I, I think I can see it," she exclaimed, "though I am not so certain as when I turn around and look with my eyes."

"Look with your heart, do not let your eyes deceive you," spoke Running Bear. "Reach out and see the Wavapata." The others saw the experiment that the three were doing and nodded to each other. They too faced the west but looked at the Canyon Lands. For a moment, all four had the same reaction as Sir Thomas.

Then, Jon spoke softly, "I see it much better when I move out of my head. I don't seem then to be so dependent upon eyes." Alison, Mandy and Darless realizing just how true his words were, moved just behind their heads and observed the vast three-hundred-sixty degree panorama open before their awareness.

Mandy's comment summed up all four's perceptions, "Why it truly is the Garden of the Gods!"

"Just how do you do this," Thea demanded a bit impatiently, determined to "see" the canyons as her mentor was seeing them.

Jon spoke gently and softly to her, "Thea just be a foot back of your head. No, don't try, that takes effort. Just decided to be there, yes, that's it. Now look wide about you. Yes, like that." Jon saw the blinders come off of the young woman.

"Oh my god!" she exclaimed, over and over and over. This moment, this scene, she would never forget as long as she lived. She also perceived Jon and the other three women, and the exclamations continued unabated.

Jon worked with Sir Thomas and Lonnie, but to no avail. Both were too fixed in their own ideas of the universe. Jon knew that both could use the gift of Fruella. Suddenly, he wondered just what it was that Fruella had done to them to "open their eyes" to their spiritual natures. He resolved to find out somehow.

Sir Thomas, though more frustrated with himself than he had ever believed possible, waited patiently, though he had to mentally recite the Code repeatedly. Finally after an hour, he spoke, "Say, it is getting late. Perhaps we should take shelter soon."

Indeed, an hour had passed! Time lost so much of its meaning to the five. Slowly, they reentered their bodies. Jon, sensing the turmoil in the paladin, said sincerely, "Thank you Sir Thomas, for letting us have this moment of time. We all really appreciated it. If I can ever find a way to help you see too, I will do so at once, you have my word on it. Yes, we better deal with life at hand."

Thanks for that, Jon, Darless sent him lovingly. *He needed the encouraging words.*

Running Bear, also coming out of his reverie, added, "Yes, we must find shelter before the night comes. Otherwise, the fell creatures of darkness may find us and eat our bodies. It is too far to my dwellings, too little light left. But you have many other horses? Where are the others of your party?"

"We seven are it; these are some extra ones we acquired along the way," explained Sir Thomas. "Perhaps we should camp here and find out more about the threat that lies before us rather than riding more yet today." Though known for his 'ever in haste, tireless riding,' it seemed to his mind that just now, it would be perhaps wise to learn all that they could about the threat of these night creatures. What were they? What were they facing? They could be more fully prepared to face them. He did not realize this subtle change in his outlook — that his perceptions of life had infinitesimally been altered.

Without further discussion, once again, Alison cast her mansion spell. Then, she spent several minutes explaining to Running Bear just how safe they all would be once inside. Though the wise man had seen many things in his long life, never had he seen an outsider's palace or such a mansion as this. Once he fully understood that they would be completely safe from attacks once inside, the growing concern of nightly dread seeped away from his mind. His conviction that these outsiders were indeed sent by the Great Spirit now solidified into a complete certainty.

Once everyone was inside and the evening meal prepared and eaten, the old brown-skinned man fell into a deep, long overdue, restful sleep. As much as Sir Thomas would have desired to question him about the dangers, he agreed that the old man needed sleep even more. He agreed to be patient until the morning. However, restless, he and Darless spent several evening hours just outside the mansion doors, staring off over the dark canyon lands. Both swore that they saw a strange flickering light far off to the southeast. Pale blue hues changed into a yellowish white and then back to a baby-blue before fading. Neither had any idea what it was or its significance, save that it was aesthetic.

Chapter 6 The Plight of the Children of Wavapata

Before the crack of dawn, the old man awoke Alison to let him out of the mansion doors so that he could honor the new day. Though not quite grasping his meaning and wiping the sleep from her eyes, she led him outside. He stood solemnly facing the Canyon Lands, facing the rising sun, staring out over his lands of beauty. She left the doors open for him but went back to bed. Running Bear said not a word nor moved until the others arose when Mandy called out "breakfast" to get their morning activities into full swing.

While Jon cleaned up the dishes as usual, Mandy and Sir Thomas attempted to find out more about the "fell creatures" he spoke of last night, but he would not say. He explained that it was not his position to do so, only the tribal leader may do such. This was the sacred duty of Morning Breeze or Many Braids, if she had usurped her mother's position. However, he did say that during the daytime, there was nothing to fear. Mandy was instructed to continue their southward journey toward the Little Bend River.

High billowing white clouds in a pale blue sky highlighted the magnificent colors of the Canyon Lands or Wavapata on their left. None of the travelers had ever had such a beautiful leisurely ride as they had this morning. Mandy now began picking up the tell-tale signs of the small party who had brought Running Bear to his death perch and then returned. To her keen ranger eyes, three rode out with one horse carrying a heavier weight than the others and three rode back the way they were headed.

At noon, Little Bend lay directly ahead; she spied a well-worn path angling down the relatively steep, eroded bank to the river. Sunlight sparkled off of the slow moving shallow waters that flowed into the Gorge of Diego just to their right. Abundant grasses and other wild plants grew thick near the water's edge. Mandy turned to her left, heading east into the canyon following the river bed and the unmistakable trail of the three riders.

Running Bear spoke now for the first time since they began riding, "Follow Little Bend for ten miles. Be wary of giant wasps or bees; something has unbalanced nature here." he would not elaborate or say more.

"What's he mean by giant wasps?" Jon asked Alison.

"Dunno," was her simple reply. "Guess we may find out. I've not told you this, Jon, but I really hate snakes and spiders and wasps. I hope we don't encounter any, let alone giant ones."

He laughed, "Yes, I hate snakes too, gives me the creeps! So do rats, for that matter. Mice are okay." She laughed glad that they shared similar phobias. They rode on. Now that they were entering the canyons proper, the sides rose steeply on either side. In just a few meandering miles, the cliffs rose several hundred feet above them, giving them a very different perspective on the land. The river twisted and turned. After a mile, smaller side canyons appeared randomly on both sides. It would be very easy to get hopelessly lost in these lands, Jon thought.

About two hours into the canyons as they passed by yet another side branch, Mandy heard a strange buzzing sound coming from this new side canyon. She halted and signaled everyone to listen.

"The demon wasps are upon us!" called out Running Bear, quite alarmed. "Don't let them sting you. Their venom is sometimes fatal."

Suddenly, a swarm of a dozen wasps flew right towards them from the side canyon. "Zagroot zounds!" exclaimed Mandy, drawing her sword wondering how best to fight them. They looked like wasps, only they were three feet in length!

Sir Henry wheeled around and charged toward them, "Leave them to me, they cannot penetrate my armor!" Mandy was only too glad to let him deal with these. However, before the paladin could reach the swarm, three balls of fire detonated within seconds of each other; the mages were taking no chances. Alison looked at Darless and Thea and all three grinned. They had all three reached the same conclusion and had acted identically, though Thea's was the last to culminate. A dozen wasps splattered randomly on the ground just in front of Sir Thomas. All were most dead. Everyone, except Running Bear, dismounted and went for a close inspection of these wasps.

Their smoldering carcasses averaged three feet in length with a wing span of four feet. The wasps looked like ordinary wasps, only greatly magnified in size. Their stingers were huge and still oozed blackish venom. Jon rolled one over with his walking stick to examine its underside. It wiggled about and he jerked back; the others laughed. "I hate wasps!" he muttered.

After looking them over, they went back to their horses, where Running Bear still sat on his horse. "I have now seen with my own eyes that you are indeed servants of the Great Spirit!" Awe was in his eyes and he humbled himself before them.

"How much farther?" asked Mandy, trying to change the subject. She did not like to be thought of as a servant of anyone other than Reylona.

"A mile on your left, you will see," he said. They mounted and continued. As they rode on, the river bed widened.

Soon Mandy called out, "Say this looks like a corn or maize field next to us!"

"Yes, we plant near the water," Running Bear explained. "Try not to damage the plants." They rode single file now. After a half mile, several riders approached carrying bows. "My people — the warriors have come to greet us." Six young men in their early twenties wearing leather loin cloths and moccasins galloped up. Jon noticed that they used no saddles and only the thinnest of leather bridles with no bits, quite unlike their gear.

The look of shock and surprise on their faces told all. "These servants of the Great Spirit have healed me," spoke Running Bear. "My leg is completely healed! Take us to the Reverend Mother at once."

One rider hastened back to let the tribe know what was coming, while the remaining five led the party slowly to their encampment. This group lived like the others in the Wavapata. The camp was made under the protective overhang of an extended cliff. High adobe walls protected the inner areas where their few horses and gear was stored. Great rope ladders hung down from the distant cliffs above them, for their actual dwelling places were hundreds of feet above in the cliffs. These were cliff-dwellers of necessity, as the party was soon to learn. Fifty people clad in leather left their work or duties and walked out to meet them. Uniformly, the men wore loin cloths and leather moccasins, while the women wore simple leather dress-like creations and moccasins as well. All hair was long, with eagle feathers in the men's hair, Mandy dutifully noted. The women uniformly had theirs braided, usually three feet long in two or three braids down their backs.

As they dismounted, Mandy noted that the men gave deference to one younger woman, who slowly walked forward. She must be the leader, she concluded. The woman spoke, "Running Bear, you have returned from the dead? For it was the time of separating, was it not?" Mandy realized Many Braids was shocked to see him alive and well. Just then, a very old woman pushed

her way though the lines and rushed forward to hug
Running Bear, tears streaked her face.

"See daughter, it was not my time, Morning
Breeze," he said softly holding her tightly. His wife said
nothing by cried and held tightly onto him. He addressed
his daughter, "Many Braids, I see you have replaced
Morning Breeze or have my eyes deceived me? Morning
Breeze has not yet gone to the Great Spirit." Jon and
Mandy detected a strong note of challenge in his
demeanor. Evidently, his daughter had indeed usurped
Morning Breeze's control or rule over the tribe.

"Morning Breeze is old and grieves yet for you. I
must lead; we perish daily, as you well know!" she said
quite antagonistically and defiantly. "Just because your
leg is healed, don't expect us to follow Morning Breeze;
she failed to heal it." She glared at him. Those around her
stood uneasily looking first at Many Braids and then
Morning Breeze and Running Bear. This shift of power
obviously was not an honorable one, though it was
expected. The father and daughter glared at one another
for nearly a minute. She had her hands on her hips
defiantly. He yielded at last.

"So be it, then, Many Braids," he spoke decisively,
"may your daughter have more wisdom than mine." It
was over, the warriors and women relaxed visibly. Their
worst fears of a nasty confrontation passed. They had
already accepted Many Braids as their leader and were
glad that Running Bear and Morning Breeze went along
with the power change.

Looking now at the party, she queried harshly,
"Who are these outsiders? Why have you brought them to
our home? Speak Running Bear."

*Hope my daughters are not this nasty to me when
I am old!* Jon sent to Alison. Using the bottom of her
staff, she punched him lightly in his rear.

"They are the servants of the Great Spirit," he
answered reverently. "This one is called Saint Jon, the

Redeemer, and it was he who cured my leg. See it is just as good as the other now."

"They are just outsiders. Can you not tell by their skin and clothing? Or do your eyes now fail you too?" she retorted.

Sir Thomas could take this no longer. Still wearing his plate armor, though holding his helm in his left hand, strode forward. "Enough of this silliness! I am Sir Thomas le Bonnaire. Holy Paladin of Ukko, the great spirit." He greatly emphasized the last two words. "This is My Lady Darless, Holy Paladin of Ukko; Lonnie Smith, Holy Paladin of Ukko; Mage Alison d'Ambrose, Holy Mage of Ukko and her apprentice, Thea; Mandy Blackthorn, Ranger of Reylona who is likewise a servant of the great spirits. We did not come here to banter words with a rebellious child!" This, of course, only made matters worse. The many warriors raised their bows forming a protective wing around Mandy Braids.

So much for diplomacy, Alison sent to Jon. *It is not his strong suit. It's why I was never really interested in him romantically.* Jon now understood Alison reasons far better.

Where is William when he would be most useful, thought Mandy, who expected it could come to blows shortly.

Darless had an idea. She stepped in front of Sir Thomas and said defiantly, "Let your warrior there shoot me with an arrow. It shall bounce off of me. For none of you have any weapon that may wound me, though bruised I may become. Come on, I challenge you. Shoot one at me. If I am not who I say I am, then the arrow will pierce my body!" Her cold black eyes glared defiantly at Many Braids.

Challenged as she was, the young leader saw no recourse. Surely, she thought, when the arrow pierces her body, the others will see that these are just outsiders. She gave a hand sign to the warrior on her right. He aimed an arrow at her chest, saw her white tunic with blue cross, became wary that metal might lay beneath it as with the shining man, changed his aim to her right forearm and fired. It bounced off of her arm and stuck in the dirt beside her. "Bruised," she muttered and held her arm up for all to see.

Gasps of awe echoed from all around. Jon now sensed fear enter into Many Braids mind, fear and uncertainty. Jon sent to Darless, *Great idea. It helped reach her. She is definitely afraid of something. That's why she is acting as she is.*

Morning Breeze spoke for the first time, softly but sternly, "Have you then forsaken *all* of our traditions, then Many Braids? Have my teachings been in vain? Are the times so bad that the welcomes due strangers are cast aside?" Her daughter could not look at her, choosing to stare solemnly at her moccasins, stirring the dirt aside. "Have you lost all faith in the Great Spirit? It is said through all eternity that 'the Great Spirit aids those of the spirit.' Can you not see here the signs of the Great Spirit's touch? Running Bear stands here healed before you. Even I could not do that. If you will not offer these spirits pava, then I will. Though old in years, I am not yet so blind that I cannot perceive, daughter." Jon sensed Many Braids's inner turmoil and her acquiescence to her mother. "Will it be your pava or mine?"

She knew her mother was right. Raising her head and looking at the party, she spoke. "On behalf of the Morning Wavas, please accept my pava, or welcome feast. Come take bread and juice with me. Pray council me with your plans that I may aid you in your journey." Her words rolled well-practiced, though a bit mechanical, off her tongue. Her guards shifted aside and lowered their bows. Jon also detected an aura of hope in many minds about him. He pondered its significance. She led them to a campfire area and signaled other women to prepare the meal. Other men took their horses and led them off to graze nearby. One by one, the party members followed her to the pava, including Running Bear and Morning Breeze, still holding onto one another.

Following the lead of Many Braids, they took seats on large logs around the fire. Quickly a large fire-blackened pot was placed before her and, using her knife, she cut the bread in it into small squares. She took one and passed it to her mother and around the circle it went. Other women brought pottery glasses filled with a clear juice. When Jon sampled the bread, he immediately recognized that it was almost like corn bread, but the juice was tangy and unusual. He'd never tasted anything like it. "Good juice," he exclaimed. "What is it made from, wild berries?"

Many Braids smiled for the first time, "No, it is cactus juice." She felt some relief that these servants of the Great Spirit did not know everything after all. It was a beginning. She was in her mid-thirties, though lines of worry already marked her smooth complexion. A pair of long golden earrings hung nearly to her shoulders. A necklace of uncut gemstones reflected many colors in the sunlight. Her distinctive headband of a golden mother and child was her badge of office, tribal matriarch and leader. She was tall and thin except that her belly indicated she had already bore many children. Her deep blue eyes contrasted with the brown of her skin and the leather dress she wore. In fact, it was her eyes that Jon noticed first. They darted from person to person, never looking directly at any of them, and for moments, she also looked at the ground as well.

"Well, I still say it is a pretty tasty drink," Jon replied and then he struck out on his own, based upon his observations of her and these people. "Many Braids, I assume that I should discuss these things with you. If I am out of line at any point, please let me know. I do not know your customs." She nodded affirmative without a glance at her mother. "Consider us as outsiders for the moment, for we truthfully do not know your customs, your ways. However, I can sense that all is not right in Wavapata. You are very much afraid for your people or do I miss the mark?" Again, she nodded. "A servant of the Great Spirit is not the Great Spirit. We are not all-seeing. Can you please tell us what has happened to Wavapata? What is or has been going on?"

Now that is the way to handle the situation. Very nicely done, Jon, Alison sent to him; she smiled.

A gleam of understanding flickered from her eyes, "Ah, the messenger is *not* the sender. When I was a child, we numbered four times our present beings and lived in harmony at the heart of Wavapata, near the center of the lands by the Great Spring. About twenty summers ago, the Evil Spirit, Daku, first appeared in our lands, bringing many evil, bird-like creatures with him. They attacked our village and Morning Breeze had us abandon the village and move farther away, for these evil winged creatures fed themselves upon our bodies and grew larger and stronger. Then, it seemed wise, for Wavapata is wide and broad — room to share, she counselled."

"After we left, the Evil Spirit built a large temple around the Great Spring and the numbers of the winged creatures with no name thrived and multiplied. At least as the summers progressed, more and more appeared in Wavapata. Evil begets evil, it is said. Further and further outward we and all of the other tribes have been forced to move to gain but a fleeting respite from their insatiable hunger. They eat not as us, ignoring deer and elk and bear. On our bodies alone do they feed. At first, we thought our cliff dwellings could withstand their attacks. For a time, they do, until they eventually claw a hole in the walls."

"Morning Breeze prayed to the Great Spirit for guidance, but I say she was never answered." She glared at her mother. "Many warriors wanted to fight back, to attack the Evil Spirits. Morning Breeze held them back saying 'these demons you have not the ability to damage.' Secretly, several warriors disobeyed her and sought them out and attacked them, but all were eaten instead; we discover their bones later. Summers pass and still we move. Now we and most of the tribes are nearly out of Wavapata. If we must move again, we must become outsiders to our land. We all have been pleading with Morning Breeze to be allowed to fight them back, to send all of our might against them. She always refused us. Always."

"Then, five summer's ago, more foulness invaded Wavapata. Great wasps and bees, a distortion of nature, appeared, swarming about the canyon lands. Their stingers are venomous, though we have saved as many as were lost to their stings. The abominations we can kill and have done so whenever they near our village. Keen are the bows of my warriors. Since Morning Breeze has only led us to near destruction, I took control and asked for many warriors to go in stealth and spy on the Evil Spirits and to choose the time and place of their attack wisely. I asked that all of the winged creatures be slain. Alas, none of the fifty warriors from our tribe and two others nearby have returned. Runs with Dogs was among them." Sadness filled her face; she could not hold back the tears. Jon surmised that Runs with Dogs had been her husband. "It seems we cannot fight them, only run. Stay and we cease to exist, go and become exiles from our own lands. Evil is either choice, I can see no other, so few of us remain. We are so overwhelmed by the Evil Spirits; we have no real choice. I've ordered fifty warriors to their deaths!" And more tears flowed, despite her best efforts to suppress them.

Jon suggested softly and gently, "Let me council you in private, just the two of us. While we do that, is it okay if my friends ask Morning Breeze and Running Bear some questions about these evil creatures?" She nodded and covering her face, led him inside an adobe horse shelter.

Darless and Alison knew what Jon had in mind; Mandy had a good guess. The other three had no idea what was happening. Alison took charge, explaining more for Sir Thomas, Lonnie and Thea's benefit than for Running Bear and Morning Breeze, "Saint Jon is going to try to help her erase the trauma she's been under, free her from her spiritual burden." Sir Thomas thought he grasped what Alison said, but whispered to Thea, who whispered back for several minutes, explaining how the technique worked. She had used it herself with many of the caravan folks.

Alison spoke to Morning Breeze directly now, "Can you describe these evil spirits? What do they look like? From what Running bear said yesterday, do they only attack you at night?"

Good question, Darless sent her mentally.

From them they learned that these creatures did indeed only attack at night and were never in all these years spotted in the daytime hours. The smallest, presumably the youngest, were about five feet tall, while the more mature ones rose to seven feet. Though their feet were similar to a chicken, they had great talons that could easily tear apart bodies. Their long spindly arms nearly reached the ground and likewise ended in even greater talons capable of eventually tearing through adobe dwellings. They had huge wings and could fly faster than many horses could run. Their ears resembled those of a bat, only many, many times larger and their faces resembled those of baboons. Their ferocious bite did kill many warriors outright.

Running Bear outlined some other startling observations. Unbeknown to Many Braids, he had spied upon them on many occasions. When they attack, a cloud of darkness surrounds them that no light can penetrate. From direct observation, these creatures were highly intelligent and cunning. "There are yet two more details of which I can speak. Our arrows bounce off of them just as it did on Darless. Perhaps, we should have told Many Braids of this. The other is very troubling to me. When our bodies return to the earth, we rest a while and are taken to the Great Spirit. Yet, many of the fallen warriors, whose remains I have found, have disappeared. They are neither waiting nor have been taken to the Great Spirit. They have vanished. How this can be, only the Great Spirit may know, but it troubles me heavily. I fear to send warriors into a battle in which, if they lose, they, the spirit, vanish. This, I am afraid, Many Braids does not understand."

"One thing I don't have clear," Alison asked, "Many Braids referred to the Evil Spirit and later to the evil creatures. Are these the same?"

"No. When they first appeared so many summers ago, I saw briefly their leader," explained Running Bear. His face grimaced as he recalled that time. "The Evil Spirit that I named him, for I have no other name for such a creature, was human sized, but not human. Black was his skin and scaly. I saw him lift a boulder that would have taken two strong warriors to move; never have I seen such strength. His face was like the black of night within a child's nightmare. His eyes were slanted upwards, his chin long and angular, coming to a point. He had large fangs where we have teeth and two horns pointed upwards from his forehead. I saw arrows bounce harmlessly off of him, just as they did you. He shot great balls of fire as you three did to kill the wasps, as well as several bolts of lightning which killed many of my friends. Yet, perhaps the strangest thing I ever saw came afterwards." He looked at Morning Breeze, "I've never even told you this. I slipped back to spy on what they were doing several days after we had moved the tribe away to safety. The huge, round stone temple was built from mud. Truly, as I watched, he shaped mud from the river bank and turned it into stone walls. Only a great spirit can do this; hence, I called him the Evil Spirit for I know not what to call him."

"Thanks, you've given us a lot to go on," Alison agreed thoughtfully. She decided that she might as well ask the single question she had wanted to ask since she arrived. "We are also on the trail of a brown dragon named Threngold. We have heard rumors that he has been seen flying over the eastern Wavapata. Here is a crude sketch of what he looks like. Have you seen him or know anything about him?" At the mention of the dragon's name, the old warrior started and looked rather surprised. His eyes showed only confusion as he looked at the charcoal sketch May had done.

"I do not know what a dragon is. From the picture, it looks like a flying lizard. I've seen none." Alison's hopes dropped. "But I know an old man, an outsider, yet perhaps not an outsider, who goes by that name, Threngold. He is brown of skin as we and claims to be from the Eastern Tribe, but I have never heard of this tribe nor where in Wavapata they may dwell. Many, many summers ago, he and I used to go for walks together. He has vast wisdom and knows many things. He comes and goes like the wind. As I now think about him, I have not seen Threngold for many summers, not since the arrival of the Evil Spirit. Perhaps he too was killed or has fled to the eastern rims as did we. Who can say?"

Just then, Jon and Many Braids came walking back to the camp seats. She was radiant, a large smile upon her face. She could scarcely contain her enthusiasm. "Mom, dad, forgive me. I love you both. I was wrong to steal tribal power from you Morning Breeze. I give it back to you; I am not yet worthy of wearing it." She took off her golden headband and hugged her mom. Running Bear's eyes shown with wonder at the remarkable change that had come over his daughter.

"No, you keep it, daughter," Morning Breeze spoke softly. "I should have given it to you many summers ago. It is I who should be forgiven." Thus it was that Many Braids retained her position as tribal leader and all seeds of discontent among the members of the group were dispelled at long last. No matter their fate, this small band would face it together as one.

Evenings come early in Canyon Lands for the high cliffs block the sun, casting deep, dark shadows long before twilight descends. Hence, the party was invited to spend the night in the cliff dwellings far above and join the tribe for their evening meal. Their horses were corralled in the adobe walled enclosures along with the pitiful few horses that yet remained to the tribe. One by one, the men and women began the long climb up the ten rope ladders. The party watched in awe as forty scampered nimbly up the ladders.

"How high do you reckon it is up there?" asked Jon, a trace of concern in his voice.

"Five hundred feet, I'd guess," Mandy replied. "Going to be some climb! Think of the view we will have! Should be spectacular as the sun sets, come on." She and Darless put a foot on the first rung and began to climb, swaying in and out from the cliff-side. "They have had more practice," she hollered down to Jon, for the natives did not move the ladders when they began to climb up.

Thea went next with Lonnie behind her, "I'm right behind you, Thea." Both were excited at the climb and anxious to do it. Then, Sir Thomas started up a third ladder taking strong, determined steps ever upwards.

"Okay, it's our turn," Alison said to Jon. "Come on." Still he hesitated.

"I don't know if I can do this, honey. What if I fall?"

"I'm not worried. I always wear my magical rings so I can fly or levitate. So a slip is nothing. But why worry, you can just step yourself right up or back down here if you fall."

"No, I need to concentrate and I don't think that is possible if I am falling!"

"Okay, silly, I'll follow right behind you so if you slip, I can grab you and levitate us both up," she promised. With that reassurance, Jon feebly grabbed hold and started to climb. At first, he made reasonable progress, but he found it very tiring. By the time he reached the halfway point, he had to pause to rest. His arms felt like butter and his legs, no better. With all his might he gripped the sides of the rope ladder. Panic seeped into his mind.

Alison felt it. "Come on, it's just a bit more," she tried to encourage him to no avail.

"I can't do this. I'm shaking!" he exclaimed.

"I know, I can feel it, I'm right behind you. Come on, you need to take just one more step." She badgered, cajoled, pleaded with him and he obeyed and somehow took another step and then another. She kept a very alert eye on him because his legs were shaking rather badly. Using a free hand, she guided each of his feet onto the next rung. Jon thought that hours had passed before he reached the top. "Little help here," she called out. The strong arms of Mandy and Sir Thomas grabbed Jon from either side and literally pulled him the rest of the way up and safely inside the entrance way five hundred feet above the canyon floor below. Jon's legs gave completely out and he crumpled like an empty sack upon the cave floor not daring to move the slightest muscle.

Many Braids knelt beside him and poured some liquid into his mouth. "Drink this. You should have said you suffer the sickness of height before you climbed. I could have given you this then. Sickness goes away." Indeed the bitter taste burned down into his stomach, but he felt strength returning to his limbs almost at once.

"What was that?" he asked, now feeling strong enough to sit up.

"An herbal remedy handed down to me by Morning Breeze, and she, from her mother and so on. It comes also from cactus, though a special one. You feel better now?"

He stood, "Ah, yes, much better. Oh yes, I feel fine, really, really fine. Oh yes indeedy! I do feel great. I maybe could even fly." The others roared. Jon was punchy already. Her potion packed a wallop.

"Don't let him fly, please! Come, I'll give you a tour of our cliff dwelling. This is the entrance room." Many Braids led them deeper into the cavern room. Side passages connected all of the rooms cradled up against the cliff. The adobe walls protected them from outside attacks and the accidental fall. As they moved deeper into the dwellings, others pulled the ladders safely up for the night. Essentially, they had taken this natural edge cavern and widened it here and deepened it there, encasing the either outer side in adobe. Twelve rooms in all comprised their home. One contained grain and other dried foods along with many pots of water. Another held a cooking fire and communal eating room. The others were the private sleeping quarters for the many extended families. She introduced them to her daughter, Fair Skies who was about twelve, and her last remaining son, Eagle Nest who was fourteen. She had lost one daughter to a sickness and her eldest son to the evil creatures, along with her husband.

After eating a quick meal, every member of the tribe then stood by the various openings and windows to watch the setting of the sun. Many chanted songs though none of the party understood the words. Predictably, Jon was enthralled with the sounds and got out his flute and played along. When the last red rays of the west lingered no longer and the brilliant stars shown down, Jon played on, improvising upon the mood of these people. The entire tribe listened appreciatively. When he finished, he had many warm compliments. Perhaps the most significant was Running Bears's: "You are the first outsider who makes the sounds of one of us. Surely you must be from the Great Spirit!"

Then, they all retired to their sleeping rooms. Many Braids and her small family moved into her mother's room so that the party could have their own room for the night. Finally they had time to discuss what they had learned. Jon first described what he had done with Many Braids. He had used his mental methods to help her erase the loss of her husband. He had been quite successful with the young woman.

Then, Alison brought him up-to-date with what they had learned from Running Bear. When she finished outlining the facts, Darless spoke with authority, looking at Sir Thomas, "Well, you are going to get your wish, My Love. We face an infestation of powerful demons, there can be no doubt. What they call the Evil Spirit is actually my counterpart, a male half demon-half human, a Cambion. From his description, this one is a Marquis at least, on par with the one who imprisoned the Air Maiden Fruella! He has super-human strength and is a powerful magic user, probably at least as good as Alison, certainly better than I am." Many exclamations followed, of which Zagroot zounds! was the least.

She continued, "Oh it gets better. From their description of the flying creatures, it is my guess that these are none other than Nabassu demons which are sometimes called death stealers!" More groans. "In essence, these demons are born in the Abyss. When they reach a certain age, they come to our world to eat humans. As they consume them, they grow. When fully grown, that is, after devouring about twelve people, they then return to the Abyss and never trouble this world again. It's their life cycle, pretty grim. Normally, their biggest problem is finding a place in this world where they can reside and eat without being killed in the process. It would seem that this Marquis has established a major breeding tower here in Wavapata. We are in for one nasty battle, make no mistake about that!"

After another half hour discussing their relative strengths and weaknesses, talk turned to the old brown man, who also bore the name of Threngold. Everyone speculated, but Sir Thomas pointed out that many dragons can change their form to that of a man and walk among men. The conclusion was this person bore further examination. Finally, Alison spoke as the party's leader, "I asked you all to come along in search of the dragon. However, I cannot ignore the dire plight of these people. I aim to do what I can to eliminate this breeding ground of demons. Will anyone back me up in this most perilous attempt?"

"Verily, my sword is yours to command," spoke Sir Thomas. "But you do not need to ask; these are demons we are talking about!" Everyone was with her, but Mandy did thank her for asking.

"Look this infestation is right on our way," Mandy added. "We have to pass through the center of the valley anyway. So let's eliminate them on our way. I say we head there at first light tomorrow. What with all the twists and turns, do you suppose they have any maps for us to follow?" she added. "We could get lost in this maze!" No one thought there was the slightest chance for a map, and they were correct.

Now the illumination in the room was dim at best, a tiny flickering candle allowed them to see the basics. Thus, they all turned in earlier than normal, trying to accustom themselves to the sleeping reed mats their host provided. None were successful, so Alison created a bit of magical light and they rummaged through their portable holes for blankets and such. Still, Jon found it very difficult to sleep on the hard stone, no matter the thin blanket and reeds beneath him. He dreamed of falling helplessly off of cliffs, of rolling over in bed and falling over the edge by accident. He slept poorly if at all. He was only too glad when the first rays of dawn came through the high small window.

The entire tribe was up at dawn's first light, once again chanting a welcome to the new day. Then, everyone headed down the ladders heading for the latrines. Jon however refused to even try the ladder; he simple stepped himself back down much to the amazement of the natives. Alison and Darless, concerned for him, levitated down rapidly to make sure he did not hurt himself. He had dark circles under his eyes and his concentration was just a bit shaky, they observed. They were right; he misjudged the ground slightly and sprained his ankle slightly. "Boy am I ever glad to be on solid ground again," he exclaimed, as the two mages floated down beside him.

"Silly, the cliff dwellings are also solid ground," Darless teased him. He glared at her, not really appreciating her humor just now.

After sharing breakfast with them, Alison outlined what they were going to do, head to the center of the canyon and find this stone temple and eliminate all of the evil creatures therein. "By any chance do you have any map that we can use? These many canyons seem like a maze to us," she asked hopefully.

There were no maps. They had no paper or writing equipment. "You are right. Outsiders only get lost here. You must take a guide," said Many Braids. "I shall give you the very best guide in my tribe. None is better than He Who Does Not Speak." She motioned toward a young warrior who hastened to her side. She told him that he was to guide the outsiders to their original home land, where the Evil Spirit now resided. He made numerous signs with his hands, evidently clarifying his orders. She turned to Alison relaying his concerns, "He Who Does Not Speak cannot talk, will you be able to follow his signs?" She now was having worries about how he would fit in with them using only his hand signals.

"Not a problem at all," exclaimed Jon. "He'll do just fine." He Who Does Not Speak grinned, proud to be able to help these mighty servants of the Great Spirit. Jon grinned back. "Oh yes, we leave you a little present of these riding horses that we found. You have need of them and we don't; we've got two extra ones." Now it was Many Braids who shook his hand in thanks, these would really help the tribe. They mounted up and rode single file out of the encampment with He Who Does Not Speak leading the way, Mandy right behind him followed by Sir Thomas and the others. Thea and Lonnie, as usual, brought up the rear.

It was cool here in the early morning; dew coated the plants, providing the moisture of life. A few billowing white clouds dotted the deep blue sky in sharp contrast to the multicolored, water carved canyon lands about them. Ordinarily, a ride such as this would have been most memorable indeed. Knowing that at the end of the ride they would be facing a host of very powerful demons put a damper on their enjoyment.

Mandy was concerned about a possible ambush by these demons in spite of Running Bear's insistence that they only came out at night. Also, there were the giant wasps to consider. She cautioned them, "If we run into more wasps, do not use any magic that creates noise. I do not want to alert the enemy of our approach. Stealth is the order of the day. I want to be able to take them by surprise." As they rode along, passing by the narrow tended fields and out into the open river bottom, Jon pondered what they should do if wasps showed up again.

Now from their general overview map, Mandy knew that this temple lay about forty miles due east of their position. However, the twisting, turning canyon bottoms made the overland distance much greater. She managed to sign with He Who Does Not Speak about this and concluded that it would take all of two day's travel to get there.

Twice during the day, swarms of wasps appeared from smaller side canyons. Jon figured out how to handle them. When they first appeared, he called out, "Stop everybody. No one move a muscle. Perhaps they will ignore us." It took nerve to stand motionless as these three-foot buzzing freaks of nature hovered about one's face, but they soon flew off in search of plants and nectar leaving the party alone. Sir Thomas felt a bit put out that they didn't slay all of these foul creatures, but went along with the stealth plan, demons were far worse than a few nasty wasps.

As the shadows lengthened, He Who Does Not Speak halted and made questioning signs about where to take shelter from the flying night demons. Needless to say, he was mightily impressed with Alison's magical mansion. Everyone got a good night's sleep that night! Jon was truly thankful for the soft bedding she created in her magical home.

By noon of the next day, they knew they were getting close. The Little Bend and the Big Bend rivers merged. The mostly dry bed extended for well over a mile to either side of the trickling water. Signs of abandoned fields lay about them on both sides, as the various tribes fled the demons in years past. Jon could sense how dismal their lives were now compared to the much wider spaces around here.

Late that afternoon, they grew close to their objective. Around the next bend, a greyish tower top could be seen. From what they could see from here, which was only the upper third, there were no windows except huge open spaces near the very top. They halted to discuss what to do next.

Mandy and Sir Thomas both agreed that they should make camp here and spy out the enemy before rushing headlong into combat. Alison agreed and cast her mansion spell. They all went inside for a quick conference. "Okay here is the plan, some of us are going to go spy out the temple and see what we can discover — like easy ways into it and such. The rest stay safely here. This mission is all about stealth. We do not want to be discovered under any circumstances or we will lose our greatest weapon — that of total surprise. If things go ill, we can send for the rest of you or retreat back to here."

"Stealth leaves me out," chuckled Sir Thomas. "In this armor, I cannot help but make a racket. I will stay behind, as much as I regret it, unless you want me to don my simple leather armor which is not altogether befitting my stature."

"No, you stay in armor," Alison requested, "If we need you, we will *really* need you at your maximum strength." He was obviously relieved by her desire. He hated wearing only light leather armor. "Mandy and Darless must go for obvious reasons. I think that I ought to go because it gives us more abilities should something go wrong. Perhaps Jon should come too, if trouble occurs, he, better than any of us, can get us all out of the tight situation in a hurry or come get you and bring you all physically to our rescue. So I think the four of us should go. Now do we go on foot or risk horses? It is still some ways off."

Mandy answered that one by making a drawing on the floor for He That Does Not Speak. She drew an 'X' indicating where they were and a cup representing the tower. She signed for him to show her how the river twisted. Indeed there were quite a few more turns before they could reach the tower proper. "We ride for a while yet. Then go on foot."

Chapter 7 Glasya

Shortly, Mandy and the other three continued their passage along the wide river bed. Only she went exceedingly slowly and very carefully. When they were perhaps five miles distant, she led them perpendicular to the river, making for the cavern walls to their left. In a concealed area, they tied the horses, making use of an abandoned adobe shelter. Next, they crept forward along the rugged walls, taking advantage of the rocky cover as much as possible. Finally, only a little over a mile from the tower, they all hid behind an outcrop and surveyed the tower.

From here they could see it clearly. It was solid rock, not built of stone laid upon stone, but a seamless stone, unseen in any of these lands, as if the hand of a god had poured the structure. No doors could be seen on the portion facing them. The only entrance was fifty feet up — the gaping holes where the flying demons obviously came and left. All about them lay utter silence. Not even a bird chirped nor a frog croaked. It was an unnatural, brooding silence. They stared for a half hour but saw nothing else.

Jon grew bored with the total inaction. He looked around at what used to be the home of Running Bear and his tribe. Though the land had reverted to wilds, still here and there the hands of men and their works could be spotted. Then, Jon saw something move. Mandy also felt the hairs on her neck tingle. *Something's out there!* she sent to everyone, as Jon pointed to where he had seen the brief movement. Yes, some person dressed in reds and yellows was also sneaking behind similar rock outcrops. Whoever it was was also spying on the tower!

"Friend or foe," whispered Mandy. "That is the question. We need to know who that is and their purpose.

The question is how best to do it. Should we go invisible, perhaps sneak up on them?" Now was a good time to not be visible, so Alison hid behind the rock and rummaged for her magical rings. She found the four she wanted and handed one to each of her friends who put them on. She was instructing them on their command word of activation, when a flash of magic appeared behind them. Startled, they turned to see the very same person they were spying upon only a moment before.

Before them stood a very, very beautiful woman, dressed in revealing bright red and yellow bikini style clothing. Her skin was perfectly smooth, a shining copper color. She used some makeup, Jon noted; her lips were ruby red and her eyes and lashes, black. She had wavy long hair and wore a rather large amount of jewelry. Alison noted five rings and a fabulous necklace with many large gems set in it. She had golden arm bands highly embossed. However, she also had a large pair of wings attached to her back, each with a menacing claw hook at the top. Two horns protruded from her forehead, mostly hidden in her lush wavy hair. Her nails were highly polished with a matching ruby red color and were at least two inches long. She was stunningly beautiful and she knew it.

"Greetings to you. It took you long enough to get here," she said in matter-of-fact tone. "We'd best hide completely behind these rocks." She gazed at Jon and commented to him, "You are not as cute as I imagined. Ah well, looks are not everything." Meantime, the four just stared gapingly at her. Such was the reaction she was accustomed to having. She thoroughly enjoyed it.

"I see you do not know me, I am Glasya, daughter of Asmodeous, consort of Mammon, friend of Dispater, the Princess of Hell, and Archmage, at your service." She bowed her head slightly. "Dispater sent me in his place; he is rather busy at the moment and could not come personally." Then, she looked Jon straight in the eyes and asked coyly, "Do you like my outfit? I chose it especially for you, Saint Jon Brown, the Redeemer."

Jon managed to mumble, "Stunning." She certainly was not what he expected devils to look like!

She wiggled her hips and chest about sexily, "Maybe later tonight if you are not busy, we can get together for some bedtime fun and play." Jon's face turned beet red. What man could resist this woman? Or would even want too?

Mandy finally found her voice and managed to feebly utter, "Zagroot zounds!"

Alison stepped in front of Jon, "Sorry, he's not available. He is with me."

Darless, shaking her head disgustingly, commented, "I might have guessed! Everywhere we go, we keep running into Dispater. What's he got to do with *this* demon mess?"

Throwing her head back, she laughed, "Okay, okay. I was just teasing him. Before we get serious, Saint Jon or do you prefer to be called just Jon. Ah, yes, Jon." She answered her own question; she read his instantaneous body language response to her question. "Seriously, Jon, it has been a very long time since I was on this plane dealing with humans. I really want to know. Do you find my outfit, my appearance — ignoring the horns and wings if you desire — do you find me attractive — make you want me?"

Still blushing, Jon meekly answered, "Do you have to ask?" Alison punched him lightly in his side.

"Ah good. Thanks for being honest. Alright, now down to business, Darless. In this matter, I have been told that it is imperative that there be no possible misunderstandings. Dispater was very insistent upon that; you know how he can be. So I will assume your knowledge is limited."

She straightened up and took on a formal air. "First, there is a universe of difference between devils and demons. We always follow the Rules of Law; demons make their own 'laws' on the spur of the moment as it suits them. While you can always trust a devil, there is no such thing as trusting a demon, unless it is to do diabolical deeds. In short, devils and demons are continually at war with each other. You cannot imagine how I have had to restrain myself from attacking and destroying yonder temple!" Her face grimaced for a moment, and a face of total hatred stared out at them but was quickly replaced by the face of total loveliness and beauty.

She saw that Darless was becoming a bit impatient. "Okay, so what has this to do with anything here? Everything. We know that you are now in search of Threngold, the brown dragon. Do not ask me how I come to know that detail; I cannot betray a confidence. Are you aware that the dragon Tiamat is the mother, the creator, of all dragon kind? Ah, I see you are well informed. That is good. Now Tiamat lives in Hell, though nowhere near where the rest of us dwell, thankfully. I detest dragons, personally, you see, too smelly. Tiamat is quite lawful in her actions, which is why she rules a plane in Hell. Thus, Threngold, being one of her consorts, yes males can also be consorts," she winked at Jon, "is bound to Hell as well."

"Remain calm, Darless, I am coming to the point of all this. I must ask you what you know about the temple yonder and who or what occupies it?"

"A Cambion Marquis is our educated guess," Darless spoke dryly and clearly. "Our conclusion is fairly simple. Number 1, this Marquis came here and established this temple driving the local inhabitants out. Number 2, he is bringing in or gating or some such method a number of hatchlings, the Nabassu. These demons are devouring the inhabitants so that they grow to adult hood and return to the Abyss. Number 3, this has got to stop!"

Glasya grinned, "Correct on all three points. I shall add only a couple details that you likely do not know. Again, do not ask me how I know these. Number 1," she said echoing the alu-demon and playing with her, "the name of the Cambion is the Marquis de Gritz." She paused to let that name sink into their minds.

"I've heard that name before," Jon said trying to remember.

"Wasn't that the name the Air Maiden called the demon that she was spying upon several hundred years ago and who imprisoned her for centuries?" Alison wondered aloud.

Instant recognition flashed in the other's minds. "Right! Oh my god!" exclaimed Jon.

"Zagroot zounds!" Mandy could not help but mutter as she grasped the magnitude of the foe that they were about to face.

Glasya smiled, thinking to herself that these humans were not as dumb as they appeared — that Dispater was correct in his observations of them. "Number 2, Threngold secretly brought the Marquis here and has aided him in getting this colony established." Again, she paused giving their frail minds time to absorb this fact. She watched their minds racing to absorb this information, to reach conclusions, to grasp its significance. It was imperative that they grasp it. She waited patiently.

"Wait a minute," protested Alison, "that makes no sense. You just said that devils and demons are at war and that Threngold is kin with devils. Why would he be aiding and abetting your enemies?"

Glasya smiled broadly, eyes twinkling. *These humans are quick to understand. Dispater maybe on to something.* She was not sure of what, just yet. "Exactly. Please realize that we have only fairly recently pieced together these facts. In spite of what you may think of devils, we are not 'all-knowing' gods. We are about eighty percent certain that Threngold had a hand in the launching of this demon outpost. If it's true, that is treasonous. So look at the situation from our point of view. A devil aligned dragon is aiding the enemy of devils. What for? How come? What are his intentions? A sneak raid upon devils? As Dispater said, 'This raises so many questions it is not even funny!' Thus, it is vital to us to find out if Threngold really has or is playing a part and what the ultimate plan is meant to be. That's why I am here — why Dispater has sent me. We must know the answers before his diabolical plot culminates."

"I hate to put the damper on this conversation," interjected Mandy, all of these conclusions were coming too fast for her liking, "but it would appear that a storm is coming soon. I suggest we get back to camp as fast as possible." Indeed, the late afternoon sun had just disappeared behind a huge thunder head. A front was moving in fast. The others noticed the change in the weather and turned to follow her back to where the horses were tied.

Jon had to make a decision. He had been silent, absorbing Glasya's words and trying to read between the lines, but a heavy spring rain was nearly on them. He did feel responsible for Glasya being here and out in the open. "Glasya, I don't know whether you have shelter you can get to or not. But you are welcome to come with us to ours. If you do, why, we would have more time to discuss your situation and such. That is, if none of you have any objections?" he added hastily, remembering this was basically Alison's mission and mansion, and that, as the leader, she might not like his inviting a devil into their space.

Alison did not surprise him, "No, Jon. Glasya, forgive my manners. Would you care to come with us and spend the night sheltered from this storm? I would like to discuss the situation with you further." Darless and Mandy also nodded their consent.

The devil smiled — her brilliant white teeth and ruby red lips contrasted with the copper skin. "Actually, I really would like that very much! I have a number of questions I would like to ask. And no, I do not have any camp. It has been a bit trying hiding out around here waiting for you to arrive. I think we should make haste."

Jon said, "Okay, to the horses really fast. Grab hold of my hand. Oh yes, Glasya, grab hold of one of us. I am going to step us there. On the count of three, just take one step forward." Without waiting for any reply, he rhythmically counted "one, two, three," and took a step forward, focusing on next being where they had left the horses. They arrived, but Glasya stumbled, taken completely by surprise by Jon's ability to travel through space without using a teleport spell.

"Was that a psi power you used? Travel or teleport?" Glasya asked regaining her balance. A large streak of lightning illuminated the area; the rolling thunder came three seconds later. "I do the Control of Energy Control and Realignment of Molecules," she added while Mandy swiftly untied the horses.

Jon faltered, "Er, no time to explain. Everyone hang onto each other, the horses and me." Just as soon as they complied, he stepped them back to where the mansion was located just in time to avoid being drenched.

Sir Thomas was at the doorway keeping an eye out for them. He'd felt a growing concern as the storm front moved into the area. "Just in time, come on it quickly," he called out as they suddenly appeared near the door. Hastily, he hurried inside himself, making way for the others leading the horses inside.

"Impressive," Glasya commented upon seeing the shimmering doors of the magical mansion. "Now this *is* a good use of magic." She was the last to enter just as the storm broke into a torrential rain punctuated heavily with lightning and thunder.

She had no more than gotten inside when Sir Thomas finally saw her and cried out, "A devil! She is a devil. Do you realize you have brought a devil inside this mansion? I fear for our safety!" Biased though he was, the paladin still could not bring himself to countermand Alison's leadership. So he phrased it as though the mage may not have seen through some disguise of the devil, some bewitchment may have been placed upon Alison and the others.

"Yes, I invited her," Alison replied, "I'm sorry I did not get the chance to warn you, but the storm broke so unexpectedly soon. Let me introduce everyone. This is Glasya, a friend of Dispater's and, I'm sorry, Glasya, I forgot all of your titles."

"Glasya, daughter of Asmodeous, consort of Mammon, friend of Dispater, the Princess of Hell, and Archmage, at your service," she repeated more slowly this time and bowed her head slightly toward the paladin.

Hastily, Alison continued, "This is Sir Thomas le Bonnaire, Holy Paladin of Ukko. This is Lonnie Smith, a fledgling Holy Paladin of Ukko as well. My apprentice, Thea Westfold. Sir Thomas fumed, but said nothing. Lonnie just stared at this most beautiful woman.

Thea cheerily exclaimed, "Wow, a real devil! Pleased to meet you. You really are very beautiful. Are all female devils as pretty as you? I've never met a devil before. What beautifully long nails you have! How long does it take to grow them that long? How did you get them painted red? They look terrific. The color blends with your skin so well."

"One question at a time," laughed Glasya. "Some devils are pretty and some are plain, just as some of you humans are comely and some are not so good looking. And yes, this is my normal appearance, Sir Thomas. I am not casting any illusions at the moment. Thanks for the compliment. I keep them about this long, two inches. It takes maybe two years for them to grow this long. When they chip, I use a simple mending spell on them. They certainly are an eye catcher aren't they? I love them and so do men, if you catch my meaning." She winked at Thea, who suddenly grasped her subtle hint. Thea flushed, wondering if she could have such beautiful nails and how she could get them painted red, perhaps not cherry red though, a more subdued red.

"Well, come on in, Glasya," Alison interrupted, "this is my magical mansion spell. Are you familiar with this spell?"

"Yes, I've used it on occasion," she replied walking into the main living room and glancing about. "I'm very glad to see that you have both style and flair, Mage Alison. That is to your credit." Then, she spied He That Does Not Speak standing solemnly in a corner.

"Oh I nearly forgot," exclaimed Alison. "This is He That Does Not Speak; he is our guide through the Canyon Lands. This is Glasya," she pointed the devil out to the dark skinned native. His eyes panned over her from toe to head; he smiled and nodded to her.

"May the blessings of the Great Spirit be upon you, He That Does Not Speak," Glasya honored him. "I'm sure the Great Spirit has noted your gift."

"Huh?" commented Alison, quite missing her point. "What gift? You know about these people and their Great Spirit?"

"An Archmage knows," she replied in a teasing fashion. "Seriously, I did my research before coming to your land. Didn't you know that He That Does Not Speak has chosen as his gift to the Great Spirit a life of no speech? It is his voluntary way to do honor to his God."

"Well, no, you have me on that point. I've only met him this morning and we really have not had time to get acquainted properly," Alison justified. "But I'm hungry. Let's eat first and then parley. I too have many questions that need answering. By the way, I am the one leading this expedition, though this current situation is not what any of us intended to find. We are on an altogether different mission. But let's eat; I am famished!"

She and Darless headed into the kitchen area to fix some diner. Glasya, not wanting to be left with alone with Sir Thomas as yet, joined them. Mandy and the paladins took care of the four horses, rubbing them down and feeding them. Thea chatted with Jon about how beautify this devil really was and how she wished she could look half as good as Glasya. He That Does Not Speak went to the doors and watched the spring thunderstorm over Wavapata; it brought the yearly renewal to the land.

The three women returned to the living room bearing trays of food and drink. Glasya noticed that He That Does Not Speak was watching the rain through the open doors. She commented to Alison, "You know, there is one little trick you can do with this spell. It is a little something extra that I invented. Let me show you." Both Alison and Darless suddenly were all ears, paying close attention. The others sat down and began to eat. Glasya uttered a magical chant and a window to the outside world appeared in the walls of the mansion. "You can make it a three hundred-sixty degree panorama if you like. Here, each of you practice it and make the small window I have created go all the away around." Patiently, the devil taught the two mages how to modify the spell and create view windows as they desired. "This is much better. We can now watch the storm." He That Does Not Speak joined them smiling and nodding his approval. He signed that this was the annual spring rains and was likely the largest amount of rain the land would see all year.

Once they had all eaten, Alison had Glasya explain to Sir Thomas all that she had told the four earlier that afternoon. She told of Dispater's deep concern that the brown dragon, Threngold, may be behind the arrival of the demons. When Sir Thomas heard that the name of the Cambion was none other than the infamous Marquis de Gritz, he swore that he would slay this demon once and for all. The paladin interrupted to outline ancient history for everyone.

This particular demon and his minions had originally occupied all of these northern lands with his main base of operations at the temple at Leeds, which was now a ruins. Of course this heyday of the demons had been over two hundred years ago. He told how his grandfather and Alison's and others who now live in the greater Verbenloc area had systematically driven all of the evil out of the more inhabitable lands. He admitted that it took direct intervention of Father Ukko and his Air Maidens to actually destroy Leeds and drive the Marquis out of the area. The presence here of Marquis de Gritz was extremely significant to Sir Thomas. He even speculated that perhaps the Marquis was behind the sacking of Castle d'Ambrose over twenty years ago.

Glasya had not heard about the destruction of Alison's family and castle. Hence, Alison took several minutes to briefly outline the sad tale of her father and the Holy Scepter of Ukko. Dispater had briefed the Princess on the four's recent recovery of that very same scepter, so Alison was spared going into an even more lengthy tale. She really did not like to even present the possibility that she was "bragging" about her adventures, especially not when Glasya was a far more superior mage than she.

Glasya then summed up her orders from Dispater, "You see, I am here to find out the truth about any possible involvement of Threngold. If he actually is or was involved, I must discover the plan, the time line, time-place-form-event, as much as is possible. We devils are constantly in a state of war against these self-seeking, chaotic animals! We certainly do not want any surprise assaults upon our lands. Sir Thomas, for the time being, we are aligned with your purposes."

Sir Thomas reacted rather badly to this declaration of alliance. "I for one would rather see all you evil beings fighting yourselves! Then, there are fewer of you to plague the world with your hatred, deceit, murder and foulness that I cannot speak of in the company of the ladies! We need no alliance with devils. Who ever heard of a Holy Paladin aligning with an evil devil! I stand for goodness!" If there had been a desk in the room, he would have pounded it into bits to further accentuate his declaration. Finding none, he fumed and glared defiantly at Glasya.

Poor Darless. She had purposely been silent, observing the others, measuring their reactions, considering carefully each position, looking for trickery — for the not quite honest statement that could come back to haunt them later. Now her betrothed had once again allowed his bias, his prejudice, his emotions to overwhelm him. She recalled Alison's statement some time back, "He makes hasty decisions that are usually wrong. I invariably make the correct ones and he recognizes that."

She had also watched Lonnie's reactions to Glasya's discussion, for he too was a Holy Paladin. She found them strikingly different. Until his outburst, Lonnie seemed to fully agree with Glasya's reasoning, finding no fault with it. Perhaps that was only due to the young lad's inexperience and training. She reached out to Sir Thomas's mind and was about to do what she could to calm his emotions, to get reason back in place of anger, when she perceived Jon was also present; he had beaten her to it.

Jon, who also had said nothing this whole time and who also observed the others, realized at once that Sir Thomas's anger had nothing to do with Glasya. He knew that an angry man seldom sees what is really there, only his imagined foe. Jon saw plainly that Sir Thomas, though looking at Glasya, really did not see her, but was looking at a picture in his mind. More importantly, Sir Thomas did not even realize he was looking at or through this image, that it was clouding his mind, his reason. So he acted, getting the jump on Darless.

Jon knew that when he needed to — he knew that he could command total obedience from others. This was such a time. Using a quiet voice, full of total command, full of his total intention that his words would be heeded by all present, he said to Sir Thomas, "I am Saint Jon, the Redeemer, and the time of your redemption is now. The rest of you be totally silent and learn. Sir Thomas, close your eyes. Good. Now look at those pictures you have there in your mind. Yes, those. I want you to go to the beginning of that time and then go through it and tell me what happened as you go along."

Sir Thomas, still violently angry, felt the total intention, the total command, such as he had never felt before. That portion of his mind that was reacting still wanted to fight against Jon, to willfully disobey his orders. Sir Thomas had no possibility of doing so, because stopping that command was like trying to stop a sled flying down an icy slope in winter. He found himself looking at the start of that time when he was eleven. His pictures, his recall, were altogether vivid in his mind. It was a dark day for him. "I'm going down the street toward the training center. Bucky, about two years older than I am, he's my enemy, waylaid me and knocked me to the ground giving me a bloody nose. I got to the class late and got a reprimand from Captain Jones. We are doing close quarters training combat simulations. We have to take out one of the real guardsmen. I protest; I'm only eleven; he's too strong and big for me. Captain Jones says we must work as a team, for a team is stronger than a single man. He orders Bucky and me to team and take out the guard. I protest. I get very angry. I leave. That's all."

"Very well done, Sir Thomas. Now I want you to go back to the beginning once more and go through it again and tell me what is happening," Jon spoke. He noticed that everyone in the room as also listening intently. He sensed a huge smile on Darless' face, though he dared not look her way, concentrating fully on his patient. He felt all the built up tension in Alison evaporate as she grasped what he was doing. He felt the total concentration of Glasya's stare on him and even the slightest touch of her mind, as she observed from a distance.

The paladin went through the incident once more. This time, he added, "I actually struck Captain Jones before I left! Boy was I mad. The gall of that man, partnering me with my enemy! He deserved it." Again, Jon thanked him for telling him and asked him to go through it yet again. This time, antagonism replaced the anger Sir Thomas felt. By the fifth re-experiencing, some yawns occurred and a distinctly conservative tone appeared. The next recounting, the paladin did not finish, instead he started laughing. "You know, that was silly of me. After I got a bloody nose, I decided right there that I would never ever have anything to do with Bucky. By the time I got into the lesson, I had completely forgotten that decision, yet it was still in effect. There was no way Captain Jones could ever get me to team with Bucky! Ha, Ha." He roared with laughter.

He looked at Glasya and laughed harder, yet tried to speak. "Forgive me, Glasya — forgive my outburst — I had you confused with Bucky — or rather you *were* Bucky there for a minute — you sure don't look like Bucky!" Now everyone roared; his laughter was contagious. Jon did not see it, but even He That Does Not Speak was smiling; the native had observed everything and understood the spiritual awaking.

Thank you Jon! Darless placed in his mind. *I owe you one.*

"Thank you for whatever you did there, Jon," the paladin managed to utter amid his laughter. "I feel so relieved that I am at a loss for words." Instead, he laughed some more.

Inspired by his success, Jon went even further. He thought it was at least worth a try. "Say, Sir Thomas, how about being a foot back of your head right now."

"Ha, ha. Okay. Yes, I'm there," he replied jovially. Suddenly his laughter stopped. For the first time in his life, he realized that he was a being and not his body. He was something separate from a body. "Oh my god! I'm me; not the body there. Oh my, oh my. This is unbelievable! I'm really me." Suddenly he understood what Alison, Darless, Mandy, and Jon had been saying about being spiritual beings. A whole new avenue of existence opened for him. The self-imposed blinders had been removed.

A tear trickled down Darless' cheek. Long had she prayed that Sir Thomas could finally see himself as a being and not his robust body. It had just happened. She whispered to him, "Now look what we can do." And she, the being, moved up close to him and they intertwined briefly as one united being. So powerful was their union, he was completely speechless. His mouth waggled, but no words came out. His eyes roamed to find her body and locked on to it. Sir Thomas had his first spiritual embrace, the first of many. Then, she separated from him, returning to near her body.

"What just happened?" Thea, containing her curiosity no longer, asked of everyone, her eyes darting from person to person in hopes someone would enlighten her.

Since Thea was her apprentice, Alison felt it was her obligation to answer. "They shared a very private moment together, a spiritual embrace, somewhat akin to a physical one. It's hard to put it into words, but it's like you both merge together into one, sharing the same space and all. It is very close, and very romantic, if I might add. Thanks, Jon. You really *are* a romantic soul aren't you?"

He blushed and smiled. "It might not have worked, you know."

Thea looked long at Lonnie and he, her. Both were wondering if they could ever be able to share such a private moment.

Glasya, outwardly showing signs of being very impressed with the entire process and particularly with the spiritual awareness and union, apologized to everyone, "You must also forgive me. I am so used to dealing with gods and lesser gods, that I sometimes forget that we, you and I, have such different realities. Let me explain. You contend that we differ because you are 'good' and I am 'evil' but please, let's define our terms. What is good and what is evil?"

"Well, that's obvious, good is good," pronounced Sir Thomas with authority but immediately realized that was not a definition. So he hastily appended, "Good is doing actions that benefit and aid mankind, things that help one's village, one's family, and even one's self."

"Don't forget about the animals," put in Mandy, "and the trees and forests and all plants as well."

"Good," Glasya continued, "But is there not a gradient scale of goodness and evil? Are not some things more 'good' than others or some more evil than others? Of course, there is. For example, let's take the destruction of Alison's home. You say that that was an evil act. But suppose that its destruction meant that one thousand other homes were spared. That is, the choice is destroy one home and save one thousand or destroy one thousand to save one. Clearly, good effects needs a better definition. My opinion is that a good effect is one that helps more broadly than it hurts. Many claim that evil is destruction or destructive acts. I do not deny that. Destroying Alison's home is a destructive effect. But Sir Thomas, do you not destroy, slay enemy hobgoblins, in the name of doing a good deed? I say you are still using a destructive effect. Yet you claim you are doing a good effect, while actually you are causing a destructive effect. A person can cause both bad effects as well as cause good effects. It depends upon the viewpoint." She paused letting her ideas be absorbed.

"Now, let's look closer at this. A person at the bottom only causes bad effects, granted. We all know such people. But is not the attitude of 'I'm to blame; I caused a bad effect' just above that? Is not just above that the safe one of 'I caused some bad things but they did too?' When you get angry, don't you feel like saying 'you are to blame; you caused a *bad* thing?' And when you are in an antagonistic mood, don't you feel like saying, 'I'm in control and I am going to *make* you do good thing?' Further, when you reach where Alison sits, don't you feel like saying 'Hey, there is a lot of bad things happening around here, let's all pitch in and go straighten them out?'"

Alison laughed so hard she could not sit, "Boy you pegged me with that one! I'm always trying to get others to get in there and help me straighten the bad things out!"

"Verily, she speaks the truth," agreed Sir Thomas, who was feeling rather bad, reflecting upon his frequent attitude thinking about others: 'You are doing *bad* things!' He now brightened up for he recognized that very attitude was precisely what Alison constantly displayed all these years he had known her, particularly when she had been his party's mage.

"Yes, we agree on all this," Darless commented, "but I fail to see where it leads us, save to prove that we are right in fighting evil."

"Touché!" exclaimed Glasya. "Now take just one step up from that. Sometimes we do kind actions such as giving water to a stranger dying of thirst in a desert; sometimes we do destructive actions such as killing a murderer who has just killed a family member. That one step beyond is to go even higher. Suppose for an instant you were a god or goddess, just suppose. You can do constructive actions and destructive actions as you choose, just like you folks. How do you judge them? Would you not agree that you might judge the results by just how *effective* that action was in accomplishing the goal at hand?" Again she paused to let them ponder this step.

"But still that doesn't help," protested Darless. "Gods can have an evil purpose in mind and yet be very effective in carrying it out using constructive or destructive effects to accomplish it."

"Ah there's the rub," Glasya countered. "How do you *know* that the purpose of the god was indeed an *evil* one? You are seeing it through *your* eyes, your viewpoint, not his! You see, you are now getting into a region ruled by reason and 'is the action effective.' Is it not said in this world that all gods have two faces? That there is a good, benevolent side of a god and also a wrathful, vengeful one?"

"You know you have a point there, Glasya," Jon interjected. "I just remembered something from my ancient history class. Back in my world in ancient times, we had gods and goddesses on Mount Olympus. Always they were depicted as having two faces, we called them tragedy and comedy. I never understood what that meant until just now. Suddenly, it all falls into place."

"Ah ha," exclaimed Darless, "and I do not ever pretend to know the mind of a god or goddess. I cannot see into the future or far into the past; I am not all knowing or even remotely. I sometimes wished that they would at least tell us what the overall plans were so we could understand better and perhaps aid them, but that is just me being vain."

"Okay, Glasya, I will accept your help in this matter," Alison concluded. "My decision is based primarily on the fact that you and I both have a high respect and regard for the rules of conduct, the laws of societies. Because of this, I deem that you would not betray us or intentionally cause us harm, nor would I, you."

"Since our leader hath so spoken," Sir Thomas agreed, "then, you have my pledge to honor it as well. Without the known rules of agreement, anarchy befalls all, and that is intolerable to everyone."

"Speak for yourself on that one," chuckled Mandy. "Ill thought-out rule followed slavishly is a bane on the group, from my point of view. However, you have no fear from me, Glasya. If you offer to help with no diabolical strings attached, I'll stand behind you."

The pretty devil relaxed for the first time since she made contact with them. "Thank you. I swear to you all that neither I nor Dispater has any devious, diabolical, devilry plans in this matter concerning any of you. In fact, we consider you strong allies against these vicious demons. Thank you."

Now actually comfortable in their presence, Glasya took up a new line of thought. "There are four main points I need to make right here before plans are made. First, it should be obvious to everyone that my help must remain a secret for the time being at least. Second and third are related. I've been watching them for several days, while awaiting your arrival. The second is that the Nabassu hatchlings only come out at night to attack and feast. Presumably we can deal with them at night. The third is that this time we may very well be strong enough to defeat the Marquis. Sir Thomas told us that it took the combined might of Ukko and his Air Maidens to overthrow the Marquis de Gritz two hundred years ago. However, then, as I understand it, he had a huge numbers of followers and demons in his employ, as well as a heavily defended location. This time it is different. Here he seems only to have the Nabassu hatchlings. I've seen no other human or demonic presence around here at all — doesn't mean that there are none, but so far I've seen none. That means we really do have a fighting chance."

"That's encouraging news," Alison interrupted. "I was actually very concerned that we were attempting to do more than we could hope to achieve here. But you said there were four. What's the fourth?"

Glasya grinned, "Ah yes. Well how should I put this? Each day, I am capable of using two of the most powerful spells that exist. Yes, I can wish for things, but normally I prefer to temporarily stop time and rectify things. You may not agree with me, but I can speak but a word and with that word slay many lesser beings' bodies. Of course, I can gate when needed, for how else would I have gotten here? Now the point of this is not to make myself look all-powerful to you, but rather another reason entirely. Neither you nor Darless have to answer this question, but Dispater believes that you both are nearing that point where you too will be able to command the magical forces required to cast these ultimate spells of power." Alison and Darless were stone-faced, showing nothing, so she continued. "Now while simple spells like the casting of a ball of fire are very commonplace, spells of ultimate power are exceedingly rare and very, very hard to find. I should know. I've spent the last three years researching for more and have come up with absolutely none for all my efforts! I think you can understand my frustrations, right?"

Both wizards grinned, for Glasya hit the mark. Alison and Darless had been exceedingly fortunate that Father Ukko had rewarded them with that large spell book with so many powerful ones in it. "On that account we agree completely," Alison chuckled. "But I don't see where this is leading. I thought the Marquis is a high demonic priest, not an archmage."

"Oh he is, he is," Glasya assured her. "However, those three years of research did give me a clue. I uncovered a little known detail. It seems that hundreds of years ago, the Marquis slew an archmage named Mingus. He kept that mage's spell book, which was in the form of an ornate wooden box, as a souvenir of his conquest."

"So you think that if we defeat the Marquis, you will find powerful spells in Mingus's spell book?" concluded Alison.

Glasya sighed, "I have to be truthful with you. For many, many years I have been searching for one particular spell, one that you have the power to use right now, but knowing you as briefly as I have, I know you would not have learned it. Yet, Mingus knew it and used it. My prayers will be answered, if I can get a look into his spell book. I would do anything lawful to have the opportunity to learn that spell. I *swear* to you that this spell is not harmful to any of you or any other people. It is something I want to use myself."

"Okay, I agree to this, but only so long as when the time comes, you must first confide in me privately what this spell is about," Alison concurred. She added, "And you must abide by my decision at that time, because if I think you could use it to harm mankind, for instance, my answer will be a resounding no."

"Thanks, Mage Alison, I know you will not think it so and I agree to your terms," the beautiful devil smiled. "You know all this talk has made me thirsty." She resumed her playful attitude, which they had not seen since their initial encounter. "What do you all do around here for fun and relaxation?"

"Hey, I'll make some tea," Darless volunteered, "if that's okay with you. We usually drink a lot of it." It was fine with the devil, so she went into the kitchen area to prepare some.

"I usually make music," Jon said, "but I don't know any devil tunes. Never heard any."

"Well how about some of your lively dance tunes? I've not heard them for such a long time," Glasya encouraged him. Jon got out his flute and began playing many of the tunes he had learned from the caravan folks several months ago. Indeed the atmosphere here inside the magical mansion changed from deadly serious to one of relaxation and peacefulness.

When it was time for bed, Glasya took Jon aside and asked him, "Can I have a private word with you?" Jon raised his eyebrows, but consented; they went into the kitchen area, which was about as private as you could get in this mansion.

"I got to tell you up front, that if anything you say impacts the others, I must tell them about this conversation," Jon hastened to add even before she spoke.

Glasya rolled her eyes in mock frustration and then smiled at him, "Of course, silly, I know that. Seriously, I've heard tales from Dispater of what you can do for people, Metrarch for instance, and Morrigan. I've just seen it with Sir Thomas."

"Oh sure, Darless is going to open up a college to train anyone who wants to learn how to do it," Jon explained. "Even Thea, here, has become quite good at helping others erase some mental traumas. Why do you ask?"

"Well, well," she faltered, she, the Princess of Hell, had never asked something from a human ever, yet she was about to do just that. "Can you do your thing on me? Mind you, I'm willing to pay your fee, just about anything within reason, of course." There she had said it, but then added as a bit of protection, "You won't mention I am asking you to do this to others will you?"

"No, not unless you tell me it is okay to do so or that I feel the others need to know," Jon answered truthfully.

"There is one other thing, Saint Jon," she referred to his title out of respect, "I know you are a master of minds akin to my own psi powers. If I let you into my mind, I run the risk of your discovering secrets that I have pledged to never divulge."

"Look, Glasya, this process only works if you are truthful about what you see. I do not need to probe your mind or anything like that. If you get stuck, I might look the images that you are stuck in, but nothing more. I have no desire to discover your secrets, Glasya, only to help you, if I am able to do so. No guarantees being successful, mind you."

"Fair enough then," Glasya took this as a good omen. "What do I do?"

"First, tell me what is the matter? I need to have some idea what we are getting into, so to speak," Jon replied.

"Well, it's like I am always tired, exhausted, these days. I get enough sleep; I eat right; I exercise, I sleep like a rock. But when I am awake, I feel so darn tired all the time. It didn't use to be this way. I used to be a veritable powerhouse, staying up for days tracking down spell research details and such. Recently, I'm so tired all the time that I sometimes cannot even concentrate properly to cast a spell! That can be deadly in my line of work," she grinned at him. He grinned back, imagining all sorts of tragic spell backfires happening to her.

"Okay then, can you recall the most recent time you felt like this?" he asked. She did and they were off. This morning when she arose, it was all she could do to get her body moving. Jon sensed her deep apathetic mood. After going over it a couple times, he asked her if she felt this way before. Naturally she had, and they ran through the previous day a couple times. Inwardly, Jon felt that this session promised to be the most utterly boring one that he had ever done, but he kept doggedly at it. A half hour later, they had covered a dozen such times and Glasya was now finding much earlier times, about a year ago. They continued.

An hour later, Glasya had recalled a time four years ago, when she had first acquired the ability to cast the most powerful spells in existence. They went over it and over it, but her tiredness, her apathy seemed unabated, though she now began to yawn heavily. Jon pressed her for an earlier time that she felt this way, but try as she might, she could find none. Jon had her go through it one more time. "Yesterday," she said apathetically, "I was full of life; I was so excited that I mastered the wish spell. When I awoke, I was so tired and lethargic. The day dragged on. I went to bed early. The next day was exactly the same, and the next and the next. Then, I had a fight with a band of demons and woke up. This doesn't seem to be working," she said apologetically.

Jon thought for a moment. Every other time, if relief did not come, there had always been an even earlier one. He did not want to go prying in her mind to find it, though. So he said, "Well, how about this one starting earlier than it did?" She looked at her mental pictures of that day and then looked slightly earlier in time.

"Oh my, yes, yes. It may indeed start even earlier. It was the day before!" Jon noticed that her apathy began to rapidly evaporate. "I see myself walking into Mammon's throne room; I was very excited. I told him that I had just mastered the wish spell! He did not seem overly enthusiastic about it like I anticipated, though. Then, I woke up so very tired." She yawned and yawned. Jon had her go over it once more.

"I was so proud, so happy of what I had just achieved. I ran to Mammon to tell him my news. But he was not pleased at all, now that I look at it. I left him, but on the way out, I heard him say to himself, 'She is getting too powerful. I must contain her.' I had no idea what he meant. Then, an hour later he came to my room and began telling me that I looked awfully tired, that I looked worn out. He said I was working too hard, not getting enough sleep. God, he said stuff like that to me nearly a hundred times in many different ways all the rest of that day! I looked up to him. God, I began to actually believe him! Maybe I was working too hard at my magic research!" She started laughing and trying to speak at the same time, which did not work too well. "I cannot believe that I actually believed him! He sure got me to stop learning magic. You realize in the last three years, I have not learned even one new spell of any kind? None, nada, zilch! Why that old devil! He sure made an impact on me. That is not a nice thing to do to your consort!" She laughed some more. "Oh, I am not tired any more, how about that?" She laughed some more. "Oh," she suddenly realized, "I am so powerful now that it is scaring him! Wow. Say do Alison's powers scare you, if you don't mind my asking something so personal?"

"First, Glasya, very well done on spotting that. Yes, I think we took care of the tiredness thing. If not, we can have another go at it later on. And no, Alison's magical powers have never scared me. We are in love, we have the highest admiration and respect for each other. I just worry that she might get hurt battling her foes sometime, you know, that sort of worry."

"Thanks, that is certainly enlightening. You have taught this old devil something about life. I do indeed owe you a big one. How can I repay you?" she asked.

"I said up front that I never charge even a penny, er a copper piece, for this. I do it willingly and because I want to help others as I can. I am just a musician," he replied in his usual fashion. Then, he thought of something. "Say do you devils have anything like music where you are at, Hell, or whatever it's called? If so, is it possible to hear any of it sometime and maybe to learn it if I like it?"

She laughed once more. This man, this human, had just given her back her life and all he wanted was music, poor as it was in Hell; there were pitifully few bards in her realm. "Sorry about that one. We don't go in much for music down there and the bards that do come play mostly the songs they learned from here. Sorry about that. I will not forget that I owe you, Saint Jon. I'm so tired!" and she laughed once more. Jon said good night and crept into the main room where the others were sleeping, snuggling in beside Alison.

She rolled over and her arms managed to surround his body, she mumbled half-asleep, "Were you able to help her?"

"Yes, it worked out fine. Night, my pretty mage," and he lovingly kissed her on her forehead and settled down to sleep.

Glasya did not turn in for another hour. She now had a great deal to ponder. Was she making the right choice? She was now more convinced of it than ever before.

Chapter 8 The Nabassu Hatchlings

The next morning, Glasya woke totally refreshed, totally alert, and totally alive for the first time in nearly four years. For her, this was both momentous and significant, though she did not mention this to the others. She spied Darless and Thea in the kitchen making breakfast and volunteered to help them.

"Sleep well?" asked Darless as she flipped some pancakes over. "You can start the tea, probably need at least ten cups worth. Fix any of the darker teas you like."

"Yes, for once. I'm really alive this morning," she answered. "Big tea drinkers, I see." She set about the mundane task which seemed fun to her this morning, for once. The magnitude of the change in her physical well-being was only dawning upon her.

"Oh yes," Thea added, not wanting to be left out of the conversation. "Jon really loves his teas. You know, as much as some men love their ales. Gosh, Glasya, you look stunning even when you just wake up!" She noticed that the devil did indeed look amazingly beautiful without combing her hair and such, if one could ignore the horns and wings. Of course, Thea did so and was more than envious of Glasya.

"Thanks, Thea," she acknowledged. Normally, she was immune to such comments, for she had on many occasions made use of her "beauty charming" ability. Few men could withstand her charm, when she cared to dominate them. Even when she wasn't, males often followed her around — rather like puppy dogs, she thought. Today, her intuition told her that Thea was being genuinely honest with her and sincere. "You are still young and developing. Be patient; you will only get prettier in the next few years."

"You honestly think so?" she asked rather incredulously. "I know my bosom is still developing; I need larger tops every so often. But prettier? Really?"

For a second, as Glasya looked at Thea, she imagined this teenager was her daughter. Glasya was as yet childless, forsaking maternity for the study of magic, romance and politics in Hell. "Well, if you styled your hair a bit differently, kind of like this," and she ran her long nails through her hair, pushing it to one side. "Yes, that would help. Perhaps I can help you style it a bit after breakfast, if you like. Another thing, just between you and me — I find some men go crazy for longer nails, such as mine. You might try letting yours grow a bit and see if you and your beau there likes them," she winked at her. *What I would give for a daughter such as Thea; she is precious!*

One by one the others filed into the kitchen, smelling the fresh pancakes. Jon, of course, was the last to get up, sleep still in his eyes. "Mornings, I hate them, always come too soon," he mumbled.

Darless thrust a cup of tea before him and a plate of hot pancakes. He ate hungrily and after getting the plate half empty, he fully woke and thanked her. She smiled back.

When all were full, Mandy, Sir Thomas and Lonnie saw to the care of the horses, while the other women sat around the table chatting and sipping the last of their tea. Jon bounded into the kitchen to wash up the dishes. "Does he always do that — wash duty?" Glasya asked rather confused. Where she came from, men were loathed to have anything to do with kitchen chores.

Alison smiled, "You bet! He's permanent dishwasher. Actually, he told me that when he was in school learning to be a musician, he had to be a dishwasher to earn his meals. I guess he is in the habit. You'll never get Sir Thomas to wash dishes! Men!"

The last chore Jon did was to make another round of hot tea, Earl Grey this time. He brought it steaming into the living room. "More tea anyone?" Mandy and Darless took a refill. Jon sat down with the others, helping himself to a cup with the pot close to him. "Nothing like a fine Earl Grey," he commented, mostly to himself.

"Well," Glasya began, "I expect that we should compare notes and abilities and skills and weapons. What we are about to tackle is going to be rather a tough fight."

"Okay, I'll start," volunteered Darless. "I am familiar with these Nabassu hatchlings, unfortunately. I don't know how easily we can take them out, really. But here goes." She began counting out on her fingers until she ran out.

"Number 1, Nabassu are born in the Abyss and grow until what might be said to be their 'teens.' Number 2, for them to fully mature, they must suck the life out of a dozen and a half or so humans. Number 3, this means that they must find a way to make the journey from the Abyss to somewhere that humans dwell. Number 4, each human they suck causes them to grow and get stronger. Number 5, when they are fully matured, they return to the Abyss and never again venture out of the Abyss. Number 6, as I understand it, a Nabassu only needs to be within about twenty feet for him or her to suck the life out of a human. Number 7, there is some chance that the human will be able to dodge the effect, but it is not a terrific chance for the average person. Number 8, yes, even we stand a good chance of getting our life forces sucked out. Number 9, if it is, then our bodies are turned into some kind of undead creature — a ghoul or ghast or some such. Number 10, if hard pressed, they can give back one of the lives they have sucked, bestowing it on a human, who is thereby instantly slain, with only a small chance of avoiding being outright killed. Number 11, their claws and bite attacks are much as a broadsword in damage, so we have not much to fear from that. No poison or such. Number 12, they are darn hard to hurt with a weapon, probably as hard to hit as Sir Thomas is in his full plate armor. Number 13, only magically enchanted weapons can damage them which, of course, is similar to me. Finally, Number 14, which is perhaps unlucky for us, they, like me, tend to have resistance to magical spells. The youngest, not much. The most mature have even more resistance to magic effects than I do. It is going to be a very dangerous business indeed." She paused pondering if she had omitted any significant detail.

Glasya laughed, "Does she always talk like that? The numbers thing?"

"Yes," smiled Alison. "I think she is more intelligent than any of the rest of us. I suspect her Mage Intelligence Factor is off of the charts, beyond genius."

"Well, I *am* bright," Darless commented. "I see right through basic illusions. It's rather hard to fool me. I've had to take care of myself in very trying situations in my life, you see."

"If they are only as hard to damage as Sir Thomas is," Mandy commented, "then I certainly can hit them even with my eyes closed." The paladin groaned, so she hastily amended, "Well, partially closed. If one is still alive after two minutes, I'll eat my hat, except I don't have a hat to eat."

"I aim to slay demons!" Sir Thomas proclaimed. "I've trained for this opportunity all my life. I shall not fail. A thousand gold coins says I slay more Nabassu than you, pretty ranger!"

"You're on," Mandy grinned, "This will be like taking a cookie from a baby!"

"Aren't you two overlooking one significant detail?" Glasya interrupted them. Both looked at her. "They are likely to suck your life out before you ever get close enough to swing your swords!"

"Oh," Mandy replied. She had not thought of that; rather, she'd forgotten it.

"Well, fortunate for us, the Nabassu have chosen to come out only at night and then they go hunting in one's and two's and not a whole pack. So with luck, we can pick them off individually," Glasya suggested. "However, we four mages are going to have a rougher time because of their inherent magical resistance to our spells."

Alison asked, "Darless, what exactly does this magical resistance you have actually do?"

"About one in three spells simply rolls off of me with no effect whatsoever," she replied, "no damage, nothing, as if it had not been cast. It doesn't make any difference what spell it is either. I've no control over this effect, though. It just happens, rather chaotic, I'd say. Since in my case the odds are not so good of it rolling off of me, I never depend or rely on its effect."

"So that means, if I've got this correct, if we shoot say four spells at you nearly simultaneously, then the odds are at least one of these might work on you," Alison asked, making sure she had this property worked out. She nodded. "So that means we wizards must concentrate multiple spells on the same target, if we hope to have any chance. It would be too uncertain if we each took separate targets. If they keep to the same pattern of only one or two together, we may yet be effective with our from a distance spells so we don't get sucked. Am I right?" She nodded again.

"I'm terribly worried about this life sucking thing. Is there no way to counter this death magic?" Alison asked. Silence answered her.

Glasya, after some thought, replied, "Well, rings of protection, or scarabs, or brooches of protection — yes, those types of magical devices will lessen the chances of doom, but none will entirely eliminate it."

"Ah ha," Darless exclaimed. "Then, we are in luck. We have several of rings of protection. Don't you, Alison, and Mandy, each have a highly enchanted ring of protection? I know we have several lesser rings of protection among us. Surely we can see that everyone has some extra measure of protection."

"Yes, we each have a really good ring," Alison assured her, "and I do have several lesser rings as well. I also have a scarab of protection but I seldom wear it because it is easily damaged. We should also wear our best protective gear. This is shaping up to be one of the deadliest battles we have fought. I'll even don my bracers of defense similar to Mandy's set."

Mandy laughed, "You know, Alison, you and I will likely be harder to hit with a weapon than Sir Thomas in his heavy armor!"

"Ah, verily, thee might at that," the paladin chuckled, "but think of the style, the honor I do for holy fighters by wearing nothing but the best armor — the way battles were meant to be fought — sans magic and all this, pardon the phrase Glasya, devilry stuff."

"No offense taken, big man," Glasya teased. "But you know, Alison, I've noticed that four of you are wearing magnificent, nearly matched emeralds. From their size, each must be worth a fortune. They have only the slightest hint of magic about them. Is there any significance to them?"

"They are a gift from a special Lady; we did her a great service once. They are magical in nature, but to tell you the truth, we have never quite found out what they actually are. All four are attuned to each other. When I was nearly killed by the Chasme bugs, my emerald somehow kept me alive when I should have been dead, or rather, it kept the body alive, I was somehow inside the emerald. The other three emeralds shone brightly, I'm told."

"Yes, several times now when one or more of us have been near to death, the emeralds glowed," Darless added. "However, we have been so busy with other things that we just have never had the time to try to analyze their powers. I do know that they were enchanted by the elves."

"Hum, would you mind if I have a look at one?" Glasya asked. "Perhaps I can determine their nature."

The three women were a bit hesitant. Jon immediately took his off and handed it to her. She noticed the amulet he wore under his shirt.

"Your amulet is self-explanatory, Jon. It is an amulet that protects life, a common magical device. Demons and such cannot possess your body, and it would house you for a week if your body were slain, giving a high priest time to heal your fallen body. Yet, I know that is not why you are wearing it. For those of us who have the psi power, it is a most invaluable device, for we cannot be mentally attacked by another with that power. Keep on wearing that amulet, Jon, for there are some extremely nasty creatures who also have psi powers and who would not hesitate to fry your synapses if they could," Glasya explained.

Next, she began a chant which was immediately recognized by both Alison and Darless. They knew the devil was attempting to identify some of the emerald's properties. Thus far, they both had failed to glean much information with this spell.

Glasya concentrated hard on the emerald in her hand. Complete silence filled the mansion. Alison did not dare to breathe for fear of breaking Glasya's concentration. "Clever creators, I'll give them that. There is only the faintest glimmer of magical energy connected to the emerald, but just enough to perk my interest. Yes, I see energy lines connecting all four together. Ah, yes, there is the effect Alison described, but there is more. It gives you additional chances to avoid magical spells, even those that always hit, like magical missiles. But there is something here much deeper." She put her full attention on the emerald. "Ah ha, there it is, its true purpose, nicely disguised, precisely what we need here. Each of these will absorb attempts to drain your life energy, your mind and soul. These are much like your scarab of protection, Alison. Wearing these, the Nabassu cannot be successful in sucking your life until the emerald's capabilities are exceeded!"

"Wow, that is what we really need now!" exclaimed Alison, a lot of the nervous tension left her. "The four of us can act with relative immunity around these nasty demons. I can lend my scarab to Sir Thomas. That makes five of us. Boy I feel a whole lot better about going after these demons. Thanks, Glasya." The devil smiled. Glasya was most definitely really enjoying their company and that she found strange indeed, humans. Dispater had warned her that she might take a fancy to them. She handed the emerald back to Jon.

"I truly thank you Mage Alison," Sir Thomas said sincerely, "now I will be free to concentrate on slaying these demons. But we need a battle plan, and there is always the Marquis. Several hundred years ago, he was so tough that Father Ukko himself had to intervene."

"Yes, we most certainly do," Darless broke in, agreeing with him. "Number 1, I think that the best we could possibly hope for is a one-on-one confrontation with him." She saw the teasing groans from Jon, alluding to "here we go again." So she cleverly said, "Corollary one, if we go after him and he is surrounded by Nabassu or other fell creatures which he might gate in from the Abyss, we may have more than we can realistically handle." Jon laughed. She concluded, "Does anyone know how we are going to get him alone?"

"We have the element of total surprise on our side," Glasya answered. "He does not know we are here or he'd be searching, scrying upon us. I've detected none. Whatever we do, we must maintain surprise."

"Oh that is an easy one," Thea spoke up. Until now, she could only try to follow the other's great leaps of logic. But finally, here was something with which she was quite familiar, that of keeping another guessing. All eyes turned to her. She almost lost her nerve, but continued in spite of it, "We seek out and find a couple of the demons and slay them very quickly. Then, we neatly bury their bodies. I can use a dig spell to help do it quickly. The result is no trace of the demons. The Marquis will be left guessing what happened to them, when they do not report back after the evening's outing. It works, I've done similar things to boys back in Freetown, not the killing, just keeping them guessing by hiding the objects."

Darless countered, "Yes, Thea, that is a good start. After the first few bunches go missing, won't he get mighty suspicious and start scrying on them, trying to find out what is going on? I'm fairly ignorant of priestly magic. What is to keep him from praying to his foul deity asking who's behind these missing Nabassu? How do we counter that?"

Undaunted by Darless' challenge, Thea enthusiastically explained, "Disguises. After we think he is getting wary, we dress up in all sorts of costumes. Like maybe make ourselves look like local natives one time. The next time we look like brigands. Next time, we look like, I don't know, say cavalry from Vyndoc. Keep him guessing each time."

"Excellent idea, Thea," Alison commended her apprentice. "Won't it look a bit strange that the raiding party is always composed of five women and three men? Even finding a single woman in a party of adventurers is unusual."

Thea had an answer for everything, "We disguise ourselves. One time, it looks like eight men. The next time, eight women. We can dress up like the guys. Oops," she realized that she was about to say that the guys could dress up as women, when she saw Sir Thomas gritting his teeth.

"How about a believable illusion?" Glasya interceded on Thea's behalf. "We give the guys the illusion of being women. Anything to confuse the Marquis for a longer time will do. Remember," she sternly cautioned, "it must always appear to be the seven of you; my part, my presence must not become known."

"After we eliminate a number of the Nabassu, do you suppose the Marquis will decide to go along with his demons to personally see what is happening to them?" queried Alison, trying to think this through. "I know that I would go along with them just to see for myself."

"Nabassu fly and Cambion do not, unlike me," Darless tossed a loose layer of her black hair out of her face and trying not to enumerate. "Since the residents of Canyon Lands are living high atop the cliffs, fly they must. The Marquis is a high priest and warrior not a wizard. While he might have an invisibility ring, I would be surprised if he had a means of flying. No, I rather suspect a priest would use various divination methods to find out the truth of a matter."

"Sounds reasonable to me," Alison acknowledged. Turning to Glasya, she asked, "One final detail. While you were waiting for us, did you see the Nabassu leave the tower? Singly? In groups? All at once?"

"Unfortunately, those that left for their hunt all left at the same time. Yet only a total of around a half dozen or so go each night. I could not tell if the same ones went each night or if they took turns. They went in different directions, spanning out over the wide canyon lands."

"I've got a question," Lonnie finally took the plunge and attempted to add to the plans.

"Ask away, Lonnie, you've got a say in all this too," Alison replied encouragingly. "After all, you are going to be risking your life here as well."

"Okay, what bothers me is how are we going to engage them? If they fly to some cliff dwelling, say fifty miles from here, how do we get there and how do we fight them when they are hovering far above us? How are we going to even know where 'there' is at? It would be late at night." The fledgling paladin spoke with a clear reality of the situation. None of these were a trivial question.

"Verily, those are crucial points," Sir Thomas backed his fellow paladin. "In my armor, I move only half as fast as the rest of you. I'm certain that I don't fly. I doubt that I could do battle while somehow flying in the air, though if you require it of me, I shall do my very best."

Alison smiled thinking to herself, "Spoken like a true paladin!" Rubbing her hands across her face, she replied, "Well, either we spy on them and follow them somehow and attack them flying or we get them to come to us on the ground. I don't see any other alternatives. Anyone?" She looked at the others in turn, but all shook their heads. "Well then, I say flying about is out. It is too risky and we are all at a disadvantage in flying combat. We must get them to come to us on the ground."

"Ah then, you need a guinea pig then," Jon added rather mater-of-factly. "Since I am not likely going to be doing much actual fighting of these demons, I volunteer to be the bait of the trap. Just don't wait too long to spring the trap on them."

"Me too," Thea hurriedly added, "I'll be bait with Jon."

"And I as well," Lonnie also volunteered looking worriedly at Thea. If she was going to put herself in dire straits, he certainly was going to be there with her and protect her as he might. It was the Holy Code and the only choice he could make.

Before Alison could rule either way, Jon quickly added, "Good. The three of us will actually look like a small party of whatever our disguises are to be. We can have a small campfire and pretend we are camping out. The rest of you be invisible or such and when they come for us, you get them before they get us."

For Alison, this was the toughest decision she ever had to make. To force the demons onto their field of play, humans would have to pose as bait. But to risk her assistant, a young paladin and her betrothed — all of whom would be greatly outmatched by even a single one of these demons — was a hard choice to make. She faltered momentarily. "No," she said resolutely, "No, I will be bait too. It will appear better, like two couples or two families. Then, if the demons get to us too quickly, I can try to fend them off. You three then use a ring of invisibility and stay hidden close at hand."

"Just be wary, these demons can move faster than we — plus they can fly away if they feel threatened," Darless added a cautionary note.

"That is the vital point," Alison stated sternly, "none must be allowed to return to the tower alive, if we are to maintain our full surprise tactics."

"Okay, gang," Mandy broke in, "if any one of the demons gets away by taking flight, I will volunteer to turn into my Pegasus form and let Sir Thomas mount me and go after it. Though, if I do this, then any we slay this way, Sir Thomas, does not figure into our wager."

This brought a round of laughter from everyone, lightening the mood considerably. "That would be quite a sight, a Holy Paladin flying into battle on his trusty Pegasus steed!"

"Mind you, no kicking me in the shins either," she added defiantly in jest. "Seriously, will one of you mages please cast an invisibility spell on us once he is mounted? Then the demon may not see us until we catch it and attack." Alison and Darless promised to retain such spells for this purpose.

They broke for lunch. Mandy attempted to communicate to their guide where they wanted to go for the first night's location. She chose a narrow canyon some fifteen miles to the north of their current location. Within a half hour, the mansion was gone and the eight rode in silence back the way they had come in order to gain entrance to a side channel. It is noted here that an invisible Glasya rode one of the spare horses, which was still being led by Lonnie. Appearances were maintained as usual.

He That Does Not Speak led them swiftly and unerringly to the desired dead-end canyon. Currently, several cliff dwellings above them stood abandoned, their inhabitants were dead or had long ago gone to a safer location. Mandy picked the final campsite with great care. Nearby was a long disused adobe corral where the horses were safely kept from harms way. Several large boulders on either side of the relatively flat open area of the canyon floor served as excellent hiding places. Yet, each could spring into the battle in just seconds.

Lonnie and Sir Thomas saw to the care of the horses, while Mandy, Darless and Alison closely inspected the general area. The others prepared a light supper. "I have to admit that I felt rather like a piece of unseen baggage," Glasya said as she helped Thea fix the meal.

"I'll bet," Thea exclaimed. "Do you suppose that they will be able to find us right away here in this dead-end canyon?"

"I'm sure that they have sort of a sixth sense about smelling out human prey, rather like animals, carnivores, I suspect," Glasya commented.

When Alison drew near, Glasya got her attention. "After dark, I will fly up high in the sky and be invisible. I will let you know when any are approaching. I will give you all as much notice as I can."

"Great! That would be most helpful indeed. Then we cannot be taken by surprise. Thanks, Glasya," she replied. As an afterthought she said, "You know you are the nicest devil I have ever heard of; I'm glad you are on our side, though I admit I have not seen your evil side."

The devil smiled, "I take that as a compliment." Inwardly, she found herself having a strong feeling of comradery with these humans, a very enjoyable union. This was also perplexing, for she was a devil. *Or am I?* she thought to herself.

Once they all had eaten and He That Does Not Speak watched solemnly as the sun sank below the cliffs, Alison cast her mansion spell once more and escorted the native inside. She made sure that all of the other wizards knew the command word to open the doors, should anything happen to her. She did not want He That Does Not Speak to end up dying, forsaken and lost in her mansion. She then gave one of her rings of invisibility to Sir Thomas. Mandy and Darless had their own such rings. Each of the three took up their positions behind the large boulders. It is noted here that Mandy placed Sir Thomas in his heavy armor in the closest position so that his slower speed would be offset by having the shortest distance to close to battle. She herself took the most distant position, though she knew that she would be the first to close to combat. She had on her special boots that she had never worn in the other's presence before — there had been no need before.

Before Glasya took flight, she asked Alison what she wanted for this night's disguise. For their first attempt, she decided they ought to look just like He That Does Not Speak, the natives. Alison caught several key words of Glasya's magical chant. She swore she heard "wish" as part of the spell. Presto, Alison looked just like one of the women she had meet at Running Bear's dwellings. She looked over at Jon, who appeared to be very dark skinned wearing a loin cloth. She could not resist a laugh at him. "You should see yourself," Jon teased her playfully. Thea and Lonnie were both looking at each other, marveling at their changed appearance.

The four stoked the fire so that it provided a good deal of light, arranged blankets for pretended sleeping. Then, the four took up their positions as bait for the Nabassu demons. Lying on his back, staring up at the splendor of the night sky, Jon felt he was in a dream. How could any danger be here amidst such beauty? Alison spoke sternly, "Now remember, don't fall asleep! Thea, if we see them, shoot magical missiles at them, not fireballs, we do not want to risk hitting the others coming to our aid."

"Yes, Mage Alison. Missiles it is," Thea replied, though she thought that Alison didn't need to tell her that. She knew all about fireballs. However, she figured her mentor was probably just worried. She snuggled closer to Lonnie, who grinned and reciprocated.

Alison lay beside Jon, his arm under her, she on her side, ready for action. "Aren't the stars just splendid out here? The heavens are spectacular!" Jon whispered to her.

"You're supposed to be looking for the demons," Alison sternly whispered back at him, rather annoyed with his lack of concern.

"Oh heck, they might not even find us the first couple of nights," Jon replied. Then he recalled Glasya's words to Thea, "They have sort of a sixth sense about smelling out human prey," and he said, "Okay, okay. I'm looking."

Lonnie had to stoke the fire four times during the evening. It was nearly two in the morning when Glasya's warning appeared in all of their minds, shocking them from semi-sleep. *Two Nabassu have picked up your scent, approaching from the south, up the way we came, about a mile from you.*

Instantly, Jon tensed and Alison whispered to Thea and Lonnie, "They are coming from the south, the way we rode in, a mile away. Get ready." Jon stared toward the southern sky. Soon he saw a darkening or obscuring of the background stars.

"I see them coming over there," he did not point though.

"Okay, pretend we are sleeping, but keep your eyes peeled, spells ready," Alison cautioned. She hated waiting as much as Mandy did, she decided. The uncertainty was very annoying to her well-ordered mind.

Then, Jon saw the fell beasts swooping down upon them like some monstrous dinosaur in horror movies. They appeared huge, their eyes frightening. Then darkness completely covered the entire campsite. Jon felt a surge of terror flow through his body. His stomach knotted and his limbs began shaking of their own volition. He could not move if he had to. Time froze for him. The events of the next minute flashed by like a strobe-lite dance.

One of the Nabassu had cast its area darkness spell over the entire campsite. Thea, also affected by terror, cast her magical missiles, but they completely missed her intended target, bouncing off of the ground. Alison's brief chant dispelled the darkness and Jon's eyes saw the two beasts landing on the ground about twenty feet from them. Surprised by the loss of their darkness, the other Nabassu cast its darkness spell and everything blacked out once more. Jon heard their steps as the demons closed the short distance. Then, from the right, Darless dispelled the darkness and caused the campfire to roar into full blaze, startling the two demons, which turned their gaze toward her. At that same instant, Sir Thomas charged toward the one on Jon's left, though he looked like he was clothed only in a loin cloth and carrying a long pole. What was surreal was Mandy. She came bounding in a high arc into the picture behind the one on Jon's right. It was rather like she came bouncing in from an enormous pogo-stick dive.

Her stick, or Zond, her new bastard sword made by Nain, sliced deep into the demon twice, causing two huge wounds to appear. The fell beast shrieked in utter surprise. This had never happened to it before. It whirled to face this native female. Shortly after its shrieks echoed in the canyon, Sir Thomas struck the other, who had by now turned to face him. He missed on his first mighty swing, but the second connected and another scream broke the stillness of the night. The horses nearby neighed demanding to be in the fight, as trained war horses are wont to do. It only added to the surrealistic scene.

Before the Nabassu on Jon's right could do anything at all, Mandy's blade clove into it once more, and then again and again. Mandy was exceedingly quick and devastating in her attack. The creature gurgled and collapsed on the ground. At the same instant, three sets of magical missiles smashed into the other demon from three angles, two of which bounced of its skin harmlessly, while the third set pierced deep into its body, startling it, distracting it from Sir Thomas. That demon turned its head to see from whence these unexpected missiles came, giving the paladin another opportunity to strike. Strike he did, thrusting his huge demon slayer, two-handed sword straight into where the creature's heart was likely to be. Jon saw the sword point appear on his side of the demon, skewed. A great cry of dismay deafened their ears and slowly the demon collapsed.

"What took you so long?" Mandy teased, rather out of breath with such a sudden, all-out effort.

"One for one," Sir Thomas acknowledged.

A shovel appeared in mid-air and at once began digging a deep pit. Thea was at work, as promised. Quickly, she and Lonnie pushed the two fallen demons into the pit. She then directed the shovel and in less than two minutes all traces of the Nabassu were gone, as if they never were.

"Thanks, Thea, Lonnie," Alison complimented. "Good work Mandy, Darless, Sir Thomas. Two down. We'd best resume our places once more in case more come." In spite of the surge of adrenalin in everyone, they quickly and quietly resumed their hiding places. Only then did Alison see that Jon was terror stricken.

"That — that — that scared the willies out of me," he finally managed to speak. "It's passed, I can move now. I was frozen there, rooted to the spot. Like some nightmare you cannot get out of! Wow. You all reacted instantly and so powerfully. Wow. Amazing. How did you all manage that?"

Thea whispered sympathetically, "I was scared too, Jon. My first missiles completely missed the target; that's not supposed to happen; magical missiles always hit. My aim was affected by my being scared stiff, I suppose. Isn't that right, Mage Alison?"

"Yes, you are right. Can you imagine the terror the poor canyon folks experienced when these demons attacked them? Horrid!" Alison exclaimed.

"Yes, horrible indeed; now it is real to me," Jon swore. "Perhaps that terror was more like one of them trying to suck my life force or something. I cannot recall experiencing such terror before. I forgot to look at my emerald thing though, to see if it lite up."

"Shhh. There may be more," Alison whispered. He tried to relax, but the night did not look so peaceful to him anymore.

About an hour later on, Glasya's warning came again. Two more were headed their way. Shortly, an almost exact repeat occurred. Only this time, Mandy slew hers with four hits, but took a couple nasty claw gouges in the process, mostly because it came at her in the darkness before its darkness spell was dispelled by Alison. Sir Thomas also killed his, but again, he had help from four volleys of magical missiles, two sets of which actually penetrated its body, severely damaging it. This time, Jon did not have a bout of terror. Instead, he managed to plant a thought into one demon's head, "The natives are coming for you." He had no idea if this was of any value whatsoever, but he thought it added to the disguise.

In less than two minutes, Lonnie and Thea had this pair buried next to the other two. "Let's call it a night," Alison ordered, "besides we are running low on spells. Sir Thomas, Mandy, Lonnie, go get the horses and lead them into the mansion. Jon, let Glasya know it's time to retire into the mansion. Ten minutes after the last battle, everyone, still high and totally alert, were safely inside the mansion where nothing could threaten them.

"Gosh, Mandy, I did not know you could jump so high," exclaimed Jon, truly amazed at her skill. "You literally came flying into battle!" He proceeded to tend to her slash wounds, starting the healing process.

"It's all in the boots," she teased. "Oh okay, magical boots that allow me to do really big jumps and strides, helps out in situations like this. Pretty cool picture of me hopping into battle, eh Jon?" she grinned.

Lonnie commented, "You sure are faster with your attacks than Sir Thomas. Perhaps he is just slowed down by the sheer weight of the heavy two-handed sword."

"No, Lonnie," Sir Thomas interjected before Mandy could answer, "she really is more skilled than I, she is faster than me, and that *is* saying something. I cannot believe I am saying this to a woman," a bit of bias yet remained in him, "but I tip my helm to you, Lady Mandy Blackthorn, well done indeed." He did so in a serious, gallant manner befitting his chivalric Code of Honor. She saw that he was really totally solemn and she accepted his compliment graciously. "I fear that I wagered too soon," he lightened up and laughed, "for without the help of the mages on my pair of demons, we would not be two to two! I have seen with my own eyes that my Alison, my party's mage, has always been in good hands with you Mandy. Thank you."

Lonnie recalled one of the Code's rules, "Always protect your mage, for they are weak yet strong." He grasped the import of Sir Thomas's pronouncement at once. He felt good that he had been by Thea's side this night, though in fact he found he could do little to help as yet. He was fulfilling his holy vows and his own personal desires as well.

"Teamwork, Sir Thomas, Teamwork," Darless added, "We work as a team and thus we are stronger than individuals. That is the real lesson here. Glasya's warnings were perfect; without them, it might have gone ill for us. We all work together."

"You know, My Lady Darless, you speak very truthfully. I will remember the lesson well. But right now, I am tired and hungry. How about a snack and some sleep?" Everyone agreed wholeheartedly; the rush of excitement had worn off, leaving a night with no sleep upon them. They ate quickly and fell asleep at once.

Just as each drifted into deep sleep, a "Thank you" appeared in their minds delivered by a deep bass voice. None took any note of this occurrence. The sole person who was not asleep was He That Does Not Speak, who had already slept. He spent the day grooming the horses; he found them good company.

One by one, they awoke around dusk. Alison opened the doors so that He That Does Not Speak could view the setting of the sun. Jon joined him, staring at the reddening world about them. He felt serene, the scene was breathtaking. He spoke softly to the native, "The Great Spirit sure has a really beautiful land here." He That Does Not Speak nodded his agreement.

Of course, the topic of conversation over breakfast was timing. It was already nightfall and they had not moved from where they had been the previous night. Some were in favor of wasting the night and moving to a new location the following day. Others wanted to try it here once more tonight. There were too many people and horses for Jon to transport them all at one time to another location. Furthermore, he would need to have some reality of the other location before he could make the attempt anyway and he was only slightly acquainted with the small portion of the Canyon Lands through which they had already passed.

Further compounding their problems, Glasya suggested, "By now they are really missing, the four you killed. Undoubtedly, the Marquis will be using divination methods to try to find out where they last were and so on. Anytime now, he or others could be coming into this spur to locate the demons. We should at least move somewhere else."

However, no one liked the idea of riding horses through the dark night. Not only was it tricky riding in these canyons, but being attacked by these demons while mounted on horseback would put everyone but the paladins and Mandy at a severe disadvantage. Yet they could not stay where they were and risk detection.

"I tell you what," Jon spoke up, "I think I can move four of you with your horses at one time. We can move to a new location in two groups. What do you think?"

"Yes, but won't that much exertion on your part leave you rather drained?" Alison protested, worried about his safety.

"True, but then I really didn't have much to do last night, for that matter." No one had a better plan, so Jon's was adopted. He decided to take them to the side canyon where they first encountered the giant wasps. It was far from here and he had some familiarity with that location, more so than any other, save being close to the tower itself. The others discussed at length who should be in which group of four. Alison insisted that one strong fighter be with each group. Darless insisted a strong mage also be with each group in case of unexpected trouble.

Thus, around seven pm, everyone exited the mansion and watched it disappear. Jon gathered Sir Henry, Darless, Lonnie and Thea together. Each mounted their horse and all held hands, rather like a strand of people instead of horses. Jon then concentrated and once again got the idea that they were all standing at the location where the wasps flew out of the side canyon at them, and they were there. The horses, startled by the sudden change of scenery skidded a bit, forcing the riders to get them back under control. All was quiet, so Jon waved goodbye and stepped himself back to where the others waited. His horse now spooked more than the first time and Jon found himself having to talk to it to calm it down. Mandy kept trying to tell him how to control the horse, but he concentrated on staying in the saddle and communicating with the horse. He knew he could do that. When his steed relaxed, Jon moved in close to the others and held out his hand. Quickly the rest did likewise and Jon stepped them to the wasp canyon to join the others. While the other's horses skidded about, this time, Jon's knew what to expect and took the change of position calmly. "Sorry, I should have talked to the horses first and told them what to expect. I completely forgot about them. I'm glad no one was thrown off."

"No, just riled up a bit is all," Mandy replied. "Well, here we are. The night is young. What now? Anyone game for another trap night like last night? We might as well since we are all fresh."

Darless cast the mansion spell this evening and they put the horses and He That Does Not Speak inside. Jon went too. By the time they had the horses safely inside, he was dozing from the exertion of moving that much weight. As they tried to move him, he woke, "Okay, I'm awake. Well, not really. I'll have He That Does Not Speak wake me if the demons come." Alison agreed and soon Jon was sleeping soundly. Alison made sure that the native knew that he was to wake Jon if a battle outside occurred. Glasya again modified the mansion spell to provide for windows to view the outside world.

Unfortunately, this time, Mandy did not have the luxury of picking their exact ambush site. She was forced to make do with where they were at — here at the junction of a side canyon with the main branch of the river. With only three people pretending to be asleep, Alison felt very uncomfortable. Only one of the lifesaving emeralds was with them — on her. She went and woke Jon and asked if she could borrow his. He gave it to her and she returned to Lonnie and Thea. Glasya had been standing guard by the two in Alison's absence. She put the emerald around Lonnie's neck. He protested that he would prefer that Thea, not him, be protected, but the mage argued that should they be attacked, thus protected, Lonnie could fight and protect them. Thea was ordered to stay behind the other two.

"Okay, then what disguise do you want for tonight?" Glasya asked as she prepared her special spell. Alison thought for a minute and then asked for rogues or bandits, highway men. Shortly they appeared, rough and uncouth looking. *I'm glad Jon doesn't see me looking like this!* Alison thought to herself. Glasya then disappeared and flew off high into the sky. Lonnie prepared the fire, leaving a large pile of brushwood close near at hand. If they were attacked, Thea promised to throw the wood onto the blaze and make it roar with light. At last, the three took up their pretended sleeping positions.

This time, there were no boulders for the other three to hide behind. In fact, there was hardly any other cover at all. But there were some abandoned crop fields nearby. The three hid among the dried maize stalks and waited, each wearing a ring of invisibility. Time passed slowly.

Glasya's warning did not come until nearly two in the morning. *Three heading your way, about a mile off.* Her words appeared in their minds as well as Jon's. He awoke with a start and got up, rubbing the sleep out of his eyes, found his trusty walking stick and joined He That Does Not Speak by the window, ready to spring into action if needed. Three dark forms appeared blotting out the stars as they approached.

Just as before, they announced their coming by casting a darkness spell over the entire campsite. Again, a stroboscopic view greeted Jon's eyes. One of the wizards immediately countered the darkness spell, bringing light back. Jon saw Thea move toward the brush to throw on more wood. Then, another cast its darkness spell and everything went black. Only to be counted momentarily by another mage's counter-spell. Jon saw Thea frantically throwing wood onto the fire before everything turned black once more as the third demon cast its spell. After a longer pause, that darkness was lifted by Thea's counter-spell.

All this occurred in less than a minute. Now Jon saw Mandy becoming visible as she sprung high into the air covering well over twenty feet in the jump. She even took a swing at one demon before it could even turn around; it squealed in agony and surprise as it turned to face this surprise nemesis. Jon saw Sir Henry clanking toward another demon who turned to face him. That left one demon attacking Alison, but Lonnie inserted himself in front of her and began swinging his sword, missing the demon.

In the next minute or so, Jon watched as two set of magical missiles bounced off of the one attacking Lonnie, but the third set, delivered by Thea penetrated, damaging it somewhat. Lonnie swung repeatedly, but only connected once, delivering some damage. The creature pounced on the young lad knocking him to the ground, slicing him in a similar to Mandy's wounds the previous night. Sir Thomas fared nearly as poorly, while he did manage to strike the demon twice with his huge sword, inflicting significant wounds, the creature dove upon him smashing him to the ground, banging uselessly on his heavy armor, causing no real harm to the paladin. Except that the combined weight of his full field armor and the demon on top of him, he could not move or get to his feet.

Mandy did better. This time she connected with her demon three times, mortally wounding it on the third blow, while the Nabassu managed to once again slice open several wounds on her arms. Jon went into action. Opening the mansion door, he stepped quietly outside, attempting to figure out how he could help either Alison or Sir Thomas. He chose Sir Thomas because he appeared to be in the greatest plight at this instant. What could he do? *Think man!* he ordered himself which, of course, did little good. "Get off him you nasty devil!" Jon spoke with complete authority to the demon. He walked boldly toward the pair, heedless of the other battles on either side of him.

The demon, startled by his sudden appearance and power of voice, turned to look at him. "Come and get me if you can, you good for nothing demon!" Jon taunted him. "Why don't you pick on someone your own size? Are you a coward?" Jon tried to utter every insult he could think of at the demon. It worked, but more than likely because from the demon's viewpoint, a man wearing only clothing is lots easier to attack than this metal-encased knight. The demon made its fatal mistake and got up off of the paladin. With a hopping, flying sort of combined motion, it made for Jon, the easy prey.

Jon's senses were keen and excitingly alert. He sensed when the demon was about to cast its death spell. At that instant, Jon, cleverly was now thirty feet behind the demon at the side of the paladin and attempted to help him to his feet. It took all Jon's strength to help the heavy knight to his feet. By the time Sir Thomas was up, the demon had relocated Jon and sprang for him once more. Again, Jon stepped some thirty feet behind him, allowing the paladin another chance to strike and this time, the paladin was exceedingly lucky. Not only did the demon slayer sword bite into the flesh of the Nabassu, the sword activated and the demon literally disintegrated in a flash of burning fire.

Meanwhile, Mandy made sure hers was dead and then took a mighty leap to help Lonnie battle his. Again, only one volley out of three sets of the mage's missiles actually impacted the demon, which groaned in pain, but didn't stop slicing into Lonnie, who managed to hit it one more time, inflicting a cutting wound in its side. He was quite grateful for Mandy's sudden landing behind the demon. It whirled but too late, Mandy's blade flashed exceedingly fast, for Zond was created for great speed. Zond found its way through the hide of the Nabassu; Mandy's aim was dead on, for Zond thrust its way through the heart of the beast, who let out a hideous death shriek as it slowly collapsed.

Now, Thea had her dig spell going fast and furious. In two minutes, she had a deep pit dug. Lonnie, thanking Mandy profusely for her timely aid, dragged the demon and threw it into Thea's pit, returning for the one that Mandy had slain. Mandy, Sir Thomas, Darless and Alison took up a watch on the four corners of their area, protecting the three others. Five minutes after the attack began, everything was done. Alison ordered everyone, including Glasya, back into the mansion. Mandy tarried attempting to remove all traces of their presence with the aid of a little magical light provided by Alison. As she stepped back into the mansion, she seemed satisfied that there was little evidence that they had been here.

Once inside, Jon tended to Lonnie's wounds which were significant. He'd fared the worst thus far. When Mandy finally came inside, Darless worked on her. Only when they had finished, did the others begin to excitedly talk.

"Jon, you have my eternal thanks," exclaimed Sir Thomas. "I was certainly pinned down by that demon. I could not move! That was awful foolhardy of you, but it worked. Thanks!"

Jon blushed slightly, "Not so foolish, I figured I could get out of the way in time. I also discovered I can tell the precise moment when they are going to try to suck at me. As long as I am alert and know that, I can just be elsewhere."

Glasya looked at him with wide eyes. *He knows when a non-verbal spell is about to be cast. How can that be?* she thought to herself.

"I have to admit, Jon," Alison said, "when I first saw you challenging the demon, I had a fit of concern. Then I realized that we act as a team. You must know what you were doing or you wouldn't have done it, so I went back to attacking the demon near me. Just don't tell me you did not know what you were doing!"

"Well, actually, I really didn't. I had to do something to get that demon off of Sir Thomas. I tried the only thing I could think of — to taunt him. It worked. I sensed when it was going to try to suck me and acted. So now it really is a good plan, but somewhat after-the-fact, sorry, dear," he apologized.

"Well, big boy," Mandy declared, "four to three. You have some catching up to do." Everyone roared with laughter. The silly game Sir Thomas had inadvertently started provided some relief from the deadly seriousness of their game.

"If I could only learn to stay on my feet," the paladin jested, adding to the laughter. For once, it felt good to make humor out of his own misfortune. Never before now had he jested about his performance.

Lonnie thanked Jon for healing him and returned his emerald, "I do believe that it saved my life out there tonight. I owe you one, Saint Jon."

"Nah," replied Jon, "you protected Alison and Thea. You nearly got yourself killed too. Good job." The young paladin smiled, he had been useful after all, though not as much as he might have wanted.

"Yes, you were very brave taking on that demon alone," Thea added. "I'm not sure I could have stood my ground before it. It is something else to be behind the lines, so to speak, casting spells at it." The lad smiled and tried to stand even more erect than he was.

"Well, everyone, I say we get some sleep now so that we can move by daylight to another location. Let's not make the same oversight twice. Jon really was taxed to move us all today," Alison suggested. They cleaned up, ate a little, and turned in for the night. Glasya removed the windows to the outside world before she lay down. Her mind pondered still just how Jon could sense when a native spell was being cast — one that had no verbal component, only force of will. Just as she fell asleep, she heard that deep bass voice in her mind saying, "Thank you." She, like the others, paid no attention to it.

As Alison snuggled with Jon, she whispered in his ear, "Did you see how I, or we all, appeared tonight? What we were wearing?"

"Er, no, I completely forgot to pay attention. I was too busy — ruffians or some such weren't we?"

"Yes," she sighed, glad that he had not seen her looking so utterly grubby. When it came to personal appearance and clothing, she preferred to look well-dressed. She admitted to herself that she was a bit vain about this, sighed and snuggled closer to him.

About five in the morning, Jon awoke with a start. He had the strangest sensation that someone or something was spiritually probing for them. He sat up and looked about. By the dim night light Alison always left on, he saw the others still sleeping peacefully. Nothing seemed amiss. *Must be a nightmare or something*, he thought to himself. He laid back down and tried to get back to sleep. Still he felt the presence of something — something he could not really describe in words. He put his hands under his head and stared up at the domed ceiling far above; then he closed his eyes. *I wonder what this is?* Spiritually, he expanded his awareness outward until he filled the room with his presence, nothing unusual. He felt the presence of the others. *This is definitely not coming from one of them.* So he expanded outward even further. The space beyond the walls of the mansion seemed utterly weird to him; it felt very strange indeed.

Then, he spied a tiny energy beam that was connected to the base of the mansion and it led downward. Curious, he followed it and arrived at their location in the Canyon Lands as the red of dawn began to break over the rainbowed lands. The presence, the probing presence was vastly stronger here. He looked about but saw no body. *Strange*, he mused. *Spiritual, maybe.* That was the catalyst. Suddenly, Jon perceived another being, a large, but very black colored being. It reeked of evil and hatred, and, whoever it was, the being was concentrating on the burial pit where they had hidden the dead demons last night. As Jon watched fascinated, he saw the being picking up mental pictures from the grounds around the area. Much like watching a movie, Jon saw the images that the being perceived. Ill-dressed, ruffians scurried about digging a whole, pitching the demons into it, and covering it up. The being noticed the magical shovel at work and seemed particularly interested in that fact. Jon saw images of some of the ugliest looking women he'd ever seen wearing dirty, ragged clothing, going about activities, but mostly looking around, while an equally filthy man carried the bodies to the pit and pushed them in. Suddenly, Jon realized that he was seeing the illusion that Glasya had placed upon them last night. Whoever this being was, he was seeing it as well.

A flash of panic hit Jon; he felt the being sense his presence — the cold touch of the being's gaze feeling about for him. Inspiration struck. He mocked up an image of the hugest, ugliest horror show creature he could think of in such short order, the Frankenstein monster, and placed the thought in it, "The Redeemer Cometh" into it; he instantaneously broke all contact, opening his eyes to see the dim light of the mansion. "That was close," he muttered to himself.

"What is it, Jon" Mandy whispered. "I've got that prickling sensation in my neck; woke me up. Danger is close?"

"I'll say — something is probing the graves we dug last night trying to find out what happened to the demons. It is a very evil being that is there. It is searching for us. Better wake Glasya; I'll wake Alison and Darless; I don't know if we are safe in here from that thing out there," Jon whispered back. He carefully woke Alison and then leaned over to Darless, who was cradled in Sir Thomas's arm. Both mages struggled for consciousness, wiping the sleep from their eyes.

"What's wrong?" Alison asked; she had a feeling something was not right. Jon never before woke her up before dawn. Mandy and Glasya tiptoed over to the three of them, trying not to wake the others.

Talking in a low voice, Jon described fully what he had just done and witnessed, though he could not explain just how he did it or knew it. "I just sensed it, kind of like Mandy and the hair on her neck."

"Darn, Jon, you are not supposed to be able to do all this," Alison sounded very concerned. "You see, this mansion really exists on another plane of existence. Only great spells allow one to move across these planes. You might get yourself utterly lost! And no one could ever find you. Promise me you won't do that alone again."

"But there was this energy line that ran from the base of the mansion all the way back down to our campsite last night," Jon tried to ease her fears. "All I have to do is follow it; I cannot possibly get myself lost.

Well, okay, I won't do that again without letting you know," he promised.

Glasya commented thoughtfully, "Little do I know of priestly matters, but my educated guess is that the Marquis has cast some form of commune with his deity spell and it was his deity whom you encountered and not the Marquis. I'm certain that a simple Cambion demon has not got that kind of spiritual powers. It is almost a certainly you encountered one of the demonic gods, Jon."

"Then, it would seem that your disguise illusion is working," Darless commented, thinking furiously. "The demon god will report ruffians with magic did the deed. Except for what Jon did at the end, leaving behind that image and message."

"Actually, that god might just believe what it perceived there, an ugly creature with the message, "The Redeemer Cometh.' I hazard the prediction that he found the image and message totally both unexpected and most oblique and baffling as well," Glasya said seriously. She added, "Especially, if he also examined the other site for what occurred there — two completely different looking parties."

"But are we in danger in here in this mansion?" Jon asked. "I got worried he might find us in here somehow."

"If it was not a god," Alison began thinking over her lore, "I would say it is highly improbably that we could ever be discovered here or attacked directly. On the other hand, if it was an actual demonic god that you encountered, I really just do not know. How about you, Glasya?"

"Certainly a god can stroll at will among the planes. If Jon saw that energy line, then why not a god too? In that case, we could be attacked or probed," she looked very, very concerned where this line of thought had gone. "Jon, can you sense him around us?"

Jon concentrated; it did not take much to detect that evil presence lurking, probing around outside the mansion. "Yes, but I don't think he has located us yet. What do we do now?" A creeping fear was setting in, once again.

"Quickly, ask me to ward it off," Glasya begged.

"I so do," Alison replied without thinking about it. "Make us safe from his probe if you can."

Glasya chanted softly; both Alison and Darless listened intently, trying to grasp the words of power that the devil uttered. Both were sure that "wish" was involved in the incantation. "There, I hope that we are protected; I really cannot afford to be discovered." The others realized that she spoke sincerely and honestly. "Jon, just do not make contact with him again. If you can, stay alert and let us know if he enters the mansion." He agreed. Everyone held their breaths, not daring to make a sound, as if sound would somehow give away their position. Glasya also felt the benevolent presence of another being in her mind, leaving her with the idea that her wish would be fulfilled. She wondered for a long time who or what said that to her. She had not the faintest idea. Such had never happened before when she fulfilled another's wish for them. She pondered this, and the incredible actions of Saint Jon Brown, long and hard, although saying nothing to the others.

The longest hour that Jon had experienced passed by like a snail. He never knew that time could move so slowly. He was sweating and nervous. However, that evil being did not enter the space of the mansion. Now the others were stirring and the women hastened to each, cautioning them and explaining their current plight. Finally, Darless muttered, "If I am going to be attacked, why I am at least going to have something to eat first. I am famished." Slowly and as quietly as she could, she went to the kitchen and prepared a light, simple breakfast for the others.

Jon was grateful for the food, because, after all the exertion of the previous night, he was ravenous. Also, this intense concentration was draining him and he welcomed a bit of a respite from his vigil.

After they ate, Mandy ordered, "We have got to get out of this location as fast as possible. I fear that the Marquis may send spies to seek us out. I guess we also have to wait until that god is gone, though." She got out the crude map and asked He That Does Not Speak how long it would take to get to another arbitrary location on the map. He indicated a long day, spreading his arms far apart. That seemed to satisfy the ranger, she would put a good deal of distance between them and their current location.

The real question was how to tell if the evil demonic god was truly gone. Alison would not hear of Jon trying to expand outward again, fearing that the god might be lying in wait to entrap him and, if so, there would be nothing she could do about it. She took the only remaining option, to open the door slightly and peer out. Rather, she had Jon peer out. He did and could no longer sense the god. Cautiously, they exited the mansion, mounted their horses just as fast as they could.

The morning sight was wondrous to behold. The heavy spring rain now brought the vast dormant plant life within the canyons to life. Greenery and flowers blossomed as far as the eye could see. He That Does Not Speak excitedly pointed this fact out to the others, though they could hardly miss it. He signed that the Great Spirit above shone on them and blessed them. Had they not been terribly worried about their presence being discovered on this exceedingly dangerous quest, the start of the day's ride would have been a most enjoyable. Instead, an unspoken fear pervaded them for a time, as they rode cautiously along the canyon bottoms amid the abundant new life of the Canyon Lands. They did, however, observe it. After about an hour's travels, their load was lightened by it.

In an hour they passed by a group from another tribe. He That Does Not Speak waved and signed a greeting and many waved back, smiling at the guide. The others now relaxed and began to enjoy the freshness of the green. By the end of the day, they had encountered seven other tribal groups, many tending the sprouting maize fields. All, without fail, recognized He That Does Not Speak. Evidently, their guide was well known through out the canyons.

Twice during the long day's ride, Mandy sensed danger was nearby. Each time, she got the travelers safely hidden making use of available cover until it passed. She swore that one particular hawk or eagle flying very high was scanning for them. Jon found this interesting since he saw many hawks or eagles, he could not tell for sure which. Soaring high above them, they appeared as specks. He trusted Mandy's senses implicitly, though he did wonder how she could tell a friendly bird from a spy.

Mandy made camp that night some twenty miles due south of the central tower. Nearby numerous rotting, raised platforms, whose poles were decorated with many ribbons and feathers, marked the communal cemetery for all of the tribes. He That Does Not Speak paused to pay his respects, so Mandy went ahead and began pitching camp nearby. Soon Thea and Lonnie had a roaring campfire going; Mandy went to hunt for some fresh rabbit for dinner, while the others tended to the horses. She returned in a half hour with a half dozen and gave them to Thea to prepare.

He That Does Not Speak hastened to the ranger just as soon as she reappeared from her brief hunt. She could tell from his eyes that something was not right. He signed away, but this time, she could not figure out what he was trying to say, the signs were strange and not easily recognizable as his others had been. So she told him to picture it in his mind and she quickly took a look at his mental images. That really didn't help much. In the end, she decided that he was trying to warn her that something here did not feel right, that something was amiss, not as it should be. Something about restless spirits, but she could not figure out what he meant by it. Over dinner, she relayed to the rest of the party He That Does Not Speak's warning. "At the moment, I do not sense any danger," she added, "but let's be doubly wary tonight."

Jon began washing up the dishes, while the others milled around tending to personal duties. He was nearly done when he picked up the traces of an awful smell. He stopped drying the plate and sniffed about here and there, wondering what was making this awful odor. Suddenly he recalled were he had smelled this before — it was in the Abyss! It was the smell of rotting flesh. At that same moment, Mandy sounded the alarm. "We are under attack! Everyone, get to the campfire immediately!" Jon, being only a couple feet away, was the first to obey.

"Where's that stench coming from? Are we too close to the graves?" he asked of Thea as she appeared at his side, followed by Lonnie.

"Dunno," she replied worriedly trying to look in all directions at the same time. "Are the Nabassu attacking us now, this early? Where are they? Do you see them, Lonnie, Jon?"

No amount of looking about showed them anything but the others scurrying to the campfire. Mandy was the last to join them, darting to and fro with her bastard sward flashing to the right and left. However, no prey or attackers were immediately visible. "What *is* that awful smell?" Alison asked as she joined them, taking up her position among the defenders arrayed in a circle about the fire.

Sir Thomas was fumbling with his armor, but finally gave it the pitch. By the time he could get fully arrayed, the battle would be long done. "The ignominy of a paladin without his armor; I feel positively naked," he grumbled as he took a position beside Darless.

"I think you look just fine," she teased him. Still nothing had appeared to be threatening them.

When Mandy finally joined the circle, she explained, "There is a swarm of creatures out there in the dark, coming from the cemetery. We are downwind from them; that's where the stench is coming from. They are moving our way. Not Nabassu. Not sure what they are. They are likely to take us from all sides." Lonnie and Thea threw more branches onto the fire extending their circle of illumination a bit farther into the darkness about them. The first quarter moon helped a bit; slow moving forms could be seen a ways off moving toward them just as Mandy had predicted, coming from all sides.

In a moment, Jon could finally see what they were facing. "What are they? This is like something out of a horror movie!" Indeed, skeletal figures waving swords moved in ranks toward them, followed by slower moving creatures that Jon would have called "zombies" and further back were many man-like creatures, obviously dead natives, but yet stealthily alive, stalking them. The stench seemed to be coming from some of those creatures.

"Undead!" yelled Sir Thomas. "This I can deal with!" he declared and began praying, holding tightly onto his golden symbol around his neck. Jon noticed that he left his huge two-handed sword planted firmly in the ground. He wondered what the paladin was doing.

"Okay, we still do not want to give away our location, so no fireballs. Use missiles and such. Protect Sir Thomas, Jon, Thea, Lonnie. He can deal with many of these, given time. We've run into skeletons and zombies before; they are easy to slay. But I am unfamiliar with the other ones — the ones that seem to be in control," ordered Alison grasping the situation at last.

"Now I know what I forgot!" exclaimed Darless. Glasya looked at her curiously. "Undead, that is the primary by-product of the Nabassu's sojourn on this plane. They make lots of undead bodies wherever they go. Glasya, I don't think they can have any real effect on us, so let's keep alert for the others." The devil nodded agreement.

Soon, the skeleton vanguard moved within the radius of the campfire light. Sir Thomas finished his chant and pointed his finger at the first group of skeletal warriors. A flash of blue light appeared and seven skeletons turned into dust, swords dropping with clanks upon the ground. He began a similar chant once more. Now Jon saw what the Holy Paladin was doing as did Lonnie and Thea. Lonnie moved out in front of him with Jon and Thea moving to his side.

Behind him, Jon heard the sound of Mandy's blade clanking upon bone and steel. Suddenly he remembered that his stick was supposed to be able to do something with "undead" and he regretted not having taken the time to actually memorize the command words. As none were yet close to him, quickly, he found his portable hole in his pocket and unfolded it on the ground and rummaged for his instruction manual. Lonnie's sword flashed this way and that. From a corner of his eye, he saw the young paladin being quite successful against these opponents. Thea discovered that she could shoot two different skeletons at the same time by splitting up some of the missiles she created with each casting. These were easy to defeat, she observed. She just needed time enough to repeatedly cast. Just as a skeleton was about to swing its sword at Jon, the Holy Paladin's chant activated. Once again, a fair number of skeletons turned into dust, including the one about to attack Jon. His hands found the manual. Quickly he leafed through the pages. He read, "Back to death." Then holding is stick in the air, he spoke the command words. Three skeletons closing upon him turned to dust and a couple retreated some distance, colliding with some zombies, who were still making their way forward.

Sir Thomas nodded his appreciation, but did not break his next prayer. Lonnie felled three more skeletons and Thea got four. Behind them, Alison watched as Mandy literally killed two or three skeletons on each attack she made; the ranger cut through them like butter. Alison and Darless, using their magical missiles, of which each of their castings contained far more missiles than Thea's, felled three or four per casting. Glasya out did them both, felling as many as five per spell. Of course, the mages were limited in the total number of spells they could use. Each mage kept doggedly at the destruction.

The next chant of Sir Thomas had an even greater effect, fully a dozen skeletons perished. Jon only disintegrated three, but three others moved hastily away from him. "I'm out of spells," called out Thea, "reverting to my sword now," she added and began hacking at any that got too close to Sir Thomas or herself. Notably, she did not challenge them as did Lonnie or Mandy. She was purely defensive in her attacks, preventing any from reaching Sir Thomas. Thus within five minutes, all of the skeletons were no more.

Now the slow moving zombies reached them and began attacking. Each chant, Sir Thomas vaporized at least four of them and Jon got consistently a pair. These were harder to kill. Thea was having decidedly more trouble with these, but she managed to kill, if that is the correct word, a pair. They did manage to inflict a small wound here and there, particularly on her arms. Lonnie continued to deflect any that got close; he was still more than a match for these, though he too took a wound here and there.

Behind them, Mandy eliminated a zombie with each attack. She was a whirlwind of motion and speed. Her new sword, Zond, always allowed her the first attack and she did not miss, though it took several hits to fell each zombie. The mages found these tougher undead required usually four missiles each and thus each only brought down a pair with each casting, compared to Glasya's three. So far, Alison had only suffered a single wound herself, nothing significant. The other two, were untouched, as they expected, for only a magical blades could penetrate their skins.

"Jon!" Thea called out, "I think I need some help right now!" He turned and saw that she had taken several more hits and was bleeding badly. Quickly he stepped to her side and touched her with his stick, speaking the command word as he did so. He watched, fascinated as always, as her wounds totally disappeared. "Thanks, I still feel a bit weak." Jon tarried at her side a bit longer, energizing his walking stick once more to eliminate another two of the closer zombies, giving her added time to recover.

"That's the last of the zombies," Sir Thomas called out. "Ghouls are upon us now, be extra careful!" He repeated his familiar chant once more. Jon took up his original position on the man's left side. Jon glanced around. He estimated that about thirty of these ghouls were all that remained of their attackers. What he did not know was these were far stronger and harder to kill. He soon found out.

The first inkling of trouble came when he fired his next walking stick spell at them. None seemed hurt in any way, but the three bearing down upon him and the paladin did move away from him quickly. He heard Glasya yell, "Jon, help Thea now!" He turned and saw a ghoul biting into her neck while she stood helpless. He dashed to her side and beaned the ghoul with his stick, forgetting to say the command word. Instead, he accidentally muttered some other word and the ghoul immediately let go of Thea and beat a hasty retreat, leaving behind an awful smell. Jon recoiled from the stench. He felt weak in his knees and stumbled, but he got a hold of Thea. She still stood motionless, like she was frozen. He did manage to get her moved closer to the fire and directly behind the paladin.

Now Lonnie was in trouble. The gradual accumulation of wounds had taken its toll combined with these stronger opponents. Jon saw him retreat slowly back toward him, bleeding from numerous wounds. At the same time, Sir Thomas called out, "Jon, tend to him. It's time I did battle." His strong hand pulled his great sword from the ground and in the same motion nearly sliced the head off of the closest ghoul.

Jon touched his stick to Lonnie and the power of Ukko once again healed Lonnie. He was still a bit weak and out of breath, and he paused a moment, leaning his hands upon his knees. "What's wrong with Thea?" He now noticed she still stood like a statue.

"Dunno, she's alive, but rigid as a board," Jon said. "I think maybe Sir Thomas or Mandy can help later on. Yikes here comes another one!" Lonnie swiftly lunged at it swinging his sword in an up thrust motion, cutting deep into its side. The ghoul clawed at him and managed to inflict more wounds. However, by now, the thirty-some ghouls were reduced to only a dozen, so Jon had Lonnie fall back and both let Sir Thomas and Darless, who had moved to his side when he took up his sword, protect them. So both men now examined Thea to see what was wrong. Lonnie decided to call it paralyzation for want of a better term. She was alive and breathing and not seriously wounded, but just not moving at all.

In another five minutes, the fight was finished. In all, only Darless and Glasya, suffered no wounds at all. Mandy looked the worse for wear, but she had taken a huge toll in undead. They were strewn in piles about her. Jon used his walking stick to heal her. Meanwhile, Sir Thomas examined Thea carefully. Then he prayed and laid his hands upon her and prayed once more. Slowly the young woman revived and the few new wounds she had suffered were healed by the power of Father Ukko.

"That was awful," she hastily exclaimed as soon as she could speak again, "I could not even move! Oh thank you, Sir Thomas! What a horrible feeling to have that nasty thing eating at my neck and I couldn't do anything to stop it! Ich!" Darless recognized at once that she had had an overwhelming experience, so she did her assist on the young mage.

"Okay, Thea, I want you to find the start of your mental pictures of this event and go through them and tell me all about what happened," spoke Darless softly to her.

"Oh, I see, I am getting an assist," exclaimed Thea excited about it. Almost at once, the images began unfolding in her mind and she followed Darless' orders and relayed what had happened. Meanwhile, Jon continued healing the others, using his cell adjusting capabilities, fearing to exhaust the walking stick's powers. He had used it rather heavily this evening.

Mandy and Sir Thomas and Glasya began rummaging through the fallen bodies. He That Does Not Speak now came out of the magical mansion, also examining the fallen bodies. Soon he signed to Mandy that he knew this one and another. They were members of his tribe who had been slain by the Nabassu. Mandy comforted him, "Well now at long last, they can go to meet the Great Spirit." He nodded excitedly in agreement and made other motions and signs that she did not follow. Hence, he picked up his fallen friend and carried him back toward the cemetery. Mandy followed him with a burning branch in one hand and her sword in the other, just in case there were more out there. He carefully placed the truly dead body on top of one of the raised platforms. "Is this what we should do with the others?" she asked. He nodded affirmative.

They spent the next twenty minutes carrying the remaining truly dead natives back into the cemetery and up onto the various platforms. With each body they brought, He That Does Not Speak directed them to specific platforms. Mandy soon realized that the ribbons and feathers denoted the specific tribes to which they had belonged in life. When the last was put upon its platform, Sir Thomas did his best to reconsecrate the grounds and bless them. He That Does Not Speak, kneeling, also appeared to be doing the same thing, although silently, just between himself and the Great Spirit. Jon watched in awe as a bluish light encased the paladin and expanded outward over the grounds. A yellowish glow appeared over the native and also expanded over the ground. Jon found this fascinating. Even though he pointed out the glows, no one else saw the energy flows. Glasya eyed him keenly, though, wondering how he could see them when she could not.

When they returned to the campfire, Darless had gathered all of the weapons into a pile close to the fire and was inspecting them. When Sir Thomas arrived back, she looked up at him and said, "All of these are demon-make, probably in the Abyss. None are magical, shoddy workmanship. Shall we destroy them?"

One by one, Sir Thomas, Mandy and Lonnie, broke the blades at the hilt, by standing on the blade and raising the hilts until each cracked in half. Darless dug a pit and Thea gathered up the shards and pitched them into the hole. Thus, no matter what else happened, these blades would never be used again.

"Okay, we are all out of spells, so no Nabassu hunting tonight. Everyone, into the mansion," declared Alison. "Let's get cleaned up, get this filth and blood washed off. What I would not give for a bath!"

"You'd have a bathtub in you mansion if you got your inflection right when you cast it," Glasya pointed out. Alison, a bit taken aback, discussed her casting with the devil in detail. She learned that she was indeed making a slight error in pronunciations. With Glasya's help, she remedied the situation, proudly announcing, "Okay, now we have a bathtub. I have a decanter of water. So I have first go on the tub!" Everyone chuckled and entered the mansion.

While the others waited patiently in line to use the tub, Glasya and Darless fixed a light snack and some tea. An hour later, everyone was clean, refreshed, and enjoying a late night snack, and a time to discuss their battle.

Sir Thomas had to explain that he had the priestly ability to impact the undead, though to a lesser extent than a normal priest might. "Some I can turn to dust, such as skeletons and zombies. But the more powerful undead, I can only turn them back for a time. Saint Jon, I am sure glad you were also able to turn them. Another walking stick ability?"

Jon sheepishly smiled, "Yes, though I admit I entirely forgot about it. I really should take the time to learn all that it can do and more importantly, learn the different command words. I keep forgetting to do so. Sorry about that." No one hounded him about his lack of learning, however. They spent another half hour discussing the fight before retiring for the night. Alison requested that they sleep in the next morning so they could be more alert that night to fight Nabassu once more. Again, no one paid any attention to the bass voice that said in their minds, "Thank you" just as they drifted off into deep sleep.

When day came, Mandy moved their location further west a couple miles, attempting to put some distance between the graveyard and themselves. They were about fifteen miles from the tower as the crow flies. They took shelter in a large, but abandoned, adobe corral. It was plain that all of those people who had lived near the central area of the Canyon Lands had moved to far distance points. It was an otherwise idle day. Those with blades, sharpened them, removing the dings and pits from the previous night's combat. Still, it was a completely uneventful day.

That evening, the disguise was pirates, though Jon had to carefully describe what they looked like to Glasya and the others. They took up their positions to await more Nabassu. They waited and waited, but none showed up. Finally, at dawn, they all entered the mansion for breakfast and some sleep. Nothing happened the next day and night and following day as well. The party was beginning to worry that the Marquis would not let the Nabassu out any longer. However, on the third night, they were once again attacked.

Glasya's warning came none too soon shortly after one in the morning. "They are coming from the north; about a mile from you. Goodness, there are six of them this time and they look larger and stronger than the others you fought!"

"Looks like they have a change in tactics now," Jon muttered, "I guess I don't blame them. It is only the prudent thing to do." After a moment he added, "Gang, we are going to have to change tactics; bunched in like this, we are no match for six at once. Thea, Lonnie, we three are going to become the Surprise Squad. I'm going to keep a hand on each of you. When I sense a sucking attack coming at us, I will move us out of the way. But I will pick a spot where, as we arrive, you two can inflict some surprise attack. Then, I'll move us away from there. Hit and run will be our tactic. Got it?" Both agreed, he could tell that both were very worried indeed. "You two stay close to me so I can grab you once the darkness falls. I must get you out of this central area immediately." Lonnie strolled over to the fire slowly and added a few branches to it and slowly moved back, trying to keep up the image of four campers.

All of a sudden, the entire area became black as night. Jon grabbed a secure hold of both, with his walking stick in his teeth. He stepped them to a point about sixty feet south of the fire, hopefully beyond the location of the landing Nabassu. His guess was accurate. They were outside of the darkness area and could see the backs of some of the demons. They had formed a circle around the campfire. Alison's spell removed the darkness and another Nabassu immediately replaced it with another darkness spell. Darless removed it and a third cast its spell. Thea began a counter chant softly beside Jon. He let her finish it and watched light reappear.

Sir Thomas now appeared behind one of the demons that was attacking Alison, his blow caused a startled cry of pain, the demon turned to face his foe. Mandy appeared behind another that was closing on Alison and quickly hit it twice, but as Glasya had warned, these were stronger and though the damage was significant, much life was still in it as it fought back clawing and biting at Mandy. Three others were on the wrong side of the fire to do any good and they flew over the fire, landing beside the other three, triple teaming on Mandy and Sir Thomas.

It took a while for the demons to realize that this buccaneer had "skin" of steel. Their clawing did no real damage to him. Once they sensed this illusion, the three flew up a bit and dove upon him, knocking him to the ground and pinning him. Jon went into action again. "We will land behind them. Do what you can to two of them; I'll get us away before they can attack back if I can." He stepped them within a foot of the demons. Lonnie plunged his blade into the back of one, while Thea let loose a volley of missiles, which unfortunately did nothing but surprise that demon. Both let go of Sir Thomas and turned to face these back stabbers.

"The heck with spells," Thea exclaimed and drew her short sword. Jon stepped them to the other side of the fire, safely out of harm's way. Here he could see that Mandy had finished one off, though having taken some wounds. She was battling away with another one, Zond flashing this way and that. However, the other one was clawing away at Alison. The sight startled Jon and Thea for a moment. She just stood there letting the demon claw at her, all the while chanting her missile spells and letting a volley go. Some hit, but most missed. What was amazing though, Alison took not even the slightest scratch from the incessant clawing and biting!

"Time to help Thomas out, here we go," Jon whispered and he took them back to the other side just in time to see Darless's spell fire. A blue glowing broadsword appeared floating in the air above one of the demons, which was pounding away on the prone Sir Thomas. Then, the sword began attacking all by itself, while Darless grinned. Sir Thomas, having learned from experience, was stabbing a magical dagger into the demon who lay on top of him. Repeatedly he plunged it in, but kept missing vital organs because of his awkward position. As they appeared, Lonnie again thrust his blade into the back of one, while Thea did likewise. However, this time, the demons managed to move sufficiently at the last instant so that the damage inflicted was not great. Indeed, so swiftly did they move, that both demons managed to counter strike Thea and Lonnie, inflicting far more wounds than they received from behind. Jon immediately moved them back to the other side of the fire once more. "Darn, they catch on real fast!" he exclaimed. "But we've got to get Thomas on his feet. Let's try it again," and he took them back.

Both swung at once at the two demons; each hit once; the demons clawed back twice, nearly doing Thea in. Lonnie hacked again and did more damage. From the corner of his eye, he saw that their diversionary tactic had worked. Between the stabbing from Sir Thomas and the magical broadsword that relentlessly hewed at the demon, in self-defense, the demon got up off of Sir Thomas and attempted to fly away and regroup. The magical blade flew after him and hit him yet again. Mortally wounded, it dropped to the ground with a thud. Darless touched Sir Thomas and both flew up into the air. Jon stepped himself and Lonnie and Thea back to the other side of the fire. Using his stick, Jon quickly healed up Thea while Lonnie laid his hands upon himself, calling upon Father Ukko for healing.

Jon saw Mandy finish off her second, though she was now very bloody. Jon sought to reach her with some healing, but she chose to jump to Alison's side instead, hacking at the one attacking the mage. The two demons that Jon had left flew up and over the fire and dove upon the trio. Jon had barely enough time to grab onto the two and step them sixty feet to the south. Even so, a claw gouged his face, tearing a deep gash across his forehead; blood gushed down his face and into his eyes, momentarily blinding him. "I can't see! Alert me if we need to move fast." Holding onto them, he had no hands free to wipe the blood out of his eyes. He was in a fine pickle. He heard Alison curse in pain; evidently, whatever magic she had employed to protect herself had worn off. He hoped she was all right.

Thea intuitively narrated, "Alison is now being clawed. The attacks are hurting her. Mandy hit the demon really hard. No, it is now dead. Sir Thomas just hit another one; there is a blue flash. That demon is slain by his Holy Sword. Now there is only one left. It is flying away. Now Mandy is a horse, no make that a horse with wings? Oh, a Pegasus. Sir Thomas jumped on her. I think she said something nasty. Alison and Darless are chanting. They are invisible." Jon felt a swish of air on his face. He knew the two were now chasing the escapee. Jon let go of the two to try to wipe his eyes, but he could not see; blood kept flowing. He had no idea where he'd dropped his stick. So he uttered its command word.

Instantly his stick appeared in his hand and he spoke the command word and touched himself. He felt the wound close, but still could not see.

He heard Thea casting her dig spell and knew that Lonnie was dragging the dead Nabassu into a pit. He heard the sounds. Then, Darless spoke softly, "I've going to fetch some water so you can wash your eyes out. All is well, though Alison has some wounds you can attend to once you can see again. Be just a minute." He did not know how long she was gone, but in the darkness, it seemed like hours. Soon water hit his face. He realized she was dousing him like a fire hose from the decanter of water. He felt a towel in his hand and began to wipe and blink like mad. Slowly his vision returned. "Golly, you are covered in blood, Jon. That one must have been a nasty wound."

"Not really, just at the wrong spot," he replied. "Thanks, Darless. I hate not being able to see." They watched as Thea's shovel scooped the last bit of dirt onto the mound covering the five Nabassu. Alison was still standing guard as was Darless' blue floating broadsword.

"Alison, I'm relieving you. Get to Jon and get yourself fixed up," the alu-demon commanded, walking over to where the mage stood. Alison complied.

As soon as she was close, Jon laid his hands on her and began concentrating, healing cells here and there. She had only a few deep claw wounds which he quickly closed and mended. When he finished, he found that everyone now stood around them awaiting Alison's next order.

"Golly, I hope Mandy and Sir Thomas are okay. Should we go after them?" Thea asked what everyone else was also thinking.

"It's night and dark, though there's some moonlight," Alison noted. "Some of us could fly in the direction they took, but I don't see how we could easily find them. If they were in any real trouble, I think Mandy would send us a mental message somehow," she thought out loud. "She knows if she sends Jon a mental picture of where they are at, he could step us all there. I think we will just wait and see." The others accepted her reasoning and began to relax.

Darless' magical blue broadsword suddenly vanished. "Oops, there it goes. Ah well, that was a terrific spell!" She commented and then had to answer a bunch of questions about her new spell.

Lonnie added, "You know, your magical blade seemed to fare much better than my real blade. You hit the demons far more often than I did and yours seemed to do much more damage than a normal broadsword. Is that true?"

"Yes on both accounts," she replied, "though I am still perfecting its use. I will get better at it. This was the first time I really put it to use. It was effective, that's for sure."

"Can you teach me that one?" pleaded Thea, looking forlornly at her meager short sword. "I mean I did hit and cut them some, but yours was really powerful!"

"Thea, this is a very powerful spell. I think you have a good deal to learn about magic yet before you could attempt its casting. I promise you, when you are ready, I'll do my best to teach it to you." That pleased the young apprentice.

Next, Alison described her new spell that she had used on herself. It made her skin tough, as Darless' and impossible to hurt. "It worked really well. All I had to do was ignore the demon's attacks on me and keep on chanting my spells at it. I just wish it had lasted a bit longer though."

Just then in a flash of magic and a puff of sulfur, Glasya appeared before them, holding on to a weary Sir Thomas and a badly bleeding Mandy. Jon went to her at once and touched her with his walking stick, speaking the command word. A blue flash appeared over her body and her wounds disappeared. "Thanks," she managed to say and collapsed exhausted on the ground. Sir Thomas picked her up and carried her into the mansion, followed by the others. He laid her on some pillows, and Darless then took over, levitating the ranger's body and floating it into the bathroom.

Meanwhile, Sir Thomas, though himself exhausted, spoke, "The demon who tried to escape is dead. Mandy flew us up under its belly and taking careful aim, I thrust upwards into it heart. Mandy over did it I think, for she was only barely able to land us by the fallen demon. I healed her as much as I could, but she was really cut up. Then, I managed to somewhat bury the demon and was wondering how I was going to get her back here when Glasya appeared and used her magic to being us back. My thanks, Glasya," and he bowed.

She accepted graciously, saying only "Teamwork." She looked at the others and exclaimed, "You all look a mess! Are you all okay now?" There was a note of concern in her voice.

"Yes, we are in good shape. We all got pretty banged up there," Alison explained. "I don't think we could have handled any more of them at the same time, thought. Jon's tactic kept the weakest members protected and still let them help out. Very good idea, Jon." But Jon was now totally asleep on the pillows. He, like Mandy, had exceeded his limits and was dead to the world.

Seeing the worried look on Glasya's face, she added, "It's okay. Jon often does way more than he should; he is just asleep. When he wakens, he will be starving. So will Mandy. Imagine her, heavily wounded after killing three of them, she still has the energy to shape-change into a Pegasus and fly after the retreating demon! I think she way over did it."

"Well, if it had gotten any worse, I was going to step in," Glasya added. "Was that a stone skin type spell you used for protection, Alison?" She nodded affirmative. "Ah, I thought so. I don't know that one, though I have researched it fully. No need for me to use it as yet. As I was saying, I was just about to intervene when Darless' blue blade appeared, turning the tables. Now that *is* a spell I would like to know! Any chance you would care to share that one with me?"

Darless grinned and called out from the bath tub, "Sure, you have more than earned it. I'll show you how first thing tomorrow. It is a rather powerful spell though, using a lot of magical energy. As it turns out, the blade is most effective indeed. By our observations, it does perhaps twice the normal amount of damage one might expect from a broadsword. I just wish it would last longer."

In a few minutes, Darless brought the floating, but clean, Mandy back into the main room and laid her gently down on the pillows. Thea covered her up carefully trying not to waken her, though she could not have done so even if she had slapped her hard. Mandy was in a very deep sleep. Next, Darless levitated Jon and Alison went along to help bathe him. Once he was resting on the pillows, the others took their turns and ate a late night snack. One by one, they also turned in. Again, just as they fell into deep sleep, the bass voice said, "Thank you," but none paid it any attention.

Chapter 9The Fall of the Marquis de Gritz

"I wonder how many more of these Nabassu demons de Gritz has left?" Alison asked rhetorically as she sipped her morning tea. Jon, as usual, was washing up the dishes. The others were lying around on pillows in the mansion contemplating their next move.

"Well, we can always move again and try another spot. You know the wait and see game," Mandy answered.

"The longer we wait, the more time he has to gate in more demons and others to defend his tower," observed Darless thoughtfully. "If that was the last of them, he might just be alone in his tower at this very moment."

"I guess there is no way of really knowing," sighed Alison. Nothing could relief the pressure of making this momentous decision, when to attack the Marquis.

"Maybe I can find out something," Mandy offered. "I can pray to Reylona for some guidance. Give me a few minutes." Alison thanked her enthusiastically and the ranger went to a corner of the mansion, knelt down, and holding her symbol of her Goddess, she prayed for guidance. She asked, "Will it be beneficial for us to attack the Marquis in his tower yet today or would it be better for us to wait yet a while?" She prayed and listened for her answer. In her mind appeared the words, *Grave danger awaits but an even greater danger comes with delay.* "Oh thank you, Reylona." She returned to the others solemn faced. She repeated the reply she had received.

"Not to be outdone, Sir Henry asked if he could pray to Father Ukko. No one objected. The paladin asked Mandy for the precise question she'd asked of Reylona. Taking out his holy symbol, he too prayed and asked for augury guidance, repeating the same question Mandy had used. Shortly he returned, his face was a bit flushed.

"Well, what guidance did Ukko provide?" asked Alison.

"Er, the same as Reylona, 'Grave danger awaits but an even greater danger comes with delay,'" he answered. "I guess both have the same opinion of our fate at this moment."

"Okay, then that settles it," Alison spoke with determination. "Make ready, for today we ride forth to challenge the Marquis directly."

"Ah, Mandy?" Sir Thomas took her aside from the others. "I don't know what the day holds for us. But in case anything ill befalls me, I want our wager settled. I do not have one thousand gold coins with me, but I do have a ruby worth about that. Would you please accept the ruby instead? You have won the match. I spoke in haste and have learned to regret it. I will never underestimate you again."

"Sure, but you don't have too; I know it was just a game we were playing," she said graciously. He insisted and presented her with a beautiful, large red ruby. They shook hands to seal the ending of the game. Mandy noted that the man felt greatly relieved and realized he was making peace just in case he was slain in battle. She wondered about herself. Should she set her affairs in order? But they were in as much of an order as she cared to have things. She fingered her nearly invisible magical ring of three wishes that Reylona had given her.

Determinedly, she spoke loudly, "Everyone, may I have your attention for a minute." Of course, everyone did. Mandy seldom, if ever, had so formally addressed them. "I have to tell you something of import." She fingered the ring. "If, if something bad happens to me, you know like I get killed, I want everyone here to know something vitally important." She held up her right hand and pointed to her index finger. "On this finger, nearly invisible, is a gift from Reylona for dire emergencies. It is a ring containing three wishes. If something ill befalls me, do not fail to take the ring and use it wisely. Cut it off my finger if you must. Please don't leave it behind."

"Wow! A real ring of wishes!" exclaimed Thea, eyes wide open in complete awe. "Can I see it?" She examined Mandy's finger and did indeed see the faint outlines of a ring. "Wow, oh wow, a real Goddess gave you such a gift! Wow!" The young apprentice could not stop gaping. Yet, she was expressing the surprise and respect the others were feeling.

"You have our word, Mandy," Alison solemnly acknowledged. "It will never be left to the enemy and we will use it wisely to somehow get you back."

Glasya added, "And I will help the user with the proper wording to make sure the wish does not turn out ill for them. I so swear." Mandy felt much relieved. Sir Thomas looked directly at this devil once more. Her actions seemed to him to be right — the correct and best thing one of her power could do for them. Yet, she was a devil; evil was second nature to her. He found the paradox still baffling, but his extremely prejudiced former self had changed significantly for the paladin to even be having such thoughts.

With the weighty matter off her chest, Mandy then suggested, "If we leave soon, we can be at the tower by noon. That gives us a lot of daylight to battle him or whatever is there." Thus, the lengthy discussion of tactics to be used began in earnest. The real question was: did they still retain some element of surprise? If they did, they could perhaps enter from the top openings, which the Nabassu used, and fight their way down to where the Marquis may be located. If they tried to bash down his door, any surprise factor would be lost. On the other hand, surprise may already be lost and they might find him outside his tower waiting for them, either defiantly or in ambush. Of course, in a battle out of doors, a completely different set of tactics could be used from those that must be used indoors. If indoors, they would be in unfamiliar spaces, giving him the advantage. At this point in time, none knew what the Marquis knew or had planned for them. In the end, it was agreed to finalize plans once they were at the tower.

Jon volunteered to step everyone from here directly to the tower. However, Mandy pointed out that if something ill befell the mages or her or him, the others would have to return on foot, which would be perilous indeed without a guide. Thus, they rode. An hour later, with spells prepared, defenses made, they set foot back into the Canyon Lands and the magical mansion disappeared. Solemnly they mounted up and followed He That Does Not Speak, who led them unerringly through the twists and turns of the Wavapata directly to the tower in the center of the land.

Around noon, the party arrived at the same location that they had first spied upon the tower and met Glasya. Here, Mandy had them all dismount. She entrusted all the horses to He That Does Not Speak, saying to him, "If we do not return, take these horses with our blessing. If we should need them, one of us will send you words in your mind." He nodded and raised his hands and began a ceremonial dance. Mandy interpreted his actions as "calling upon the blessing of the Great Spirit." In actual fact, she was entirely correct.

"Again, I will be nearby but invisible," Glasya caution. "Remember, my involvement must remain a secret, especially if you all fail in this attempt. But I will try to do what I can to help out and yet not give my presence away, if you follow me."

"Thanks," Alison said, "any help is greatly appreciated. Mandy, lead on."

"Okay, single file, Sir Thomas, you bring up the rear. I am going first because I can go very, very stealthily. I do not want us to fall into any kind of trap.

You in your armor will be anything but silent on this rocky ground. Darless, you follow me, but stay at least five hundred feet behind me, just in case."

"Thea, you and Lonnie stay way back. Only help out if you really see something you can do safely. This demon can slay you with a glance; he has powerful priestly spells that we may not be able to counter. He is going to be fighting for his life, no holds barred. I don't want you two needlessly exposing yourselves."

"Yes, Ma'am," Thea replied, a bit huffily. She was her assistant, after all, not some dummy. She knew the danger and had no intention of unduly risking her life. She knew full well her limitations; her skill was no match for this demon. It had not been sufficient for even a single Nabassu.

"Here," Alison softened her tone. She handed both of them a ring of invisibility. "When we close to combat, stay well back and put these rings on so you will not be visible. That may give you some working room. But remember, once you do anything of an offensive nature, the invisibility effect is destroyed."

"Wow!" Thea's spirits rose once more, and she excitedly took the ring in her hand, holding it as if it were a mighty treasure.

"I shall not fail you, Mage Alison," bowed Lonnie. "I will protect your apprentice with my life, if need be." Alison smiled; she knew that he would do just that. It was a small comfort to know that her apprentice had someone watching over her.

Mandy set the pace at about half her normal speed so that Sir Thomas in his heavy armor could keep up with them while on foot. She assumed that he normally rode into battle and that he was not enamored of hiking a couple of miles on foot. Hopefully, he won't be tired out, she thought and slowed her pace even more. Both fighters were going to be needed against this deadly foe. She moved quietly and nearly unseen, Darless had a good deal of trouble keeping her in sight, as she moved from brush to boulder, taking advantage of what the land had to offer as if she were stalking a deer.

Finally, she had to halt about five hundred feet from the tower. Here the broad river plain was wide open all the rest of the way to the tower, that rose upwards of fifty feet. The tower measured at least fifty feet across at its base. She assumed the walls were very thick to support the heavy weight of the stone. Still, she sensed no trap, saw no sign of the enemy. No hairs on her neck twitched. One by one, the others came up to this last large bounder before the broad open space. All stared forward at the tower. No sounds could be heard, not even crickets or frogs. Utter silence, broken only by Sir Thomas's heavy breathing; it had been physically challenging for him to have hiked this far on foot. Mandy resolved to give him time to rest up. "Now what?" she asked.

"At least there is not a visible army awaiting our arrival," Jon whispered in jest. "Maybe no one is home. Wouldn't that be something to find the place deserted?"

"He may have some warning devices or spells between here and his door just waiting for us to trigger them," cautioned Mandy, who was now getting down right apprehensive about the unnatural quiet of this place. "I don't like it; too silent; as if he is just waiting for us."

Glasya, invisible, flew high overhead and studied the area but also saw nothing amiss. *It appears empty from way up here,* she placed in their minds. Instinctively, all heads looked up into the sky, but saw nothing, of course.

"Okay, let's cross the river and make for the door; Thea, Lonnie, you stay here for the time being. See how it goes for us," Alison decided. Mandy and Sir Thomas led the way, spread some twenty-five feet apart. Alison and Darless followed about ten feet behind them, while Jon brought up the rear behind the others. Some fifty feet into the open they had to wade across the shallow river stream. None did this quietly, however.

Just as soon as they set foot on the far bank, Mandy sensed danger approaching. "Danger! I feel it, be alert everyone," she called out. Her trained eyes, swept across the land from left to right and back again. Something was out here, but she could not locate it. Suddenly, something invisible grabbed a tight hold of the paladin. He cried out in alarm and began struggling against its vice grip on his shoulders. Mandy turned and saw a large mostly invisible creature, which seemed to be made out of air particles, for want of a better description. She yelled to the others, and ran to help the paladin. Just as she got to his side, the paladin was now aloft, being born swiftly towards the door of the tower. She gave a mighty leap and jumped after it and did manage to get one swing of Zond. She hit the creature and felt it hurting as a result. Then, she concentrated on her landing for she had just jumped nearly fifty feet!

Just as soon as Mandy yelled, Darless spied this aerial creature swooping down on Sir Thomas and gripping his shoulders. She chanted and let loose a volley of magical missiles directly at the eight-foot tall air monster. She observed it recoil in pain from her damaging blast. Alison too now saw dimly the creature, but was slower reacting and getting her missiles away. Her even larger volley connected, causing the creature to momentarily falter in its swift flying motion. Finally, from her concealed location, Thea let fly her magical missiles. Though her volley contained drastically fewer actual missiles, they, nevertheless hit it weakening it further. Still the creature flew towards the door.

Mandy ran as fast as she could after them, unwilling to leave the paladin to his fate. Alison and Darless stood still conjuring up another volley of the missiles. They fired. Again, the creature faltered and swayed nearly dropping Sir Thomas. He sensed it was severely wounded, and using his brute strength, he attempted to break free. His large, strong arms groaned at the intense strain he forced on them and suddenly, he did indeed break free and began falling. Only now did he realize that he was about fifty feet above the ground. He muttered a curse and braced himself for the hard landing, hoping he would not break too many crucial bones that would put him out of action.

Jon watched the situation as it occurred, unable to do anything to help out. The second he saw Sir Thomas break free and begin falling, he acted. He stepped himself to the falling man, grabbed a hold of him and stepped them both to just in front of the running Mandy, landing them both safely on the ground.

"What the," the paladin only managed to say, completely disoriented. His fighter instincts quickly took over; he hunkered down and turned to face the unseen aerial creature. Now he could see it flying directly at him to grab him once more. Mandy also saw it coming. As the creature swooped to pick up the paladin again, both attacked, Mandy was faster and again sliced into the creature. Her damaging blow was followed by the paladin's equally powerful swing with his huge two-handed sword. This time, he connected and mortally wounded it. Both ducked out of the way as the large creature fell to the earth with a resounding thud. It was still mostly invisible as it lay dead on the ground. From the corner of his eye, he spied the two mages running their way as fast as they could run flat out. Jon guessed that they were only about a hundred feet from the door, which now suddenly opened!

Out stepped the Marquis de Gritz fully dressed for battle. He had been expecting them. His aerial servant had attempted to bring him the powerful fighter, but it had failed in its attempt. *No matter, just pesky humans are all these are,* he consoled himself. He stood about seven and a half feet tall; his skin was black and as shiny as ebony. Two long, slender horns protruded from his forehead, arcing upwards. He had medium length black hair that stood straight up in the air — a rather bizarre effect to his liking. But it was his face that captivated Jon — ugly and distorted — definitely not human in origin. Deep, up-slanted, piercing red eyes glared at him, while his narrow, pointed mouth dripped saliva between huge fangs — razor sharp teeth that could shred flesh. He wore a magnificent looking black plate mail, highly enchanted, though no one knew this fact at this time. A huge mace hung from a belt at his side and his right hand wielded a magnificent looking broadsword — its jewels gleaming in the sunlight, particularly from the pummel. Jon could not help noticing his upper arm muscles; they were huge, perhaps the most powerful he had ever seen, nearly twice the size of Sir Thomas's arms. No doubt, this was a very strong man, or demon rather, that they faced. A couple of rings glimmered in the direct sunlight as did other jewelry he wore. He confidently strode toward them, chanting all the while.

Now, Sir Thomas quickly gathered himself to do battle. Uninjured actually, from the aerial servant, thanks primarily to Jon, he shut his visor. With the two-handed demon slayer sword raised before him in challenge, the Holy Paladin strode forth to challenge this demon. Mandy, however, like a crouching tiger, circled around to de Gritz's right intending to bring physical combat to the demon from two sides. Jon felt definitely out of place, standing but fifty feet directly in front of the Marquis. When asked why he said what he next did afterwards, he could only reply, it came to me on the spur of the moment — instinct perhaps. He could tell the demon was about to cast a spell, but said softly to the demon, "The Redeemer has arrived. Redemption or death; you choose."

Suddenly the heavens above the three opened up in flames, flames gushing like a blast furnace downward onto their bodies. His flame strike, as he called it, was designed to turn these pesky humans into cinders. *Why always fire?* Jon mused to himself as he countered the heat with an ever increasing flow of coldness that he mocked up like a fire hose spewing forth liquid nitrogen. *Ah, these are the most powerful flames I have ever encountered!* He discovered that he was unable to keep up with the incredible intensity. In the end, his hair got singed, but that was the extent of the damage. The Marquis looked at him with a strange look in his eyes, a look of "How is this possible? Not even a counter-spell uttered?"

Sir Thomas, now close enough to strike, attacked him with his sword and completely missed twice! Mandy with Zond, her bastard sword of speed, attacked twice, hitting him both times, inflicting enough wounds to have slain one of the youngest Nabassu demons. The wounds merely annoyed him. Jon watched as simultaneously the largest concentration of magical missiles he had thus far witnessed bounced harmlessly off him, as he roared with laughter, intending to demean the mages.

He began chanting once more, only this time, the spell culminated almost at once. Jon heard the harshest, not-understandable words, uttered in a totally commanding, domineering voice. He watched in utter dismay as the words hit Sir Thomas, who cried out in agony, dropped his sword, and grabbed hold of his ears through the helm. Immediately, the paladin was blown back off his feet and sent sprawling some fifty feet behind him, still all the while attempting to cover his ears. Jon wondered how on earth mere words could have that effect on someone. The words, though harsh and ugly sounding, were to him, just words. Jon just did not understand that one at all.

He did grasp Mandy's impact; she got off three attacks this time, hitting him twice giving him a nearly identical amount of wounds. Still, he showed very little sign of weakening. However, she finally had gotten his attention; he turned his face toward her. "Female?" was his only word and he brought his mighty sword to bear on her, hitting her twice. The second had such force behind it that Mandy was sent flying backwards nearly fifty feet, bleeding rather badly because she had just taken more wounds than she had inflicted on one of her pairs of attacks! She hit the ground hard and was stunned, recoiling from the single attack's ferocity. Never had she faced such a powerful opponent!

Now Jon saw Darless' blue bastard sword appear close to the demon attacking him. Against his powerful protections, she just could not hit him with her blade, though it did distract him slightly. Alison knew she had to do something fast or the game was done. She cast a rarely used spell at him. This time, his resistance to magic failed and her spell connected. Jon watched him cry out and grab his eyes, rubbing them. The demon temporarily had been blinded by her spell. Jon instantly took advantage of this fortunate turn of affairs. He grabbed the very heavy two-handed sword the paladin had dropped and stepped over to him. He helped pull the heavy armored man to his feet. Jon noticed that Sir Thomas could not hear, but he could fight and grabbed his sword and charged toward the Marquis. Jon also saw that the paladin was not hurt, though his armor was somewhat dented. He then stepped to Mandy and pulled her to her feet and used his walking stick to heal her numerous wounds. While she was not near death's door, considering how badly she was wounded in just one attack, Jon thought it prudent to take this opportunity to get her back to one hundred percent, just in case. She thanked him and rushed back into battle uttering, "Zagroot zounds!"

Jon saw that Darless had slowly been moving closer and was now only about a hundred feet from the Marquis as was Alison, but they kept a good twenty-five feet between themselves for protection against area wide spells. Alison sent him mentally, *Good thinking, Jon!* All the while, Darless' blue magical broadsword kept attempting to hit the Marquis. Now that he could not see, she finally did manage to connect and delivered some more wounds. Jon did notice that the bleeding had stopped somehow. *Is the Marquis able to adjust cells like we do?* he wondered. Darless later explained that his body has the ability to regenerate itself. Killing him would be difficult at best.

The Marquis began another chant just as soon as he was blinded. By the time that the two fighters had gotten to their feet and had closed to attack, his spell went off, completely dispelling Alison's magical blindness. He glared first at the paladin rushing toward him and then at Mandy, evidently deciding which was the deadlier foe. He had assumed all along that the Holy Paladin with his Demon Slayer sword was the one, but in fact, this upstart of a woman had cleanly, consistently penetrated his defenses and delivered significant wounds. He bought time for himself and drew his deadly mace and prepared to meet her head on.

Both attacked offensively, with little regard for their own defense, and both attacks by both hit. She delivered another huge number of wounds to the demon. However, while the first blow of his crushed her ribs with a horrible cracking sound, his second was more of a wild swing intended to eliminate the opponent. Mandy again found herself flying wildly through the air in a huge arc. She would have landed some hundred feet away had she not reacted and changed into a large eagle to stop her fall. As soon as she landed, she changed back and gasped for air. Breathing was excruciatingly painful, all of her ribs on her left side were cracked and some on the left as well. Holy cow! Jon thought as he immediately stepped to her side. He had never seen such pain on her face ever. Quickly he used is walking stick on her to heal her. Yet, she was still stunned from the utter viciousness of the blows. She needed time to regain her focus.

Darless and her blade, more like a pesky wasp, kept buzzing around his head, distracting him slightly. Hence, she let loose with another volley of missiles, which again his magical resistance warded off. Jon observed that this person was depending upon that resistance, quite the opposite of Darless who never depended upon it. He sent this observation to her and Alison, figuring the mages might find this useful somehow. Alison had now created a huge boxing glove over the Marquis and the fist in glove was attempting to punch him out cold. It actually hit him squarely in the jaw, jolting him slightly, causing some damage to his jaw. During this time, Sir Thomas managed to hit him once more with his attacks and the huge sword caused even more wounds. Jon noted that at last he was beginning to weaken, but he also heard the Marquis begin another chant.

This time, de Gritz was faster than any of the others. His spell went off and all of his wounds disappeared. "Ah, that's better!" the demon exclaimed. "I feel fine, now for a good fight!" Uff. The glove smashed into his head once more. The blue blade missed again. This time, Darless let loose a very nasty spell. Jon recognized it, for he had heard it before. She sent a disintegrate beam at his head. Jon watched fascinated as one of the brooches on his neck seemed to energize in a bluish glow and sucked the spell into it. He wondered if Darless also saw that. Though she was staring right at him, she did not see the effect, only that the spell had no effect.

The paladin again attacked twice but only hit once, delivering significant, from Jon's point of view, wounds which were only a trifle to this demon. Jon also realized in a flash that had the Marquis had only a few others to help him out, this battle would have ended long ago in all their sudden deaths! At that exact moment, Jon heard the Marquis begin another chant. The words were familiar once more to him; he'd heard and experienced that spell before. *He's gating! Do something fast!* he sent to Alison and Darless and Thea. Jon immediately heard the also familiar counter chants from Alison and Darless. "Mandy, are you okay now? Please get up. We need you badly. You are the only one having a major effect on this demon."

"Zounds, Jon! Give me a break! I last for one round and then get myself splattered across the universe. He crushed my rib cage last time. What's next, my head?" She tried to focus and found it very hard to do. Her long hours of training and vast experience seemed to vanish into thin air. She felt fear, real fear. She had only rarely felt such an intense emotion. She tried deep breathing but nearly hyperventilated. Jon tried to massage her shoulders, desperate to get her back into control once again.

Now the Marquis spell went off and he exclaimed loudly, "Now let a few play things come forth to end this battle now!" A gate had just been opened into the Abyss, Jon assumed. A glowing pentagram appeared on the ground beside de Gritz. And bam, Darless' counter-spell went off; it failed. Bam, Alison's spell to undo the gate went off; it failed. Jon's hope sank. The paladin attacked twice more missing both times, in spite of the Marquis's concentration on his spell casting. Sir Thomas was becoming more than annoyed to say the least. The demon was incredibly hard to hit! Just as some creature was about to appear, Jon saw the faint outline of a beastly creature appearing, another counter-spell landed upon the glowing gate. This one worked, the gate vanished just as suddenly as it had appeared. Thea, Jon thought. Against incredible odds, this young apprentice had somehow been phenomenally lucky and pulled off the dispel magic against magic that was far, far above her current level of skill. The Marquis looked stunned, but only for a couple seconds. "I guess I shall just have to finish you all off myself," he declared and proceeded to lay into the paladin.

Sir Thomas again attacked twice, scoring a hit finally doing some damage to the man, enough damage to have sent Jon to the houses of healing, if there were any. The demon swung his huge mace striking a counter blow that nearly took Sir Thomas's head off. Jon wondered if perhaps the violence of the blow had broken his neck. The paladin was sent reeling, staggering to keep his feet. The Marquis then picked him up with one arm and threw him high through the air. Sir Thomas landed in a crush of steel and ground nearly fifty feet from the demon, who let out an "Ah, that's better." Jon could do no more for Mandy. Now he had to get to the fallen paladin. He again stepped himself the short distance to the man.

The Holy Paladin was moaning in pain. "Do you need curing fast?" Jon asked unable to ascertain the severity of his wounds because he was encased in now badly dented full armor. He did notice that his helm was twisted sideways at a weird angle.

"No, but my helmet is killing me. Can you get it off of me without breaking my neck?" he begged.

Jon fumbled around. He had never observed how the man put it on in the first place. Now that it was bashed into a twisted shape, he had even less ideas. "Let me at it," the voice of Lonnie spoke from behind him. The younger paladin had come running as fast as he could, when he saw Sir Thomas take that blow. Quickly he saw that it was now impossible to remove without cutting some support leather inside. Carefully, he used his long, narrow dagger, inserting it carefully beneath the plates at exactly the right spot, cutting the leather. Sir Thomas then managed to pull his head out of it. His neck was very black and blue, but he was otherwise all right.

"Thanks, Lonnie, I owe you. One of the benefits of such armor, Jon, is that it can take a significant amount of damage that you would otherwise incur. Darn, I've lost my sword again," the paladin exclaimed dismayed. "Look at that!" he suddenly pointed to Mandy and Alison.

Alison had rushed to Mandy to give her some support. Before she could cast the spell she had wanted to use, the Marquis had unleashed another of his flame strikes from the sky above onto the pair, intending to fry them both. They saw this huge cloud of intensely hot flames come rushing downward onto the two only to be sucked straight into Alison's magical staff. She had countered that attack successfully. "May I borrow your sword, Lonnie? I'm a bit desperate at the moment," asked Sir Thomas. Lonnie unsheathed it and lent his less magical blade to his mentor. Sir Thomas, now helm-less, charged back into battle.

"Gods, if he takes another mace blow to his head, it will kill him," worried Lonnie. Jon felt a sickening feeling in his stomach. The young lad was right. He had to do something.

Meanwhile, Darless fired another powerful spell at him, this time it impacted him, giving him some wounds. He growled back at her. "You are on the wrong side, alu-demon!" he yelled at her. Ignoring him, she began yet another chant.

Alison likewise. Only Mandy was the beneficiary this time. She had turned Mandy's skin into a stone like toughness that would ward off any injuries for many attacks. This was just enough to raise Mandy from her depression. "Thanks, I'm off to slay this demon!" She charged back into battle.

Now the paladin attacked twice again, missing both times. Again, one sweeping swing of the mace smashed into the paladin's chest, throwing him backwards another fifty feet, landing him on his back. Jon heard all spell casters chanting at the same time. Just then, he had an idea. "Lonnie, go help Sir Thomas to his feet. I am going to try something or we are all going to get the crap beat out of us." The young paladin rushed unhesitatingly to his mentor. Meanwhile, Jon's eyes searched for where the heavy two-handed sword lay. It was very close to the Marquis at the moment. "Timing is everything. Now while he is occupied chanting." He stepped to the sword, picked it up, and stepped away, all in a flash before the Marquis could have reacted had he thought that Jon posed any threat whatsoever. Instead of arriving with the sword where Sir Thomas was now on his feet, Jon arrived at a distant point near the river bank.

He turned and watched Mandy attack him twice, inflicting what would be grievous wounds to another but hardly phasing this demon, and then with a sweeping swing of the mace, saw her again flying through the air, undamaged of course this time, just the wind knocked out of her. Now he saw a terrifying sight coming from de Gritz. His spell had somehow called forth thousands upon thousands of biting bugs, swarms of them covered the entire landscape, all making for the party members. The shock caused Alison's spell to malfunction. Darless halted hers and began a counter-spell hoping she would be in time to prevent major bug bite damage. Jon had seen pictures of swarms of African fire ants that swarmed over a cow leaving only white bones in its wake. He saw Sir Thomas and Lonnie backing up to avoid the slow moving swarm. "Well, here goes nothing," he said to himself as he concentrated and stepped yet again, carrying the heavy two-handed sword.

His destination was altogether strange. He arrived at where he had intended, four hundred feet above the Marquis. No one noticed him up there at all. *So far, so good. Here it goes.* Of course, he did not have magic he could call upon or rely upon, unlike Alison or Darless. He began falling. The heavy two-handed sword seemed to pull him down even faster. He fell upside down, holding the sword in his right hand, pointed straight down; his feet were flailing uselessly above him. He concentrated on his aim. His course corrections were minuscule and he kept over compensating. He had only seconds to accomplish his task. As the ground neared, Jon was vaguely aware that the others were now watching him. *Okay, sword, time to do your thing, if you can. I trust in you*, he sent to the sword. He did not know if it was alive like the Holy Scepter of Ukko that he had used before and which had actually taken control over his body and actions on a couple occasions. He concentrated only on maintaining the proper trajectory, straight down onto the top of the Marquis's head.

Clear up to the point of impact, Jon was fiddling with course corrections, trying to get it right. He knew that this trick would only work one time. He had to get it right on the first try. At the very last instant, the Marquis, seeing the others looking up over his head, looked up himself, only to see the sword about a foot above his head, dangling Jon behind it. Wham, the sword and Jon hit directly on his head, the sword rammed straight through his skull and deep down through his body finally sticking deep into the ground. Jon smashed hard into the ground, heard bones snapping, felt a rush of pain in his limbs, and blacked out as he crumpled to the ground. He did not wake for over an hour. Thus, he did not see the Marquis's body completely disappear from this universe just after the impact.

Sir Thomas was the first on the scene. "Well I'll be, a musician actually slew the demon! But where'd the demon go?" Looking all about, seeing only his companions running toward him, he examined Jon's crumpled body. "Broken bones galore. Wonder he is still alive." He chanted to Father Ukko and laid his hands upon Jon, and the mending process began. The others arrived as he finished.

"Is he alive?" asked Alison frantically, worry lined her face.

"Yes, broke a lot of bones. He's out cold. Probably for the best, he'd be in a lot of pain. I've done what little I could for him. Perhaps you all can do more," he answered her fears.

Darless took charge, "Okay this is work for Mandy and me. You all scout the area, make sure that we are not attacked. We will be quite defenseless while we heal him. Mandy, you want the top or bottom half?"

Teasingly, Mandy said, "The bottom half, it's more interesting." Both chuckled and then went to work healing him, tiny step by step.

The others fanned out and carefully searched the entire area, but saw no sign of the Marquis. Meanwhile, Glasya landed and cancelled her cloak of invisibility. "Congratulations everyone on the most incredible fight I have witnessed. Is Jon alive?" Alison explained that the two were working on healing him. The devil went over to Jon to see what she could do as well.

Darless looked up as Glasya approached. "How's it coming? Need a hand?" she asked genuinely interested in helping.

"Rather daunting. He has eighteen bones broken in the upper half," she replied.

"Four in his legs," Mandy added. "Any help would be appreciated. This is going to be quite a challenge. I wonder if anyone else can make use of his walking stick to heal him."

"Allow me," Glasya replied, and she began a chant. Darless recognized it at once, but thought better of protesting. If this devil wanted to cast this spell, it was her choice and hers alone, though she personally knew what it cost the caster. "A moment later, Jon opened his eyes, straightened his body, relaxed, said thank you, and promptly fell into a deep sleep. "There, let him rest. You can check him over first and see if I missed anything."

Both, of course, did exactly that. They inspected his body carefully, but found no trace of any wounds, damaged or broken bones. However, Darless did see a new mental picture Jon had involuntarily created of the fall. She also saw that it was connected to a number of other "falling" mental pictures. Thus, she knew that one day soon, she would have to give Jon a therapy session. *No wonder he is afraid of heights*, she mused.

Meanwhile, Sir Thomas gathered the two fallen weapons: the mace and broadsword the demon had used on them and brought them to the others near Jon. "I put the evil, cursed weapons by the door," he proclaimed.

"Be not so hasty in your conclusions, Holy Paladin," Glasya cautioned. "Both are most likely highly enchanted, but they may not, in fact, actually be evil. Let we mages examine them." He accepted her criticism; inwardly, he knew she was right. *If only I didn't blurt out things so without thinking them through*, he thought to himself. He and Thea reconnoitered the area, looking for anything amiss and found none. Lonnie had gone back for the horses and a half hour later came riding up, leading them, along with their guide.

Neither Thea nor Sir Thomas could find any traps or devices on the flat lands about the tower. Hence, they then joined the others standing around the sleeping Jon, discussing what to do next. "We cannot go searching the tower and leave Jon out here alone," Alison said, "What if the demon is not slain but is hiding or recovering? What if there are other creatures inside? We might as well give Jon time to sleep and let us make whatever preparations we deem necessary."

"Look," Glasya offered, "you are about to enter his sanctum. No doubt he has many traps lying for the unwary to protect his domicile. We must approach this search with the utmost caution. Be ever on the vigil for traps. Make sure we still have fast access to counter dispel magic in case we accidentally trigger one. I have a wand that can be used to detect traps. I think this is the time that I really made use of it!" Following her suggestion, the mages rested up and prepared their various detection and counter magic spells. Meantime, Glasya walked to within about fifty feet of the single door and stood examining it closely.

After Lonnie returned, Alison had Thea fix them a brief lunch with plenty to drink. She really was thankful to have something to do for everyone, since she knew that she would have little to offer in the main search of the tower. The young apprentice had no ideas of what a trap or magical trap even looked like, let alone how to disarm the thing. Instead, she remained jubilant that it was her dispel magic spell that had actually worked, undoing the gate spell which would have defeated them all had she failed to counter it. Her accidental victory was enough for her today. Efficiently, she made lunch for everyone. However, she resolved to keep her eyes and ears open so that she could learn what she could from the others. In fact, she kept a very good record of the ensuing search.

While they were eating, Jon finally woke. "Is he dead?" was his first words, followed by, "I remember intense pain, neck broke too. Funny, nothing hurts now? What happened?"

"You got him, silly," Thea explained. "And that was positively a brilliant move, if I do say so myself! I know that I would never have thought of that!" She would have continued had Alison not interjected.

"Yes, Jon, you saved the day. Very well done. As Sir Thomas's sword pierced completely through his body and stuck into the ground, some magical energy flashed and his entire body disappeared, we know not where. Darless speculated perhaps he went back to the Abyss. Glasya suggested he might be inside recovering, healing himself. We just don't know. It's been about an hour now and no sign of him or anyone else for that matter. Glasya healed you fully using her magic, so have something to eat and drink. When you are done, we are about to try to enter the tower and give it a thorough search."

"At least he does not have those two weapons anymore," Darless added. "He dropped them when you skewered him. Sir Thomas has them over there awaiting our analysis."

"Analysis done," Glasya spoke, "I took the liberty of studying them while I was examining the trap on the door itself. Both weapons are very highly enchanted and none are evil. Neither appears to be demon-forged. If I were you folks, I would keep these and use them."

"Let me touch them," Mandy put in. "I can sense their history. Perhaps that will shed a bit more light on them." She did so. Again, horrific scenes of their history poured into her mind; this time she knew what to do and kept pushing further back into time. Finally, the grim countenance gave way to a smile. She opened her eyes, "Both of these once belonged to a priest and a fighter. Both men were slain by de Gritz, who confiscated their weapons. I believe if you bless them for some time, you can purge from them all traces of the evil abuse that they have been force to bear and then make good use of them." That totally satisfied the Holy Paladin, who swore to see to that task no matter how long it might take to clean them.

After Jon finished eating, he stood up, this time using his walking stick for support. He found that he was still a little wobbly on his feet. Sir Thomas gave him an arm to lean upon, saying rather privately, "I want to thank you for all you did to help me and the rest of us out. I realize now that I have a whole lot more skill to learn before I can slay demons! That I actually saw the Lady Darless slay Lord Jarred now seems even more monumental to me. My admiration and respect for her just keeps growing."

"She's one terrific person," Jon answered. "You are one lucky man to have her love!" The paladin beamed as the two brought up the rear as they approached the door. Glasya, still standing some fifty feet from the door itself, was pointing out the signs of the trap to Alison, Darless, Mandy, and Thea, who had a notebook and was rapidly taking notes of everything.

"See that pale glowing arch around the entire door frame?" Glasya pointed out. "That is a magical symbol that will do something most unpleasant to us if we get too close."

"What will it do?" asked Thea, curious of course.

"No way of knowing, unless you want to experiment for us and tell us what it does," she poked a little fun at her. "Seriously, if we had a high priest among us, he probably could tell us."

"I'm no high priest," Sir Thomas spoke somberly, "but Father Johnas is and he has told me about such protection spells. According to him, if you get much closer to it, you either feel utterly hopeless, surrendering on the spot, or you become wracked with massive pain for hours or you even may decide to join up with the demon! No matter what, it is demonic."

Glasya began a magical chant, which Jon recognized was a dispel magic counter; he had heard Alison and Darless use it any number of times now. He was starting to get the hang of recognizing what spell was being cast from the foreign words, even though he did not understand a single word being chanted. Her spell detonated and countered the Marquis's symbol. Everyone saw the faint symbol entirely disappear. Still, Glasya studied the door carefully before she suggested she get closer and touch it. Finally, she pronounced it safe and the others moved up to the door.

Now how to open it was the problem, for the door had no handle, no knob, no key hole, and no visible connection to the outside world. Perhaps it was designed to be opened only from the inside. But then how would the Marquis ever get back in once he came outside? Finally, Alison could see no other way of opening it except by using magic. She had everyone stand way back just in case opening it triggered another trap. She chanted a brief spell that knocked or forced the door open. It swung open and stayed open. No other trap fired. Glasya, again in the lead, carefully approached the opening and examined the inside of the door. It was magically enchanted to open upon speaking the proper command word, she pronounced. That explanation satisfied everyone except Thea, who asked Alison when she could learn how to so enchant doors; it seemed to her a really useful, cool spell.

The inside of the first floor of the tower was well lit by numerous lanterns adorning the walls. The circular room held a combination kitchen and study. Numerous books lined a bookcase. A desk and chair stood near the shelves. Various supplies were chaotically stacked against the walls opposite the entrance. In the exact center, a circular stairway led upwards but not downwards. Immediately to their left, curving around the sides of the tower was a staircase leading to the basement. No sounds of any kind, except the breathing of the party, could be heard. Mandy felt no prickling on her neck and so pronounced it safe to enter.

"Do not touch anything!" Glasya ordered; Alison seconded it. They all entered. "First order of business, find out if any other demons or creatures are in here. We do not want to get surprised by some monster while we are searching."

"Okay, I can do that," Jon found himself whispering, not daring to intrude on the utter silence of the place.

"How?" asked Glasya, most curious. In fact, her impressions of Saint Jon had arisen tenfold during the events of this day.

Jon concentrated, expanding his senses, ignoring his body. He heard Darless whisper an explanation to Glasya, including her tease of "Just don't be surprised if he contacts you when you are using the bathroom!" He smiled; he would never live that one down. Now he perceived the familiar glows, or perhaps auras some might call them, of his dear friends. He spied the devil as well, only she did not look quite as black in color as he expected. For a minute, he began wondering. Then, he forced himself back to the task at hand. Slowly, he widened his zone of awareness until he covered the room. Then, he probed upwards until he felt the brilliance and warmth of the sun above the roof. He'd sensed nothing. Now downward he sent his awareness, down and down. He had no idea how far to go down. All was dark as far as he could go. After going down the same distance he had gone up, he decided that the place really was deserted. Slowly he opened his eyes and reported, "It is all clear. Nothing above us. I don't know how far it goes down there, but I probed fifty feet down. Nothing here but us at the moment."

"Well, that is good news," Thea spoke and wrote dutifully in her notebook: After opening door and stepping inside, try to detect presence of other creatures in tower. She looked up to see what they would do next.

"Ordinarily, I'd say, let's split up and thoroughly search this place," Alison spoke. "But the likelihood of further traps is quite high. Perhaps we should stay together?"

"Well, we can cover more ground if we break into teams," Glasya observed. "I know, let me use my wand and scan this floor for traps. If none, then you can fan out and very carefully search this floor. The Nabassu probably lived upstairs, so after I scan this floor, I'll go up the circular stairs and scan up there. That will give a lot of area to safely search." She spoke a command word to her wand and began pointing it at the library portion of the room. She observed that a drawer on the desk glowed, as did some volumes on the shelves. She moved to the kitchen and then to the storage areas. Nothing else glowed. She climbed the stairs and was gone a couple minutes. She returned to say that nothing seemed booby trapped upstairs, that it was more like an eerie than a room.

She, Alison and Darless chose to examine the library with its traps. Mandy took the supplies and kitchen area. Sir Thomas and Lonnie climbed the stairs to examine the Nabassu quarters. Thea flittered between the different groups, trying to make reasonable notes on what each was doing. Jon just hung out; his idea, be useful when someone needed him.

The two paladins stomped up the circular stairs and promptly came back down. There was no light in the upper rooms. Following Alison's orders, Jon went outside and found several short branches and brought them to her. Then, Alison and Thea placed several light spells on them and the two paladins clanked up the stairs once more, each armed with two bright lights. The others next heard some muttered, awful condemnations from the two men.

The upper forty feet of the tower was devoted to the Nabassu roost. It was entirely open save for a dozen giant nesting boxes molded into the walls at different elevations. A stone staircase arced its way around the circumference of the tower, ever rising higher. A landing was beside each of the nesting boxes. The floor was literally covered in guano a foot deep. These demons defecated just like birds, thought the younger paladin. They had to walk through the feces to get to the stairs going up. At least the tower was empty. Dutifully, they searched each nest. "Ah, the ladies are going to want these," said Lonnie decidedly. Inspecting the first box, he found numerous gems in its bottom. The two men got out a couple of sacks and began collecting gems. "This is rather like collecting chicken eggs," teased Lonnie, remembering how he had helped his uncle with chickens one summer to earn some spending money.

"Only these eggs are a lot more valuable. I found a really big red one, probably a ruby. This will certainly help Alison pay for her village upkeep," said Sir Thomas. "Normally, I stand guard while Slickster does all the gathering. He's our party's handyman, but I swear he is a glorified thief, never been able to prove it, though."

"He doesn't steal from you, does he?" asked Lonnie.

"No, never that I can tell, though I have tempted him numerous times in the past, trying to get the goods on him, so to speak. But he seems to know an awful lot about traps and such for an ordinary person. I guess it isn't so bad doing all this scrounging after all," he added.

"Actually," replied Lonnie, "it's kind of fun, really, although I only really need a couple of these to pay my expenses for the year. I guess if she gives me a share, I can make a substantial donation to the Church of Ukko. Say do you know of a worthy church to donate to? Where I come from, I think even the church is a bit seedy."

"Well, I'm sure Father Johnas can help you out. He is always seeking funds for the church. I usually give him my extra," Sir Thomas answered. It took them an hour to fully search the eerie. The found one hundred and thirty gems, which later were valued at about one hundred thirty thousand gold coins, an impressive amount.

Mandy, searching through the supplies, discovered a water system. Using her detect magic spell, she ascertained that the bulbous portion was magical. She detached it and water gushed out until she quickly found something to plug the opening. "I'll bet this is another decanter of water." Her search turned up ten bottles of very fine wine, still in their packing crate. There were two empty slots, so he had evidently drunk two bottles. In one corner she found a curious coil rope. It had a card attached to it. She read the words out loud. Unfortunately, it was the command word. Instantly, the rope straightened out and flew through the air to the nearest person, which was Thea. At once, the rope entwined itself about her coiling around her body so quickly that the young mage could do nothing about it. She found herself tied up securely. Mandy had a chuckle as did the others. She read the bottom words and the rope released the teenager and recoiled itself at Mandy's feet.

Recovering her dignity and straightening her hair, Thea commented, "Now that *is* a useful item! One of us should carry that with them at all times." She picked it up and put it over her shoulder. "Hum, I need to practice using this." She looked around at the busy people and saw Jon was just watching. "Hey, Jon, can I practice this on you?" Jon suddenly got very busy helping Alison move a box.

Now Glasya first examined the books on the shelves. She cast a detect magic on the lot. One had the aura she was looking for and she used a set of thongs to pull it out, explaining to the others, "Sometimes curse spells are cast on valuable books so that if any one touches them, the curse fires. I'm playing it safe." She managed with difficulty to get the large volume down. However, the writing was illegible to her until she cast another spell enabling her to decipher the title, "Brinker's Tomb to Heighten Your Destructive Capabilities in Five Easy Lessons." Reading the title aloud, she commented, "I think that this one should be destroyed."

"I concur," said Alison with no hesitation.

"Yes, added Darless, "we've seen quite enough of that lately."

Gingerly, the devil carried the book outside so that it could be more easily destroyed without any repercussions on them. She had visions of the book exploding or something equally nasty. Standing back a good distance, she first shot a huge lightning bolt into it, tearing its binding. She followed this with a ball of fire which did the job. The dry, brittle parchment turned to ashes in short order. The devil then returned to her search.

"Look at this," Alison pointed out to Glasya, when she had finished destroying the evil book. "I've found a secret compartment. The width of the drawer indicates some extra space in the back of the desk."

"Yes, but look more carefully. See, there is another protective spell on it. You might have gotten fried if you tried to open it," the devil pointed out.

"Not a chance," she replied. "I've encountered this type of thing many times before. Stand way back. There is only one way to deal with diabolical traps." She chanted and her spell forced it open, springing the trap. Several tiny needles shot out in all directions, but found no target within the expected three feet and fell harmlessly to the floor. Darless pointed out that the darts were coated with a dark liquid, "Probably poison," commented Alison.

"That means he really did not want us to get inside this secret compartment. Which is why we really do need to inspect it carefully," added Darless, intentionally not speaking the word, "Number," for Glasya's sake.

The three looked closely inside; Jon craned his neck to see over their shoulders but couldn't see anything. Neither could the three mages. "All right, another spell," Glasya muttered and then chanted. Jon now caught a glimpse of something glowing slightly, lying flat on the bottom of the secret compartment, concealed to look as though it was part of the wood. Glasya picked it up and brought it out to the desk.

"A portable hole?" asked Jon, realizing it looked a lot like the one he was using to store the party's supplies and Sir Thomas's extra gear.

"Yes," Alison replied. "Now comes the really tricky part. We need to unfold it and go through its entire contents, any piece of which could be highly cursed or worse."

"And," added Darless, "either we dump the entire contents out, risking breaking something or we stick our hands in and grope around, which is highly dangerous."

The three considered their options for several minutes before deciding to risk a third approach. Darless cast a light spell and placed it on her hand. Then, she took a deep breath and slowly lowered the top part of her body into the hold, using her light as a guide. She stayed partially inside for several minutes before she backed out. "Yes, there is strange stuff inside, breakables I believe. Jon may be very interested in some of the stuff. I am going to risk bringing them out one at a time." The others muttered the usual "Be careful's."

Darless first brought out an ornate, polished mahogany box with many jewels on its lid. It was just less than two feet long but only three inches in the other dimensions. Inside, snug in the velvet lining lay a recorder, probably alto in pitch. Jon eyed it eagerly. "Don't touch!" Darless was firm. Next, she brought out a magnificently made lute, it even had several jewels imbedded in its body. She repeated, "Don't touch!" It was all Jon could do to obey her; he longed to 'touch' and play on them to hear how they sounded, but he knew he had best follow her guidance, at least for the moment. He restrained his impulses to try them both out.

She brought out a coin pouch; coins jingled inside. Next came a set of gauntlets that tied about one's wrists. These were followed by metallic bracers that also strapped upon one's wrists; these looked remarkably similar to those that Mandy always wore to give her much better defense against attacks.

Finally, grinning broadly, she stood up holding in her hands a very large, expensively bound, spell book that no longer looked like a box. Across the front of the leather cover, embossed in gold was 'Mingus Volume 9.' "Eureka!" cried Glasya. All three mages grew intensely excited with this find. For them, this leather volume was utterly priceless because it should contain the casting instructions for numerous exceedingly powerful, high level spells. However, Darless knew that if they stopped the search and began looking at the spell book, Jon would immediately begin playing around with the two instruments. She said, "For now, I will put it back in the empty portable hole for safe keeping. We should attempt to analyze these other items. They may be useful." The other mages concurred. Both Glasya and Alison picked up an instrument and chanted their magic detection and identification and spells.

Glasya spoke first, "Thea write this down for Jon. I think he is going to like this lute. It is called The Lute of the Traveling Bard. Besides being a high quality lute, the player can cast seven magical spells via the lute by using the proper command word while playing. Let's see, it can cast a Hold Animals spell, a Protection from Fire — seems to be a circle of protection about twenty feet in diameter. It can Neutralize Poison, that's interesting. It can cast Protection from Evil, again in a twenty foot circle — please, don't do that while I am around," she jested. "Ah, you can go Invisible, Levitate, and also Fly. Here are the command words for these." She carefully told them to Thea who dutifully noted them expertly in her notebook.

Alison then gave her analysis of the recorder. "This is the Recorder of Charming. If you play the tune and think the command words, it can Charm a Person, Charm an Animal or Monster, Create Light or Dim Light, and Cause Sleep. Ah, this is nice, it can Detect Invisible Creatures — useful. It also can cast a Forget spell or Remember. I think I like the latter form better. Now this is interesting, it can Hold a Person or an Animal or even an Undead Creature. We should have had this a few nights ago. While playing it, you can implant a Suggestion in the listener; be careful with that one, Jon! Finally, it can detect if someone is magically Scrying on you. This is a useful recorder." She also carefully noted each of the command words; Thea wrote them all down precisely. She made a copy of both instructions and gave them to Jon.

"Now can I play with them? I promise not to fiddle with the spells," Jon pleaded. They agreed and the sweet sounds of the alto recorder soon echoed through the tower. Then, he tried the lute. It was still in perfect tune, which he thought rather amazing; back home, stringed instruments were always going out of tune. He soon discovered that he would need a good deal of practice to make respectable music on it.

Meanwhile, the mages continued their analysis of the other items. Darless identified the gauntlets as providing the wearer the strength of an ogre. Mandy, quite excited about this discovery, just had to try them on. Immediately, she felt the magical strength boost. "Wow! This will aid my attacks big time indeed! Mind if I wear them?" No one objected. Indeed, Alison thought that this was a very prudent thing to do. Little did she know just how fortunate this minor action would turn out to be.

Alison identified the bracers as being what they expected, providing magical defense against attacks. She insisted that Jon put them on and wear them. He did so, but really did not want to stop playing with his new instruments. The mage noted that they were not quite as good as those that she and Mandy wore, but only by a little bit. She felt more relaxed since Jon would now be harder for a fighter to hit with a sword or other weapon.

"This one is peculiar," Glasya commented. "The coins are not from this land nor are they from the Abyss; the coins, one platinum, five gold, six silver and three coppers, are not magical either. Yet, the pouch has a faint magical glow about it. Do any of you recognize the coin's mint?" Each took a look, but none did. While they were looking, Sir Thomas and Lonnie joined them, each carrying two bulging sacks, full of the gem stones they had found.

"Ah, I do," the Holy Paladin commented. "Those come from the southern lands, Alison, from where our grandparents' came. I have a couple keepsake coins just like them."

"Well, we need to do an experiment with this pouch to see if it is what I think it is," the devil said. "Here, Sir Thomas, hold on to all these coins. Look everyone; I am leaving just one copper coin in the pouch. Tomorrow, let's all remember to look inside the pouch. If I am correct, tomorrow we shall see that there are one platinum, five gold, six silver and three coppers back inside it. If so, always remember to leave at least one single coin in the pouch over night for the magic to work."

"Clever, a traveler might never run out of spending cash," commented Lonnie. That would be most useful." Glasya gave him the pouch for safekeeping. "Thanks."

Sir Thomas and Lonnie opened their bags showing all of the gems, large and small, that they had found in the Nabassu nests above. Thea and Lonnie had never seen so many gems at one time. Thea had to finger, touch and examine a great many to satisfy her curiosity.

"Now for the basement," Alison ordered. "I don't think we all need to go charging down there at once. Jon, why don't you and Lonnie and Sir Thomas stay up here and keep an eye on things. If we run into any trouble, we'll give a shout." Jon was only too agreeable, for he kept right on playing tune after tune on the alto recorder; the fingering was not too different from his flute. The paladins went outside to check on the horses and to make sure no other creatures had approached while they had been preoccupied inside the tower. They found nothing amiss and came back inside and sat down and relaxed.

Suddenly the peace was broken by a dark shadow appearing in the doorway. He spoke, "I thought I would find you all in here." The Marquis de Gritz had returned. Jon nearly dropped the recorder in shock and surprise.

Both paladins jumped to their feet crying out as loudly as they could, "The Marquis is back. Help!" They were trying to let the others, who had just gone down the stairs, know. Jon sent them the message mentally.

"Silly human," sneered the Marquis at Jon, "you think a High Priest is so easily slain? Hah! I was prepared for that. A contingency spell simply activated, taking me home where I could heal myself, resupply and return. Now you all are low on spells, 'course they don't affect me anyhow. The ball is in my court now, Redeemer; prepare to meet the wrath of the Marquis de Gritz!" Although he had dropped both of his weapons when Jon had attacked him from above, he obviously had other weapons at his home in the Abyss. He wielded another broadsword and a mace hung from a belt at his waist. He looked just as fit as when Jon first saw him. He began a chant. Sir Thomas struck the first blow and actually it him solidly, causing a bit of damage, that Jon though would be enough to kill himself, but it had almost no effect on the chanting demon, who completely ignore it. Lonnie jockeyed for an opening to attack but failed to hit him. Jon tried to calm his mind, preparing to counter another batch of flames or such. He knew he would only have an instant in which to counter, but he got no clue as to the nature of the spell.

When the chant finished, the Marquis uttered some foul words that they did not understand, but its effect was felt by all three men. A great weakness came over them, as if they were somehow cursed. Jon found himself now standing on the green grass of his Urbana estate near Crystal Lake Park. "What the heck? How'd I get here? Ah, the spell!" Immediately, he stepped back into the tower. He had been gone perhaps only thirty seconds. He arrived in time to see Sir Thomas vainly try to attack him, but the weakness caused him to not even come close. Lonnie could not even seem to raise his weapon, either in attack or defense. Fortunately for the youth, the Marquis had no intention of wasting time on him. He went after Sir Thomas. Two mighty attacks found the paladin lying smashed up against the opposite wall, stunned from the violence of the collision and from so many wounds that Jon felt that if he had taken that many, he would be one dead musician.

Mandy, running far ahead of the others, reached the top of the step and ran into the still extant spell, recoiling and staggering from the sudden unexpected weakness. Jon sent to Alison and Darless, *We need some magic dispelled up here real fast. We are all recoiling from a fantastic weakness. I even ended up back home in Urbana. How's that possible?*

It was Glasya who answered him. *He cast a Dispell Good Creatures on you. Let me cast through your body, Jon.* He agreed. At once, he felt Glasya move just inside his head looking out through his eyes. Jon heard his voice chanting unfamiliar magical words and he watched as the counter-spell instantly removed the weakness that they all felt. She thanked him and left him standing with his mouth open. *What an experience!* he thought.

Meanwhile, the Marquis's next chant ended. The entire room filled with searing flames raining down from the ceiling upon one and all, including the Marquis, on which it had no effect. Jon tried to counter the heat by mocking up an intense cold, but the attack came so fast and in such a huge volume, Jon faltered. He realized that if he did not counter it, Lonnie and he would likely be roasted alive. Perhaps, Sir Thomas and Mandy may survive it; they seemed to be able to withstand a whole lot more than he could. But he knew he could not counter this one. Yet he had to do something. He did the only thing he could think of in that instant. He concentrated and stepped himself safely outside the tower, bringing the flames along with him. By the time he arrived outside, the tip of them had reached his head. He felt the intense heat melting, sizzling his hair and realized this was probably the end for him, a fiery death indeed.

As he was watching and sensing the flames hit his head, he saw the devil walking rapidly toward him. He tried to move to warn her away, but his arms did not seem to move. He tried to yell at her but his mouth did not respond. In fact, he found he could not even move his body. The flames did not seem to be falling down upon him anymore, though, and he found that a bit bewildering. The more he struggled, the more frustrated he became that his body would not work. Then, he wondered if perhaps his body was already dead. Glasya then reached him and put her arms around him and flapped her huge wings, lifting him into the air as if he was nothing but a stiff statue. *What's going on? Am I dead? I cannot move,* he thought to her.

No, you are in the middle of my spell, she answered in his mind. *I have stopped time. Strange how you are not effected at all and can still talk to me. That is not supposed to happen, though in truth, I have not actually attempted to communicate before now.* She sat him safely on the ground just outside the area of the flames and flew back inside the tower. *I've only got a bit of time left! Got to rush it.*

Now inside, just as the flame spell began, Mandy closed to battle him and managed to hit him twice, only this time, the damage she inflicted was much greater; she was still wearing the gauntlets of ogre strength. The Marquis stumbled and reeled backwards from her fierce onslaught, gravely wounded by the ranger. He back peddled toward Sir Thomas who was struggling to his feet.

Alison and Darless reached the edge of the room and cried out in dismay. The flames would fry everyone; they were too late. Then, Alison heard Glasya's brief chant behind her. She watched as Glasya brushed past her. She tried to move her body out of the way, but found that it was frozen to the spot. Darless, likewise; the alu-demon tried to move but could not; her limbs felt like lead; she was glued to the spot and nearly fell over when Glasya passed by. Both watched and Glasya rapidly ran out the door. Alison felt a wave of sickness surge; *the devil was abandoning them.* Darless thought only, *Hum.*

No, she's back, Alison though, as she watched the devil fly back inside in haste. She tried to turn her head to see, but could not, so she just turned herself and looked. Glasya went over to Sir Thomas, who still had not regained his footing and she lifted him up, stood him up straight. She placed his huge two-handed sword upwards at a particular angle. *What are you doing? Why cannot I move?* Alison placed into Glasya's mind. Darless echoed her. The devil glanced over at the two mages — a startled look appeared on her face. Neither mage's face was facing her. In fact, she could see neither of their eyes, yet both were talking to her!

Glasya knew she did not have much time left. *Spell,* she thought back to the two mages and she quickly reached the demon, which was frozen, mid-stagger. She moved his body closer to the Paladin and straightened it up. Then, she gave him a push backwards. At that instant, her spell ended. Alison and Darless felt their bodies continuing their previous rush into the room as if nothing had happened. All of the flames were suddenly not here. Glasya stood before the demon, which saw her as he fell backwards. Instant recognition flashed on his face, as his arms flailed wildly in a vain attempt to keep from falling over. As he fell backwards, there was Sir Thomas's Demon Slayer sword pointed straight at his back. No one was more surprised than the Paladin as the demon impaled himself for the second time this day on the huge sword. Only this time, the Demon Slayer itself chose activate its enchanted powers, to slay demons, of course.

Just as the Marquis suddenly realized he was falling onto a sword in his back, he felt a cold, devastating energy flooding from the blade. It started as a small area just at the puncture location. Rapidly, the piercing cold seeped ever outward. He tried to scream and managed to make a hideous sound before the cold completely encased his body. A flash of magic occurred and his body turned into dust flakes that floated downward, landing on the floor. Sir Thomas stood gaping as did all of the others. "Exit one vile demon," Glasya commented cheerily. Dull thuds and clanks sounded as the empty shell of his armor and rings and other possessions fell on the floor.

Jon appeared in the middle of the room, stepping here just as fast as he could, but he found the Marquis was gone. "What happened? Where's the Marquis? Gone again? How come I am not dead, fried utterly? Why are you all gaping?" Thea, disobeying her orders to stay put downstairs, poked her head into the room, her eyes trying to take in everything at once. To her, Jon's questions seemed to echo her own thoughts.

"Sir Thomas has just slain the demon Marquis de Gritz," Glasya announced, "with a little help from yours truly," she grinned. The paladin could not doubt her words; it was his sword in his hand that the Marquis had fallen upon.

"Teamwork," the smiling devil continued. "Okay, okay. I used my favorite spell, Time Stop. I had no choice. Somehow, don't ask me how, but Jon managed to take the entire flames outside, where they would do no damage to anyone, except kill himself, leaving you all unharmed in here. Jon, how on earth did you pull that one off? That was unbelievable! Anyway, the demon had already smashed Sir Thomas into the wall and was about to slam into Mandy. You all weren't here yet, so I acted. I stopped time, dashed outside, pulled Jon from the flames just as they singed his hair, flew back in here, helped Sir Thomas to his feet, got his sword up, and gave the Marquis a little helpful push so he would fall backwards. I didn't have time to do anything more. The Marquis and

Sir Thomas with his Demon Slayer sword did the rest. I assume that that is what we saw — the Demon Slayer doing its magic?" She looked to the paladin for confirmation, though there was hardly any other possible explanation for the demon being turned into dust.

Shock and stun; those were the operable words describing the look on everyone's faces as Glasya glanced at the others. Sir Thomas coughed to give himself a moment to grasp what had just happened, "Yes, Demon Slayer activated and disintegrated the Marquis."

Darless adjusted herself rapidly to the changes, "Yes, Number 1: the Marquis de Gritz is now actually quite dead. Number 2: he was not a Demon Lord so his death here was permanent, not like Lord Jarred, who was simply returned to the Abyss. Glasya, welcome to the team! I have never been so grateful to welcome anyone as I am now! Wow. I thought we were really doomed this time. He was one very powerful demon! Thank you!"

"That's an understatement!" added Mandy recovering from the sudden surprise. "The strength that man had was ungodly! Are you all right, Sir Thomas? You took a major bashing again I see."

"Verily, I did indeed! Never in my adult life have I been so thrown around like a sack of fodder. I guess I was fortunate that he only cast a Dispel Good on me this time. Last time it was an Unholy Word that did me in." He paused a moment, looking at the gorgeous devil and then at the dust on the floor, which was all that remained of the demon, "While I would have preferred to defeat the Marquis in combat, if I am to be perfectly honest about it, I do not think that Mandy or I working together could have taken him down alone. I am thankful for your intervention, your assistance. I never, ever, thought I would be saying that to a devil, mind you." Darless smiled, her paladin was growing.

"Well, I could not have done it without you, Sir Thomas. It was your strength to hold the sword and apply the force to thrust the blade into him. Without your inherent skill and strength, nothing much would have come of my intervention, save the saving of Jon," Glasya wisely complimented him. She knew she was on very delicate ground; she strove to make him a significant part of the outcome. The devil succeeded.

"Thanks, Glasya," Jon took this opportunity to add his thanks, "I'm sorry everyone, his fires this time were too strong, too sudden for me to counter. I did the only thing I could think of to get you all out of harm's way. I took the whole falling fires outside where they would damage nothing. I, er, just did not have enough time to get myself out of the way. Say, how's my head look? It got really singed."

Darless looked him over, "Smells like it, but no real damage. Be glad you have short hair!"

"I must say everyone," Glasya added sincerely, "I thought I knew all about teamwork, but today you all have shown me that I really only had the vaguest understanding of the word. Thanks to all of you; I really mean it. Before I go, I will make sure that your two mages learn how to use this Time Stop spell. As you can see, it can be very useful and I know you would never abuse this spell, unlike some other mages that I have known." Alison and Darless could not conceal their joy and excitement with her pledge; to know one of the most powerful spells in the universe was the ultimate!

"But I have a few questions," the devil tossed errant strands of her long hair out of her face. "First, Jon, how did you manage to teleport the flames from the spell outside? I cannot even imagine what you did. He cast some kind of flame strike, conjuring an intense set of heat and flames falling from above. Yet, you took it outside? How is that possible?"

"Yes, Jon, how *is* that possible?" Alison added just as baffled as Glasya. "Do you realize that you interfered with priestly magic, which is totally another thing from wizardly magic, totally."

"Er, sorry, I didn't know I wasn't supposed to do that," Jon mumbled a bit taken aback. "You are right; I just didn't sense what he caused until the flames actually began. This time they were way too intense for me to counter in so short a time. How did I do it? Well, flames are flames, I thought. Once they were real and present, I sort of figured that if I can step material things, like the sacks of your brother when he was moving to your village, why I ought to be able to bring the flames, they are objects too. So I did. It's just that there was not enough time. There was only a second or so between the first appearance of the flames and their falling on us all. I guess I need to learn how to react faster."

"React faster?" exclaimed Glasya in total disbelief. "My gods, Jon, you did what no one else I know of could have done. I doubt very much that Dispater himself could have pulled that one off. As you say, not enough time. You are just incredibly lucky that my spell went off when it did or I might not have been able to get to you. I only made it by a tiny fraction of a second anyway! You are amazing. But that brings up the second question."

She looked at Jon and then Alison and then Darless, "While I had time stopped and was frantically rushing about trying to set things right, did you three talk to me mentally? I swore you all three did."

Jon was the first to answer, "Yes, that was the weirdest thing I have experienced. My body felt like it was a statue, I was completely unable to move it, not even twitch! Yet, I was able to chat with you mentally."

"That's exactly what it felt like," chimed in Alison and Darless.

Darless added, "I could not move, like I was glued to the spot, but as I recall, I was not even facing you, yet I could see you and talk to you mentally. Conclusion: I believe that we were using spiritual powers, not physical ones. Would you agree, Jon?"

Jon nodded, but Alison interjected, "Some spiritual powers are so akin, so similar to magic effects, that the line blurs. Father Ukko has me exploring that aspect. I think that is what happened with Jon and the flames — the two blurred, became one and the same. At least that would explain it."

"That is most intriguing — most!" Glasya commented thoughtfully. "How does one go about increasing or even discovering one's spiritual powers?"

No one spoke, no one had an answer, At last, Darless broke the silence, "That is one thing I am going to research at my new college that is being built in Alison's new village. It is second only to spreading the word, teaching others how to do the mental assists we've been doing." That satisfied the devil for the moment, though she still intended to contemplate this further.

"Well, I guess we had better examine the things the Marquis had on him," Alison changed the subject, looking at the empty shell of armor on the floor, along with several rings and such. "Sir Thomas, will you do the honors of seeing if any of this stuff radiates evil? Anything inherently evil should probably be destroyed to prevent it from ever being used again."

"Gladly," he replied only too eager to do so. His consideration all along was that all of the Marquis personal possessions were likely highly evil in nature. Holding his holy symbol of Ukko, he said a brief prayer and his spell was granted. He surveyed each item very, very carefully. The three rings and a scarab were neither good nor evil; likewise to his surprise, neither were the broadsword nor the plate mail. Only one small talisman radiated an evil glow. "Okay, I was wrong. Only this demonic talisman is actually evil in nature. Permit me to destroy it." No one seriously objected, so he smashed it into fragments using the Marquis's own mace.

"Men!" Glasya commented. "Great, now you have hundreds of tiny bits that are evil. You really didn't get rid of it. Here, let me show you how it's done." She chanted briefly, pointed to the fragments. A flash of magic and all the tiny bits of the talisman vanished.

"Where it go?" he asked rather surprised.

"I let them go a few miles from the surface of the sun. That should completely annihilate them, don't you think?" He nodded his approval. He was beginning to like her style!

Next the mages worked on identifying the remaining articles. The plate mail, though indeed too large for normal men, had been highly enchanted, some four times and was excellently made. One ring granted invisibility, another, protection, but the third was unusual. Darless identified this one as a ring of regeneration, explaining that if one lost a hand to a blade, placing this ring on the other hand would energize its magic to regrow a new hand. This was a very powerful treasure indeed! "No wonder he has always been so hard to actually defeat!" exclaimed Sir Thomas as he realized that any wounds given to the Marquis would just be automatically healed in time via this ring. "That explains a lot to me." The others concurred.

"The scarab is like mine," Alison then said, "it offers protection, just as mine. It is very valuable too."

"Hadn't we ought to finish checking out the basement?" Darless remembered. "We had only reached a door down there, when all the commotion occurred up here. We were going slow looking for traps." Once more they set out for the basement. Only this time, everyone tramped down the long spiraling stairs to the basement. No one feared a return of the Marquis anymore.

The stairs led down about twenty feet ending at a locked door. "We had just discovered the door is booby trapped," Glasya explained. "I'll show you again." She chanted a short spell and a yellow band of shimmering energy appeared outlining the door frame.

"What would happen if we tried to enter?" asked Thea, a bit naively, though curious.

"Only a priest could say for sure," Alison answered her apprentice. "Probably the spell would inflict pain or actual wounds and probably quite a large amount, since the Marquis was the likely caster. Please, stand way back. I am going to try to disarm this guarding spell." They did and she chanted her counter-spell. Jon watched fascinated as the energy from her spell counteracted the power of the guarding spell. It vanished.

"Now is it safe?" asked Thea, after dutifully noting what Alison had done in her notebook.

"My rule of thumb is a bit pessimistic, Thea," she replied thinking this was as good a time for a lesson as any. "Where there is one trap, there are likely lots of traps. For good measure, I will check for traps once more. If I still feel uneasy about it, I'll have Darless try it too," she replied and cast her Detect Traps spell. "Ah ha. See, there is yet another one there." Everyone now saw that there was a small symbol glowing just above the door handle and lock mechanism.

Again, Alison chanted a counter-spell, unfortunately it failed to disarm the demon's symbol. Darless gave it a try and she too failed to counter it. Finally, Glasya, the most powerful of the wizards cast hers and at last the demon's spell vanished. This time, Darless checked for addition traps. "Well, look at this, there is also a mechanical trap by the lock," the alu-demon observed. "If we try to open it, I'll bet we get hit with poisoned needles or such."

"Ah ha," Thea duly noted in her book, "so now what do we do?"

"When up against mechanical traps," Alison instructed, "I have everyone stand way, way back so they have no chance of getting hurt. Then, I cast a Knock Open

Doors spell. It forces any locked door open, springing the trap harmlessly. Everyone get way back this time." All retreated back up the stairs a good distance, Alison did as well. From a distance of fifteen feet, she cast her spell and the door flew open with a noisy bang. When they approached it, Darless' suspicion proved correct. Three small needles with a black liquid dripping from them were clearly visible. She retrieved the decanter of water and let the gushing waters wash the poison off the door. Then, she broke the needles so that no one could accidentally get stuck. Thea dutifully documented all this in her notebook.

Only then did they enter this basement room. Both Alison and Darless provided the initial light from atop of their wizard staves. This room was obviously a workshop of some kind. All around the sides were various tables and even a tiny furnace with small metal crucibles on top, some filled with something golden. One cabinet held many drawers that were very small in height, reminding Alison of the map drawers she had seen some time ago when she went in search of maps. Another table had rows of tools, all relatively small in size. Another desk had a few drawings and papers on top of it. In the center of the room covered with a canvas tarp held up from a pulley from the ceiling stood something large and bulky on top of a table.

"Well, this is totally unexpected," commented Glasya. "What was he doing down here?"

"Is it safe to raise the canvas?" asked Thea, as she quickly sketched the room in her book.

"Better check for more traps," cautioned Alison. "I'm out of spells at the moment. How about you, Glasya?"

She had not yet exhausted her higher power spells, so she immediately cast yet another Detect Traps spell and moved about the room inspecting things. Finally, she said, "Well, the only one I see is the bottom desk drawer there with the papers on top of it. Everything else looks okay. So I guess we risk raising the canvas. Sir Thomas, would you do the honors?"

"Certainly, ma'am," he replied without hesitation, "I'm very curious about this. What was he doing down here?" He went to the side wall and undid the rope and pulled the canvass tarp up toward the ceiling and tied it securely.

No one was prepared for what they now saw. Sitting in the center of the table stood a four foot tall golden statue of a dragon with five heads. Great matching jewels were set for each head's eyes, some red, some green, some clear, some blue, and some brown. Other lesser gems dotted the body of the dragon, giving it a shimmering body. "It's a four foot statue representing Tiamat!" exclaimed Glasya. "Ignoring the fact that it is a nasty dragon, the statue is a wonderful work of art! The gems alone in it must be worth a fortune! I think we are seeing a side of the Marquis no one ever saw before. From the looks of it, it is probably finished, or nearly so. I don't see any flaws in it so far."

Everyone drew up close and examined it. Truly, it was a magnificent work of art, very impressive indeed. No one said anything; they just stared in disbelief at the dragon. Finally, Jon muttered, "Why would he be making such a fine work of art? Darless, are demons known for this kind of craftsmanship?"

"Some are; he was a Cambion, half-breed, and highly intelligent. I would say also he was a highly skilled craftsman. Look over the tools and see if they are appropriate for making this statue." They milled around the various tables and workbenches. Now the usage of the small tools became apparent. Some were for gem cutting, some for setting stones, some for working gold, and so on. "If any of you have a hankering for learning gem cutting or jewelry making, why here is a complete laboratory. I suspect that all of the tools are of the highest quality as well, though I am just guessing," Darless observed.

Meanwhile, Glasya explored the papers on the desk. They were detailed sketches of the statue during various stages of construction. All were drawn by the same hand, except for one. The sole exception was a beautifully done sketch of the final product with measurements and specifications neatly done in the legend at the bottom of the page. "Well, look here, this one is signed 'Threngold'," she noted. "A connection at last!"

Thea, of course, had to compare the writing of this one with the others. "Ah yes, I can see that the Marquis has an ornate style of writing. Threngold writes in more my style, practical and plain," she commented. Alison smiled.

"Okay everyone stand back," Glasya requested. "I'm going to try to open this trapped drawer. The others just have pens and ink and paper in them." Everyone retreated all the way back to the door, some forty feet from the desk on the opposite side of the round room. Glasya tried to disarm it. Unfortunately, her attempt failed and the trap sprung. Suddenly a grey gas gushed forth from the drawer engulfing the mage as she stood close to the drawer. She gasped and choked and fell back quite dizzy.

"What do we do?" cried out Jon alarmed.

"Okay," Mandy, ever practical said, "Jon, you step in there holding your breath, get her and step her outside the tower. I'll head there right now. Then, I can attempt to neutralize the poison, unless you want to try it with your new instruments. The rest of you, get out of the tower fast."

"Oh no, I need to practice first!" Jon protested. "I'll get her." He took a deep breath and stepped the short distance to her side, grabbed a hold of arm and stepped them both outside the door to the tower, out into the fresh air and sunshine. Momentarily, Mandy came running up to him. Glasya was now unconscious and Jon had her lying on the ground. Clutching her holy symbol of Reylona, Mandy began a lengthy prayer. When she was done, she touched Glasya on the forehead. Jon saw a bluish energy flow from down from the sky into Mandy's body, out from her finger and flow over the entire body of the devil. Glasya coughed and coughed and then stirred. She opened her eyes staring up at the smiling Mandy.

"That was a close call," Mandy said softly. "I think you will be fine. Rest a bit. You got a good whiff of those noxious fumes." The devil coughed for several minutes, though progressively less and less. Finally, she got her voice back and sat up.

"Thanks, Mandy. I really blew that one! I owe you," she said intensely.

"Nah, teamwork," Mandy replied. "But I wonder what is in that drawer that he would go to such extremes to protect?"

During this time, Darless created a strong gust of wind spell and methodically blew fresh air into the tower and the fumes out. She figured that, thus diluted, the fumes would be harmless. However, she took no chances and did not let anyone back in until she could not even sniff any of the foul odor any longer. At last everyone hurried back inside to see what was in that drawer!

Since Glasya was the one who triggered the trap, the others let her do the honors of opening it, though all crowed around to see too. Inside was a rolled up parchment tied with a brown ribbon. Otherwise the drawer was completely empty. "Strange," muttered Glasya as she untied the ribbon and unrolled the parchment. It was a letter or document of some kind. Two signatures were at the bottom, that of the Marquis de Gritz and Threngold. However, the writing was in a foreign language none understood. Glasya quickly remedied that with a simple spell.

She rapidly read aloud for everyone to hear, "We hereto enter into this bargain. . ." It was filled with many heretofore's and such, very legal, very proper, very hard to decipher. "In essence," Glasya summed it up when she finished reading it, "this is what I was after. Evidently, Threngold hired the Marquis to make this statue of Tiamat in exchange for the construction of this tower and aid in setting up the place for the Nabassu. There is no indication that the Nabassu were to be used to attack the Hells. Now that is indeed good news, just some kind of private deal."

"Well, why would Threngold want this statue made?" asked Thea, not quite grasping everything. "Why go to all this trouble?" No one answered her, though they thought about it.

Jon finally speculated, "Well, from what all you have told me about brown dragons and their mating cycles with Tiamat, I think it is to be a present to her to ensure Threngold is picked by her the next time she wants to mate, kind of romantic, in a way. After all, aren't you ladies impressed when we give you very expensive, artistic presents?" he teased. Now that he had said it, it did seem to fit logically.

Alison and Darless smiled at him. Alison said, "Yes, Jon, I think you have it. This statue has got to be worth a fortune, maybe even as high as a couple hundred thousand gold coins, maybe more."

"Well, what do we do with it?" asked Sir Thomas, wondering how heavy it was and how delicate. "How are we going to move it anyway?"

"Hum," Glasya thought, "there must be some way. With this much gold in it, it is likely to be very heavy. You cannot just go carrying something this valuable around outside. Look around; see if you can find any kind of carrying case or box or something." They all went scurrying about but found nothing.

Meanwhile, Glasya examined the table on which the statue was sitting. "Hey, look here." She pointed to a lever at the side of the table. She pulled it down and watched as the four sides suddenly flew upwards forming a box around the statue. The base of the table floated in midair, under some kind of permanent levitation spell. Jon found the lid lying in off to one side; he slid it over the top. The lever she pulled then snapped into a closed position firmly encasing the statue inside. Tentatively, she pushed the box. It floated gently away from her. "Impressive!" she commented. "We can put it into a very large sack or maybe it will just barely fit into a portable hole," she added. Jon fetched the one that they had found earlier and indeed it just barely slid into the opening. "That's that!" she clapped her hands in finality. "Now what?"

"Well, I guess we should pack up all these tools and stuff and all the rest of the things we want from here," Alison decided. "It is getting late. Should we spend the night in here or should we make another mansion?"

"I'd feel a whole lot safer in your mansion," Jon answered.

"I think that's wise," Sir Thomas added. "Lonnie and I found a pentagram, probably the gate that the Nabassu use to get from the Abyss to here. I have no idea how it's activated, but I can see no reason why more Nabassu demons might not try to arrive here at any time. I wish there was some way we could destroy it or disable it. It's built into the floor, actually. I guess there isn't any way."

Curious, they all headed up to the Nabassu roost to see the gate mechanism. Squarely in the middle of the room was the golden pentagram, rather similar to the terminal that Nain had created back at Castle d'Ambrose. The mages held a discussion on how best to destroy it. "Actually, I would rather like to totally undo this whole tower," Alison said. "Since it was created with a mud to stone spell, I had in mind to cast the reverse and stone to mud the tower. However, it is going to take a whole lot of those spells. I cannot do it in one day. With my staff, I can manage one such spell today, though. What do you think?" she glanced at Darless and Glasya. "If I take out the surrounding stone, the gate pentagram will crash down stairs. Will that be sufficient destruction to halt its gating properties?"

"Dunno," said Darless, "I've never had any experience with this spell, although I can cast it, I have not yet done so."

Glasya thought for a moment, "Yes, I think that would undo the magic properties to prevent its further use. Give it a try. Tomorrow, I will prepare some of those spells as well. Between us three, we ought to be able to undo this tower in a couple days. Besides, that will give us time to study that spell book and for me to teach you two some spells." That settled it. When everyone had gotten far back from the gate pentagram, using her staff for the power, she cast her spell that turned stone back into mud. A ten-foot section of the floor gave way and the entire pentagram stone portion crashed into the floor below them. Quickly everyone dashed downstairs. A pile of mud covered the central portion of the floor and the stone gate itself was smashed into six pieces. Smiles graced all faces; no more Nabassu would come here by this magic.

Once outside, Darless cast the mansion spell. It took a half hour to cart everything inside, along with the horses and their guide. As usual, he watched the setting sun by the open doorway. Thea rushed to fix some dinner, while the others cleaned up. Poor Sir Thomas, his armor was incredibly smashed up; it had sustained major damage in the fights with the Marquis. Furthermore, when Lonnie removed the armor, Sir Thomas noted many black and blue spots all over his body. He still hurt and assumed he would be rather stiff and sore the next day; he was. He and Lonnie had a lengthy discussion on how best to temporarily repair the armor until a proper armorer could be found. Alas, here in the field, there really was nothing significant that they could do to repair the damage to the magnificent armor of the Holy Paladin. Sir Thomas would have to resort to his leather armor for the duration of this trip.

Over dinner, Alison explained to He That Does Not Speak that the Marquis was finished, that no more Nabassu would come to attack them, and that tomorrow, the wizards would destroy the tower, melting it back into the original mud of the river bed from which it came. From his gestures, she thought that he was delighted to hear the news. His huge smile was contagious and he kept nodding his head in agreement.

After eating their fill, everyone was really quite exhausted. Fatigue and the aches from the day's combat took their toll. Everyone went to bed shortly after eating, except Jon, who still had to clean up the dishes. He was the last one to lie down. Just as soon as he did, he fell asleep as well. Once more, everyone heard a deep bass voice say, "Thank you," in their minds, though none paid it any heed.

The next morning, Mandy and Sir Thomas rose quite stiff and sore. They had taken a substantial pounding from the super strength of the Marquis. Today, they paid the price. "Man, I feel like I've been smashed into little bits and put back together upside down!" declared Mandy as she sat down very slowly to eat. The Holy Paladin was perhaps even stiffer, as he grunted a morning, and refused to sit to eat. "I hope your plans for today involve resting up," she added looking at Alison.

"Yes, we mages will research our spells this morning. I think around noon, we will take a crack at bringing or melting down the tower. The rest of you can relax and sharpen your swords and such. Take the day off, so to speak," she relied.

"Great! I can play with the new instruments," Jon interjected. He was really quite happy to have undivided time to experiment with them. Alison knew he would do just that.

They finished eating and Jon had barely begun washing up the dishes, when Sir Thomas let out a yell of surprise. Alarmed, everyone rushed over to the corner where he had left his equipment the night before. "Just look at this!" he exclaimed, holding up a breast plate. It looked like a breast plate as far as Jon could tell, wondering what all the commotion was about.

"We are, My Love," Darless said softly, "It looks fine to me. What's the matter?"

"That's just it! It is just fine!" he was exceedingly perturbed. Even Lonnie was beside himself, sorting through the other parts, holding up arm sections and leg portions, showing them to Sir Thomas as fast as he could.

"So?" Darless asked confused, the others were just as confused as well.

"Yesterday, my magically enchanted full plate armor took the worst beating in its history, saving me from many far greater wounds, perhaps even having my neck broken. When Lonnie and I put them down here last night, they were very beat up; some parts were almost locked into a fixed position! Now look at them. The whole suit is back in perfect shape as if some armorer has already done a superb job of repairing them!"

"Don't look at me," protested Glasya, "I swear I had nothing to do with it."

"None of us did, Sir Thomas," Alison said gravely. "Are you sure that the armor is not magically enchanted to repair itself?"

"No, I've never ever heard of such kind of magic," the paladin shook his head in dismay.

"It really takes the skill of a master armorer to repair very damaged magical armor," Lonnie put it, backing up his master. "We were discussing who we should entrust the repairs to last night. It is not a light matter, you see. And now, it is completely repaired. How?"

"Well," Darless said, "Number 1, none of us here could do it. Number 2, considering we know nothing about armor, it would take a wish spell on our part to get it done as well as you claim it has been done. Number 3, we can safely rule out all of us. Number 4, we are inside an extra dimensional mansion. Number 5, only Gods can easily get in here. Therefore, my conclusion is you have had some outside godly intervention." Jon looked at Glasya, who was grinning at Darless and her enumeration. Darless spied their playful grins, and quickly added, "Be thankful it was countable on one hand!" She chuckled along with them.

Her voice full of concern, Alison asked, "Perhaps it was Father Ukko. Has he ever done this for you before? Are you sure you didn't pray for it to be repaired?"

"No and no," he said sternly. "I would never ask such a mundane thing from Father Ukko!" That satisfied her curiosity. She had no other explanation either.

"Lonnie, help me put all this on and we'll see if it all fits correctly, that nothing has been fouled up in the repairs." The two set to work while the others returned to their tasks. In about twenty minutes, Sir Thomas, dressed in his shiny armor, strutted around the mansion testing his movement. He could tell no difference whatsoever; a perfect repair job. Not even the slightest dent remained.

The men and Mandy next led the horses outside of the mansion. Jon brought both of his instruments with him, leaving the four mages by themselves inside, studying diligently. They exercised the horses, fed them, and established a picket line for them to move around a bit so that they did not spend the whole day confined. Then, while Jon sat leaning against the shady side of the tower playing on his new recorder, the other four took a leisurely stroll around the area, noticing the damage to the environment that the demon had done. Fortunately, it was not much, since the Nabassu had kept pretty much within the tower as had the Marquis, who obviously now had spent a great deal of time fabricating the dragon statue. When they returned from the walk a couple hours later, both Mandy and Sir Thomas felt much better physically, having worn off some of the stiffness. Much of their soreness had also ebbed away.

Mandy felt slightly bored and contented herself with sharpening up Zond and her other weapons. The paladins did likewise and Lonnie also took care of Thea's short sword. Mandy did admit that Jon's soft background music was really quite good and very enjoyable. She resolved to make sure that she acquired some musicians for her castle, a royal wind band.

While they were all thus engaged, the four mages walked out ceremoniously from the mansion. "I have a formal announcement to make," Darless said formally. It got the other's attention, for none could recall Darless being so serious. When she was sure that she had their undivided attention — Jon even stopped playing — she said, "I would like to announce that Alison d'Ambrose has finally risen to the rank of Archmage; she has mastered one of the highest power spells known. I present to you Archmage d'Ambrose." Alison, blushing slightly, and wearing her magical mage's robe, stepped forward and bowed ceremoniously. Darless started clapping and the others joined in; Alison blushed even more. Then came a round of hand shaking and congratulations from everyone.

"I always said you would do it, remember?" Sir Thomas patted her on her back. She did, he had many times told her that she would succeed. There were times in her early career when she was down in the dumps and really needed the encouragement. She smiled at him and nodded.

"I hate to be so ignorant," Jon said, "but what does this mean exactly? I really don't know quite what to make of this. I assume it means you are a very powerful wizard. Is Darless also now an archmage?"

Alison fielded this question. "Let's say for example that magical spells can be rated in terms of the amount of magical energies needed to be controlled for their successful execution. If we look at them that way, then all known spells can be classified into power ranges from one to nine, with one being the smallest. A beginning wizard can manage one of these lowest ones per day. It takes a lot of training to rise to the level where one can command the necessary magical energies to cast a level nine spell. When a wizard can finally do so, they are accorded the status of Archmage. That's why there are so few of us around."

"Thea has just now mastered her first fourth level spell. She now too can make skin hard as stone, warding off all attacks for a time. It's the spell I keep forgetting to cast on you fighters," Alison announced. "So now, my apprentice can do it too, when I forget." Thea beamed with pride at Lonnie; and he, her.

Darless answered Jon's other question, "I'm afraid that Alison has always been a couple steps ahead of me in magical effects. Yes, I am still behind her. I still do not quite grasp the highest level spells, but I am getting very close. I'll keep studying and it should not be too much longer before I too reach the stage of Archmage."

"Verily, having two, no, make that three archmages in the same party," Sir Thomas corrected himself as he remembered Glasya, "is nearly unheard of! Having one of such power is phenomenal enough! But three, it boggles the mind!"

"My mind is easily boggled!" declared Mandy. "Look over there and there and there!" she pointed in all directions that they could see. The inhabitants, the various tribes of Wavapata, were in the process of assembling all around the tower, maintaining a mile's distance from them. He That Does Not Speak signed to Mandy. She relayed to the others, "Ah, he says that the Great Spirit has called all his people here to witness the destruction of the tower."

"But how could all of them have known about it?" declared Alison, most confused. The final destruction of the Marquis was less than a day old. Yet, some of these folks would have had to had traveled all night and then some to have gotten here.

"Oh yes, he says not to fell the tower until after lunch. Not everyone is here yet. I think Running Bear and his tribe are not here yet," Mandy added. He That Does Not Speak nodded that she got it correct.

"Okay, we had better go get our spells prepared," exclaimed Alison. She rarely liked an audience of watchers watching her perform, she was not a performer, and she hated to be the center of attention. Quickly the four mages went back inside to prepare.

Jon resumed his recorder practice. Mandy got out her "Eyes of the Eagles" and watched the gathering of the people of Canyon Lands. Sir Thomas and Lonnie stood on guard in a formal manner befitting their paladinhood ideals, for they believed that they were being watched and judged. In a little while, Thea brought out a light lunch for them. She said excitedly, "I think that they are about ready, though Alison said that it might take several days of casting to totally transform this tower back into its original mud. I do hope that they are not too disappointed if it doesn't all go down at once!"

"I think they understand patience, Thea," Mandy suggested wisely. "I think that it will be great therapy for them to see the tower's demise. After all, they have suffered enormously from the evils of the demons." Now the beating of drums floated across the space between them and the tower. All around, each tribe added to the rhythmic sound. Jon stopped playing and began listening. This was fantastic as far as he was concerned. They all stayed together across the vast space. Sounds echoed off the tall cliff sides, reinforcing the patterns.

Jon noticed that He That Does Not Speak began dancing, pounding steps into the ground. Mandy reported that others in the gathered tribes were also dancing in a similar manner. "I guess they think it is time or else they are just celebrating," she suggested. The three mages also heard the drums and came out to see what was happening.

"Well, I guess it is show time," said Alison. "I want you all to know that I really hate this, you know, being on display so to speak, with everyone in the world watching me. I hope I don't screw up!"

"You won't, love," Jon encouraged her. "Try not to think about them. Concentrate on your spells. You can do it." She smiled at him. According to their plans, the three mages walked to three equidistant points surrounding the tower, standing perhaps a hundred feet from it. Darless called out "One, two, three." Jon just barely heard their soft chants above the music of the drumming. The spells went off at the same time. All three had positioned the detonation point of their spell near the top of the tower. Their calculations suggested that twenty-five of their transformation of stone to mud spells would be needed to reduce the entire tower. Each was prepared to cast five such spells today. They figured they would need two days to do it fully.

The spells culminated nearly simultaneously. Jon watched in fascination as the top portion of the tower's stone turned into mud and slowly melted and began flowing downwards, much like a melting ice cream cone. Their first volley lowered the tower from about fifty feet tall down to forty. However, just as they were about to begin their second volley's chant, the next section of about ten feet in height melted and slowly slid downwards, gathering speed as it fell. And then the next ten feet of tower followed suit. "This is not supposed to be happening this way," Alison exclaimed. Then the next ten feet gave way. Finally, the entire central portion of the tower collapsed in on itself, clear down to the basement. A great inflow of river water gushed into the vacuum and then splashed outward nearly drenching the three wizards.

The drumming took on a fevered pitch and the pattern was now exceedingly fast, as if echoing the rapid demise of the tower. A great clap of thunder suddenly echoed overhead. As all eyes turned upwards, Jon noticed something was falling ever so slowly downward toward them. The others noticed it too. "What is it?" Jon yelled above the commotion, for the drumming and chanting of the natives, though still a mile distant, was very loud nevertheless.

"Looks like falling feathers?" cried Mandy. They were; eight feathers were falling, one above each party member, including Glasya. Mandy and Thea tried to catch theirs; Sir Thomas and Lonnie tried to get out of the way of theirs. It did not matter what each did, for the feathers had a mind of their own, or were being controlled by another. Each feather landed and stuck itself into the hair of its new owner. At that instant, a deep bass voice echoed across the canyon lands, audible even to the tribesmen, "Thank you." In their minds they also heard, "I grant you each one wish. Use the feather's wish when you need it."

"Oh my!" exclaimed Alison totally surprised at such an incredible gift and at a total loss of words.

"There really *is* a Great Spirit!" yelled Mandy. "Sir, you have a *great* land here. Glad we could help!"

"Wow! Wow! Wow! A *real* wish! Wow! Thank you!" declared Thea, truly at a loss of words for once.

"Well, I'll be. . ." Glasya commented and then added, "Thank you, Great Spirit."

In unison, everyone gave a chorus of thanks up towards the sky, presuming that was the right direction of the Great Spirit. All except Jon, that is. He looked outward across the vast spaces of the Canyon Lands and saw him. He thought to him, *You really are huge. Thank you.*

Later when they were discussing this event, Jon described what he saw. "It was like that time with Fruella. I could see him, or better perceive him. He seemed to be occupying a sphere at least a mile in diameter, totally encompassing this whole area. Maybe that is why the natives stayed a mile distant, do you suppose?"

Jon also sensed the Great Spirit rising up into the sky, signaling that the event was complete. The waters had calmed down now and Mandy saw some of the folks slowly making their way toward them. Using her binoculars, she announced, "Here come Running Bear, Morning Breeze and Many Braids."

In a half hour, they all were chatting gaily, expressing their thanks for saving the all the Children of Wavapata. Sir Thomas had to relate their many battles in detail at least ten times as different tribal representatives arrived at different times. Every one of them wanted to know what had happened to the demons and all about the Marquis's downfall. That afternoon flew by. Alison was only too glad that Sir Thomas did the telling, because she hated relating her adventures to strangers. On the other hand, the Holy Paladin felt that this was part of his duty to humanity and took it very seriously, much to her relief. Quickly, the native women, bored with the tales of combat, gathered about the five women staring wide-eyed at the gift feathers and at Glasya. None of them had ever seen a devil. Her wings were a big hit among these women, because with them one could fly out over all of Wavapata.

Jon and He That Does Not Speak both quietly moved out of the crowd and sat down near the tethered horses. Jon took up his new lute and began picking out a soft tune. Of course, soon they also had an audience, children. Many gathered around him just to listen to the pretty music. So the afternoon passed as freedom returned to Wavapata.

Chapter 10 Crossing the Canyon Lands

By suppertime, most of the folks had departed for their homes. Although Alison had suggested that Running Bear and his family spend the night with them, they refused saying that they now had a lot to do; they all would be moving back into the central areas where they used to dwell. Many plans had to be made quickly. They departed as well in the late afternoon. After Alison cast a new mansion spell and Thea had supper ready, they were back down to just the nine of them, including He That Does Not Speak, who still had to guide them to the far western rim of the Wavapata.

While they were eating, Thea, still excited, said, "How about that. We met a real god today! I'll bet he made your spells extra strong and powerful so that the tower went down really fast. Don't you think so?"

"Yes, that is the only explanation," Alison concurred, adding, "I'll bet anything that he was the one who repaired your suit of armor as well, Sir Thomas."

"Verily, I do believe so," he replied and paused reflecting on just how to say what he was thinking. "Strange as this may seem to all of you, but I swear that I've heard that voice these past several nights just as I drifted off to sleep."

"Say, you are right! I did too," said Jon, realizing the connection once it had been pointed out to him, and so did all the others, who were annoyed with themselves for not having spotted it when it occurred. Jon chuckled, "A god was talking to us and all we did was ignore him. Doesn't that take the cake?" Everyone laughed. They felt rather sheepish; laughter vented their feelings of foolishness.

"Well, I still can't get over it; he gave *me* the gift of a wish! Say, I'll bet you, Alison can now cast a wish spell, can't you?" Thea continued with her rush of thoughts.

"Well, I have that spell in my book, Thea, but I do not intend to actually cast it. There are side effects, major and bad ones." She looked sternly at her apprentice, "Each casting prematurely ages the caster about a year. I for one do not want to grow old and feeble before my time!"

"Amen to that," Darless could not help interjecting. She'd had all of that magical aging that she cared to when she was a pawn of Morrigan and been forced to use a wish spell.

"Oh," Thea replied somewhat downcast. She brightened right up, "Ah so that makes the Great Spirit's gift even more valuable then. I bet gods cannot age like we do, so it is safe for him to dole them out to the worthy. Do you suppose?"

"Never try to predict the gods, Thea," cautioned Glasya. "I know, been there, done that. Your conclusions would always be based upon how you look at things, not how they do. It is the same kind of thing between good and evil with the gods. What you perceive as evil may in fact be good from a totally different point of view." Thea frowned slightly; she did not really understand her, but did fully respect her message. She filed it away for later thought.

"Actually, what I want to know, Alison," Mandy chose this time to change the topic, "is what are our immediate plans? Do we travel once more tomorrow or what?"

Alison looked at Darless and Glasya and then Thea before she met Mandy's gaze. "I'm torn. Yes, I really want to get on with attempting to locate the dragon. However, we have this incredible spell book with us. It contains many very powerful spells that I believe may be of assistance at some point to us. Glasya has taught me that the Time Stop spell can be a life saver. I really ought to practice that one a bit more to have it down pat. The longer we stay put and we mages study, the better prepared we may become. On the other hand, I do feel some urgency to get on with it. I know you and Sir Thomas and Lonnie are itching to hit the saddle once more."

"Glad I am not the leader," joked Mandy. "Look at the tough decisions! True, my swords cannot get any sharper. After that last combat, I think I could teach Sir Thomas a few finer points that may help him — Lonnie too. If the men are willing to learn from a woman, then we could spend a day or two at it. What say you men?" she teased and smiled playfully.

Lonnie nodded eagerly; he saw what a sword master she really was and knew she could teach him much. However, the Holy Paladin was slower to answer. "A year ago, even after the events of the Marquis, I would have insisted that there was nothing a 'woman' could teach me. At this moment, I know that to be the height of conceit. Sometimes I saw her get in three attacks, where the very best I can do is two. That is saying nothing of actually striking and causing any damage. Damage-wise, we are nearly equivalent, taking the weapons into consideration. Yet where I consistently missed him, this Great Ranger hit. I am truly humbled by the experience." He bowed his head.

Oh no, I've done it again! Mandy thought to herself. *I teased him too far.* "Don't berate yourself, Sir Thomas. You are neglecting one major, major factor: I have had far more training and adventure experience than you have. I know not how you rate rank or skill levels in the paladinhood. If you were a ranger like me, there would be a substantial gap between our skill levels. It is much like the difference between Darless and Thea, though not quite that big a difference, if you follow me."

"What you are saying," Lonnie tried to summarize for his own understanding, "is that it is more the lack of skill and training that accounts for the rather extreme difference in impact with the fight with the Marquis?"

"Yes, Lonnie," she was thankful he saw the point she was trying to communicate to Sir Thomas. "If Sir Thomas and I were fighting hobgoblins, and ignoring that fact that I tend to go rather ballistic when fighting them, you would see very little difference between us. Remember the bandit surprise attack? We were both about equally devastating on them. It is only when the person we are attacking has a terrifically high defensive capability, whether magically enhanced or not, there is where the skill level difference becomes most apparent. Not so much in damage inflicted, but in the ability to actually hit the opponent in the first place. This is what I will try to show you both when we practice — how to hit more accurately; the resultant damage will take care of itself." Lonnie beamed; this was just the thing he most desired, for if he could actually strike and hit better, he would be far more effective in combat, which was his goal.

"Wisdom from a ranger!" Sir Thomas finally smiled. "You speak honestly and truthfully. If you will teach, I will endeavor to learn. Never let it be said that Sir Thomas is unwilling to learn." Moving close to Darless, he whispered, "How could you have ever fallen in love with me before now? I was so arrogant, so haughty."

She smiled lovingly at him and whispered back, "I saw the real you beneath that veneer and I liked what I saw there."

He smiled back at her, "I think that meeting you was the catalyst for all these changes in me. You are the best thing in my life!" She kissed him gently. Oh if only they could go for a walk, she thought to herself.

Glasya had been watching them from the corner of her eyes. For a moment, the devil felt rather envious of

Darless; it only strengthened her resolve to follow through with her plans.

Alison decided that they would stay here another day or so. Hence, everyone went to bed early, ready to begin at the crack of dawn — learning spells and fighting techniques.

In actual fact, they spent two more days here doing just that. The four mages learned many spells, sharing some with each other. Glasya became quite animated and flushed when she finally mastered the one spell for which she had been looking these last many years. Alison asked her about it, a Clone spell, one that made a replica of your own body. She had visions of numerous more powerful devils running around and was just a bit concerned that maybe she was now responsible for multiplication of devil adversaries. Glasya, sensing her deep concern, put her mind at easy, "I solemnly swear to you that I have no intention of cloning more devils! That is the last thing I want to do. What it is that I really want to do, I am not at liberty to say at this moment, for it may not work at all. I promise you, if it does work, I will let you know; you may even approve of the spell's use at that time." That was enough for Alison, but she spent half a day wondering what Glasya was really up to.

Outside, Mandy, Sir Thomas, and Lonnie spent the day practicing their fighting skills until the sweat poured down their faces. They, then, took a brief cooling off respite before jumping back into the strenuous regimen Mandy set for them. After two days of this heavy training, Mandy noted a significant increase in both men's skill levels; she knew she had been successful. Both men also knew it as well. In fact, Lonnie was now nearly as good as Mandy had been when she first met Jon. She smiled to herself as she watched him carry himself taller and straighter. He had more respect for himself now. That was very good indeed.

On the third day after the fall of the tower, the party set out once more on horseback, making for the eastern rim of the Canyon Lands. Of course, due to the numerous twists, turns, and switchbacks, the overland distance traveled was double that as the crow flies. It felt good to have the smooth feel of leather beneath her as Mandy and He That Does Not Speak broke trail. Darless and Sir Thomas followed immediately behind them; Jon and Alison, next; Lonnie and Thea brought up the rear, still leading two spare medium warhorses.

Glasya had departed this morning before they set out. Actually, her departure bought sadness to everyone. Each one had not only grown accustomed to the beautiful devil's presence, but had grown to like her as a person, if a devil can be so considered. She did promise to come visit them later on, so it was not like they would never see her again. For that, everyone, including Glasya was grateful. As Glasya chanted, opening a gate back into Hell, no one saw the two tiny tears form slowly in her eyes and trickle down her cheeks. However, she had to report back to Dispater and she now had to work on her new spell. Perhaps her dreams were not in vain.

It was a lovely, warm spring day. Now that the evil had been removed from the Canyon Lands, they rode in a very relaxed manner. Still Mandy kept a wary eye out for the giant wasps. In the past, they had ignored them, leaving them for the natives to handle. They did encounter on swarm of about a dozen giant wasps. However, they followed Jon's advice and simply halted and froze. The wasps quickly flew away. Perhaps the Children of the Wavapata and these wasps might get along. Mandy decided to leave that up to them.

Now the only other thing worthy of mention on this day's travel occurred around two in the afternoon. When they rounded a bend, they saw what appeared to be a very old man, bend over carrying a heavy sack over his shoulder. From a distance of five hundred feet, he looked like just another older native of these lands. However, the hairs on Mandy's neck twitched and she felt uncomfortable approaching him.

Slowly, he walked up to the party, which halted, more or less waiting for him. Mandy did not like their location. Tall canyon walls rose on either side. Here the river valley was only about fifty feet wide, a great place for an ambush. "I don't like this. Darless, Alison stay alert; could be an ambush. The two mages kept a sharp eye on the canyon rim far above them.

When the man drew close, he spoke in what sounded like a raspy, old man's voice, "Hail mighty warriors, pity on an old man in need of survival funds. I must sell my treasures. I even have some magical weapons to sell. Here, have a look. I am sure you will find them quite to your liking. They are yours for a small sum, just enough to help out an old man." Without waiting for any reply, he opened the sack and arrayed its contents carefully on top of the sack.

Sir Thomas and Lonnie saw two beautiful broadswords, a gem encrusted dagger, a well-made knife, a good looking long sword, an ornate two-handed sword, and many pieces of armor. Both men stared at this unlikely find. "Yes, all of these are magical or so I am told, but I am no expert. Perhaps you can tell better than I what exactly these all are. Perhaps some of these are finer weapons than those you bear. Please help an old man pay his expenses and not starve to death out here in these desolate lands."

"Yes, they do look beautiful. I am Sir Thomas, Holy Paladin of Father Ukko. This is Lonnie, also a holy paladin. And you are?"

"I am Rad Brown," he answered. "Indeed, then I am in very safe company. Out here, you never can tell. Pray, help yourselves, examine them," he motioned them. The two men definitely were keenly interested in the magnificent weapons. Mandy stayed mounted as did the other women. Her eyes darted about looking for any wayward sign, but saw none. Evidently, he was what he appeared to be; still, she did not let her guard down.

"Mind if I ask you where you got these fine blades?" Sir Thomas asked, concerned about an old man having such valuable weapons. Had he stolen them? Robbed some graves?

"My son had them, but he died many years ago from a black scorpion bite," he replied rather dejectedly. "Kept them all these years, but now I have no use for them."

"Oh, can I see too?" inquired Thea, dismounting and drawing close to Lonnie. "I'm Thea, a fighting mage. Do you have any short swords perchance? No, I don't see any my size," she sighed, answering for him. But undaunted, she continued, "Where around here do you live? Can't you sell them in your town? Well, maybe there are not too many towns out here," she added remembering the distinct lack of such. She continued chatting, never really letting the old man answer.

When she finally took hold of one of the daggers to inspect it, Rad smiled and replied, "You are mighty young to be a mage and fighter, Thea. I live far to the west of here. No, there are few towns. That's why I am on this journey. I've just got to get some money to pay my rent. I am too old to do much work. I am not asking for a handout, no ma'am." This seemed totally plausible, especially to the paladins. He then changed the subject, "Say, I'm heading the way that you have apparently come. Is the way safe for me?"

"Oh yes," exclaimed Thea. She was just about to blurt out all that they had done, when something inside her resisted. Something was not quite right, she felt. "Yes, quite safe. How far are you going?" This she thought was a good counter question.

Had Thea said one more word about what they had done, Mandy, growing edgier by the minute, was prepared to telepathically order her to keep quiet; Alison, likewise. She did not know what was wrong; the old man seemed harmless and good natured. No bandits attacked. Still, she refused to let her guard down; she did not examine the weapons.

Now the old man, scratching his chin asked, "I've heard that there is a gentleman in some tower not too far from here who might be interested in buying some weapons. Perhaps it is only a rumor. I've seen no towers in these canyon lands as yet. But who can say, I've only see a small portion. Perhaps you have seen such a tower?"

Thea's eyes darted to the old man; she forced them back to look at the dagger in her hands. She knew Alison would not approve of an outright lie, but she thought that this question was just a bit unusual. Did others know of the tower — others beyond the Canyon Lands? She answered, "No there is no tower any longer. I believe the Great Spirit had a hand in melting it. Anyhow, it isn't there anymore."

If Rad was genuinely surprised, he did not show any outward sign. "I had such high hopes of selling my wares; but then you know how rumors are. You never can be sure of them. Are you interested in any of these?" he shifted focus to the paladins.

"Well, while these are very nice blades, we really don't need any more," Sir Thomas admitted. He watched disappointment fill the old man's eyes and added quickly, "but I will give you a hundred gold coins for this fancy dagger here."

Rad's eyes gleamed with happiness, "Oh thank you sir paladin. Thank you." Sir Thomas retrieved a pouch from his saddle bag and counted out the coins. So few coins remained that he put those into the saddle bag and put the hundred back into the pouch and handed it to the shaking outstretched hand. "Thank you. Thank you." Quickly, he put the remaining items back into his sack and threw it over his shoulder. "I bid you all good day, then. I must continue my journey. Thank you for helping me pay my rent for a month." He walked past Mandy and the other women. He nodded as he passed Jon in the rear holding onto the spare horses for Lonnie. Still no attack came.

Mandy twisted around and watched him slowly walk around the bend and out of sight. "That man gave me the creeps," she exclaimed.

"Yes that is what I think too," Thea added, "creepy. Something is not quite right with him, but I don't know what it is. I almost felt like he wanted me to tell him all about our adventures, but I resisted it. Creepy, that's a good way to put it, Mandy."

"Look what I bought, Darless," Sir Thomas smiled as he walked back to where she was still standing guard. "This is a fine looking dagger indeed. I gave him a fair price though."

She looked down at the dagger and frowned, "What on earth are you doing with that filthy, rusted dagger?"

He grimaced, "What do you mean? It is a gem encrusted dagger."

"No it isn't! Look at it Alison," she asked, seeking another opinion.

She too took a look and said, "Why it looks like a gem — hey, wait a minute!" She rubbed her eyes and took another look. "You've been bewitched! It is a rusted piece of junk!"

"Ah, one second," and Darless proceeded to chant a spell. A small flash of yellow energy burst over Sir Thomas and the outstretched hand with the dagger. Now he could see clearly that it was a rusted piece of worthless junk. "It was under some kind of illusion spell. You've been had, Sir Thomas!"

Anger flashed in his red face. Veins grew large. He mounted his horse and galloped back the way they had come, obviously to confront the old man, Rad. Quickly, the others mounted up and rode after him. They rounded the bend and rode hard for ten minutes before Sir Thomas halted, letting the others catch up to him. He was fuming still. "He's disappeared!" he called out as soon as Mandy got in range.

"How could he just disappear?" asked Thea as she reined in by Sir Thomas. "Shouldn't we have caught up with him long before now?"

"Right, Thea, long before now," Mandy answered. "Come on, let's backtrack. Our galloping has probably erased all signs of him, but let me go first, just in case." Slowly they rode back to where they had first met the old man. Unfortunately, their hasty ride had wiped out all traces of the man on foot.

"Well, now what?" asked Jon. "That was one strange man!" They discussed it but no one had any more of an idea than when they first met him. Finally, Mandy ordered them to resume their original course once more. In the rear, Jon and Thea continued to talk about Rad, for some reason, Thea just could not put him out of her mind. She talked on and on to Jon. Finally, she said, "That's it, Jon! Now I know what bothered me from the start. Remember he called these lands 'desolate!' But they are anything but desolate. He That Does Not Speak's people are all over and are very friendly! It's not desolate!" Now that she had spotted it, she was content.

Mandy, who could not help but overhear her, yelled back, "Well done Thea. That is exactly it. Something was bothering me from the first, and you just pointed it out. Very well done!" The ranger, too, was greatly relieved, her certainty in her observations restored. "At least it was not a trap. I thought for sure we were going to be ambushed back there — that Rad was just a decoy. Guess not, though."

"But I feel like such an idiot," Sir Thomas said meekly. "I felt sorry for him; I thought I was being kind and doing him a favor."

"Pay it no heed, My Love," Darless replied. "If he did not know that they were junk, he was taken too. If we confronted him with it, he'd probably just deny all knowledge of it. He might be on the level. Yet, somehow, I doubt it. How did he just disappear like that? If he was a wizard, he could have teleported away. Or maybe he used some priestly or druidical spell to transport himself. Guess we'll never know that one." The paladin relaxed and seemed satisfied now. They rode onward with no further surprises.

For five more days, the party rode through the canyons, twisting and turning, but always making progress westward. They met a dozen more tribal groups, many of whom were moving back to their original dwellings now that the demons were gone. Other than an occasional group of the giant wasps, they encountered nothing of any great interest. In fact, after nearly a week most had become bored and contented themselves with viewing the magnificent scenery. Mandy, however, did not once let her guard down, nor did Sir Thomas.

Finally, late that afternoon, He That Does Not Speak halted the party and signed that the journey was done. He pointed to the dim trail that now climbed steadily upwards just in front of them. The canyon rim lay in that direction. He bid them farewell and everyone thanked him, shook his hand or hugged him. He left knowing that his guidance had been well appreciated. Solemnly the party rode up the rising trail out of the Canyon Lands, making the rim top at sunset. Once again, the reddened view was spectacular and all watched the sun set in silence and deep appreciation for this land.

After dinner, everyone gathered around Alison and the maps. Mandy attempted to make her best guess as to their location on the western side, but it was only an estimate; the rudimentary map was of little help for that matter. Their guess put the southern portion of the Desolation Range some fifty miles further westward. Whether South Wash, the stone giant community, lay north or south of their current east-west position remained mere speculation.

Eventually, the burning question was raised. Thea asked inquisitively, "Alison, how do we now find the lair of the brown dragon?"

Jon replied a bit sarcastically, "I think we are now embarking on a looking for a needle in a hay stack operation — especially, if the dragon doesn't want to be found. He's probably got his lair concealed and we may walk right by it without noticing." Then, he noticed Alison's dower face; he'd never seen her look so dejected and wished he had not opened his mouth.

She sighed, "Okay, I'll admit it. I am just as stumped by this as you all are. Secretly, I had hoped that somehow by this point in the trip we would have some solid clues which we could follow. But we got zip, zero, none. Worst, I just don't see how we are going to get any either. Suggestions?" she asked very near tears. She had gotten this close to finding the dragon that had stolen away her parents, but could get no closer. She was dejected, to say the very least. Everyone else shared her keen disappointment. Silence answered her back.

At long last, Mandy tried to sound encouraging, "Well, maybe tomorrow, as we close to the Desolation Range, something will turn up, a town perhaps or some traveler who has seen the dragon in flight." She really did not expect to find any towns out here, nor travelers, but it could happen, she thought to herself. With that tiny prospect of hope, they all somberly went to bed early that night. Alison did not sleep well, fidgeting all night long.

By eight the next morning, the party was on the move once more, heading due west. The rim terrain quickly gave way to a series of gently rolling hills. The land was still semi-arid, tufts of hardy grasses grew in scattered patches; the ground was rocky and dry; a few gnarled oak trees grew in patches, rising only to perhaps a dozen feet in height. Little rain fell on these lands. The water laden clouds dropped all their moisture on the far side of Desolation, leaving little for this no-man's land. From hill tops, no signs of any towns could be discerned, even using Mandy's Eyes of the Eagle. When they stopped for a lunch break, Mandy shape changed into an eagle and flew high in the sky looking for signs of a village or other habitations. Her great plan fizzled; she only spied the Desolation Range looming before them, like a black monster with jagged teeth.

"Boy this is the biggest wasteland I have yet seen," commented Jon, sipping his after lunch tea. "Nothing around for miles and miles. Jeesch." The others dejectedly echoed his sentiments. Sitting and moping, Jon felt something brushing his mind. He instantly recognized that someone was trying to spy on his memories. Interestingly, he also sensed his magical amulet repel that intruder. He mused upon who might be trying to spy on him. He was startled from his thoughts by the cries of Thea.

"Iee," she jumped up, holding her head in both hands, screaming, "Get out! Get out!" Her face, terror stricken. Everyone jumped to their feet looking for an ambush that did not come. Alison, Darless and Jon went to her side at once, Alison hugging her, providing support. The young girl took some comfort in the gesture, but terror still radiated from her shaking body. She was quite terrified.

Curiosity rose within Jon; quickly, he concentrated and moved into Thea's space and beingness, planting the thought in her mind, *It's Jon. I'm here. I'll get him out of your mind.* Actually, he had no idea how that might be accomplished. He sensed Thea grasping his thought and felt her fear subside slightly. Now he could sense that other probing mind; he saw the pictures in Thea's mind that it had forced into view — images of the golden statue of Tiamat. He sent toward that other mind, *Get out of here now!* Vaguely, he heard the distant chanting of Darless. Then, as suddenly as Thea had been stricken, Jon felt the other mind's contact with her evaporate. It was instantly gone.

"There, it was a spell. I have dispelled it," the mage commented. "Thea, are you okay? Did he do any damage to you?"

Tears rolled down the still scared face of the young mage. She could not speak yet, only nodding she was alive. "Here, put this around your neck," Jon said sternly, unfastening his magical amulet. "This will keep him out of your mind, guaranteed. He tried to get into my mind just before he invaded yours, Thea." She brightened up considerably and finally got her voice working.

"Thanks. It — it — it was horrible! He just forced his way into my mind! I couldn't stop him. I feel so utterly *dirty* all over!" She threw up her lunch then and there; she felt violated and sick.

"Jon, I'll take over now," Darless said softly. Instantly, he knew what she intended to do. He let Darless' strong arms gasp Thea and move her now weak body well away from the group, to get a little privacy. He heard her say, "Okay Thea, find the pictures of where this thing first began." He knew Thea would get a timely assist over her fright.

"Anyone else attacked?" Jon asked quickly. No one else had been as yet. "Okay, gather close to me. The instant any of you feel someone prying in your mind, give a yell." They agreed.

Lonnie, his voice speaking his deep concern for Thea asked, "Will she be alright?"

"She's getting the best assistance I know of, Lonnie. Darless is terrific with trauma," Jon reassured him.

"It was a wizard spell, that is certain," Alison added. "The instant any of us is attacked, I'll cast a counter-spell."

"Yes, but what if it is you that is attacked?" Sir Thomas asked, growing more worried by the minute. "Who'll cast it then?"

"He can't get me. I'm wearing my Green Gem. Plus I have other protections that I've activated. I don't think he can penetrate my mind," Alison explained, reassuring the rest of them.

Several minutes passed before Lonnie said, "Hey, something strange is going on with my mind. I keep seeing all these recollections of that golden statue we found!" Instantly Alison chanted her counter. Just as soon as her spell triggered, Lonnie let out a sigh of relief. "That did it! I am not thinking of that any more. So that is what it feels like to have someone probe your mind. Rather nasty, if you ask me. I can see why Thea felt so upset about it. I'd sure like to get my hands on whoever is doing this to us!" He was definitely more than a little angry.

They huddled together for another ten minutes, but no further attacks came. Eventually, they relaxed their guard. Jon was still deep in thought. "You know, Alison, I believe I know who is doing the scrying. It has to be Threngold himself. It is the only answer that makes any logical sense." He explained his line of reasoning; the other's smiles and nods only further convinced him that his surmise was correct. "Threngold is searching for his statue!"

"Hum," thought Alison out loud. "Then that means he knows that the statue still exists and that we have it and that it is safe and undamaged," she concluded. The others nodded in agreement. "But where does that get us?"

"I think we have a way to get to Threngold," Jon said slowly, thinking the idea through. "Would we be willing to trade the statue for knowledge of what he did with your parents, you know, his side of what actually happened that night — who he was working for and such?"

"Well, I don't know," Sir Thomas answered. "What if he hurt them or killed them? As far as I'm concerned, that would be a death sentence in my book. I'd have to slay that dragon."

"Yes, if he killed them," Alison agreed, hesitatingly, "my first impulse is to get revenge,".

Jon looked at her and asked, "Alison, revenge or justice? There is a huge difference between the two." As usual, Jon's insight was spot on, she brightened up as his words struck home.

"Absolutely, not revenge!" she declared, "Justice! Nothing is gained by revenge; I'd only feel sick afterwards. Justice is what I intend. Thanks Jon. How do you always see so clearly?"

"Verily, I agree with you. I mis-spoke, justice is desired, not revenge. I will pray to Father Ukko for forgiveness tonight," humbly spoke Sir Thomas. Once again, his fiery temper had gotten the better of his reason. This time, he noted that his reason triumphed rather quickly over his passion of the moment. *This is a good omen!* More than anything, he wanted to become truly worthy of Darless.

Darless and Thea, who was smiling once again, rejoined them. "What's this about justice?" asked Darless. Jon explained who he thought was behind this spying upon them.

"Threngold! Now that does make sense," she declared. Thea nodded her agreement too, contemplating on the idea that a dragon had entered her mind and violated her. Somehow for her that a dragon had done it made the impact less than it would have been if a human had done it to her. Perhaps that was because she considered a dragon nothing but an overgrown lizard. She had never seen dragons, only drawings of them.

Darless' mind raced down avenues of potential responses that Threngold might make. Sir Thomas gazed lovingly on the deep lines furrowing on her face as she concentrated solely on the possibilities. He loved her expressions, so intense. By now everyone knew that she was about to illuminate them and waited patiently. Finally, she announced, "Number 1, Threngold now knows that we have the statue he commissioned. Number 2, he knows that it is in good shape and finished. Number 3, and this one is the pivotal one, he very likely knows that it was we who eliminated all of the demons. Number 4, if any further actions come from Threngold, we shall know conclusively that he still greatly desires this statue. Thus, Number 5, he will not act hastily or brashly for he must consider us a formidable foe. And that is on our side of the ledger, by the way."

"But what will he *do* to us?" asked Thea, the conclusions of Darless seemed utterly obvious to her, the essence of simplicity. Of course, she had not had to figure them out herself.

"Well, I know what I would do in a similar situation," Lonnie answered, "I'd go to them and try to see if I couldn't buy it from them or trade them something for it."

"But he has already paid and likely paid dearly for it," Alison cautioned him. "Is he likely to want to pay for it a second time?"

"Er, no, probably not," Lonnie answered crestfallen. He had not thought that through.

"Well, I'd send my minions to fetch it," Thea broke in, answering her own question. "Send in a big force and tell them to slay everyone and get the statue."

"Does he have minions? Is he willing to possibly risk damaging the statue? Does he want others to know about the statue? Can he trust said minions?" Darless countered. Thea's excited face turned into a big frown. She figured the answer was "no" to each of them. "Further, he knows that some of us are unscryable, that we have protections guarding against magical spying. He probably assumes that we mages can cast similar spells to ward off any further attempts on his part to gain information that way," she added, counting them out on her fingers instead of verbally enumerating them, "which is correct, by the way. If he tries that again, Alison and I will cast a defensive spell on the rest of you. No more violating your minds!"

"But aren't dragons capable of using magical spells like you all do?" Jon interjected. "Won't he do something to counter your counter?"

"Some do, Jon. I would assume Threngold does use magic, probably at a fairly high level — that would be my guess," Alison answered, twisting a long strand of errant hair around her finger, thinking furiously. "He knows where we are; we do not know where he is. I'm sure he will use that to his advantage."

"It would seem to me that the only option we have is to wait for him to send his minions to attack us and for us to just keep on defeating them until he himself finally decides to come and talk to us," Sir Thomas attempted to formulate a conclusion.

"I certainly cannot contact him," Jon explained, "I have to know the person whom I am trying to reach. So yes, he has got to come to us. It'd be so simple if he would just come and talk. We could get the information we seek and be on our way. But I don't suppose he would see it that way."

"I'm afraid that he saw that we are looking for him," Thea said meekly. All eyes turned to her. "Sorry, but he just pulled that right out of my mind. I really was helpless to stop him." Tears welled up in her eyes once more.

"That's okay, Thea," Alison quickly acted, "There was nothing you could have done to prevent his mental invasion. If there is any fault, it is mine. I should have anticipated his attempt and protected all of you. My only defense is that I did not see it coming."

"None of us did," Mandy consoled both of them. "I for one should have anticipated some action on Threngold's part. A ranger should, but I didn't. You can kick me in my rear if you like."

"Hold on everyone," Darless interrupted them all. "This is an important fact Thea has revealed. He *knows* that we are *looking* for him. Thea, did he discover why we are looking for him? Folks, you have to follow the critical line of query." At times, she felt like she had to educate her friends — how could they not see the really important ramifications? Time enough for recriminations later on. "Think, Thea, did he see images of yours that show why we are looking for him?"

The young apprentice squirmed and thought and thought. Since the assist Darless gave her, she could at least review her recollections of the intrusion. From the seriousness of the alu-demon's question, she reflected very carefully. She grasped the ramifications of such a revelation before she found the actual answer to the question. "Well, no, I don't think he did. He was so intent in looking at all my images of the statue and the tower's destruction that he did not get to our basic interest in him. You all got him out of my mind at that point. So, no, I don't think he knows really who we are or why we are seeking him. That's very important, right Darless?"

"You betcha," she said, adopting Mandy's phrasing. Looking up at the others, she said, "Can you all see just how critical that is?" She looked at the mostly blank faces and knew that she was way ahead of their mental deductions. She explained. "As it stands, Threngold thinks we are after him because we have his statue. What if Threngold knew we were after him to find out what he did twenty-one years ago, seeking justice? Can you see how critical that detail actually is?"

Thea had already figured this out and eagerly added, "If he thinks we are just trying to find him because we got his statue, he might want to talk, trade, buy it back or something. But if he knew we were after him for a nasty crime he did long ago, he'd just disappear. Well, I know I would just high-tail it out of the area. Or maybe hide in my secret lair. Avoid them at all costs."

"Or come in for the total kill," Lonnie added, "that is, if he thought he could easily defeat us. He did see your memories of us defeating the Nabassu and the Marquis, right?" She nodded affirmatively.

"Then, the question he must be attempting to answer at this very moment," Mandy concluded, "is 'Am I strong enough to kill them all or are they strong enough to slay me?' Right?"

"Yes, that about sums it up nicely," the alu-demon confirmed.

"So are we?" asked Jon.

Sir Thomas beat everyone else, "Before meeting the Marquis on the field of battle, my answer would have been 'Certainly we can defeat a single dragon!' But after being so badly manhandled by the Marquis, I am now not so certain. Never have I been tossed about like I was an ant! That was most humbling!"

"You said it! Zounds, that was incredible," Mandy added. "I'd expect a dragon to be able to throw me just about anywhere it wanted to."

"Don't forget, we are a team. A team is always stronger than anyone of its individual members," Alison counseled. Jon's question remained unanswered, though.

"Well, we have tarried here long enough," declared Mandy. "Let's hit the trail!"

Somberly, they mounted and resumed their westward journey. Clumps of trees passed by. Yucca plants blossoming white flowers grew in isolated groups.

Here and there, the fresh, green, hardy grasses grew, waving in the mid-afternoon, southwesterly breeze. Hills rose and hills fell, and time drifted by in a monotonous pattern of horse footfalls. Still no villages appeared.

However, near sunset, Mandy called a halt. "Look yonder, to the south. Smoke." A thin curling wisp of grey smoke twisted skyward, reddened by the low hanging sun. "Should we investigate?" Alison nodded, they rode towards the smoke. In five minutes, they crested an oak clad hill overlooking a somewhat darkened glade.

"Looks like a farmstead," Mandy called out and slowly rode down into the small valley. Neatly tended rows of corn, barely six inches tall lay to the right of the trail, while a log fence kept sheep rounded up, along with one old plow horse. The smoke was drifting up from a stone chimney in a log cabin nestled against the hillside. However, their arrival was announced by six huge dogs that came bellowing loudly their way, when they were perhaps five hundred feet from the cabin. The two front windows on either side of the plain door were shuttered only a small crack of lantern light from the inside was visible.

The door opened and a tall, burly man stepped out, "Heel! Heel!" his deep voice bellowed commandingly. The well-trained dogs dashed back to his side, sitting three on each side. They continued to stare intently at these unwelcome visitors. "Travelers?" he said directed at the approaching riders.

"Hail, stranger," Mandy answered him. "Yes, travelers. Just passing through these lands. We saw your smoke and followed it. You are the first person we have seen since the natives of the Canyon Lands. There are not many villages around here that I've seen, none in fact. We were a bit surprised to find your place."

He raised his lantern and cast its pale beams slowly on each of the riders in turn before he spoke. "You do not look like you are more of the Riders of the Black

Scorpion. I'll take the chance and welcome you to my humble farm. Tie your horses in the corral back yonder and come inside. However, I do not have chairs enough for all of you, nor food for that matter. I can offer you crude shelter from the chill night air. Come on in," he beckoned. Mandy and the paladins took care of the horses, while the other women and Jon followed the pioneer inside his log cabin.

As they entered, his wife and two children were just replacing six heavy crossbows back in their fittings on the front wall. Jon noticed that the cracks in the windows were just enough to allow a quarrel shot from inside. Their host spied Jon's eyes on the cracks and crossbows, "Protection. Out here, we stand alone against raiders. I am Herbert Winterhaven and this is my wife, Elizabeth and our three children, Thomas, Betsy, and Samuel." Herbert was approximately thirty, Jon judged, while his wife was possibly slightly younger. Both their faced displayed weather-beaten lines indicative of a hardy, outdoors life. Thomas was in his early teens, Betsy, slightly younger, and Samuel, likely ten, Jon guessed. All five wore grey homespun woolen and leather clothing. Plain was their attire as was the interior of their cabin. All five had long, straight black hair, but Herbert sported a bushy beard as well.

The cabin consisted of one huge central room with storage alcoves added on both sides and the back. Their sleeping quarters lay above the room on all four sides; movable ladders gave access to them at night. A large stone stove with crackling fire was in the center of the left side and a stew pot was simmering. An oak table and five chairs marked the center of the room. Various gear, spinning wheel, and numerous sacks lined the other walls.

Each of the Winterhaven's nodded as they were introduced. The excitement of seeing strangers clearly reflected in all of the children's eyes. Jon glanced around, but since the others had not yet finished stabling the horses, he figured it was his turn to do the introductions, especially since Herbert was looking at him expectantly. "Thanks for your hospitality. I am Saint Jon Brown, the Redeemer, and a simple musician. This is Alison d'Ambrose, a Holy Archmage of Ukko and our party's leader. This is Darless, a Holy Paladin of Ukko and a powerful mage, almost an Archmage herself. This is Thea, apprentice mage of Alison. The others looking after our horses are Sir Thomas le Bonnaire, a powerful Holy Paladin of Ukko, Lonnie Smith, also a paladin, and last but not the least, our expert guide, Mandy Blackthorn, a mighty Ranger of Reylona. We have just come from the Canyon Lands and are just passing through here on our way to the Desolation Range. We were about to camp for the night when we spied your chimney smoke. Actually, you are the first people outside of the Canyon Lands we have come across and I guess we are just curious." Jon shrugged unsure of what else to say.

Apparently startled by something he said, Elizabeth whispered to Herbert, "These must be the ones!" Jon noticed that the children uniformly looked quite worried; he thought he detected a note of fear in their eyes.

"Oh my!" Herbert exclaimed taken aback.

For a moment, Jon could see him wondering what to do — what to say next. He decided to probe a bit. "We are the ones what?" he said in a quizzical manner. *Good reaction!* Darless placed into Jon's mind. *Where's Mandy when you need her?* Jon thought back to her.

Sizing up the situation took Herbert only seconds, "Ah, now it makes more sense. Let me explain. Earlier this afternoon, six Riders of the Black Scorpion gang came through here with a dire message. They ordered us to be on the lookout for a party of adventurers containing four women and three men. They said that there is a reward of five thousand gold coins on your heads. If we see you, we are to send word to them and maybe get the reward. Now I see why they are plenty worried! You have no fear from us. We despise those brigands. Clearly you folks are a threat to their evil out here! You are plenty welcome here," he grinned broadly. "The Riders of the Black Scorpion are one of the nastiest cults that I have ever seen. They are ruining this entire virgin land with their evil."

"Who's ruining what?" asked Mandy, as she and the paladins entered followed by the six large dogs. "Oh, are the dogs supposed to be inside? Hi, I'm Mandy."

"Er, yes. That'll do," he ordered the dogs, who playfully made for the children. Herbert repeated his introductions and told them about the reward on their heads. Of course, this interested Sir Thomas and Mandy. Herbert spent another ten minutes explaining what he knew about the cult. Their numbers tally at least a hundred and their main center of operations lay due west, near the foothills of Desolation. From their stronghold there, they have been wreaking havoc on all the lands between the mountains and the Canyon Lands. They raid homesteads, take captives, especially young women, and ransom anyone who has any funds. They are led by an evil high priest, and they all worship black scorpions. Rumors say they poison people with scorpion bites, a nasty bunch.

Mandy grinned when she heard where they were located. "Ah, good, their headquarters lies directly on our path!" She looked at Sir Thomas and added, "What say you? Shall we pay them a brief visit? I do believe they need a lesson in manners."

The paladin, realizing she was teasing, added, "Verily, scum like that need to be paid a visit! I think they need more than manners!" Facing Herbert, he said, "If our path crosses theirs, I swear to you that I, Sir Thomas, Holy Paladin of Ukko, will see to it that they trouble you no more!" He bowed low to Herbert, sealing his promise.

"Well, if you can do that, all of us pioneers out here would be most grateful," Herbert replied, hope filling his eyes, "of that you can be sure. None of us around here like them."

"Wait a minute," Mandy interrupted. "We've not seen any villages out here. Yours is the only homestead we have seen at all. Where are all these others?"

"Oh, scattered about. Hamstead is about twenty-five miles to the south — that's a village of about five hundred. Out here, we are all around ten miles from our neighbors. The Lucas family is the closest to us, about nine miles north," he explained. "The land is dry and it takes a good deal to support much. Besides, we like our privacy," he grinned at his wife, who returned it.

Elizabeth said rather apologetically, "I'm sorry but we are not really able to host seven of you. I've only enough stew cooking for us. I've told Herbert to build some more chairs, but he never seems to find time for it as yet."

"We don't want to impose," said Alison. "We've got our own provisions, though perhaps we can blend ours with yours and make us all a feast." She went on to relieve her host's unspoken additional concerns, "Either Darless or I usually provide our nightly shelter. We create a magical mansion, which is like a huge palace, plenty of space and accommodations for us all with no fear of outside attacks. Jon was right, we really would just love some friendly company for a while before we retire. Most of us are from the greater Verbenloc area, far to the east of here, past the Canyon Lands. While we were in those lands, we had a fine time with some of the tribes there. Do you know of the natives of that magnificent land?"

Her concerns eased, Elizabeth relaxed, "Oh yes, we trade with them several times a year. They make all of the leather goods that we have. Sometimes when our harvest is poor, we have gotten corn meal from them. Herbert is a retired fighter and something of a weapon smith. He often swaps knives he's made for leather goods with Tired Bear. But things have gone ill for those people of late, we hear. Some evil has descended upon the park land — that's what I call it — it's the most spectacular land I have ever seen, but a bit harsh in climate."

Alison grinned; her eyes sparkled, "Oh, well next visit, you will find that the evil is totally obliterated. Nothing remains, save some giant wasps. We have eliminated all of the demons that had invaded their lands. Probably by the time you take your next trip there, things should be back to normal." Gasping, Elizabeth put her hands over her mouth in total disbelief.

Herbert exclaimed, "Incredible! Demons, no less. Oh my! You must — you must be really powerful people to have done that! When I heard from the nasty gang that they were hunting for a party mostly composed of women, I thought they were crazy. Honestly, I've only heard of women in an adventuring party once in my life. When they said your party had four, I figured you must just be travelers or some such, but to take out those demons, why you'd have to be incredibly strong folks!" He looked anew at each one of the seven long and hard, as did Elizabeth and the children. "I'm a mid-level fighter myself," he added, "so I have some inkling of just how formidable a foe those demons can be, but only three fighters among you?"

"Two really," Sir Thomas attempted to set the record straight. "Lonnie here is a young lad, still learning the ropes, so to speak. While he did fight, the heavy fighting was handled by me and Mandy. Let me tell you, this woman is the most powerful ranger I have ever run across! I suspect she could even defeat me! And that is saying something." Mandy beamed, Sir Thomas acknowledged her skill for what it actually was.

"Well, we both got more than a little bunged up fighting those demons," she interjected. "That was the toughest fighting I have ever experienced, ever! But don't forget, we also had the total assistance of three mages! And Jon too," she added.

"Hey, leave me mostly out," Jon interrupted. Looking at the family, he added, "I'm really just a musician, really." Alison, Darless and Mandy chuckled at that.

Alison, her stomach growling, interrupted them all, "Come on; let's get some supper going. I'm starving. We can tell them the story over dinner, how's that?" So Thea, Alison and Darless, joined Elizabeth in fixing a much needed feast. Alison suspected that these folks lived rather frugally, so she added as many extras as she dared to the feast pot. In a half hour, the women sat at the table, while the men and children sat on the floor and everyone had all that they could eat. Enough remained in the pot to feed the Winterhavens tomorrow evening, which was what Alison had in mind.

After dinner, Jon got out his instruments and entertained them, while Elizabeth and Thea did the dishes. Then, he played soft background music while Alison, Mandy and Sir Thomas took turns relating the highlights of their adventures in the Canyon Lands. Jon saw that this time was like Christmas for the children who sat eagerly listening to every word.

A hour later, when they had finished their story, Herbert asked, "Mind if I ask you a simple question? If you think it is none of my business, just say so. But where are you going? Where are you headed? You are a very long way from home. It must be some very serious business that brings folks of your powers to these nearly empty lands."

Alison sighed, "It's a long story. We are looking for a brown dragon named Threngold." She spent another half hour briefly outlining her past and her current quest to find this dragon.

"Mommy, we've seen him, their brown dragon, haven't we," Betsy enthusiastically said.

"What?" exclaimed Alison totally surprised. "When? Where? This is great news!"

"Mind you, we don't see him very often," Herbert explained. "Once in a while we see him flying high in the sky, usually at night, heading east of here or west of here. I think Betsy saw him most recently, right?"

"Yes, dad. About two weeks ago, mommy and I saw him flying against the full moon, very high in the sky, flying to the west," Betsy explained. She really felt important as she described what she had seen.

"That is terrific news indeed! Thanks Betsy. Now we know we are truly on the right path!" Alison added for the young girl's benefit.

"Say, are the Black Scorpions in league with the brown dragon?" wondered Mandy out loud, yawning heavily as sleep drew near.

"I doubt it," Herbert answered, "I don't think dragons take kindly to humans."

"Truly, dragon-kind would be more likely to feed off us," Sir Thomas added. "It's probably just a coincidence in direction, that's all. But I'm falling asleep myself. How about putting the mansion up, Alison?"

"Can we watch?" echoed all three children in unison, wide-eyed, though fighting sleep.

"Well, I was going to put up our mansion outside, but actually, it can be just about anywhere. Would you mind if our doorway was temporarily just about here?" Alison asked.

"Would we run into it?" wondered Elizabeth, who had no idea at all what this was all about.

"No, it will be completely invisible; you could not even tell it's there when I shut the doors," she replied. With no objections, Alison began her chant and in a moment the shimmering doors of a new mansion stood open, here inside the cabin. Of course, the children just had to see inside. Alison took the entire family inside for a royal tour. Naturally, the children wanted to spend the night inside too. In the end, everyone spent the night inside the mansion. For the Winterhaven adults, it was like a honeymoon suite. For their children it was the most exciting night they had ever had. Alison's spell brought wonder and happiness to others instead of just safe sleeping quarters. All got a good night's sleep, that is, once the children finally fell asleep.

Darless and Thea rose first and, as usual, fixed a hearty breakfast including pancakes especially for the children. While they were eating, Betsy said to Thea, "Boy I sure would like to be a wizard and cast mansion spells. I bet it is terribly hard to learn magic."

"Oh yes, it's hard. It will be a long time before I know enough magic to be able to make one of these mansions," Thea explained, eager to have someone to talk to about magic. "I'm only a beginner, myself. If you want to learn, I'm sure Alison could probably teach you what she first taught me, how to start a fire."

Realizing that she could not quickly learn how to make a mansion, Betsy protested, "Gee, I already know how to start a fire. I can start one with two rocks, with two dry sticks and a bit of rawhide, and with a piece of steel and a rock. Why would I want another way?"

"I could start one those ways too, Betsy," Thea explained. "But as it turned out, that was a very important spell for me to learn. I ended up having to start dozens of fires in the middle of winter with three feet of snow covering the ground and with all the wood waterlogged and covered in ice and snow. That's when the spell was most useful."

"You cannot start wet wood on fire," she protested. "You'd have to have some dry kindling to start it."

"There wasn't any and besides, our fingers were nearly frozen after riding all day," Thea explained. "The whole caravan would have frozen to death had I not been able to start all those fires."

"Wow!" Betsy's eyes rounded. "Around here we only get a little bit of snow, just enough to make the ground look white for a short time. There is snow in the mountains, though."

"Yes, that's where we were, trying to cross Desolation in the winter," Thea added.

"Wow! No one can cross the mountains in the winter time," Betsy commented, "at least we have never heard of anyone being able to do it. Dad says that the snows get deeper than I am tall. Is that right?"

"Probably. We did not stay through the winter, but it was three feet deep after the first snowfall!" Thea recalled with a shiver.

"Well, maybe you don't want to be a wizard after all. Too much studying," Thomas, her older brother interjected, "you'd rather run and play in the woods!" She nodded in agreement.

"Thomas wants to be a fighter like dad," she changed the subject.

"In that case," Thea smiled at him, "you should ask Sir Thomas for a lesson. I learned my fighting skills from him. I use a short sword when I run out of magical spells."

He ran over to the paladin, who was packing his gear, getting ready for the day's ride. "Please, Sir Thomas, can you give me a fighting lesson? Thea said you taught her how to use a short sword. I'm old enough. I've practiced a lot. Please?" He pleaded with the warrior.

Sir Thomas saw Herbert begin to protest at his son's actions, but waved him off. Looking at the young lad, he said, "All right, one short one, because we are about to hit the trail." Thomas could hardly contain his enthusiasm as he eagerly waited for the paladin.

"Son, the first lesson is this: the best fight is the fight that you can avoid, especially if it is a fight you cannot hope to win," he explained. The boy looked crestfallen, while Herbert smiled. "Look, Thomas, fighting is a last resort when all else has failed. Fighting rarely solves any problem, unless you slay your opponent. However, then you inherit what your foe has left behind. You are forced to pick up the pieces, and there are always consequences." He could see that he was not reaching the lad, so he tried to think of a simpler analogy, remembering his youth.

"Let me give you an example. Suppose that there was a gang of thugs around and one day one of them challenges you and orders you to walk around him through a mud puddle. While you could fight it out with him, think of the consequences. Suppose that you defeated him. The next day, you would have all of the other thugs challenging you! Are you strong enough to take them all on at one time? Or would it be better to just walk through the mud puddle and ignore him? Or would it be better to defeat him and then seek out the next thug in the gang, get him by himself and defeat him, and the next, one at a time? Suppose that he was much bigger and stronger than you are and that you could not hope to defeat him? What good would it do to come home all cut up or with broken bones? Think the situation through, then act, act in a way that does the most good to everyone." Thomas said he was beginning to see what he meant.

"A few days ago, we killed the last of the demons in the Canyon Lands. We therefore inherited the Canyon Lands. We were able to give control over the lands back to the local people, fortunately, and they were ready to receive it. However, suppose that they all were destitute, starving because all their crops had been destroyed. Now I would be responsible for feeding everyone, finding them all a place to stay, helping them to build new homes, and so on. Remember, you inherit what your vanquished foe leaves behind."

Herbert commented, "Now that is a very good lesson to learn! Thanks for telling Thomas." The boy was lost in thought, pondering the significance of Sir Thomas's words.

"Yes, I think I see what you mean," the lad said, "If I had shot my crossbow yesterday and killed one of the six thugs that came here, like I had urged dad to let me do, then the other five would have attacked us all. Five to one is not good odds for dad. If one got away, he'd bring a whole bunch of them here and probably kill us all! Sorry, dad, for being so angry with you yesterday," he apologized. His dad just gave him a hug.

"Hey, guys, it's time to go," hollered Mandy, eager to get on the trail once more.

They all said their farewells. The children watched as the mansion disappeared and watched as their new friends mounted up, waved good-bye, and rode off heading eastward. "Look Betsy, Mandy is leading them," exclaimed Thomas.

Herbert explained, "Yes, she is a ranger and it is her responsibility to guide the others safely on the trail. It is a very important job indeed, one I never ever tried to do, way too hard for me. See, the fighters are up front in case of trouble. The wizards are in the middle and a fighter brings up the rear. That's another lesson for all of you." The children smiled, this had been a most interesting visit indeed.

Mandy, following Herbert's directions, quickly found the east-west trail. Once they were beyond sight of the cabin, she dismounted and examined the trail. "Yes, six riders passed here heading eastward yesterday. Tracks are but a day old." Satisfied, she mounted and led them eastward. Only now she kept all of her senses totally alert. She knew trouble lay ahead of them. Sir Thomas wore his full plate armor; he was ready as well.

Since this cult was not on her itinerary, Alison chose to let Mandy and Sir Thomas lead. "What's the plan?" she asked the paladin, when they stopped for a stretch break.

"Well, we could see if we can sneak up on them and take them by surprise," Mandy began, "but you know how I hate doing that. Perhaps we should just ride in and arrest them."

"However, you know we really do not know their true intentions," Sir Thomas added. "Perhaps we should just ride on in to their fortress and see what they do in response. If they attack us, then we are obliged to take them all out. On the other hand, maybe they want a parley. Or maybe even will tell us how to get to the brown dragon himself."

"Or maybe they will ambush us or try to poison us," added Darless. "At least we do not have to go out of our way to find this cult." She was trying to be a bit more positive about this excursion.

"A ranger should know before she goes. That's my motto, anyway. When we get closer, I am going to change into an eagle and do a bit of reconnoitering to see what we are up against, if no one has any objections," Mandy declared, pinching her lip. She did not want to lead them into an ambush or worse; she'd never live it down. "Come on; let's get going. We might get close enough yet today." Again they mounted and rode due eastward.

By lunch time, the track they were following grew wider. Now it was obvious to even Jon that this trail was heavily used. Mandy explained that these men probably rode straight out from their fortress and then slowly fanned out in an arc, as they traveled about this hilly land between the Desolation Range and the Canyon Lands. It made sense, Jon thought.

While they were milling around eating a light lunch and resting their horses, Mandy heard the telltale sounds of approaching riders and sounded a warning. Jon marveled that she picked up that sound, for he could not hear it for at least another minute. Since they had their gear out and spread about for dining, they couldn't really just pack up and hide; there was too little time. The approaching riders were galloping from the direction from which they had just come. Further, it could be anybody, not necessarily evil cult riders. Mandy and the paladins quickly tied the horses into a string that Jon could hold and then took up defensive positions with the mages in the center. It was not long before the riders came into view between the stunted oak trees.

Six Riders of the Black Scorpion, riding in pairs, came rushing into the little clearing where the party stood awaiting them. Each wore a head piece fashioned from leather to resemble a scorpion's head and dyed black. Mandy surmised that this was supposed to instill fear in the beholder, but she thought it rather humorous. *The things men will do for attention!* she thought to herself. The lead pair, galloping fast, took only a few seconds to realize that here before them were the very people they were seeking. Jon spied the sudden jerk one man had, knowing that his body motion spelled recognition. What would they do, he wondered.

In a flash of thought, Jon saw that they could choose to attack, using the advantage of fast moving, mounted cavalry or they could attempt to kill or wound their horses thus slowing the party's travel tremendously or they could stop and talk or they could ignore the party and ride off or they could reign in and simply surrender. He wondered if the paladins and Mandy had similar thoughts. Then the lead pair was upon them, their horses not breaking their stride. Hot air flashed by Jon's face, followed by splatter from the lather dripping off the overly hot horses. Each of the three pairs of riders merely looked at the raised two-handed sword and the bastard sword and the cluster of mages as they swerved around them and then edged back onto the trail ahead. They said nothing. Just as fast as they came, they left. Mandy kept everyone still for some time as she listened to hear if they halted up ahead. Satisfied that they didn't, she explained that they rode hard until she could no longer hear any sound of hooves.

Mandy commented, "Smart of them. Not too bright, though. They are wrecking those horses!" She wiped horse sweat from her face. "I could use a wash now!" Alison got out her decanter of water and everyone washed the splatter from their faces and arms. "Well, the cult leaders should now know where we are and where we are heading. Forget the surprise factor."

"They certainly were wise not to tangle with us," Sir Thomas spoke encouragingly. "I'll give them that much credit, but their horsemanship is terrible. Either the cult headquarters is very close or they are going to ride the horses into the ground!"

"Maybe they have a rest area up ahead where they can swap mounts," Lonnie mused. "If I knew I was to ride that hard, I'd have several sets of mounts spaced at critical intervals."

"I see, like the Pony Express!" Jon interrupted, grasping what the lad implied. Unfortunately, he then had to explain what that term was to the others. All agreed that that would be an ideal way to go if they needed great speed and not harm the horses.

They finished their meal and, when the horses were cooled enough, they continued their eastward ride. Even Jon could now see the heavy imprints from the galloping horses ahead of them. It was that plain and obvious. They had not gone more than two miles, when Mandy spied a curl of smoke among the trees up ahead. The trail headed straight for the smoke. The fighters drew their swords in preparation, while Alison and Darless got their magical staves out and into their right hands, ready to cast volley after volley, while still riding. Mandy slowed their pace though; she did not want to rush into an ambush.

In a minute, they entered a small clearing. A small cabin stood just ahead off to the side of the trail. Smoke from a cooking fire rose, twisting this way and that in the heat currents of the day. To the right of the cabin was a corral. There panting heavily were the six horses that had passed them only a few minutes before. There was no sign of the men. As they rode even with the cabin's door, they spied and embossed Black Scorpion at eye level on its door. It was also obviously bolted from the inside. Mandy noted that there were several arrow slits in some of the windows; she pointed them out. As they rode on by the cabin, both mages pointed their staves toward the door, mostly as a dire warning to those inside not to try anything.

Once they had passed the cabin, Mandy noted fresh tracks of six horses galloping eastward, ahead of them still. "Looks like Lonnie was spot on. I'd say they swapped horses here. They must have done it pretty darn fast though. It's only been a few minutes. Good show, Lonnie!" The lad and Thea both grinned in appreciation and nodded to each other.

Two miles further east, at the top of a hill, the distant sight of the Desolation Range of mountains became clearly visible along the horizon line stretching as far as the eye could see north and south. The ground, Jon noted, became rockier; boulders at least three feet in diameter occasionally lay in their path. The trail twisted around them. Until now, the trail had been straight as an arrow. As they paused to view the scene before them, Jon also noted that the land continuously rose toward the mountains, now some twenty miles away. They had reached the foothills of Desolation. Overhead, several hawks alternately floated and soared, ignoring them entirely. Under normal circumstances, this would be a marvelous sight to view, but Jon knew ahead only lay trouble with the scorpion cult. He tried not to let that thought dampen his appreciation of the view. "It's much prettier down here than it was way up north," he commented, remembering their passage across the northern section of this land last year.

"Yes, here the foothills are really kind of nice," Mandy acknowledged. "Well, I suppose that the headquarters probably lies either in or right by the actual mountains. I'd say that it is at least another twenty miles. We might get there by dark. Quarter moon might help at night a bit. However, I say camp tonight and tackle them tomorrow morning. What do you say, Sir Thomas?"

"I agree with you ranger, though that does give them plenty of time to prepare for us. It is far better to attack in the daylight," he replied. "Let's go about three-quarters of the way there and then stop." They continued their easy ride.

As they moved along, Mandy pointed out various side trails that veered off to the north or south. The general conclusion was that this was the main road out from their encampment. Now that he had some idea what to look for, Jon could see signs of many riders both coming and going down these side trails. However, in another five miles, the ground became rockier and the obvious heavy hoof prints evaporated for him, but not for Mandy's experienced eyes.

They were about halfway across the foothills when Mandy halted them atop a rise. "Look there, far off. Dust clouds. That would be our six riders, I'll wager. They are at least ten miles ahead of us now and very close to the mountains. Let's pause and see if we can discern their destination." She got out her Eyes of the Eagles, the pair of binoculars Jon had given her last year, and watched. After another ten minutes, the dust cloud thinned and disappeared entirely. She could not tell if they had stopped or had begun a climb into the mountains ahead. Both were equally likely as seen from this distance. Once more they continued their eastward ride.

The sun was getting low when they halted still some five miles from the actual mountains. A chill was in the air. Jon could tell that the air was thinner; he guessed that they were nearly a mile high. Once on foot, they discovered quickly that they had to be observant where they placed their feet. Not only was the ground rocky and uneven, but also numerous cactus plants grew low to the ground, sharp spines sticking out for the unwary. "I can see why scorpions live out here," Jon muttered.

"Yes, ideal climate," Mandy replied, missing Jon's sarcasm. To her, all animals had an ideal climate in which to thrive. This was just what scorpions needed.

Alison quickly cast her mansion spell. One by one, they led their horses inside, though the doors remained open for a while yet. Mandy used her binoculars to scan the horizon, while the paladins took care of the horses who, as usual, were kept in the anteroom by the doors. If she saw anything, she said nothing about it.

Soon, the delicious odors of supper greeted everyone, compliments of Thea. When Mandy finally came back inside shutting the doors, she complimented Jon, "Looks like you finally have your riding legs. You are not stiff and sore."

"Hum, you might be right. I had not noticed it," Jon replied as they all sat down to eat. "It kind of crept up on me," he added. She smiled at him.

The evening passed uneventful. After cleaning up the dishes, Jon played on his new lute for a while until sleep came to one and all.

Chapter 11 The Black Scorpions

Over breakfast the next day, no one discussed any battle plans. Jon assumed that the others thought that this expected confrontation today was not anything to be particularly worried about. However, Alison did tell Sir Thomas, Mandy and Jon that before they went into actual combat, she intended to cast a spell on them that made their bodies immune to several physical attacks, giving them a healthy edge. Little did she know just how crucial this minor action would prove to be.

Once spells were prepared, armor donned and weapons made ready, Alison modified the mansion so that a window opened onto the foothills. They saw no evidence of anyone lying in ambush waiting for them to leave their mansion. Mandy opened the door and peered out. As soon as she smelled the air of the hills, the hairs on her neck bristled. Though she said nothing, her raised arm signaled Stop and Quiet. Only a cursory glance at the ground about the entrance of the mansion told her much. Handing the reins of her horse to Sir Thomas, she bent low and studied the tracks very carefully. Finally, she spoke softly.

"As I suspected, we've had company during the night! A large group of horsemen came by here — probably expecting to find us camping. See here," she pointed out, "someone on foot carefully followed our trail right up to where we disappeared into the mansion. From their jumble here by the doorway, I'd say that they were at a loss to explain what they saw, probably something like, 'They rode up to this point and dismounted and led their horses a few feet and then horses and all entirely disappeared.' Next I'd say they fanned out and rode in all compass directions search for us. Finally they came back here and then left. It's a little hard to tell just how many

339

riders without actually going outside myself. Suggestions?"

"Well, as I remember from yesterday, there are enough trees and boulders around here to hide behind — though none are nearby," Sir Thomas answered thoughtfully, sizing up the possibilities. "If they are hiding and waiting for us to appear, it might not be too wise for us to lead our horses out one by one. Ambush and all — we'd be dismounted. We could mount up here inside and ride out the door prepared for an attack. If we go quickly, we would certainly gain surprise and we could be in formation before they could respond in any way." He paused and looked at Alison, "By the way, thanks for the mansion. Had we been out in the open, surely we would have been attacked while we slept!" She smiled back at him.

Mandy heeded his advice. Issuing orders to mount up inside the entrance doorway, she and the paladin rode quickly out of the doors, followed by Alison and Darless. Jon followed next, dragging the two spare horses. Finally, with drawn swords, Thea and Lonnie exited the mansion. The moment the last two cleared the door, Alison cancelled her spell and the mansion disappeared. No attack came.

Mandy kept them walking eastwards at a slow gait still on the trail, but all eyes glanced around in all directions looking for the unseen enemies. They did not have long to wait, for within three minutes, far off to their left and right flanks, many riders appeared from their hiding places. However, they did not attack nor make for the party. Instead, they paralleled their forward progress, obviously monitoring them. "I make twenty-five or so on our right," Mandy called out. The paladin added that he thought that at least that many rode on their left. "We have about five more miles to go to reach the more mountainous area ahead. I'll bet that they intend to close the distance as we near Desolation proper. Keep your eyes peeled." Somberly, they rode on.

From here, the rising, tall grey granite mountains made an impressive view, but only Jon admired it; the others were too intent on the coming danger. The two groups of riders paralleled them for the first mile, and then slowly began to close the distance between them. "My guess is that they will close about the point that we reach the actual mountains ahead," Mandy surmised. The paladin agreed with her conclusion. When they were about a mile from the protruding range, Alison canted a spell and gently touched Mandy on the shoulder. The ranger felt a surge of bluish energy flow over her body. Alison then did the same to Sir Thomas. At last, dropping back a bit, she did the same to Jon.

"It tickles," he exclaimed. "So I don't have to worry about getting hit with an arrow or blade, right?"

"Yes, my love," she answered, "when it no longer tickles even a tiny bit, the spell is likely used up. It should block a dozen blows or so before it wears off. Got your walking stick handy?"

Jon had it tied to his saddle. "No, but it comes to me when I will it to do so, so I'm ready. Look, I can see something ahead."

In the distance ahead, where a valley between peaks ran down and met these foothills loomed a massive fortification. Something black lay at its center. However, from this distance, no one could say what it was. They did not have time to contemplate it either. For at this point, the riders that had been paralleling them now broke into a canter heading their way. Several of the lead riders bore long lances, while the rest waved swords that glinted in the morning sunlight. Both groups were coming at them from a forty-five degree angle from their front — a perfect V-shape. "Dumb move," Mandy commented to Sir Thomas.

"They should have come from side to side or front and back," he answered, "then they would have us at a disadvantage."

"Probably just testing our strength. We are within sight of their encampment. Their leaders are probably watching," Mandy observed. "I wish that we didn't have to give away our attack strength so soon, though."

Meanwhile, Darless looked at Alison who looked at her. Both smiled simultaneously. "Are you thinking what I'm thinking?" asked the alu-demon.

"A pair of v-shaped walls of force out in front of us should do nicely," Alison answered, grinning.

"From the staffs?"

"Yes, save our inherent powers," Alison ordered. Both chanted briefly. Two shimmering walls of force appeared in front of the party. Each locked together at the leading point, about five feet in front of Mandy and Sir Thomas, flairing outwards so that the entire party was behind the safety of the ten-foot tall walls. Of course, there was no protection from above or from their rear — that was province of Lonnie and Thea, the rear guards. Naturally, they halted or they would have run into their own walls. To the charging riders, this looked like a miracle. Their opponents were taking the worst possible reaction to their charge. The Riders of the Black Scorpion would cut them to pieces.

Actually, the opposite occurred. The lead riders with the lances detected the shimmering walls far too late to do anything about it. Their outstretched lances hit the walls and shattered into pieces, as did they and their horses, when a split second later they hit the walls with the full force of their galloping charge behind them. The carnage was total and complete. Only a half dozen riders on each side — who were in the very rear of the charge — survived by frantically pulling their horses wildly to the right and left. They kept right on galloping away from the devastating scene.

Just as suddenly as the walls of force appeared, they vanished. "Whoa! Hey gang! We did not cancel out spells. They must have some powerful wizards of their own up ahead! Be wary," yelled Alison. Mandy now led them forward at a trot, anxious to get the real fight underway.

When they reached the top of a small rise before the fortress, the enemy's preparations became obvious. The cult had built a thousand-foot long stone wall, fifteen feet high across the entrance to this narrow V-shaped valley here at the start of this portion of the Desolation Range. Fully five hundred riders stood arrayed across its frontal area awaiting the signal to charge into battle. Several hundred others manned the battlements proper. The black object was the entrance gate, formed in the shape of a giant black scorpion. The trail led directly into its mouth, a giant stinger arced over the entrance way, menacingly. Jon wondered if it was for show or was some kind of diabolical device to poison those who entered unbidden.

Alison's keen eyes spotted the magic users centrally located above the scorpion along with a man dressed in black, priestly robes. "Darless, we take on the magic users. See them?" She did. Turning in the saddle, she told Thea, "While we distract the two magic users, you blast the riders with balls of fire. Try to get as many as you can with each spell to lower the numbers our fighters will face. Okay, Darless, here goes a lightning bolt at the one on the left." She chanted and sent one arcing toward the distant mage. Only a second after that, Darless' bolt arced toward the other mage. Just as she suspected, both spells were nullified by the mages, who appeared to have absorbed the spells in their staves. However, just as she had calculated, while thus engaged, Thea's spells worked unimpeded, and so they did! Her first fire ball blasted into the line just to the right of center.

Giving their opponents no time to counter-spell them, both mages let loose another lightning bolt, which, again, the opposing wizards had no choice but to absorb. This time, Thea's fire ball detonated just to the left of center. All the while, they continued to close to combat range. Alison could now see the enemy mages cursing her, because they knew fair well that if they did not counter-spell, they'd be struck — yet they had to protect their own forces. Twice more, Alison and Darless shot bolts toward them, and twice more, Thea's spells detonated, felling many riders.

At this point, Jon could see the priest taking some action. Actually, Jon was bored since he had little to do. So watching Thea's spells go off, a germ of an idea formed. Jon decided to dabble. As Thea's fourth fire ball exploded, Jon created an identical illusion of a fire ball on the other side. He made the illusion look exactly like Thea's real spell. To his wonderment, several riders fell off their horses, some patting themselves as if they were on fire. "I'm out of fire ball spells!" yelled Thea.

Alison knew this instinctively — she knew just what Thea's capabilities were. "Here catch," she tossed her Staff of Power to her apprentice, commanding it to be caught by Thea, just in case. The young woman grabbed it with her free hand, dropping her reigns. Fumbling, she managed to sheath her short sword. Lonnie, bending low leaned over and retrieved her reigns for her, a riding skill he had long practiced. "Okay, hold onto the staff and cast away. When it is drained, you'll know. If a bad spell comes your way, say 'Suck' and it will absorb the spell." Thea's eyes opened wide. For a lowly apprentice to actually be using her master's Staff of Power was a high honor! Quickly, she cast a fifth ball of fire. Jon paralleled it on the other side.

Alison spied the weird effect. She turned around and stared at Jon. He smiled back at her. She shook her head in disbelief. *He is casting illusion spells now! But that cannot be! He is not trained like my sister. Ah, must be a mental thing that he's doing. I wonder.*

Now they were getting quite close to the enemy. Jon saw the priest chanting. Already his mind and beingness were wide open, sensitive to all that was going on around him. Intuitively, he sensed a wall of flames about to appear above them all and he began a counter-creation, a sea of ice rising upwards. The priest's spell culminated. Fifteen feet above them, a great sheet of flames appeared, just like the Marquis had done. Only this time Jon had the time to prepare. He created more and more rising flows of ice. A searing, melting sound filled the air about five feet above them, steam rose in a billowing cloud above them. The look on the priest's face was that of complete and utter disbelief. Never had he ever seen anything like this happen to his most powerful spell! Neither had Alison, for that matter.

The remaining enemy riders galloped into close combat, charging into Mandy and Sir Thomas. Those unfortunate to attack the pair first met an instant, early demise, as the ranger and paladin cut them to pieces. Each was taking out two or three men with each attack! Within seconds, all of the party's forward progress halted. Mandy and Sir Thomas hacked this way and that, veterans of close combat from horseback. However, Alison now had to throw batches of magical missiles at those that chose to get too near to her. Darless, heedless of those riders trying to hack at her with their non-magical swords, continued to blast spells in the direction of the two mages and priest. At the rear, Lonnie turned and fought off those that attempted to get past him to Thea, who now move to Jon's side. All were bunched tightly together, sitting ducks for the spells of the enemy. Still Thea managed to launch two more fireballs toward the rear of the riders. Amusingly, Jon kept still more at bay by commanding their horses to retreat, which of course totally distracted those riders. The body count rose alarmingly in front of the party.

Now, a huge number of missiles flew from those manning the walls, heedless of hitting their own men. The rain of arrows produced only three hits, one in Alison, one in Thea and one in Lonnie's back. All others simply bounced off of the others in the party. However, twenty of their own men fell victim to the rain of arrows. Only after this tactic failed so completely did Jon heard the words appear in his mind, *I wish all of their weapons, armor and gear was ten feet to their right.* However, he could not tell from whom the spell came. He only saw that his newly acquired bracers of defense that Mandy insisted he wear now lay on the ground to his right. So was all of the paladin's shiny armor, their swords and wizard staves!

It was quite a shock to Mandy and Sir Thomas, both mid-swing of an attack, to suddenly find their arms holding nothing. Sir Thomas was clad only in his skivvies! Their opponents blades now landed upon their defenseless bodies, but bounced off, thanks to the spell Alison had put on them before they rode into combat! However, Jon knew that her spell had worn off of him after the rain of arrows fell; he did not have that tingling sensation any longer. They were doomed, he thought.

Alison and Thea still had their spells, each shot magical missiles. Alison tried to keep as many riders off of Sir Thomas as she could, while Thea did her best to protect Lonnie. Darless flew out of her saddle and dove onto those hacking away at Mandy, who by now began taking nasty wounds from the striking blades; her's had worn off as well. Hovering above the men, the alu-demon, smashed heads, tore bodies from saddles, and generally wreaked havoc. Blood-lust filled her eyes; she had even forgotten to cast her fancy magical blade spell!

Then, given this slight reprieve, Jon heard Mandy speak slowly and carefully, "I wish all of our gear was back where it was before it was taken from us." Her wish feather floated out of her headband and slowly fell to the ground. When it landed, it vanished completely without a trace. In that same instant, all of their armor, weapons and gear was back where they belonged, once again, startling Sir Thomas. He was now totally spooked! He stared at himself, while several swords smashed into his solid armor. On the other hand, suddenly finding his sword back in his hand, Lonnie instantly reacted by a strong attack.

Both opposing mages let loose a huge volley of magical missiles at Darless, many bounced harmlessly off of her, but several broke through her innate resistance to magic and inflicted wounds. She ignored them completely. However, with Sir Thomas finally hacking away once more and Mandy felling others around her, Darless calmed down. Jon spied her looking straight at one of the magic users, who in turn was looking at Alison, chanting a spell. He knew immediately what the alu-demon would cast. He was right. He watched as a tiny beam of energy flew from her pointing finger. It flew straight at the mage who suddenly had a one inch hole through his head. Jon saw the death expression of utter surprise and shock frozen on his face as the lifeless body slowly collapsed. Never cross an alu-demon, Jon concluded with a smile.

Now, with a moment's breathing room while the remaining two enemy casters tried to grasp what had just happened, that is the priest and other mage, Alison choose to cast her special, fancy lightning bolt spell, the multi-fingered one. It first hit the remaining mage knocking him completely off of the platform on which he was standing. He never reappeared. It forked and spun the priest around, heavily wounding him. Then, it arched on down the line of the defenders, throwing archer bodies this way and that off of the walls. She let loose her final one down the other line of archers. Again, a great many were hit and fell to their deaths.

In any battle, there comes an unspoken point where the opponent's will to fight breaks. Here the enemy was taking massive casualties yet giving almost none. With the nearly simultaneous loss of both their mages and their leader, the remaining cavalry routed. No words were spoken; the men simply turned their horses around and galloped off, out into the foothills, not even looking back. Just as fast as the battle had started, it ended. An eerie silence fell upon the battlefield, filled only with sporadic moaning from the badly wounded. Mandy, Sir Thomas and Lonnie sat in their saddles gasping for breath; they had put forth a tremendous exertion of strength.

Darless, covered in her opponents' blood, slowly flew back to her horse. She and Alison said nothing, but looked all around, totally alert for treachery. It would not do for a wounded enemy to stealthily rise up and stab them in the back. None made any such moves, rather the opposite. Some of the less badly wounded came to the assistance of those less fortunate. Slowly Mandy had the party move to the right and then forward, bypassing the huge number of fallen fighters, who lay in their direct forward path. Slowly they rode closer to the ominous entrance, the black scorpion.

She instinctively halted the party when they were about five-hundred feet from the gaping mouth entrance. From here, the stinger arced menacing overhead, as if poised to strike. Jon's fears about this device were well founded. The scorpion's tail was a metal contraption that could move, striking downward onto any that entered the single-file, tunnel-like door. There seemed to be no other way into the fortress. "Suggestions?" she asked wearily.

The blood-lust gone from her eyes, Darless leaned over toward Alison and whispered. The archmage nodded and turned around toward Thea, "I need my staff for a moment, Thea." She barked her command word; the staff flew out of Thea's grip and landed precisely in Alison's outstretched hand. She and Darless faced the granite fortress wall and the black scorpion entrance. In unison, both began a magical chant; both were using stored magical energies that still remained in their staves to power the spell. Though Jon did not understand their language, he remembered hearing those sounds; by the time their spells discharged, he guessed their intended effect.

A glow of magical energies illuminated twenty-foot sections of the granite wall on either side of the black scorpion entrance. The perilous entry way was double illuminated by the intentional overlapping of the two transmute rock to mud spells. For an instant nothing happened. Then the intricate stonework turned into a vertical wall of soggy grey mud. Unable to sustain its weight, the sections collapsed downward and outward in a gushing flow of mud. Like a bursting dam, it swept bodies and boulders before it. A minute later, only the remains of the metal scorpion's tail could be seen some twenty-feet in front of where the entrance had been. Black and grey mud swirled together forming an intricate chaos pattern on the ground. They heard cries of "We've been breached!" echoing from the remaining defenders, who dashed toward the forty-foot opening in their impenetrable wall. Valiantly, some hundred archers attempted to form into a line to prevent the party from entering.

"Yahoo!" cried Mandy, "That's what I call a breech! Well done mages!" She was about to charge when Sir Thomas cautioned her.

"Wait yet a moment, Mandy. Someone in authority is still giving orders. See, they have enough command value to muster a defensive line in a very short span of time. Let's not be hasty," the paladin observed. His tone was deadly serious. She watched as the archers all notched arrows, preparing a deadly flight. However, the rain of death did not come. It became obvious that the defenders intended to let the volley fly when the party was much closer, where the damage would be far greater.

"Mandy, Sir Thomas," Alison barked, "what range do you estimate they will let them fly?" She was thinking rapidly. Sure, the three of them could soften the defenders up with several fireballs. However, there had already been sufficient carnage for her liking. Surely the defenders must realize that further resistance was utterly hopeless. She hated unnecessary use of force, deadly force.

"Well, if I were in command," Sir Thomas began speculating, "I'd give the first order to fire when we were about a hundred-fifty yards away. That way, they could have a good chance of getting three flights of arrows off before we are on top of them."

Mandy speculated slightly differently, "If I were giving the orders, I'd have them fire just as soon as we make any forward motion, hoping that a well-trained archer could get off four volleys before resorting to hand-to-hand combat. Either way, we are looking at a rain of three or four hundred arrows coming our way." Jon and Thea both uttered a curse, imagining that they could end up looking and feeling like a pin-cushion.

Meanwhile, Lonnie kept watching their rear. Stress lined his face; he fretted that the cavalry that had fled the battlefield would regroup and charge them from the rear, forcing them forward into the deadly hail of arrows. To his relief, such did not materialize; he could see no sign of them.

Alison glanced behind them at the senseless carnage. She hated this part. For a moment, she pitied the poor soldiers who lay wounded or dying behind them. There were hundreds. "What's this all for?" she muttered. As she turned her gaze back to the line of archers before her, she took a deep breath. She was the leader; the others were waiting patiently for her orders. In a moment, she knew she had little choice but to issue the attack command. There would be no hope for the line of archers; their fireballs would put an end to their threat before a single arrow was shot. "Why?" she asked herself. Her purpose was crystal clear with Metrarch and the demons. Likewise, with the Vyndocian cavalry attacks upon the caravan from Freetown, protection of lives made no other choices possible. But here, here they were fighting an unknown cult for unknown reasons. Men were dying, and for what purpose? Still she hesitated to give the final assault order.

In this long pause, Jon sensed her deep feelings, her hesitancy. For him, his mind still wide open, the pain and agony of those sprawled on the dry earth behind them screamed full volume. This was the part of adventuring he despised the most — all the killing — to his mind, needless killing. Jon first looked toward Mandy, her thought reflected in him: *What kind of a fool so orders his own men?* Instinctively, he moved his gaze to Darless: *Demons in human form.* Just then, from the corner of his eye, he saw a prairie dog wiggling their way, just in front of them, off to their right. As he watched it, the dog grew rapidly in size. By the time it approached Mandy, it had changed into a wart hog, slowly walking toward her, ever growing. He blinked only to see a wild horse stepping up beside her horse.

This unexpected appearance took but perhaps three seconds from start to finish. "Zagroot zounds! Where'd this horse come from?" a very startled Mandy wheeled her horse around in an attempt to block it. Too late, the wild black stallion had already moved into the center of the party passed her. Incidentally, the appearance of another horse in their midst did not cause swords to be raised nor drawn. Once somewhat hidden from the distant archers, the horse continued its transformation. All eyes saw the horse turn into middle-aged man carrying a staff.

Grave concern bordering on a panic, he said softly looking quickly at each of the party members, unsure who was in charge, "Friends, do not be alarmed. Hide me from prying eyes. I must have a word with you, quickly, before it is too late. I am Michael Sustarrie, the Brown Protector of the Dry Hills. I do not know who you are, but I do thank you for all you have done for my people trapped inside. But now you must flee before the Black Death is unleashed! Please, flee before it is too late!"

Alison spoke first, "I am Alison d'Ambrose, Archmage, leader of this party. We are on a long journey, just passing through here when we were attacked by these Black Scorpion thugs. This whole thing makes no sense to us. What could we possibly have done to get this cult into such a wanton bloodlust? And what is this Black Death you speak of?"

"It is the most unspeakable horror!" He kept glancing toward the line of archers some five hundred feet away. "Oh no! Look, it is too late. The Black Death has already been unleashed!"

All eyes turned to the breech in the fortification. Indeed, the long line of archers had already retreated back behind the walls. In their place, was a black wall. Whatever it was, it was moving. "Zounds! What is it? It is moving toward us, albeit very slowly," called out Mandy. Never in all her experience had she seen anything like this. Neither had any of the others, for that matter.

In a controlled panic, Michael urged, "Quick. Flee while there is yet time!" Since no one moved, he hastily tried to explain. "It is thousands and thousands of black scorpions — all under his control. They fan out and poison every living creature in their path! Now flee, please I beg you!"

"Hold on a minute," Jon asked incredulously, "You mean to say that that is a giant mass of scorpions?"

Michael nodded hastily. "And one man is somehow controlling them?" Jon added.

"Yes, the High Priest, Hector Bastiano. Please, there is still time; horses can outrun them!"

"I am not fond of scorpions, mind you. In fact, I have never really seen one up close, just dead ones in a museum," Jon explained. "I didn't think insects, I guess they are bugs, had spiritual beings in them. I guess they have a mind; all life forms have some kind of mind. Well, if he can do it, I guess I can too. Alison, if they get too close, let me know. We can flee, but let me take a stab at this."

"Okay, Jon. You've got a couple minutes before we have to flee. The rest of you — get ready to head west by south. Lonnie — continue keeping an eye on our rear, please," Alison requested. She whispered to Jon, "Good luck," but he was already concentrating, eyes closed, spanning the distance between them and the slow moving, mass of scorpions.

Jon let the pain and anguish of the fallen cavalry behind him slip into the background. He reached for the scorpions. *When I reach for a person, I can sense their beingness, the spirit that is the person. Horses are similar, though not much beingness there. Do insects have individuality? I cannot find anything, no minds! Now what?* Panic crept into a corner of his thoughts. *What if I cannot communicate to scorpions because there is nothing there to communicate with? Concentrate, Jon.* Still he found nothing. Suddenly, it dawned on him. *Wait, not concentrate! It is observe! Look, you fool, look at what is!*

Jon saw the minds now, thousands of scorpion minds, low order minds capable of just running an insect body. He perceived what was happening, those minds were being dominated, controlled, forced to the will of another person. He could not tell whether the mind in control had gotten into that position because of a priestly spell or whether it was a direct contact such as Jon often did with horses. The result was the same in any case. This other person was forcing this mass of scorpions to do his bidding. Jon attempted to intervene, to block that control, but to no avail, the person had a strong, solid line into the scorpions.

He realized that three things needed to be done simultaneously, if control was to be wrestled from his opponent. Jon placed into minds of Mandy and Darless: *Need help. Flow me your power. Mandy, please concentrate on throwing a barrier to this black communication line from him to the scorpions. Yes, like that. Darless, drill some energy beams back at the sender, the one at the other end of this black line, yes, blast him. I'll take over control of the scorpions.*

Nearly simultaneously, Mandy threw up a solid, mental blocking wall, chopping the solid line of communication that their opponent had with the mass of insects; Darless blasted energy back toward their unseen opponent back up that black line. Jon inserted himself as the new terminal on the solid line to the scorpions. Jon quickly sent the concept of: *You are now free of control. Escape. Run. Flee far from this place. Go resume your lives in peace.*

Alison, Thea, Sir Thomas and Michael watched the ominous approach of the Black Death. When the sea of scorpions was but a hundred feet from them, they could make out their individual bodies, moving across the terrain as a single unit. Alison muttered, "There are thousands of them! Get ready, Sir Thomas to lead Mandy's horse and her away when I give the signal. I have Jon's reigns. Thea, you get Darless' horse." The swarm of scorpions edged their way to within fifty feet of them. "Okay, everyone get ready. This is not working. Another twenty feet and we are out of here!"

Suddenly, the swarm stopped in unison. For an instant, to Alison, it seemed that time stopped, that the scorpions were thinking, if such creatures are capable of thought. Then, a chaos of dispersal occurred; scorpions crawled off in all directions avoiding any close contact with the large horses. Alison watched and the single unified motion was replaced by individual actions and movements. The scorpions scattered away from them in all directions, save back from whence they had come. "You did it!" she exclaimed. Sir Thomas sighed in relief. Thus far, he had come up with no ideas whatsoever on how to fight off thousands of deadly scorpions on the rampage and he was relieved that he did not have to do so.

Michael was dumbfounded. His voice failed him completely, though he tried to say some words, none came out. His eyes were very wide open, blinking excessively as if to try to disbelieve what he was seeing. The three broke their mental contacts and moved in their saddles, relaxing muscles that had tensed up under the strain.

All three looked at one and then the other. In unison, Jon, Mandy and Darless voiced their mutual revelation, "Communication goes by means of solid lines between us and the other person!" Jon tried to explain their new found observation to the others, "You see when we communicate with each other, we actually put out a line of intention toward the other person. We can actually perceive that line! It is truly amazing. I wonder how come no one else has observed that before. But it is really there, really!"

Jon's gaze met blank faces of non-comprehension from Alison, Thea and Michael. He saw at once they had no idea what he was talking about. "Save explanations for later," Sir Thomas interjected, "We are not through here. Something else comes. In the name of Ukko, what is that?"

"Oh my god!" cried Alison, glancing toward the breech in the fortress.

"Zagroot zounds!" exclaimed Mandy.

"What demonic creatures are these?" cursed Darless. The others merely gasped in shock.

Crawling their way swiftly toward them were twelve huge black scorpions whose bodies were at least twelve feet in length, not counting the arched stingers. Their claws were enormous, sufficient to crush even a horse! Where the scorpion heads should have been were the torso and arms and head of humans! Each monstrous creature moved on its own, picking its way around or over boulders, but still moving rapidly toward the party.

Scorpions of this size could move very quickly. In less than a couple minutes, the first of these monsters was within fifty feet of them. This close, Jon could see the immense agony in its face. The nearest freak of nature begged them, "Please kill us. Have pity on us, slay us. Kill me now! End our torment, I beg of you!" Tears trickled down the cheeks of the man and onto its scorpion lower body.

For an instant, all had to work to control their war horses, who too were quite shocked at the sight. These horses were highly trained for combat, but facing such formidable, never seen monsters, they needed some convincing to stand their ground. Still they pawed the dirt restlessly with their front hooves. "Slay us fast; we cannot control all of the reactions of the lower bodies. The sting is deadly poison. Kill us fast," begged the half-man-half-monster sized scorpion.

"Zounds," exclaimed Mandy, "you can step on a normal scorpion. But these, I'll wager anything that they will take quite some doing to kill. Jon, get your instrument out and be ready to neutralize the poison if we get stung. It'll probably be a very fast paralyzation type poison." By now the other scorpion monsters were also quite close.

Michael thought he recognized one of the females, "Elaine, Elaine Rostdam, is that really you?"

Jon saw one female form begin to cry, she nodded and sobbed, "Michael, kill me. Kill me fast. I cannot bear this any longer. Please." Quickly, the fighters and mages conferred on how best to slay these hideous creations, how to kill them fast and avoid getting stung in the process, how to be the most humane.

Thea saw Jon quietly take out his feather from the Great Spirit, she heard him whisper, "Oh Great Spirit, it's Jon. I am ready to make my wish. I wish these poor folks and any others like them still trapped inside the fortress yonder were back in their normal human forms. Please undo this diabolical, inhumane transformation they have undergone. Thank you." Of course, the second the others heard the words "I wish," all turned toward Jon, knowing instantly what he was attempting to do. Jon had never cast a wish spell before. Jon never did any magic. Yet, he was using his most precious gift from the Great Spirit and using it on these total strangers! Alison instantly regretted not having taken the time to train Jon in the proper methods of stating a wish to the gods. Darless, likewise.

"Jon, what have you done?" asked Darless, though Alison wanted to ask that very question herself, but for different reasons.

"I'm trying to help these poor people. It's like some Frankenstein doctor's work. I'm trying to undo it, give them their lives back. Why? Did I do it wrong?" Jon replied.

Before any could reply to his question, a great ball of yellow light and energy descended upon the whole area surrounding the scorpions. An incorporeal voice asked, "Jon will you take on the responsibility of their mental states?"

"Oh yes I will! I swear to do anything in my power to help them all recover from this," Jon exclaimed without hesitation, directing his voice toward the yellow glow, not knowing where else to point it toward.

The deep bass voice said, "I knew you would. These are all that remain alive." The yellow energy grew so bright that none could look straight at it, all eyes turned away. In a minute, the glow vanished just as suddenly as it had come. When the party looked back, they saw twelve men and women lying naked on the ground. No signs of scorpion bodies were to be seen. All were unconscious.

Mechanically, Jon put his feather away and dismounted. The others followed suit. He ran to the nearest man and felt for a pulse. It was strong. "He's alive." The others quickly joined him. "We'd better get them some clothing or blankets. If they wake up this way, they will be embarrassed on top of everything else."

Michael quickly went from person to person, "I know about half of these folks. They are from around these foothills. I believe that they all were reported missing quite some time ago. I know for a fact that Elaine here has been gone for nearly two years. She just disappeared one day from her homestead, leaving her small baby behind."

"Here, start wrapping them up with these blankets," Lonnie interrupted; he had quickly retrieved a pile of them from their spare gear on one of the spare horses. Carefully, the dozen were wrapped up, while Mandy and Sir Thomas carried them to a central area fairly clear of small stones. All remained safely asleep or unconscious, she was not sure which.

While they attended to these rescued people, Thea stood guard, watching the horses, the fallen defeated enemy cavalry, and the as yet untaken fortification. Interestingly enough, she saw many of the remaining archers throw down their bows and walk out of the breech in the walls. In small groups, they went north or south; none made any advance in their direction. Thea thought it best to just let them go.

When Jon came close to the horses to get some water, she pulled his arm, "Jon, did you notice one important thing about your wish?"

"Er, no, Thea. It did work though," he replied, fetching several cups and a canteen from a saddle bag.

"Your feather," she pointed out, "Your feather is still intact. Your wish did not use your wish gift. I think that you should have Archmage Alison examine it to verify that it will still work. I think you still have your wish feather."

"Hum, Mandy's turned to dust after she used it, didn't it," he said realizing the import of her observation. "I wonder how come mine didn't?"

"I think," she said stretching out her words, "that you got a free wish from the Great Spirit! That's what I think."

"Well, I did promise to help these people overcome lingering mental anguish aftereffects," Jon mused. Then, a flash of insight hit him. "That's why, I'll bet anything on it!"

"What's it?" Thea enthusiastically and eagerly asked — all ears.

A small pout appeared on her face when Jon replied, "Later, I got to get them some water just now. Later, I'll explain." He hurried back to the group just in time as one man was rousing.

Michael, who knew him, offered him a drink. Shock lined the middle aged man's face. Though very weak from the ordeal, he felt his legs and lower body, even pinching them just to be sure this was not a dream. "Here, take a drink, Sam." The others remained unconscious.

He accepted the cup and drained it. Glancing at the others lying beside him, he asked feebly, "Are — are they okay as well?" Michael nodded. "How? How is this possible? I don't understand." Sam was completely confused.

"Don't know," was all Michael could say. "Are there others inside the fortress?"

The subtle reminder of the Black Scorpion brought a dire sense of worry to Sam's overstretched mind. Animatedly, he cried out, "Hundreds of others, they are imprisoned inside. Are they freed? My wife is in there." Michael shrugged an "I don't know" answer.

Hearing this, Sir Thomas whispered to Alison, "We should really head on into the fortress and finish this once and for all."

Tossing an errant hair back from her face, she replied, "I know. I've been kind of waiting to see what the enemy proposes to do next. Thea observed that the archers have deserted. If we are lucky, there may not be much left inside to fight, save their high priest and perhaps a mage or two. Jon and Darless are going to be needed here. Though it looks like the fallen cavalry are helping each other somewhat, I still don't trust them to not seek revenge. I am hesitant to leave Jon and Darless here by themselves. I hate splitting up our meager forces. We are strongest when we act as a team. But you are right, we need to finish this. If there are still hundreds imprisoned, we have to set them free! Suggestions?"

Sir Thomas was never short on these, decisions such as this he'd had made time and time again. "I'd suggest that you, Mandy and I go on ahead and finish the job. Lonnie can act as rear guard here protecting the others. I know Thea also knows how to help the others with Jon's mental process. That would be three of them doing that with Michael tending to the others and as a go-between. He seems to know them. Lonnie should be able to handle any surprise treachery from the defeated cavalry. We would have our two strongest fighters and archmage to flush out any enemies left inside."

"Your archmage is nearly out of spells," she grinned, "but I think you council wisely. I'll leave Thea my staff, just in case and take Darless's staff. You and

Mandy get ready and I'll tell the others." He nodded, eager to finish this business.

Alison explained to the others what they intended to do next. Darless raised the only cautionary flag, "If you run into trouble, let us know and we can be there instantly. You take care; there may be many traps waiting for you." Jon just gave her a kiss.

Next, Jon sat down beside Sam, while Darless and Thea did likewise with two others that had just awakened. "I'm Saint Jon Brown. I'm going to help you recover from this nightmare you have been under for so long. What is your name?"

"I'm called Sam Burgess, Your Holiness," he replied, uncertain just how to address a saint.

"Nah, just Jon, if you please, Sam. Now all I want you to do is to recall just when your misadventures with these Black Scorpion men began. Got the mental picture where it begins?" The man nodded, grimacing and clenching his teeth. "Okay, now I want you to move through these events and tell me what is happening as you go along." So it began. He heard Thea and Darless softly saying similar words to two women nearby. He knew that this would be a long and arduous therapy session. He placed the thought into Lonnie's and Michael's minds to prepare a large dinner. Though he could not see the young paladin's face, Jon knew Lonnie had already thought of this. Jon smiled encouragingly and listened intently to Sam's description. It was not a pretty tale; he knew it would not be.

Two hours later, the three ended their sessions for a lunch break. The abject horror that their three patients had endured for the last twelve to fifteen months had been diminished, but only somewhat. However, this was all that the three patients were capable of handling for the moment; they were totally exhausted — mentally, physically, and spiritually. Further, their bodies were overly tired and malnourished, prompting Jon to issue orders to Michael to make sure that all twelve victims were given plenty of nourishing food for the foreseeable future and to get plenty of sleep. At this moment, he had no idea how this would be accomplished out here in the middle of nowhere.

Jon, Thea and Darless greatly appreciated the lunch that Lonnie had prepared, quite timely indeed. Since, the others had not returned from the fortress as yet, the three began their assists on the next three victims. The sun was slowly sinking, when they finally finished their initial assists on the last three. All twelve victims had been able to at least take the edge off of their mental horrors. Meantime, Alison and the others had returned and the smells of dinner filled the chilling air. Jon noticed that their numbers had grown over the afternoon. Well over a hundred folks now formed a rather large encampment here on the high plains. Several bonfires crackled enticingly.

During the afternoon while the others were occupied, Lonnie assigned himself the task of cleaning up the cavalry battlefield, burying the dead, salvaging weapons, valuables, gear and stray horses. He found enough undamaged clothing to fully clothe the twelve victims plus many others in need who had come later in the afternoon — prisoners whom Alison had freed. On her return trip from the fortress, Alison brought out a great store of food and firewood — two wagon loads, in fact, along with cooking utensils and the like. Sir Thomas drove another wagon loaded with bedding and firewood, but he could find no tents for shelters. Camping under the stars here in the chilly high plains was not a serious problem for these people who lived in this realm. They were accustomed to it, as long as they had bonfires and blankets aplenty.

The party sat on stones in a circle around a crackling bonfire eating dinner and discussing what they had discovered. Jon related what they had learned from the twelve victims.

"Essentially, they all tell the same basic story. At least a year ago, cult riders kidnaped them from their homes and fields bringing them to this fortress, which is called Shill, headquarters for the Cult of the Black Scorpion. The evil priest, Hector Bastiano, rules the cult with an iron hand, poisoning or stinging any deserters. Together with his right hand man, Mage Alberto Hortus, he invented a procedure for turning a human into a giant half-scorpion by coupling magic with his "healing arts." Only one in ten actually survives the process, and those that do survive the surgery generally went mad and had to be killed. Only recently has Hector managed to keep his victims from going crazy. Apparently, he found that if he drove them into a deep mental apathy, they would tend to obey his orders, barely. The nightmare that these folks have endured has left the deepest psychic scars that I have ever seen, short of the Abyss!" Jon continued, "We have them slightly stabilized at the moment, but they are going to need a whole lot of assist sessions, if we are going to get them back to anything resembling normal."

Thea added in a very somber voice that lacked her usual unbridled enthusiasm, "A very great deal of assisting, I should say. *Never* have I heard of such barbarism. How could one human being ever *do* such a thing to another?"

Her answer came from Darless, who said in a soft, low, serious voice, "You have to loose all of your own self-respect first — all of it. Jon, we are going to be at this a very long time indeed."

"Let's give them another day or two," he suggested, "that will not really slow down our mission that much. If we can get them fairly stable, they can return home. Later on, we can check up on them and continue as needed. How does that sound, Alison?"

"You got it!" she replied without hesitation. "After what they have gone through, we have no choice but to do what we can to get them able to at least live again. Perhaps once Darless has her college going, we can bring them all there for as long as it takes to erase all this madness. This has been a day of profound opposites. We have seen the lowest levels a person can sink to and the highest level one can achieve in helping his fellow man. Jon, Thea, Darless, I am so very proud of you; you are working miracles! Thanks. I'll help out tomorrow as well."

"We all will," Mandy volunteered, gesturing toward the paladins, "if only you will show us what to do." Jon could not turn down their offer, the faces of Lonnie, Sir Thomas and Lonnie told all.

Michael looking totally perplexed ventured, "How come you are doing this for my people? You don't even know us? Why? You were even granted a wish from the Great Spirit. I just do not understand you. Are we to repay you? If so, how?"

Sir Thomas was about to launch into his Holy Paladin explanation; Alison opened her mouth intending to explain good versus evil, but Jon beat them all. "Michael, we are indeed strangers here in this land, just passing through on a mission of our own. Until yesterday, we had never heard of this Cult of the Black Scorpion. When I saw what Hector Bastiano did to these poor people, when they begged us to be slain and put out of their misery, I just could not pretend I had not seen it. It offended me so deeply that I would never be able to live with myself if I had not acted to try to rectify that horrible act. I used my Wish Spell from the Great Spirit to undo their physical transformations. I am called Saint Jon Brown, the Redeemer, because I have discovered a method of apparently erasing bad memories from a mind so that they have no further effect on the person — in essence, redeeming their lives."

"Though I really am just a musician, I find myself also in a position to be able to *really* help another person. And is that not the true measure of a person? Can they and do they help their fellow man or woman? At least I think that is the measure. You see, Michael, I and my friends are doing this to help these twelve survivors recover and be able to live a fruitful life, free from the terror of their experience, free from hideous nightmares and such. We do it because we *are* able to help and because we want to help others in need, nothing more — no ulterior motives, no personal agendas, no remuneration expected, no future commitments, no godhood adulation, no IOUs, no nothing. A simple 'thank you' is more than enough." The women glowed admiration toward Jon; even Sir Thomas smiled, he could not have put it any better.

Humbled, Michael replied, "I call that 'greatness.' Out here in these lands, survival is tough at best. I'm afraid to say that we don't see enough 'greatness' in men. After today, I will personally see that the tales being spread about you properly reflect your motives. It stands as a lesson to us all. We shall never forget it."

With the air cleared, Sir Thomas proceeded to describe what they had done and found earlier in the day. Entering the fortress through the drying mud breech, they found the town nearly deserted. The high priest, Hector, was dead, stung to death by well over a hundred scorpion stings, his face and hands swollen to twice their normal size by the poison. His mage Alberto had been killed by collapsing rubble. The other mage, who had been in charge of the defense of the fortress, had been slain much earlier by Alison's magical lightning bolts. Fully fifty bodies lay dead within the walls, all were carefully searched. Once the three were convinced that no one still defended the fortress, they began to explore the small town which lay behind the walls, cradled at the mountain's edge.

Most of the town lay underground in vast caverns. There, caged like rats, were nearly a hundred prisoners. Some, they learned, had been marked for the "Holy Conversion" into giant scorpions. These prisoners they freed and sent them out to join up with Michael.

They found vast stores of food and other living needs for probably six hundred people. Siege mentality ruled; the paladin estimated that the cult could hold out for at least six months!

However, when they got to the deepest underground rooms, the going became perilous. Guards and traps lay everywhere. Sir Thomas even got his hand slightly burned when opening a door before Alison defused the fire trap. "Truly, Slickster is a thief by training; I realize that now, though I never could admit it before. My ego. Today, I learned just how much I owe him for his services in the past! He does have a good heart and he certainly knows his traps!" He continued his explanation. "The treasury was heavily guarded. Alison had to defuse at least three different traps. However, when we found the 'operating room,' I smashed all of the equipment into rubble." Several chuckled at this point.

In the two mages' rooms, we found numerous books on magical things and some other gear. In the priest's room, we found many documents among other items. One of these, I hold here." He held aloft a parchment scroll. "This explains a lot. It is a letter from Threngold himself, probably in his own hand, requesting the cult to capture or kill all of us. The brown dragon was offering a reward of five hundred thousand gold pieces for us, dead or alive. So that explains why they were after us, greed."

"I think that Threngold not only knows about us, but is also very, very worried about us!" Alison commented. "I just hope he doesn't fly the coup before we can find him."

"I don't think he will leave just yet," Mandy observed. "We have something that he really wants." She didn't mention the golden statue — too many ears were around.

"Anyway, it is going to take us several days to sort out all of the stuff we have acquired, decide what to do with it all and so on," Alison observed. "To say nothing of the treasury we found. How much was it, approximately, Sir Thomas?"

"I lost count several times," he apologized, "but at least three hundred thousand gold coins worth, not counting the gems and few pieces of jewelry."

"Michael," Alison turned to the mage, "all this money probably originally comes from your people — from raids and extortions and the like. We would like you to take all the coinage and find a way to return it to those who need it. Help compensate the victims for their torture and such."

"I — I — I don't know what to say!" he blurted, dumbfounded at the incredibly generous offer. No one had ever made such a noble gesture to him before.

"Then, just say 'yes'," the archmage answered for him. "Besides, we really don't have any need for the money. Also, there is still a huge amount of ordinary stuff in the fortress complex. Perhaps tomorrow you can take some of the more able folks and see what of it may be serviceable. Spread it around to those that can use it. There are many wagons, grain, blacksmith supplies and horses — we got more horses around here than we could possibly use! We are only going to keep the magical items we found and the gems. The evil magical things have already been destroyed. None of us want those items to ever again be used against men and women! Sir Thomas and Mandy were most effective in destroying them," she grinned at them. They both smiled back. Jon caught a brief glimpse of a mental image from Sir Thomas — the Holy Paladin had chopped a evil priestly staff in half with his Holy Blade. He'd used far more gusto than had actually been required. Jon smiled.

"And now it is presentation time," Alison could scarcely contain her excitement. "Thea please step forward." Her apprentice did so, her eyes humbly staring at the ground, uncertain of what her mentor intended. She was not used to being singled out like this, she fidgeted a bit nervously. Something was up and she did not know what. "Mage Thea, for your services in the name of good, I hereby present you with your first Staff of Power!" Alison handed her the staff that previously belong to Alberto. "It is currently drained of all power and has no evil about it. Charge it up and have it serve in the cause of good." Thea's eyes opened wide, her mouth opened but for once, no words came out. "Staff, bond now with Mage Thea; serve her well," commanded Alison. She handed it to Thea.

As Thea's fingers grasped the highly polished mahogany, she felt a tingle of magical energy. In her mind, Thea thought she heard the staff say, "I am yours to command; I serve Mage Althea Westfold." Tears formed and trickled down her cheeks. She, Thea Westfold, was now a force to be reckoned with — she was truly a mage of power. Finally, she found her voice sufficiently to mutter "thank you."

"And here are two magical rings, Thea — one confers invisibility and the other stores up to four magical fire ball spells or their equivalent in power. May you seldom need them, but in times of need, my you never lack such spells," Alison teased her apprentice. This was one magic user who truly excelled in the use of fire-based spells. She knew that each mage preferred their own particular types of spells. Thea was enamored of all kinds of fire-based spells, more so than any other mage Alison had ever known.

Alison continued, "Mandy, you get this decanter of endless water; I know you can use it in your castle."

Mandy grinned; it would be a very useful item to have indeed. With a twinkle in her eye, Alison said, "Darless, Thea, we've got more spell books here!" Both knew what that meant; a chance to learn some new spells, broaden their knowledge of the mystical arts.

"Jon, I have a very special item for you." She swung a greyish cloak over his shoulders and fastened it at his neck.

Jon muttered, "It's not very colorful — a weird fabric — not very warming."

"Silly, it is magical cloak that makes your position in space appear different from where your body really is. Sir Thomas, try to throw a punch at him." She had to really coax him to do so. Reluctantly, he took aim and swung the gentlest punch at Jon's chin. However, his fist missed completely, as Jon was not where the paladin's eyes told him Jon as located. Both men began laughing.

Mandy also took a swing at him and missed. "Now that is pretty darn amazing!" she exclaimed. "Wearing this, you are going to be very hard to hit in a fight, Jon. Great protection indeed!"

Not to be left out, Darless got up and walked over to Jon. "Mind if I try?" she asked.

"Sure go ahead and hit some air," Jon teased. He was really enjoying this new cloak, feeling completely impervious. She closed her eyes and landed her fist on his chin. "Ouch, that hurt!"

"See silly, you are not impervious," she teased back, "just harder to hit. The secret, you guys, is to close your eyes and not be deceived by what your eyes tell you." She sat back down with a smug look on her face. Everyone roared with laughter; Darless could not hold her serious mein any longer and laughed along with them.

Alison then distributed several magical rings of protection, some arm bands of defense, and let the others pick from a pile of assorted magical weapons and several wands. "It never hurts to have a spare blade in case one breaks," she added. "The ones you don't want, I'll take back to arm our castle guards, if you don't mind." Finally, she gave everyone a small pouch filled to capacity with gemstones. Jon had no idea of their worth, so Alison whispered, "Each one is about twenty-thousand gold coins worth, as near as I can estimate." Jon was speechless.

While they were stowing their new gear, Michael approached Alison. "May I have a word with you?" She nodded. "You are the leader, correct?" Again she nodded, wondering where this was leading. "I could not help overhearing that you are looking for Threngold, a brown dragon. I've seen a brown dragon flying east or west a dozen times or so. I have a fairly good idea of its general flying origin point up in the Desolation Range. I don't know if this brown is the same one you are looking for, though, but it is the only brown I've ever seen anywhere. I just had an idea that might help. May I see that letter from this Threngold, or smell it actually?"

Hope surged in her, "Sure!" She retrieved it from Sir Thomas, and handed it toward Michael. She wondered what he meant by smelling it, though.

He refused to take it. "No, you open it and hold it out toward me. I am a master of the art of transfiguration — that's my magical devotion. Let me change for a minute and smell the scroll." Before her eyes, his body quickly morphed into that of a large mastiff, a large black war dog with huge fangs and enormous feet. He cautiously approached her outstretched hand and the scroll and sniffed and sniffed. Then, the huge dog morphed back into the familiar human form. "Ah, yes, dragon scent is strong. We can follow it."

"What do you mean?" asked Alison, who was not quite sure what he meant by his pronouncement.

"I am also a breeder and trainer of dogs. You see, I love dogs — all kinds of dogs. They are my best friends —

my sole love in life. The dragon's scent is still strong on the parchment. I can direct my trackers to that particular scent and order them to follow. No matter how the brown has disguised its lair, my dogs and I will eventually find it. Please allow me to contribute to your cause as I am able. I would be honored to be of some small service after all that you have done for us."

"Thank you!" she replied without any hesitation. "You don't know how good that sounds to my ears!" Another idea struck her, "But do we need to go quickly or do we still have time to help all these folks here? I mean does the trail or scent diminish with time? I'd hate to lose this opportunity to easily find his lair. But I will, if it means abandoning these people just now when they really need our aid."

"We've plenty of time. The main thing is to not contaminate the scroll with other scents. Don't let others handle it any more, if you can," he replied. "I live a good twenty miles south of here. It is going to take a couple days to get everyone sorted out, the gear, the supplies, the money and so on divided up. Most of those you have freed are in pretty good shape. We can let them be the bearers of the goods back to their respective farmsteads. Still, it is a long day's ride to get to my home from here. I did not bring a horse with me because I was spying on the cult. I flew here as a giant falcon. Besides the dragon scent is overpoweringly strong. My dogs will have no trouble tracking it."

"Terrific, Michael, just terrific!" she replied. "You know I think that you should know why we are seeking this brown dragon. Got a half hour to spare?" she teased. She relayed the highlights of the destruction of Castle d'Ambrose and the abduction of her parents and their current quest. He sat spellbound throughout, amazement plastered over his face.

Then it was time for sleep. All the mages were completely out of spells, all three staffs held no charges.

Tonight, there would be no magical mansion. Sir Thomas and Mandy quickly setup bedrolls for everyone. The paladin kept saying, "See, I told you we would need all this extra gear, and you kept saying why bring all this stuff?"

Jon teased, "Yes, 'Be prepared' — that is a good motto. I've heard it used before in my world." He carefully did not say by the Boy Scouts. Still, he found sleeping outside under the stars both elating and painful. In every position he assumed, a rock found its way into his body. Further, the starry heavens were so spectacular that he found it difficult to fall asleep. He realized that he had been missing gazing at the heavens. Jon resolved to do sleep under the stars more often.

With everyone sleeping outdoors, Sir Thomas efficiently setup three hour watches for himself, Mandy and Lonnie. He was glad to be on home ground, familiar ground once more.

Chapter 12 Threngold

The next day, Sir Thomas and Michael led some twenty-five of the fittest men back into the fortress to scavenge for anything useful. By day's end, they had confiscated two dozen wagons and had them filled with salvaged goods. They also made plans to divide up the spoils among all persons who had been harmed by the cult over the years. A council was formed to handle the details.

Jon taught Lonnie and Mandy how to deliver an assist session and together, the six continued the previous sessions on all twelve victims finishing the last by lunchtime. After eating and comparing notes, they began another round with each. It was during the first afternoon session that Thea ran into trouble with her patient. She broke to get help from Jon.

"She just keeps saying 'I can't see anything' — over and over. We were doing well until we hit this barrier. What do I do now? Is this a failure?" she asked confused and a bit letdown because she was not succeeding.

Jon took a break from helping Sam and visited Thea's patient named Elaine. "Hi Elaine, I'm going to have Thea continue and I will watch. Is that alright with you?" The woman, who was in her late thirties, looked like she had been crying. Her face was contorted from the pain of her ordeal. Her eyes stared vacantly at the ground, but Jon thought he saw her nod her head slightly. "Okay, Thea, continue where you left off." She did and asked Elaine to go to the beginning of her ordeal. Yet, all she got for a response was a whole body jerk followed by a wailing of "I can't see it." He thought for a moment. Her body motion was evidence that she had contacted the mental images. Like the others, they were still running through the long months of their body mutilation and transformation. "Oh how silly of us!" Jon thought suddenly grasping what was happening. He whispered to Thea, "Ask her if she can see an earlier image that is similar to what that she is looking at. It's coming from an earlier one."

Thea did as she was told. Elaine brightened up at once, "Why yes, yes. Something's there, but I don't know what it is. I keep hearing 'I can't see it' over and over." So Thea had her run through it and tell her what was going on. Jon stepped back leaving the session in Thea's hands, but he kept alert to see what happened. "It's dark. I can't see anything. It's warm. My head hurts worse and worse. I feel pressure all over my body. I hear someone saying 'It's coming' and another voice answers 'I can't see it!'" Suddenly, Elaine opened her eyes wide in total surprise! "It's my mother and her mid-wife, Rose. They are talking. I'm being born! Now it makes sense. I couldn't see anything. Mom was saying it's coming. And Rose kept saying she couldn't see it!"

Thea had her run through the images several more times; she found herself getting a lesson on child birth. All of a sudden, Elaine began laughing uncontrollably. Between fits of laughter, she explained how she had been terrified all of her life about going blind. She would get these migraine headaches along with the certainty that she would soon not be able to see a thing. And now all that was totally gone! No more headaches, no more panic and no more worry over her eyesight. She laughed on and off for the rest of the day. Thea beamed and glowed for the rest of the day. She had just performed a major miracle and was proud of her accomplishment.

While the others did not have such huge wins as Elaine had, the remaining eleven did improve substantially, bit by bit. By dinner time, all felt calm and at peace for the first time in nearly eighteen months. While the horrors were not totally eradicated, they were greatly reduced. Jon knew in time they would be completely gone, another day or two, he hoped.

That was indeed the case. In three days' time, all were on the road once more. Jon had charged the others to look after each other and the twelve. He promised that he would return later in the year to check up on them. Anyone who had any lasting effects from their captivity was promised additional assists at that time. He explained that Darless was setting up a college to teach this method to others so that there would be enough people to deliver the assist sessions to all that needed it. This sufficed. Many others had been asking about also getting some of these assists, after word spread about the phenomenal success Elaine had had.

On the third day, the party, along with Michael, mounted up and watched the dozen wagons roll off in all directions, save toward Desolation, accompanied by hundreds on horseback. No one had to walk home. Like the spokes in a tire, they spread out over the high plains, these foothills of the Desolation Range. Michael, now riding one of the confiscated horses, at last led them off southward toward his home. A day's ride it was, though quite picturesque, paralleling the start of the tall mountain range.

Dusk was drawing near as they crested another ridge and spied the thin curl of smoke coming from Michael's chimney. Cradled in a craggy notch with a grove of stunted gnarly oak trees stood his large stone house and kennels. When they were withing a half mile, numerous dogs announced their arrival. He had left his assistant dog trainer, Sam Trueblood, in charge while he was gone. As they approached, Sam stood beside the open door awaiting Michael's arrival.

"Hail Michael," he called out over the din of the dogs, "All's well here. I see you have brought company. Should I kennel the dogs?"

"Hi Sam. No, they'll want to greet me," he replied. Turning to the others, he added, "If you don't like dogs, stay mounted. If you dismount, you will most definitely get a warm greeting." Just as soon as he set foot on the ground, twenty-five dogs all rushed him to say hello. As usual, he was besieged with numerous, slurpy dog kisses. He loved it. Jon, too dismounted. And at once, three dogs came to sniff, wagging their tails rapidly. Jon petted them so more came to see him too. Now he had six dogs all wanting attention from him at the same time and he did not have enough arms to go around. Jon laughed as he attempted to pet each one. He noticed that all were very well behaved. None growled at the others. Michael had done a really good job with them.

Seeing Jon doing well with all these dogs, the others decided to dismount as well. Of course, they were dutifully sniffed as well. Unlike Jon who had knelt down to the level of the dogs, they stood tall avoiding their friendly tongues. Jon laughed as he had both of his ears thoroughly washed and his chin cleaned several times. "These are great dogs!" he exclaimed. Michael smiled.

"Watch this," Michael said, unable to resist showing off just a bit. "Seth, Fred, stable horses," he commanded in a normal tone of voice. Instantly, two black and white, medium sized, long haired dogs rushed into action. By barking and nudges, in less than a minute, all ten horses were standing in their own stalls in the barn, ready to be unsaddled and fed.

While Michael stooped to pet Seth and Fred, the others echoed, "Amazing! Unbelievable!" and similar kudos. Neither Jon nor the others, save Alison and Mandy, had ever seen a working dog at work. To them, this all seemed almost unreal, magical indeed. "These are my two best herding dogs," he explained. "We'll use others for the tracking tomorrow. After you take care of your horses, come on inside and wash up. We'll see what we can do for dinner." To the dogs he ordered, "Okay, dogs, kennel up. Dinner's coming." Twenty some dogs bolted for their own dog house. Jon noticed nearly none of the kennels had any doors or latches to keep the dogs inside.

Jon followed Michael, who paused beside a washbasin just inside the door. Both men washed off the dog kisses. The women merely smiled at them and looked around. This was obviously both a bachelor's and a dog lover's home. While the fireplace warmed the main central room, it nevertheless smelled like dogs, because two female mothers and their litters were curled up in opposite corners on straw bedding. "Ah Molly, you look well," Michael spoke to the black and white mother, who was washing her six puppies which definitely were not cooperating with her. They were trying their best to climb over the walls to get to Michael, tails wagging furiously. Bending down to them, he introduced each one. "This is Molly and her litter. The pups are about six weeks old now, doing well as you can see." They were all chewing on his shirt sleeve unwilling to let him leave them. "In the other corner is Betsy. Best not to bother her just now; hers are only a week or so old; the pups eyes have not yet opened. She's overly protective of them with strangers." As he stood up, the pups began whining and protesting noisily.

"Okay, okay," he consented finally. To his guests, he explained, "Look, the usual routine around here is: when I come in, I let the pups roam around freely for a while. Would you all mind it if they run around under foot, until they get tired?" He looked at their grinning faces. Seeing no objections, he opened the exit slat and out bounded all six. They began by happily sniffing his boots. Then, they fanned out to greet all of the guests. The pups were so cute that everyone just had to pet the young pups, they were irresistible.

However, one with three white paws and white rings around its eyes came over to Jon and literally adopted him on the spot. Jon, of course, gave the pup his full attention, talking softly to it. "I think this one likes me," he exclaimed. Whenever he moved the puppy followed him relentlessly.

"That's little Bessy," Michael replied, "I've never seen one take such a fancy to a stranger. I do think she likes you, Jon."

"Sup's ready," Sam called out from an adjoining room. Everyone made another trip to the wash basin before heading into the side room. Sam had managed to crowd enough chairs and boxes around the table to seat eight. He had already eaten and decided to play host and not crowed the table any further. Everyone took a seat, with the women claiming the chairs. As Jon sat down on a box, Bessy followed him and laid her head on his foot. Michael smiled at Jon who insisted on talking to Bessy. Alison could see that Jon was really falling for this puppy.

Sam served up a chicken stew. Everything was cooked in one large kettle, but it did taste excellent. To cleanse the palette, a glass of berry wine was the drink he served. "Don't worry about all the dishes, Sam," Jon said between mouthfuls, "I'll wash them. It's rather my job." He also snuck small pieces of chicken down to feed Bessy, who was enjoying herself enormously. True to his word, Jon washed up the dishes, while the others sat sleepily by the warm fire in the main room. Left alone, Jon picked up Bessy and put her on a chair beside him so she could see what he was doing. The puppy watched his every move as he did up the dishes. Finally, Jon with Bessy at his heels joined the others by the fire.

When he lay down on the floor, Bessy crawled up onto his lap and promptly fell asleep. Jon did not have the heart to move her. "I'm afraid I don't have remotely enough beds for you, only two, mine and the spare that Sam uses," apologized Michael.

"Actually, a few blankets and right here is just fine," Alison said dreamily. In spite of the chaos of bachelor's pad, it was warm, safe and somehow homey. She was relaxed and nearly asleep. Lonnie fetched their sleeping gear and they all curled up for the night. Bessy was still snuggling with Jon.

"Should I put her back with Betsy, Jon?" Michael whispered.

"Nah, she is fine here with me, if that's okay with you. If she wakes up and needs Betsy, I'll go put her in the kennel," he answered, rather unwilling to lose his new found friend. Jon and Bessy slept soundly together. Only in the early hours of the morning did Jon finally carry her and put her gently beside the other puppies and their mother. It was feeding time for the pups.

Jon awoke the next morning with Bessy licking his face. Startled at first, Jon began to say sternly, "Bessy!" At that same instant, several others began laughing at him. He snuggled Bessy instead.

"No peace with her," explained Michael. "Ever since the sun came up, she's been yapping and yapping! Had to let her out," he chuckled, obviously enjoying the effect. "Looks like she has really adopted you, Jon."

"Do you ever sell your pups?" Jon asked. "If you do, I would love to purchase her. She is adorable."

"In your case, I think there will be no living with her if you don't accept her! Yes, sometimes I do, but she is not yet weaned from her mother, needs a couple more weeks yet. Can you come back and pick her up later on?" Michael asked.

"You bet! You hear that Bessy, you are going to be my dog! Good girl!" Jon petted her and she snuggled him even closer, as if she understood.

"Well, you best find a way to explain to her that you will back to get her when she gets a bit older. Otherwise, there'll be no end to the troubles for Sam here!" he replied teasingly to Jon.

While the others held a brief council around the table, Jon explained to Bessy that he was on a trip and would come back to get her in a few weeks, when her body was just a bit larger. To his surprise, he found Bessy really did seem to understand what he was saying. Still, while he was still here, the puppy followed him incessantly.

"I'll bring six of my best trackers with us. From here, it's probably a good twenty miles to the entrance valleys of Desolation. I suspect we can narrow the search to the nearest four gorges, based on where I've seen the brown dragon flying," advised Michael.

"How do we get the dogs there?" asked Mandy. "Isn't that a bit far for a dog to travel? Can we carry them on horseback?"

"I can see you have never 'handled' a dog," he smiled. Sam choked a laugh in the background, as he was preparing the dogs' breakfast. He'd pictured Mandy on her horse valiantly trying to hold onto a wildly struggling dog. "The dogs can walk it, but we would have to go at a slower pace for their sake. I think I'll take a wagon with us to carry their food and them. When we get close, I'll ride and let the dogs roam to pick up the scent. Besides, I want to bring Buster along and he is way too old to go it all on foot. He's my very best tracker. If any can pick up the scent, it'll be him. It will be a good day's journey to the first gorge to try. I'll also bring along two guard dogs to protect the wagon while we are away from it."

By nine that morning, Michael was ready to leave. One draft horse pulled a strange looking wagon. Its bed was divided into dog sized bed boxes and one large supply chest. He brought along Buster, Billy-Bob, Hammer, Jen, Gus, and Rob to do the tracking. Fritz and Hummel were the guard dogs, both of which were two of the largest dogs Jon had ever seen! Their temperament was vastly different from the six trackers, decidedly unfriendly. Michael tied his riding horse to the end of the wagon, leading it along until he needed to ride. He gave some last minute instructions to Sam, telling him he expected to be back within eight days at most. Finally, they were off, slowly heading due west toward the distant sharply rising Desolation Range.

The lands around Michael's farmstead were fairly flat, though the land itself was always slowly rising toward the mountains. Rocky outcrops dotted the landscape along with stubby trees. A good deal of a hardy grass and other plants that Jon did not recognize gave a greenish hue to the land. Michael explained that this was the green part of the year. Up here on the High Plains, melting snow from the peaks of Desolation trickled down and out onto the plains. Flush with life giving water, all plants grew abundant here in spring. By early summer, most of the streams would dry up or flow only the barest minimum of water. Water holes would then be in great demand. Only those who were familiar with the High Plains dared to travel long distances during the hot summer and fall months.

As they rode slowly along, Jon, always curious, asked, "Michael, how come all of you live out here in this rather desolate or harsh environment? People are so far apart."

"We like it that way. We call ourselves the High Plains Pioneers. Out here, meeting another person is an important occasion; it's special. Bet you can't say that about where you are from?" Michael teased. "Besides, we are all pioneering spirits; we like fending for ourselves — builds character, self-reliance. Most of us High Plains folks hate towns. That is one reason towns are scarce around here; we like it that way. Also, I can practice my magic transformations undisturbed. Just try changing into a lion in a town!"

After a pause, he added, "I guess all this freedom has its drawbacks. Because we live so far apart, it was particularly easy for the Black Scorpion Cult riders to wreak havoc upon us. I've been thinking that perhaps we should form up a voluntary militia group to serve as a defensive force when needed. I would have tried to make one up before now, but because of the overwhelming strength of the cult cavalry, I figured that I would get no volunteers. Yet, now I think the idea might just work."

A little later, Michael changed the topic. "Jon, I've been meaning to ask you about Bessy. What kind of training do you want her to have? I mean, she could be trained for just about anything. She is a very bright pup. It does look like she will be a constant companion, you know; where you go, she goes. Do you know anything about training dogs?"

"Er, no I don't actually," he admitted. "But I just thought of her as my furry, faithful companion, a friend. I don't think I need a tracker or guard dog. Perhaps just let her be a companion dog. I'm sure she and I will work it out."

"Probably for the best," Michael agreed, "though I suspect that she will be somewhat protective of you in the end. From what I've seen of her so far, I'd say she'd give her life for you. Be a bit careful what you ask of her, she'd die trying."

"I know. I could tell that at once. Faithful, that's Bessy's goal," Jon acknowledged. "I lost my parents when I was very young; my late grandfather raised me and we moved around a lot. I only had one dog when I was a lad. Just being around all of yours has brought back to me just how much I miss having a pet."

"Well, she comes from herding stock," Michael explained. "Her lineage is that of a working dog. Her mother used to herd sheep, when I had some a few years back. Don't be surprised if Bessy tries to herd everything in sight." Jon grinned, it was an amusing scene he could not help imagining.

Steadily, the forbidding, stark granite peaks grew across the horizon before them. Ever the land continued to rise. True, they rode down one rise, but the top of the next rose ever so slightly higher. Michael skirted the occasional boulder fields to avoid any possible mishap with the horses or the wagon. Though he did not say anything about it, Mandy assumed that he intentionally avoided any homesteads along the way. Though if there were any, then they certainly stayed miles apart. Twice she thought she detected the faint traces of smoke clouds from a chimney.

While the ground tended to be relatively rough, hardy grasses waved in the slight breeze, growing rapidly while the abundance of spring moisture was plenty. Here and there, meadows bedecked in a rainbow of colors contrasted sharply with the ever-present grey granite walls rising straight ahead. Four times, they spotted herds of elk and deer migrating toward the high country. Game was plenty. Mandy constantly flushed rabbits and such from her path through the grasses. If they were not headed into a confrontation with a powerful brown dragon, she thought that this could have been a most enjoyable ride. The air was crystal clear and invigorating to her senses. She was out in the wide open spaces, which she dearly loved, second only to forests and rolling meadows.

Near sunset, they halted for the night. Alison cast her mansion spell and led them inside for protection. While Thea and Darless worked on fixing dinner, Michael let the dogs roam freely. Jon watched, admiring their grace and beauty as they playfully romped about. After dinner, Jon, inspired by the day's riding, gave them all a concert of recorder and lute music, while they relaxed and sipped their tea. This had been a remarkably relaxing day for one and all.

Sir Thomas and Darless even took an hour's walk about the area where the mansion's doors opened, enjoying a brief private time to themselves. They had covered nearly thirty miles. The actual search would begin sometime the next day.

By noon the next day, Michael led them unerringly to the southernmost gorge that he had intended to search first. He explained to the others, while parking the wagon and getting the dogs ready, that he had brought them to the southernmost possible valley entrance into the high Desolation Range. "We are probably south of where I suspect his lair might be. This way, if this is not it, we just move northward and try the next. If my hunch and observations are correct, one of these four should yield positive dragon signs. Now, Alison, give me that parchment please. It's time to scent the dogs and turn them loose."

Alison retrieved the scroll letter from Threngold and handed it to Michael. He called the six trackers to his side and spoke a number of strange words to them, letting them sniff the paper as much as they needed. He explained that, when he trained his dogs, he used a local dialect; most of those that purchased trackers preferred their own rustic language. Then, with a sharp command, all six dogs bolted off toward the entrance of this valley. Michael and the others mounted up and chased after the racing dogs.

Jon found the tracking dogs' behavior quite fascinating. "Watch ole Buster," Michael hinted as he saw Jon intently following them. While the younger dogs raced this way and that around the entrance of the narrow valley, the old veteran dog, Buster, walked toward the middle, raised his head and sniffed long and hard. The others were now way ahead of him; still he stood motionless, inhaling the scents of the area. At long last, he let out a yowl. The dog turned to look at Michael. "Look, Buster thinks this valley offers no scent. He wants to know if I want him to continue anyway." Michael hand signaled Buster to head on up the sharply rising valley after the scampering younger dogs. Buster obeyed, but only walked deliberately up the middle of the gorge. After an hour of fruitless search, the valley had narrowed into a steeply sided V-shape. Fresh snow melt trickled down its center. On horseback, they could go no further.

Reluctantly, Michael issued his stand down orders and the dogs, tongues hanging down, panting from their excited searching, walked slowly back down the valley. "On to the next one," commented Michael.

However, by the time that they got back to the wagon and traveled northward to the next valley entrance, the sun was getting low partially hidden behind the towering mountains. Shadows loomed long and ominous. Here they decided to camp for the night; this time, Darless did the spell-casting honors providing a safe mansion for the night. Another routine night passed uneventfully.

Bright and early the next morning, Thea announced, "Well, gang, it's May Day. Today we were supposed to all get married!" She had been keeping careful track of the days in her journal. The others joked a bit about their unusual wedding day. She added, "I'll bet this will be a very lucky day for us." Without further ado, they headed into this second valley.

Initially, this one was broader. Grasses grew tall on either side of a boulder-filled, bubbling stream the wound its way down the middle. When the dogs were turned loose this time, the younger ones darted off sniffing helter-skelter. Once again, old Buster stood at the entrance, head held high, sniffing long. This time he let out a solid bark and began moving determinedly up the center near the stream. "Ah, Buster has picked up his scent. While this valley may or may not be the one we want, the dragon has certainly been here at some time in the past. Buster has picked up his scent." Once Buster's confirming barking sounded, all the other dogs began barking, as they also recognized the scent of the dragon. Still they dashed this way and that sniffing and trying to follow the scent.

Jon watched Buster. The old dog moved slowly up the middle of the valley. Soon Jon noticed that he was taking the easiest, smoothest route up the valley, one which even he would have chosen had he been riding up the valley. "Say, Buster is really smart! I do believe he is searching along the route that one of us would most likely take," Jon exclaimed.

"Right!" Michael smiled, "Spot on. That's ole Buster for you. Smart one, he is. Best tracker I have ever come across. No wasted motion or effort. Sometimes I swear he really uses his brains!"

Unlike the previous valley, this one did not play out. While it did slowly begin to narrow, it twisted left and right, but always headed upwards. On and on they went, with the barks of the dogs drifting through the stillness of the land. Jon figured that if the dragon was anywhere about, he certainly would know they were coming!

After two hours, the dogs grew more excited; the scent was growing stronger. However, the valley grew more and more rocky and its sides pitched more steeply upwards. Progress became significantly slower and slower. The horses panted heavily from the exertion and the higher altitude. Try as they might, the horses continually lost ground to the more nimble dogs. Around noon, Michael called for a much needed break. Jon was exceedingly glad to dismount; for the last few miles, he had been clinging tightly to the saddle horn in a desperate effort to keep from sliding off of his horse. Mandy, he noted, along with Sir Thomas and Lonnie, rode normally, as if they were on flat lands. He spied Thea and Darless clenching their saddles as tightly as he, while Michael and Alison occasionally held on when their horses pitched upwards. So Jon asked Mandy, "I'm glad we stopped. Just when I was sort of getting used to riding a horse, we go up. How the heck do you keep on the horse? I keep sliding off the rear!"

Mandy looked straight at Jon and said as seriously as she could muster, "Glue, Jon. Glue. I put glue on my butt." He looked at her wide-eyed. He had not seen her putting anything on her rear, but then maybe she had when he was not looking. Suddenly, she could contain her mirth no longer. She and Sir Thomas roared with laughter. She laughed so hard her sides hurt, gasping for air.

"Great one!" the paladin managed to compliment her between laughs of his own. "Positively brilliant!" Soon, everyone joined in this relief of tensions, though Thea, Jon and Darless spent a good deal of time rubbing their arms, hands and legs, trying to relax taught, tense muscles. Still it was funny and they laughed too. Mandy never answered Jon's question, though.

While Thea fixed lunch, Michael proposed that they go the rest of the way on foot. Jon heartily agreed, before anyone could disagree. Of course, another round of laughter followed. It would be far easier on foot. The horses could rest up and the dogs could go slower as well.

Around one o'clock, they saw the first warning signs that they were on the right path. By now the dogs had just rounded a bend ahead of them and made a horrid racket, an incessant barking, which Michael said indicated that they had found something. The rising valley made for painstakingly slow going, and all were heaving for breath as they rounded the bend and saw what the commotion was about.

A giant mound of sun-bleached bones rose from the valley floor, entirely blocking passage. "Zagroot zounds!" exclaimed Mandy breathily, "What *is* this? Hold on, let me go first and examine it." The ranger paused for a moment to catch her breath and started her close examination of the pile. Michael called the dogs back and he and Jon petted them lovingly, acknowledging them for having done a good job of tracking.

"This one is a strange one to read," she explained as she worked her way around the pile and then into it, occasionally moving lifting a bone for closer examination. "Herd animals, deer, elk, horse. Bear too. No foot prints.

Some show deep teeth marks; some bones have been crushed by teeth. It looks like they were just dropped here from above. I'd wager a guess and say we have stumbled upon his garbage pile! You can come look for yourselves." They all did. "Probably over a hundred creatures. Guess we know what he has been eating for dinner."

"It's encouraging that he is not eating people," Jon said trying to sound encouraging as the stark reality of facing a powerful dragon loomed suddenly much closer.

After stumbling over the barricade, they continued their upward climb. Michael kept the dogs fairly close to him now, fearing for their safety should they encounter the dragon. An hour later, everyone stopped and fell silent. Yet another pile of bones lay before them. Here the valley ended and a nearly sheer granite wall rose to their left. A small stream fell down from above; a small waterfall so steep was the land. To their right, the rock rose but not quite so steeply and a trail like passage led twistingly upwards. What caused the sudden hush was the second pile of bones. Two rows of human skulls affixed to tops of rusting spears lined either side. The remains of the bodies lay piled in the center on either side of the rushing stream.

Mandy broke the silence, "I'd say this is his final warning to trespassers. You know, travel from here at your own risk. Michael, I'd say what we are very close to our destination. Well done to you and your dogs. We'd probably have spent weeks and weeks looking for this place."

"Well, here I leave you. The dogs can go no further. Buster is facing that steep, winding path, so that is the way to his lair, I'll wager. He's never wrong. What now?" he asked.

Alison issued the orders, "Many, many thanks, Michael! We should take it from here. You head back to the wagon. Take our horses with you and wait there for us. If we are not back by tomorrow night, you head home for we have likely joined these poor fellows."

They all shook hands with Michael and thanked him. Solemnly they watched as he and his dogs disappeared back the way they had come. "Now we must prepare."

"How on earth am I going to climb up there in my plate armor?" moaned Sir Thomas.

"First, we need to know where the entrance is at," spoke a determined Alison. "Then, we can teleport ourselves up or Jon can step us all up."

"Ah, it's time for a ranger to do her thing," teased Mandy. "Give me a few minutes." They watched as she concentrated mentally. Jon stared fascinated as she turned into a giant eagle right before his eyes. He really wondered just how she could do this transformation. With a great flap of wings, each nearly six feet across, she took flight, circling, spiraling ever upwards. She spiraled down a few minutes later. After a pinpoint landing, there was Mandy standing, smiling.

"Well, just up there a ways is a level patch of granite and yet another sheer wall. No sign of any opening anywhere around here for miles in all directions. If this is his lair, there is no visible sign of it," she reported.

Alison bit her lip. This had to be the right place, but where was his entrance? "Well, it's likely that he has it disguised or concealed. After all, when he is not here, what's to stop any intruder from ransacking his treasures? It must be up there," she said determinedly.

"Join hands, everyone. I'll get us all up there," Jon replied soberly. He wondered just how bad this encounter with a dragon would be. Would they meet their doom right here? "Mandy, concentrate on what that level area looks like, please. Okay, I got it. Here we go." He stepped them upwards. Sir Thomas was not quite ready for this and managed to stumble and clank headfirst onto the rock surface. Lonnie helped him back to his feet.

They stared at their surroundings. It was rather like being in an eagle's nest, Jon assumed. They were about ten thousand feet high on a ledge some hundred feet in length by fifty wide. On three sides, sheer drops loomed for an unwary foot. Ahead of them rose a nearly vertical granite wall, while far above them crested the peak of this mountain perhaps another five thousand feet upwards. "Well, there's the entrance," said Darless mater-of-factly. They all stared where she pointed, but didn't see anything but the sheer rock wall. "It's an illusion," explained the alu-demon. "Can't you see the opening ahead? It's about thirty feet high and twenty wide, rounded at the top." No one else could see it, try as they might.

Darless attempted to dispel the magic of the illusion, but to no avail. "Zounds," declared Mandy, "Are you sure it's really there? I sure don't see any opening. Looks like a solid wall to me." She stomped up to the wall and pounded her fist on to the observably solid granite cliff face. To her and the other's total amazement, her fist disappeared. So unexpected was the non-resistance of the obviously solid rock face, that Mandy lost her balance and fell forward onto the wall. Only her quick reflexes kept her face from meeting the ground just inside the tunnel entrance. Meanwhile, the others saw her fall into the rock and the top half of her body disappear completely. Only her dangling feet remained visible, like she had been cut in half. The ranger leaped to her feet, drew her sword and confronted the dimly lit tunnel. Of course, she was now inside the dragon's lair.

"Ah ha!" exclaimed Alison, "Okay, let's go." Sir Thomas needed no further encouragement; his steel clad shoes clanking on the rock surface, he walked straight into the wall, found himself inside the dimly lit tunnel and nearly fell over the ranger, who was nearly on her feet, knocking her back down onto the floor once again. She muttered another "Zounds." The big paladin managed to maintain his balance and fortunately didn't fall on top of her.

However, in the next instant, Alison followed closely by the others stepped into the tunnel, colliding with the immovable Sir Thomas. "Ouch! My nose," she whispered in a nasally sounding voice. "What's the hold up? Should I risk a little more light?"

"I ran into Mandy," he whispered back. "What *is* that stench?"

"Dragon, I reckon," Mandy whispered back in a disgruntled tone, rather annoyed at the circumstances. "You might as well shed some light on the tunnel. Only a small amount of sunlight is coming through the illusionary wall. Besides, he must know we are coming."

Alison chanted a command word; a dim globe of light appeared at the end of her staff, which she held aloft, slowly increasing its output as much as she dared. "Okay everyone, take your positions as agreed upon. Remember, if the dragon launches his breath weapon at us, remember to bunch up behind Darless and myself. We will get the force wall up in time, we hope." Thea and Lonnie fell behind them; their job was to bring the statue still inside its shipping crate within the portable hole. Jon came next. Alison and Darless stood in front of Jon and close together to coordinate their spells if needed. Only a short distance in front of them strode Mandy and Sir Thomas — both had their swords drawn and were ready for action.

The tunnel was likely the remains of an old volcanic vent with rough and uneven walls. It sloped slightly downward as it bore deep into the mountain side. Spider webs hung close to the sides; occasional unnamed bugs scurried out from underfoot. Their footfalls, especially those of the paladin, echoed noisily as they walked, amplified by the narrow confines. Jon heard

Thea whisper, "I'm really scared, Lonnie!" Jon could sense the fear in her voice. "I am too," was the young paladin's reply.

Jon turned to face them, "I think we all are!" He could sense it. Worry or fear emanated from all, just in varying degrees. "In the end, Thea, it is just how we deal with it and still press on is what matters," he attempted to comfort her.

"Like rats in a maze," whispered Mandy. "If he's asleep, we have a good chance of success. If he is just waiting to ambush us, look out." She shuttered recalling how she had been thrown about like a sack of potatoes by the demon d'Gritz. However, her simple observation sparked an idea in Jon.

Slowly Jon expanded his awareness outward, stretching forward into the darkness ahead of him. Though he could not actually see into the inky blackness with his physical eyes, he found he could sense the pressure or gravity or the solidity of the tunnel walls versus the openness of the tunnel proper. He later referred to it as a sort of mental groping along. Some distance ahead, two side passages opened up, one on either side. "Ahead of us, there are two side tunnels. Which way do you suppose we need to go," he both informed and asked. He quickly added, "I'm trying to provide an early warning detection system."

"Good going, Jon," whispered Mandy. "Tell you when we get there." It took them several minutes to actually arrive at the junction. The one on the right rose slightly as it arced off nearly thirty degrees from this tunnel. The left passage was quite small and dove down sharply. "It's either straight or right. The one on the right is probably too small for a dragon to navigate, but both of these look entirely plausible. I guess it is fifty-fifty."

"Wait a minute. I have an idea," Jon requested solemnly. "Let me see what I can perceive down each. I don't relish walking into a trap." The others were only too pleased for the brief respite. Alison didn't even think to tell him to be careful. Jon pushed his perceptions on down the tunnel straight ahead. After going a considerable distance, he pulled back. "Ahead goes on for a very long way. I think it gets hotter, and there are more adjoining passages. I'll try the right one." Again, he expanded his awareness down that tunnel, again finding nothing. "Same thing with this one too. More branches. It's like a maze, only it gets worse the further into it you go. One second longer, let me try the narrow one." Mandy was about to protest, but bit her lip, deciding better of it — of interrupting his concentration.

This smaller tunnel descended sharply at a thirty percent grade and it twisted and turned. Also, the air in it grew warmer the further down it he sensed. Suddenly, he felt the presence of a mind, a cold, foreign mind, and it felt him as well. He knew at once that he had felt that mind before, only he could not place it. Since it had detected his presence, any element of surprise was gone. Undaunted and willing to take a gamble to spare his dearest friends from a deadly combat with this dragon, Jon opened up a telepathic communication line to this mind. *Threngold, I presume. Saint Jon Brown, the Redeemer, here. May I have a word with you?*

Impressive that you found me so easily. Okay, I am curious. Say your word.

Jon chose his thoughts carefully, reminding himself that a dragon was a huge, powerful beast. *Despite appearances, we come in peace. We wish to return a golden, bejeweled statue of Tiamat to you — that is, if you are its rightful owner. In return, we wish only to ask you a few questions about an event to which you were party a long time ago. No matter what your part in that situation was, I promise you that we will take no actions against you.*

Connected so intimately was he that Jon could not help be read the flood of thoughts rushing through

Threngold's mind. Jon also realized in that moment, that, if he was so connected, he would know about any sudden attack that Threngold might decide to take even before the dragon began to execute it. That was a small comfort, a small security blanket. Thoughts of anger, rage, hatred and deep loss accompanied the receipt of the fact that they had his statue. That they were in fact returning it to him baffled him, confused him utterly. This situation had never, ever occurred to Threngold. He had not planned for this eventuality; he had never conceived that this could be. No one ever had obtained his property only to return it, ever. This caused Threngold an enormous amount of confusion. His reply was long in coming as a result. Questions? All they wanted was to ask questions? What kind of questions. About something he had done? But a long time ago? How long was that? He was one thousand, four hundred, sixty-three years old. At this point, Jon interjected the thought: *About twenty-one years ago or so.* He hoped it might calm the confusion of thoughts.

A catch. There must be a catch. He said they would not harm me whatever I did in it.

No catch. We just need some questions answered. I believe that they will in no way compromise you, but I cannot guarantee that. He hoped he was being honest.

After a long pause during which Jon picked up an enormous sense of total disbelief on Threngold's part, the dragon though, *All right. I consent. Come down the first small passage that heads steeply down. But wait five minutes before you start the descent. I will disarm all of my many traps. If you are lying, I believe you have seen the graveyard of all those who have dared to enter my lair. You will join them after I've eaten your meat.* Jon shuttered slightly as he received that thought, grim indeed.

"Okay everyone, I've found the dragon, talked him into meeting with us. Told him we were returning his statue to him in return for answering our questions," Jon finally hastily explained to the others, once he had broken his connection with Threngold and returned his awareness back onto his body and the others.

The exclamations were many and varied, but with all came a deep sigh of relief. The heavy veil of unspoken fear lifted from the others. "How'd you do that?" asked Mandy, before the others could collect their thoughts. She always reacted swiftly to changing circumstances as only a well-trained ranger could.

"I ran into his mind. He seemed to recognize me as soon as I recognized him, I think. He has a very foreign or strange mind, that much I can tell you. He was waiting for us behind a large number of deadly traps. I told him what our intentions were. I also promised him that no matter what he told us of his involvement, we would not harm him. I think that he does not really believe me on that point, though. Also, all those bones we found — it is the grave yard of all those who have entered here before. He said that he ate them first and tossed the bones into that pile. Grim sense of humor." Jon looked at Alison, "So Love, even if he did eat your parents, we cannot retaliate; I gave him my word." She nodded, though she found it difficult to do. The idea was so utterly despicable, but she did agree. He added, "He also told me to wait five minutes before we head down the small side passage. He said he was disarming his traps."

"I knew it! I knew it! Traps! He just had to have lots of traps!" exclaimed Mandy quite relieved to hear her worst fears confirmed. "If he leaves, something must be guarding his lair and treasures. I suspect we'd been all dead before we ever got to him! I *hate* traps!" she declared vehemently.

"Thank you Jon!" declared Sir Thomas. "For once I am eternally grateful for our musician. Lord knows what we would have run into in these other, more promising tunnels before we ever descended this one. It goes down so steeply that we surely may lose our footing and slide down to our untimely deaths! Jon, you probably have saved all of our lives. I owe you one." He was quite sincere. Jon nodded an acknowledgment.

Darless, who had been very quite ever since Mandy had accidentally fallen into the tunnel, finally opened up. She hugged Jon. "My thanks as well. I had a terrible feeling about this ever since Mandy fell through the illusionary wall. Call it a foreboding if you will. I feared to say anything that might add to our plight. I've never really felt much fear before, but I have just discovered how awful it is to be so afraid. It's rather disconcerting to a logical mind."

Alison, who needed this small passage of time to fully recover from the imagined images of the dragon devouring her parents and her finding out about it and having to restrain herself from seeking instant revenge, added, "Teamwork. We all do what we can to forward the group. When we confront him, I'll do the asking. Jon, you make sure he is telling the truth. The rest of you, feel free to jump in, if I falter or if you think of something that I've missed. I hope I don't falter now. I've waited twenty-one years to find out what really happened. Give me strength to succeed!"

"You'll do fine," Mandy comforted her, "Just fine. We'll all back you up."

"I know you all will," she answered softly, "it's just that I'm scared and worried that I might blow my *one* chance to discover what really happened."

"Relax, take a deep breath," Jon said. "The only thing that will defeat you is yourself. Just do not react to what he says — ask and get things clarified instead. Since I made the contact, I'll begin the conversation, open the door, and pave the way. Say how do we know when five minutes are up?"

"Hum, you know that is an awfully steep descent. If he greased a section of the floor, we would all slide down out of control. Perhaps we should rope ourselves together, just in case," observed Mandy, still not at ease about traps. They spent over ten minutes roping themselves together for the descent. Sir Thomas, the heaviest because of his armor, went first. That way, if he hit a greased patch and fell, the combined strength of the rest could arrest his fall. Mandy took the rear for her newly acquired gauntlets of giant strength could hold many of them if they fell. Jon went just behind Sir Thomas so that he could greet the dragon. Alison was right behind him. After fifteen minutes, they began their descent down this small side tunnel.

It was narrow, only about six feet wide at the widest. Worse, the tunnel was nearly circular in shape, an old volcanic tunnel flow, making footings awkward at best. Mandy was correct. After they had gone perhaps a quarter of a mile downwards, Sir Thomas encountered a greased section. His feet went out from under him at once and down he went with a loud crash of armor on stone, arms flailing uselessly in the air.

Like dominoes, the rope bit into the others, the heavy weight of Sir Thomas pulled Jon off his feet and down into the greased section as well. Only the combined strength of Lonnie, Darless and Mandy managed to arrest their fall. "Didn't I tell you!" gasped Mandy, as she pulled with all her might, holding the line firm until Jon and Sir Thomas regained their footing. Slowly she lowered each of the others over this treacherous passage. At last, Darless, casting her fly spell, transported herself and Mandy over the greased path. "Thanks. I'll bet he expects to see us arrive in a sliding rush at his feet. Well, I won't give him *that* satisfaction! Okay, lead on, Sir Thomas." They continued on down.

They did not have far to go. In a few hundred feet, the tunnel suddenly opened up into a very large cavern, well lighted by some twenty globes stuck in torch holders on the distant walls. All blinked, as their eyes adjusted to the sudden, unexpected increase in illumination. They arrived, in fact, right into Threngold's treasure room, work room, and bedroom, all rolled into one enormous cavern. The ceiling rose to several hundred feet at least, lost in the distance far above them. The chamber was roughly circular about three hundred feet across with three other exits, each much larger than the one they entered. In the center of the chamber lay an enormous mound of gold and silver coins, bracelets, cups and candelabra. Resting on top of the pile stood the largest dragon any had ever seen, fully two hundred feet from head to tail tip, fifty feet in girth and nearly seventy-five feet from toe to his back. He was exceedingly long and spindle shaped, unlike the white dragons Jon had seen.

His teeth were simply enormous. The claws on each of his feet measured a deadly six inches and sharp enough to slice armor as though it were butter. Although his wings were folded against his sides, Jon could see that two sets of smaller grasping claws grew from the bony supporting structure midway down the wings. The power deliverable by his massive seventy-foot tail could not be guessed. Here was a foe of enormous strength and power. Jon sensed the awe his companions emanated and knew that he had to speak first, giving them more time to grasp the situation. However, he nearly choked on the vile, sulfuric fumes from the dragon's breath. He cleared his throat and tried again.

"Greetings, Threngold. I am Saint Jon Brown, the Redeemer. Allow me to introduce the others." Threngold's deep brown eyes, unblinkingly, drilled into the fabric of each person as they were introduced, as if he could see their very souls. "This is Alison d'Ambrose, Archmage and our leader, who has the questions for you. This is Ranger Mandy Blackthorn, Holy Paladin and nearly an archmage herself, Darless. This is the Holy Paladin Sir Thomas and his fellow paladin, Lonnie Smith. Last, is Mage Thea, Alison's apprentice, though a strong mage in her own right. We have journeyed a considerable distance to meet with you and ask you some questions. On the way here, we seemed to have picked up something that we believe belongs rightly to you. Lonnie, will you and Thea bring out the shipping crate?"

While Jon was speaking, Mandy's eyes darted about the huge chamber, memorizing details, particularly the exits, should she need to lead them in a hasty escape. Along the wall to their left stood several book cases and the largest scroll rack she had ever seen, all overflowing with books and rolled up parchments. After a exit tunnel opening, came some kind of workshop. She was too distant from it to tell exactly its use, but she could see wood and stone tables with hand tools neatly arrayed. After another tunnel exit opening, to her right, ancient tapestries adorned the walls, along with chests and boxes overflowing with gems and jewelry of all shapes and sizes. They shone with a spectacular brilliance, rather painful to the eye. The third exit lay between tapestries and the crates. She also noted that she was standing on a crack in the floor, which ran in a straight line across the entrance they had just come down. Threngold noticed her noticing the crack.

He spoke for the first time in a very deep voice, but with an inflection they had all heard before but couldn't place. "The floor rises to make a wall; on the other side facing the tunnel are innumerable three-foot spikes. Any that has ever made it this far have been skewered, ready for roasting on the fire. Yes, I am Threngold, the Brown, Consort of Tiamat. Let me see the crate and its contents." His words, his tone of voice, though foreign of human emotion, yet held a power of command, of authority, not to be challenged.

Lonnie and Thea got the crate out of the portable hole and carried it before the dragon. Thea stepped back, holding her nose and grimacing from the stench so vile and strong this close to his mouth. Lonnie opened the case revealing the fabulous dragon statue in gold and gems. While Threngold did not say a word, Jon swore that if dragons have tear ducts, then he thought he saw a teary film come over the dragon's eyes, but only for a moment.

"You see, it is undamaged," Jon said seriously. "It does belong to you, correct?" They all knew that it did, that he had commissioned the Cambion demon to fabricate the statue. This was just a formality to avoid any misunderstandings.

"Yes, it is my statue. You speak truth — so far at least. Wisely I shall not ask how you acquired it, nor shall you ask my intentions behind it. All right. Ask your questions. No wait a moment." He spoke a command word and flash of magic encased his body. To their amazement, Threngold shrunk to approximately one half his size. "I don't like being quite that big; but the larger I am, the more dangerous I become. There now. This feels better. Ask, though I may not know the answers nor may I give the answers you seek."

Alison cleared her throat and took a deep breath trying to quiet her nerves. She wondered if Threngold could sense her knees banging against each other. This was the moment she had been seeking, searching, waiting for all her adult life. "Castle d'Ambrose, twenty-one years ago, nighttime, in Verbenloc. You were there and assisted in its destruction. You bore two humans away with you, male and female — my parents. Do you recall that time or need I refresh your memory further?"

Jon saw what had to be a flinch or grimace from Threngold when the words "my parents" reached him. No other outward sign did the dragon make. "Hum, you know much. Where is this castle?"

"West of here across the Canyon Lands, across the Red Lands. You flew by way of Fitzgerald Castle and down over Edgeway. The attack came near midnight," she replied, eyeing him. "I point out that Jon here can tell whether or not you speak the truth."

"Ah, you did not say you were a priest," Threngold commented wondering if this was a deceit.

"I'm a musician, not a priest. I was given a gift from Father Ukko; so let's assume that I can tell a lie when I hear one," Jon replied trying to avoid any upsetting of the dragon.

"Before I answer, may I ask how you know this information?" Threngold obviously was testing them.

"I was inside in my bedroom that night. I survived. We have recently excavated the collapsed ruins and found the remains of those that died there that night. We have seen what they saw during their last moments of life. However, my mother left a message, telling us what happened and that she and dad were being abducted by a large brown dragon. You were seen flying to and from the area that night by another Archmage who lives further north. We have assumed that the brown dragon in question was you. How many other brown dragons live in this area?" she added taunting him slightly.

"Impressive," he commented dryly. "At first, I thought you must have used divination methods, but now I see that my original thoughts at that time have borne fruit. They did not listen to my council. I warned them that collapsing the castle would allow many inside to escape. Underground, I expect. Castles always have extensive underground tunnels. I find it fascinating that the woman, tied up as she was, could have left a message. How come it took twenty-one years to reach you?"

"She dropped it just as you took flight. Unfortunately it was then trampled into the soft earth by other riders that night. Only with the keen eyes of Darless here has it finally come to light just a while ago," Alison explained without giving away too much. This was a boxing match; say only enough to convince the opponent you know the truth, yet not reveal the precise details; give the opponent nothing of which to attempt to dispute its voracity. Threngold was being a worthy opponent.

He stared at her a moment. "You must have been but a baby, if I know humans. Hum, doom from a baby, how interesting. That I would *not* have predicted. Okay. You may assume that I was the dragon in question. Ask your questions. What is it you have come here to ask me?"

"Based upon your answers, there may be several. First question, what did you do with my parents after you took flight from the castle with them aboard your back?" she held her breath. This was it. Now she would finally know, she hoped.

The dragon did not hesitate, "I brought them here as instructed."

"And then what happened to them? Were they still alive?"

"Yes, but in a drugged state of helplessness. She arrived on schedule the next day and took them away, but only after leaving the balance of my fee."

Alison felt a great relief. Her parents had made it this far unharmed. The dragon had not harmed them — had not eaten them. Jon had not interrupted, so he must be telling the truth. "I don't suppose that you want to tell us the entire story from beginning to end? No I suppose not. Okay. Then, who came and took them away? Do you know where she took them or why?" She was desperate to get some clue where to look next. Surely her quest must not die here. She had to avoid a dead end.

"Archmage Sarah le'Garde. I was not privy to where she was taking them. However, most likely she was taking them to her tower up north," came the cold reply.

"Was it she who hired you to take part in the castle's destruction and kidnaping?"

"No."

"Who?"

"Lord Jarred. She was at one time his human consort."

The very mention of that name shocked everyone present, visibly so. Threngold's eyes did not miss this fact. Actually, the folds above his eyes rose, rather like that of a human who has just witnessed something of great and unexpected interest. No one spoke for a minute as the magnitude of his pronouncement sank into their consciousness. Lord Jarred once again! Or was it for the first time. Alison's mind was racing. *So Lord Jarred was the real culprit behind it all along and not Metrarch!*

"How do we find her tower up north? Can you give us directions to it?"

"I have not seen nor heard from her in well over five years. However, I can draw you a map. It lies north of the main path that crosses the Desolation range up there." He spoke a command word of power and a blank parchment and quill floated over to him from his desk area. Using no hands, just the power of his spells, the quill quickly sketched out the map in less than a minute.

"Nice trick," Alison commented. "I'll work on that spell. Thank you for your assistance. You have been more than helpful." Turning to the others, she indicated that she was finished and that they should leave as soon as possible.

"That is all that you wanted to ask?" Threngold seemed rather amazed. All along, he had been waiting for the bomb to be dropped. This mage was finished and no tricks, no traps. All they really wanted was information. He still found this completely unbelievable. However, he could afford to take no chances. "All right. I will tell you this that in all of the time I have lived here, you are the first to see me and the treasure here. I have been purposely testing you, taunting you with it, but you do not seem to be after it. I leave you with these parting words. Do not ever attempt to come back here. I have many, many traps in this place. No one in the last eleven hundred years has ever made it to this room alive. Do not even try. Further, after you leave, I will have to devise even more traps, since you have seen my inner sanctum here. I bid you good day."

Jon mentally sent to the others, *Grab hold of me; join hands quickly. I'm getting us out of here fast.* Just as soon as he sensed the connection of everyone through to him, he stepped forward landing them all in the valley just below the enormous pile of animal bones they had first discovered. No one spoke. Each sucked in the fresh air. The stench of dragon breath had been almost overwhelming.

Threngold's mouth opened wide in surprise. He had intended to watch them carefully leave, half expecting the mages to utilize a simple teleport spell. "What was that?" he finally muttered to himself. He reviewed his observations. "They all took hold of each other's hands. Then, this saint fellow appears to be taking a step toward me, and they were just gone! How can this be?" He thought long and hard. "Ah, the real question is 'Is my lair now safe?' Perhaps it is time that I should be moving. I've been here for far too long. But then, this is a cozy, ideal location. Perhaps another tunnel complex." He went in search of his maps of the area.

"If one of you can manage, could we get to where we left the horses rapidly?" asked Mandy, her voice full of concern. "I do not trust that dragon. The farther we get from here and the sooner, the better I am going to like it."

"Grab hold," Jon replied. A few seconds later, they all stumbled into the tethered horses. Another minute and they were heading back down the steep valley. "Oh man!" exclaimed Jon, "Going down is worse than going up! I'm sliding into the horn. Ouch!" He distinctly heard several laughs. Thea and Darless were dead serious, trying valiantly to keep from sliding into the protruding horn. Neither found the laughter encouraging either.

Finally, Mandy turned in her saddle, "Look at it this way, going down takes less than half the time going up."

"Yes, but after this, I may not be able to father any children!" retorted Jon.

"Angle your feet forward and down like mine; push back and lean vertical. Yes, now you got it," Mandy answered, grinning at Sir Thomas, who grinned back.

Thea, grimacing as well had the last word, "See, I told you today would be our lucky day! It was supposed to be our wedding day!"

An hour later, they galloped out onto the high plains and headed for Michael's wagon now clearly visible not far ahead. Smoke from his campfire drifted into the late afternoon sky. The tall mountains behind them cast enormously long shadows before them. Even the air took on a chill. It was still early spring in the mountains.

"Hi all, back so soon?" Michael greeted them as they galloped into camp. "Success?" He need not have asked as the broad smile on Alison's face told him they must have had a great success. He saw no battle wounds and that was very encouraging from his point of view.

"Yes, better than I had dreamed possible," Alison answered as she dismounted and walked to the fire to warm her hands.

"Gods, you stink like dragon!" exclaimed Michael, rolling up his nose. Even the dogs slunk away from the fire and Alison and the advancing others.

Thea moaned, "I'll never be able to get this stench out of my hair! My clothes are full of it! What ever will we do now?"

"Well, a nice warm bath in a bath house would be great, but I suspect we'd not be let inside one smelling like this," teased Mandy.

"Okay, don't panic," Alison teased back. "Darless and I both will create magical mansions. Remember, it has a nice bathtub in it. We take turns. Women use my mansion; men, you get Darless' mansion. Throw the stinky clothes outside the doors. One of us gets the job of washing clothes!" Her eyes twinkled as she mentioned the washing job. The men groaned anticipating that one of them would get this thankless job. "I get first bath and so does Jon. He really saved the day for us, so he goes first, guys!"

"Yes'm!" exclaimed Sir Thomas in mock dismay. Soon everyone was inside and throwing the smelly clothes out the doors into two growing piles. Poor Michael had to move downwind from the laundry piles. It took the men less than an hour for all of them to emerge cleaned up and wearing their spare clothes. On the other hand, the women didn't come out for nearly two hours. Long hair and dragon stench did not mix; each wore a towel turban over their hair to fend off the night chill. Meantime, the men discussed ways and means of cleaning the clothes. While a good washing would handle some, the woolen items and leather garments, particularly Mandy's would take special care.

"Well, don't look at me," proclaimed Jon mockingly, "back home, I just throw them all into the washing machine and let it do its thing." Unfortunate choice of words, next he had to explain washers and dryers to the others. "Magical machines" communicated best to these men.

"It's women's work," Sir Thomas protested. "At home, women do all the laundry. I am at a loss, guys."

"The woolens will shrink, if you don't use cold water," offered Michael, used to doing his own laundry. "The smell is going to be hard to remove in cold water. Perhaps it is best to wait for the women and get their opinions. I wouldn't want to be the one to tell Mandy 'Gosh, I shrunk your fine leather top.'" he added playfully, "though it might be amusing." This brought several chuckles. "But let's boil a large pot of water. At least we can do that much." When the women finally came out into the chilly early evening air, the men had the largest pot Michael had brought boiling away. They also had fixed supper, albeit nothing at all fancy.

Jon volunteered to be the spokesperson, "Alison, we fixed some dinner and have a pot of boiling water ready for the laundry. We thought it best to wait for you more knowledgeable folks to give instructions on how to do the washing. There's cotton, wool and leather garments. We didn't want to shrink or damage them." He hoped he was being diplomatic enough and that having the food ready would count in their favor. The others looked sheepishly at the ground, while Jon said his rehearsed speech.

Ever the keen observer, Darless teased them, "Ah, so you hope to buy us off with dinner, hoping we will feel more like doing the laundry because you fixed the food?" Even Jon looked sheepishly at the ground. "Men!" she added in mock jest. The women roared.

"Seriously, Jon, you acted wisely," Mandy finally stopped laughing. "If you had shrunk my fine leathers, I'd have shrunk you. Our mages have thought up the answer to smelly clothes. After we eat, they'll take care of it. Come on, serve us some food! We've got lots to discuss." They all grabbed a plate; soon all were sitting on the large boulders that Michael and Sir Thomas had rolled up to the fire.

Finally, sipping her after-dinner tea, Alison related their encounter with Threngold to Michael. Jon had to try to explain how he located the dragon and got him to agree to meet, instead of fight. Then, Alison talked of the question and answer session with the brown dragon. Right in the middle of her explanation, Jon suddenly interrupted her, "Now I know where we've met Threngold before! I knew I had encountered that mind before. He was the old man that tried to swindle us with the fake magical weapons!"

"Well, that makes sense; he must be a powerful mage in his own right," Alison added.

"It's a good thing I didn't challenge him on the spot!" proclaimed Sir Thomas. "That might have been a total disaster for us!" Alison then continued with her recollections.

"It appears that the infamous Lord Jarred was behind the entire destruction of Castle d'Ambrose in an attempt to acquire the Holy Scepter of Ukko for himself. He hires his one-time concubine Archmage Sarah le'Garde to lead an assault on the castle and he hires the dragon, apparently a friend of hers, to both help smash the walls and to ferret away my parents. The only good thing from it all was that the Scepter was not found. Anyway, we know that she came here and took my parents, who were still alive and in good health, away — most likely to her tower. Threngold even drew us a map. One thing still puzzles me. He said that he has not heard from her in the last five years. Now implicit in that is he has heard from her for at least some fifteen years after the attack on my castle. I'm a little concerned that when we get to her castle, she may be long gone."

"She might be back down in the Abyss," offered Darless, "or even dead. We never asked Threngold how old she was. Could be she died of old age."

"I've thought of that too, Darless," Alison answered, "but even so, we might find something useful if we search her tower. So far, we have been pretty lucky in our searches."

"The next thing is to figure out where this tower is and how best to get there," Mandy interjected, getting to the heart of the matter, as far as she was concerned. "Can we see it?" Alison spread the map out on a rock and raised her globe of light above it so that all could see, increasing its intensity to better illuminate the yellowing parchment.

"Ah, there's Deadman's Pass," exclaimed Jon, finally getting oriented to the crude map. "Funny, when we emerged from the underground passage with the gnome, we were only about a hundred miles more or less from her tower. Had we only known."

"Sorry folks," Michael said disappointedly, "I've never been remotely that far north. I cannot help you further."

"No problem, Michael," Mandy answered, "We've been through Deadman's pass last winter. Man was it cold! And the snow was three-feet deep after only the first snowfall! Glad we are heading there in the springtime." Turning to Alison, "How are we going to get there? Ride all the way?" This was what she really wanted to know.

"Well, while we could teleport people, moving the horses via spells is going to be really challenging, if not impossible," Alison mused. "Jon, if we take the people, could you transport the horses, say in small groups? Is that possible? I know you did a jump, when we were charging to the caravan's rescue."

"Yes love, I can maybe take three horses at one time. These are a good deal heavier than the ones we rode then. Say three or four trips. Doable," he answered.

"Okay. Then here's the plan. First, we all get teleported to the desired spot, say near where we came out of the gnome's tunnel. Then, Jon makes as many trips back here as needed to bring the horses. Michael can watch them until Jon gets the last ones, if that's okay with you, Michael. Then, you can head home." He nodded his full agreement.

"And I'll come by later on to get my puppy," Jon added. The dog breeder smiled.

"Then, we ride north looking for the mage's tower. It should not be too hard to find given the map and assuming Threngold was fairly accurate in his sketch. Maybe three days ride, right Mandy?" The ranger nodded, relieved that they did not have to spend several weeks riding along the edge of the Desolation Range. "Okay, then that's settled. Tomorrow we ride forth on the next step of the quest. The rest of you, go get some sleep. Oh yes guys, Darless cancelled her mansion spell, so we all stay in mine. It's aired out by now. Thea, Darless and myself will be along later on; we want to experiment with magical cleaning of the laundry," she added smiling coyly. They had long ago worked out how to de-odorize their clothing, but had carefully not spoken any word of it until now.

An hour later, the three satisfied mages entered the mansion and closed the doors behind them. Their work was finished and a total success. The laundry, fresh and clean, was drying outside. Inside, they found all the others asleep, only the guard dogs kept one eye open and saw them enter, smiling to one another.

Chapter 13 The Tower of Archmage Sarah le'Garde

Breakfast was thoroughly enjoyable, nearly festive. "All that worry over fighting the dragon and, poof, we only talk. Boy do I feel relieved!" Mandy commented to the others while eating pancakes. "I feel a hundred pounds lighter!"

Even Sir Thomas was in a particularly festive mood, "I'll second that one! I have to admit that, ever since we began this journey, I have been worried sick about actually having to fight Threngold to the death. I figured it likely would be ours. I didn't say anything," he said apologetically, "for fear of worrying you more than you already were. We actually *talked* to a dragon, er well you did, Alison. After that encounter, the rest of this journey ought to be relatively easy. After all it is only an Archmage we are going to track down, right?" He looked to Alison and Darless for confirmation. He didn't get it exactly.

"Dear," Darless explained, "Threngold may have an evil streak in him, but he does follow the accepted rules or guidelines for behavior. It is not too surprising that he chose to talk not fight. Besides, we had a powerful bargaining statue, but this Archmage may be another story. If she really was a concubine to the demon Lord Jarred, she probably acknowledges no rules, save what she makes up. We've no bargaining factor with her. What makes you think she will tell us what she did with Alison's parents?" She paused for dramatic effect and then added, "No, we may very well have to force it out of her and that may take quite some doing."

"I'll bop her on the head to convince her," declared the paladin. Though several laughed at the idea, Darless sternly answered, "What if she has used the same spell

Alison does to make one impervious to many blows? While you are pounding away doing nothing, she may be frying you, blasting you full of missiles, disintegrating you or your armor, boiling you, freezing you, stopping time to do you in. No, I would be very, very careful when dealing with an Archmage. I think it wise to adhere to the philosophy: Never challenge an Archmage, it may be your last." With that, the three mages and Michael laughed loudly, Mandy and Jon smiled as well.

"Well, first we have to find her tower," Mandy spoke up, ready to get moving. She hated just sitting around doing nothing, especially when a formidable task lay ahead. "So how do we go about getting there? What's first?"

"Okay. Okay, I can take a hint," Alison said, sitting her empty tea cup down and rising from the table. "First, pack up. Then, Darless and I will teleport us all to just outside the entrance to the gnome's underground passage. Jon studies the area and returns here and brings the horses in as many trips as he feels necessary. Meanwhile, the rest of us scout the area. In case of trouble, dive into the tunnel. Remember, my sis put a permanent illusion over it to hide it from the eyes of others. If all goes as planned, we mount up and ride north. Simple."

In a half hour, they all stood outside the mansion and Alison dispelled it. Michael had his dogs in the wagon for the return trip. The friends bid him a farewell. He had never been hugged by so many women at one time before and was a bit embarrassed by all the attention. Then, he took the reins of the nine medium warhorses and watched the seven join hands with Alison and Darless. He recognized the familiar teleport chant, for he often used it as well. The next instant, a bit of aloneness drifted over him as he sensed they really were gone. He realized that he had actually become close friends with them in this short space of time. He missed their company already. He signed and waited.

In less than a minute, Jon appeared just in front of him walking slowly toward him. "Boy, your arrival is startling and no magical energy flashes," he commented to Jon.

He smiled, "I guess so. Well, now for the horses. I'll take Mandy's and Sir Thomas's first." Michael handed him the reigns and watched him closely, hoping to learn a bit more about how Jon moved them across space without using a teleport spell. He heard Jon muttering soft words to them as he led them forward a few feet. Jon then nudged them to start walking. As they stepped forward, both horses and Jon completely disappeared. Michael still had no idea how Jon did this.

Though he watched Jon intently on the next two trips, which were just a few minutes apart, he still saw nothing more. Man and beasts just started walking and were gone. Finally, Jon reappeared for the last time. "Well, this is the last one," Jon said. "I'll be back in about two weeks or so depending on how things go with the quest. Say, when I come to get Bessy, I can take you with me to see Alison's new castle and town under construction. That is, if you are interested in seeing where we live."

"You got it! I'd love to. I've heard your place is surrounded by tall green grasslands. I've never seen such. Should be most interesting. Well, so long for now. I'll look after Bessy until you can come get her." The two shook hands, then Jon and the remaining horses were gone. Michael and his dogs began their slow trek back to his dog ranch. This time, since he was not in any rush, he paused long enough to let all the dogs off the wagon. On foot, he led the wagon towards home, dogs frolicking in the warmth of the spring day.

When they all arrived safely some thousand feet from the entrance of the gnome's tunnel, Alison cautioned them to not go near it, as a safeguard. They did not want anyone getting any clues that the entrance was here. While Jon was fetching the horses, Mandy changed into her eagle form and flew up for a scouting view. Lonnie and Sir Thomas stood a watchful guard, but no sign of any living thing could be seen save hawks and eagles soaring in the blue sky.

Instead, all eyes went to the scenery. This far north, the Desolation Range still held significant snow fields. White capped peaks contrasted with the barren granite and blue sky. Under foot, the spring rains and snow melt caused the annual growth cycle to commence. Green lay all about underfoot, in stark contrast to their last visit during the early winter, when all was barren and dry. These arid plains would be green for only a month, before slowly wilting under the relentless sun and low rainfall. Yet at this instant in time, it was magnificent to behold.

In six minutes, Jon had brought all the horses. He was now tired and as they mounted up to head northward, Jon fell asleep in the saddle. They rode slowly at a walk for his sake. Mandy reported that no trace of the hobgoblin hordes could be seen for miles. In fact, she had seen nothing but birds and a few herds of deer. From her viewpoint, this was indeed a good omen. Perhaps they would have an easy passage northward after all.

They made twenty miles this day. Most of the time was spent enjoying the spectacular scenery to their right, the mountains. On this trip, not burdened with the utter survival of the entire caravan, they could relax and admire the tall, craggy, snow packed peaks. Jon woke up after an hour and he too could not take his eyes off of the view.

The next day, Mandy saw signs of a small band of roaming hobgoblins, but they did not actually see them. She estimated that six of them were about, hardly worth worrying about. About midday, they spied a farmstead to their left, but chose to veer to the right to avoid any possible contact. Otherwise, the day passed uneventful.

The third day out was different. In actual fact, they were about ten miles from the Archmage's tower, though they did not know it. "Okay everyone, we are getting close now. From now on, everyone concentrate on trying to discover the location of the tower. We really don't know what it looks like or its precise location, but it is nestled in one of these valleys of the mountains. So keep your eyes peeled. She could have some kind of illusion over it to hide it. I'm counting on Darless to stay alert for that. Mandy, you look for any obvious signs of inhabitation," Alison ordered. The ride began once more and the early morning air was crisp and refreshing, though not too cold. They began the ride in silence, all eyes scouring the mountains on their right for any signs of the tower.

About ten o'clock, Mandy called a halt. "Something doesn't feel right," she muttered. Although she didn't feel the hairs on her neck prickle, a sure sign of imminent danger, she felt uneasy. Though the others looked carefully all about, nothing seemed amiss. Mandy finally resorted to sniffing the air. Finally, she asked, "Do any of you smell it?"

"Smell what?" came many replies. "Death. I smell the distinct odor of death on the light breeze blowing on my face. Can you smell it?"

Everyone sniffed and shook their heads. Only Darless, who was altogether too familiar with decay and rot of the Abyss, said, "Well, perhaps I do. It's pretty faint, if that's what it is."

Without further discussion, Mandy nudged her horse forward once more, but she kept all her senses totally alert. In a half hour, they rounded a large spur of granite and a valley opened to their right. Mandy estimated that this was at the approximate distance the tower should be from Threngold's map. Again she halted and surveyed the deep valley. After several minutes, she pointed out, "There it is! See way up this valley, near the steep cliffs. That's got to be a stone tower." They others gave a cheer and urged her on.

"The odor is getting stronger," commented Darless to Mandy.

"Yes, I know," came the dark reply, sobering everyone's spirits at having found the Archmage's tower so easily. Slowly she led them up the valley. Her keen eyes picked out a long unused track leading in the general direction. She pointed it out and followed it. A half hour later, they rounded another bend in the valley and got a clearer view of the tower.

Though they were still five miles away, they could finally make out some details. The tower was built up against the sharply rising granite mountain side, rising some fifty feet tall. Around its base was a small village with a stone wall perhaps ten feet tall arcing around it in a protective semicircle. One entrance beckoned them from squarely in the middle of the wall. The nearly invisible track that Mandy was following led straight for this point. After a pause, she led them forward once more. All was ghastly silent save the occasional bird calls far off in the distance. Mandy felt ill at ease.

Another few minutes and they halted once again, this time just before the entrance. It was spooky. The wood and iron gates that had at one time barred entrance lay sundered on the ground; wood rotting. Through the opening in the walls, they could see small buildings to the right and left of the main road, which led straight to the tower. Still no signs of life appeared. Alison's heart sank. The place looked utterly deserted. For a moment, no one spoke. Then, the words of Mandy resounded cold and harsh in the silence, "Sir Thomas and I will enter and reconnoiter. You stay out here at the ready in case of trouble." She and the paladin rode through the entrance side by side, very, very slowly, swords drawn, just in case of a trap.

They rode about five hundred feet inside and paused, looking slowly in all directions. "It appears to be abandoned. Dust lies thick in here, undisturbed, except by rodents," she reported. The hairs on her neck prickled. "Something is watching us!" she whispered to Sir Thomas.

Now the paladin acted on a hunch. He fumbled about and retrieved his holy symbol with his left hand, just in case. It turned out to be a wise move. No sooner had he got it out, than the sound of clanking bones rattled both to their left and right. From out of the small huts came skeletons armed with meat cleavers, pitch forks, knives and an occasional rusting sword. Slowly they moved toward the two mounted riders. More and more funneled out of the small homes. Instantly, Sir Thomas began his holy chanting. Ten skeletons to his right turned into dust, weapons clanking on the ground. "Skeletons!" yelled Mandy back to the others. "Hundreds. Stay back, we'll take care of them."

Jon got to see firsthand just how a medium warhorse with competent rider attacked. Mandy moved away from the paladin to gain fighting room. Her sword swooped down right and left, shattering a skeleton with each swing. All the while, her horse reared and crushed others before it, which were attempting to slash into the horse. The horse deftly spun to the right and left, knocking others down and trampling others in its wake. It was hard to tell who slew more, Mandy or her horse.

Sir Thomas continued his chanting relentlessly. Dozens about him turned into dust with each chant. Those that got too close were smashed by his warhorse. Jon marveled at the skill these two warriors displayed. To his eyes, they seemed to be controlling their horses with no hands — just their knees. In five minutes the combat was over. A huge pile of bones of all sizes lay around Mandy. On the other hand, enormous dust piles surrounded the paladin. Smiling, they rode out of the village to rejoin the others.

Jon and Darless dismounted to heal their wounds, but found surprisingly few, mostly minor scratches. Instead, they found themselves tending to the two warhorses, which had received the brunt of the skeleton's attack. It took them ten minutes to get the horses back to normal.

While they were handling the horses, Mandy and Sir Thomas took a well-deserved break, chugging water and catching their breaths. "Most peculiar," the paladin said to Mandy and the others.

"Sure was," the ranger replied. "Some of those skeletons had to have been children! I'd swear that those were the villagers!"

"How can that be?" asked Alison incredulously. "The whole village turned into undead skeletons? How? When? Why? By whom?"

"No idea, but good questions," Mandy commented.

"Do you suppose there are more of them?" Alison asked worriedly.

"We'll go checkup as soon as we catch our breath and make sure the horses are ready," Sir Thomas spoke with authority. He added, "For once, Alison, I went with a hunch. Somehow I just knew that there may be undead around and took the time to get my holy symbol at the ready. Only just in time too. Maybe it was Mandy's suggestion of the smell of death that did it."

"Well, good going on following your hunch," Alison answered good-naturedly. For as long as she had known him, he'd been a "man of action," act first, think later. Thus, for quite some time now she had been working on getting him to trust his hunches, his intuition. She smiled thinking that perhaps he finally was doing it. He grinned back, suspecting this was what she must be thinking.

"Head's up!" Lonnie called out; he was still performing his duties as rear guard. "Someone's coming up on us rapidly."

Everyone's demeanor instantly changed to total seriousness. Mandy and Sir Thomas quickly remounted and took the point facing the oncoming rider. The mages formed up in the middle, staves in hand, while Lonnie and Thea pivoted around to the rear closest to the village gate. A small dust cloud marked the coming of a lone rider, who was either following their trail or heading to this village. There was no other target in sight.

A minute later, Mandy, shielding her eyes from the suns glare hollered, "Well I'll be! It's Rufus! What's he doing here?" Everyone relaxed and dismounted, waiting for their friend to arrive. Another minute and a puffing pony and rider galloped up and reigned in.

"Hi there, Rufus! Good to see you," called out Mandy. The gnome, like his pony, was completely out of breath and hastily dismounted. Mandy gave the little man time to catch his breath by giving the others an introduction. "This is Rufus Quickenbroadbeam, Inventor Extraordinary." The little gnome stood only about thirty inches tall with a long brown beard. He was perhaps thirty-five pounds in weight. From the total disarray of his clothes, he had obviously left in a very great hurry. His shirt was only partially tucked in; his socks did not match; one suspender was not fastened. Mandy presented the others to Rufus, who had never met Sir Thomas or Lonnie.

"Ah, I am just in time to warn you I see; you haven't entered this village," he said still a bit out of breath. "Be very careful; this place is haunted by many undead creatures!"

Sir Thomas grinned, "Yes, we know. Mandy and I eliminated all of the skeletons, hundreds of them. You just missed it." However, the gnome's worry and concern did not evaporate as the paladin thought it would.

Alison said, "Welcome Rufus. Thanks for the warning. How come you knew we were here? I must admit you gave us quite a surprise when you showed up."

"Ah well, you will pardon my half-dressed appearance; I was a bit rushed. I was using my latest invention, the Very Far Seeing Tube — just gazing out upon this deserted plain, when I spied you all. I did not expect to see you so soon. Then as I followed your path with my invention, it became quite clear you were heading to this abandoned village. I had to warn you. I grabbed some traveling clothes, teleported my pony and myself just as close to you as I dared and we galloped the rest of the way here," Rufus explained in his typical detailed manner.

He went on, "My dear friends, skeletons are the least of your worries, if you desire to explore this abandoned tower. It used to belong to a powerful mage; she was in league with demons, it is said. I have to warn you, something like five years ago, the whole village was abandoned, or at least all of the people who lived here vanished without a trace. Three years ago now, I came here to explore, figuring I might find some useful objects to barter with others. Oh my, dear me. So many undead, so many. I managed to elude the skeletons that you conveniently destroyed and spent several days trying to find a way into the tower. The ground level doors are fused. Melted metal, even. I've speculated long and hard upon how that could have happened. Mind you, I've even done some experiments myself to see if I can reproduce that effect."

Seeing that they really were not interested in hearing about his experiments, he resumed. "Okay, as you can see, there are no windows. Peculiar. I hate it when something defies all my attempts to get inside. And that *is* saying something. However, on the roof, I did find a hidden trap door. There is an observation platform on the roof, you see. She was interested in the sky as well. I

420

got the door opened and went inside, hoping to explore and find all sorts of useful stuff she had left."

"I says to myself, 'Rufus, old boy, this is going to be your lucky day. Look at all the stuff she left behind!' I had barely begun to search through the books, when I swear ghosts and other creatures drifted up right through the floor and tried to attack me! I only just got out without being killed! Ever since, I have been working on a new potion, that is, when time allows. I believe I have it perfected. Actually, I have not yet had the courage to come back here and test it myself. However, with you all here now, we can try out my new potion. I call it the Elixir of Invisibility to Undead Creatures. Sounds rather catchy doesn't it? Er, I only have one slight problem. I have only enough for one person made up. If it works, I can make some more for all of you, if you like and are not in a hurry." He finally paused.

"Slow down, Rufus," teased Alison. "First, let's move inside the village, establish a camp of sorts. Sir Thomas, Lonnie and Mandy were just about to go house to house to make sure the village is totally safe. While they do that, I'll explain why we are here and we can make plans. I'm glad for the warning and you are more than welcome to tag along with us. I have every intention of doing a thorough examination of this tower from top to bottom! We are looking for something." Without further discussion, they all walked their horses back through the village gates, tethering them just inside. While the mages and Jon set about the tasks of establishing a camp of sorts, Rufus rubbed his pony down and unsaddled it and set about straightening his clothes.

Once settled and while Mandy and the paladins began their door to door search, Alison outlined their adventures and her mission here. She began with a quick update on the castle and village construction, the finding all of her brothers and sisters, except one, their discovery of her mother's long lost message, their journey westward through the Canyon Lands, their defeat of the Cambion demon, the brief encounter with the Cult of the Black Scorpion, and finally the discussion with Threngold, the brown dragon. Rufus, naturally asked many questions, and was quite attentive. Indeed, Thea and Darless served up lunch during the discussions, which took several hours to complete. When she had finished bringing the gnome up to date, the thorough search of the village was complete and the warriors reported in for lunch as well.

"Village is all clear," Sir Thomas reported. "No sign of any other creatures, living or dead."

"It's like everyone just up and left everything behind. Some homes still had food on the table. Something happened here really, really fast. I even tried to pick up any physic residue of the folks who used to live here. All I can get is some kind of black energy cloud seeping over the entire village. When it crept into a home, the people just vanished — gone — no trace — nothing. It is the strangest thing we have ever encountered," Mandy pointed out, with the paladins nodding in complete agreement.

"Evil necromancy, evil necromancy at work!" declared Rufus, who always seemed to have a theory. "Well, if your parents were here when the black cloud came, we are not likely to find them. However, chronologically speaking, they would have had to have been kept prisoner here for what — say fifteen years before this necromancy event. Unlikely, unlikely. Take hope. Take hope. Maybe the Demon Lord has them. We should go explore the tower."

"Hold on, there is no rush," Alison cautioned. "Now that we know that there are more powerful undead creatures inside the tower, we mages need some time to prepare our defenses."

"Also, figure into your calculations," Sir Thomas added trying to be helpful, "that via Father Ukko, I can encase us all in a protection from evil ward as long as you all stay say within fifteen feet of me. I do have a good deal of power over the undead, compliments of Father Ukko. I can turn to dust even wraiths, but against real ghosts, if ghosts they be, moving through walls and all, those I can at least keep at bay. I guess what I am trying to say, Alison, is to count on my acting as Father Johnas, our priest, would act and not as a fighter. I cannot do both."

"You keep them at bay, and Lonnie and I'll chop them to bits," declared Mandy. Lonnie agreed with his elevated status of "involved" paladin. He was tiring of being the rear guard.

"Er, Mage Alison," Rufus interrupted, "I came here in such a hurry that I did not have time to fully equip myself. I only can teleport once. While you are making your preparations, do you suppose that someone could take me home so I can get my stuff and bring me back here?" The forlorn look on his face — an illusionist caught without the tools of his trade — was almost more that Alison could handle without bursting out in laughter.

"I got nothing to do," Jon quickly volunteered. "I'll be glad to take you, Rufus. It will give me something to do for a while. Sometimes, I feel just a bit useless on these adventures. Come on, let's go." He gave Alison a hug and kiss.

"Give us an hour, Jon. Thanks," she replied.

Jon took Rufus's hand and together they appeared just outside his front entrance. "Whoa!" exclaimed Jon as he landed on the melting, but packed snow. He slipped and landed on his butt with a thud. Shivering from the cold, he looked around as Rufus opened his door. Here in the high country, snow still lingered. The gnome still had several feet of drifted snow covering the entire lands about his home. The blinding whiteness forced Jon to squint just to see. He staggered inside the gnome's home, glad to be out of the blinding sunlight and into the warmth. "Warm yourself by the fire, while I get things together," Rufus suggested and scooted into back rooms rummaging for useful items. Jon needed no further suggestion. He stood before the fire and rubbed his rear, reflecting on just how lucky they had all been to have gotten the caravan out of these mountains before becoming snowed in for the winter.

About a half hour later, Rufus emerged from his back rooms. All sorts of things were fastened to his clothes and about his belt and over his shoulder. Further, he struggled carrying a heavy sack brimming with other items. He was coming prepared, that was obvious. "What's the pick axe for?" asked Jon, glancing at the axe sticking through the gnome's belt.

"Ah, there is nothing like a good pick for exploring things — most useful tool indeed. I believe I have everything. Shall we go? Oh, do you have a weight limitation on what you can teleport?" he asked as an afterthought.

Jon chuckled. "I don't know how to teleport, Rufus. I just transport us. You certainly don't weigh as much as three of our horses. So, no problem."

"Three horses? You can teleport three of them at once?" he asked unbelievingly, eyebrows rising quizzically.

"Yes, that's how we got here this morning from just beyond Threngold's place far to the south," he replied. With Rufus's mouth fluttering, trying to figure out what to say next, Jon took his small hand and stepped them back to the warm village.

After they arrived, Rufus finally managed to say in protest, "But I watched you just now. You didn't even say a word!"

"No, I never do. What has words got to do with it?" Jon answered. "Well, if it makes you happy, I suppose next time I can say 'Hocus Pocus.' Would that help?" Jon joked. Rufus looked at him speechless.

Since the mages still needed more time in their spell preparations, Rufus decided to explore nearby deserted homes in search of useful items to confiscate. Soon he had an ever growing pile of things: cooking utensils, pots, pans, work tools, and so on. Notably, among the collection of 'useful stuff' were no items not made of metal. Fabrics and such things as leather and rope had rotted away long ago.

Spying Jon observing his pile, the gnome hastened to explain, "Someone always needs a new pot or a new hammer." He was a trader at heart, adding, "It is going to take days to search through each of these houses here! I guess I had best get myself ready to go into the tower too." With Rufus off making his own preparations, Jon got out his flute and played tunes to pass the time.

Around two everyone seemed ready for action. Lanterns were distributed to Jon and Thea, just in case the mages' magical lights were extinguished. With Sir Thomas and Mandy in the lead, the group walked up the road to the tower proper. It was an imposing stone structure some fifty feet tall and perhaps forty in diameter. Composed of hewn granite mined from the mountainside directly behind it, the tower blended with the sheer side of the mountain face it stood before. From the rear, it was unapproachable, save for birds; the sheer walls rose for nearly two hundred feet, dwarfing the singular tower. Yet, it was well constructed, though not of dwarven make. From the outside, there was no way to tell the thickness of the walls, but later estimates would place the thickness at approximately three feet. Even more striking was the singular lack of windows. The walls just rose up fifty feet in a sheer stone wall. The only visible means of entrance were the main doors, which of course, everyone had to examine.

These massive iron doors stood six feet tall; each was five feet wide. An intertwining vine motif was etched into the metal, twisting and turning. In their day, these were quite aesthetic doors, which gave a clue to the demeanor of the tower's original owner, Archmage Sarah le'Garde. It was, however, the seam between the doors that attracted all their attention. Just as Rufus had said, something had fused the iron halves together, like a blast of incredibly hot air. These doors would never open again; they were now a single piece of iron. After a few minutes examination, Alison concurred with Rufus. "Yes, these are sealed shut, so it is up to the roof. Okay, everyone, break into three groups. One with me and one with Darless and one with Thea. We are going to levitate our way to the top."

Quickly they formed up, held hands and the three mages spoke their ring's command word. Slowly and gracefully, the party rose up the side of the tower. Two minutes later, everyone set foot firmly on the tower's roof. "This is an observation deck," Alison immediately commented. "She probably studied the stars from here."

"Ah, you can also see anyone coming for miles," noted Mandy, ever the more practical. "With the Eyes of the Eagle, one could see perhaps for forty miles. This is a very defensible location."

"Keeps out thieves too," added Sir Thomas.

"Yes, but it is so isolated," Jon protested. "She must have been very lonely out here all by herself. I don't think I would like it one little bit."

"Me either," Rufus added.

"Jeesh, and no town nearby," put in Thea, who came originally from Freetown. I'm sure I would not want to live here."

Darless felt the need to clarify for everyone, "Number 1, she was originally a consort of Lord Jarred, the Demon Lord. Number 2, she was also an Archmage possessed of arcane lore. Number 3, as such, if she resided in a large town, undoubtedly, she would have been constantly pestered by others seeking advice. Number 4, I would guess she was researching or practicing all sorts of evil magic. This would be an ideal place for such. I do agree with you, Alison, this is an excellent observation area. See how the small barbicans do not really interrupt the line of sight? And here," she pointed to a lone three-foot tall granite block, "is where she placed her equipment for studying the stars."

"You mean she had a telescope?" asked Jon. "I didn't know you had invented such things."

"What's a telescope?" she asked. Crestfallen, Jon then had to explain. Rufus, of course, thought that that was a better name than Very Far Seeing Tube and decided to adopt it.

Meanwhile, Sir Thomas, Rufus and Lonnie examined the trapdoor. It was made of heavy iron. One side was hinged and a large pull ring lay on the opposite side. "It's very heavy," Rufus commented, "I can just barely open it without resorting to magic." When the others gathered around, Sir Thomas grabbed the ring and pulled the door open; Mandy, sword drawn stood opposite him, ready to attack anything that might sail out.

Only a strong odor of death and decay seeped out. "Yuck! That smell!" exclaimed Thea, making a grim face and holding her nose. "This is going to be awful. It's like a whole lot of things died down there!"

"Tisk, tisk, my dear young lady," Rufus chided. "Once we enter, your nose will soon cease smelling it. You will get used to it in no time." She glared at him, but realized he was right.

Surveying the darkness inside for a minute, they saw nothing emerge. No sound, no light, nothing but the odor. All three mages created a globe of light on the tip of their wizard staves and held them over the black opening. Now they could see a set of stone stairs leading down. Actually, the stairs was built into the wall and curved as it descended. From here, they could see a floor some ten feet below them. "See all the books!" exclaimed Rufus. Indeed, two sets of bookshelves rested against one wall opposite the door. Both were brimming with books, scrolls, parchments, and sketch pads. There appeared to be no occupants.

Darless went first, holding her staff aloft so she could see. Sir Thomas followed her, his sword drawn, armored boots clanking on the stone steps. One by one the others followed. Jon found the descent a bit hair-raising. The steps were no more than thirty inches wide and no handrail, no protection on his right. One stumble meant a ten-foot fall onto the hard floor below. Instinctively, he kept his left hand lightly touching the wall as he went down. Thea, coming behind him, did likewise.

Once everyone was safely on the main floor, the wizards spread out, illuminating the entire large room. Going vertically up the exact center of the circular room was a three-foot pillar of stone, supporting the weight of the observation deck above. On the side with the two bookshelves, were two oak tables and two padded chairs, done in royal purple velvet. A thick rug covered the entire floor. Six oil lanterns made of burnished brass in the shapes of demons lined the walls at regular intervals. Rufus proceeded to see if they worked. "Hey, the lanterns still work," he exclaimed as the first one lit. Quickly the others were turned on as well, providing a uniform illumination.

On the opposite side of the room were numerous crates and a very large table with bins above it holding many rolled up parchments. On the table lay one very large star chart now quite yellowed with age. "Okay everyone. It's search time. Now here is how we are going to do this. Mandy, Sir Thomas and Lonnie — you stand guard. We don't want any surprise attacks by Rufus's ghosts. While they provide protection, we wizards are going to systematically look for any traps, concealed or otherwise. I don't want anyone getting hurt. Once we have verified there are no devices, then we can all take a portion and search for anything useful."

However, Rufus didn't wait or rather follow orders. He found himself standing beside one of the large chests, just his size. Curiosity got the better of him. "I wonder what is inside."

"Rufus! Don't touch that chest!" Alison commanded him sternly, catching him kneeling before it and guessing his intention. Startled, his hand, which was just about to fiddle with the lock, froze in mid-air. "Remember, traps." She began her chant. Once she pronounced the last syllable, she then began a slow gaze of all of the objects in her immediate vicinity, beginning with the chest the gnome was about to open. In a monotone, she pronounced, "Rufus, lock is trapped. Gas I think. The chest to your left is also booby trapped. Third chest is clear." And so it went with the three wizards.

In five minutes, they had surveyed the entire room. Each had also covered the same objects the others did. They were making triply sure of traps. When they finished, six more traps had been positively identified. One was on the trap door leading to the room below. One was on the wall beside it — a double whammy to anyone venturing below this room. Another two lay upon what appeared to be a pair of very ornamental, jewel encrusted swords hanging on the wall over the back of one of the two purple chairs. The other two were traps protecting the handling of two books on the shelves.

"I have these two disarmed," proclaimed Rufus, who Jon noted had some small tools in his hands, similar to those that Alison's brother, Mat, the master locksmith used. Jon guessed that Rufus was also trained as a thief, albeit a well-intentioned one like Mat.

"Good going, Rufus," Darless commented. "These two on the trap door leading down will have to be dispelled. I'll see what I can do about them." She moved as close as she dared so that she could examine their exact nature before attempting a counter-spell.

"Thea, those two on the swords seem to be rather simple ones. See if you can disarm them. These two on the books are quite complex. I'll tackle them. The rest of you stand way back in case we goof and the trap activates." Thea went over to the ornamental swords to see if she could handle them. Though she was still an apprentice and impulsive, when it came to her spells, she was methodical in the extreme. Carefully, she went down the checklist of observable magical trap traits, which yielded their nature. "Electrical discharge," she concluded aloud to herself. Next, she reviewed the counter-spell in her mind until she was satisfied she had it right. Only then did she verbally cast her spell. Holding her breath after she spoke the triggering syllable, just in case it failed and the electrical blast triggered, she watched as a yellow magical energy engulfed the sword's blue trap energies. Both dissipated in a flash. "Whew," she muttered. However, like a good, cautious wizard, she then examine the swords to see if the traps were really discharged, again going down the checklist item by item. Only then did she announce, "Okay, these are cleared." With a proud expression on her face, she walked over to Lonnie and gave him a hug. "I did it! Disarmed my first *real* trap, well, the others were only practice traps, really." He smiled back at her.

Meanwhile, on the other side, Darless was not faring as well. Her traps were far more diabolical. Obviously, the prior occupant, the Archmage Sarah le'Garde did not want uninvited quests gaining access to the lower levels of her tower. These two that she faced were far more intricate and complex. A bead of sweat dripped down from her forehead into her right eye breaking her concentration ever so slightly, but it was just enough. "Duck!" she yelled as she dove for the floor. One trap defused, the other discharged. A streak of powerful electricity arced its way upwards from the trap door toward the ceiling and back down once more. Had she not dove out of the way, she would have taken the blast full-force. Fortunately, no one was hurt, only her pride. "I should have had that one too. This Sarah is one mean wizard with traps!"

"Okay, everyone pay attention. This green tomb is clear. However, this black volume I cannot disarm. I think only someone truly evil in nature can dare touch it. Under no circumstances does anyone touch this black volume directly. I am going to knock it onto the floor and slide it under the table way back out of the way. I don't want anyone to touch it. Now that we think it is clear of traps, gang, let's search away. Remember, we are primarily looking for clues to what happened to my parents some twenty years ago. Maybe one of these is a diary or such. Remember to use caution. There may be other, as yet undetected, traps." The search began in earnest.

Rufus eagerly opened the chest that had commanded his attention. Actually, it was the same chest he was trying to open years earlier when the ghosts had attacked him. Now he eagerly opened it up. "Hey, look at this stuff! Star gazing equipment of the finest grade! What a find!"

Catching his excitement, Jon took a look at the various high quality instruments the gnome was bringing out of the velvet lined chest. "Hey, I recognize that one. It's a sextant and that is an astrolabe. I recognize them from pictures in my history books!" The two began chatting about what you could do with these. Meantime, the three mages began a systematic examination of the books, tombs, parchments and scrolls. "This is going to take some time," muttered Alison. There were hundreds and most were written in a foreign language. Alison had to cast a spell just to be able read the titles.

While the others were going about the search, Sir Thomas, Mandy and Lonnie stood with their backs to the central pillar, each watching over about a third of the space of the room. It was rather a boring task, but all three took the job seriously, and not just because of Rufus's tale of ghosts. For Mandy, something-someone-someones had died in here. It was unsettling to say the least, which more than made her edgy. Besides, she almost felt the hairs on her neck rising. For the paladins, it was duty — their duty. Their leader had given them a task to perform and duty demanded that they carry it out to the fullest, as long as they agreed with the order, that is. So it was that all three were alert and prepared for the danger when it came.

And come it did. The others had barely spent five minutes in their examinations, when Mandy detected something moving up into the middle of the room. It was seeping up through the floor beneath her feet. Now the hairs on her neck rose sharply, but she did not need the warning. "Something's coming!" she called out. Another one had simultaneously appeared just in front of Sir Thomas.

"Make that two somethings!" he yelled. Simultaneously, he launched his huge two handed sword straight through the middle section of the ghostly specter before him. Mandy did likewise only a split second behind him. The others turned around to see both mighty swords pass clean through the creatures doing no damage whatsoever.

"Ieee, it is the ghosts again. Flee, flee for your lives!" screamed Rufus. He dropped everything and bolted to the stairs and flew up the steps as fast as his short legs could carry him, figuring the others would be right behind him. They weren't.

Alison and Darless were both exceedingly quick in reacting, seasoned veterans in surprise attacks. No sooner had the swords finished their wide sweep through the air, when Alison's volley of magical missiles flew to the one before Mandy. To the mage's astonishment, they did absolutely nothing to the ghostly creature, which continued to seep upwards into the room. Only its lower extremities had not yet come through the solid wooden floor. Darless's spell was more intense and took somewhat longer to come into being. Jon recognized the beam of disintegration as it left her finger heading toward the one before Sir Thomas. It went through the specter and eliminated a chuck of the stone column to the side of the paladin, missing his head by a mere foot. Darless cursed.

Lonnie moved into striking range, protecting a totally terrified Thea, who slowly edged her way toward the stairs, unsure whether to stay or flee and only barely able to make her legs work. Sir Thomas took command, "Flee now! Mandy slowly give way. Do not let them touch you. Everyone move!" So strong was his intention that in spite of herself, Alison found her feet moving toward the stairs. The others followed suit. Slowly, the paladin and Mandy edged their way backwards toward the others. They heard the scuffling of frantic feet and knew the others were on the way to safety.

Fascinated by these spectral beings of which he had never heard nor knew existed, Jon, however, moved only reluctantly and was the last of the group to reach the stairs, just behind the two fighters. He could not resist the temptation to try to establish communication with them. Figuring they could not speak, for they had no corporeal bodies, he chose instead to place his thoughts into the mind of the one nearest him. *Who are you? What do you want? We mean you no harm.*

He was not prepared for the violent, angry response he received on the back flow of his communication line. *Death! Your death! Slay all living creatures!* Only a short moment later in a soft voice, both timid and pleading, came, *Alicia, Servant of Sarah. Please, please slay me!* And then the contact was broken. Jon turned and stumbled his way up the stairs, followed by Mandy hot on his heels, spurring him on. He heard the clanking sounds of Sir Thomas right behind them both, so he concentrated on scrambling up the precarious stairs with no guard rail.

When the three made it to the root top, they found the others already forming into the three groups, ready to levitate off of the tower and to safety should the ghostly specters follow them outside. Jon quickly joined Alison as well as Mandy. Sir Thomas stood rear guard about ten feet from the opened trap door. He waited, but the ghostly beings did not pursue them. "I think they do not like the light of day," he commented. He also put his sword back into its sheath across his back and took out his holy symbol. "Bear with me a moment," he ordered. "I need to check something out to be sure." Without waiting for any acknowledgment, he began chanting a prayer to Father Ukko. Then he reentered the trap door and started down the stairs toward the two ghostly creatures, holding his holy cross prominently before him.

Both ghosts were now fully in the room and about a quarter of the way up the winding circular stairway, but they had halted. When they saw the paladin coming back down, they at first eagerly floated upwards toward him. Then the flash of his holy cross burned them and they both even more hastily retreated. Careful of his footing, the paladin slowly moved down the stairs. The two ghosts had retreated to the opposite side of the room as far as they could get from the menacing symbol of Good. Sir Thomas still holding his symbol before him continued to approach them. At last both began descending back through the solid floor from whence they came. Two minutes later, they were gone. The paladin then yelled upwards, "All clear. You can come back down now." The others needed no further encouragement.

As they others cautiously moved toward the trap door, Thea whispered to Alison, "Excuse me. I've, er, had an accident. I must go change my clothes." She was holding her hands in front of her, but Alison spied the wetness anyway. Thea looked totally embarrassed.

"I'm sorry Thea, it is really my fault. I had no right to let you get so close to this kind of danger. Really, it is all right. Go change. I won't tell the others," she whispered. Thea looked grateful and quickly used her magical ring to head down to the ground and back to their camp.

Alison was the last one back down. When she arrived in the room, Sir Thomas explained, "Undead spectral ghosts. They are undead ghosts. Rufus, you are absolutely right. These are terrible foes indeed. I was able to turn them back and force them back through the floor for the time being. I do wish Father Johnas was here. He would know how to defeat them."

"Well, my disintegrate beam did nothing. Perhaps magic does not affect them," Darless suggested coldly, attempting to size up the situation.

"My magical missiles are useless, too," moaned Alison, who had yet to encounter a foe on which the missiles inherently could do no damage once any protective spells had been eliminated. "This is serious — immune to spells and to weapons. How do we defeat them?"

"More to the point," put in Mandy, "how many more of them are there?"

"So far, only the two," Sir Thomas declared getting rather perplexed, "but I really do not know much about these creatures. I've only heard of them from Father Johnas — as yet, I've no training in their combat." His face cringed with annoyance; he was used to being able to supply others with such critical information. Alison was depending upon him and he had no answers.

"Well, I've never run into such creatures either," Mandy said consoling the paladin as best she could. She needed him fully alert, not dwelling on some imagined failure. How could anyone know about all the nasty creatures in the entire universe?

"I know something of them," broke in Rufus, who had been abnormally silent up to this point. Seeing he had everyone's attention, he continued, "They are very evil undead creatures. Their driving purpose in existence is to kill any living creature, man or beast! Often just the sight of them fare scares some folks into their grave! If they touch you, they try to suck all of the life energy out of your body! I've seen what's left of a gnome who accidentally ran into one; he was all shriveled up, wasted like. His body looked like that of a five hundred year old ancient gnome. But they also attempt to steal your body — sort of take control over it from you! Can you imagine what would happen to the rest of us if one took over Sir Thomas's body or Mandy's? Why we'd all get chopped into tiny pieces! If one took over Alison's body or Darless's, none of us would have any chance at all of surviving! These are very, very nasty creatures. Perhaps we'd better just forget about exploring this particular tower."

Alison was worried. Never had she faced an opponent that was apparently immune to everything. Yet, her whole quest led to this tower. Inside just had to be the clues she sought all of her adult life — what happened to her parents? She just could not give up. However, as the leader of the party, she had to think of everyone's safety as well. These were not just mere mercenaries, but her dearest friends. Her reverie was interrupted; she suddenly noticed the complete silence and looked up to find everyone was looking her way for guidance. Her face reddened and she tried to speak but only a gurgle came out. She cleared her voice, giving her time to think.

Jon sensed her plight and ventured his observations. "Er you guys, if I might interrupt Alison for a moment. I think I should add just a bit to the observations. When we were fleeing up the stairs, I tried to mentally contact the one nearest me. I asked it who it was and what did it want — that sort of thing. I got back the most violent anger imaginable. It's like Rufus says, it wants only to destroy the living. Yet, I don't know what to make of the rest of its reply. It did say that it used to be Sarah's servant, Alicia, but it also whispered pleadingly to slay it. Does that mean that it really wants to be killed? I don't quite understand it. How can something that is dead be alive? How can something that is dead already, but alive, be killed again?"

"Allow me," Sir Thomas who also quickly answered in order to give Alison more time to recover. "The how's and wherefore's are really the province of very high priests, of which we have none. Normally, when I am adventuring, I bring along Father Johnas, High Priest of Ukko, for just such situations, to say nothing of his healing powers. As a paladin, I do have some small training in these matters, but my ignorance is certainly showing today. As near as I can say, it is in the power of high evil priests to bring the dead back into an ungodly life. How, I don't know. You've seen it with the skeletons, zombies, and ghouls that we've seen both here and back in the Canyon Lands. We call them the undead because they are not energized like we are. Perhaps they are driven by some kind of energy that is the opposite of what powers us. I just don't have that knowledge. Father Johnas would be able to answer that for you, I'm sure. However, a body is a body and all bodies can die. It's just in this situation we do not know the proper way to slay them."

Jon nodded and pondered his words. Just what was an opposite life force energy anyway? That sure didn't fit in with his grasp of the world.

"And that is just what we must do," Alison finally found her voice. "We must pause for a spell, while some of us go and consult with Father Johnas. While we are gone, the rest of you stay well clear of this tower. I do not think that the spectral ghosts will come out into the world after you, or Rufus here would not be with us. I think you will be safe enough while we're gone. We must find out how to deal with these nasty creatures." Sighs of relief came from one and all.

Alison continued, "I'll take Sir Thomas with me, and, Jon, you come too," she added as an afterthought. "Mandy, I'm leaving you in charge of the defense of the rest. Darless, if any trouble comes, get everyone safely into a magical mansion and ride it out in safety. Okay, let's get out of this tower and back to the safety of camp." Slowly they all filed up the stairs."

"Say, where's Thea?" asked a worried Lonnie, who noticed she was not nearby.

Hastily, Alison replied, "She's safe. I sent here back down to camp for something." She intentionally didn't say more. It was not a lie, she told herself; she was just not offering a full explanation. Besides, Thea would probably tell him when they were alone.

Thea was just finishing putting on a clean pair of pants, when she spied the others slowly walking toward camp from the tower. There was no time to hide her dirty clothes. When they got closer, she timidly said, "Those ghostly things really scared the crap out of me. Sorry to let you all down." She stared at the ground, humiliated.

"Ah fair Thea, that is nothing to be ashamed of," Sir Thomas gallantly proclaimed. "We've all had such embarrassing moments in our adventures." Her eyes met his and he winked at her, adding softly, "It's just we don't talk about those times, if you follow me." Both grinned. Thea felt relieved, particularly when everyone seemed to not look at her dirty clothes.

Alison took Jon and Sir Thomas aside. To the paladin she said, "I'm depending on you to carry the conversation with Father Johnas. He and I, well, you know, I am not so religious as he expects and all."

The paladin smiled, "I know. He knows. But yes, I will gladly do so. How are we to get there? Teleportation? I'm not sure where he is, but probably he is somewhere near his church. At least that is a good starting place to look. I'd better change out of my plate armor before we go. Lonnie, can you give me a hand with this?"

Relieved, she replied, "Thanks. I owe you." When the paladin was ready to go, she commanded, "Okay, everyone, hold on to me." When she felt their secure grip, she spoke a command word to her staff. Magical energies flashed and Jon watched fascinated as they floated three feet to the ground before a stately, brown stone, Church of Ukko — one that he had never seen. It had to be such a church, because there was no mistaking the elaborate carvings on the massive oaken doors that stood before them. The building's design was not as elaborate as the Church of Ukko in Freetown or Alison's new church that the dwarves were building. Jon surmised that this priest believed in function not grandeur. He was correct.

Hymnal singing greeted their ears. They were in luck; Father Johnas was conducting the evening worship. Quietly, the three opened the doors, which were quite heavy, but moved easily on well-oiled hinges. They tiptoed past the entrance way, where the parishioners' jackets were hung neatly on pegs that were chest high. The singing grew loud and full of passion as they entered the chapel proper, taking seats in the rearmost pew which was empty. Jon guessed that the chapel could hold perhaps two hundred worshipers, but just now he estimated there were maybe a hundred in attendance. He recognized Father Johnas in his ceremonial white robes with the familiar blue cross emblazoned on its front.

Off to the left, another priest was moving his arms about obviously directing the people in the hymn singing. From the man's highly exaggerated mouth motions, he was a music conductor at heart. Jon grinned. On impulse, he got out his flute, assembled it and then began to play along with the voices. Once he had the tune down, he added a bit of ornamentation here and there, spicing up the sounds. His flute was indeed heard and Alison noticed many people were smiling in appreciation of the extra musical quality it added. Jon was not particularly religious himself, but music was music, and the beauty of the hymn was compelling. He was at peace with himself.

The music ended all too soon, as far as Jon was concerned. Then the deep bass voice of the bushy bearded Father Johnas echoed through the church. "Finally, let us pray together." After a short pause, he continued, "Father Ukko above, we humbly give thanks for all that you have done for us. Always do we honor you in both our hearts and minds. At all times do we endeavor to do what is right and just for all, though that path sometimes seems so very hard to follow. Continue to guide us along the path of righteousness that we may not fall into evil and sin. Though we, your children, are not always here in your church," he looked straight at Sir Thomas and Alison, whose cheeks reddened slightly, "know that you are not out of our minds, our prayers. In the name of Father Ukko, I now bless you all for another day." As he spoke the ending words, Jon felt the tiniest tingling of an energy flow over him. He closed his eyes and concentrated on that energy. Then he saw. Everyone in the room now had the same blue aura or energy glow about them. So there was something to this Bless Spell after all, he concluded, a different kind of magic.

The service complete, the townsfolk began chatting among themselves; most stood up and began heading for the rear entrance. "Before you go, on your way out, you might say hello to our own Sir Thomas le Bonnaire, Holy Paladin of Ukko, and Mage Alison d'Ambrose, Holy Mage of Ukko, and her fiancé, Jon Brown, who provided the impromptu accompaniment. We are blessed with their company this evening." Sir Thomas arose and bowed humbly toward those in front of him, Alison rose and curtseyed. Jon also stood up and nodded.

For a moment, a hush fell over the entire room. Then, whispers began in rapid fire. Jon caught several "Is that *the* Saint Jon Brown?" from many corners. Somehow he was known even here, although he had never been to this town, as far as he knew. Father Johnas also heard the whispers and piped up, "Yes, it is *the* Saint Jon Brown, the Redeemer." Now folks hesitatingly came up to the trio. Some wanted to shake the paladin's hand, but most just wanted to look at Saint Jon.

He felt rather awkward. Being a center of attention was the last thing Jon wanted. "Really, I'm just a musician." He waved his flute above his head, as if that would dispel doubts. The most common comment from the well-wishers was "Thank you for doing what you can." He smiled graciously, wondering what they meant by it. Finally, the last couple said their hello's, and Father Johnas, who had been following them, rather ushering them toward the rear, greeted them.

"Sir Thomas, so glad you could drop by," and they exchanged a hand shake and a hug. "And my dear Alison, I'm so pleased." Again, a hearty hug from the older man in his early forties, who stood just over six feet tall and weighted perhaps two hundred fifty pounds, all muscle. Jon felt that this was a priest who made things happen by force, if need be. "And Saint Jon, so glad we meet again. Welcome. I hope I didn't embarrass you too much there. It is always good for ordinary villagers to meet those of us who bear the power of Father Ukko. They can see that we are real people. It strengthens their beliefs and helps them to always do right actions in life. I'm sure you do feel such responsibility."

"Certainly, but I'd rather just play some music in your church," Jon replied, shaking his hand. "To be honest, Father, I just don't like being the center of attention."

The big man smiled, "That is as it should be, my son." While Jon pondered his statement, he continued, "So, Sir Thomas, to what do I owe this visit? Will you not come partake of dinner with me and tell me what you have in mind for this humble servant of Ukko? Millicent always prepares more food than we can possibly eat."

Before the paladin could answer, Alison smiled; she knew that there was no turning him down and said, groaning in mock protest, "Oh, I always over eat at your house!" The priest laughed. "His wife is nearly as large as he, and she insists you eat to get to their size," she added for Jon's benefit. Father Johnas led them through a side doorway, down an elaborate hall and into his private quarters, a small home that abutted the rear of the church.

As they entered his frugal home, the aroma of fresh baked bread and steaming chicken dwarfed all other senses. Jon immediately felt hunger pangs and was very glad for the chance for a proper home cooked meal for a change. Millicent was just as Jon had imagined from Alison's hints. She was a large woman, very practical, a good house keeper and mother, though Jon learned that all of their children had now left the roost in seek of their fortunes. She was very glad for their company as she bustled about adding three more places for dinner. Jon took an immediate liking to this plain woman, they spent an enjoyable hour at the table.

Once the meal was finished and Jon's offer to wash the dishes turned down by a surprised Millicent, Father Johnas declared, "All right now. Let's hear what you need, Sir Thomas." While his wife busied herself in the kitchen, the paladin explained what they had encountered. The rather jovial expression on Father Johnas' face turned altogether serious, as he quickly realized what his friends were up against, spectral ghosts. Clearly, he was worried and concerned.

"My son, you did right to retreat from these foul foes. I apologize for having failed to educate you properly on these types of undead creatures. My only excuse is that they are so exceedingly rare and we were concentrating on the more commonly found ones that you might encounter. Yes, your gnome friend is very well informed. These are exceedingly nasty creatures. You are all very lucky that you were able to turn them aside when you did, otherwise they would very likely have attempted to take over control of a pair of your bodies. With all of you being so powerful, that would have been an exceedingly bad situation. It would seem once again Father Ukko has smiled upon you all!" He paused for a moment reflecting and then continued.

"As to how to slay them, ah that is a good question. They can be attacked in only two ways; both are fraught with peril to you. When they attempt to strangle the life out of you, during that period only are they vulnerable to attack by weapons. However, the life is being drained out of their victim at the same time. Hence, this is not a really good way to defeat them, far too costly. There is another way. They can be attacked mentally. Jon, I believe you possess the mental powers that can destroy them. Their undead minds must be crushed utterly. Only a strong willed individual can hope to overcome them this way. I must truthfully admit to you all, I have never faced such opponents and I know that, like Sir Thomas, I only have a chance at making them turn away as he did. In some ways, Rufus's suggestion to turn away makes good sense. However, our calling is such that once we have discovered such vile creatures, we must do our very best to remove them from our world, if only for the sake of other innocent victims. So when do we leave?"

"Huh?" replied Sir Thomas, taken aback by his sudden volunteering. "We cannot ask you to come to aid us. You yourself have said that it is far too dangerous."

"Nonsense, my young man, duty calls. How could I possibly sleep at night knowing that there is a pair of spectral ghosts out there just waiting for their next hapless victim? No, with the two of us attempting to keep them at bay, this gives Jon a better chance at actually crushing their minds."

"Wait a minute! I don't think I know how to crush another's mind, Father Johnas," Jon protested. "How do I do that?"

"I'm sure you will figure out a way, my son," was the non-helpful reply.

"Well, maybe Darless or Mandy will have some idea. Maybe I should get some kind of mental training," Jon mused. This was the first time he had thought that formal training might be of critical value to him. Of course, now there was just no time for that. He did feel a bit more hopeful with two of them keeping the ghosts at bay, while he worked out how to destroy them. At least the others would not be in mortal danger if he failed.

Alison spoke up, "We can go just as soon as you are ready. I am forever grateful for your help, Father Johnas, really I am. We are getting so close to finding out what happened to my parents! I just cannot let this go."

Millicent had finished up the dishes and had heard the last few minutes of their conversations. "I'll pack you a bag, Johnas. Now mind you Sir Thomas, I expect to get him back in good condition," she teased, hiding the deep concern she always felt when her husband was about to embark on a dangerous mission.

"You have my solemn word, Millicent. I have never failed to protect him yet." She smiled at him, knowing quite well just how far the paladin had gone for her husband over their many years of adventuring. They said their farewells.

"Okay, how do we get there?" the priest asked, slinging his pack over his back.

Alison did a quick mental calculation and turned to Jon. "Can you do the honors? Together, we weigh too much for a single teleport spell."

"Sure thing," Jon answered. "Okay, grab hold of each other and me."

"Wait a minute," broke in Father Johnas. "Don't we need to go outside or something? I don't know what to do."

"Ah don't worry, it's child's play," Jon explained. "Yes, take hold of Sir Thomas. Now everyone just take one step forward, and, yes, here we are." At the beginning of the foot step they were in his dining room and at the end of the step, their feet landed upon the dry ground just outside the deserted village near where the others had setup camp. The sun was just going down behind the mountains. Of course, the priest stumbled; his senses could not adjust so fast. With Sir Thomas holding on to him, he didn't fall down.

"My, that is an interesting way to travel, my son. Very indeed!" he exclaimed, as he regained his footing and looked around. "This land looks very much the same here in spring as it did last winter, desolate, devoid of life, fitting place for spectral ghosts. Ah that must be the deserted town."

They arrived at the edge of the town. Mandy had a nice campfire blazing and Thea was just finishing up the evening dishes. Lonnie, standing guard duty, hailed their arrival, as the four walked into camp circle. Sir Thomas introduced the High Priest. Darless responded by promptly producing a steaming pot of tea; she knew that they would all gather around to share news. Jon was most appreciative; he nodded his thanks to her. While the tea was brewing, Sir Thomas pointed out the town and the tower, before the twilight failed altogether. Next, the paladin had Father Johnas explain the details of fighting spectral ghosts. Needless to say, when he finished, everyone was very glad the priest had chosen to come to help them. He received many thank you's.

But the real news came from Mandy. "I decided to help Rufus in his thorough search of all the deserted homes. It was very strange indeed. After inspecting a dozen homes, it struck me that whatever happened here occurred around meal time — supper I'd guess. It happened to all of them within a very short space of time. None, it would appear, were expecting the catastrophe that befell them. Traces of their last meal abound in nearly every home."

"Now I could not resist seeing if my mental powers to 'see what happened here' would shed any light. Well, I began touching objects but sensed no physic traumas." She paused with a twinkle in her eye, as she watched Alison's face fall from expectancy of something important to that of "darn." Mandy, ever the tease, then continued, "Not until I picked up a metal fork with which some woman had been eating when it happened to her. Then, I saw what she saw in those last seconds. It was horrifying. I really do not know what to make of it or what it was. I've never seen or heard of anything like this. Perhaps Father Johnas can make some sense of it."

"Pardon me, My Lady," the priest interrupted, "but I don't quite know how you saw into the past. Can you elaborate? And how could I see too? I'm not following you." He looked rather perplexed, as if one who has been given a problem but not the data with which to solve it.

"When I touch objects, sometimes I can pick up latent images that are somehow still affixed to the object, but only if they were traumatic in nature. I think the images come from the person that is being affected. I see them in my mind. Thus, I can replay them for all to see. Jon, will you help me out here. I'll show them to Jon and he has the ability to put the images into other people's minds." Jon relaxed, concentrated, and one by one, made contact with the other minds. Once he had everyone connected up to him, he sent Mandy a go ahead signal. She slowly replayed in her mind the salient portions of what she had seen earlier that afternoon.

It was gruesome and scary. The images began with a family being served dinner. Then, a cold, black energy seeped through the walls, creeping slowly toward the family, who stood terrified, frozen to the spot. A sense of curiosity gave way to stark terror in these people. When the wave of energy hit them, unimaginable pain wracked their bodies, driving them into complete unconsciousness. After a long blackout period which the ranger cut short, everyone received the same horrid shock that these people had when they finally regained consciousness and saw their bodies stripped of all flesh; they stared down at their own bleached white bones. The poor people could not even scream. Then, they sank into a deep unconsciousness once more. Mandy halted the projections; Jon broke his connection to the others, staggered and fell onto the ground, so great were the reactions of the others to seeing these vivid images. Jon had picked up not only the scene, but also the seven other's emotional reactions to it all. It temporarily overwhelmed him.

"Jon, Jon, are you all right?" Alison reached his side, propped his head up, looking for any injury from the hard fall. He had a swelling bruise on his forehead.

"I — I — I'm okay — just a little shaken. I got all your reactions in a sort of feedback. I'll be all right in a minute," he offered. "Oh, my head!"

"You all discuss it, and I'll help Jon out," Darless took charge, helping him stand and moving him off some distance from the fire. "Okay, Jon. You know the drill. I want you to go back to the start of this event. Move through your mental images and tell me what happened as you go through them." Darless, once more, got the opportunity to practice the mental assist they had perfected. Ten minutes later, they returned to the others.

Jon was all smiles and all trace of the bruise had vanished.

"That was a most humbling experience, Mandy," Father Johnas commented, deeply moved by the images. "You realize that this is the first time that I have ever seen the living made into undead skeletons. Those poor people! Words cannot thank you enough for the visions you have given me. I have much to ponder. There is one thing I can tell you. That deadly energy field was not clerical or priestly in nature. It must have been conjured from the arcane magical arts. We are not dealing with an evil priest, rather it is more likely an evil magician."

"That's what I was trying to say, necromancy," piped up Rufus.

"That seems highly suggestive, given the circumstances," Alison concluded, biting her lip in thought. "It is the tower of the Archmage Sarah le'Garde, apparently deceased for five years. She was likely very evil in nature, since she was at one time a consort to the Demon Lord Jarred, who we know is altogether evil. He is very likely the culprit behind the abduction of my parents and the destruction of our castle. Do you suppose that she destroyed her own villagers? If so, why?"

"Who can say with such evil, chaotic beings," Father Johnas answered her solemnly. "But the pieces are beginning to make sense. Apparently, the death energy even killed her servants, if Jon's mind contact with one of the spectral ghosts is to be trusted."

"Yes, but she also disappeared never to be heard from again," Alison added. "What happened to her?" No one had any ideas. At this point, Jon and Darless rejoined them. Quickly Alison told the two what they had concluded thus far.

Since the hour was getting late, full darkness lay upon the land, and the bonfire had died down, Alison cast her mansion spell, and they moved the horses and gear inside. This was the first time that Father Johnas had been inside a magical mansion, and he was very much impressed. His comments were similar to Sir Thomas's when he first stayed inside. "Now this sure beats sleeping on the cold, hard ground! Such luxury. Is it safe? Should I worry about anything?" Alison smiled and explained the basic operation and its safety.

Meanwhile, Jon took Darless and Mandy aside for a conference. "There is only one flaw in the Father's plan. I have no idea how to attack these ghosts. I know, I know, Mandy, I should really get some training. Honestly, there has not been much time for it." Mandy glared at him. "Oh, okay, there was during the winter, but I just didn't want to do it." She smiled; she had gotten the truth of the matter out of him.

"Well, both Darless and I know how to do such attacks, right Dar?" The mage nodded. "However, I don't have anywhere the overall power or energy that either of you have. My psi ability is rather limited."

"No question, Jon," Darless confirmed, "you have so much power that ours pales in comparison."

"Hey, wait a minute. Why don't we three join forces? We've done it before to extend our capabilities? Three are stronger than any one of us," Jon suggested in a flash of insight.

"Hum, there is a great deal of merit in that idea," Mandy mused. "I'm nearly totally useless at this point. They are immune to weapons."

"I like this idea," Darless added, thinking quickly. "I didn't raise the issue as yet, but what happens if both spectral ghosts appear at the same time? Jon could not fight them both simultaneously, at least not very effectively. But if Mandy and I are both fighting, we can each take one and suck as much power from Jon as we need. I think it makes perfect sense!"

"Well promise me one thing," Jon insisted very seriously, "promise me that you will use energy from me first, before you tap into your own reserves. That way, when I run dry, you will still have some left to help get the others out of harm's way if needed. Promise me that." Both assured him they would. The three hugged each other and then joined the others as they were retiring for the night.

As Jon lay beside Alison, he whispered to her their plan of action. "My love, if I start to feel too drained, may I suck energy from your newfound powers? I won't unless I have too. I just don't want to pass out and force all of you to have to carry me out, while keeping those ghosts at bay."

She kissed him lovingly, "Of course, take all you need."

"Promise me that you will let me know when you are also running low. I don't want to disable you either, promise me that."

"Of course, Jon, I will," she whispered back, but she was still thinking long after Jon fell asleep. Only she saw the converging, parallel lines of energy between the psi mental disciplines and her magical incantations. She kept thinking of her last conversation with Father Ukko. Until now, she had only thought of how similar mental skills were to her magic. What if it worked in reverse as well? If she could convert her immense pool of magical energy at her command into mental energy, Jon would find her a veritable dynamo. Grinning to herself, she finally fell into a sound sleep.

Everyone slept soundly that night, save Father Johnas. He was nearly asleep, when he heard the unmistakable voice of Father Ukko in his mind as he so often did when the God answered his evening prayers. Ukko said, "Johnas, stay with them to the end. Your services in my name will be sorely needed at that time."

He woke with a start, looked around at all of the sleeping forms, and assured himself he was not dreaming. Carefully he prayed, "Thank you Father Ukko for the guidance. I will see it through to the end. I am only glad to be of service to you once more. Thank you for the opportunity." It took him another hour to calm down sufficiently to get to sleep.

The next day, once breakfast was finished, everyone made their personal preparations for the battle. Father Johnas gave to Sir Thomas further instructions in the proper prayers to hold the undead at bay. Next, he gave each person a vile of holy water. "If one of these foul creatures begins to attack you, throw this holy water over your face and neck. It may help keep them from getting a strangle hold on your life force for a very, very short while. Perhaps that brief time will be enough for the physical attacks of ours to have an effect on them." The others found this slightly reassuring.

It was about nine o'clock when they all joined hands and Jon stepped them onto the roof of the tower. The sun shone brightly in the deep blue sky; it was another beautiful late spring morning. When Sir Thomas opened the trap door, the putrid odor of death and decay once again assaulted their olfactory senses. For this battle, a new marching order arose, once Jon explained how they were going to handle the mental attacks.

Thea and Rufus were in the rear, guarding from any possible surprise from that direction. They were to stay on the stairs proper. Besides, should attacks on the creatures materialize, their spells could be cast from this position; they would have a great viewpoint. In front of them were Jon and Alison and then Mandy and Darless. All four were also instructed to stay on the stairs proper. Only Sir Thomas, Father Johnas and Lonnie actually set foot on the floor. Lonnie stood between them. While they chanted and prayed to keep the evil ones at bay, should either fail, Lonnie was to intervene as best he could until help arrived. Lonnie found this a great honor, for once he was in the thick of the confrontation, and his masters were both depending upon him utterly. His was a great responsibility, and he recited the Paladin's Code of Honor quietly to himself several times.

"Wait a minute!" called out Alison, just as the three men were about to descend the stairs. "The lanterns are out. We left them burning. Please let me check for traps before you go much further." Jon marveled at how fast her reaction had been. He'd not even realized the lanterns were out yet. That meant someone other than they had put them out, and that same person could very well have reset some of the traps that the three mages had defused yesterday! She had deduced all this in less than an instant. Hence, Jon's utter amazement and respect.

"Ah, yes, yes, that is a very wise idea," Sir Thomas replied, catching up with Alison's train of thought. He thought to himself, *She always is faster than I am on these things. I'll never be as sharp as she is!* He watched as all three mages commanded their globes of light on top of their staves to glow even brighter, compensating for the scant illumination coming in from the trap door above this top room of the tower.

Quickly, Alison and Darless both began a short magical chant. Thea was too far behind to actually search this time, so she waited patiently, committing to memory the situation that led her mentor to suggest a re-searching operation. Jon watched as their spells activated. He could see nothing occurring with his eyes, but the mages could. As they systematically moved their gaze about the room, traps should be outlined in a bluish energy glow, if such were present.

"Ah, the pair surrounding the trap door to the next lower floor has been reset!" exclaimed Alison a bit dismayed.

"A new one is set to trigger, when someone steps on the last step!" declared Darless. The two mages then verified each other's findings. "We concur, two have been reset and a third added since we were last here yesterday.

Number 1, that implies someone with the ability to set magical traps has been in this room since then. Number 2, though we did not set a watch on the trap door, it is highly unlikely that someone from the outside world entered here and reset them, though it is possible, especially if they cloaked themselves with an invisibility spell. Number 3, it is more likely that the magic user is still within this tower somewhere. Number 4, I have a very bad feeling about this magic user, for how can any living thing avoid the attack of the ghosts?"

Father Johnas spoke up for the first time. "Now I have a very bad feeling about this, Darless. You are correct, but maybe we are wrong. Let's hope for the best, I do not want to scare you all needlessly. So can the traps be removed easily?"

Both mages began another very short chant. Sparks flew as the two opposing energies briefly cancelled each other out. "Clear," spoke the two mages in unison, smiling broadly. "It's safe to continue down now," added Alison. The party resumed their orderly descent into the top room of the tower of the Archmage Sarah le'Garde. Quickly, Father Johnas and Sir Thomas began their prayers, both holding their crosses of Ukko boldly before them. They were standing about five feet apart with Lonnie, sword drawn, between them and slightly in front of them ready to protect them. On the second step from the bottom stood Mandy and above her on the next, Darless. Both were relaxing and letting their minds encompass the space of the room. Right behind them and above them, Jon stood. He had already made contact with their minds and setup a union with them so that he could supply the mental power or energy they needed for their attacks. Behind and above him stood Alison. She felt Jon's presence in her mind; she hoped that she could figure out how to give him any needed mental energy boost he may need. Really, she didn't have a clue about how to do it yet. Curving even more around the side and above her stood Rufus and Thea.

Thea used one of her clever fire spells to ignite the six lanterns located systematically around the room. Combined with the three glowing staffs, the room was now reasonable well illuminated, she felt. She resigned herself to waiting; she, too, hated waiting and inaction. Thea wondered how Mandy could have the patience to wait as well. She grimaced and stood still.

It wasn't long before the pair of spectral ghosts began floating up through the middle of the room's floor. "Here they come!" exclaimed Thea, fighting hard to restrain the utter feeling of terror that began to flow over her once more. She desperately hoped she could control her body this time. Her "accident" the day before was humiliating enough. Straining with all her might, she prepared her magical missile spell. If one so much as tried to attack the men, she would start launching them, volley after volley in hopes that it would do some good.

The two priestly prayer spells culminated just as the two forms had completely gained the room. Both cringed back against the wall as far from the two men as they could get. For a minute, they hesitated. Thea swore that they were looking for a way to get around the two men to get at her! Now both ghosts began rising above the floor. *Surely they are coming after me now!* she screamed to herself in her mind. "Steady there, Thea, steady," reassured Rufus, though he too felt his legs shaking so violently he could hardly stand up. He leaned against the wall for support.

Jon felt a huge mental jolt as both Mandy and Darless made mental contact with the two ghostly minds. He felt both women sucking energy from him. Realizing that that effort was really going to waste, he began flowing his energy down the energy pathway that they had set up, straight into their minds. He felt their relief and felt them place all their concentration out onto the pair of minds. Now Jon connected with Alison's mind and began to draw a gentle flow of energy from her, passing it on down the line as well.

Ah ha! thought Alison. *So this is how it is done. This is easy. Hum, I wonder if I can send him more? Wonder if magical energy will suffice? Well, why not?* For months now, she could see only a minor amount of difference between her mental energies and her magical energies. She sent the equivalent magical energy of a magical missile down the line to Jon. She detected only a slight "What's this?" from him as he sent it on to the two women. So she continued sending a little bit extra every half minute.

Mandy and Darless both experienced nearly identical reactions because they were really connected to each other via Jon. With their minds totally open, they could sense the presence of the ghosts when they arrived. They needed not their eyes and in fact, once they began their attacks, both found it easier to keep their eyes shut so that they could concentrate on the attack fully.

Die foul undead creature! Mandy sent it as she mentally smashed into its mind. Darless merely smashed into hers. As their mental energies hit the opposing minds, both felt the ghosts raise their own mental defensive barriers to counteract the attack. Both women drew on more power from Jon to press down on the ghosts even harder. The harder they pressed, the harder the ghosts' defense grew. A stalemate resulted. In unison, the two women changed attack modes. This time, they shaped their energy into a sphere around the ghost's minds and then began to compress the minds, intent on squashing their minds into pin head size, thereby killing them in the process.

Ah, once again, the defending ghosts also changed tactics and setup a repulsion flow, forcing the collapsing spheres of pure energy slightly outward. Both women drew even more power from Jon to keep the pressure on.

Another stalemate. Next, they drew double the amount of energy from Jon, who lurched at the suddenness of the energy drain. Alison also felt the backlash. However, Darless took a bit of her awareness and took a look at the attack from outside the immediate arena. Then she saw it. Another supporting energy flow was helping to back up the two ghosts! *More power! Someone is helping the ghosts!* she sent to Jon. However, so loudly did she send it that Alison heard it too.

Alison sent back, *Okay. Here comes a big one.* She hoped the others were prepared. She mocked up the energy required for her ultimate Time-stop spell, her most powerful spell, which required the most energy of any magical spell she could cast. Wham, she sent that bolt down the line. Prepared by her warning, Jon relaxed even more and allowed the humongous pulse of energy to flow on through him to the two women. Likewise, the two women prepared their minds to just let whatever came through to flow on out onto the crushing spheres. Both women jerked violently in spite of their relaxation as the giant wave of energy passed through their minds and out onto the crushing spheres. Instantly their spheres collapsed into tiny black dots of nearly solid energy. All resistance to their attack instantly ended so suddenly, that both women lost their balance and fell forward onto the backs of the priest and the paladin. Jon lost his footing and fell down the stairs. Alison fell backwards from the sudden disconnection, landing on her butt on the edge of a step. "Ouch, that hurt!" she exclaimed.

Just as the two women fell onto the two men, the men saw the two ghosts suddenly become exceedingly transparent and then vanish without a trace. Father Johnas thought he heard an echo in his mind saying merely, "Thank you," but he lost it as he took the full weight of Mandy landing on his back.

The two men caught off guard also fell to the floor, cushioning the fall of Mandy and Darless. "Er, sorry about that," Mandy exclaimed, as she picked herself up off the floor and Father Johnas. Darless gave a loving kiss to Sir Thomas before she got up off of him.

"What happened anyway?" asked Father Johnas. "Look out, Jon has fallen too. Nasty fall. He's not moving. I'd better see to him at once. Excuse me." He rushed up the couple steps to Jon's prone body. Indeed, he had hit the stairs hard and was unconscious, bleeding profusely from his nose and mouth. He'd smashed them on the stone steps, breaking them badly. The robust priest lifted Jon up and carried him to the floor and laid him gently down. Everyone else rushed down the steps to see what had happened. Alison cringed when she saw Jon's face, it looked gruesome. However, Father Johnas merely began another chant, a rather long one though. When he finished his lengthy prayer to Ukko, he touched Jon's face with his hand and held it there for a minute. The hushed watchers saw a bluish glow encompass both the priest and Jon. Right before their eyes, the smashed face healed up completely. Only the fresh blood showed that he had even been hurt. He stirred.

"Oh. I don't feel so good," he muttered as he regained consciousness. He opened his eyes, "Well, no, I don't feel as bad as I thought I would be feeling." He seemed momentarily confused. His hand wiped his face; he saw the blood and a very worried look came over his face.

"Relax, my son," Father Johnas spoke softly, "You took quite a nasty fall there, but now you are fully healed. Can you stand?" He helped Jon get to his feet. Alison quickly brought out her decanter of water and a rag and cleaned up her man. Jon smiled and let her wipe off the blood. Father Johnas pleaded, "Now then, can someone please tell me what happened? Both ghosts are now deceased, to use a terrible pun."

"Well, we crushed them, just like you said to do. It was tough going though," Mandy tried to figure out how to explain what they had actually done.

"Actually," Darless added dryly, "it was a total stalemate until the very end there. Someone was backing up the ghosts just like Jon and Alison were backing us up. What the heck happened at the end there? Was it you Alison that said 'Here comes a big one?'"

"Er, yes, I'm the culprit. I sent you a big one," she said rather sheepishly.

"Now wait just a minute here!" Darless said her voice full of surprise and disbelief. "You do not have the kind of psi mental power reservoir that Jon has. How did you do that trick?"

"I don't know," Jon replied. "I am so tired! I gotta have a nap." He tried to move to the stairs, but then ended up just lying down on the carpet, sound asleep.

"Now that is totally predictable, Father Johnas," Darless explained. "When he uses up too much mental energy, he just collapses into a sound sleep. Of course when he wakes, he'll be famished. Thea, that's your cue."

She laughed, "I know, I was already thinking what I can fix in a hurry. I reckon he will sleep for a while yet. I want to hear what happened."

Mandy broke in, "Come on, Alison, you have been strangely silent. How on earth did you give us that tremendous pulse of energy? Spill it. On my best day, I cannot muster but a fraction of what I got via you in that single instant!"

"I, er, ah, don't quite know how to put this," the Archmage muttered. "Remember me saying that I could see a great parallel between my magical energies and the psi mental energies you all use? Remember me saying the border between the two seems to me to be rather gray? Well, to put it bluntly, you both received the full amount of magical energy that I use to cast my ultimate, highest, most powerful spell, my Time-stop."

"Zagroot zounds!" declared Mandy, now completely staggered. "I had no idea how much magical energy that took. Compared to what I can control and cast, you are a giant and I am an ant! I have a new, profound respect for Archmages!"

Darless, however, said nothing. She was lost in thought. At long last she spoke to Alison directly, "You know, I think that I can actually command and control that much magical energy now. When we get a chance to return to our magical studies, can you let me have a try at doing that spell? I believe that I now can handle it."

"You got it," Alison agreed wholeheartedly. "You realize Darless, that if you can handle it, you too have reached the Archmage status!"

"Unbelievable!" declared Mandy. "A party with two Archmages in it, now that would be something to tell our grandchildren about! I've never heard of an adventuring party with two Archmages in it, ever! Congratulations, Darless!"

"Hey, I haven't yet learned that I can do it, so hold off on the congratulations, please." Intense pleasure and satisfaction radiated from the face of the alu-demon. She knew of no other alu-demon that had ever risen to Archmage status — or even as far as she had already arisen in her magical usage.

"Wait a minute," Mandy, who had been pondering what Alison had done. "Alison, you sent just one blast, the equivalent of one spell, right?" Alison nodded affirmative. "Zagroot zounds, Alison. Do you fully realize what you can do? What if you also sent the equivalent of all of your spells? How much would that be?"

Alison did a quick calculation, "Well, if I did no other magic in a day, I could deliver that amount about fifteen times," she said meekly, suddenly realizing just how much power that represented.

Mandy could not help teasing her, "Zounds! Remind me never to cross you!" Everyone laughed at that, even Alison.

Rufus, who had been completely silent this whole time, very uncharacteristically, finally had to speak, "I don't think it is ever wise to ever cross an Archmage! However, is it safe in here now? Can we continue our searches?" The riches of the room loomed large in his eyes.

"I believe it is safe enough for the present," declared Sir Thomas. "I will personally stand over Jon and guard him while he sleeps. Lonnie, you guard the others. The rest of you, search away. We do know that someone was helping the ghosts, so stay alert for him." They broke into smaller groups once more resuming their thorough search of the room.

"Oh, yes, Father Johnas," Alison remembered that evil book that she had found yesterday and had kicked under the table. "We found what I think is an evil book. Whatever you do, don't physically touch it. What do you make of it?" She used her staff to slide it back out from under the table. The priest stooped to examine it visually. Then, he spoke a short prayer and examined it more closely.

At last he spoke, "This is an anomaly. I thought you said the tower was owned by an Archmage?" Alison nodded. "Well, this is a highly evil priestly tomb that should never be allowed to ever get into the hands of an evil priest! The havoc they could raise with it is terrible to contemplate. How is it that a wizard has it? Now that *is* the question." She had no answer. "Do you mind if I confiscate this and see that it is either destroyed or sequestered so that its evil can never see the light of day?"

Much relieved, Alison replied, "No. It is *all* yours! It's one less thing I have to worry about. Thank you, Father Johnas." He pulled out a pair of gloves and a sack and carefully put the book into his sack for later disposal.

The detailed search continued for over two hours. Much of the equipment in the room concerned the study of the heavens, as did many of the books. Since all mechanical pieces were of the finest make, Alison's rough estimate of the value of the contents was about one hundred thousand gold coins! However, the room yielded no clues about the fate of her parents so long ago.

However, one book was a financial log book with various numbers neatly scribed by a feminine hand. On a whim, Alison thumbed back some twenty years and came forward. Most entries concerned the villagers, their taxes, and her expenses in village upkeep. However, one entry pricked her interest. It read rather cryptically:

20 Aug 1222 Project S Income: 1,000,000 Outlay to D: 500,000; Outlay to A: 200,000; Profit: 300,000

It was sheer speculation, but Alison recalled that the brown dragon had said that he had been paid 500,000 gold coins for his services. 'D' for dragon maybe. But what was 'S' and 'A'? She showed it to Darless, who pondered it for a time before suggesting that 'S' might be Scepter, though she had no idea what 'A' could represent. Mandy looked at it and suggested 'A' for army. It all seemed to fit, but then, maybe they were reading into it what they wanted to see.

Meanwhile, Rufus had gathered all of the valuables into a well-organized pile near the center stone pillar. He decided against taking the rug. Getting the odor of death out of it would be a challenge not worth the effort.

When Jon finally awoke it was lunch time. Thea had left them about a half hour earlier to fix something for Jon; everyone took a much needed break. All were grateful for Thea's hot lunch. Being outside once more in the fresh, clean air and the light of day was refreshing to everyone. After lunch, they would have to descend to the next floor. Alison secretly wondered if they would have to fight their way down each level. She hoped not.

While Jon did up the dishes, under the guidance of Rufus, the contents of the top floor that were considered valuable were air lifted down from the roof and safely stowed in an empty house near the village gates.

Chapter 14 The Descending of the Tower

By one o'clock, the adventurers congregated by the trap door that led down to the fourth floor. To be doubly safe, Alison insisted on checking it for traps once more. Finding none, she gave Sir Thomas and Mandy the go ahead to actually open it. While the strong man proceeded to pull it open, Darless and Alison held their glowing staves close by.

No sooner than the paladin got the door fully open than three things happened nearly simultaneously. First, the next room was pitch black. No light from the wizard staves penetrated the inky blackness. It was as if they were staring into empty space. Second, the stench of death, of rotting flesh, flooded out of the long closed room, causing everyone save Darless to momentarily gag, choke and gasp for breathable air. Third, a massive lightning bolt arced out from the depths of the room striking the paladin squarely in the chest, fully discharging itself on all his metal armor. The force of the blast knocked him off his feet, sending him flying backwards ten feet, bowling over Mandy, Alison, Father Johnas and Lonnie. The big man lay motionless, not even breathing.

Darless sprang into action, slamming the trap door shut, while Jon rushed over to the fallen warrior. Lifting his front plate cover to expose his face, Jon saw a very pallid skin tone. He felt for a pulse. Finding none, he immediately used his trusty walking stick. "In the name of Father Ukko, he spoke softly and touched the man's face gently with the end of his stick. Father Johnas was just getting to his feet, when he saw the blue energy glow flood over the fallen paladin. Recognizing what it was, he smiled to himself. Musician or not, Father Ukko had blessed Jon with the ability to heal — of that the priest was certain. Sir Thomas, in a panic, took a giant intake of air, gasping for breath.

"Take it easy for a bit. You took a nasty shock" Jon spoke softly to the paladin. Father Johnas helped him sit up. "Thanks for being quiet everyone," Jon added. While Jon was handling the paladin, Darless cast a lock spell on the trap door, so that whoever was below could not get to them. Now that the dire emergency was over, everyone began talking at once.

"What the heck was that?" exclaimed Thea. "Was that a lightning bolt?"

"Zounds! Who the heck is down there anyway?" put in Mandy. "That was vicious! Why was it so black anyway?"

"Man, that was some attack," added Lonnie. "The force of the blast was incredible."

"How can anyone be alive down there anyway?" Rufus wanted to know.

"That, my friends, was a Darkness Spell," Darless attempted to explain. "It's the opposite of our Light spells. Probably a Continuous Darkness spell at that. I've run into them before. The Dark Elves often use it to hide their sneaky attacks or to vanish without a trace." However, only Rufus knew what a Dark Elf actually was. She let it go and continued, "That was indeed a lightning bolt spell. I just caught a glimpse of its triggering perhaps a fraction of a second before it detonated. We can all be thankful it was not the fancier chain lightning bolt spell like we used on the Cult of the Black Scorpion. Otherwise, all of us might be lying on the floor and not just Sir Thomas! Further, the power behind that spell is indicative of a very powerful caster." As an afterthought, she added thinking hard, "Almost what I would expect delivered in one of Alison's bolts."

"But what does this all mean?" Thea wanted to know. "Are we facing a powerful magic user who lives down there? If so, why doesn't he show himself?"

"But how can a magic user stay alive down there, Thea?" Rufus protested. "You know — those two nasty spectral ghosts. They rose up from this very room, that's for sure."

"Well, it could have been an ancient defense mechanism that the Archmage Sarah left activated to prevent anyone from entering from above," Alison surmised, trying desperately to put the pieces of this puzzle together. She was the leader and shortly they would want to know what to do next. "I've heard about such and actually seen much lesser traps. It may have been just that — a trap that we sprung. I was able to only check for traps on this side of the door, mind you. But Darless is right, if that had been a chain bolt, we all would have taken the blast."

"Why didn't it hit me?" wondered Mandy. "I was right there beside Sir Thomas. Why him and not me?"

"Well, that's clear enough for me," the paladin finally got his breathing under control. "I'm a perfect conductor of electricity in this armor suit. Probably the wizard figured I was the most deadly of his foes. Besides, look at the damage that bolt did to me? By the way, thank you Saint Jon. I do believe you saved my life there."

Jon, a bit embarrassed by the sudden shift of attention squarely on himself, shuffled his feet. "Er, actually it was Father Ukko's spell, not mine. I was just the first to get to you, that's all." Desperate to get the attention off of himself, he added, "So now what do we do to get around this?" He also hoped Alison had had time to think of an answer.

She had had barely enough time to work it out. "Okay, the darkness can be dispelled by counter magic.

However, I shall not risk anyone's life. None of us are going down there until it is safe. I think I have just the right spell for this situation. Will you give me a minute to confer with Darless?" They did so and began milling around the now nearly empty room, discussing the situation among themselves and wondering just what Alison had in mind.

Alison quickly explained her idea to Darless. The alu-demon concurred, adding, "Let me handle the dispelling of the darkness first, then cast yours. I'll stick my staff down through the door to provide the necessary illumination. If the light is somehow dispelled, remember: if I can dispel his darkness, he may just dispel my light. If that happens, you cancel your spell and let me cast one. I can see in the dark a bit. If there is a living body down there, I should be able to see him, unless he's cloaked in some form of invisibility. However, if he attacks, then I can see him."

"Okay everyone. Here's the plan. When I say 'Okay,' Mandy you open the trap door, but do it from the side so you provide no possible target. I don't want you getting blasted. Then, Darless will attempt to dispel the darkness spell. If she fails, Thea, you give it a go. You only need to stand here, just so you can see the very edge of the darkness. Once the magical effect is gone, Darless will poke her light staff down, but staying well back so she cannot get attacked. Then, I will use my Magical Eye spell. I can create a big floating eye that I can move several hundred feet away from me. I can see what is in there through the eye. That ought to do it." Everyone thought that was a sound plan, especially since there was no risk to be taken by remote observation. Jon found the idea of looking through a magical eye rather fascinating and he paid close attention to what Alison was doing.

Standing to one side, Mandy opened the door. Darless chanted her counter-spell. Again, Jon noted the effect of two opposites colliding. Hers won, the inky blackness dissolved into a darkness one might expect in a very dimly illuminated room. Next, she poked her staff down through the door. Those nearby could now see the curved side wall of the tower just below. Evidently, the stairs down was like this room, built into the side of the tower, curving, spiraling downward. Finally, after a rather lengthy chant, Alison's magical eye appeared in front of her face. Once she adjusted to looking through it, she concentrated on moving it over the doorway and on down into the room.

She went painstakingly slowly, methodically scanning all about. "It's a bedroom," she whispered to the others.

"Gosh, it sure does stink down there!" Thea whispered to Lonnie. She held her hand over her nose in a vain attempt to block the stench. He nodded agreement, but held his finger to his lips, telling her to be quiet and not disturb Alison. She glanced back at Rufus; he was holding his nose as well.

Ten minutes later, Alison had convinced herself that the room was indeed totally empty. She cancelled her spell. "Okay, everyone, it is a master bedroom with a huge bed, several wardrobes, night stand, writing desk and a bunch of chests. It appears empty at the moment. However, it is likely full of traps. This time, I am going down first, but I will go prepared. I will put a major globe of invulnerability around myself so that, if I get attacked, the normal spells will not affect me at all. Once I believe it is safe, you follow me down, but use the same marching order. I think we should have our fighters up front, just in case."

Thea whispered to Lonnie, "Now *this* is one spell I just *have* to learn as soon as I am able! Imagine, being impervious to fire balls, missiles, and lightning bolts! Isn't that just super?"

He had to agree with her on this one. "Can a wizard put that spell onto another?"

"Search me," Thea shrugged, "but I would suppose so. Alison put the spell that made one impervious to physical attacks onto us before, so why not this one too? Seems perfectly reasonable to me, but then I have not yet learned the spell. Once I do, I'll let you know. It could be a very useful spell, don't you think? You go into a battle and the opposing wizards cannot get to you, pretty nifty I'd say."

Soon, Alison was beginning her descent into the fourth floor room. Carrying her staff with her globe of light shining at its maximum and with Darless holding her light at the top of the stairs above her, she could see fairly well. Slowly, she began her magical search for traps. She had no intention of accidentally triggering one. One step down, and then another, slowly, slowly she went. Midway down, she halted. A footstep onto the very next step would trigger a spring mechanism hidden in the wall. She assumed that the idea was to push the person off of the side of the stairs, letting gravity do the damage. A short chant later, the trap sprang harmlessly and she descended further.

Finally she reached the wooden floor. The central stone shaft supported the floor in an identical manner to the one above. However, near the center was yet another booby trap for the unwary. Her alert eyes caught the slight difference in the rug. Using her staff, she pushed down on this small section of floor and up shot three two-foot long spikes. "Cleared that one," she thought to herself. The only other trap seemed to be on the door handled of the closet. Again, to be safe, she forced the double doors open with her shaft. This time, two small needles sprang out, oozing what she assumed was some kind of lethal poison. "Okay, it is clear I believe. Darless, you come next and recheck my work. I believe all are now disarmed."

The alu-demon did as instructed, casting her detection of traps spell and descending slowly and methodically. Finally, she also gave the all clear words, and the rest of the party crept down the stairs. "Master bedroom, I assume," Alison explained. The others concurred and began a thorough search.

"Mind if I help out?" asked Father Johnas. "I want to see if anything in here is actually evil, you know, something that would harm others."

Alison gave her blessing, "Oh yes, please do. It has been so long since we've had someone along who can easily do that." The priest, after a short prayer to Father Ukko, began surveying the room.

Rufus, finding nothing of much interest to him in this ladies bedroom began tapping here and there looking for hollow areas, secret compartments. Sir Thomas stood guard over the trap door leading down to the third floor. The rest began a thorough search.

"Oh, I do like this ornate mirror," Thea exclaimed. "Full length, no less." She stood in front of it, imaging herself in fancy dress.

"Get away from that mirror!" called out Father Ukko. "It is radiating evil." Too late. As Thea swayed her body this way and that admiring herself in the mirror, the magic in the mirror activated. Thea was instantly sucked into the mirror's extra-dimensional space. The others just saw Thea vanish right before their eyes.

"Thea!" cried out Lonnie. "She's gone! What happened?" He was extremely emotional; his fiancé had just disappeared. He hated things happening for which he had either no idea what was going on or that were beyond his control.

"Zounds! What mischief have we here?" Mandy cried out as she bounded over to the mirror, inspecting its back side.

Alison quickly cast a detect magic spell on the mirror. "It's magical. I had better try to identify what this evil thing actually is right away. Silence everyone." She quickly chanted a long complex spell and then touched the mirror itself. For three minutes she stood concentrating on the mirror. Finally, she said, "Ah ha! It is actually another fiendish trap of sorts. If anyone gazes into the mirror without saying the password, the mirror sucks them into an extra-dimensional space. Jon, see if you can reach her mind. If so, tell her to use her magical door spell to escape."

"Yes, but where do I search for her? What space? Where?" Jon wondered mostly in protest. He had no idea what Alison was talking about.

"Never mind, Jon, I ask the impossible. How could you know where she is," Alison apologized. "I'll get her." She quickly cast a spell that caused a magical door to appear before her. She opened it and stepped through. A moment later, she stepped back out of the door, leading Thea by the hand. The young apprentice looked scared to death. Her face was quite pale and her legs were shaking slightly, but she was listening to Alison's explanation, trying to concentrate on her words. "So remember, use your magical door. It's always a good thing to try first. If that fails, try a teleport." Thea nodded, and Alison then dismissed her door, which vanished as fast as it had appeared.

Lonnie rushed to Thea's side, "Are you all right? Really? No harm?"

"No, mostly my pride," she said downcast. "I am still an apprentice; I have *so* much to learn." She held on to Lonnie tightly.

"Nothing else appears evil in here," the priest confirmed. "So the question is what to do with the mirror. Can it be destroyed? I would not want others to be trapped by it."

"It can be destroyed, but I expect that if you just smashed it, that action would release some pretty devastating magical energies, maybe an explosion. However, it is too big to get through the trap door. It may be that one can dismantle it somehow. For now, let's just leave it alone. I'll throw a sheet over it." The search continued.

The master bed, which stunk worse than anything else so far encountered, showed signs of recent use. The sheets were filthy beyond belief and messed up; the covers, in disarray. "I'd swear that someone has been sleeping in this bed!" declared Mandy. "But they must be a pig!"

The closet contained numerous dry-rotting women's clothing and shoes. Sometime in the past, someone with wealth had purchased a great deal of fancy outfits. However, left unattended for so long, they had either molded or rotted. None were of any value.

The writing desk held a dried out ink pot and quills and parchments, all unusable. The chests contained sheets and covers, all worthless at this point in time. An hour later, Mandy declared, "What a waste of time. A room that stinks to high heaven, with absolutely nothing of value in it, but which someone thought valuable enough to blast Sir Thomas with a lightning bolt, and important enough to have set all these traps — very strange indeed."

"Ah, not so fast, ranger," Rufus spoke up. For the entire time he had been carefully and systematically tapping the walls and central pillar looking for secret cavities or compartments. "Come look what I have found." Naturally, everyone moved to his side beside the central pillar. Enjoying all the attention, he proceeded to tap here and there. "Hear any difference between this spot and this one?" Everyone did; one sounded hollow. Rufus had found a secret compartment hidden in the supporting stone column. "Now the real question is how does it open and what is inside?" he proudly proclaimed.

"Well, I do have to admit that I sorely miss the talents of Slickster," Sir Thomas acknowledged to Father Johnas. "Though I swear he is really a thief, he sure knows how to get into these kinds of things." The priest nodded; he knew Slickster was indeed a thief, but a good one. Because of Sir Thomas's bias toward thieves, the priest kept that information to himself.

"Allow me," Rufus continued. He fiddled here and there. Suddenly as he pushed on the side of the block of stone above the hollowed out stone, everyone heard a loud click and a fake stone door opened, revealing a hidden compartment. Rufus looked very pleased with himself. The others called out "Good going, Rufus!"

However, when he looked inside, his expectant face soured. He had hoped to find jewels or gems or at least something valuable. Inside was only a lever; it was in the upwards position. "It's only a lever!" he said downhearted. The others peered in around him to see as well.

"Why would someone go to all this trouble to make a secret chamber and hide in it only a lever?" Mandy asked. No one had any answer.

Finally, Rufus said, curiosity getting the better of him, "I wonder what it does?" Before anyone could protest, he pulled the lever down.

"Don't do that!" exclaimed Alison. "We don't know what it does!" Everyone held their breath, expecting the worst calamity to befall them, but nothing observable or hearable happened at all. Silence, nothing more. "Well, no harm done," she added. "I guess it doesn't do anything anymore. Come on, we best be heading down to the next floor." They all moved over to the trap door in the floor.

Alison had in mind to tackle this next one exactly like the previous one. She began her preparations. Bored, Jon stared down at the wooden floor, wondering if anyone lie below waiting to attack them. "Idiot!" exclaimed to himself. "I'll take a peek." He closed his eyes, took a deep breath, slowly exhaled and concentrated. His mind, his awareness, expanded. He felt Alison, Mandy, Darless and the others. Now he pushed is awareness downward beneath his feet. He did not expect to "see" anything, because his perception of other minds, other beings, was not done using his body's eyes. Besides, he had no reason to suspect this room was any different than the other two, pitch black, no windows, no lights. He sensed what he expected to sense, a vast, dark empty space.

By now, Alison cast her protective spells on herself and readied her magical eye. Darless had her staff with its globe blazing brightly. Mandy stood by the side of the door awaiting Alison's signal to pull it open, while staying well back of anything that might come out at her. Alison, using her fingers, counted down from three to one and on cue, Mandy gave a mighty pull, throwing open the trap door. It crashed as it slammed fully open. Immediately, the two mages inserted their staves throwing light down into the room. Nothing happened.

Now Alison began moving her magical eye over to the opening in the floor and started it down the stairway. "Library," she called out in a monotone adding, "seems empty." Systematically, she floated the eye about the entire room, but it was devoid of people. She saw only walls lined with bookshelves, hundreds of books and scrolls, several tables, chairs, and soft couches. Unlike the other rooms, twenty golden lanterns shaped like various demons from the Abyss lined the walls. On the walls, rich tapestries hung, in part to dampen sounds. Satisfied that no one was lying in wait to attack her, she dispelled her magical eye and moved to head down the steps. The others quickly moved into the same marching order as before, ready for the descent, once Alison had checked for traps.

She slowly descended five steps. Jon felt her move into this space he was watching. She felt warm and comfortable to him. Suddenly he detected another, more distant mind. It was black, cold, and lifeless. Nevertheless, he picked up its intentions. Instantly, he placed in her mind, *Alison someone is about to attack you.*

Where? she fairly screamed mentally back to him.

Down maybe fifteen feet and to your right some forty or so, he sent back, realizing that his estimations of distance were only a wild guess. He mused, *How does one measure distances between minds? What has distance to do with it?* In the next instant, Alison caught the tell-tale energy streak of a spell launching her way. Confident that her protective spells would work fine, she was not too concerned just yet, but tried to spy where her attacker was located.

No good. The spell arrived extinguishing both globes of light. Alison was plunged into near total darkness. *This is not good,* she thought to herself. In the next instant, she felt a large volley of magical missiles bounce off of her protection globe. She could not see from where they were launched. She knew that she ought to change her position so that the attacker would not know where she was. While she was contemplating her next move, a lightning bolt reflected harmlessly off of her invulnerability globe. *He's testing me, probably has determined that I'm using a globe of protection. So the next spell I would cast would be its removal. I have to do something. Jon, I cannot see him. I've got to move. I'm going up into the middle of the room.* She did just that. She leapt high into the air, jumping off of the stairs out into the room. Instead of falling to the floor and perhaps breaking her neck in the process, she energized her flying ring, hovering high above in the room, looking down to where Jon had indicated the attacker was located. Still, she saw nothing.

Jon, however, did. As he watched the one-sided battle, he noticed the unmistakable energy streaks from the other caster outward to Alison. A thought formed. Again, he perceived the streaking flow of yet another spell heading toward the mage. This time, he experimented. In short, he pushed it to one side. The spell detonated on the wall, disintegrating a chunk of the tapestry and stone wall behind it. *He must not be able to see me,* Alison sent back to Jon, *he missed by a mile.*

Er, no he was dead on; I deflected it, he answered back. *Cast one of your magical missile spells towards him.*

But I cannot see what to shoot at, she protested. Jon insisted and so Alison sent forth a large volley of missiles down and to her right. Jon saw her spell's energy arc and gave it a nudge in the right direction as it streaked down. It hit something, for Jon felt the foreign mind record some pain.

We hit him, he sent back. *Wait, he's gone.* Startling, but true, Jon no longer sensed that mind. It had just disappeared in a flash. One second it was reacting to Alison's missiles and the next, it was just not there. *All clear; I'll keep watch.*

Darless had not been inactive during this brief time. First, she stuck her head down inside using her special vision to search for the heat given off by living bodies. Finally, satisfied she saw none, she re-cast her light spell and stuck her staff back in through the door in the ceiling of the room below her. She spotted Alison flying in little circles near the center of the room, only ten feet from her. Now that she could see again, Alison quickly re-cast her light spell and landed safely back on the steps near where she had last been standing. She had no intention of missing a trap. She picked up her trap scanning from where she had been interrupted. "Jon's been helping me. He thinks that my missiles hit the magic user and drove him off. Leastwise, he is no longer here. I'm continuing my traps scanning. I never did see my attacker. He's one tricky mage." Some of the others above her yelled, "Be careful." She smiled, as she remembered that Sir Thomas in the past had teased her about being overly careful.

This time, her search for traps yielded so many that she began to lose count. "Gosh, there are traps everywhere down here. Thea, start taking notes on these before I lose track of them!" Quickly, her apprentice took out her quill and her notebook and yelled an okay. It took Alison another thirty minutes to completely detect all of the traps and for Thea to get them all duly noted in her book. Once done, Darless then cast her detection spell and joined Alison, while Thea methodically called off of the ones she had written down. Twenty different traps protected this room! However, Darless also found two more that Alison had missed. Thea added these to her list. Then, Alison had Thea join them. She gingerly came down the first five steps. Alison then had her cast her detection of traps spell and read Thea's notes back to her apprentice and had Thea verify each of the traps. For the young apprentice, this was on the job, real live training. Though scary and dangerous, it was very illuminating. She really learned a great deal from her mentor during that half hour.

Next, came the painstaking defusing of each trap. "Since this is a library, I would guess that the trap setter is not going to launch fire ball spells at us; that would destroy all these books. I suspect electrical discharges and poisons and mechanical type traps would be the rule. Gosh, I have never seen so many traps set in one space before!" Alison commented.

"Must be tons of good stuff down there," yelled Rufus encouragingly, "probably many really valuable books!" He sounded very hopeful; after all, who would go to all of the trouble and expense necessary to set twenty or so traps in one room, if there was nothing of value in it? He smiled thinking of wonders to see just as soon as the wizards finished their work.

The three, working together, had just defused the seventh trap, when Jon detected the presence of the cold mind once more. *Attacker is back. Same place as before,* he frantically placed in all three women's mind. Darless had time to throw a protective force wall in front of the three wizards, hoping to fend off any electrical bolts. However, the attacker's spell detonated high above them, near the center of the room. A cloud of noxious yellow gas billowed down onto the three women. "Poison!" screamed Alison, as she started choking. All three held their breath and rushed for the stairs hoping to get out of the room just as fast as they could.

Sensing their plight, Jon sent to Darless, *Cast a lightning bolt ahead of you, say just out there into the room! I'll guide it.* The mage did not hesitate, although she had never ever heard of any mage ever actually "guiding" their spells. It only took a few seconds for her chant to trigger a rather large amount of magical energy, sending it around the edge of her force wall. Jon watched the energy streaking out into the room. This time, it took more than a nudge to get it to their attacker. He had to physically man-handle it, twisting its direction nearly forty-five degrees. He saw it hit something and felt that cold mind recoil from the electrical discharge. *We got him!* he sent back. Once again, Jon felt the mind totally vanish just as fast as it had appeared.

"Zounds!" cried Mandy, "They are not going to make it. Thea's down. Darless's down. Now Alison's down. We gotta get them out of there fast!"

Sir Thomas and Lonnie took a deep breath, held it, and rushed down to the women's aid. All three women had gotten nearly half way up the stairs before the poisonous fumes had weakened them. Each had slowly slumped against the side of the wall. Quickly the paladins reached them, grabbed a hold of them — Lonnie got Thea, while Sir Thomas grabbed Alison and Darless. Bearing their burdens, both rushed up the stairs. Just as soon as they both cleared the door, Mandy slammed it shut.

Meanwhile, Mandy and Father Johnas had prepared their prayers. Kneeling beside the unconscious women, they prayed and began to neutralize the poison's effects. Soon, all three women began choking, a sure sign of life. Mandy looked at Father Johnas, who looked back at her. Both grinned, "Just in the nick of time," she said, "sure glad you are here!"

As soon as he heard that they were being poisoned, Jon remembered that one of his new instruments could help neutralize poisons. The three were on the road to full recovery before he got to their side. "Oops, I see I'm too late. Sorry, I only remembered that this instrument here can wipe out the poison. Bit slow. Never had a chance to try it out," he explained sheepishly.

Between coughs, Alison said, "Thanks all of you. We were nearly goners in spite of all the preparations! That is one tricky magician down there! Did anyone see him?"

"No, he just appeared," Jon explained. "Darless got him with her lightning bolt." "No I didn't," she protested, "I just shot the spell off blindly. I did not see anything to target. Jon made it hit the wizard. Now how the heck do you do that? Even magicians do not see the energy streaks all that often. Once shot or pointed, they are beyond your control. They just do their thing."

"Sorry, I just see them, that's all and I just pushed them around a little bit — well, okay, a whole lot on that last one. I don't know how I did it, I just do it," Jon replied.

Groaning to himself, the others heard Rufus mutter, "Now how will we ever be able to get into that library? The poison will be there for days, maybe weeks. No windows, it can only seep through the floor cracks or back up here. Darn." He looked gloomy, but only for a second as an idea formed, "Maybe I can build a fumes-sucker-upper machine. Now let's see, what would I need?" He was off enthusiastically making sketches on Thea's notebook.

Jon got out his Lute of the Traveling Bard and the instructions Thea had written down on how to get it to play the neutralizing of poison spell. Satisfied he had it down, he began to play. "Okay Mandy. Open the trap door and let's see if this thing will work. Shut it real quick, if it does not get rid of the noxious vapors." Mandy did so, and all of the others stopped to watch and see what would happen. As the trap door opened, the yellowish fumes tried to rise upwards, but the magic of the lute's song dissipated them.

"I think it is working," Mandy encouraged him, so Jon played on. Periodically, Darless did a visual progress inspection by sticking her head and staff down the opening. Each report showed less and less vapors remaining. However, it took Jon nearly a half hour of continuous playing to disperse all of the gas. By then, he and the others were sick of hearing that same tune over and over.

When Jon had finished, Rufus commented, "Well, Jon, good going on clearing out the poisonous fumes. But I think I will still work on my fumes-sucker-upper machine. I cannot stand listening to that song over and over. The maker should have picked a more interesting piece, don't you think?"

Jon smiled at him, "What do you think it is like playing that same tune over and over all that time?" Everyone roared with laughter. "My fingers are sore!"

Alison once again cast her preparation spells as did Darless and Thea. The three re-entered the room and once more resumed the detection and removal of the traps. Jon remained focused on his mental detection of their opponent and the others tried to stay alert for any sudden surprise attack. But their mysterious attacker did not make another appearance. Finally, most of the others became extremely bored and took to sitting around. With so many traps in this third room, they dared not go down and had to wait for the mages' all clear signal.

That did not come for another three hours! By then, Alison, Thea, and Darless were totally exhausted, physically and mentally. For all those hours, one slight mis-step, one slight loss of concentration, could mean the accidental triggering of a trap ending in their death. It was exceedingly grueling work. Often, Alison wished her old traveling companion, Slickster, was here. He would have made short work of all these traps. Finally, Mandy, detecting their fatigue, suggested that they quit for the day, since it was starting to get dark outside. "Clear!" Alison finally exclaimed. "Done! I'm, no make that we, are beat. Let's call it a day. We'll search it again tomorrow." Wearily, the three mages climbed up and Mandy shut the trap door. They all filed up onto the roof, where Jon stepped them all back to their camp area just outside the deserted village gates.

"Can someone one else fix our supper tonight?" Thea pleaded. "I'm really awfully tired. I never knew handling traps could be *so* exhausting!"

"Well, I am not the greatest cook," Mandy volunteered, "but if the guys help me, I'll take care of it." She looked at Jon, who had fallen asleep; he'd spent way too much energy this afternoon. "Lonnie, I think you get the dish patrol tonight!" he chuckled.

"I'll lend a hand," Sir Thomas volunteered, "though you will like my cooking even less." He grinned. But between them, supper was fixed in less than an hour. In spite of her disclaimers about cooking, the meal was quite good.

The hot meal revived Darless sufficiently and she cast her last spell of the day creating the magical mansion. Alison was greatly relieved because she had forgotten to save that spell and had been trying to find a way to break the news that they might have to spend the night out here in the open or have Thea cast it from one of the scrolls that she had given her apprentice. "Thanks, Darless. I totally forgot about saving a spell," she whispered. The alu-demon smiled back, she had guessed that might be the case.

This evening, the three mages went to bed almost as soon as the spell had built the mansion. "I guess they really are tired!" Lonnie said to Mandy, as they mulled outside about the small campfire he had made. Both were watching the stars in the sky.

Sir Thomas came outside to join them, after having bid Darless good night. "Rufus and Father Johnas also turned in. Beautiful night," he commented adding after a reflective pause, "This is the part I miss. You know, when we spend all the nights in the mansion, we miss such a simple thing as gazing at the heavens."

"Yes, it's what I miss the most too," Mandy mused. "But then, the safety of the mansion has been a godsend on our trips. It sure is beautiful isn't it? I wonder if William is watching the sky tonight." Her thoughts drifted off toward her fiancé. She could sense that the two men were also thinking of theirs as well. When the fire died down to red embers, the three silently entered the mansion shutting the doors behind them.

The next day, once breakfast was handled and the mages had time to prepare their spells for the day, the work of exploring the tower began once more. Again, being overly cautious, Alison took the lead, checking for any new traps that might have been setup during the night. Rufus wondered if that was really necessary, because he was really excited about examining the library. Surely there must be highly valuable stuff in that room to warrant so many traps to protect it. Indeed he was not the only one grumbling at the slow descent back to the third floor room. Cautious Alison ignored them; she knew she was up against a powerful, tricky opponent.

"Ah ha, will you look at this?" she suddenly pointed to a glowing spot on the side of the wall beside the trap door leading down into the fourth floor. "Our antagonist has setup a new electrical frying trap here. If we had just walked own down to where we left off, one or more of us would have been fried!" Darless did the honors of disarming it. That brought a very solemn countenance to all faces.

Jon, though, smiled at Alison. *You sure know your business! Thanks love*, he placed in her mind. She smiled back.

"Ahem," Sir Thomas cleared his throat, "I admit you are right once again, Alison. Had I been leading, I would have walked right into that one. Thank you." She smiled even more broadly. Once the trap was disarmed, she continued with her descent into the fourth floor and then on down to the third floor. She found no more traps. Darless also re-scanned the entire library, but none of the traps here had been reset.

"Okay, search time. Paladins and Jon, you are our guards. Father Johnas will be on the lookout for anything radiating evil. Everyone else search away!" Those were the magic words for Rufus! He was off scampering here and there, looking at this and that, like a child in a toy store.

Shortly he exclaimed, "Bookworms! Rats!" Sure enough, left unattended for so long, a colony of bookworms had made this room their new home, slowly devouring the pages. However, all were now quite dead, thanks to the poisonous gas cloud of yesterday. "We are going to have to be quite thorough here; we must save as many of these books as possible," declared the gnome, who obviously placed great value on them.

Three hours later, they took stock of their findings. They had discovered some seven hundred books, of which about one hundred were damaged by the worms, ten of which were completely destroyed. Rufus volunteered to rescue the remaining ninety. Of these, fifty related to arcane magical spells and research, most valuable to the three mages. Fully two hundred related to general knowledge of such things as the heavens, herbs, spices, healing arts and so on. However, many were considered light reading — the travel journals of various persons, mostly unknown to all those present. Yet, a hundred dealt with matters of interest to the goings on of life within the Abyss. Darless decided to take charge over these because they would make sense to her. In the end, there were books of interest to everyone, including Jon, who found several dealing with music and its effects upon people and animals.

Rufus, who was the most knowledgeable in these matters, appraised the total value of the book collection at somewhere near twenty thousand gold pieces. Not huge, but significant. Next, they examined all of the bookshelves. These were of excellent craftsmanship and worth salvaging, if some means of getting them out could be found. The tapestries, depicting springtime debauchery with many of each sex gaily cavorting about in blossoming fields of flowers, spoke loudly of the Archmage Sarah's tastes. These Rufus volunteered to attempt to sell for them. Alison gladly accepted his offer. The men assisted in taking them down, while the gnome stored them in ever growing large sacks. The tables and chairs were of very high quality. Rufus estimated their total worth at nearly a thousand gold pieces. These were comfortable and useful items, so Alison decided to keep them for the party's use. The plush couch, though, was another matter. It stunk of death and decay. Why? No one could explain. Torn seams and worn out patches told of heavy use. This they decided to leave.

Among the scrolls, Darless found a dozen contained, in fact, magic spells, ready to be cast by any reader. Most spells were rather common ones, though, such as putting people to sleep or magical missiles. Several other scrolls were actually maps. These Alison found most illuminating as did Darless. Some were detailed maps of this northern region of the Desolation Range. Some were maps of places in the Abyss. "These may prove very useful indeed," proclaimed Alison.

Thea found a large stash of writing supplies, all in good shape. One particular quill was magical. One talked to the quill and it wrote down what you said. This item, she confiscated. Since she was the official note taker for the groups, she figured it would come in very handy indeed.

While the others sat back surveying what they had discovered, Rufus became annoyed once more. Muttering unintelligible words, he began levitating up to the many golden lanterns with the demonic shapes, examining them. "Well, these lamps appear to be made of gold," he called down to the others who were sitting on the chairs. "Probably worth twenty coins each. I'll take them down." He fetched some tools from one of his many pockets and began systematically removing each from the walls. As he removed one in particular, something metal fell off of the top of the lantern. The agile gnome managed to grab it, as it began its fall to the floor. "What have we here? Look!" he held up a large key. "I've found a key. Has anyone found something that is locked? I wonder what it fits." Nothing had a lock on it in the entire room. Dejected, Rufus finished up removing all twenty golden demonic lanterns. No further "keys" appeared.

Although the others were now getting ready to tackle the floor below them, Rufus insisted on making a thorough search for secret compartments. An hour of tap-tap-tapping here and there produced no such find. Now the gnome got positively angry, "What is going on here? All those traps to protect just this? It does not make any sense at all!"

"Calm down, Rufus," Alison attempted to console him. "It doesn't make any sense to the rest of us either. Maybe if we find out who put them here, then we may make some sense of it all. At the moment, to me, it seems totally out of place."

"Ah my small son," Father Johnas added, "Alison is right. Patience. In time, it may be revealed to us."

"You know," Darless butted in, "it is almost like someone is trying to keep us from descending further into this tower. We got by the ultimate weapons, the spectral ghosts, so now it is a multitude of traps. Take heart, perhaps our opponent has run out of creatures with which to attack us and is resorting to trap tactics. I find that a bit encouraging, if true."

Rufus calmed down, "Say, you might have something there, Darless!" he commented, thinking it through. "I kept thinking of valuables, but maybe that is the wrong interpretation of the traps." He took his position in the rear of the party once more, while the others headed for the trap door leading down to the second floor.

"No traps," Alison reported. "Okay, Mandy, open it up." The ranger obliged. This time, loud clanking, mechanical noises greeted their ears. Cautiously, Alison inserted her magical eye into the opening, peering safely into the room, while Darless poked her staff into the opening to provide light. Alison was not prepared for what she saw!

The room had been the servant's quarters. The remains of two beds and other furniture lay in shambles, smashed into small pieces. Flying about the room were huge scything blades on moving arms. A great machine lay on top of the trap door leading down to the first floor and it was completely across the room from her. Great flying arms sliced this way and that about the space of the room. Jon whispered that he detected no one's presence, so Alison risked more light and let the others peer down.

One by one, each took a look; each face showed signs of complete disbelief in what their eyes saw.

"Zagroot zounds!" Mandy declared, "What the heck is that? A killing machine?"

"Le'me see! Le'me see!" cried Rufus, impatiently waiting his turn, which was last. When he finally got his turn to look, he said, "Wow! Will you look at that marvelous machine! We must not damage it! The amount of work it took to build it! Oh. Oh. Oh. Such a find!"

"Rufus, how are we going to get around it without destroying it?" Alison said sternly. "Notice that it has already destroyed nearly everything in the room. Nothing remains larger than about a foot in length. We have to get by it, you know."

Each took a turn of looking and appraising how to get around it. None had any answer. While one might duck a flying blade here and there, across that large a space and with the seemingly random pattern of slicing motions, sooner or later, a blade would connect. The best idea was Sir Thomas's. He suggested staying in one place and attempting to smash each blade or arm as it came near. However, there were at least twenty arms with which to deal and all at one time. Sometimes, three arms moved together, and that was the flaw in his idea.

Rufus became annoyed with them, "It's only a machine! You are talking as if it is alive. It's not; it's just a beautiful piece of machinery! Okay, so you want through or by it. All we have to do is to turn it off. That's all."

"But Rufus, we do not know how it runs — how to turn it off. Where's its off switch?" protested Alison, just as baffled by this as the rest.

"Well, just give me some time to study it," the gnome begged. "It has to have an on-off switch somewhere. Now, if it were mine, I'd put that switch where we could not get at it, say on the machine's body way over there. That way you'd be cut to bits before you could turn it off."

"Yes, that is the problem," Alison glared. "How do we turn it off without getting killed in the process? I don't relish being diced like a carrot!"

"Hum, if I am not mistaken, Alison, we can rule most magic spells out," Darless commented dryly. "Do you see that magical shield spell surrounding the machine or am I seeing things?"

Alison cast a short detection spell and looked crestfallen, "Yes, good work. I missed that; I got so caught up in this unexpected machine that I missed that detail. I guess we are going to have to attempt to dispel that magic, if possible, before any of our spells will get through."

"Well, we certainly cannot hack at it with our weapons," Sir Thomas added. "I think that those strong metal arms may break our blades. Perhaps we could smash it with a footman's mace, though, except I didn't bring any along." Lonnie had not either.

"Well, then," Thea added in her cheerful way, "we are just going to have to use our brains on this one. Let's see, it's just a machine, right Rufus?" The gnome, who was still admiring the device, nodded affirmative. "So don't all machines have an on-off switch?"

"Ah, yes, Thea," Rufus replied excitedly, "you have hit upon it. All we need to do is to turn the switch off. I have spied what must be that switch. Everyone, look at the base of the machine. See that little lever there? It is up. I bet if it is pulled down, the machine goes off."

"Very good, you two," remarked Alison, as she spied what he had found.

"Only problem," added Mandy, after she stuck her head down the trap door for another peek, "is just how do we get to that lever? Those blades are cutting everything in the room into small pieces!" He had no immediate answer; neither did anyone else.

Daunted by this setback, Thea cried, "Darn, nothing smaller than a mouse can get through that room. Nothing is left larger than about a foot in size!"

"Thea! Bless you! That is precisely the answer," exclaimed Rufus. "A mouse can get through! And I aim to turn it off! Alison, if I get it turned off, may I claim the machine, please? I'm begging you!" He got down on one knee. She looked down at him and his pleading face, her heart melted. She could not refuse him and agreed. It was only a machine, after all.

Quickly, the gnome began a rather complex magical chant. Jon had never heard this one. By now he learned to recognize the musical quality of the mages' chants. He watched fascinated, trying to pick up on the rhythm of the gnome's spell. Nothing happened when he finished, instead, he fished around in his pockets, emptying out bits of this and that. Finally, he found a long piece of string and formed a lasso on one end. Then, he stuck it in his mouth.

Next, he moved over to the trap door and snapped his fingers. Right before their eyes, the little gnome began to change or rather transform. First, he began to shrink. Jon was alarmed because he was so small anyway. He shrunk down until he was only about six inches tall. At that point, he got down on his hands and knees and slowly turned into a large rat, with string hanging from its mouth. He then began his descent of the steps. The rat was just the right size to barely make it down each step without falling down each one. Because of his very small size, none of the wicked blades ever got sufficiently close to him to harm a whisker on his face.

In just a couple minutes, the rat had reached the floor. Scampering over the massive debris that totally covered the floor was another matter. While he need not worry about the blades swinging wildly above him, the uneven mass of wood, bedding and other stuff made movement difficult. He kept stumbling and slipping and sliding. The rat took nearly ten minutes to cross the room to the machine.

Once in place, he had to be very careful. A pair of very short arms kept slicing and whirling about very close to the machine's on-off switch. Obviously it was designed to prevent any hand from trying to pull the lever. Twice he nearly got his tail removed and once his head. But he made it and had his forepaws resting high on the side of the machine. Unfortunately, a rat cannot effectively operate a lasso. Further, the lever was nearly a foot and a half above his outreaching paws. Rufus sat back down close to the base of the machine, out of harm's way and thought. Jon watched him turn back into a very tiny gnome. He pressed his little body tightly up against the side of the machine and began to grow back to his normal size, but very slowly.

Rufus kept looking in all directions, gauging how close the pair of short blades were getting to his increasing sized body. Finally, he reached his normal size and the two blades just barely missed slicing him into small pieces. Carefully, he looped the bit of string over the lever and slowly pulled it down until his entire body was hanging from the string, feet just off of the floor. He had not thought of this detail — what if his weight was not sufficient to pull the lever down?

"Rufus, it's not working!" called out a very worried Thea. "You don't weigh enough to pull it down! Can you shrink back down and come back here?"

"Er, not today," he said in reply. "I, ah, can only do this once a day. I'm rather stuck here, if I cannot get it stopped."

Thea was going to say "Well, pull harder," but bit her lip instead; she realized he was hanging on with his whole body. Suddenly, she had an idea. "Hang on there, Rufus, I think I can help you out!" She knew that any kind of magical attacking spells would be nullified by the protection spells. But not wind. Obviously, air was moving all about the room. She chanted her spell, which she had not really used before in front of others, only while playing around by herself. Jon watched her cheeks bulge into enormous balloons. Then, she let loose a giant puff of air, rather like blowing out a candle, but with an enormous puff of air. She directed it down onto the head of the gnome, as close to straight down as she could from way up at the ceiling and opposite him. The blast of air hit the gnome nearly causing him to lose his grip and fall, which would have been disastrous if a blade should be there as well. He held on with all his might.

Clank! The lever suddenly fell into the down position. The string slipped off of the lever causing Rufus to fall onto the floor. The whining noise stopped. Slowly the blades stopped their wild motions. Rufus watched fascinated as the blades retracted, the arms telescoped down into very small sections. Finally, the whole mechanism clinked into a shut off position with the arms in a small, compact form, barely three feet beyond the machine's cylindrical main body. "Whoopee, Thea, we did it!" yelled Rufus, hugging his new machine.

"Well done indeed, Rufus," called down Alison, "but please stay where you are. Let me search for other traps. I don't want you to get hurt." After his harrowing experience, the gnome had no intention of moving. Besides, he wanted to examine his new machine close up. In five minutes, Alison and Darless gave the all clear sign and everyone descended into the second floor room.

"What a mess!" exclaimed Mandy. "Sure glad I don't have to clean it up! I don't suppose that there is much of value left in here."

"From the amount of bed parts," Darless commented, "I would guess that this used to be the two servant's rooms. Under all this litter might be some small valuables, such as a golden hair brush or some jewelry, I suppose. But how do we find it without cleaning up this mess?"

"Cursory inspection, that's all let's do," declared Alison. "We mages will check for anything that might be magical. The rest of you do a bit of poking around. But be cautious. We don't know what is under all this pile of wooden bits, shredded bedding and such. Jon, you keep alert for any more surprise attacks." The quick search began. It yielded nothing of value and neither mage found any additional traps. Satisfied, they decided to break for lunch.

Instead of just climbing up out of the tower, Jon merely stepped them all back to their camping area. It is duly noted here, that Rufus held on to his new machine and Jon inadvertently transported it to their camp as well, much to the surprise of all, including Rufus. Actually, Alison commented that this was actually fortuitous, because their opponent could have started it up again while they were away, and then they'd have to do it all over again. The gnome felt vindicated.

Fresh air poured into everyone, revitalizing them, for the tower continued to reek with the stench of death. It seemed the further down they went, the stronger the smell became. Jon wondered if perhaps they would find a cemetery on the main floor. However, he forgot about basements.

Lunch and the clean air livened their spirits and all were ready to tackle the last floor with some enthusiasm. Most felt the end of the quest was near at hand. In no time, the group scampered down the four stairs to the messy second floor room from the rooftop. Still, Alison was careful to the possibility their unseen opponent may have reset some of the traps along the way. None had been. All was as they had left it.

One by one, they took up their positions around the trapdoor that led down to the main floor. However, Mandy distinctly heard scratching sounds coming from the other side of the door. Using hand signals, she motioned for complete silence. Now everyone could hear the distinctive sound. The hairs on her neck prickled; she whispered, "Zounds! I don't like the sounds of this. I'd swear that it sounds like an animal clawing its way out of a box. Do we dare open this door?"

In spite of her strong desire to get on with the search for information on what had happened to her parents, Alison forced herself to exercise caution. "No, prudence. Let's see, we need to open it and shine light down so we can see what is there and yet not let whatever is trying to get out actually get out."

Darless, thinking out loud, said, "Perhaps as we open it a crack, we could slide a wall of force just under the trap door. Light could go through, but creatures could not."

"Yes, Darless, that's it," added Alison, "brilliant idea. We can slide it under and have everyone else stand on it. That should hold it down, while we see with what we are dealing. Let's do it!" Darless cast her wall of force. To the others, it appeared as a shimmering transparent rectangle. She purposely kept its dimensions fairly small. She and the others picked it up as though it were a sheet of Plexiglass and slid it to the edge of the trap door by the side wall. Mandy stood on the hinged side of the door, ready to pull it slightly open, while Alison readied both staves with their lights. "On the count of three," she said and called the numbers out at an even pace.

Mandy pulled the heavy door up just enough to allow the others to slide the wall of force under the edge. Then in a rush of action, she swung it completely open as the others slid it across the opening and jumped on top of the shimmering sheet. Alison stepped into the middle standing directly above the opening. All eyes stared down. "Zagroot zounds!" exclaimed Mandy.

"Rats, I do hate rats!" added Alison.

"Will you look at the size of some of them!" cried a shocked Thea, "Some must be at least two feet long! Giant rats!"

Jon muttered, "The whole place is swarming with them. There must be hundreds and hundreds of rats down there!"

"Why?" put in Father Johnas. "It is almost like someone was raising rats. Why?"

Several tried scratching at the wall of force to no avail. "Well, there are so many that we cannot launch fireballs and roast them. There are too many and we'd destroy whatever evidence might still be down there," added Alison.

Mandy concentrated her thoughts and extended her sense of perceptions toward the rat clawing at the invisible barrier. "Hum, they seem to be trying to find a way out. I get the sense that they are trapped." The others looked at her questioningly. "Animal empathy," she added, "I can feel their emotions, well sort of."

"Well that makes sense," observed Thea. "Look at them. Some appear to have been slightly eaten by the others. See, that one is missing an ear; that one, a tail. I bet they are starving too."

The effect of blinding light into a room that had been pitch black for so long started to wear off. More and more began climbing up the long spiraling staircase along the wall. "Okay, let's see if we can get the door shut again," Alison ordered. Mandy lowered the door and carefully, they slide the nearly invisible barrier out until finally she stood on top of the door as it shut completely. "Excellent work, everyone. Now how are we going to get them all out?"

No one had a workable idea as yet and they discussed it for some time. Certainly, they could not just open this trap door. While the rats could climb to the roof, they would be just as trapped there — some fifty feet above the ground with no way down. "If only we could open the front doors," grumbled Rufus, "then they could all just leave."

"My friend," Alison agreed, "my sentiments exactly. Come on everyone, let's go have another look at those doors. It's either open the doors or blast a hole in the side of the tower. Either way, we have to let them out." Everyone held hands and Jon stepped them all to just before the front door; it was a familiar location to him. These short steps really took very little effort on his part.

"Well, we could certainly turn a section of the stone wall into mud," Darless commented. "Make it sufficiently small and the structural integrity would not be compromised."

"Well, maybe we can just do it here and here," Alison pointed to the slight indentations where the iron hinges turned inwards. "They are probably bolted into the stone itself. If we can get just the right sections of stone turned into mud, we should be able to pull the welded doors outward."

"Yes, but then the rats will swarm out and have us for lunch," Mandy commented, envisioning the hundreds upon hundreds of starving rats attacking them. We need a good distance between us and the rats."

"Well, we certainly can cast the spells from a distance," Alison conceded. "Accuracy is not going to be that important, but won't strong hands be needed to pull the whole assemblage out?"

Mandy and Sir Thomas tested the giant door rings again. During their first examination of the doors several days ago, they had tried to pull them open. Now another plan was forming. "You thinking what I'm thinking," Mandy teased the paladin.

His eyes twinkled, "You bet. These are very strong rings. We have rope and solid horses. Let's get three of them. We'll be back in a couple minutes, Alison. Come on, Mandy, Lonnie. We have horses to prepare."

Soon the trio returned leading three of the larger horses. Carefully, the men tied the ropes to the door pull rings and then to each of the three horses who stood patiently some fifty feet away. Then, the three mounted up and took up the slack. "Okay, we are ready. When we pull the door out and the rats charge out, we will cut the ropes and ride off. I do not want to risk the horses being attacked either," Sir Thomas explained. "The rest of you, get to some place safe."

"Okay, Darless and I will simultaneously cast the rock to mud spells on the hinges. Just as soon as they are cast, Thea will teleport us back to the roof of the tower. Jon, you take Father Johnas and Rufus and get up there now. When Thea has us moved, that will be your signal to pull." They all went into action. Standing some twenty feet from the doors, the two mages, with Thea just behind them, began their chants, coordinating and timing their spells. Thea held her staff at the ready; her spell would take almost no time to cast. The pair of spells detonated, turning the stone about where the hinges ought to have been fastened into the stone of the tower into mud. The fused doors creaked and twisted. Thea barked her command word and latched onto the two mages and in the next instant, all three joined Jon, Rufus and Father Johnas safely on the roof.

They heard the three riders bark commands to their war horses, which strained and pulled. The doors creaked and the hinges gave way. The massive stone doors collapsed onto the ground with a deafening boom. Immediately, the riders cut the ropes and cantered off out of the village, veering to the north. Only when they had put a good quarter mile between them and the tower did they reign in and turn around to see what was happening.

What happened was just as expected. Long unused to light in any form, the rats stood motionless, blinking at the blinding daylight. After a couple minutes, a few dared to scramble out into freedom. Then others followed. Soon the entire swarm scampered out of the tower, scattering in all directions about the village and then out onto the vast empty plains beyond, thinning out as they went. They were free at last and could only think of running as far away as possible. The three riders found that they needed to put another mile between themselves and the horde. It took nearly a half hour for the swarm to disperse across the plains and for the trio to decide it was safe to head back to the tower. When they rode up, they found the other five standing before the opening looking into the first floor of the tower.

"I don't know whether that death stench or the rat's stink worse," Thea commented to Lonnie when he dismounted. "It smells just awful. Alison thinks some of the worst of the smell might dissipate, if we give the air a little time to get in there." He turned up his nose as he got a strong whiff of the odor. He was grateful that Alison was not going to ask them all to charge straight in just yet.

They waited another half hour, standing just outside the gaping entrance, peering into the dark interior. They could see some objects, but could not really tell what they were without getting closer and without shining direct light into the room. Alison waited until her nose could tolerate the smell before she began slowly heading inside. At last with her staff with its light held before her, she motioned for the others to follow. "I don't think we have to worry much about traps. If there were any, surely the rats would have triggered them all by now." They entered the tower's first floor in search of Alison's long sought answers.

This circular forty-foot diameter room was divided by a central entrance passage, shaped like a pair of long counter tops. To the right side lay the kitchen area, complete with stove, sink, and cupboards. A wooden preparation table was centrally located in that hemisphere with numerous pots and pans hanging from ceiling hooks. To the left was the dining area and lounge. The eating section was dominated by the huge mahogany table with six matching chairs. The remnants of tapestries hung on the walls but were mostly devoured by the rats in search of anything edible. Three sofas lie in ruins, torn to shreds by the creatures. A small writing desk and chair was positioned against the rising circular stairs; both were well gnawed. The rats had definitely made a mess of this room.

"Look, they even chewed the legs of the chairs!" exclaimed Mandy, who systematically observed the details of the room. "Strange, by I'd swear that these rats had only been in this room relatively recently, perhaps just a few hours. At least that's the way I read the signs. What say you, Sir Thomas?"

The paladins had also been examining the room. "Yes, for that large a number, the droppings are so few. Someone or something let them out. That's my guess," he replied.

"And here's where they came from," Rufus enthusiastically interrupted, sliding a fallen desk aside. Now it was obvious to all. At the back of the room opposite the entrance doors, a narrow set of stairs led to some underground chamber. The overpowering stench drifted up from down below this area. "I wonder how the rats were kept down there. Must be a door here somewhere." The mechanical aspects now consumed the gnome's interest, and with his small hammer, he began methodically tapping, searching for the door's operating mechanism.

"Ordinary kitchen stuff," Darless and Thea reported. "I wonder where their food pantry is located? It certainly is not in here."

"Well, if there were any clues in here, they have been chewed by the rats," Alison gloomily added. She and Jon had made a cursory examination of the dining area and lounge. "I suppose there must be some basement rooms," she added hopefully.

"Ah ha, here it is!" exclaimed Rufus, who proudly slid open another secret box like chamber in the central pillar. It was just like the one he found two floors up. He slid the concealed lever down and a soft grating noise followed. A granite slab slid across the doorway to the rat's room, concealing it perfectly. Unless one knew that there was a door there, one would assume it was just the side of the tower. He pulled the lever up and the door slid open again. "Clever. I wonder if I was the one who let the rats out. You don't suppose?" His voice trailed off into silence, as a bit of guilt surged. After all, it was he that moved the lever.

"Don't worry about it," Alison answered. "I think you left it up. Besides, there really is nothing of any real value here that was destroyed. Mandy thinks the rats were only let out hours ago, so it was probably not your doing." The gnome definitely felt relieved to hear this. Alison continued, "But everyone stand back. If there is one secret chamber, there must be more. I'm going to find them all at once."

Sir Thomas knew immediately what she had in mind. He had seen her do this trick many times before. He said, "Thea, watch and learn how a master works. Alison is most impressive, when it comes to finding hidden doors and such. Most impressive. She's often saved us hours of searching." The apprentice needed no further encouragement. She focused her full attention on Alison, who began a lengthy chant.

Her spell culminated with her barking out one word with a solid forceful command, "Open!" Immediately, the stone door to the rats' room crashed open, as did the sliding door that Rufus had found which concealed the lever. From the kitchen side another door slid open and further off in the distance somewhere beyond the rat room, yet another door opened violently. "Now that's more like it," she muttered to herself. "Come on, we've got several to explore now. Could be even more rooms further on down."

"Which should we do first?" asked Mandy, who was peering into the dark depths of the rats' room, "this one or the one in the kitchen?"

"Trust your nose," teased the wizard. "Let's let the rat one air out a while. I really don't want to go wading in rat manure just yet. Let's see what the kitchen has to offer." One by one the others headed into the kitchen half, peering into the dark depths of a three-foot wide stairs that led down into inky blackness.

"Alison, this one smells like some decaying carcass is down there," protested Thea. "Why can't these people keep a clean house anyway? Sir Thomas, does it always smell this bad, I mean at all those other places you've been?"

He laughed, "No my child. We've been in some stinky places, true, but nothing like this tower. This one has to rank the highest on the repulsive scale, that's for sure! Come on, Lonnie and I will lead the way." But then, he thought better of that and said to Alison as he passed her, "Unless you think we should check for traps once more. Do you suppose?"

She and Darless inserted their staves with the light into the hallway leading down trying to see what lie ahead. Their light only revealed a long corridor with several opened side doors some hundred feet ahead.

Mandy was at the rear, her attention was still on the rats' room. Somehow, she could not pry her attention off of it. Now the hairs on her neck began to prickle. "Guys, hold on. I think you'd better get over here. Now! Zounds! Now! Like really now!" Her voice rose steadily in pitch. "I hate snakes!" The others scrambled over one another to get to Mandy's side. With the light increase from the two staves, Mandy let out a shriek the likes of which Jon had never ever heard from this ranger. Then, he saw why.

Slithering slowly from the inky blackness from the most distant portion of the rats' room came snakes — lots and lots of snakes. The nearest was now about twenty feet from Mandy, slowly climbing the short stairs to the door to this first floor room. Mandy stood transfixed, eyes staring at the vipers.

"Those are hooded vipers!" exclaimed Sir Thomas quite alarmed. "Highly poisonous. Whatever you do, don't get bit!"

"Look, there are more of them," put in Darless. "Hold on, we have got to see what we are dealing with far better than this!" She gave a quick chant and threw a conjured, brilliant light globe into the farthest point of the rats' room that she could reach. It arced through the air like a flare and slowly fell to the ground. No one spoke, but several gasped.

There was not one or two of these vipers slithering their way, but hundreds of them. The black splotches on their brown bodies glistened in the light. Their heads were shaped like a diamond and the nearest one now reared up forming a hood about its head. Its tongue flicked about sensing them, while its eyes seemed to stare at nothing. These vipers had a poor sense of sight compared to other snakes, but their sense of taste or smell on their tongues were highly sensitive, leading them to their prey.

In a flash of insight, Thea remarked, "Well, now we know why all the rats. Someone was raising vipers, feeding them the rats. Makes sense once you know the whole picture."

"What do we do about these?" Jon asked, getting rather nervous about the swarm slowly heading their way. "If these all get outside, the country side around here is going to be endangered with this many snakes."

Alison said decisively, "Okay, the snakes will have to be destroyed; there really is no other viable alternative. Darless, Thea, fireball time." Quickly the three mages began casting their spells, but since fire was Thea's specialty, hers ignited at least a second before the others went off. Alison managed to yell "Duck!" just in time as the giant blasts of fire expanded to fill the rats' room and then blew out into the first floor flaring over their heads narrowly missing everyone. Jon had to pull Mandy down to the ground because she still stood transfixed before the snakes. The fall jarred the ranger back into reality.

"Thanks, Jon. I do hate snakes! I don't know what comes over me, but I just freeze up," she said rather ashamed of her reactions. "It's my most vulnerable thing." If the stench was bad before, now it was even worse, sizzling snake bodies added to the odors.

"You know," muttered Darless, "this Archmage Sarah's tower ought to be called the Dark Tower of Death! Everything about this place is deadly. It appears to be clear now. I think we got them all, but we had best go inside and check."

"My Lady, allow me," Sir Thomas offered, "I'm armored head to toe. If there are any snakes left, they cannot harm me. But I need more light." Rufus quickly brought him a lantern. Armed with a lantern in his left hand and his two-handed sword in his right, the paladin clanked down the stairs into the rats' room.

To everyone's surprise, his feet sunk nearly six inches. "Biggest pile of dung I have ever heard of!" he called out. He poked about here and there and finally returned. "I found several drain pipes in the floor. Rat feces are really thick. Can we perhaps wash it down the drain?"

"Brilliant!" exclaimed Alison, who retrieved her portable hole from under her shirt, opened it up and rummaged inside it. "Ah, here, Sir Thomas. Use my decanter. Just uncork it and use it as a hose." She handed the paladin her bottle. He sheathed his sword and took the decanter. Under its forceful blasts, the dung dissolved and slowly went down the drains. It took the man nearly an hour to get the room clean enough for his satisfaction. All the while, Mandy stood on the lookout, this time armed with her short bow. If any viper should appear, she'd nail it before it could harm the paladin. None came.

When he was done, two hundred charred snake remains lay by the six drains, too large to go down them. He looked most pleased, because now his Lady could enter the room and not get soiled. That meant something to this man. He re-corked the decanter and gave it to Alison as she joined him in the room. Even the foul odor had mostly gone away, much to everyone's satisfaction. "Well done indeed, Sir Thomas," she prided him, very thankful that she had not had to do this dirty job.

They were about to head further down the hallway from which the snakes had come, when Darless, who had been deep in thought the entire time spoke up. "Stay a minute. Listen, I've been thinking about this. If this Sarah had been raising all these snakes, she must had had a purpose in mind for them, and not that of surprising a thief in the night. If I were raising them, there would be a reason. I've invented about a dozen possibilities. One obvious one is that the snakes were guarding something of value — probably immense value to her. If this hypothesis is correct and I, her, there would be even more backup systems to protect it. Of course, there are eleven other possibilities. Do you want to hear the others?"

Chuckling, Alison said, "No. Point well taken, well made. Okay, let's get a good defensive marching order as we head down this corridor. I think we can go two abreast, but no more. Sir Thomas, you take point; Darless and I will follow right behind searching for traps and the like. Mandy, you and Lonnie follow us. Thea, you are rear guard, keep Jon and Father Johnas ahead of you and well protected from a rear surprise." Thus they set off down the corridor.

Now this very straight corridor was carved from the bedrock beneath the tower and was six feet wide and six tall. It sloped gently down. They cautiously crept forward some hundred feet with no sign of traps nor side passages. To be certain, Rufus, tagging along in the rear with Thea, kept tapping here and there looking for secret side doors. He found none but was not discouraged by this in the least.

They reached the end of the corridor at last. An open door, one that Alison's spell had opened they presumed, stood gaping before them. Beyond lay another room, the snakes' room full of boulders and smaller stones formed into crevasses under which the snakes made their homes. The room was about forty feet square. A dozen lanterns were affixed to the walls about six feet above the floor. Directly opposite the entrance door stood yet another door. This one was made of stone and had no handles or visible means of opening, but did look like a door. Rufus exclaimed excitedly, "Now this is some door! I wonder how it works. Shall I try to find out, Mage Alison?"

"No, that won't be necessary, Rufus, I have not got the patience. Stand back everyone, I shall open it." Once more she chanted her spell of opening, barking forcibly the final word. The door slid open to the right, revealing another dark room. A strange odor greeted their nostrils. Suddenly, all of their magical globes of light extinguished and the three lanterns went out, leaving them all in pitch darkness. Jon had never experienced such an absolute loss of light. Even the stars produce some light at night. It was so dark he could not see his hand in front of his eyes. It was as if he were suddenly totally blind. Panic crept into his mind. He sensed it creeping into several other's as well.

Mandy's hair on the back of her neck tingled. "Danger! Something's out there!" she called out, and very carefully drew her sword, trying not to hit a nearby companion.

In the next few seconds, several things occurred nearly simultaneously. First, Darless, who could see in the infrared spectrum, saw their opponent outlined in a reddish glow. It took her only a brief moment to recognize what it was. "It's a demon guarding something. Middle of the room. I can see its form."

How? Can I see what you see? Jon placed in her mind. She beckoned him look with her eyes and Jon also saw the strangest sight he had ever beheld, the infrared image of a demon. He wondered if he could learn to perceive as Darless was. However, he saw instead a beam of magical energy arcing its way toward the group.

Everyone heard the cold, high-pitched screech, "Die Tin Man!" coming from somewhere distant above them yet from within the room they faced. Jon reacted instinctively; he contacted the beam and gave it a slight push to the left. It detonated with a resounding blast. Bits of rock flew in all directions, hitting many in the party. "I'm hit!" several called out. Just as he was giving the beam a shove, he also saw the streaking of flames heading their way. He was still connected to Darless and saw the demon's gaping mouth with flames pouring out. Unfortunately, he could do nothing about it, there was no time left. He felt the searing heat flood over his body, burning his exposed skin.

Mandy charged into the room heedless of the flames and flying stone bits, nearly knocking the paladin over in the process. She could see nothing, except the cone of flames drenching her. That was enough for this ranger. Suppressing the burning pain, she focused her attention on the origin point, the mouth she assumed, and attacked. She had some skill in "blind fighting," although she hated those lessons. Yet, she forced her thoughts to focus on that mind-set and began her systematic assault on this demon, visible or not, she intended to make it pay dearly. Two of her four blows connected to its body, of that she was sure.

The paladin, recovering his balance, charged as well, chanting a brief prayer. Mandy heard him mutter, "Now that's better. I may not see you, but I can see your evil aura. Take this you demonic beast!" He attacked with his huge two-handed sword; Mandy heard the sound of breaking bone and knew that the paladin's forceful blow had connected as well.

Jon saw three sets of magical missiles arcing to the demon, but missing the two fighters, he assumed, for he could see their infrared forms dancing about the tall creature. However, Alison's curse told him that the missiles did nothing to the demon. That demon must be protected or immune, Jon thought.

Now Jon heard both Darless and Father Johnas chanting counter-spells. Both were attempting to create desperately needed illumination. For reasons he could only guess, both spells failed utterly. Now yet another magical blast headed their way, arcing down from the ceiling of the dark room before them. This time, the party was very unlucky; the spell was a forking lightning bolt of immense power. The first targets were Mandy and Sir Thomas, both of which were caught completely off-guard and took the hit full-force. Both were sent flying across the room. Mandy hit the wall with a dull thud, followed by the tell-tale sounds of bones snapping. The paladin crashed into the wall with a mighty crash of steel bashing on stone. Both, in fact, took double damage: a massive electrical discharge and a uncontrolled smash against the wall.

However, the arcing, forking bolt continued its journey, heading straight for the rest of the group. Since the spell had already activated, neither mage could suck its energy into their staff. Almost in slow motion, Jon watched the streaking pair of bolts coming at them. It continued to fork into several smaller bolts, each heading toward the other party members. Jon did the only thing he could think of in such a short period of time. He simple stepped himself into the room with the demon and unseen attacker. Behind him, he heard the resounding cries and thuds of the others being hit and thrown back against the walls. He hoped that they would survive.

Glancing around in the dark, he noticed that he was no longer looking through Darless' eyes and thus he was totally blind. However, he did spy Mandy's magical bastard sword lying on the floor, where she had dropped it. It had a bluish glow about it. Instinctively he picked it up. *Stall, I gotta stall for time!* "Oh Demon, you know that your master is now long gone, quite dead. There is no need for you to stay here. Leave now while you still can," Jon tried.

A deep voice from just before him laughed and replied, "Ha. You wish. She is still here. Die!" Jon saw another cone of fire beginning to emanate from a mouth just before him. Jon waited until the demon committed his flames toward his location and then just stepped to what he thought would be behind the demon. He stumbled and fell, sticking out the sword to attempt to catch his balance. The sword stuck into the back of the demon instead, who whirled around, totally surprised by this unexpected, unintentional back stab. So sudden was his whirl, that Jon nearly lost his grip on the blade. At the same time from somewhere above him, he heard a cold voice call out, "Die!" He spied another magical beam heading his way. He was physically trapped. His feet kept slipping on loose objects on the floor and he could not regain his balance. His left arm ached from the twisting demon's pull on the sword he still held. In short, his position was precarious indeed. So he did the only thing he could, he just pushed the beam away from him, a couple feet to his left.

A huge flash of magic momentarily illuminated the demon. From the corner of his eye, Jon saw the huge eight-foot form outlined in a bluish energy glow. Then the entire demon just vaporized. At that same instant, Jon heard Father Johnas's prayer activate, heard the High Priest command, "In the name of all Goodness, banish all Evil from this room!" Jon heard that cold voice far above him cry out as if in pain. Then total silence.

Jon's senses were dulled. He could see nothing. He felt his aching body; parts had been hit by flying debris, parts burned, and his arm holding the sword twisted by the demon. His other arm flailed about trying to gain his balance, but lacking sight, he could not tell up from down. At last, he fell with a resounding crash onto the floor and whatever lay upon it. The sounds of sliding coins echoed off of the walls in the room. Then followed total silence, save for labored, pained breathing coming from many directions.

At long last, Rufus got his lantern lit. "There that is better. Oh my," he said as he shone the lantern to his left and right. Various party members lay moaning against the walls in the outer hallway. Then, he shone it inside the chamber where Jon lay on the ground, sliding in all directions on the slippery objects. "Oh my," he said once more, but for a different reason. Jon could finally see what had tripped him. He lay in a huge pile of coins. Thousands of them; he was nearly buried in them. He stopped struggling. "That was nasty indeed. Say what have we here?" His attention, as usual, was drawn to a lever just inside the door. It was up, so he pulled it down. Jon was too confused to yell at the gnome to stop. He prayed that nothing ill would come from that action.

Instead, six brilliant ceiling lights turned on. The brilliance nearly blinded everyone. Jon blinked uncontrollably for several seconds. While he was lying amid a huge pile of coins, he paid them little attention. The others would be in terrible shape; he struggled to his feet and barked a command to his walking stick. A short while later, his stick appeared in his hand. He headed toward then nearest fallen comrade. Father Johnas had already rushed over to Sir Thomas because the paladin was closest to him. Jon heard a prayer to Ukko and then the moan of Sir Thomas regaining consciousness. Jon reached Mandy, who lay in a crumpled heap against the side of the wall. Badly burned, gouged, electrically fried and smashed into the wall, she was unconscious, but still breathing. An arm and leg lay at a weird angle; he knew instinctively both were broken. Gently, he moved her onto her back and straightened her body out and then used his walking stick, muttering, "In the name of Father Ukko." He touched her with it and watched the familiar yellow glow appear over her body. Shortly, she regained consciousness.

Jon did not wait. Nearly simultaneously, he and Father Johnas, who also looked the worst for wear, headed into the other room to tend to the others. "You look a mess," Jon muttered to the priest.

"So do you, my son," he managed to smile. "I think the others will be in better shape. These two took the brunt of the attacks." When they entered the snake room, Rufus had already begun to help the others. He had Darless sitting up, surveying the damage. Jon went to Alison, while the priest tackled Thea, who was nearly dead; he felt only a small pulse. Again, his prayer for full healing was granted. The young mage stirred. Meantime, Jon used his walking stick on Alison, and she began to regain consciousness, moaning as well. Finally, the priest healed Lonnie as he did the others, though he needed several smaller cure spells to fully repair the young paladin's wounds and broken bones.

"How about you, Rufus?" Jon asked, "do you need some help?"

The gnome had fared the best of all of them, due in part to his small stature. "If you could be so kind to heal these infernal burns, I'd be most gracious," he replied. "The lightning bolt missed me entirely, but I got fried by the demon." Jon used his walking stick on the gnome.

"Looks like we now have everyone healed up," Father Johnas called out to Jon. "Many thanks; I've never had a party this badly in need of so much healing all at once ever before!"

"Wait a minute, we forgot us!" Jon was suddenly reminded by the burning pains in his face and hands. Both men laughed, for they had thought only of the others and not of their own plight. "I'll fix us both up." Jon once more commanded his walking stick, touching it gently to the priest. At last, he did it to himself. Once the sharp pain from Jon's burns was gone, the priest shook his hand, a broad grin upon his face.

Now, one by one, the others got to their feet. From the other room, they heard Mandy's voice, "Zounds! I'm alive. Where's my sword? Oh, my!" Jon guessed she saw her sword atop the huge pile of coins.

He yelled to her, "Sorry, but I borrowed it. I stuck the demon in its back with it. Hope you don't mind."

"Not at all," she replied, "how's the others? Zounds, I am stiff. Oh, zounds, I remember now, I hit that wall!"

"We all did," Alison groaned, now fully on her feet, but still a bit stiff. "We sure got blasted that time. Everyone all right?" she added a bit fearfully.

The deep voice of Father Johnas answered her. "Yes, dear mage. All are alive and now well, though I am certain I don't know how that came about."

Mandy joined them, helping Sir Thomas along; he leaned on her, still a bit unsure of his balance. He held his helm in his other hand and looked very haggard indeed. "What happened?" she asked. "I know we got blasted, but then I remember nothing."

"Well, I believe we were hit by one of the high powered, forking lightning magical spells," Alison surmised. "Then, I remember nothing."

"I dodged it," Father Johnas put in.

"I stepped in front of the demon and it missed me," Jon added. "Mandy, do you know your sword glows in the dark? Well, I saw it lying there in front of the demon, so I picked it up. But the demon tried to fire blast me again, so I stepped behind him. Unfortunately, I landed on the pile of coins, lost my footing and accidentally stabbed him in the back. I don't think he liked that. You know, if you are totally in the dark and lose your footing, it is darn near impossible to regain it? Well, as I was falling, that other person yelled something about me dying and shot a spell at me. So I deflected it. It accidentally hit the demon who disappeared. I, ah, think it might have been one of those disintegrate spells again."

"Verily, I believe I owe you my life!" Sir Thomas suddenly interrupted. "Alison, didn't one of those beams get fired at me right at the start?"

"I think so," she replied. "But it was all so dark."

"Yes, but look at all the stone fragments lying around," the paladin continued.

"Well, I saw it coming at you, Sir Thomas, and just nudged it out of the way. I guess it hit the door frame," Jon said meekly. "Glad it didn't hit you."

"Ah then that is what hit me in the face," Thea exclaimed. "I think my jaw got busted by the flying stone bits! Now it makes sense."

"Wait a minute," Jon interrupted. "We forgot about that unseen opponent. He just suddenly disappeared."

"My doing, my son," the priest broke in, "I sent the Evil from this room, banished it, at least temporarily anyway. It could come back, though."

Rufus, who had been standing first on one foot and then the other, grew impatient. "Say, can we go see what all is in the treasure room? We know now that the snakes and the demon were here to guard the Archmage's treasury. So please, can we go have a look see?"

"Okay, okay," Alison ordered, "let's go inside and see. My, the lights are bright." She took a step into the room and her voice trailed off, "Oh my." The others gasped.

The room was about twenty feet high with highly polished stone walls, illuminated by six magical globes hanging from the ceiling. The treasury room itself was square, forty feet on a side. In the center a huge mound of gold coins lay, their neatly stacked piles in complete disarray, due to Jon's having fallen on them in the dark. To the right side lay a much smaller repository of silver coins and some coppers. In the rear of the room were three boxes, each three feet long, two feet wide and a foot tall. All lids were opened. One was brimming with uncut precious stones of various sizes and types. The two others were brimming with jewelry and golden objects, such as pitchers, candelabra and so forth. Never had any of these seen such a huge pile of wealth in one place.

Later, when they had time to sort it all out, appraise the gems and such, the total worth yielded each of the nine companions well over a quarter million gold coins. Alison insisted each get an equal portion. When Rufus heard that, he was speechless for a short time. "You realize that I will no longer have to be a lowly trader merchant! Oh thank you, Archmage Alison!" Vast new vistas of life flooded his mind, unlimited possibilities.

"What do we do with all this treasure?" wondered Darless. "Is it safe to leave here until later?"

Alison thought for a minute while the others rummaged about the piles. Finally, she said, "Okay, the three chests contain the most valuable items. Darless, Thea and I will teleport the three chests back to my treasury and return. I think we can safely leave the coins until we are finished here." That met with everyone's instant approval. "Meanwhile, the rest of you, search for any hidden chambers in here, just to be sure and thorough. There are no magical items in here, and this is an Archmage's tower. This is only her treasury room. There must be more somewhere around here. Just don't go off exploring any other tunnels while we are gone." After this last battle, no one would have even thought of doing such!

Rufus, Jon and Father Johnas did a thorough inspection, but found nothing. Meanwhile, Sir Thomas and Mandy, whom had taken the brunt of the battle, sat down and rested up. Although physically healed of their wounds, both were quite fatigued. The big paladin said, "You know, I am beginning to find this suit of armor may not be the best thing to wear when I go exploring. At least not when there are all these magic casters intent upon either electrocuting me or blasting me to bits."

"Well, your armor saved you some broken bones," the ranger replied. "I really hit that wall hard. I know I broke my arm and leg; I've got some mental images sitting here. Being half-naked has its disadvantages, and I also got badly burned."

"Well, we both were so intent upon destroying that demon that we failed to see the magic user's attacks. If we had known it was coming, we may have dodged or deflected some of it," he consoled her. "You know, we do make a powerful team, Ranger Mandy. I'm proud to be by your side." She grinned at him.

The others had just finished their search when the three mages returned. "Hi Alison, welcome back," Jon cheerily said. "We didn't find anything. I think this room is solid and carved from bedrock."

"Thanks for looking everyone," she replied. "Would anyone object if we called it a day? Frankly, your mages are more than a bit done in." Cheers arose spontaneously from all sides. Hers was something of an understatement. This time, the nine slowly walked out of the tower and back to the edge of the village. Darless did the honors and cast the mansion spell. All entered without a word. "Women get the bathroom first," Alison declared. No one objected. The women greatly desired to get the smell of burned hair out of their hair and see just how bad they looked. Besides, their clothes were quite the worst for wear.

Lonnie helped the paladin out of his suit of armor. "Looks like it absorbed a great deal of damage," he commented.

"Yes, my lad. That is one of its advantages," he explained. "A good suit like this one can take quite a punishment that is meant for the wearer." Once out of the armor, he sniffed and embarrassedly said, "Gosh, I do smell. I hope the women hurry up." Both men laughed.

Father Johnas, on the other hand, heedless of his burned clothes, knelt down and began a long meditation to Father Ukko. Jon heard him pray for his blessings on this valiant group. Jon smiled. Then, he looked at his clothes. They were not too badly ruined. He headed to the kitchen to fix some dinner. He figured he would bathe last.

The women took an hour to clean up, while the men, only a half an hour. By then, the smells of dinner reminded everyone of their hunger. All were most grateful to Jon for fixing it this evening.

While they were sitting around sipping their after-dinner tea, Alison questioned Jon. "All right buddy, just *how* do you see these magical spells and how do you *deflect* them anyway? You know you are not supposed to even perceive them, unless you are a highly trained mage and then it is not very likely. I've never seen *any*."

"Dunno, my love," he replied, "I just do. You know in that inky blackness, I was totally blind. I never really knew what it might be like to not be able to see anything. That was an awful feeling."

"You can say that again!" Thea exclaimed, listening in on their conversation.

"Yet Mandy was able to fight. Mandy, how do you do that?" Jon asked, deftly sliding the topic away from himself. Alison, though, noticed what he was doing, as did Darless. Thea missed it because she too wondered just how Mandy and Sir Thomas could continue to fight in the total darkness.

"Blind-fighting training," she said quickly, but found that only the paladins knew what she was talking about; so she added, "Sometimes we train that way. You know, don a blindfold and then try to fight. Makes you use your other senses. Personally, I always hated those practice sessions, but now, for the first time, that training came in handy."

Sir Thomas nodded his full agreement and then added, "It takes weeks and weeks of practice to get really good at it. Unfortunately, I never did get really good at it. Glad Mandy was by my side or it may have been quite grim indeed." He yawned. "I guess I am really tired." Taking that as a clue, the group turned in for the night.

However, once all the lights were turned down, leaving only a night-light glow, everyone grew very nervous and worried. Jon did not need to sense their minds to know. It was that obvious. "Okay, I think we all need mental assists tonight or we are never going to be able to shut our eyes." Several nervous laughs signaled that he hit the mark. Jon began with Alison, Darless, with Sir Thomas, and Thea, Mandy. When those three were laughing and feeling perfectly at ease in the dark, they moved on to help out Lonnie and Rufus. At last, Jon aided Darless and Alison, Thea. Unfortunately, Jon fell totally asleep before anyone could run him through the events of the day, erasing any ill remnants left in his mental pictures of the day.

Jon slept ill. He kept finding himself in a totally black vacuum with that cold voice above him crying out,

"Die! Die, Saint Jon Brown!" He awoke with a sweat in the morning.

Over breakfast, Alison summarized her theories. "After yesterday, I am convinced that a powerful mage still inhabits this tower. All those spells had *immense* power behind them. Only a high level mage can come and go so easily, to say nothing of defeating so many of our counter-spells. Somewhere, probably where we have not yet explored, lies that mage in waiting. We have seen his powers several times now. It is not going to be easy to defeat him. I expect that we should find a room with all his magical stuff down below. There hopefully we will find some answers that I have been looking for all my life. I guess, I am just trying to warn you that today might be even more dangerous than yesterday as we perhaps corner this mage. Any questions?"

"Er, I have one," Rufus hesitatingly spoke up. All eyes looked at him, flustering him slightly. "This is or was the Archmage Sarah le'Garde's tower, right?" Alison nodded. "Well, then my question is: who is this mage that is fighting us? Could it be that the Archmage Sarah le'Garde still lives? Or has some other mage taken over this tower?"

"I don't know how to answer you, my friend," she replied slowly. From the apt attention of all of the others, she knew that they were just as interested in her answer as was the gnome. "Since our arrival here, we have seen nothing human alive, only rats and snakes. No food, no water, nothing of which we would need just to survive. This place is totally isolated, no town to go to for supplies or to grab a bite to eat. Further, we have the presumption of the brown dragon is that she is long dead. Honestly, I just do not know how to read this riddle, save only that we are dealing with one very powerful spell caster of magic as opposed to the priestly spells. We can rule out druids, evil priests and even illusionists — wrong kind of spells. Beyond that, I cannot say. I've never run into anything quite like this before."

Solemnly, they gathered their gear and left the mansion heading back into the tower. However, Father Johnas was thinking hard. Alison's speech started him thinking. He did not like the direction his thoughts were taking him. Thus far, he could not see why Father Ukko had requested him to stay with these people to the end. But now, this strange thought began forming in his mind. He hoped it was not so, that he was being overly paranoid.

Chapter 15 The Confrontation

When they arrived at the entrance to the tower, Alison cast her spell that enabled her to detect traps. She checked the gaping hole where the iron doors had been. "Good grief!" she exclaimed. "Someone has setup another trap overnight. Look here, had we just walked inside, we'd have triggered it. Give me a minute to defuse it."

"Zounds!" exclaimed Mandy. "This guy just doesn't give up!"

"Thank you for being so overly cautious," Sir Thomas added. "I promise never ever to tease you about this again!"

She smiled back, "Okay it's now safe to pass the doorway. Let me check on ahead. Darless, it might be a good idea for you to double-check me." The pair of mages quickly scanned the first floor for new booby traps, but no further ones were found. Instinctively, they retraced the route to the treasury room and found it in the same state that they had left it yesterday: coins scattered over the floor and with no new traps set for them. Confident that all was well thus far, they headed back to the secret tunnel opening that led down from the kitchen.

As they set up their marching order, Mandy had a sick feeling in her stomach, "Guys, I think this is going to be the proverbial big one. I just have this feeling." The happy mood of the others instantly turned sour. "Always trust your ranger" was burned into their minds.

"Oh dear," was all that Thea could muster for a reply.

"Gather round," Alison took charge. She had to change their mood. It was no good heading into danger this way. "We mages have given this some thought, especially after the beating we all took yesterday. First of all, everyone is going to get the benefit of the skin of

516

stone spell. That means, you probably can take nearly a dozen 'hits' that would have wounded you — take them with no effect at all. When the tingle sensation has left you, the protection is gone. Mages, front and center. Use the charges in your staff to cast these. The rest of you, line up in front of us."

"Now this is more like it!" exclaimed Lonnie to Thea, who was about to cast the spell on him. "I can be invincible for a short while and really help out!" She grinned and proceeded to cast the spell. He felt the tingle flow over him, but then he remembered something she had said about not being able to cast this spell yet. "Say, you've learned how to do this one!"

She beamed. "Yes," she proudly said, "I've learned quite a bit in the last few days! Thanks for noticing it!" He gave her a hug and stepped back so Rufus could get his protection spell.

Once everyone had theirs, Alison continued. "Next, Darless and I have cooked up a scheme we want to try out. It is a contingency plan or set of spells. In other words, gang, should a particular event occur, the spells we setup now will automatically be cast with no effort or thought on our part. First, Mandy. If we encounter sudden darkness, like yesterday, I'm going to have a globe of light appear on the top of your head to counter it." The ranger smiled, now this was a good idea, she thought. Once Alison had cast the pair of spells, she continued, "Sir Thomas, should the lights go out like yesterday, from the top of your helm will fire a dispel magic spell headed in the direction you are facing. Remember, if all goes black, face toward the opponents, if at all possible."

"But what happens if I am not?" he protested slightly. "Won't I accidentally cause some of your other spells to malfunction?" He sounded very worried about this.

"Don't worry, if that happens, it happens. I've never tried this sequencing of spells before, so we will just have to see how it works out. You cannot harm us by this spell so don't give it any concern at all." He seemed a bit relieved, although he was still not totally comfortable about this. Since Darless did the casting on him, he felt better about it, just as she had predicted to Alison earlier when they were discussing this idea.

"Finally, I'm moving Thea up in the marching order. I want her beside Jon and behind Darless and myself. If the lights go out, Thea, from your head will come a wall of force. You only need extend your hands to control it. The idea is to throw up a barrier to any incoming spells or fires so that all of the rest of you are immune to it and can then respond."

Thea happily accepted the pair of spells cast onto her head. "Didn't hurt a bit; hardly felt it," she cheerily whispered to Lonnie.

"Finally, Rufus, Lonnie, Jon, and Thea, each of you are to carry a lighted lantern and a box of Jon's magical stick lighters. If all goes dark, you can relight them if need be. I want lots of light today! Any questions?" she paused mentally checking off each step to make doubly sure she had omitted nothing.

"No! Let's do this!" exclaimed Sir Thomas enthusiastically, and they set off. The secret door was on the opposite side of the tower from the entrance doorway or on the south side. Cleverly, part of the floor slid out of the way revealing a set of steps leading downward into a darken passageway. Once they had gone down the ten steps, they reached a long corridor six feet wide and seven tall. Like the other one they explored yesterday, the sides were hewn from the bedrock and highly polished. This was no quickly made tunnel.

Every ten feet alternating from side to side, lanterns in various demonic shapes were fastened near the ceiling. None, of course were lit. However, Lonnie lit each one as he passed by; he was in the very rear and could take the time to dally. The corridor or tunnel was pitch black, save only for the lights they brought, four lanterns and three magical globes atop the staff of each of the three mages. However, they were still only able to see clearly some thirty or so feet ahead.

Progress was slow because of three ongoing actions. First, Mandy was examining the floor as they went, looking for signs. Dust had accumulated here for many years and was a quarter of an inch thick in places. Anyone passing through here would leave a clear trail. What bothered her was the dust was entirely undisturbed. This she continually pointed out to Sir Thomas, who could not help but notice it himself. He had no explanation for it either. Second, Alison and Darless both were continually checking for traps. They found none in the first hundred feet. However, they had to be looking ahead of the two fighters in front of them. Third, Rufus, in the rear with Lonnie, was continually tap-tapping here and there checking for hidden side chambers. The gnome's worst fear was to pass by a concealed chamber and then have some monsters come out and attack him from behind.

The tunnel sloped gradiently downward. At the hundred foot mark, side chambers opened up on either side, both quite dark inside. Mandy halted by the one on the left, while Sir Thomas did likewise, but facing the one on their right. The two mages squeezed close and shown their lights inside the rooms. The paladin announced, "We have found the pantry," while the ranger added, "and the supply room. Shall we split up?"

This was Alison's worst fear: that they should split up and then be attacked at one-half their strength. "No, I am in no hurry. Mandy and I will go check out the supply room. The rest of you stay right here and keep guard on the other three directions." The two entered the supply chamber.

This room was about twenty feet square, but its ceiling rose to ten feet. Along the walls stood several wooden, floor-to-ceiling shelves full of household tools and items. Brooms, hammers, saws and such were neatly stowed on the shelves. In the middle was a huge oak work bench. Clearly, here was where repairs were made and new things built. Mandy and Alison examined it rapidly, even scanning it for anything magical. Alison found nothing of any real interest. She knew Rufus would have fun in here later on. They rejoined the others in the passage way, giving the all clear.

Now Darless and Sir Thomas carefully entered the pantry. This room was identical in size to the other supply room. However, in here, the many shelves were packed with food items. An ugly mold grew everywhere and on nearly everything. "Be very careful not to disturb this mold!" cautioned Sir Thomas. While exploring an underground dungeon several years ago, he had had a very bad experience with mold. In fact, he had gotten so sick that Father Johnas had to cast a cure disease spell for him to even recover. It didn't take them long to rejoin the party.

"Mold is everywhere in there," Darless announced. "Nothing is fit to eat. I think we can safely say that no one is using the stored food. It matches the other homes that we searched, when we got here. I'd say people stopped using this room and its food stuff many years ago, at least a half dozen. It fits the overall pattern."

"Okay, let's continue on down the corridor," Alison ordered and they resumed their slow march. The tunnel continued on downward, straight as an arrow for another fifty feet. Then the tunnel ended at a tee. Similar passage ways led to the left and to the right. They stopped.

"Well, darn," said Alison to herself. "But it's what I would have done." She explained to the others, particularly Thea, Lonnie and Jon, that with a split like this, any raiding party would be forced to split up or be constantly worried about being attacked from behind.

Jon now understood. "Say, I'm not really doing anything. How about if I expand my awareness in all directions and scout about and see if I can detect any minds? If I find any, why I can sound the alarm, though I might not know where the mind is in relation to us." Alison thought that was a terrific idea, it greatly lessened the chance for a surprise attack from their rear.

"Okay, everyone, time for a little lesson in maze traversal," Alison assumed her teacher approach. "When you are not familiar with the layout, as we are not here, and when passages go off this way and that, one can easily get lost or miss things. The trick is always stick to a predefined sequence, always. When presented with a choice, continue on straight, and, if that is not an option, go right. If we get into deep trouble, every one of you can find your way out by reversing our steps, follow me?"

Sir Thomas added, "Listen to her! Her ideas have saved my party on several occasions!" Jon chuckled and attempted to burn her words into his mind — straight else right. They promptly turned down the right tunnel. After an uneventful fifty feet, the tunnel turned ninety degrees, resuming their northerly direction once more. They had gone only twenty more feet, when Mandy called a halt.

"Do you all see what I am seeing? Is that light coming from way up ahead of us?" she asked incredulously.

Everyone began whispering. It was indeed a faint light ahead. Cautiously they continued on down the tunnel. After another thirty feet, another tunnel connected to this one coming in from their left side. The light was coming from this tunnel, and they instinctively turned to see what they could see. "Shh. I think I can hear voices coming from down there," cautioned Mandy. In the stillness, low mumbles could be clearly made out by everyone. "I think I see people moving about," she added in a whisper.

Jon, of course, had been letting his awareness expand all about him. It was lots easier to do with his eyes closed, though. As long as they were standing still, he shut his eyes and moved his attention toward the light, trying to sense the minds of those that were obviously there. *I must not be really aware or alert today,* he thought. *I don't sense any minds, but I think I can see some people down there.* He concentrated all the harder, trying to reach those minds.

The hairs on Mandy's neck twitched and Alison gave the order, "Let's go see who's there. Careful now." They began a relative quiet march down this side tunnel, relatively, because the full plate armor of the paladin made echoing clanking sounds with every foot step. More than once, Mandy gave him a side-long stare, like "can't you walk more quietly?" He did his best to go as silently as he could. They went only some ten feet before a huge, well-lit room opened before them.

This giant chamber was fully eighty feet across and square. The ceiling was at least twenty feet above their heads. Six great hanging lanterns, each with six radiating spokes that each held six huge lanterns. Jon heard Darless mutter, "6-6-6, very unlucky number." Far across the room and straight in line with this one, another tunnel exited the room.

In the precise center of the room rose a huge ornate altar. Many pews formed a semicircle about the southern half of the room and the altar. To the north side, great tapestries hung down from the ceiling. It was not the lanterns or the tapestries that commanded their full attention, rather the occupants. Standing at the altar was obviously a High Priest; he wore rich robes and had a long, grey beard. To either side of him stood two middle aged mages, each bearing a staff similar to Alison's; these were obviously powerful wizards. Just behind them towering over all the men stood a dozen of the vulture, bird-like demons that the group had faced last year when they confronted Demon Lord Metrarch's High Priest. They had nearly all perished from the violent attacks of these demon creatures from the Abyss. Here were fully a dozen more!

Uncontrollable surges of recognition followed by fear crept into Jon's, Mandy's, Alison's and Darless' minds. Sir Thomas had arrived at that battle just in time to see these creatures gating the foursome down into the Abyss. It was the worst moment of the paladin's life, standing there watching his Alison being gated away, when he could do nothing to prevent it. Fear crept into his mind as well. They had only barely survived the bird demon's attacks, because Jon had discovered how to slay them via their minds.

Why can't I sense the priest's mind? Those demons, I remember how I got them. I'd better begin to contact their minds just in case they attack. Jon strained but found he still sensed no other minds present. Sweat trickled down his forehead, so hard did he strain. This had never happened to him before, ever!

Now, the High Priest waved to them and spoke. "Hail Thieves! I am Cain, Master of the Dead, High Priest of Faruko, God of the Underworld. To enter this tower means only one thing. You wish to become Undead. So be it. I give you a choice: do you want to be a skeleton or a zombie after the Unholy Conversion Ceremony? Be advised, that in this Unholy Chamber of Cain, all magic is nullified — your spells shall have no effect upon us, the Unholy — no blade can harm our bodies. Do not think of attacking us, because then you lose your choice; I will choose the most despicable form for your here-after undead life as my servants."

All this was not anticipated by any member of the party. It was so wildly unexpected, that everyone stood rooted to the spot, trying to mentally grasp the situation.

Thea even blinked, as if this was all some kind of dream. The pale complexion of her face belied that idea. Mandy was the first to offer any reaction. She merely charged toward the High Priest, her highly enchanted bastard sword poised for the first strike. The High Priest did not flinch nor move, but watched her rush towards him. She swung, intending to end his unholy days right now. To everyone's amazement, the High Priest somehow avoided her blade with nary a scratch on him. He said, "For you, I shall craft a rotting zombie body full of pussy facial blobs, totally ugly. So be it. You have spoken." Mandy tried to get another swing at him and once more completely missed the priest.

At this precise moment in time, several things happened nearly all at once. The catalyst was Darless, who screamed loudly, "Don't believe any of this! It is all an illusion. The room is completely empty!"

Well, now it all makes sense, Jon though and he added, "There are no minds here. It isn't real!" He blinked twice and saw a well-lighted, but totally empty room. Mandy had been swinging at empty space. Just as the others rubbed their eyes trying to block out the illusion, Jon sensed that cold mind appearing somewhere in the room. He tried to sound the alarm, "That wizard is in here!"

But as his words came out, all lights in the entire room, including their magical globes and the four lanterns they were carrying, went out. It was once again utterly pitch black, a total and complete darkness. Panic hit everyone; this was just like yesterday all over again.

Only this time, Alison's contingency spells instantly activated. In the next instant, a globe of light appeared on Mandy's head providing some visibility of the vast, empty room. Sir Thomas just happened to be looking toward Mandy, when the spell on his head triggered. This, of course, was exceedingly fortunate for both Mandy and himself. For at that same instant, another one of those massive forked lightning bolts that had nearly killed them all yesterday came streaking straight at Mandy and Sir Thomas. But the dispel magic forces collided with that streak of intense magical energy completely nullifying it, to the total amazement of Sir Thomas and Mandy, who were already bracing for the inevitable lightning strike.

Thea detected the wall of force in front of her and held on to it. "Which way? Which way do I position it to protect you all?" she called out, but no one answered her confusion.

Which way is that mind? Jon heard in his head. It was the solemn voice of Darless.

He answered her back mentally, *Dunno. Somewhere above and to our left.*

To this alu-demon, who could see through illusions, the wizard could not be an illusion. It must obey laws of the universe. If his body mind was above and to their left, then his body had to be there as well or so she assumed. One glance told her all she needed to know. Above and left, there was only one place that this wizard could be and that was in or on or hanging from that distant lantern group. One second later, she teleported herself to that space, hovering in the air using her bat-like wings. There she detected the shimmering of space that denoted something magically invisible. Without further thought, she lunged at it, grabbed a hold of the wizard and teleported them both to the floor, wrestling with the creature.

She felt for its throat. The shape was all wrong, but she found what she assumed to be its neck and attempted to throttle it using her inhuman, demon-spawn strength, much as she had done to kill Lord Jarred's body last year. Unfortunately for her, as her hands made contact with its neck, an intense coldness such as she had never know flowed through her hands, freezing her steadily. Now its hands fumbled for her throat and that intense freezing cold began choking the very life out of her!

The cold voice uttered a command word. Wham! Darless lay totally stunned, inactive on the ground, totally and completely helpless, unable to move a muscle. She stared up at the grisly demonic creature, the likes of which she had never seen before. She watched helplessly as it cast a spell back toward the others. She knew that it had just cast an enormously powerful ball of fire.

The others had not been idle. The instant that Mandy saw Darless falling down from the ceiling bringing something with her, she dashed across the room, putting her magical boots of striding to their maximum jump. She arrived just after the mighty ball of fire was loosened upon the others. So fast and unexpected was her appearance that the wizard was taken by surprise, her bastard sword plunged deep into its form, wounding it severely. It rose up to its full height and stared at Mandy. The ranger's body let out a high pitched shriek all on its own, so hideous was this creature's appearance.

Sir Thomas was only a couple seconds behind Mandy. He chose to come at it from its rear and just as Mandy took the creature's stare full on, the Holy Paladin's blade thrust through the tattered, rotten robes and into its body, wounding it further. At that same instant, the prayer of Father Johnas activated. Now he was sure of what they were facing. He took solace in that he had cast the right spell. Boom! Waves of energy flooded over the creature, knocking it back and away from the trio, some fifteen feet, straight into the poised staff of Alison, who had used it to teleport herself behind the action. So violent was its motion that the creature became skewered on her staff as if it was a spear. At that instant, Alison's spell activated and a huge volley of magical missiles penetrated its skull, causing the creature to writhe in agony.

The creature's giant ball of flames erupted on the others. Thea still held the wall of force between the flames and the remaining five. So strong was the blast that she could not physically hold the wall up and slowly she fell over backwards, still fending off the worst of the erupting flames. Jon neutralized the rest of the flames that moved around the wall by creating a great volume of cold energy. Thus, the five suffered no damage at all from the enormous blast that had been destined to kill them. Lonnie helped the stunned Thea push the wall up off of the five, now prone, adventurers.

Jon, however, did not get up. For the first time, he had finally made good contact with that cold, evil mind. He was not going to let go of it without a fight. Thus he began bombarding that mind with energy balls. More and more and more he sent to that mind. He did not know if he was having any appreciable effect, but if he could cause it to delay, to hesitate, perhaps the others could slay it.

The next moment, three things occurred nearly simultaneously. Mandy, now on her opponent, was able to chop her blade into its body three times, while the paladin managed another solid blow himself. At that instant, a contingency spell of the creature's activated and the creature disappeared. It was physically no longer where it had been standing. But distance and location meant nothing to Jon's mental attack. It was just space that he was crossing. Now his energy balls were becoming quite large indeed. He used the same trick that he had done over a year before, when attacking a white dragon mentally. He just kept gradiently mocking up more and more and more energy balls and blasting the cold, evil mind with them. In the distance, he heard Alison cancel her spell, the wizard was nowhere to be seen.

Just then, everyone's attention was drawn to a loud explosion overhead. All eyes rose to see what it was. Thus, everyone witnessed the last energy ball of Jon's explode about the head of the creature. A cry of utter agony pierced the silence of the room. The undead creature died. The damaged remains of its body fell back to the floor in a crash of bones and robes. Sensing the mind was no longer present, Jon stopped and relaxed and dozed. It was now peacefully quiet. No sound was heard save the heavy breathing of Mandy and Sir Thomas.

The bass voice of Father Johnas was the first to break the silence, "That, my friends, was a lich, one of the most deadly and powerful of all the undead creatures in existence. Congratulations one and all, you have actually slain a lich! This is nearly unbelievable!" Then he remembered his duties, "Is anyone hurt?"

From a distance, Darless could only squeak, "Help, over here. I'm not doing so well." Rufus was the first to reach her; he had been running full speed toward her once the fire ball had gone out. He sat the lantern on the floor so that he could examine her. She had great grey patches around her neck. It looked like a pair of grey hand imprints. He took her hand to feel her pulse and noticed both her hands had turned deadly grey. Father Johnas arrived at her side and Rufus pointed out the grey areas. "No circulation," he ventured to say.

"This is grim, my lady. You tangled physically with the lich. Let me see what I can do for you." He began a lengthy prayer to Father Ukko and then touched her gently. Rufus watched fascinated as the color quickly returned to her neck and hands.

She cleared her throat several times before she could speak properly. "Thank you. That was rather horrible. Is it really dead?" The priest helped her up.

"Yes, thanks to all of us, particularly you, my dear. You realize that it was your stroke of genius that made it possible? If you had not found him and wrestled the lich to the ground, it may be a very different story we have to tell. You are very brilliant and also very lucky to be a live mage!"

"It was Jon's doing," she protested. "He located the lich for me. Glad you intervened when you did, Mandy, or I may have been a goner." The ranger and the others were now standing around her as she sat on the floor.

"Liches are very powerful and darn hard to slay," the priest added. "We all helped out. The blade strikes did much damage. My prayer caused it great pain and confusion. It actually stabbed itself on Alison's staff and her missiles did great damage, but how did we actually slay it?"

"It was definitely a magic using lich," Alison volunteered. "I believe it had contingency spells of its own. I think that, when it felt it was hurt sufficiently bad, that it was teleported away from the danger. But how did it die? Who cast those yellow energy balls at its head? The ones that seem to explode, but did not really explode?"

"Not me," Darless said, "I could not even speak."

Both looked at Thea. "Not me, I was too busy deflecting that fire ball, falling down, and trying not to land on Lonnie."

Alison looked bewildered and then said, "Jon?" All eyes darted about to see him, but he was not standing among them.

"Oh, he's over there," Thea volunteered, "sleeping I think."

Hearing his name mentioned, Jon raised his head up, "No, just dozing. It is very peaceful in here now. Quiet too. Restful." Suddenly he sat bolt upright. "Wait a minute! You *saw* my energy bolts? That's not possible — at least I don't think so."

"Verily, we all saw these yellow balls come out of nowhere and detonate, or appear to detonate, about its head," the priest confirmed. "Are you a wizard too? Some spell?"

Jon looked very embarrassed. "Er, no, I was just attacking its mind. Perhaps I just got a bit carried away with it. I sometimes do that." His voice fell away.

"Well, then, my son, it was your energy blasts that finished the lich off. Well done," Father Johnas complimented. "Come on every one, let's go have a look at the lich's body. These are exceedingly rare. I've never seen one personally." Everyone followed the priest over to the remains. He explained as they walked, that only exceedingly powerful, but evil, beings can, upon their body's death, transform themselves into eternal undead life. The mere physical touch of such creatures begins to suck the life force out of living creatures. Indeed, Darless had been fortunate to have the others distract the lich from extinguishing hers.

"That's not a man!" exclaimed Thea as they looked at the remains of the lich. The body itself was nearly skeletal. Black spots replaced eye balls in their sockets. But the clothes, once very expensive but now rotten and torn, were most definitely female. She wore a blue satin gown under the rich purple robe. Several rings were on her fingers and a pendant in the form of a demon from the Abyss hung about her neck.

Recognition came to all nearly simultaneously, but Alison spoke the words first. "Allow me to present the late Archmage Sarah le'Garde. Now we know what happened to her."

"Well, she is now quite dead at last," added Rufus.

"Who'd want to be living looking like this?" Thea added incredulously. "Skin stretched over bone. No eyes. Hideous to look at. Rotting. Gosh, she stinks! Oh! So it was her that we have been smelling all this time!" She suddenly connected the smell and its maker. The others smiled.

"Thea, my child," the priest tried to explain, "some people cannot accept the cycle of life. That is birth, growth, decay and death. This is one way to attempt to cheat death. Such a route is only possible for the most powerful, evil people."

"What I don't understand," Jon mused, "is why she just didn't go pick up a new baby body and start over? We are spiritual beings, after all."

"Ah, my son, that is easily explained," the priest smiled at his naivety, "when was the last time you saw a new born baby get up and walk back to its former house and reclaim it and its bank account as well?" Everyone laughed, save Jon. This was something to think about — to give serious thought to.

"Wait a minute," exclaimed Thea, suddenly very worried about a thought that just struck her. "Can she get reborn as a new undead lich once again? What's to keep her from just reforming or whatever tomorrow?"

The priest chuckled, "No she is gone for good, my child. You see, on her death bed, she must have performed great unholy magic to bring about such an unnatural change. I recall that you said she was at one time a consort to a demon lord, so that is probably where and how she came unto the knowledge to bring about her transformation. You may relax, this lich is permanently gone."

"Well, she may be gone, but this is her tower. Who knows what other traps she has set for us? We had best be continuing our exploration. It is a shame that we could not question her about what she did to my parents. Maybe we will find clues she left behind. Come on, let's continue as before. Jon, if you are up to it, please keep alert to any other minds heading our way. Gosh knows what else we may yet encounter down here," Alison requested. They resumed their explorations.

Being methodical was Alison's middle name. She led them back out the way they entered this large chamber and continued on straight. After another fifty feet, the tunnel turned left. After another hundred feet, left again. After another fifty, a side passage with light emanating from it junctioned on their left. They could see back into the large chamber they had left. So the other exit led here. She continued straight ahead and after another fifty feet, it veered left once more and after another fifty feet, a side passage opened on their right. "Ah this is the tunnel that we originally came down from the first floor," Mandy called out. Even Jon could easily see their footprints in the heavy dust.

Alison had them march back into the large chamber, glad that they had left the room's lanterns blazing. "Well that was fruitless," Alison commented. "Okay it is time to search for more concealed chambers. There just has to be more!"

"Where should we search first?" wondered Thea. This was her first experience in underground tunnels. She had just mentally got the tunnel plan firmly in her mind. "Why would she have a tunnel that goes completely around this room?"

"Symmetry would suggest there is a hidden passage just opposite the entrance tunnel into this large square tunnel," Alison proposed. "But who knows if she had symmetry in mind when she designed this tower complex. If there was one there, it would be rather obvious where it was." They held a discussion on where to start looking first.

Meanwhile, Darless glanced over at the remains of the lich, the Archmage Sarah. She swore that she saw a finger move slightly. But no, maybe it was just the light. Still, ever curious, she walked over to the bones to have a closer look. The skeletal form looked just as it had fallen. *No wait, one finger with that ring on it is more solid than the others. It's regenerating!* She called out urgently, "Gang, we have a problem over here. This lich is regenerating, coming back to life or unlife or whatever you call it." Everyone dashed over to the body, the fighters had their swords out, just in case. Sure enough, one finger was reforming itself.

"That cannot be," Father Johnas complained. "It's not supposed to do that. At least I've never read that regeneration was a power of a lich undead creature."

"Hum, I have a theory," Darless concluded. Using her staff, she knocked the ring off of the finger by pretty well smashing the finger to dust. Then, she slid the ring over the floor, and using a handkerchief, she picked it up and put it in one of her pouches. "I am going to attempt to identify this ring tonight when all's quiet. I think that it is the ring that is doing it, Father Johnas. But to be on the safe side, while you all look for secret doors and chambers, I'll keep my eye on the lich and see if anything else happens."

"Best get all of the rings and items off the body," Alison concluded. "Take care not to actually touch anything with your skin. It might be harmful. Collect the lich's things and put them in this bag here and we'll study them tonight." Darless took the large sack from her and went back to smashing finger bones to dust so that the rings came free easily without her having to physically take them off of the lich's body.

All the while they were studying the lich's remains, Rufus had been slowly moving around the room's walls, tap-tapping with his little hammer. "Hey, Alison, come over here. I think I have found something." All, save Darless, quickly walked over to the north wall. Rufus was standing midway along the eighty-foot wall.

"Listen to this," he said enthusiastically, when everyone gave him their full attention. First he tapped way to the right and then right here in the middle. "Notice any difference in sound?"

"Oh, I get it, Rufus," Thea exclaimed. "Over there it sounds rather muted, but here it sounds, well sort of lighter. Does this mean the wall's hollow?"

"Means that something lies behind here," he explained. "Now all we have to do is figure how it opens up. Must be some mechanism around here." The room was exceedingly bare of things. Only the lanterns hanging from the ceiling and a switch on the wall were visible. "I must admit, I'm not sure where to look for the control switch. I bet it is hidden inside a concealed little box like the switch I found up on the third floor."

"We have not got the time to spend searching," Alison concluded. "Stand way back, I'll open it." When they were back some twenty feet, she chanted her spell ending with a barking "Open" command. Boom. On side walls near the entrances, a small concealed box appeared hewn out of the rock walls; inside each was a lever, now both in the down position. More startling was the loud noise of grating stone, as part of the floor and the central section of the wall parted, revealing a sloped passage leading further underground, a new tunnel network.

Sir Thomas and Father Johnas smiled at each other; they had seen her do just this so many times in the past they had lost count. This ability was one of the reasons Alison had her former adventuring party's complete respect. She made the laborious task of finding secret chambers a breeze. On the other hand, Thea cheered her mentor, "Way to go Alison. I've got to remember this. Brilliant."

Darless joined them, "The lich seems to be staying dead, so let's go down and have a look." She was getting a bit excited as well for she, like Alison, realized that they had not yet discovered the mage's magic study where she kept her spell books and other items most valuable to wizards.

So using the same order, with Mandy and Sir Thomas leading the way, they headed down the sloping ramp, which was actually the floor of the chamber when the doorway was closed. The passage went down twenty feet in depth in about fifty linear feet, so footing was a bit slippery. Once down, the passageway leveled off much as it was above, that is six feet wide and seven, tall, with nicely polished granite walls. As before, lanterns were spaced evenly on either side twenty feet apart. Lonnie lit each of them as he passed by.

They had not gone but another fifty feet when a pair of doors appeared on each side of the tunnel. Both doors were made of enchanted stone and a bluish energy glow outlined the circumference of the each door. "These are obviously trapped or magically protected," Rufus pronounced the obvious. "I believe a dispel magic spell is in order here."

"Let's not be hasty, Rufus," Alison cautioned her little friend, "after all, she was an Archmage. She probably has these very well guarded indeed. I know I would. Darless you and Rufus study that one, and Thea and I will examine this one. Then, we will swap doors and then compare findings. Four sets of keen eyes are better than one. Expect trap upon trap." They began their examinations. Each mage cast various detection spells, commenting to the other what they discovered. Meanwhile, Mandy and Sir Thomas moved on down the tunnel a short distance and then sat down to wait it out. Jon, Father Johnas and Lonnie did the same guarding the rear.

The wizards were taking no chances with these doors. Fully an hour passed before they conferred about their mutual findings. Several points were missed by each and another fifteen minutes passed while they went back to verify what they had missed. Finally, Alison summarized their findings to the others. "As we suspected, both of these doors are very well protected against unauthorized intrusion. The good news is that we believe both doors have exactly the same enchantments laid upon them. If we get one open, we merely repeat the same steps for the other. What we have going for us is the fact that we have four spell casters present, not just one. So if you all will stand back, we will attempt to open one of them. Which one will it be first? That is what we cannot decide."

"Let me check for minds," Jon volunteered. He closed his eyes and expanded his awareness into both rooms simultaneously. After a couple minutes, he opened them and said, "Nope, no minds in either space. So pick one, how about the one on your left?"

Alison smiled back, "All right then, it's this one first. Everyone, stand well back. If we goof the sequence, there is likely to be a severe energy backlash — probably electrical in nature, or else poison gas. However, we think because of the depth, if gas were released, it would be very hard for the owner to clear it out." Everyone now went further down the tunnel until they were about thirty feet from the doors. Alison alone stood before the door, she would attempt this one, while Darless would later try the second one. The sequence of spells was demanding and used up a fair number of the spells that any one wizard would have prepared for a day's work. Yet, they still had magical energy in their staves as a backup should even more be needed. Five minutes and five spells later, the bluish glow disappeared and the door opened inward of its own accord. She had been successful. A bead of sweat dripped into her eye, she rubbed her forehead with her sleeve. "Okay, clear I think. Let's have a look."

All hurried to peer inside. Alison and Darless poked their staves with the magical light into the room. No one said a word; all mouths stood gaping wide open; eyes blinked in total disbelief. The room was twenty-foot square with a ten-foot high ceiling. However, all the walls, save the one opposite the door, were lined with tables. Crates of all sizes lay under them, but it was the stuff that so awed them all. Against the opposite wall were piled ten suits of armor, still shiny, some ring mail, but most plate armor. One was actually full field armor similar to Sir Thomas's now battered armor. Swords abounded, all in scabbards, some jeweled, some plain. Nearly every type of sword was represented. There were maces and hammers and even a pole arm. Four different kinds of bows lay on one table.

From some of the chests, the glint of golden rings and jewelry could be seen. At last, Father Johnas managed to regain his sense of perspective, "Allow me to cast a spell." He gave a short prayer to Father Ukko and uttered his command phrase, "Show me what's magical." All eyes turned to him, but his eyes nearly popped out of his head. His lower jaw kept involuntarily opening and closing, but he could say no words. The four wizards could stand the suspense no longer. In unison, they chanted their spells that would show them what was magical in the room. Their eyes too blinked unbelieving, their mouths wagged.

The others grew even more impatient. "Oh come on," protested Jon. "What is it?"

"This — this — this is unbelievable. Jon, look at what I see and show it to the others who cannot see. You will understand." Jon moved inside of Alison's mind, picked up her vision, gaped, and then contacted Mandy, Sir Thomas and Lonnie. In their minds, they now saw what Jon saw who saw what Alison was seeing. No one said a word.

Finally, Rufus managed to squeal in a squeaky voice, "Everything in the room is magical! How can this be? Rings, staves, wands, scrolls, potions, armor, weapons, everything! We have found the mother lode of all mother lodes of magic items! We are rich beyond our wildest imaginations. You cannot believe what all this would be worth. It utterly dwarfs the entire treasury twenty-fold at the very least! Darless, please say this is all an illusion! This cannot be!" He blinked and blinked.

"I — I — it's real!" was all the alu-demon could muster. "We'd better check for more traps!" Sometimes the mundane things help bring one back to reality. Going down their methodical checklist of trap detection, the four wizards finally recovered. "No traps. It's clear,"

Darless finally commented. "So let's get a closer look," and in they all went.

"Wait a moment before you touch anything," cautioned Father Johnas. "Allow me to check for anything that is inherently evil in nature." He prayed and then cast his spell and methodically examined each area. It was impossible to examine every item, for that would take days and days. Fortunately, things seemed to be somewhat organized. Several blades and one suit of armor radiated intense evil. On these, he placed a small bit of cloth to warn the others. Then, they made a cursory survey of the immense find.

Jon finally said the obvious thing, "Say, how could one person possibly carry and use all this stuff? You can only wear one suit of armor at a time. I've never seen a wizard wear armor, though I don't know why."

"Interferes with magical energies, Jon," Darless explained. Jon got the image of an electrical short. "I believe you are on to something. Either this is her hoard ready to be doled out to those that will protect her tower from an assault or these all belonged to someone else. Well, maybe some of it is hers."

"If that is the case," Alison estimated, "at least fifty adventurers could be outfitted in royal fashion, don't you think?"

"At least! We all have quite a collection of stuff," Darless added. "Yes, probably somewhere between fifty and a hundred could be well outfitted. Ah ha! I'll bet all this gear has come from all of her victims over the years! That would explain it. She's downed warriors and wizards at the very least."

"Ah, I do believe you are right," Alison commented. "That sure would explain all this stuff. Golly, we will take months and months just to identify all of this! We'll be weeks just transporting it out of here!"

They walked about the room gaping at all the myriad items, wondering who owned them originally and what had become of them. Suddenly, Alison let out a shriek. Instantly, fearing the worst, everyone rushed to her side. She was holding an ornate cross done in gold with silver inlay. It was the holy symbol of Father Ukko. "What's the matter, my child?" Father Johnas asked, not seeing any real danger about.

Great tears welled in her eyes. She held up the cross and then turned it over. "Look," was all she could say without completely breaking down. There etched in the backside was some lettering. He bent closer to read it, saying out loud, "Basil d'Ambrose." Her tears flowed; hearing those words, she could not suppress her grief any longer. Mandy's eyes clouded over as did Jon's, Darless', and Thea's.

"Come, sit down, my child," the soothing, comforting words of Father Johnas broke into the sniffling silence. Alison fairly collapsed into his arms as he gently helped her sit down. No one spoke; they all had their own thoughts.

At last when her sobbing quieted, Father Johnas spoke again, "Well, look at it this way, my dear, this is the first really solid evidence you have that your father was here or at least captured by this Archmage. You finally have proof. That is something. I would never ever have predicted that you would have found anything after so many years. Well done indeed." His words comforted her and helped bring her back to the current reality.

"I know," she said, "It's just the sudden shock of finding dad's holy symbol. I'll be all right in a minute. The rest of you, see if you recognize anything else in here. It must have belonged to someone else long ago." There, that would give them something to do while she regained her composure. Jon sat beside her and put his arm around her; he kissed away some of her tears. Then, he helped her up to her feet.

Lonnie announced, "Say, I recognize this herald. Isn't this the crest of the great Sir Egmont of Flaxton?" Sir Thomas took a good look at it.

"I do believe you are right. He was a Holy Paladin, who lived some thirty years ago. Met his end in the Abyss War, as I recall," Sir Thomas declared.

Mandy, who had been rather silent, spoke up, "Shouldn't we try to return these to their rightful heirs? I mean, if that suit of armor and shield did belong to this Sir Egmont, wouldn't the right thing be to return it to whoever is still living in his line?"

"Absolutely!" declared both paladins in unison. They laughed at their identical, instant answer.

"Okay then, I can help out by using my mental abilities to view the last owner of each of these things. Maybe that will be of use. Golly, it will take me years to go through all these things item by item," she declared.

"Oh thank you, Ranger Mandy!" Sir Thomas replied enthusiastically. "You know, returning the possessions of the departed can help bring final comfort to grieving relatives, even if it has been so very long."

"Yes, he is quite right," put in Father Johnas. "It would be the most honorable thing to do, and very rewarding to you, spiritually, that is. I'm very pleased you have remembered your teachings, Sir Thomas." He smiled at the paladin.

"Okay, everyone, I think I am back with it," Alison broke in on their conversation. "What say we open the other door?"

Quickly, they reassembled in the hallway and then moved quite distant as before, just in case something went wrong. This time, Darless cast the complex web of trap disentanglement spells. While Alison was a master at trap disarming, having done it so many times in the past, Darless was not. She spent a grueling ten minutes weaving the necessary spells together. At long last, the blue energy glow around the doorway disappeared, and with a grating sound, the door opened.

"Ah, the magic user's laboratory at long last!" pronounced the alu-demon with certainty. "Let me check for traps." She went carefully about the room and found and disarmed five traps before giving the all clear word. The non-wizards found this room rather dull. There were many tables full of scrolls and parchments and opened books. One wall was lined from floor to ceiling with books about the arcane enchantments. Hanging from the ceiling was another of the great lanterns with six arms with six lanterns on each arm. A lever by the door switched on the lighting. When Rufus did the honors, this became the best lit room they had encountered, as fitting long hours of study and reading.

"Well, this room may likely hold the clues I have been seeking," pronounced Alison, "but it will take months to go through all of this to find the scrap of data we seek. Let's leave it for now and see what else is down here."

The others agreed; it would be intensely boring for them to stand around, while the wizards examined all of these materials. Without further ado, they reassembled in the main tunnel and continued their exploration. After another fifty feet, the tunnel ended, opening into a huge room approximately sixty feet across. Six columns helped support the ceiling some twenty feet overhead. Once again, lighting was provided by a pair of the fancy lantern fixtures. Rufus did the honors flipping the lever down fully illuminating the room.

Since someone could be lying in ambush behind the columns, Jon closed his eyes and expanded his awareness seeking minds. He found none. They entered the chamber confident that there would be no surprises.

Just as soon as they entered this room, things began happening. First, Mandy shrieked and held her hands to her ears, dropping her sword on the stone floor.

Myriad voices screamed their torture in her mind. Sensitive to the physic residue, the sheer magnitude, the sheer volume of the pain and suffering that occurred in this room totally overwhelmed her. Images flooded through her mind.

Sir Thomas, on the other hand, felt like his skin suddenly was on fire. He was burning up from within his suit of armor. In vain, he dropped his sword, flailing his arms in a hopeless attempt to cool himself off.

Just behind them, Alison felt the burning of evil. Instantly, she recognized it for what it was. This same sensation had overwhelmed her last year when she had been gated into the Abyss. There, she had been nearly incapacitated by the suddenness of this horrid burning of pure evil. While there and with Jon's aid, she had managed to use her mind to gain some semblance of control over it. Since that time she had grown; now she instinctively began controlling the effect the burning pain of this evil area had over her.

Darless recognized the evil at once; she had grown up in the Abyss. This room held some kind of tight connection to that plane of existence, though she had no idea yet what it was. However, her immediate concern was for the two fighters in front of her. She stepped to their sides place a hand on each and cast her teleport spell, bringing them both back outside of the room, just behind Lonnie in the tunnel. Alison simply stepped back a few paces until the burning of evil subsided.

"What, what was that? My skin was burning!" exclaimed the paladin, very disoriented.

"Pure evil, my love, pure evil," Darless spoke seriously and solemnly. "Are you okay? That burning sensation should have stopped by now; we are safely beyond the portal of that room."

"Yes, nothing seems to be damaged," he said humbly, checking himself over as best he could. "I feel awfully silly, though. A Holy Paladin shirking from the Evil I've sworn to defeat."

She smiled back at him. "Evil can be hard to confront, to face, my dear, but we were taken completely by surprise here, there is no shame in that."

Meanwhile, Jon was at Mandy's side, flowing cool, calm thoughts her way. To sooth her mind, he placed an image of fresh air blowing across a blossoming meadow. She signed and relaxed and finally calmed down. At last she spoke, "Thanks, I needed that. Took me by surprise. Zagroot zounds is that room ever evil!" She paused, "No, Jon, it is not the room that is evil, but rather what has gone on in that room is evil. The torture, the pain and suffering, the torment — absolutely hideous — and so many of them." Her voice trailed off to a whisper.

"Are you all right?" Alison asked her dear friend. "That must have been really rough on you, so unexpected and all."

"Yes, took me by surprise, that's all. I'll block it all out next time. Rats, we've left our swords in there. If someone wanted to attack us, now would be a perfect time — both key fighters disarmed," she joked.

"Not for long," Thea proclaimed, "I'll fetch them."

"Don't go in there!" Sir Thomas protested.

"I'm not, watch," she gaily smiled, eager to show off her talents. She walked as close to the entrance as she dared and then chanted a spell. "Come!" she barked and Mandy's sword slid across the floor right up to Mandy's outstretched hand. Then, the two-handed sword of Sir Thomas slid out of the room and over to the waiting paladin. The apprentice smiled in satisfaction. "I am a wizard, you know." She received a round of thanks and a nod from Alison.

"Perhaps I can help protect us while we are in the room," Father Johnas spoke up. "I assume we intend to fully explore it."

"Any help will be most welcome," Alison formally answered. "First, can you tell us anything about what you saw, Mandy? Jon, can you say for sure that there is no living people or creatures with minds still inside that room? I'd hate to be taken by surprise in there; it could be nasty for us."

Still a bit confused, Mandy began, "Gosh, Alison, I really cannot say for sure. It was all a massive jumble of things, so many of them; their thoughts and emotions and pains all got mingled in my mind. Generally, they all have one thing in common, she was there doing something horrible to them, something which I cannot describe — I — I don't have any words that fit. Whatever it was, each of her victims thought it was about the most horrid thing imaginable, that's for sure," Mandy did her best to answer, but this time, what occurred was so far beyond anything she had ever heard about, she was completely at a loss to describe it. Besides, it was only vague images of the people being tortured to near dead and then surrounded by some massive energy field and finally they disappeared somehow.

Jon interjected, "I'm still not picking up anything, Alison." I'll keep on scanning all the while we are inside there, just in case."

Now it was back into the room. As they passed by Father Johnas, he touched each person on the shoulder, transferring onto each a priestly protection from the evil of the room. Mandy also set up firm mental barriers to block all the residual trauma from the victims. Once she set foot inside, her comments resembled those of Sir Thomas, who said, "Ah, now this is much better. It's working, Johnas," he called out. The priest nodded, he knew it would work.

As soon as the gnome entered, he flicked on the lights; he just could never resist the temptation of a switch beside a door entrance. Now the massive overhead lantern complex fully illuminated the room. As they entered, some equipment lay neatly up against the wall just to their left. This they examined first, in part to make sure Rufus did not tamper with something deadly while they were elsewhere. The three devices were all torture machines, a rack, an iron maiden, and a barrel with holes for one's head and feet and hands to protrude. These, everyone decided needed no further examination. The traces of dried blood disabused even the curious gnome from touching them. The priest made a note to see to it that these were destroyed before they left.

They followed the walls around the left side of the room and against the opposite wall. Here they paused. Before them was an ornate pentagram fused into the granite bedrock floor. "This is a magical gate, probably to the Abyss," declared Darless. "Whatever you do, do not, I repeat, *do not* stand inside the ten-foot pentagram. That central gem in the floor is the activator. It is highly likely that all one needs to do to activate this permanent gate is to touch the gem. It is purely mechanical in nature. Press the gem, you arrive somewhere in the Abyss. Just where, we really do not want to find out. My guess is that it is likely to lead somewhere close to the palace of Lord Jarred, if not inside it somewhere. Whatever happens in here, stay away from this gate!"

Alison thought she was being a bit melodramatic about it, but then she did not relish the idea of having to visit the Abyss again to rescue Rufus. As they continued their walk around the room, a desk and chair came into view, having been hidden partially by the tall columns of granite supporting the ceiling. The desktop was bare, but it had several drawers, one was locked and a greenish glow outlined its front edge, trapped for sure. This had to be checked out fully.

While the others backed off a safe distance, Alison and Darless cast their magical examination spells and then defused both the guard spell and the poison needle spring trap. Alison used another spell to force the lock and all the drawers slid open as far as they could go. "Well, let's see what we have here," she declared, pulling out a small ledger book. The protected drawer contained nothing else but this six inch square, small volume.

While she leafed through the book, Darless examined the other drawers. Six high quality pens and eight bottles of a special kind of ink were in the top drawer. The middle one contained a set of keys to lock the iron maiden and a set of hand and foot shackles. "Not much here," Darless commented.

"Now why would she keep an empty ledger locked away under such powerful enchantments?" Alison interrupted her. "Come look at this, you too Thea. See, all the pages are completely blank. This makes very little sense." She flipped through several pages so the others could see.

"Let me see it close up," Darless requested. She examined it in minute detail, even sniffing it.

"Why on earth are you sniffing it?" asked Thea in complete disbelief that she was witnessing a powerful mage sniffing a ledger book. Alison also wondered why; so she was glad that her apprentice had asked the question instead of herself, just in case the answer turned out to be a silly one.

Darless frowned and sniffed several pages near the end of the book. A smile slowly formed, "Ah ha. Just as I thought: invisible ink. She's used invisible ink to write the entries. Here, you two. Take a sniff of the first page and then take a sniff of the last page. Smell any differences?" The two mages took turns sniffing.

"It might help if I knew what I was trying to smell," declared Thea, still baffled.

"Okay, close your eyes and take a whiff when I tell you to," Darless ordered. Both mages shut their eyes. Darless opened the ledger to a page near the front and put it by their noses and then repeated the process with one near the end.

After several times, Alison commented, "I think there is a different smell, very faint, between these pages."

"Oh now I smell it!" Thea's excitement grew, "Boy that sure is a faint difference. Why do they smell different?"

"Think, Thea," Darless said didactically, "What would make two identical pages of a book smell differently?"

"Oh I see, one has ink on it and the other does not! Now that is pretty amazing! How did you know that?" she asked, but then quickly added, "I'm still an apprentice that's for sure."

"You have more senses than just sight, learn to use them," Darless commented. "Now the real question is just how do we make the writing visible? That is the real question before us. Alison, I think that this book might be very important. We should see what it contains before we do much else. I have a hunch about this. Mages of the Abyss tend to be a bit methodical, when it comes to vital records of their personal deeds; no one else will bother."

"I agree," Alison concurred. "Okay the rest of you, relax, but keep alert for a while. We think we need to try to get this invisible writing visible."

"Why don't some of the rest of us explore the rest of the room?" Father Johnas asked. "My protective spell will not protect us indefinitely. Perhaps Rufus can search for further hidden doors. It'll speed things up. Jon can warn us if anyone suddenly appears, right Jon?"

"Sure thing," he replied. "I'll just sit here and observe." He had sat down on the hard floor, resting his back against one of the four massive pillars.

Alison thought a moment. There really did not seem to be anything at all in this room, save the ledger. "Okay, why not. Have at it. Keep a sharp eye out for traps or trouble." Gladly, the three fighters, accompanied by Rufus, began walking about the remainder of the room that they had not yet surveyed. Meanwhile the three mages put their heads together to find a way to make the writing visible.

Darless first experimented with the ink. Using a scratch piece of parchment she fetched from within her portable hole, she drew several lines over the page using the fancy pens and ink they had found. Strong black lines formed as she drew. However, as the ink dried, it totally disappeared. "Ah ha," she exclaimed, "I'm right; this *is* invisible ink." She tore the parchment into thirds, giving each of them a sample on which to experiment. The three began their attempts to make it visible once more. Time passed slowly.

Jon grew bored. Sitting here doing nothing but feeling the vast expanse of the room did not hold his interest. He began daydreaming about his new puppy and quickly pulled himself back into the present. *No good, not paying attention; she'll have my head if we get surprised again. Concentrate. Okay, expand outward again. Ah, there's Mandy.* One by one he located each of the other's minds. Still no other minds were present. Then, he had a horrible thought. *What if there were other secret tunnels and chambers somewhere around here? I know, I'll just expand my space in all directions. See if I feel any presences.* Jon began enlarging the space of which he was aware. All was black of course. He was looking for spiritual beings and their minds with their mental pictures. *I wonder if I have any limits on just how far away I can be aware of? I remember that fabulous bath house we went to last year. I wonder if I can sense that place.* His awareness greatly expanded by hundreds of linear miles. He found himself actually viewing the bath house. It was rather crowed at the moment. His face turned beet red, so many naked women. He still had really not gotten used to these public bath houses. Quickly, he retreated back to this underground chamber, glanced around to make sure that

Alison had not seen him become so embarrassed. She was still busy with the invisible ink, so he went back to his task of searching for minds.

Still, he was bored. *I wonder how far down I can go? I should not get into trouble going in that direction. Maybe I can sense the hot, molten core of this planet.* He began expanding his awareness downward. Suddenly he encountered something. Then more somethings. Lots of somethings. Jon had never before sensed anything like this. They were minds, he assumed, but something was very wrong with them. It was like the minds were frozen on a totally black image. *This is really weird! What have I found? Some kind of underground race of things? Bizarre. They have no thoughts at all. Weird indeed.* He was brought out of his musings by the excited voice of Alison crying, "Eureka! It works!" Jon decreased his awareness and opened his eyes, got up slowly, and went to see what worked.

He saw the three mages closely examining one piece of the torn parchment of Darless' experiment. Even from a few feet away, he could see the broad black ink line she had drawn on the page. "All right, here goes. Page one here we come. She chanted a spell and writing appeared filling the page. Jon could not read it, for him, it was a foreign language. Alison frowned. "I don't recognize the tongue. How about you, Darless?"

"Ah, yes, it is Abyss slang. Use your read spell and it will translate," suggested the alu-demon.

It was a list on names going down the left side of the page. The next column showed one of two things: a monetary amount or a large 'X'. Most of the monetary columns had a third column that also contained a monetary figure. Most of the two monetary entries agreed, but a couple showed a slightly larger value in the right most column, while a few showed a lesser amount. Fully twenty names were on the first page. Alison flipped to the next page, one entry caught her eye, that of Sir

Egmont of Flaxton. An 'X' was beside that name. She flipped more pages and then let out a shriek, nearly dropping the book. Jon heard the others running over to them as fast as they could go.

Alison stared at the page, tears swelled uncontrollably. Darless read it out loud for the benefit of the others. "Basil d'Ambrose, Anna d'Ambrose. Both have 'X'es after their names, just like Sir Egmont of Flaxton has. If there were ever any doubts that Archmage Sarah got her hands on them, this proves she did." Jon put his arm around Alison for moral support. Her hand found his and she clenched it.

Finally she muttered, "Well, at least I finally know. They are both dead, probably tortured in some hideous way by Sarah. It's just the reality of it — seeing their names here. It's so hard," her voice trailed off. The room was totally silent, each absorbed in their own thoughts for a time.

Sir Thomas at last broke the stillness, "This room appears to be a dead end. We have searched very thoroughly, but there seem to be nothing hidden at all. Perhaps you could use your spells in here just to make double sure that we have not missed anything. Then, we had best leave the room. I think the protective spell is starting to wear off. I'm beginning to get uncomfortably warm, if you know what I mean."

"I'll do it, Alison, you head for the door," offered Darless. She knew that Alison desperately needed some time for herself. The alu-demon spent another two minutes using her magical detection spells, but likewise found nothing. "You men did well, I concur. No secret doors in here. It looks like no minds. No surprises. I like that part. I guess we have eliminated all of them. The lich was the last denizen of the tower complex."

"Well, that is not entirely true," Jon added hesitatingly. "Say, are there strange people or creatures that live deep underground in the solid rock?" She frowned and stared at him.

"Not that I am aware of," she replied. "Rufus?"

"Oh well there are all sorts of beings that live underground in tunnels and caves and such. Some are the dark elves, some are dwarves, and there are some other creatures as well. But nobody can live inside the rock itself. I suppose you meant to say living in tunnels, right?" the gnome insisted.

"Er, no, I mean *in* the rock. Very strange," Jon mused.

Alison's interest was pricked. "Why do you ask, Jon? Have you sensed something?"

"Well, yes, but I don't know what I sensed. There is a bunch of somethings far down there," he pointed to the floor. "Way, way down there, in the rock itself, I think. Like minds, but not. It's the weirdest thing. It's like every one of them is frozen into a picture, a totally black, solid picture. No thoughts, no nothing, just frozen. Weird. You say there cannot be anyone living inside the rock, but something sure is there."

Alison's curiosity rose. This was something new, something she knew nothing about. "Just how many are down there? Did you count them?"

"Er, no, lots of them though. Shall I count them before we go?" he asked.

"Wouldn't hurt, Jon, this is very perplexing. There shouldn't be such a thing. I'd like to know more, if you don't mind."

"Please Jon," Darless added. "This is totally baffling. I, too, want to know more. Can I sense through you while you count them?"

"Sure thing, but the rest of you had better get out of the room before the spell is gone. We'll be all right in here, I can handle the evil," he added.

While the others exited to the safety of the tunnel, Jon focused his attention once more on the strange things deep beneath the floor of the chamber. He sensed Darless in the back of his mind, seeing what he perceived. This was about as intimate as two beings could get. *Ah, there is one,* he thought. She looked too. Jon began his count. He could also see Darless trying to communicate with the minds, but he sensed that she sensed just what he had before: a complete solidity of mind. *That's it, twenty-five. Let's get back to the others.* He felt Darless slide out of his mind, but only after giving him a mental thank-you kiss. He blushed, but managed to give her one back. She beamed; Jon had finally broken through his own barriers.

"We counted twenty-five," Jon reported. Darless concurred and verified all his previous statements regarding this phenomenon. "Now what do we do?"

Alison, walking ahead of them, turned to face her friends. "Well, we must examine very thoroughly the mage's room we found. That is going to take us quite some time. It's getting late, so why don't some of you head back and fix dinner. I think that we have slain all the evil in this tower. We are now probably safe. Besides, you all will be bored to death while we search the mage's study."

"I've a better idea," suggested Darless, "why don't we all take a breather, a much deserved one, and get dinner. We can come back this evening and take our time going through her room. It may take us days to unravel the many mysteries surrounding this hermit Archmage." Alison was secretly thankful for the alu-demon's suggestion. In truth, after finding the names of her parents in the ledger, she felt emotionally drained and really needed time for herself. They all headed outside into the fresh air once more. It was still light and Darless and Mandy prepared dinner, while the others relaxed, sharpened their swords and handled the horses.

Alison sat away from the others on a rock. She still had the ledger. Idly she opened it and recast the read spell. The names appeared once more. *At least she has legible handwriting, almost elegant,* she mused. *This ledger must be very important to her. I wonder what all these monetary figures mean.* She thought a while, trying to picture herself as an evil archmage. Suddenly, she had a flash of insight. "Hey you guys, I'll bet that these figures are ransom amounts. The right column gives what she received for the person. That would account for the huge treasury we found. Ransom money. Well, we shall just have to see that great good comes from it. That would be the greatest irony of it all!" She received many kudos for that observation. It did cheer her up a bit.

"The 'X'es she probably tortured and killed," she added.

"How many did she kill?" asked Thea mostly from curiosity, though actually she had a twinge of intuition in back of her question.

Alison counted them page by page, "twenty-three, twenty-four, twenty-five. Yes, looks like twenty-five in total." Suddenly, everyone was completely silent. "Oh my god!" Alison uttered. She had the same count as Jon had from the weird, frozen minds.

"You don't suppose," Thea began following her intuition, but she never got to finish her thought. Everyone had the same thought at the same instant. "She has trapped them somehow!"

Alison was so excited that she started jumping up and down, shaking Thea's hand. "You did it! You did it!" Thea was slightly embarrassed by this sudden complementary attention. "You realize that all these people might still be alive somehow? Maybe we can actually rescue them!" Tears of joy, of hope, flooded down her cheeks. Her parents might not be dead after all! She was so excited, so charged up, that she could barely eat. She just had to get back down into the Archmage's study and dig through everything. She had to find out just what Sarah had done to these twenty-five people.

Just as soon as the mages finished eating, they rushed back into the tower, leaving Jon and the men to clean up the dishes and make camp. However, before they headed into the tower, Darless cast the nightly magical mansion. "You can rest up, take a bath, whatever. We'll be back later. I'll send Jon a signal if we encounter anything bad." Sir Thomas felt better after that, because he was more than a little worried that another spectral ghost of which they had not yet found might attack his bride to be. However, the horses needed to be walked and tended. He, Lonnie and Mandy handled that, while Jon cleaned up the mess. Rufus tinkered with the guardian machine.

Chapter 16 The Chamber of Horrors

The three mages quickly retraced their steps back to the Archmage's magic study room. As they entered, Alison cautioned them, "Thea, you are to look for correspondence, letters, diaries — anything that might prove our theories. Darless and I will look for her spell books. We must be very, very careful of those. She was thoroughly evil. If we find them, do not physically touch them with your hands. It could be fatal." They set to work. It was a challenging task because the room contained hundreds of books, scrolls, parchments and such. Days would be required to sort it all out.

While there was a fantastic amount of things in this room of intense interest to the mages, they willed themselves to stay on track. A half hour of searching later, they had found the spell books, all fifteen of them, bound in green dragon hide and guarded by wards from being opened. Another half hour was used in cancelling all such protections. Still, Alison and Darless used spells to open the books and turn the pages.

Meantime, Thea began her search. Buried under a pile of papers, she found a little red book. She opened it. "Hey, looks like she kept a diary. I found one book. I'm going to try to see what all it says — gives me a chance to practice." For once, Alison did not warn her to be careful; Thea noted its absence. *She trusts me!* thought Thea and she straightened up and began her study of the volume. A while later Thea called out, "Hey listen to this! Last night the r came for Fred Rustlebeam. Was short 25,000. H was wrong once again. His estimates are running about 90% correct. I'll bet that 'r' stands for ransom! We are on to something, if this Fred fellow is on one of the pages in that book." Alison quickly flipped through the pages. Sure enough, there was an entry and the two monetary columns differed by 25,000. Thea felt very pleased indeed.

"Terrific, Thea, well done indeed!" praised Alison. She resumed her study of the eighth spell book. A short while later, she gasped and put her hand over her mouth. "Dar! Dar, is this what I think it is?" Her friend left the book she was examining and looked at what Alison had found.

"Oh my god! This has to be it! My god, Alison, they may be alive! Your parents may be alive!" she said. Thea let out a whoopee yell and rushed over to have a look. Unfortunately, she could not comprehend what they were reading. "Bit over your level, Thea, I'm afraid," Darless commented. "It is the directions to imprison someone. Only an archmage can learn to cast this one; it is a very, very complex spell, Thea. Now all we have to do is figure out how it works and then figure out how to undo it. Tall order, but then," her voice suddenly trailed off as she realized fully the implications of her being able to read and understand the magical writing. The way that the spells were written into a spell book, only a mage of comparable or higher power can read and decipher any given spell. Darless had just had not the slightest trouble reading this imprisonment spell. That could only mean one thing. She, Darless Thornapple, was really now an archmage herself — beyond the slightest doubt.

Alison had a twinkle in her eye. She reached for Darless's hand and shook it. "Congratulations, Archmage Darless. I thought you had reached this level, but this proves it beyond any doubt. We sure do make a power house team now!" Thea had to shake her hand too.

"Okay, now let's get back to this spell," Darless insisted. "Thea, keep looking for any information to confirm our theory that she has imprisoned these people. We are going to see if we can learn how this spell works and then see about undoing it."

"But you are not going to have to actually imprison someone are you?" asked Thea just a bit concerned and wondering if she should volunteer to be a guinea pig for them.

"No, we need to know totally how to do it so that we can devise its opposite," explained Alison. Thea was greatly relieved and went back to her work.

The hours dragged by and at long last the adrenaline high evaporated, leaving three exhausted wizards. Thea had stopped reading and had gone in search of more diaries and found three more. At last, Alison said, "Okay. I'm falling asleep. I think we should call it a night. There is always tomorrow." They turned out the lights and headed back to the outside world and the mansion.

Of course, just as soon as they entered, the others insisted on knowing all that they had found, but first, Alison introduced Archmage Darless officially to everyone. She received many "well dones!" Best of all, she got a warm hug and affectionate kiss from Sir Thomas.

With the formalities out of the way, Alison had Thea read that passage she had found, confirming the ransom theory. Finally, she said, "Most important of all, we think we have found out what she did with the twenty-five others. We believe that she has used an imprisonment spell upon them, imprisoning them in the stone beneath that room. I think that Jon has detected their location. If, and this is a big if," but there was such hope in her eyes, "if the spell is reversible, which we believe it is, we ought to be able to free them all." There, she actually said it.

"You mean," Mandy fumbled for words, "you mean that they are still alive? Your parents? Buried alive in the stone? Rescue-able? Zounds! That is fantastic! Wow!"

"Oh dear me," exclaimed Father Johnas. All eyes turned to the priest. Seeing everyone staring expectantly at him, he explained, "Some days ago, Father Ukko told me that I was to stay with you and see this thing through to the very end. Until this moment, I just could not imagine why? You all are more than able enough to take care of yourselves. You really do not need an old High Priest slowing you down. Now I fully understand. All praise to Father Ukko!"

"Hum, I don't quite understand," Jon interrupted. "How does this imprisonment thing fit in?" No sooner had he asked that question than he knew the answer. Before the priest could reply, Jon blurted out, "Their mental state! My god, what state will they be in after all this time?"

"Precisely my son, precisely. That's why you desperately need a High Priest. If we are very lucky, perhaps they will only be insane," he declared solemnly. "Think of the shock of suddenly appearing a hundred years into the future." That was a very sobering thought.

"Are you suggesting that we should not try to free them all?" asked Alison slightly confused by the priest's hints.

"Oh no, no. Free them we must, but slowly and with care. I can, with Father Ukko's aid, handle most any physical injuries, but only a couple a day. We may need a week to free them all. No, it is the distinct possibility of insanity about which I am terribly concerned."

"Wait a minute," Thea interjected, a new thought had just occurred to her. "She was an evil mage. What if some of those she imprisoned are actually evil people. Should we free them as well? Might not we be releasing some unholy terror on the world?"

"I say we free them all," Jon replied before anyone else could. "No being, good or evil, deserves that kind of treatment. Besides, it is possible for people to change their ways."

"I believe that I am starting to see some of what Father Ukko sees in you Saint Jon Brown, the

Redeemer," complimented Father Johnas. "You have spoken like a true high priest."

"Er, I'm not a priest," Jon protested. "It's only common sense."

"What's common sense to you may well elude many, many others," cautioned the High Priest. "But enough of this, we had all better get some sleep. I believe we have our labors cut out for us tomorrow. Bless you all!"

Alison tossed and turned; she was so excited about her parents that she could neither relax nor get to sleep. Thus, Jon gave her a long back rub, which ended when she finally fell asleep. She awoke refreshed and ready to tackle the complex spell to undo the imprisonment of these people.

All the next day, the two archmages poured over Sarah's spell book, examining every detail of her extremely complex imprisonment spell. By midday, both were convinced that they could cast that terrible spell. However, the undoing of one so imprisoned was another matter and they had no guide, no mentor to query some of the finer points of the reverse spell. "We really have only two choices as I see it," declared Alison irritably, "either we intentionally imprison someone and then free them or we just attempt to do it for real on one of the imprisoned people and hope we get it right."

"I really don't like the latter choice," mused Darless, "what if we get something wrong? We could never live with ourselves, if we free you parents only to accidentally kill them in the process. Say, I have another idea, let's try it out on one of those rats. I still keep seeing a few around the village. We can imprison it and then free it. If it works, we know that we are ready to try it on those that are imprisoned."

Alison was a bit hesitant at first, "Yes, you are probably right. I hate mistreating even a rat, although I don't like them, but we absolutely must practice this before we actually do it. I totally agree with you on that point. Okay, a rat it is. I wish we could get its agreement to participate, but how do you communicate with a rat? I surely don't know, nor am I really all that interested in knowing, for that matter."

"Hum, you know, I think I came across just the spell we need, Alison. It was in one of the other spell books I looked through yesterday. Let me see, where did I put it?" and she rummaged through several of the green dragon hide covered books. "Ah here it is, this spell allows a mage to communicate with animals. It is not a difficult spell, give me a few minutes to learn this one. Then, let's go find us a rat." A half hour later, the two mages were back inside the magic study room — volunteering rat in tow. Darless promised the rat all it could eat for letting them experiment on it. The rat thought this was a good deal because it was exceedingly hungry.

At dinner time, both mages walked confidently out of the tower to the campsite where the others were about ready to eat. "We are ready," announced Alison, "we have both been able to imprison a rat and then free it without any glitches. Tomorrow we do it for real on those that are imprisoned." They were congratulated and handed plates of steaming stew. Over the meal, Mandy brought them up to date on what the others had done that day.

The others, save Thea, had spent the day doing an exhaustive search for any overlooked secret chambers and had found none. Now everyone was confident that the entire tower complex was known to them. Additionally, the massive treasury had been sorted into manageable piles and was now awaiting some means of transport.

Thea was keenly interested in reading the diary of the Archmage. First she searched for as many of the volumes as she could find. Next, she arranged them into chronological order, all ten of them. That took a bit of reading to sort out, because the Archmage used several different calendar years with which Thea was unfamiliar and still was. She still was not totally sure of the exact order of five of the volumes. "She details many of her experiences in the Abyss as Lord Jarred's consort — sometimes she gets rather sordid. Sometimes, it's, well, let's say it gets pretty perverted. But I think that we may glean some very revealing information on Lord Jarred and his realm, though it may well be a bit out of date. For sure, she has been ransoming people for a very long time. I did find out a bit more about it. Seems she is always working with this person called 'H' and no one else. H gathers all the intelligence, so the way I figure it, H must be some kind of thief or spy who certainly must travel around a lot."

"Could be an assassin," interjected Darless, "we know that there is a major, powerful group of them not too far from here, just over the mountains and south. H could be an assassin."

"Hum, had not thought of that. It makes even more sense," Thea pronounced. "As I was saying, H seems to always get a portion of the ransom, ten percent of the take. She kept very good records of the money. I had thought that maybe we could figure out who these people were and go and return their money, but the records are not sufficiently accurate to do that. Anyhow, just before dinner time, I finally found a section that deals with your parents. It is rather cryptic, but here's the gist of it." Alison sat bolt upright, all ears; her apprentice had just scored a major success. "It seems Lord Jarred for years had greatly desired to possess that Holy Scepter, but could not muster the forces to openly steal it from Metrarch. However, Sarah documents that he had many spies within Metrarch's royal court. When Basil and his party snuck into his palace to steal it, they were seen by one of Jarred's spies. Lord Jarred saw this as his golden opportunity to get the scepter for himself. Unfortunately, the other spies he sent to follow Basil were caught and slain by members of Basil's party, who thought they were Metrarch's followers coming after them. Jarred could not risk being directly involved in stealing the scepter from Basil for political reasons, so he hired Sarah to get it back for him and paid a huge sum to her in advance. Well, we know the rest of the story," Thea omitted the additional grim details.

Alison inquired, "Didn't she write anything about capturing mom and dad? Surely she must have mentioned them?" She was pressing the issue. Thea knew that sooner or later, Alison would also go read the diary. She said, "Well, yes, it was pretty nasty. She described how she had tortured him, broken his arms and legs, cut him open, threatened your mom. Basil refused to tell her anything about the scepter. She said she imprisoned him, when he was in massive pain and close to death so he could savor the pain for all eternity. She was pretty evil if you ask me. How could anyone actually do that?" Alison was very near tears once more, but managed to thank Thea properly.

Everyone went to bed very early that night. Tomorrow was the big day — the day of freedom for these long imprisoned souls. Father Johnas prayed for a long time before retiring that night. Mandy and the two paladins, likewise.

The fateful morning arrived. Alison was very on edge, barely eating any breakfast. She had a case of nerves that steadily grew. Darless insisted she eat more and Alison tried her best to force more down.

By seven o'clock, the party, once more under the priestly protection spell, arrived in the bottom-most chamber, the chamber of unspeakable horrors. Alison had the ledger open. "Okay, the first question is whom do we free first?"

"Shouldn't we rescue your parents first?" Jon quickly answered her. The others concurred and nodded agreement.

"I cannot decide whom to do first, mom or dad? If I get dad, I'm sure he would say that I should have rescued mom first. But if I get mom first, she'll say I should have done dad first. I thought, okay, silly, you get one, while Darless gets the other. We get them both at the same time, but if they are in bad shape, Father Johnas can only handle one at a time. So what do we do?"

"My child, you are right, I can only take care of one person at a time," Father Johnas agreed with her, "but Jon can use his gift from Father Ukko if needed. However, have you given any thought to their physical and mental states when they are suddenly freed? I have. Thea has suggested that your father, in particular, may be near death's door physically. I'm sure I can heal his body; Ukko has never failed my healing prayers. I've thought all day yesterday about their mental states and prayed to Father Ukko last night for guidance. I'm confident that I can cure any temporary disorientation that has arisen from their imprisonment. I can do so three times each day. However, what about their spiritual well-being? Has any of us considered that detail?" Total silence.

He went on, "Imagine how you would react suddenly being released from a catatonic imprisonment and waking up hundreds of years in the future. All your possessions lost to time. All your family and friends, long dead. You'd find yourself a stranger in your own land. How would you react? Short term and long term, eh? I find their prospects are pretty grim. Perhaps freedom has a terrible price for these folks to pay. If nothing else, the shock of discovering a hundred years has passed may kill them on the spot."

"Why don't we just use our wishes from the Great Spirit?" Thea burst out. "If it is going to be so bad, why not use a wish? Let the Gods make it all better. I'll let you use mine, Alison."

She was sorely tempted. Yes, they probably could use all of their fabulous wishes granted by the Great Spirit, she calculated. She thought better of it. "Thank you Thea. Your generosity is tremendous. However, the way I see it is this. A human misusing magic has caused this condition, and, by golly, another human using magic ought to be able to undo it without divine intervention. Those wishes are very, very precious, immensely valuable. I want to save them for a time when only the intervention of a god can save the day — like when the Goddess Morrigan interfered and killed me instead of Jon. When things are beyond our control, that's the time to use them. Besides, both Darless and I can now cast our own wish spells, as long as we are prepared to pay the steep price of said casting; our bodies age physically a year every time we cast a wish spell. Surely, we can undo what Archmage Sarah has done without divine intervention. At least I hope we can."

"I'll help all I can," Jon declared. "We fared pretty well with those poor people that the Cult of the Black Scorpion experimented on and turned into giant half-scorpions. They seem to be recovering from their ordeals, thus far any way. Perhaps, their mental images of their capture and long imprisonment will be erasable with my assist methodology. I'll give it my all."

"So will I," Thea added.

"I think the answer to your question, Alison," Darless commented, "is to free both your parents at the same time. That way, they can see each other. There must have been a fantastically strong bond between them for them to have survived their ordeal. Seeing each other alive ought relieve their most immediate fears and worries. Think about it for a moment, the last thing they ever saw was each other being imprisoned. That horror has to have been on their minds all these years. They will not even recognize you. Even saying you are their grown up daughter might be enough of a shock to send them over the edge in their likely delicate state. I council you not to even mention who you are until we get them stabilized and ready for it."

Father Johnas suggested, "Free them both at the same time, I will assist your father first, because we already know that he is in dire need of immediate healing. Perhaps Jon can see to your mother, if she needs any emergency healing,"

"Thank you one and all!" gushed Alison. "Okay Darless, let's do it. I'll take mom and you take dad." The two mages took their positions just outside the burial area of the floor of the chamber. Jon stood by Alison and Father Johnas, by Darless. Sir Thomas and Mandy stood off either side of the four. Lonnie and Thea along with Rufus stood behind them, as usual, protecting the rear. The two mages began the lengthy complex chants. Jon had never heard a magical incantation take as long as this one did. Nearly two full minutes elapsed before they climaxed their spells by pronouncing the full name of the victim followed by the word 'free.'

However, just as the spells began to activate, Thea cried out in alarm, "It's another trap. There is another trap about to go off!" Thea had been practicing what Alison had taught her, always check for traps. Sure enough, Archmage Sarah had booby trapped any attempt to free her imprisoned souls. From the floor in front of the mages arose two giant creatures made of iron. Each stood nearly twelve feet tall; this is why the room's ceiling was so high. Sarah had thought of every detail. She knew that any mage attempting to free her prisoners would be totally helpless for nearly five minutes afterwards, because the mages would have to concentrate on bringing the trapped victims to the surface. Her iron monsters would slay the mages long before they successfully freed anyone.

These iron golems were magically created at a very great cost to Archmage Sarah. Made completely of a malleable iron, they stood twelve feet tall. A warrior's battle helmet covered each head, but was mostly for show. They had bulging muscles and carried an enormous crude iron sword, which they really did not need to use. The force of their fists could potentially inflict more damage than one of Mandy's sword attacks. Each weighed nearly a thousand pounds. Further, against these golems, magical spells had virtually no effect; they could only be slain by physical damage, and these could take a great deal of that before they would expire. Indeed, Sarah had planned well.

Instantly, Sir Thomas and Mandy rushed to get themselves positioned between the two mages and the two creatures. Lonnie circled wide around them, intending to engage one from its rear. "Oh my!" exclaimed Rufus. "I know what those are. Those are iron golems. They are mindless destroyers. Oh my, oh dear. We'd best get some spells flying, Thea." However, Thea had already loosened a volley of magical missiles. In dismay, she watched the missiles bounce harmlessly off of the iron giants. "Oh yes, I forgot. They are immune to magical spells. A lightning bolt might slow them down a bit, but I'm afraid that is all the magic that will bother them. Oh dear, oh dear. I think we are in trouble. Yes, I'm afraid I do." The giants had now completely surfaced, gotten their bearings and spied the magic users. Each opened their mouths and out came a cloud of poisonous gas heading straight for the mages. "Oh dear, I forgot, they also shoot out poison gas. Hold your breath everyone!" He pinched his nose with one hand and pinched his lips shut with the other.

The two fighters, spying the yellow, expanding gas cloud, dodged around it and delivered two powerful blows, injuring the golems slightly. The mages held their breaths, but maintained their concentration of their spells. Jon immediately tried to attack the iron golem's minds, but to his dismay, he found no minds. These were preprogrammed destroyers, nothing more, mindless robots. The situation looked very grim indeed.

Rufus knew he had to do something for the mages, since they gave no indication of cancelling their spells. He did the only logical thing he could think of on such short notice. His spell was a zephyr wind, a gushing spring breeze blew from his mouth, blowing the gas away backwards. The two clouds lost much of their potency by the dispersing winds of Rufus. Unfortunately, Lonnie, now moving in behind then, got a huge whiff of the gas and began choking. It burned his lungs, but much of the deadly potency was diluted, fortunately for him.

Now the golems swung at the two intervening fighters. Their goal was solely the elimination of the two mages. Both golems connected with the two fighters giving them both severely crushing blows that sent both sprawling across the floor. "Zagroot zounds!" echoed through the chamber, followed by "Not this again!" Sir Thomas said nothing audible.

Jon reasoned that the mages could perhaps withstand only one of those massive blows. He had to do something. But what? They had no minds to attack. He had no real weapon that could harm them. In a minute, one would be close enough to smash Alison! He did the only thing he could think of, which was to move them away from here. Into Lonnie's mind he placed the thought: *Hold it back from hitting Darless.* He stepped himself just behind the golem that was closing on Alison and touching its back leg, he stepped them both outside of the village. Instantly he let go of the golem and stepped back to where he had been. He arrived in time to see that Lonnie had managed to get himself between Darless and the remaining golem. He saw the young paladin strike another blow to the golem before the golem swung its huge sword smashing into Lonnie, hurting him and, more importantly, sending him flying out of the way. Jon ran to the back of the golem, touched it and stepped them both outside to where he had left the other golem. Again, he let go and stepped back into the chamber and collapsed onto the floor. Those golems weight half a ton, he was completely exhausted from his frantic efforts at moving them.

"What just happened? Where'd they go?" asked Father Johnas, shocked by their sudden disappearance. He had just gotten his heavy mace out and was about to join the fray.

"Oh, Jon just told me he moved them outside the village gates," said a very surprised Lonnie getting to his feet, nursing his sore side that had taken the brunt of the golem's slam. Mandy and Sir Thomas staggered to their feet and moved to Lonnie's side.

"Outside you say? Okay, come on, Sir Thomas, Lonnie, we got us some monsters to slay. Thea, look after Jon will you?" Without waiting for an acknowledgment, Mandy ran out of the room. Hastily Lonnie followed after her. The clanking of Sir Thomas's metal clad feet echoed more slowly after him.

"Oh my, look Thea, I think something is happening. I think it's working," exclaimed Rufus. Indeed, two heads had appeared sticking out of the floor. As they watched, the catatonic bodies of Alison's parents slowly rose up fully out of the stone floor. At last, the spell was complete, at which point the bodies instantly collapsed onto the floor. The mages finally moved, their spells complete. Father Johnas rushed to the side of Basil. Thea's description of his treatment at the hands of Sarah was an understatement. He was nearly dead. Besides the four broken appendages, he was bleeding profusely from numerous slashes inflicted about his chest and face. Anna, on the other hand, had only suffered a bashed up face; she did not look in too bad a physical shape.

Sizing up the situation, Darless acted. *Alison, connect to me, yes like this. Now we flow energy to Jon. Jon get up, get back outside. Heal up the fighters with your walking stick.* Jon stirred, new found energy flowing within him. Then, he recognized the boost's source. He smiled and stood up and said out loud, "Thanks, they were awfully heavy," and he was gone. Jon arrived back outside ahead of the charging fighters. He commanded his walking stick to appear, and in the next instant, his trusty stick appeared in his hand. "Thanks!" he said aloud to it.

He spied the two golems slowly moving back toward the tower. "Single minded creatures!" he muttered to himself. The only positive thing about these creatures was their very slow speed. Due in part to their massive weight, they moved about half the speed of a person. It would be some time before they could get back down to the Chamber of Horrors and continue their attack on the two mages. Before long, Mandy came charging out of the tower toward him.

"Ah you are back," she said and added, "where are they — ah there they are. Nasty creatures. Good thinking getting them out here away from the mages. Brilliant, I'd say."

Lonnie now caught up to Mandy, who was standing beside Jon surveying the situation. "Yes, it was all I could think of doing. I'm under orders to heal you all when you need it, so let me know."

"Okay. Lonnie, let's observe them a minute until Sir Thomas gets here. Maybe we can spy something to our advantage."

"Well, they sure are single-minded," Jon spoke up. "They seem to ignore everything except the two mages."

"Hum, maybe we can use that to our advantage," Lonnie said. "Mandy, what if we circle around them and come at them from behind. We can time our blows to cause maximum damage. Undoubtedly, they will only take a swing at us and continue on their mindless task and not stop to fight us. What do you think?"

"I think you have hit the nail on the head, as my blacksmith teases me sometimes. Let's give it a try. I'll go right, you circle around to the left. Jon, you come around to the rear to help us, if we get hit too badly." She was off using the maximum speed her magical boots generated. She literally came upon the back of hers twice as fast as the fleet-footed Lonnie. Again, she gave it a mighty slice with her powerful bastard sword. She swore it bellowed in pain just before it swung back at her; once again the force of its blow sending her flying backwards. These were strong creatures. "Okay, Jon, heal me," she wheezed from several cracked ribs. "I think we are making progress on this one," she added enthusiastically. Jon stepped to her side and using his walking stick, fully healed her wounds, particularly the cracked ribs. Her gasping returned to a normal breathing.

Lonnie did the same to the back of his golem, injuring it further before it tossed him off like a fly. Jon went to his aid immediately healing him. Now Sir Thomas arrived. Mandy yelled out their plan to him.

"But I don't like attacking from behind," he protested. "It's not honorable."

"They are not alive!" she called back, disgust in her voice. She did not have time to waste arguing honor with the paladin. She watched as Sir Thomas took his position before one of the golems. It ignored him. In fact, it would have just marched right over him had he not taken a mighty swing, damaging it further. In reaction, the golem swung his huge sword striking the paladin squarely in the chest. The sheer force of the blow sent him sprawling once again. A huge dent in the front of his armor made breathing difficult. The golem continued it slow march back toward the tower.

Jon dashed to the paladin's side and used his walking stick to heal the fighter. Because of the smashed chest plate, Sir Thomas had Jon loosen some of the straps. "Okay, that's good enough. Thanks," he said, and he headed back into the fray, only now he had to catch up. His speed was just barely greater than the golem, so whether he liked it or not, he was forced to attack from the rear.

"Jon, if they get back into the tower, go on ahead of us and close the secret doors. Maybe that will slow them down," Mandy ordered. The golems were now only about a thousand feet from the opening into the tower. Again, Mandy and Lonnie stabbed them from behind; again, the creatures simply swung a defensive blow to get them off their backs. Both fighters were momentarily stunned but recovered rapidly, signaling Jon that they were still okay.

Sir Thomas finally caught up to the nearest golem. This time, he plunged his mighty two-handed sword deep into the golem's back. He too swore he heard a moan. The golem staggered and then slowly fell to the ground. The force of the impact bounced the paladin several inches off of the ground, ripping his sword out of his hands. The blade snapped as the golem fell on it. However, Sir Thomas was quite pleased that he finally felled the beast. As Mandy rushed by him, he called out, "Go get it, my weapon's broken. It's all yours."

Once more Mandy plunged her bastard sword into the back of the remaining golem. However, she was very quick to pull it back out again, having seen what happened to Sir Thomas, who had delayed slightly. The golem staggered and swerved but did not fall until Lonnie reached it and stabbed it again. Then, the last golem came crashing down hard onto the ground, lifting up a small dust cloud as the other had done a moment before.

"We did it!" exclaimed Lonnie, quite out of breath but elated with victory.

Mandy gave him a hug, "We make a good team! Come, we better get ourselves cured up a bit and see to Sir Thomas. I hope he has a spare sword handy."

"I do, but it's packed away in Darless' portable hole. I guess I don't need it at the moment. Lonnie, can you help me out of this armor? I think it's time I made use of some of your magical protections, Mandy. This suit is going to have to be completely repaired before I can wear it again."

Seeing the major bruises about the paladin's chest, Jon inquired, "Should I use my stick on you again?"

"No. Let's not waste the precious gifts of Father Ukko. I can pretty much fix myself up. Give me a few minutes." The paladin said several brief prayers to Ukko, touching himself after each. Jon watched the bruises slowly disappear. Meanwhile, Mandy had retrieved her portable hole from within her bra where she kept it close to her chest. She stuck her head and arms inside the hole that was now laying on the ground. She looked rather funny with the top half of her body not visible. Bits and pieces of armor and protective bracers came flying haphazardly out of the hole. Then, she emerged.

"Okay, let's try these on for fit." She fastened a pair of bracers around his wrists and put a ring on his finger. "There, that ought to hold you for now. You should be almost as hard to hit as before. Just don't go taking any blows to the chest." She grinned. He profusely thanked her.

Picking up the battered pieces of Sir Thomas's armor, Lonnie asked, "What should we do with your armor?"

"Oh, just leave it here. No one else is around. I'll get it later and pack it in my horse pack," the Holy Paladin replied. "Come on, we've dallied here long enough. We had better get back to the others."

Jon said, "We walk. Ordinarily, I'd just step us back in there, but I am running on borrowed energy at the moment. Darless and Alison are flowing it to me." The four began walking fast back to the tower.

"Say this *is* much better than clanking around in the armor," the paladin admitted.

"Freer motion too," Mandy noted, pleased with herself. However, she had a nagging worry that he would continue to accept chest smashes as he was prone to do, expecting the armor to deflect it. Such was the difference in their fighting styles. If he did not change, he was destined for a painful lesson in cracked ribs.

They had just entered the tower when Jon received a mental message from Darless saying that they were teleporting out to the usual campsite just outside the village walls. "Hold it, everyone. They are teleporting out. Back to the campsite we go, come on." That was very good news.

While all this was going on, back inside, the priest knelt beside the bleeding Basil, who was just barely conscious. He prayed to Father Ukko for a minute and then touched the wounded man. The energy glow of healing spread over Basil. Alison spied a small smile on her father's face. She was sure that he had recognized that prayer and realized he was now in good hands.

Darless reached the side of Anna, whose face was swollen and black and blue from her repeated beatings. Her eyes were barely opened and the woman looked utterly dazed. The alu-demon spoke very softly to her, "You are amongst friends now. Basil is being fully healed by prayers to Ukko. Let me attend to your wounds. Just relax; all is finally okay." She felt the woman grasp what she was saying, but was not sure she had relaxed. Then, using her mind, she began adjusting Anna's facial cells, promoting healing as best she could. Into Father Johnas's mind she placed the thought, *Anna can use some healing when you can get to her.* The priest, unused to other's thoughts appearing in his mind, jumped with surprise. He looked over at Darless and Anna and nodded.

"Okay, Basil, you lie there and rest a bit before we move you. I must see to Anna's wounds. She is otherwise in good shape." Basil nodded; he was too weak to move anyway. Quickly, Father Johnas chanted to Ukko once more and then healed Anna. Darless watched fascinated as Anna's face slowly healed fully. However, the alu-demon was still conscious of the energy drain Jon was using. Fortunately, he was not requiring much from her. She looked over at Alison to see how she was holding up.

During this time, Alison, unused to flowing spiritual energy to another, was concentrating diligently on assisting Jon. Thus, she was only barely cognizant of what was happening about her — just enough to realize that her father had been healed as had her mother. Darless realized that this was just perfect; Alison had something vital to do, which kept her mind off of her parents for the moment.

Rufus and Thea felt a bit useless at the moment. "I guess we are the rear guards now," Thea explained to the gnome.

"The only guards, you mean," he replied back in jest. Both watched the healing operations. "We are going to need to get them out of this room pretty soon, I think. Johnas's protective spell doesn't last too long."

"I can use my teleport spell when they are ready," Thea proposed. "Alison and Darless are pretty much occupied helping out Jon, although I really do not know how they are doing that, do you?"

"Er, no. Jon is definitely a strange one, but then the world is full of strange things," he answered. "That's what I like about it so much. Everywhere you go, there are new things to see, new things to learn. Exciting isn't it?"

"Well, I never thought of it quite that way," she answered politely, "but I can see your point, I think."

"Okay everyone, Jon reports that the golems have been slain. We need to get these two out of here pronto," Darless spoke up.

"I'll teleport us," Thea declared enthusiastically. "Oops, there are too many of us to do with one spell." She looked quite downcast.

"Thea, you take Rufus, Alison, and Anna. I'll take Father Johnas and Basil. Target is our usual campsite," Darless ordered. Alison looked quite drained from her support of Jon and was very glad her apprentice was able to handle the spell. At last she let her connection to Jon go and grabbed Thea's hand and then her mother's hand.

The two mages chanted briefly and the next instant they all arrived safely at the campsite. Darless immediately used the stored charges in her staff to cast the magical mansion spell. "Okay, let's get them inside right away." The strong arms of the paladins and Mandy carried the weak forms of Alison's parents inside the safety of the mansion.

"Where are we? Who are you?" Basil managed to speak, his first words in over twenty-one years. His voice cracked from long non-use. Father Johnas held his hands to his lips, indicating to Alison not to blurt out anything. His patients were very weak and likely confused and most importantly subject to shock, if they found out too much too quickly.

Father Johnas spoke softly, but with authority Alison seldom heard him use. "You are totally safe. All danger has been eliminated. You are amongst the largest assembly of Holy Paladins and Holy Mages of Father Ukko that I have ever heard tell of — five of them, in fact. You could not be in safer hands. At the moment, you are in a magical mansion safe from all possible dangers from the outside world. By the blessing of Father Ukko, both of your bodies have been fully healed. I know that there is much you want and need to know, but first you must eat and sleep. Your bodies and you have been through quite an ordeal. We must take things slow and easy. Time is on our side. Ladies, could we have some light broth, perhaps with the chicken bits in it?"

"Coming up!" exclaimed Thea, eager to be of use. She and Lonnie darted to the kitchen area. Meanwhile, Jon found a soft pile of pillows and collapsed, asleep at once. Alison found herself very tired; she now fully appreciated what Jon had endured so many times after using so much of his energy. She looked at his sleeping form, brushed an errant lock back into place. She looked at her parents, who were also lying comfortably side by side, holding each other's hands, gazing at each other lovingly. Tears trickled down her face; her knees gave way, and she laid down beside Jon, gave him a kiss, and promptly fell asleep herself. Later, she would declare that this was the best sleep that she had ever had.

An hour later, she and Jon were aroused by the smell of food. She had a craving for food, a craving she had never really felt before. As she sat up, she realized this was how Jon had felt so many times before; only now it was very real to her as well. Mandy stuffed a plate into her hands as Darless did likewise to Jon. Both ate rapidly. Finally, frantic hunger satiated, she looked at her parents. They had already eaten a good deal of the healthy broth. It seemed to revive them a good deal. They looked much more alert she thought.

Finally, her father seeing her finish up an enormous plate of food, said, "Greetings, Fair Mage. I am Basil d'Ambrose and this is my wife Anna. I don't know how we can ever thank you enough for our rescue. Whom do we have the pleasure of addressing?" Alison looked at Father Johnas. What should she say?

Fortunately, Father Johnas had had an hour to think about this eventuality. "Let me do the introductions, My Lady," he said to Alison, who was immensely relieved. She steeled herself to go along with whatever introduction the priest thought best.

He began slowly, "Let me begin by saying that you are now twenty-one years into the future. Yes, you have been imprisoned for twenty-one years by the Archmage Sarah le'Garde." He paused to let that bit of information slowly sink into their minds. Both gasped.

"That long?" whimpered Anna, tears forming. She held her husband's hand tightly. After a minute or two, she looked quite startled. "What of our children? Basil we have to get back to — no," she fumbled as she tried to grasp the reality. "No it's too late, isn't it?"

Before Basil could try to say anything to Anna, Father Johnas spoke, "Don't worry about your children. I believe most are alive and doing well. They all miss you, of course. Now that you know the date, let me introduce you to your rescuers." This consoled them sufficiently. He could see their relief at knowing their children were somehow safe. "Allow me to introduce the leader of the party, the Holy Mage of Ukko, Archmage Alison d'Ambrose. Yes, your youngest has actually been the one to rescue you." He knew that they would have to face this sooner or later. Both seemed to be taking thing well, so he went for the biggest factor first.

The parents stared at Alison; tears flowing down her face, Alison stared back at them, hoping against all odds, they would not go crazy or worse. Anna was the first to speak, "My Runtkin? Baby Allie? Is that really you? You have her eyes and hair."

"It's me, mama!" she could contain her emotion no longer. She rushed to her mom and held her tight; both women were crying uncontrollably with joy. In fact, there was not a dry eye in the mansion. Even Sir Thomas, had to wipe his eyes several times. Darless hung onto his arm for support. Then, her father insisted she come to him and he hugged her for dear life, whispering in her ear, "My little one! You are alive! We thought you were all crushed to death."

It took over five minutes for the emotions to die down. Alison sat down between her parents, one hand around each of them, and they, hers. "I've missed you both so much," she blubbered. "I never gave up hope of finding you, never."

At last Father Johnas could continue the introductions. "And this is Alison's fiancé, Saint Jon Brown, the Redeemer. He holds the key to your full recovery, I might add. Oh yes, he is a musician." Jon smiled and nodded. "And this is Sir Thomas, Holy Paladin of Ukko, a mighty warrior and lifelong friend of Alison's. This is Archmage Darless, Holy Paladin of Ukko. Yes, she is an alu-demon, Father Basil, but it was Ukko himself that bestowed paladinhood on her! And this is Mandy Blackthorn, Ranger of Reylona, the mightiest ranger and fighter I have ever seen! And this is Lonnie Smith, Holy Paladin of Ukko and Thea, apprentice mage of Alison's. And this is Rufus. Oops, sorry I don't know your full title. Accept my apologies, please?"

Rufus stood up so he could be seen, "Rufus Illusionist and Invertor Extraordinary, at your service. I live not too far from here. Met Archmage Alison last year, and we. . ." He did not get to finish his speech; Father Johnas cut him off.

"If you let him, Rufus will talk for hours at a time. Later, my good gnome, you can talk all you want," chided the priest. "And finally, I am Father Johnas, Holy Priest of Ukko and also lifelong friend of Alison."

"You are so grown up!" Anna said trying to grasp it all. "And an Archmage? Basil, doesn't that mean she is a wizard?"

"Allie, Archmage?" he asked her incredulously.

"Yes, daddy, Archmage; Darless is too. We made it together."

"Anna, our daughter is one of the most powerful wizards in all the lands, if this be so!"

"Yes, daddy. It took two Archmages to free you from the imprisonment spell of Archmage Sarah. We had to kill her first, though to get to you."

"Then it's true, that evil wizard is dead! Well, that is truly a reward. She was such a bitch!" exclaimed Anna.

"There, there, Anna. Remember we are now in the presence of very holy people," chided Basil. "But can you tell us about the others? What of the twins?" That changed the topic as far as Anna was concerned.

"Both just fine. Both are quite impressive. May is an illusionist of some renown and Mat is monk and master locksmith. They salvaged an entire city, but that is a long story. Christina is a healer of Ukko and she is married to a blacksmith and have three children already. You are now grandparents! Stephen is a Castle Steward and is married with two children. Ruben is a wealthy banker and Lennard is still recovering and is planning to be a beekeeper, if you can imagine that. Only Heinrich remains unaccounted for. I have not been able to track him down. Thanks to Mandy here, we know he survived." She caught herself from blurting out any reference to that night and the destruction of their castle.

"Our children are all grown up," Anna began crying as that reality struck home.

"Ah, Anna, look on the bright side," Father Johnas was quick to point out, "you now have five grandchildren that need your attention. That is, as soon as you are able." That seemed to console her sufficiently.

"I feel so old, so awfully tired," Anna finally said.

"You both should get some sleep now. Enough excitement for one day," the priest replied. "You have yet many days of joy ahead of you. There is no need to rush your recovery. Sleep now. In the morning, we can talk more." With that, Alison helped tuck her parents in and put a blanket over them. Both fell asleep holding each other. Alison spent several minutes just watching them. She could see the deep love both had for each other.

Finally, she got up and went over to Jon and Father Johnas.

"Let's step outside," she suggested. They followed her out. "They took everything very well, didn't they? They are going to be okay?" she asked pleadingly.

"Yes, so far so good. But beware, all of those frightful memories are still present in their minds and can activate at any time," the wise priest replied. "Best to give them as much time to recover their physical strength as possible. Besides, we must still free many others."

"Thank you so much!" Alison said, and give the priest a solid hug. He beamed and went back inside.

It was only late afternoon, so the two decided to take a walk together. In the distance, they heard a metallic tapping sound. Rufus was already ahead of them, exploring the fallen iron golems. The two wandered over to him. He looked up and said, "Yes, indeed, made of iron. Heavy too. Solid as far as I can tell. Never seen one before, though. Have you?"

"No, Rufus, I've never seen any kind of golem, though I have studied about them. By the way, thank you for dispersing that poisonous gas cloud. It saved the day," she added. He smiled back and went on with his examinations.

Nearby, Mandy and the paladins were walking the horses. Darless and Thea, finished with the chores, came outside as well. "Father Johnas is watching over them," the alu-demon told Alison. Congratulations Alison on a job very well done indeed!" Both women hugged each other.

"Say, I didn't know you are called Allie," Thea spoke up.

Alison looked at her sternly before replying, "That is a baby name. I am Alison. Don't ever call me Allie!"

"Yes, Archmage Alison," Thea said in mock sternness. "Really, I prefer Thea and not Althea. Who has ever heard of anyone being named Althea anyway." She scampered off to find Lonnie. In the distance, Alison heard her say to Lonnie, "She's Allie, but don't let her hear you call her that!" She also heard the couple chuckling.

Jon then broke the silence, "Say, do you suppose that we should let your brothers and sisters know that we have rescued your parents? That they are alive and doing reasonably well?"

"I've been thinking about that very thing. How did you know? Read my mind? I just thought of doing that," she asked.

"No, I just thought of it just now," he replied. They both looked at each other and said in unison, "How amazing." They hugged each other gently; they were becoming very close indeed.

Alison shared her thoughts, "Well, I just don't know. If we do, I'm worried that they will all want to come here right away. I know I would, but that might be too much of a shock for them to handle. Besides, with all of those horrid memories they have in their minds, anything can happen. Remember how bad I was, you know, screaming terrified in the late morning? They might still go insane over all this."

"Well how about me letting them know and telling them in no uncertain terms not to come just yet, that they need time to mentally recover?" Jon asked. "I think I can explain it to them."

"Can you? That would be wonderful. I was thinking about teleporting home to bring them the news, but I going to have my hands full with all the imprisoned others."

"Good. I'll make contact with them tonight before I go to sleep. I should be rested up enough for that by then. By the way, thanks for all your energy flows today. Worked perfectly." She radiated back at him, before they embraced lovingly.

Later that evening, true to his word, as they both lay down to sleep, Jon expanded his spiritual awareness once more and reached the minds of Mat, May and Christina. (Stephen was already sound asleep.) Jon placed various thoughts into their minds and showed them his images of what their parents looked like just before they fell asleep earlier. The back flash of joy they sent him nearly overwhelmed him. He slept exceedingly peaceful that night as well.

The next morning, Basil seemed quite cheerful and alert. Over breakfast, he asked, "Allie, how soon can we head home? Is there anything we can do to help out? I am a priest, if you haven't forgotten, that is unless Father Ukko has forgotten about me. What is the situation at present?"

"Dad, Ukko has not forgotten about you, I'm sure. Give it some time, you need to heal fully. The situation is really a tough one. We have slain all of the evil creatures here. We believe the tower is completely secure. There are no neighbors for many, many miles in all directions. But the real problem is you two were not the only people she imprisoned. There are still over twenty others that need rescuing. Only Darless and I are capable of undoing her awful spell. Her imprisonment spell was one of the most powerful spells any wizard can cast. Realistically, we cannot head home for some time yet."

Unfortunately, the word home triggered an avalanche of ill memories for Basil. Alison saw what had happened at once. "Jon, help!" she called out.

Jon came over and sat down beside him. Basil's eyes were staring off into space; his mind was reliving that horrible night. "Okay Basil, I see you are looking at your mental images of the night your castle was destroyed. Now what I want you to do is go to the very beginning of that time, just where you first noticed something was wrong. Yes, there. Now I want you to go through your images and tell me what is happening as you go along through them. Yes, like that." Basil was off, reliving in vivid detail, with excruciating emotions and pain, that fateful night twenty-one years ago.

Unfortunately, Anna had overheard all of this and she too suddenly found herself reliving that night. Darless and Thea both rushed over to her. "I'll do it," Thea insisted. "You need to rescue the others. I cannot do that, but I certainly can do this."

"Thanks, Thea," Darless complimented her. Thea softly told Anna the same thing that Jon had just said to Basil, and she was off and running, so to speak, through the events of that night as she had seen them. At times, both screamed wildly at the now non-existent persona, so strong, so vivid were their memories of it all. Thea concentrated on persevering and four hours later, both had desensitized their memories of that night considerably — at least they were not screaming any more. They broke for lunch and then resumed later that afternoon. Indeed, as one might expect, these two had a lot of mental energy, mental charge, bound up in these horrible memories. All of it had to be discharged. She hoped that it would go quicker than poor Lennard's therapy.

With her parents being looked after, Alison decided it was time to free another pair. However, after brief consultation with the other members of her group, she decided to leave Lonnie behind to guard the mansion just in case of unexpected troubles. In truth, he insisted that he pull guard duty this time. The rest headed back into the Chamber of Horrors to free two more that were trapped.

As they paused just outside of the Chamber of Horrors, the priest questioned, "Have you given any more thought about whom to free? Some may well be very evil people; some could even be demons or worse. All we have is a ledger name to go on, my child."

"I know, I've thought a great deal about it but have no real conclusion. I can argue it from many approaches. What most worries me is to free one whom should not be released, one that will in the future cause great harm. That's what terrifies me the most — to be the person responsible for unleashing great evil upon others. I thought today we'd release the one's I'm pretty sure about, that is the paladin and the holy warrior," she answered very reservedly.

"I have a proposition for you then," Father Johnas proposed, "make me a copy of the names on the ledger. I cannot read that script she used. Tonight, I will pray for divine guidance from Father Ukko. Let us pass that responsibility on to him to make the choice of whom to free and whom to leave imprisoned."

A great weight lifted from her shoulders, "Would you? That would be really best I think. I know you know just how much I hate placing decisions of mortals into the hands of gods. We should be able to deal with our own affairs. But in this case, I just don't have enough information to properly make the call of whom to free and whom to leave imprisoned."

Alison went into the magical studies room, found a parchment and ink, copied the ledger list, and returned in less than five minutes. By then, the priest was ready to cast his protection spell on them so that the horrors of this room would not affect them. Mandy and Sir Thomas stood much closer to the mages this time. Mandy wondered, "Do you suppose that another trap will spring when you free more people?"

This time Darless answered, "Nothing about this Archmage Sarah would surprise me anymore. She has had contingency spell after contingency spell. It is certainly possible that our attempt to free another will trigger yet another trap of hers. This time, I will also stand guard just in case. If all goes well, then Alison can guard, while I free the second. Okay, everyone, battle stations."

Alison looked at each person to verify they were ready. Then, she began her very complex chant. As before, the ritual took her minutes to fully complete. The others recognized her final words, "Free Sir Egmont of Flaxton." Magical energies flashed as they had done the day before. She concentrated upon raising the paladin from his tomb far below.

This time, no iron golems rose up out of the stone floor. Instead a scroll suddenly appeared floating in the air. It moved straight across the room to the pentagram gate. As it floated over the pentagram proper, the gate energized and the scroll disappeared. The whole event took only a few seconds. "Zagrot zounds! That gate still works!" declared Mandy moving into a defensive position placing herself between the gate and Alison. The paladin did likewise.

"Oh dear," exclaimed Rufus to no one in particular, "this is not good either!"

"Cheer up," Darless teased, "look on the bright side. We now know that the gate is fully operational without having to gate ourselves to the Abyss to find out. Rather, we should be wondering what was on that scroll."

"Hum," Rufus pulled on his beard a few times, "the only reasonable assumption was that the scroll tells someone that mages are releasing people that Archmage Sarah had imprisoned. I wonder whom she is telling this to anyway? Lord Jarred?"

"If so, he cannot make a personal appearance to do anything about it, Rufus," Darless was quick to point out. "Remember, last year I killed his body form on this plane. He cannot come back to this plane for many, many years. No, if it is directed to him, and I cannot think of any other likely candidate considering she was his consort for a time, he will likely send spies or messengers or a combat group to do us in."

"But might that take some time to prepare?" wondered Rufus. "This was only a possible foreseen future event — not one that was known to be about to occur. Maybe he will take days to respond, if at all. Maybe he won't care at all."

Unfortunately for Rufus, Lord Jarred did care. Alison had the man fully freed by now and the priest was kneeling beside him healing him. In the total silence of the room, everyone heard the paladin's whispered voice. "She's poisoned me with strange worms that are eating my insides out." He coughed and spat a pile of blood on the floor. Father Johnas immediately began a second prayer and then touched the prone man. Suddenly hundreds of small, white, worm-like creatures poured out of his body onto the floor. They wiggled out of his mouth and nose and ears and through the pores of his skin. Egmont cried out in agony.

The priest began stomping on the worms. Quickly Darless and Alison joined in. "Don't let any of these vile leeches live or we all may become infected," cautioned the priest. Even Rufus got into the action, stomping here and there. Soon the worms were eliminated and the priest once again performed additional healing on the man.

All the while, Mandy and Sir Thomas maintained their watch on the gate. Sure enough, the gate began to activate once more. "Zounds! Gate's opening, heads up everyone, could be really bad," called out Mandy, her bastard sword at the ready. The hairs on her neck rose up in warning, though she needed it not. The gate opened, magical energy flashed, and the gate shut down. But Mandy could see nothing there. "What?" she cried out confused.

Darless cocked her head to one side, as she was prone to do when attempting to discern if something invisible was before her. She thought she detected the tell-tale shimmer, so she quickly cast a detection spell. "One invisible man is there; on guard." Quickly she chanted a second spell; as she was chanting, the gate reactivated once more. Her spell fired and the visitor became visible to everyone.

Standing before them in the middle of the pentagram was a magic user, who was in the process of making a hasty exit back into the Abyss. "Stop him," yelled Darless. Mandy dove for him, but was repelled by a wall of force the man had about him. From her now prone position on the floor she looked up at him and saw him sneering wickedly down at her. A volley of magical missiles from Alison merely bounced off his protective spells. "I know you," called out Darless. But the gate activated at that instant and the mage disappeared back into the Abyss.

"I've seen him before too," Mandy declared getting to her feet. "But where?"

"He was one of the six witnesses that Lord Jarred had with him at Metrarch's Council last year, when we were playing bodyguard, remember?" Darless suggested.

"Oh yes, that's right, Darless. So Lord Jarred knows we are here. Zounds, that is not good news," Mandy continued.

"Well, he was bound to find out," Alison added. "Really, there was nothing we could do to prevent that contingency spell of Sarah's from triggering. I just hope that that was the last of her tricks!"

Father Johnas had Sir Egmont sitting up and sipping some water. The others heard the soft gentle voice of the priest explaining to the man that some hundred years had now passed since his imprisonment. He was being as gentle as he could with the man.

"Well, I'm glad that I still live and am now well, that is the most vital thing, I suppose," Sir Egmont acknowledged hesitatingly. "How has the world changed while I have been away?"

"Well, your exploits are legends in your lands, I'm told. In my land, we have even heard about some of your adventures. However, I'm sorry to say that I've never been to your part of the world, so I cannot answer you. But here in my land, it's the same old evil actions to thwart. So I expect you may still find much to champion — to set to rights."

Egmont thought for a minute, trying to get a grip on the new reality in which he now found himself. "Ah so then there is still a vital need for Holy Paladins of Ukko?"

"Ah my Holy Warrior, yes indeed, most certainly. Your rescue party has three Holy Paladins, a Holy Mage, a Holy Priest, and a Holy Redeemer in it, to say nothing of the Ranger of Reylona and others. So your skills are yet needed in the world, my son."

Sir Egmont smiled, that seemed to clinch his grip on the new reality. He tried to stand up, Johnas assisted him, steading him. "All I need do now is find my armor and Holy Blade. Then, Sir Egmont shall ride forth once again. Say, you have not come across my gear, by any chance have you?"

"Welcome back, Sir Egmont," Alison broke in on their conversation, "Holy Archmage of Ukko, Alison d'Ambrose, at your service. Yes, we have your gear safely stored in a vault not too far away. If you can walk, we will take you there immediately. But I would suggest that you pause for food and some well-earned rest to get your strength back."

"Ah, I am forever in your debt, Archmage d'Ambrose. If there is ever any deed you need done, you only have to ask and Sir Egmont will carry it out! Please, lead the way. Though I am weak, I shall not rest at peace until I am once again reunited with my Holy Blade." Alison looked at Father Johnas for confirmation that it was all right to do this right now. He nodded his approval and the group slowly made their way out of the Chamber of Horrors into the tunnel and shortly into the room of magical gear.

Just as soon as the paladin entered the room, he spied his sword against the far wall. "Erlingrass! You still exist. I have returned!" He rushed over to the scabbard, drew forth the blade holding it up high in the air. Alison thought she spotted a small magical or priestly energy exchange between the man and the blade. Indeed, Sir Egmont now seemed steadier on his feet. "Ah, my armor is also intact. Praise be to Father Ukko. I am yet whole!" In fact, he found all of the gear that he had with him when he was captured. It took him several minutes to collect all of his things. "Okay, now I'll partake of refreshments," he declared. Sir Thomas carried the armor for him, and they chatted as they exited the tower heading for the magical mansion.

Because the mansion spell was due to expire within a few hours, Darless cast another one. It took only a few minutes to transfer everyone out of the one and into the new mansion. Meanwhile, Lonnie and Sir Egmont chatted as only Holy Paladins can. Sir Egmont did ask Lonnie about what was a Holy Mage and Holy Redeemer; of these, he had never heard tell. Lonnie was only too eager to explain.

During the short break, Alison told those that were outside the tower about the visitor from the Abyss. "Lonnie, you and Sir Egmont guard the mansion and those inside. We have to return below to free a Holy Priest. If anything gates in from the Abyss, Darless will alert you and you may come and join the battle. But perhaps, Lord Jarred only wanted to see what was going on, perhaps," she tried to sound as hopeful as possible.

"Sir Lonnie, lead me to the food!" declared Sir Egmont, realizing now just how famished he really was.

"Please, Sir Egmont, just Lonnie. I have not yet earned my title," Lonnie humbly said, as he led the warrior towards the kitchen.

As they walked back into the tower, Alison asked, "Sir Thomas, what does Lonnie mean the he has not yet earned his title?"

"Only experienced paladins are qualified to be awarded that title. They must have performed some heroic feat to be worthy. Their liege then bestows the title, bestows a Holy Sword, if possible, and usually grants him some small parcel of land on which the paladin can then build a very small keep or castle — nothing extravagant, mind you, just enough for their needs. Lonnie certainly now has acquired the experience, but he has no liege as yet, I'm afraid." Alison thanked him for the explanation and smiled to herself. That detail would soon be rectified.

As they approached the Chamber of Horrors, Darless called a halt. "Let me check for ambushes." She put on a ring of invisibility and stole quietly into the room. Since the lights were off, she made effective use of her infrared vision, but detected no one. Double checking herself, she cast a brief spell to spy on any possible invisible persons. Again, none. Assuming it was safe, she took off the ring and became visible and signaled the others. Still Mandy and Sir Thomas were on guard, fully expecting an attack by creatures and/or persons from the Abyss.

Now, Alison handed the ledger to Darless, pointing out the name, Father Joshua de Fleuree. At once, everyone moved to their familiar places, with Darless doing the complex spell casting. This time, the process went without any alarm being sounded. Five minutes later the High Priest of Ukko lay on the floor, Johnas administering the healing.

Joshua was a very elderly man with thinning, long white hair and beard. He wore the familiar white robe with blue cross, indicating his status as a High Priest of Ukko. However, he was very old, approaching eighty and rather feeble in physical form. When he recognized

Father Johnas as a fellow priest of Ukko, he whispered, "Do not waste your spells on me, Father. Please, I am old and ready to let the body depart. Please, leave me as I am."

"But I can heal your body," Father Johnas protested.

"To what end? You give me a few more weeks, a few more months? Rather, tell me who you all are? What happened to the Evil Mage here? When is it? I know I have been imprisoned, but I know not for how long."

Father Johnas understood and motioned for the others to help him move the old man out of this room. When they were safely in the tunnel near the two side chambers, Joshua was gently laid up against the side wall and given as much water as he desired. Then, Father Johnas introduced those present and told of those who were outside. "The Evil Mage has been slain by these people and we are in the process of freeing those she entrapped. As near as we can tell, you have been imprisoned for about a hundred years."

"Please to make all of your acquaintances. Praise be to Ukko that I have been spared eternal darkness of that prison. I come from San Louis de Grall, a small town far, far to the south from here, where this tower is located. In my youth, I and my friends were instrumental in the total destruction of numerous Evil Temples and made, I'm afraid, some terrible enemies in the Abyss. Finally, an army of demons, men, and fell creatures attempted to take back some of the territory they had lost. Although I was nearly on my death bed at the time, I arose and helped in the great battle. I was in the rear, healing the fallen, resurrecting those that died, when this Evil Mage came upon me. Even in my youth, I would have been no match for her. She brought me here and took my rods and imprisoned me." He coughed from the strain of so much talking. He was getting weaker by the minute.

"Can't we do something for you?" pleaded Alison, grieved by his tale and plight.

"No my child," he said, but then a light flashed in his eyes; he brightened up. "Yes, yes, there are two things that you may be able to do yet for me. My body is not long for this world. Before it fails, I would dearly love to view these mountains. When I was brought here, I found them spectacularly beautiful. We have no near mountains where I came from. And when the body passes away, please bury me with my feet toward the mountains, that symbolically, I may see the mountains."

Holding back her tears, Alison said, "We so promise!"

"The other thing, by any chance did you come across a pair of magical rods? They look like two brown sticks about two feet in length carved with many crosses of Ukko?"

"We found a room with tons of stuff in it; we have not yet taken time to identify any of it. We'll go look for them right away." Everyone headed into the room to search for his rods, while Father Johnas stayed at the old man's side. Johnas bade them to make haste, for the priest was weakening rapidly.

They all entered the room that was packed with all sorts of items. "It'll take days to search through all of this stuff!" Sir Thomas groaned.

"Well, let's split up; each take a section and search for the pair of rods," suggested Alison.

"Okay, so it will be only a few days search," complained the paladin as he surveyed his allotted section.

Mandy stood by the door looking into the room. "Oh this is silly, gang. We'll be hours and hours trying to find them this way. All right, here's how it's done. First, you decide you know what you are trying to locate; that's done, two matching rods. Second, you decide that you will just walk over to where they are located. Three, you pick them up."

"Sure, Mandy. We all have mastered the first one. But the other two? Get real!" Sir Thomas bellowed slightly antagonistically.

"Like this, Big Boy," teased Mandy. She shut her eyes and concentrated, making the decision firm in her mind. Then, she opened them and walked over to the back left corner, stooped and extended her arms. When she stood up, she held two matching sticks, both about two feet in length. "Are these what we are looking for?" she asked naively. Sir Thomas's mouth wagged in disbelief; no words came out.

"How did you do that?" asked Darless incredulously.

"I just told you," she teased and began walking triumphantly out of the room. The others followed, asking each other if Mandy was for real, if they saw what it was that they had just seen. None of them believed she had actually just done what she had done.

Alison caught Mandy by the arm. "Seriously, Mandy. How *did* you find them?" She was so earnest that Mandy stopped teasing.

"It is a trick that I learned when I was a little girl. My dad would hide things and I would find them. I got so good at it, that he had to let me learn to handle a sword. Good thing I can still do it." She smiled coyly.

Mandy gave the rods to Joshua. "I think these are what you are wanting, but I'm not sure."

The old man took them in his outstretched arms. He spun them around in his hands using his fingers to rotate them. "Ah, tis a good feeling to have them in my hands once more. For half a century, I wielded these at the rear of battles, raising the worthy of the fallen. I was rather famous for it, as I recall. Here, Father Johnas, I want you to take them on behalf of your party here. Give them to whomever you choose. Put them upon your altar and Father Ukko recharges them, though it takes about a week to get them fully back to battery again. May they serve your people as well as they have mine. Now I can let go of this old, old body. Know that I am at finally truly at peace." His voice trailed off and his eyes shut. Mandy swore that she could see a yellow colored being float up and out of the body, up through the solid rock above them. Later, when they compared notes that evening, Darless and Alison also believed that they too had witnessed it. They decided it was due to their heightened familiarity with their own spiritual being.

No one said a word for several minutes, but Father Johnas said a lengthy prayer. Quietly, Sir Thomas picked up the Holy Priest and carried him outside back to their camp. Then, he and Mandy went in search of a proper burial site. When Thea heard what had happened, since she was finished for the day with Anna's therapy, she went in search of the two. "Hi there, is this the spot?" she asked, when she found them about a quarter mile from the tower. From here, one had a great view of the mountains. It was late afternoon.

"Yes, this is a good spot, it matches his wishes," Sir Thomas solemnly answered.

"Then, please allow me to dig his grave," and without waiting, she cast her dig spell and dug a picture-perfect hole. When she was finished, she said, "Thanks, I wanted to help in some small way." They both thanked her and told her that Joshua probably appreciated her helping hand. Thea then went to fetch the others for a proper burial. Twenty minutes later, with a full ritual befitting a High Priest of Ukko, Father Joshua de Fleuree was laid to rest, facing the towering mountains.

In silence, everyone walked back to the mansion. As they neared the open doors, Father Johnas spoke softly to Alison, "Do not weep, my child. We have done well by him."

"I know Father," Alison sighed, "but I had somehow hoped for more, I guess. But today, we saved a soul, a being, and that I believe is vitally important, though just how, I am not certain. Jon would probably know." They all went inside.

She found her parents looking much better than when she had left them in the morning. True, both were still exhausted and a bit peeked in complexion, but the sharp edge of their horrid memories had been dulled. She did not fail to profusely thank Jon and Thea.

"I don't know what they are doing," her father told her, "but it is sure working. The heavy burden is lightning somehow. Saint Jon says we just need to keep at it a while longer. Right now, for some unknown reason, I feel like I have not eaten in weeks!" Anna wholeheartedly agreed with him. Jon smiled, handling one's reactive mental pictures took a great deal of effort. He had seen this phenomenon many times now. Thea and Darless headed for the kitchen as fast as possible. The Archmage was very pleased to find that Thea had most of dinner nearly ready and gave her a worthy compliment.

After dinner, while sipping their tea, Jon cleared away the mess and headed off to the kitchen to handle the dishes. Anna noted this and asked, "Allie, does Jon always do the dishes or is he just being polite?"

"Yes, mom, he does. He claims it is only fair that he does half the work," Alison explained.

"Allie, honey, you have here a gem of a man!" Anna still addressed her daughter as if she were barely able to walk. "You take note of this, Basil. It wouldn't hurt you one bit to help out in the kitchen."

"Yes, Anna," he replied half-heartedly. "Come sit with us, Allie. We are dying to know all about you. Last time we saw you, you were just out of diapers, and now you are an Archmage no less. How on the face of this earth did you ever find us? Jon has said that it is okay for you to tell us about yourself and adventures."

Alison was dying to tell them everything, but she restrained herself a moment. It was one thing for them to say it was okay, and quite another for Jon to do so. She looked at Jon, who was carrying another pile of dishes into the kitchen. He nodded it was now safe. Alison sat down between her mom and dad and began her tale. "Where to start? Ah yes, I'd best start at the beginning." She told them of her escape that fateful night, hiding in the dungeon under the protective eye of her nanny. She described her early resolve to become a magic user so as to be able to find out what had happened to destroy her castle and family. She then skipped over her early adventuring years merely pointing out that she began her career with Father Johnas and Sir Thomas and several others who were not present.

Then, she told of her quest to find the magical picture books and how those clues had led her to running into Jon and Mandy. The hour was late by the time she finished up with her dying by taking the spear thrown by Morrigan, Goddess of War, who had intended to slay Jon. Both parents gasped. She continued with what she was told of her resurrection by Father Ukko and of their triumphant arrival back in Zaire at the Church of Ukko."

Both parents had tears in their eyes when she finished this portion of her life story. Her mother said, "You must really love him to have given your life for him."

Alison smiled, "More than you know, mom, but that will have to wait for tomorrow night. It's late and I have to get my rest. We still have twenty-one more to free. And you need your rest too. Jon's giving you more therapy sessions tomorrow. I promise that tomorrow's saga will cast more light on what Jon is doing with you two." She gave them hugs and kisses and helped them turn in.

When that task was finished, Sir Egmont and Father Johnas came up to her, "I hope you didn't mind our listening in on your tale. I've never heard some of it. Most impressive indeed," the priest commented.

"No, you are welcome to listen, both of you, but tomorrow's portion will be much more elucidating," she promised.

Later that night, Father Johnas placed the parchment with the names of those who were imprisoned upon his small portable altar and prayed long to Father Ukko. In the morning, he examined the parchment. He smiled, his prayers had been answered. Now he was even more certain why his God had asked him to stay to the very end. Over a dozen names had been scratched off of the list. Only ten names remained.

When Alison finally snuggled in beside Jon, her last action was to fire off a final magical spell for the day. A parchment appeared in the air above her, a quill appeared and began writing words. When the quill finished, it disappeared and the scroll rolled up. Then, it too vanished only to appear in the hands of its recipient, Nain Anzulbizar.

After breakfast the next morning, the priest took Alison and Darless aside and gave them the parchment. "Father Ukko has shown us who should be rescued and who should not. No specific order of rescue is indicated, so I guess be methodical about it. Start in at the top of the list."

"Wow! Thank you!" exclaimed Alison. Then she added, "Gosh, at least half of these people must be evil and beyond redemption. Without your guidance, I may have loosened well over a dozen evil beings back into the world. I'm forever in your debt." He smiled at her.

As they were preparing to leave, Lonnie took Alison aside for a brief word. "My Lady, Sir Egmont has recovered a good deal. May I suggest that he remain here guarding the mansion and let me accompany you. I fear that you may be attacked by forces of Lord Jarred and you'll need all the fighters you can muster."

"Point very well taken, Sir Lonnie Smith. Granted," she paused watching his face. As expected he began to protest, but she put her finger to her lips to silence him. "May I have everyone's attention. I have a matter of importance to announce." Of course, this got everyone's full attention. When she was sure she had, she continued, "From this day forward, be it known that this is now Sir Lonnie Smith, Holy Paladin of Ukko. I, his liege so declare. Unfortunately, his Holy Sword is still in the forging process, but he shall one day soon have his Holy Sword as befitting his high stature. Further, I grant him five acres by Ringbottom Hollow, there to build his keep. It is only a few miles from our new town, by the way — a very picturesque location, I might add." Lonnie was speechless. He had never dreamed that this would be happening to him. He got down on one knee and recited his chivalric code of honor as befitting such an occasion.

When he had finished, Sir Thomas whispered to Alison, "You are supposed to now tell him to arise as Sir Lonnie."

Alison formally said, "Arise now, Sir Lonnie Smith, Holy Paladin of Ukko." He rose and stood tall and proud. Thea giggled and ran to his side to congratulate him and hug him. Sir Lonnie was a bit embarrassed by all the attention, but he felt that he could now conquer the world. With great pride, he accompanied them back into the tower once more.

As they walked through the tunnel complex, Darless wondered, "Alison, what do you think of rescuing the ones that have been trapped the longest? Those may well be the hardest cases requiring more therapy and healing to keep them from going insane or worse."

"I think that is the best approach, lacking any other data. However, length of imprisonment may not have all that much to do with their resultant mental state or their physical state. We've seen just how brutal she could be — imprisoning them near the point of death.

Would you agree with that, Father Johnas?" Alison looked to him for confirmation. She was rather out of her element; she had never paid much attention at all to spiritual matters.

"You are probably correct, my child," he answered, but added, "but another reason to go in that order is they might be related or know one another, like your parents. Perhaps she trapped several party members at the same time, or nearly so. Those freed would take great comfort that their buddies were here with them, sharing in the new situation."

"That makes a lot of sense. Okay today, there are three, if this ledger book is accurate. One Elrohir Elvasser, a Valadmir Velacoffskii, and Ellineana Evenstar. Strange sounding names," Alison commented.

"The first and last sound sort of elvish to me," Mandy commented.

As they approached the entrance to the Chamber of Horrors, they paused so that Father Johnas could once more provide them with protection from the massive evil aura the chamber contained. "One more thing everyone, I communed with Father Ukko. I really hate all of these sudden surprise attacks and actions that we have been encountering when we free someone. I didn't want to alarm unduly the others who are recovering. But I believe that we are to be attacked in the chamber sometime today. So let's be ready."

"Well, in that case, we had better prepare before we enter. Thanks for the council!" exclaimed Alison. Perhaps having a priest in the party was a good thing after all. She began by using some stored magical energy from her staff. Onto Sir Thomas, Sir Lonnie, and Mandy, she place her skin of stone spell, while Darless did likewise for Father Johnas, Rufus, and Alison. Both mages then cast major globes of protection onto themselves so that they would not be affected by lower level type spells such as magical missiles and fire balls.

"Say, I have an idea," Mandy suddenly got their attention. "Why not play hare and snare?" Of course, no one had any idea about what she was talking. "It's a kid's game we used to play. When trying to catch the illusive hare, lay a snare instead. In other words, instead of us going about freeing someone and likely being caught in the middle of it in a very vulnerable position, let's lie in wait for them to arrive and snare them first. After we deal with the surprise party from the Abyss, we can then rapidly go about freeing the three for today."

"Well, I don't know if it is honorable to lie in wait and surprise the enemy," Sir Thomas worried.

"There is no absolute right and absolute wrong; the world is not laid out in pure black and white," Mandy countered. "There are millions of shades of grey, some whiter than others. I'm not proposing a sneak raid into the Abyss, rather, let's take up our defensive position and wait a while and see if the raiders show up. The instant they do, we attack, snare them."

"Well, when you put it that way, it does seem honorable enough," the paladin replied. "I certainly don't want Father Johnas here hurt; I promised his family I would look after him."

"The only drawback to your plan, Mandy," the priest countered, "is my protective spells only last a short while. If we wait too long, the protection would have to be renewed rather often. Should the spell wear off while we are under attack, it would go very ill for some of us. Otherwise, I think that your plan is quite prudent indeed."

"Ah, had not thought about the protection wearing off," Mandy agreed. "Well, then, the other possibility is to go in quickly, cast the spells and get the people out of the chamber and into the tunnel here as fast as we can. You know, minimize the time we are in there."

"But out here in the tunnel, we are very vulnerable to area of effect spells. One fire ball spell of necessity will be constrained by the walls. Thus, it will cover a huge length of tunnel, getting us all in its blast," pointed out Darless.

"How about teleporting them directly outside just as soon as they are freed and before he heals them?" wondered Mandy.

"Too much sudden shock might disorientate them or even worse, give them a breakdown," cautioned the priest. "It is safest if I heal them first and give them some time to adjust to their sudden release from the prison."

"During those ten minutes or so, we are terribly vulnerable. Those freed are in grave danger should a fire ball explode around them. You are tied up seeing to their needs. During that time, we don't have freedom of movement," Mandy pointed out to herself, trying to find a workable solution.

"I have a counterproposal," Darless volunteered. "What if we place a pair of force walls at ninety degrees to each other so they support themselves. Have them between the mages, priest and those just freed. The rest of you stand beyond the walls ready to attack anyone using the gate. If anything harmful comes toward those that are most vulnerable, the walls of force would likely deflect it."

"Would the walls be big enough to actually protect everyone that needs it?" wondered the ranger. She was mentally picturing the other walls of force they used last year in the defense of the caravan of Freetown folks they had escorted.

"I believe so, it's better than nothing," Darless added.

"Okay, then let's go that route. Come on everyone it's show time," Mandy said and she headed into the chamber. Rufus was right behind her, turning on the lights using the wall switch. He loved machinery, of course.

Once Alison was in position to do her first casting, Darless constructed two walls of force and positioned them in a large V about the area. Father Johnas and Alison would then be behind the wall of force, which stood between them and the pentagram gate. Darless took up a position outside the wall just behind the three fighters. Rufus was ordered to stand at the edge of the wall so that he could either go help the priest or help the fighters as needed.

Alison made sure everyone was in place and then began her lengthy chant to free another. After two minutes, she spoke commandingly, "Free Elrohir Elvasser!" She then concentrated on bringing him to the surface of the stone prison.

The elf's body had only risen half way out when Darless yelled, "Gate's activating! They must be able to sense when we are freeing someone!" Quietly, Rufus took out a small curious looking wand and petted it lovingly, just in case.

The only factor that benefitted the party was that the gate was so small only a few people could come and go at the same time. Sure enough, magical energies danced around the pentagram and shortly two large warriors appeared. Each wore black plate armor and carried a shield emblazoned with the seal of Lord Jarred. They wielded wicked looking broadswords in their other hand. They came to fight and charged straight into Mandy and Sir Thomas. It was as if they knew exactly whom they were to face, as if it had been pre-arranged.

Just as soon as they left the pentagram gate, it activated once more. Two more fighters appeared and rushed into the battle, one taking on Sir Lonnie, the other double teaming Sir Thomas. Then it activated once more and another pair fighters arrived. In the space of two minutes, all three fighters were facing two opponents each! Still the gate continued to activate! "Oh my," said Rufus to himself.

Mandy instantly connected with her opponent. However, her blade did no damage on either strike. By the time that she had hit him for the sixth time, she realized that these fighters also had stone skin protections of their own. She remembered what Alison had told her, that they provided protection for a finite number of hits. She kept at it, hoping Sir Thomas and Sir Lonnie fared better.

In fact, they were in the same pickle as Mandy, their blows bounced off the black clad warriors as well. So ferocious was their attack, that the three defenders were physically being slowly forced back towards the wall of force. At this point, Alison finally had Elrohir fully freed and Father Johnas ran to the elf's side. He was sitting up and looking about wondering what was happening. All these strange people fighting one another. Quickly, Father Johnas explained that Alison had just freed him from his long imprisonment and that it was now about sixty years in his future and asked if he needed any healing.

The elf was about five feet tall with a greenish hued skin, dressed only in a loin cloth. He had long black hair, which was rather dirty and tangled at this point in time. He had no visible wounds and appeared remarkably fit. It took him a minute to comprehend events before he spoke, "I am fine. No harm done. I placed myself in a trance at the moment of her spell. Ah, I see you have a wall of force to protect us here. Good. Can you free the others, Valadmir Velacoffskii and Ellineana Evenstar? They can aid the fight right now if you can get them free."

Alison looked at Father Johnas raising her eyebrows trying to ask "should I?" He nodded affirmative, so Alison began chanting another freedom spell, using the last remaining charges in her staff for the motive power. Meanwhile, the elf began singing a mellow song, yet full of hope. Father Johnas assumed that its purpose was to assist and encourage the fighting trio, but he was wrong. Two minutes later, a large pile of the elf's belongings came floating into the room up to the elf. "Ah, this is much better," he said, putting on his bracers of defense, his various rings of power, and strapping on his various knives and swords. Thus five minutes into the fray, Elrohir rushed to join the battle.

Meanwhile, Darless watched as the first two fighters took no damage from Mandy's or Sir Thomas's blows. Instantly, she suspected they were also protected. She sought a way to counter it. She reasoned that a dispel magic might or might not work in this case. On the other hand, the spell would only protect against a finite and relatively few blows. She could damage them with a fire ball, but the close proximity of her fighters ruled that out. There was not enough distance between her and them to launch a lightning bolt. "Why waste powerful spells on simple warriors?" she declared. "I'll just hasten the end of their protective spells!" Thus, she began shooting magical missile volleys at all six of the fighters; each missile strike lowered their protective defense by one. Sooner or later, their stone skins would end and the fighters would begin to take damage, rapidly, she assumed.

Still the gate continued to activate. Next, a High Priest and a mage appeared. The priest stepped back out of the way, putting as much distance between himself and the fighting as he could. He began a very lengthy prayer. Meanwhile the mage took up a position in front of him to protect him while he cast his spell. The mage spied Alison and immediately shot a huge volley of magical missiles at her. As expected, the missiles bounced off of the protective wall of force she was behind. Darless heard the mage say, "Ah ha. Good move. Well, so much for your wall of force." He began chanting once more, this time he'd use the counter-spell to dispel the wall. Darless acted.

She assumed that the mage would likely be well protected, if the fighters were any indication of just how well protected this raiding party was. No, she would waste missiles or even a fire ball if she tried to use them to stop his chanting. It had to be something to force him to lose his concentration, to break his casting. Darless spoke her command word. "A huge fist the size of a giant appeared directly in front of the mage and immediately punched him extremely hard right in his face. She knew the stone skin would protect him from punching damage, damage was not the effect she sought. No, the force of the blow caused him to lose his train of thought. His spell sputtered into nothingness, he staggered three steps backwards in order to keep his footing. Darless made her giant magical fist pursue him repeatedly punching him, keeping him off guard. She felt something wet hit her face. She wiped it, it was blood. She turned to see from whom it came. One of the fighters, who was attacking Mandy, was now bleeding profusely. That was very encouraging, she thought.

Alison now had Ellineana Evenstar freed; she was also an elf, scantily clad, but none the worse for her ordeal. Seeing Elrohir buckling up his gear brought her instant relief, a bit of normalcy. "Where's my stuff? Where are all my magic wands?" she asked. Father Johnas did his best to explain the situation to her.

Alison hearing "magic" word, quickly asked, "Magic user?" The elf nodded affirmative, though she also added softly, "and priestess." Father Johnas smiled at that.

"Here, use my staff of power, not many charges left, so absorb some as fast as you can. Here catch this one," and she shot a spell toward the elf, who sucked it into the staff. "Darless, come free this Valadmir Velacoffskii fellow." Alison headed around the wall of force to join the fray.

The two elves now appeared by her side. One glance at the fighters told them all was going well with them. Mandy had slain one of her opponents and was about to finish off the other. Lonnie had one nearly gone. Sir Thomas finished one of his off even as they watched. Darless was walking backwards, maintaining her fist spell on the opposing wizard as long as she could. As she passed Alison, she handed Alison her staff. "You need it more than I do at the moment. Watch that wizard, he's on to the wall. Priest is doing something." As she slipped behind the wall, her giant fist disappeared.

Darless took a deep breath, cleared her mind and began the lengthy freedom spell. Father Johnas moved to her side, readying his healing spell just in case. He thought, *Elves have a remarkable makeup. All this time being imprisoned has not really bothered them all that much as far as I can see. Interesting.*

The evil priest's spell activated just as two more fighters appeared on the pentagram. The priest had opened a larger gate to the Abyss. Alison saw two huge vulture-like forms appearing. *Not them again!* she thought to herself, but matters took a turn for the worse. Even as Alison shot a huge volley of missiles at the vulture demons, the priest, and the mage, she watched them bounce harmlessly off of the two men. The demon creatures were hit, but ignored them; they were concentrating on using their own native abilities to gate in others of their kind.

"Zagroot zounds," Mandy exclaimed breathlessly. She had just eliminated the second fighter, who had attacked her, and she helped Sir Lonnie dispatch his second opponent. Sir Thomas finished his second one at nearly the same time. The three fighters took a needed moment's break to catch their breath. "Looks like you get your wish, Sir Thomas, you now got nasty demons to fight!"

The two new fighters moved into defensive positions in front of the mage and the priest; they took no offensive action. They were following their orders. For a moment, neither side did anything, save survey the other, which was exactly what the raiders greatly desired. The gates continued to activate, now there were six vulture demons, then twelve, then twenty four. As they continued to arrive, the mage shot a counter-spell at the wall of force. What he did not realize was that there were two walls. His spell only eliminated one. The other leaned and began to fall down on top of Father Johnas and Darless. The priest and Rufus reacted quickly and held it up with their hands. Now Darless's spell culminated and the form of a very, very large man began rising from the stone.

Seeing that their companion was appearing, both elves gave a quick chant and several of the fallen fighters blades began sliding across the floor over to the elves. Alison realized that they were obtaining some weapons for this Valadmir fellow. She decided that it was now time for some serious dispelling of magic protections. She began casting her dispel magic spell. First, she concentrated on the mage. Each time, she detected some protective spell of his dissipate. With weapons at hand, the two elves also began chanting, following Alison's lead, they shot theirs at the priest, double teaming him. Even more rapidly, his protective spells vanished. More importantly, the vulture demons were now having their gating spells disrupted as well.

Their mage once again attempted to shoot missiles this time at Darless, who nearly had Valadmir freed. He was rather surprised to see them bounce off of the second wall of force. Grimacing, he once again cast the counter-spell. Suddenly, Rufus felt nothing in his hands. "I guess it's gone now," exclaimed Father Johnas, "Watch my back, Rufus — got to heal Valadmir."

Valadmir was a huge man with enormous muscles. He looked like a wild man, though, with long hair and beard, clad in a leather loin cloth. The priest tried to break the news of what was happening to the man, but he only grunted, looked around, spied the elves, who saw that he was freed. They sent a pair of swords his way.

Valadmir grunted once more, got up unsteadily on his feet. Father Johnas cast his heal spell on the man anyway. The huge man grinned, nodded approval, grabbed the swords and charged full blast toward the demons. The elves now followed him and closed upon the nearest demons.

Alison had planned to order a retreat back down the tunnel as soon as Valadmir was rescued. She thought that there were just too many of these powerful vulture demons for them to fight. However, the newly freed trio charged straightaway into the melee. Seeing them charge, Mandy and the two paladins joined them. Now six of the demons were under attack. That left the other eighteen free. Their priest ordered loudly, "Gate more!" The eighteen vulture demons bellowed and began their chants, following orders.

"Oh dear, oh dear," exclaimed Rufus. The tiny gnome was dwarfed by these creatures. He was more afraid of being accidentally stepped upon than anything else. Eighteen times two, seemed a rather large number to him. Thus, he fired off his wand, directing its rays at the chanting demons. Six charges he used in rapid fire succession, then aimed a seventh at their priest and mage. Alison, who had just launched her last dispel magic that she had available, saw the gnome's wand activating, but saw no immediate fireworks. She wondered what he had done.

One demon had scored a direct hit on Sir Lonnie, who fell to the floor from the force of the blow. The huge creature lunged forward to stomp on him when a tiny beam of energy from Darless removed the top half of its head. The instantly dead body swayed this way and that before it collapsed to the ground with Sir Lonnie crawling like mad to get out of its way.

Alison now saw that something weird was going on. Several of the demons began arguing with each other and quickly they began fighting each other. The mage started screaming at the demons. Several other nearby demons began yelling obscenities at the mage. Their priest cast a hold monster spell on several of the fighting demons, temporarily halting their argument or brawl. But then two others got mad at the priest for having done that and began attacking the priest. Next, two others began attacking those that were screaming at the mage, so three more attacked those two. Next, three more came to the defense of the priest and began tearing away at those attacking the priest. The priest now was screaming orders until Alison shot a simple spell that clamped his mouth shut. He was not looking her way and took the spell full force. The mage, now in a rage, began to chant a dispel magic spell to counter Alison's, but Ellineana paused briefly in her battle with her demon to point her finger at the mage and hit him with several magical missiles. He didn't see what hit him, assumed it was the nearest demon, and he whirled around and blasted it with a volley of his own missiles. The neighboring demon then trounced on top of the magic user and began jumping up and down on him, until his body was pulp.

Father Johnas, seeing the time was right, cast a hold person spell on the opposing priest, who had completely ignored Father Johnas, because he was desperately trying to regain control over the demons. Instantly, the priest froze mid-action, like a statue. A nearby demon accidentally bumped into him and knocked him over.

Suddenly it was over. First one demon, seeing all was lost, seeing that the opposing fighters had just killed five of their kind, simply gated home, back to the Abyss. As soon as one left, the others said something that sounded rather like "Huh?" and they too gated home. In less than a minute, all that remained was the frozen priest and a number of dead bodies. The remains of the two body guards were found trampled to death by the chaotic demons.

"Yahoo!" yelled Mandy. "We got them! Congratulations everyone. Oh yes, welcome, you three," she said to the elves and barbarian, "Mandy Blackthorn, your friendly neighborhood Ranger of Reylona, at your service."

A deep bellowing howl joined her victory chant. Valadmir, who had discarded these inferior black blades, had wrestled and pummeled his demon with his bare hands and eventually he had broken its neck by sheer muscle power. He was standing on its chest, arms upraised, adding his war hoop to that of Mandy's. He was, however, bleeding from several claw marks across his back where the demon in vain had attempted to dislodge him. Ellineana moved quickly to his side, chanted briefly and touched him. His bleeding stopped and the wounds slowly disappeared. "Last one I had — was saving it," she said to Elrohir. The other elf nodded.

Father Johnas walked around the bodies to get over to the priest that his spell still held. "Well, we've captured their priest or maybe leader. Not sure."

"Verily, let me disarm him, Father," Sir Thomas hurried over to him, "remember the drill." Quickly, the paladin began removing rings, amulets, bracers, mace — anything that could possibly be useful or a weapon. Satisfied, he said, "Okay. Release him." The priest cancelled his spell. The enemy priest stirred, looked about at the one-sided carnage, and lowered his head. His raid had been a complete failure.

"Who are you and why are you attacking us?" questioned Sir Thomas. He added, "Remember, Father Johnas, here, can tell if you are lying or not." He didn't bother to add that Johnas had not yet had time to cast that spell. The others heard Johnas quickly praying.

"I am Eldrich, now ex-High Priest of Lord Jarred, supreme ruler of the Abyss." He sneered, "Our purpose was rather obvious don't you think? We came here to kill you all — Lord Jarred's orders."

Sir Thomas remembered that Alison was still the leader of the party, so he asked her, "What do you want us to do with him? Take him back with us and put him on trial for all of his crimes against humanity?"

This was not something Alison was ready for — one part of being the party's leader that she had mostly ignored. For a moment she was at a complete loss about what to do with him. Stand trial sounded good, but no one knew what his crimes actually were. What should she do, she wondered.

Darless, on the other hand, had had a good deal of experience with the Abyss, having lived there in her childhood. She picked up on what the priest had said, "ex-High Priest." She knew what that meant. She spoke up, "Alison, perhaps the best thing to do with him is to send him back to the Abyss to face his leader's wrath. Perhaps have him deliver a message to Lord Jarred, say from his slayer on this plane, Archmage Darless, Holy Paladin of Ukko."

When he heard those words, he visibly shook from fear, not from the alu-demon, but from who she was. If he was very, very lucky, Lord Jarred would slay him instantly as he spoke the message.

Alison saw him flinch and smiled, "Say also, that Lord Jarred should be wary. Saint Jon Brown, the Redeemer, is now after him. So beware."

On hearing those words, he whined and sank to his knees. "Please, please don't send me back. I'll do anything you ask. Put me into prison. Put me on trial, I'll plead guilty to whatever you charge. Just don't send me back to Lord Jarred this way! Have pity on me."

"What pity did you show us?" countered Alison. "No, you have made your own future. Now live it. Put him on the pentagram." Sir Thomas dragged the struggling priest, still pleading and begging for mercy, to the desired spot. Nodding to Alison, he pressed the jewel activation button and quickly stepped back out of the way. In a few seconds, the man's wailing and begging ceased, he was back in the Abyss, his home.

"Now then, who here needs some healing?" asked Father Johnas. He need not have asked, the three fighters were all three sorely in need of healing. He went about it methodically, healing each, until he ran out of spells. Then, Darless and Mandy took over using their cell adjusting skills. By then, everyone was in pretty good shape.

"What a mess. Now we got all these dead demons and men to dispose of," complained Mandy. "I don't think we want them lying around here. We still have seven more people to free."

"I know," Darless smiled. "First search them and them drag them over to me here by the pentagram." Grinning, Mandy caught on to what Darless had in mind. The others quickly began a thorough search of the fallen, tossing anything of value to one side. It took three strong people to drag one of the vulture demons. Thankfully, the pentagram was not a raised dais but merely built into the stone floor. When each was fully on the pentagram, Darless pushed the activation button sending the dead back into the Abyss. Lord Jarred would get some reminders. It took them a half hour to send all the dead back to the Demon Lord.

"Now, you three need some introductions," Alison finally said. "I am Archmage Alison d'Ambrose, Holy Mage of Ukko, leader of this party." One by one, she introduced the others and then named the others back at the mansion. She explained that Archmage Sarah was now dead and that their gear was likely in a nearby room. They only had to claim what was theirs.

After the lengthy introductions, Elrohir introduced his small group. He was a wood elf from the northern reaches of the Greenway. He was not only an accomplished fighter but also an even more powerful magic user. Elrohir was really an archer, but would use swords at close quarters such as this. Ellineana was a grey elf from East Havens, located near the southern edge of the Druse Woods. She was both a priest and a mage and had served as their party's healer. Valadmir was a barbarian from the Northern Steppes, whom they had befriended some years back. They were the sole survivors of a raiding party, who had discovered Lord Jarred's stronghold at Hoar Frost and attempted to destroy it some sixty years ago. They had underestimated the size of the stronghold. They had been captured and the rest was history.

They all headed to the gear room to locate what still remained of their gear. Needless to say, it took nearly a half hour for them to find everything. Once that was handled, they all left the tower and entered the mansion to meet the others, to clean up, and to feed their rescued new friends who were exceedingly hungry. On their way, Alison finally remembered Rufus. "Say, I saw you use your wand back in the battle. What did it do? It was after you used your wand that all the chaos broke loose."

He chuckled, "I thought that things were getting a little out of hand. My wand just introduced a little more chaos into the picture, if you know what I mean. Sort of confused them." She did and gave him a rather stern look, though she did not say anything yet. "I only use it as a last resort," he added hastily, for he guessed that she was about to say that the confusion could have just as easily worked against her party.

Instead, she said, "Well, thanks, you saved the day, Rufus." He smiled appreciatively.

After eating their fill, the elves and barbarian longed for any news of what was currently happening. Alison did her best to relate what she knew, but it wasn't much. Neither she nor her friends had ever been that far north.

Resolved to having to find out for themselves about the current state up north, Ellineana said, "In the morning, after we restudy our spells, we will teleport Valadmir back to his lands and see for ourselves what changes have occurred. We are eternally in your debt. If ever we can repay you in any way, you only have to let us know. I live not far from your new town, Alison, though when I last passed that way, it was an empty green land. Will be nice to see your town."

After seeing to their guest's needs, Alison finally had time to ask Jon and Thea how her parents were doing. His reply was highly encouraging to her, "Great progress, I think. A lot of pain and grief dissolved today, I think. I know they are most anxious to hear more of your story tonight."

First, everyone took a turn in the bathroom cleaning up. Next came dinner. Finally, over tea, Alison began relating the next part of her adventure to find her parents. She began with the attack on her life by the Chasme demon swarm that nearly killed her. Her dad made her repeat several times just how it was that Jon and Mandy came to her dungeon home in time to rescue her. Jon filled in some details. "There is a connection between us, somehow," he tried to explain, "I just knew something bad had happened to her and came at once." Both her parents stared at each other for a minute, thinking the same thing. Jon didn't know what that was and didn't ask.

She described how Lady Ursla had been instrumental in healing her and how the others had greatly helped. Her father had never heard of healing by using one's mind and had Mandy, Darless and Jon try to explain it to him. They were not very successful. Then, Alison described how they had figured out what the true path of the demon bug swarm was and had set off to track them down. Alison next hesitatingly explained her "nightmares" that nearly ruined her entire career and life. Each morning at the same time the attack had come, she became temporarily insane. Her mother gasped and her father lowered his head. Alison explained what Jon had done using his "therapy" and what the results had been, complete erasure of the nightmares. "That's what Jon and Thea are doing with you two. When they get done, hopefully none of this will leave any permanent mark on you either."

She then described their ride across the country after the demons, arriving at the abandoned Leeds Tower. She had to explain the part about how Jon had detected the imprisoned Air Maiden, Fruella, several times. When Basil heard that they had actually freed an Air Maiden of Ukko, his opinion of his daughter rose enormously! Then came the battle with the High Priest of Metrarch and the demons, just like the ones they fought today. Both her parents cried when she got to the part where they were all nearly dead and suddenly found themselves being gated into the Abyss. Her father, in particularly, cringed; it brought back all his images of the foul place when he went there to steal back the Holy Scepter of Ukko, which had, in fact, caused all of the rest of the events in his life to occur.

Both parents stared at Darless, when they heard that she had swan dived into the gate to be with her friends and try to save them. Darless blushed. Alison described how Jon had healed them all during the short gating transit into the Abyss. Basil halted the story at this point, demanding to know just how Jon had managed this.

"Well, it's more exciting to find out as we did, bit by bit," Jon teased. Seeing that Basil was not amused, Jon said, "That walking stick I picked up was none other than the Holy Scepter of Ukko, in disguise. It has an intelligence of its own. It even spoke to me on occasion, but none of us knew that then nor even suspected it."

"You found the Holy Scepter of Ukko!" he exclaimed, standing up. He was truly amazed and very excited. "Come, please, just tell me what happened to that most holy relic. I must know now!"

"You are getting way ahead of our story, dad, but if you must know, Jon personally handed it to Father Ukko, when we next visited him. Ukko gave Jon his current walking stick in return. Satisfied?" she asked.

"You hear that, Anna?" the man said beside himself with happiness. "The Holy Scepter is back in Ukko's hands! All praise be to Father Ukko! And our Alison, or Jon, rather, did it. Personally?" Suddenly the magnitude of Alison's words sunk in. "You were in his realm?" She nodded. Basil sank back down, completely overawed at his own daughter. Meekly, he said, "Please continue, Allie."

She then described their meeting with Metrarch and Dispater and the subsequent bargain that yielded them another picture book and her brother, Lennard, who was hopelessly ill and totally insane from twenty years as a prisoner in the Abyss. Both parents cried over the fate of their son. She described how she had taken him to Lady Ursla, the Great Druid, and how she had healed his physical body, but could do nothing for his insanity. For the benefit of her parents peace of mind, she jumped way ahead in her story to explain what Jon's therapy utilized by Darless had accomplished with Lenny during the winter months. He was now back to being a happy young boy interested in raising bees. Both parents were greatly relieved and both prolifically thanked Jon and Darless. Jon could see the respect her parents had for him and Darless was growing by the minute.

At long last, she got to the council at Freetown or Twinstown. She delightedly told of running into Mat and May. She spent an hour telling them all about how the twins had survived and began changing the town's unlawful nature. However, it was getting late so she ended here. "Tomorrow night, you will hear about the redemption of Metrarch at the hands of Jon. I think this is why Father Ukko has named him 'the Redeemer,' though I am only guessing." Both parents stared long and hard at Jon, until he became red faced and excused himself to use the restroom.

Needless to say, both of her parents worked even harder during the next day's therapy sessions, particularly now that they had some idea of the great benefits it had. Actually, when Alison entered the mansion for supper, she found both of her parents laughing nearly continuously. First one would utter something, which would set them both laughing, and then after they quieted down, the other would mutter some trivial statement, trivial as far as Alison could tell, setting them both laughing once more. Their cheerfulness really changed the mood around the supper table and for the entire evening.

This morning, the elves and Valadmir prepared to leave. Alison insisted that they take several hundred gold pieces each as traveling money. Thea gave them a grub sack with food for several days, just in case they ran into trouble. After exchanging information about how to locate each other, they all shook hands; and then the elves teleported themselves and the big barbarian back up to the northern wastes from which Valadmir came.

The others next assembled in the tunnel just outside of the Chamber of Horrors once more. "Today, first up is one Francine Stillwater; she's been trapped here something like fifty-five years, something like five years after the elves," explained Alison. "And then a pair who have been here for about forty years are next, a Johannes Alvarade and Rebecca Tuthill. So Father Johnas, should we be prepared for another attack today?"

"Well, if my commune spell worked, for once, we should not be bothered with surprises, at least I hope so," he answered, voice full of encouragement. He cast his protective spells upon those that needed such and they once more entered the chamber. The odor of yesterday's battle was still strong and pungent. Still, it was better than the stench that the lich had created.

Alison cast her freedom spell and soon Francine appeared up out of the stone floor. She was weak and dehydrated, and she had obviously been tortured for information. This time, the priest's healing spell was greatly needed. Sir Thomas carried her out of the chamber and Darless gave her a water flask. Once she drank as much as the priest thought best, he explained who they were and when it was.

The woman, disoriented at best, tried to grasp what he was saying. At last, confident that these people would not hurt her, she offered, "I, I'm Francine Stillwater, a Healer Priest of Tannersville. I had gone for a foray here by the mountains looking for various healing herbs when I came across this tower. I did not know someone had built a tower out here in the middle of nowhere, so I went to investigate. There was this Evil Woman, I think she called herself Sarah. She was meeting with another man, a demon I believe; he had horns. When he saw me looking at him, both of them went ballistic. I do not understand why. They tortured me, beat me — kept asking me for whom I was spying — why was I here, they didn't believe me for the longest time. Then, when they finally accepted the fact that I was herb hunting, the man insisted that I should never leave here. Something about my having seen him here greatly alarmed him. She imprisoned me here. I begged her to know why it was so important that I not tell and who this demon was. I even asked her why she did not outright kill me to keep me quiet. Only that question did she answer. 'You may yet be useful to me one day.' That was all I remember before everything went utterly blank."

She paused, then added, "Well, that is not quite all. When she was not looking, doing her spell casting, I managed to get off a prayer to Lord Hector. He told me that I had seen the Demon Lord Metrarch and that now he knew about it thanks to me. He said for me not to worry, I would be all right and he would arrange for my rescue. Did Lord Hector send you?"

"Er, no, I'm sorry," Alison replied, "We came to rescue my parents, actually. We are all followers of Father Ukko, but who knows the workings of gods," she added. "Lord Hector may have worked out something with Ukko." This explanation seemed to satisfy the healer.

"I could use something to eat," she became more aware of her body every minute. That was a good sign.

"We'll take you outside to our magical mansion. There you can eat all that you desire and rest and regain your strength," Alison told her. "On the way out, there is this room that has tons of people's possessions in it. We can stop there and let you see if you can find your stuff."

"Really?" she asked in disbelief. "I thought I'd never see my priestly artifacts ever again." Sir Thomas helped her to her feet and then let her lean on him for support. Soon, she was searching about the room full of possessions. It took her fully forty-five minutes to locate her few, but treasured items. She had a golden holy symbol, several magical rings, a rod and a staff. She found her back pack still the way she had left it some fifty-five years ago. The herbs she had already gathered were, of course, totally dried out.

When she had her things, Father Johnas asked, "Do you have family back in Tannersville or those who may have greatly missed you, loved ones?" He was searching for the impact that the long imprisonment might have on her. Was she married? Children? It could be rather upsetting and confusing for her if she did.

"Not really," she said rather downhearted. "I donated my life for the good of Tannersville and the Church. When I am not doing my healer duties, I teach school, or rather I used to teach school. I don't suppose I can do that anymore."

"Sure you can, kids still need to learn to read and write and compute figures," encouraged Alison. "That has not changed. Your only weakness now would be history, and that you can catch up on rapidly I think."

Hearing Alison's words, did cheer her up a bit. Perhaps it was not going to be so bad after all, but so much time had gone by. No one would recognize her, would they even remember her? Then her faith in Lord Hector returned. She was still his priest. He would look after her. She held her head high as she walked out of the tower, a free woman, a free priest.

After seeing to Francine's immediate needs, and after having Thea, who was on a break from her therapy sessions with Anna, cast a number of spells into her staff to recharge it, Alison was ready to head back to the chamber. When they were all reassembled, she said, "Now that was rather nice; no surprises, no ambushes, no attacking demons. I hope our luck holds."

It did. Since both Johannes and Rebecca had been imprisoned nearly at the same time, the mages decided to rescue them both at the same time. Since no attacks had come when they had freed Francine, they assumed none would be forth coming today. After all, they had delivered a significant setback to the demons yesterday. Thus, ten minutes later, both Johannes and Rebecca appeared on the stone floor of the chamber.

Rebecca at once looked over at Johannes, weakly she advised, "He's a bard. She cut out his tongue. He can't talk." Both showed signs of having been in a desperate battle that had gone ill for them, but their injuries were not life-threatening. Methodically, Father Johnas went about his task of healing their physical wounds. As expected, both were weak from their long imprisonment.

"I'm sorry that I cannot do anything for his tongue, my child. At least his body is now otherwise healed of its wounds," the priest explained. He went on to tell them about their rescue party and the demise of the woman who had imprisoned them. Finally, he told them how much time had passed. The bard, who was thirty-five, made gurgling sounds, but could not speak. A great sorrow came over him. For him, this was a fate worse than death. Everyone could sense his despair. She, who had great sympathy for the afflicted bard, was thirty.

"I am Rebecca Tuthill; I was or may be still am, I'm not too sure, a High Priestess of Reylona. He's a famous bard, Johannes Alvarade. We are both from Greyton." She saw the totally blank stares and quickly added, "It's a large town far to the south of here. I assume we are still in the tower near Desolation. We were part of a great expedition to the Hoar Frost. Our forces were dedicated to the removal of the demonic influences there. We rather underestimated their forces, though, and were soundly defeated. When this Evil Mage found out that he and I were the most powerful members of the assaulting force, she imprisoned us, saying one day she might yet have a use for us. Johannes refused to bed her, so in spite, she cut out his tongue. It is horrible. A bard is known for his singing, his music. She has ruined, destroyed his entire life." Tears of sympathy trickled down her face.

Darless retrieved a small pouch of rings that she kept safe in her bosom. She picked out one particular ring and quietly went over to the bard. She put the ring on his finger, magically it enlarged to fit his big fingers. Then, she whispered in his ear, "Wear this ring at all times for the next few days and you will have a new tongue, you'll be good as new. You can give me the ring back when you have regrown your tongue." Shock and surprise filled his eyes as he looked up at her. He tried to speak, but of course couldn't. She added, "You can thank me properly later when you are recovered."

Everyone could see the hope flooding back into the man, where none had been before. All wanted to know what Darless had done. "Oh just a little something. We'll see how well it works in time." That was all she would say. The ring was in fact Metrarch's specially modified ring of vampiric regeneration, a rather unholy ring at best.

On their way out of the tower, they stopped at the room of possessions and let these two try to find all of their gear. It took them about an hour to find everything. The bard had a portable hole filled with musical instruments as well as swords and other equipment. He also had a large flask of wine, which was now totally soured.

Soon these two were sitting at the kitchen table eating their fill. Francine had finished earlier and was now taking a nap, still recovering. The bard found it difficult to eat properly without his tongue and was very embarrassed. Rebecca kept comforting him, encouraging him. However, after she was full and had sat back to relax, the reality of her situation smacked her rather hard.

She had left two young sons at home. Now they would be middle aged. Would they even recognize her? She had missed out on their entire lives. She began crying softly to herself, pitying her awful plight, her doomed fate. It was all Lord Jed's fault. He had insisted — no, had ordered her to go on this quest. She wailed. Of course, Father Johnas had been expecting this sort of reaction to occur to one or more of those that were freed. He immediately went into action.

"There, there my child, it is not as bad as you might think. One must always have hope. Now, tell me all about this Lord Jed and what he ordered you to do."

Everyone listened to her brief tale. She had been opposed to taking the strongest men at arms away from the town and castle and sending them on this quest way up north. In fact, he had actually been forced to deliver her a direct order to accompany the war party. Ever curious, Darless asked her what his full name was. "Lord Jed Rar. Well, he was Lord Jed Rarold, but he was very sick last year — no I guess I mean a long time ago now. It was about a year before we all marched up here that he took ill. Then one day, he miraculously recovered, but he seemed a different man after his near death sickness. He even shortened his name, claiming he was not old anymore. Shortened it to just Rar. Illness can do that to a man, I'm told."

Darless muttered, "Lord Jed Rar, Lord Jed Rar." Suddenly she jumped up, "Oh my goodness, he did it again! Hey everyone, what else can you make from these letters, Lord Jed Rar?" She didn't wait before answering her own question. "Lord Jarred! He's done it again!" Various curses echoed about the room. Darless then went on to explain how Lord Jarred had disguised himself as a merchant and started a war between the dwarves and Vyndocians, a war that nearly annihilated both groups. "You've been betrayed by the Demon Lord himself, Rebecca. I think you have a new purpose. You have got to return to your town and set matters right, if they have not already been rectified!"

She sat there rather stunned, absorbing all that Darless said. "Well, darn. Now it all makes sense. It is so clear to me now! Why didn't I see through it back then? Well, just as soon as we recover our strength, Johannes and I must head home and see what ill has befallen our town. How can we ever thank you enough for all you have done?" Now this was more like it, thought Father Johnas feeling rather pleased with her new goals and purposes. Having and following a strong, worthwhile purpose, he felt was the key to a holy and satisfying life.

She yawned and now felt sleepy, so Alison helped her to make a comfortable spot in which to doze. The bard, scratching at his neck, also joined her for a nap. Fortunately, the therapy sessions going on were relatively quiet ones now and would not disturb the sleeping folks.

"Well, we still have half a day left," Alison mused. "What should we all do?"

"I still have quite a few healing spells left," Father Johnas answered. "Perhaps we could rescue another person?"

"I can utilize the energy in my staff and do it," Darless seconded the idea.

"Yes, let's go for it," added Mandy. With no fighting going on, she found all this magical rescuing work rather boring. The sooner all were rescued, the sooner they could all return home. Besides, she found herself missing William rather badly.

As they paused by the entrance to the chamber, the priest said, "I'm rather short on the protective spells. I wasn't watching them all that closely. I'm afraid I cannot protect everyone this time."

"You don't need to do me, I can use my mind to compensate," Alison declared.

"Me too," put in Mandy.

"Me three," teased Rufus, "I can manage without. Make sure the holy paladins get it. We may need them to fight. You never know about demons, they are unpredictable." Darless thought that was a gross understatement, but kept her mouth shut.

Within a few minutes, Darless had Herbart Von Schultz freed and resting upon the stone floor. No surprise attacks came. However, there was a different problem. Herbart had been tortured and his body showed the usual signs of Sarah's ultimate torture, imprisonment while in pain. However, the man also had two prominent horns protruding from his head, was dressed entirely in black leather clothing, and sported a long tail with a little bush of hair at its tip. Herbart was some kind of devil! Faintly, Rufus's "Oops!" echoed in the still chamber, and reflected everyone's immediate reaction.

Father Johnas, who, as usual, was the first to reach the side of the freed person, suddenly faced a moral dilemma. From the priest's viewpoint, he based his life and actions on Law and Good. Yet here was nearly his opposite, a devil, which stood for Evil. Well, true, they likewise stood for Law and Order, but they were anything but Good. Should he attempt to heal this devil who obviously needed healing. Had they errored in some way? Could Father Ukko have made a mistake? All these questions suddenly flooded his mind, preventing any immediate action on his part. At that moment, his memories of a conversation he had had with Jon several days ago replayed in his mind. *We are all spiritual beings. There is an infinity of good just as there is an infinity of evil; it is a gradient scale. In this world, absolute good and absolute evil are not achievable by us. A man doing more evil than good, I have found, used to do good, but something happened to him and he can no longer trust himself. He has lost his self-respect.* "I am Father Johnas, Holy Priest of Ukko. Here, first let me heal your grievous wounds," and he chanted his prayer to Ukko.

The devil raised his eyebrows. "What's this?" he wondered. "How is it that a priest of Ukko is healing the likes of me? Well, I do need it at the moment. Thank you, Holy Priest." The healing aura flowed over the devil and his wounds began healing rapidly. Ukko had granted his prayer, that was very hopeful sign to the priest.

Feeling better about his decision, he continued, "You have been freed from your imprisonment by Archmages Alison and Darless, Holy Mage and Holy Paladin of Ukko. As far as we can tell, you have been trapped here for about twenty-five years."

"I see. Well I am in deeply in your debt," he nodded, since he was still sitting on the stone floor. "Two archmages?" his eyebrows raised once more. "I am Herbart Von Schultz, but you already know that to have freed me. I am a devil from Hell, but you already know that. I serve the Lord Dispater. I came here to spy on

Archmage Sarah le'Garde. Unfortunately for me, I was discovered and summarily imprisoned. Well, she did give me a choice: be killed outright or be entrapped. Not much of a choice, if you ask me, which she didn't. But, say, I have one question for you, did Dispater send you to rescue me?"

Here, Alison stepped forward, she would have rather had Jon be present to answer, for he was the one who had the dealings with Dispater. So strong was her thoughts about having Jon here, that he picked up her intention. "Well, it is true that we have met Dispater on several occasions. As far as I know, Dispater has never mentioned you or that you needed rescuing. But Saint Jon Brown, the Redeemer, has been the one talking with Dispater. He may be able to answer you more fully."

At that moment right on cue had it been planned, Jon suddenly appeared in the chamber. "I got the idea you needed me?" he asked Alison and looked at the devil, who had recovered sufficiently to get to his feet. She quickly explained to Jon what had happened thus far.

However, Herbart stared wide-eyed at Jon as if Jon was some kind of god or supernatural being. Jon stepped over to him, "Hi, I am Saint Jon Brown, pleased to meet you — thus far anyway. No, Dispater has never mentioned you, sorry." He held out his hand to shake the devil's hand. Very hesitatingly, as if unsure whether or not to meet his hand, the devil extended his.

He finally spoke in an awed voice, "Then it is true! You have come just like Dispater prophesied! I am humbled to be in your presence!" and he bowed as low as he could safely manage, a sign of the greatest respect, though none of those present realized the significance of his gesture. He shook hands with Jon and added, "That you actually have chosen to shake *my* hand is one of the most momentous occasions of my entire life! I shall cherish this moment forever."

Most of the others were completely stunned by the devil's seemingly sincere and deeply felt remarks. However, Jon was dismayed, he had no idea what the devil was talking about. What had Dispater prophesied anyway? What had it to do with him? Here was a person who had been imprisoned for the last twenty-five years, and yet knew of the existence of Saint Jon Brown, probably before Jon was even born! The devil continued, "And would you, Saint Jon, offer redemption to me right here and now if I asked it of you?"

Redemption? Is he talking about my therapy? Jon thought, trying to understand what the devil was saying or alluding to. *Help Darless! Is he talking about our therapy sessions?* he sent to her.

I'm as dumbfounded as you are, Jon. But that must be what he is asking about, must be, she sent back.

So Jon took a gamble and replied, "As I see it, we are all spiritual beings, we all have minds full of images of everything we have ever done. Some of these gain power and control over us, dictating our actions. I'm not sure how just yet. Anyone can be redeemed as you put it, they only have to be willing to see what they have done, to look at what is really there in their own mental images. It is a simple thing, but one which most of us cannot do all by ourselves, or we would have redeemed ourselves long ago. If this is what you mean, then, my answer is yes. However, just now, I have my hands full with others, but if you want it, come by Darless' college, say half a year from now when it is fully built, and we'll do what we can at that time. Dispater can tell you how to find it." True enough, Jon was not familiar with this world to be able to give directions on how to find Alison's new town. He had no idea how to explain to this devil how he could manage to get around using his mental powers, and he certainly did not want to put Alison on the spot and have her divulge the location of her new town to her potential enemies.

To everyone's utter amazement, a tear of joy trickled down the devil's right cheek. He bowed low to thank Jon. "I will indeed, if it is possible. I may be tied up with other duties, but I will plan on it. And now, I must be on my way. Say, by any chance is my trident still around? It is about twelve feet long, prongs on one end?"

Utterly confused, Alison grasped onto this request; it was something she understood. "Yes, everyone's gear appears to be stored in one nearby room. We'll show you on the way out."

"Thank you again, honorable Holy Mage," he bowed to her, "but I only need your permission to retrieve my things." He spoke a command word and presto, his trident and net, along with a backpack stuffed with sundry items, floated from the storage room into his outstretched hands. "And now I should be off, I seem to be quite late in reporting back, some twenty-five years too late."

"Wait a minute, please. What do you mean about Dispater's prophecy? What prophecy? What is this all about? I wasn't even born that long ago," Jon finally managed to utter what had totally confused him about this conversation.

"Oh, perhaps I have said too much; perhaps I have errored by even speaking to you. Oh dear me. I do hope Dispater is not displeased with my actions here!" He looked positively startled by Jon's questions. "I'd best say no more. You can ask Dispater about it sometime. Yes, that is the best answer, ask Dispater. And now I had best be going. Oh yes, I am deeply indebted to you for your rescue. If there is ever anything I can do to repay the favor, just call on me. Thank you once more." He snapped his fingers and vanished leaving a tiny cloud of sulfur floating in the air where he had just stood.

"What — what just happened with this devil? Does anyone know what he was talking about? What prophesy?" Jon asked just as confused as before.

"Jon, I'm sure I don't have even the slightest idea what he was talking about," Alison consoled him.

"Jon, that has to be the most unnerving conversation I have ever heard," Darless added. "Truly, I have no idea what he was talking about, but he seemed believable and totally in awe and totally sincere. Devils are lawful in nature, so I don't think he was playing mind games with you. But how he knew of you some twenty-five years ago, golly, this is mind-boggling. I promise you, Jon, that I will research this we get back home. I'm just as confused as you are."

Father Johnas shook his head, "His words took me by total surprise as well, Jon. I've no idea what he is alluding to either. This has been a strange day; do you realize that I have actually cast a healing spell upon a devil? What I find even stranger is that Father Ukko wanted us to free *this* devil. Either that or we somehow made a mistake."

A sudden panic came over Alison. She got out the ledger and the parchment and compared the two lists. Relieved, she said, "No, his name is definitely on the list to free, Father. We are doing as Ukko has bidden us; no mistake that I can see."

"Well, Saint Jon," the priest declared, "strange things occur around you, that's for sure."

"But I am just a musician," his protest fell on deaf ears.

"Come on, let's head back to the mansion. I think we've done all that we can do for today, unless some of you want to continue sorting out the treasury room," Alison pronounced. She had too much to think over now. Did Dispater know about Jon? How? Was there some devilish plan in the works? Herbart's news was definitely unsettling her.

Jon returned to his therapy session with Basil. The three mages poured over other documents that they lifted from the magical study room, looking for any information that might clarify anything. Mandy and the paladins, accompanied by Rufus, continued to sort through the enormous mountain of treasure, attempting to get it fully ready for transport.

Father Johnas retired to a very quiet corner just outside the walls of the village and prayed to Father Ukko for some guidance; he was still somewhat confused. In his head, he heard the voice of Ukko responding with a solitary, simple statement, "He brings redemption for us all." The priest was left to ponder its significance. He noted that Ukko has used the phrase "us all." That would include himself, perhaps the greatest among the gods. This was unsettling for him.

When the mages came into the mansion for dinner, both of Alison's parents were laughing gaily. She knew that Jon and Thea had been quite successful. If she had doubts about her parent's mental state after their long imprisonment, they were dispelled by hearing the sound of their laughter. She gave both Jon and Thea a huge hug. "Thank you both! It is just incredible what you have done for them."

All that evening Father Johnas kept a careful eye on Basil and Anna, marking and noting the many changes that had occurred to their personalities, their outlooks on life and other factors he considered their imprisonment could have on their long-term well-being. He constantly found that mention of certain events, which he expected to cause both of them much heartache and pain, now was of no great concern to them. By the end of the evening, it struck him that perhaps the qualifier "redeemed" may be placed upon them, and the priest thought long and hard about the significance of this.

Over dinner, Darless asked the bard, Johannes, how he was doing. To the complete shock of everyone present, he replied, "Well pretty good actually. It is definitely working." He had a slight lisp, for the new tongue was not completely full-sized. "I owe you my life,

Archmage Darless of the coal black eyes and raven hair!"
He was a lady's man at heart, he was an entertainer, and
he knew how to treat a woman, especially those of a royal
court.

"You should be back to normal by morning,"
Darless replied. The others had stopped eating and were
gaping at the two. Yesterday he had no tongue, but this
evening he did. "Oh just a little of Darless' magic, that's
all," she cleverly said. Everyone accepted her explanation,
everyone, that is, except Alison.

She whispered, "You did didn't you?" Darless
merely smiled back at her, but eventually gave her a nod
to the affirmative.

When everyone was relaxing with their after-
dinner tea, Alison continued her tale from where she had
left off the previous evening. She told of their meetings
with Metrarch in Freetown and of the assassination
attempt on Metrarch at the council. She described the
charging demonic armies, whose goal was the capture of
the main town well. With the help of Mat and May, she
told how they had discovered the history of the town, how
it had been founded by followers of Father Ukko as a
bastion of hope amid the surrounding lands devoted to
demonic activities. The discovery of the ancient
mechanism for the defense of the town fascinated Basil
and she had to dwell at length on it. She figured he would
be keen to know about that priestly artifact. Then came
the huge battle. They had to protect the town and keep all
of the armies at bay. Alison gave a thorough account of all
that had happened, especially the roles Mat and May had
played in the saving of the town.

However, when she then went on to describe the
arrival of the Air Maidens to bring them all before Father
Ukko personally, her father broke down and cried tears of
joy. "All these long years and I have never met Ukko! I
am one of his holy priests — yet my daughter, a mage, not
even a priest, has seen him twice! Unbelievable. Such

honor do you bring to our family, daughter! It is beyond my wildest imaginings." When he had finally collected himself, she continued with what Ukko had said and done for them during that visit.

This too, her father had her repeat several times. He had many questions for her, but Anna interrupted her husband, "Basil, dear, you and Allie can talk to your heart's content later about all this. Please, let her continue her tale, I want to know what happened next."

He began laughing, "You know you are right? I can spend the next twenty years discussing this with Allie. Continue, please." He then muttered happily to himself, "My little Allie did all this!"

Next Alison described how some six hundred of the Freetown folks had just had enough demon invasions in their lives and formed a hodge-podge caravan, intending to migrate to greener pastures. They left just before the armies were to assault the town. However, the lands in all directions were occupied by forces loyal to one of the various Demon Lords. That they would make it was highly dubious. Fortunately, William, the Baker of Blackthorn Village, was with them. Here she had to stop and explain a bit about William and the fact that he was now Mandy's fiancé. "At the time, none of us knew what William's gift really was. We soon found out. He can make two people who are arguing, simply stop and go away. When Reylona, Mandy's Goddess, told her to ride like the wind, we figured the caravan was in big trouble. It was. Seems William had been holding off bands of raiders for two days non-stop by his sheer willpower alone!"

An hour passed as she described the various battles with the Vyndocian cavalry regiments that were intent on wiping out the cavalry. "We didn't know why these people were so intent on killing Jon and wiping the caravan out until much later." She described how they found the stone giants and had become great friends. She told of how they all freed a dozen captured stone giants and also of their discovery that the nearby dwarven city was being attacked by these same Vyndocian cavalry regiments. "Naturally, dad, we had to go help them out. William kept the caravan going through Deadman's Pass in the high Desolation Range, just south of here. We all went with the dwarves to help them out, to help defend them from these savage cavalrymen."

She described the siege of the city and their incredible victory over them all. When she got to the end and told of the arrival of the Goddess Morrigan, gasps were heard all around. "Somehow Jon figured out the real reason that the Vyndocians went to war against the dwarves. It was all Lord Jarred's doings done behind the scene in disguise. I don't know how Jon figured it out, but he was right. As soon as the dwarf leader and the Vyndocian leader saw who really was instigating the conflict, in less than a half day, they were good friends once again. But Morrigan tried to personally intervene. She, of course, tried to kill Jon again, throwing both her magical spears of death. I'm still not sure how he did it, but he made her miss him completely. And he even ran his therapy on her, discovering that she had him confused with Vainamoin. She apologized to Jon in her own fashion. Pretty darn amazing, if you ask me."

Basil, naturally interrupted her at this point, directing his questions to Jon, "How is it possible that you could avoid her magical spears of death this time and Alison took the spear for you the first time? And how can you avoid them at all? Our records indicate that once she throws them, they never miss."

Jon was afraid of this, "The first time, I did not know or realize what she was doing. I also had not worked out just what all I could do. After Alison saved my life by giving freely of her own, I swore that I would never, ever put her in that type a situation ever again, ever. I avoided them simply by being ten feet past them as they came at me. It's kind of hard to explain. But if you imagine the spears moving in slow motion toward you, to have them miss you, all you need to do is to then be in the space through which they have already passed, if you follow me."

"I don't, but I'll accept that for now. I won't ask the obvious question of how do you be in that other space just now," he acquiesced; Anna had poked him in the ribs.

Alison then went on to describe how they then recovered within the dwarven underground city and of the visit of Dispater to Jon. Since the weather had turned really bad in the high country of the Desolation Range, they hastily departed from the dwarves and rejoined the caravan only to find them stranded on the high trail. Three feet of snow made progress nearly impossible. None of these desert dwellers had alpine winter clothing. They were nearly all freezing to death when the party rejoined them. If it had not been for Thea and her magical fire starting skills, they would most likely have perished.

Next, she explained how the dwarves had told her of a side valley that may offer them some shelter. Of the brother and sister who lived there, she did not mention their lycantropy disease, but chose instead to dwell on how alike they were to Mat and May and how they fell in love with each other. Then, she had to explain the swarming of the hobgoblins and how Rufus brought them the news. Thanks to Rufus, a way was found to move the caravan from the high country down to the plains unnoticed by anyone. Purposely she did not mention his secret tunnel, not with so many other ears present. Once they reached the plains, it was a race to get past all of the thousands and thousands of hobgoblins that lain in wait for the caravan.

Again, a hush fell when she told of Lord Jarred's involvement, just as it seemed they would elude all of the hobgoblins. She described the ensuing battle, hopelessly outnumbered, and how it went. She carefully described how, at the very end when all was nearly lost, Darless had personally and physically killed the Demon Lord himself with her bare hands. This brought the praises and compliments Alison felt the alu-demon should have for her actions. Darless seldom blushed, but she did on this occasion. At long last, she told of the arrival of Sir Thomas and the army he had hurriedly assembled to come to their rescue.

"What you also need to know, mom, dad, is that through all these years, I have saved up enough money to afford to have the castle rebuilt — well, sort of. I hope you approve of what I did. I assumed that you both were dead and that as the sole heir, I had the right to rebuild our claim to Verbenloc." Her father nodded his approval. She continued, "I had discovered the spell that brought down the castle. I also discovered a way to cause that spell to malfunction. The entire castle and city walls are being built with this very special stone that is being quarried by my stone giant friends. My dwarven friends are building the entire complex to my specifications. They are working triple shifts in order to have most of the town and castle built later this spring."

Anna exclaimed, "Town? What town?"

Basil exclaimed, "Dwarven engineers? Triple shifts? How on earth could you even get a dwarf to consent to building it and do you realize what that speedy construction is costing?"

Rufus answered him before Alison could figure out how to explain it. "The dwarves owe her far more than that. She could have asked for a king's ransom and gotten it without even the slightest hesitation. But she is also now a very good friend of a friend of mine, Rolf, a stone giant. He and his people would gladly do the quarrying for her out of friendship, but she is paying them what they most desperately need. So everyone wins."

"Yes, dad, it took a million gold coins paid in advance. I was expecting to pay far more than that, so my treasury still is well supplied." Both gasped loudly at the sum, but Alison shrugged it off, continuing, "And mom, I decided to have a free town adjoining the castle. A town where people can live in freedom. Many of those who left Freetown are settling in my new town. I expect we will draw in many more as the word gets out. Dad, we are building a magnificent Church of Ukko and Darless is building her college, where anyone can come and learn Jon's therapy methods from her. Jon has helped design the church so that music will be as magnificent in it as it was in the Church of Ukko in Zaire!"

Anna asked only one question, "What's the name of your new town, dear?"

"It's called Chateau d'Ambrose et Ville Bon Liberte or just Castle d'Ambrose and the Good Free Village in the common tongue, although I have already heard some folks shortening it to just Ville d'Ambrose," she answered proudly.

"I think it will just be marvelous to have so many good neighbors so close, don't you Basil?"

He smiled as he recalled just how many times she had had that complaint, no neighbors for miles. "Yes, dear," he said and they both burst out laughing. He recovered a bit and asked, "I am surprised you didn't call it Castle Brown. You are changing your sir name when you marry aren't you?"

Alison had never given this the slightest thought. Jon broke in before she could think of anything to say. "Heck no! Look, if I were to suddenly change mine to Jon d'Ambrose, everyone would be completely confused. They think I am Saint Jon Brown. Imagine the confusion. Same is true for her. She is the well-known Archmage Alison d'Ambrose. I won't condone her even thinking about changing her name. The last thing I want in either of our lives is more confusion. I've seen and experienced enough confusion to last me three lifetimes! No thanks." Alison's hand found his and she gave it a loving squeeze to show her total approval of his point of view.

Jon then added, "Okay everyone, it's getting late. Tomorrow morning, I think it is time for you parents to be reunited with Mat and May. While you all are freeing the last of them, I will fetch the twins here. Alison still has much more to tell you, especially about the finding of her other brothers and sisters and just how we ended up here with the ability to rescue you. Mandy has a big part in that too. After tomorrow night's tale, I will bring the rest of your children here for a visit. We want to take it slow and easy on you two. I know you want to go home, but remember home as you know it has not existed for over twenty-one years. Everything was lost in the castle's total destruction. Plus with all the construction going on right now, living arrangements are a bit tight. But I do have a way for you to see what it looks like right now."

"How Jon?" asked Alison, amazed that she had not thought of trying to find a way to show her parents what the new town looked like.

"Get your picture book out, dear," he said with a grin. Instantly, she saw what Jon saw. From her portable hole, she fetched two of the magical books. Quickly she opened one to the page that used to show the ruins of Castle d'Ambrose. Now it showed the town and rising walls of the new castle. It also showed numerous tiny figures engaged in construction. Hundreds of them.

Everyone gathered round the two books to have a look. It was impressive. Anna's comment was, "Allie, it is rather plain looking, squarish in fact."

"Yes, I like squares, but the stone of the castle and the town wall is very special. See how polished it is, it reflects light well. It has streaks of silver in it which make it really, really beautiful. Dad, I'll let you see if you can figure out what it really is," she teased.

"Anna, you hear that, she is challenging me. Okay, you are on, just wait til I get a close up look at it."

"Here, dad," she handed him a small piece of that special stone, a sample piece she carried. "This is the stone that will cause the spell that helped bring down your castle to fail utterly, by my personal experimentation even. Let me know when you have figured it out," she challenged him. He took the stone and began studying it. She quickly added, "And no fair going and asking Father Ukko what it is, that's cheating," she teased. She had given him something to occupy his mind, which was a brilliant tactic at this point in his recovery.

The next day brought a great deal of excitement to the camp. Just after breakfast, Jon gave Alison a hug and simply vanished. Ten minutes later, he reappeared holding hands with the twins. Both had hastily dressed; they came just as fast as they heard that they could. It was indeed a joyous reunion. Both sides stared at each other for a minute as reality sunk into each. For the twins, their parents looked exactly like their childhood memories of them, which strained their reality. For the parents, their children were long grown up and they had to adjust all of their thinking. Once the shock had subsided, it was hugs and tears of joy all around. Non-stop conversation then followed.

Alison, wiping tears from her eyes, quietly led the party out of the mansion and back into the tower. Three remained to be rescued. Jon and Thea stayed behind just in case any assists were needed. None was, for they had done a very thorough and complete therapy job on both of them.

"Zounds!" said Mandy, wiping tears from her eyes. "It's times like this that make all the hardship and trouble we've endured more than worthwhile!"

Sir Thomas and Darless walked hand in hand as did Sir Lonnie and Thea. As they neared the tower, the bard, Johannes, came rushing up. "Oh great mage of the magnificent black eyes, I return this to you. It has done its job." He handed her the ring. "I feel perfect, yes indeed. I want to stay and hear the rest of your tale, but I will have to return for that later on. Today I must take Rebecca home and see what the world looks like these days. But I promise to return soon, oh fair lady of the long black hair." He winked at her and turned to Sir Thomas, "You take good care of her. There's none finer in all the lands."

Just a bit embarrassed, Sir Thomas meekly answered, "That I already know, though I suspect she thinks that she has to take good care of me." Darless gave his hand a loving squeeze for this was precisely her point of view. She thought that he was coming around rapidly, making good strides, from what he personified only a year ago when she first met him. Of course, the bard did not fathom what the paladin actually meant, and he took his leave.

The party turned to watch the pair depart. Johannes got out his lute and she held onto him. He strummed a merry tune, his lute activated its teleport spell and they were gone. Jon, hearing the music and recognizing in it the rhythmic patterns of Alison's teleport spell, stuck his head out of the mansion in time to see them go. "Fascinating," he commented, "I'll have to remember to ask Alison about this later." He was beginning to see a pattern between music and her magical spell casting, both had a great deal in common.

Fifteen minutes later, Willow von Stallstadt lay on the floor of the chamber. Father Johnas recognized the tattered remains of her cloak as being a Priest Healer of his church. Other than minor wounds, she did not seem to be in too bad a shape. "I'm Father Johnas, Holy Priest of Ukko. We have freed you from your long imprisonment. Allow me to fully heal your wounds." The woman made no move one way or the other, letting him cast his healing arts upon her.

"The evil mage that imprisoned you has been slain. You are now safe, Willow," he went on looking for a response from her. She grunted what sounded like "okay." So he added, "From our calculations, we think that you have been imprisoned about twenty years." She gave a small sigh. Something was terribly wrong here, he thought to himself. "Can you tell us who you are and what happened to you?"

After a long pause, she said very slowly and with no emotion in her voice, "Willow von Stallstadt, she was once the High Cleric Healer of Ukko, but is no more. Willow is dead." This was all she said, her tone was a total apathy.

"Can you tell us what happened to you?" the priest ventured, figuring it would be good for her to at least talk about it.

Very slowly in a voice that showed no life, she said, "My husband, Count von Stallstadt, and I were on a holy quest to find a trapped Air Maiden somewhere around the abandoned Tower of Leeds. Only it was not abandoned. A party of demons and evil men were there doing something in secret. We were surprised and captured. Evil mage Sarah shrieked at us wanting to know who we were — why were there. We said nothing. She cut off my husband's head before my eyes. Ukko abandoned us to the demons. I could not cry. I was numb. Night came. I was here. All went black. You came." And she quit speaking. Father Johnas's heart felt numb, this was what he was most afraid would happen to these prisoners. He was at a loss about how to heal her.

Darless took charge, "Father Johnas, leave her to me. I'll take her to Jon and Thea. Her hope lies with them." Sadly, the priest stood up and Darless stepped to the side of the woman, chanted and teleported them to the mansion. She carried Willow inside, temporarily ending the festive mood inside. She quickly related what Willow had told them.

"Leave her, Darless, Jon and I know what to do," exclaimed Thea. The apprentice mage immediately went to rustle up some healthy food and drink, while Jon made her comfortable in an isolated corner of the mansion. Darless headed back into the tower. Her mood was somber; so much evil in one person was her thought.

By the time Darless made it back into the chamber, Alison had freed Able Wolf Runner and Father Johnas was attending to his wounds. He had also been tortured before being imprisoned by Sarah. Soon he was able to drink and talk. She noted that he looked like he came from the Canyon Lands. Now that she saw him, even his name fit the native. She realized that she should have been able to deduce that before seeing him.

He explained he was long ago actually the highest trained ranger in all the Canyon Lands. He had undertaken to track the brown dragon, who occasionally stole cattle from the natives. After a year of failed attempts, he finally found the dragon's trail and had followed it to its lair. Unfortunately for him, an old man had spotted him snooping around the outside of the lair. The next thing he knew he was taken prisoner by a female magician, who tortured him and then imprisoned him. "She never even asked me a single question except for how many others knew of the dragon's lair. Nothing else. Weird. I guess the Great Spirit has looked over me. It is good that this woman is now dead."

Since he seemed well-balanced, Alison explained a bit about this dragon. Then, she told of the demon invasion and how ill it had been on his people, ending with a brief version of how she and these others had destroyed the evil and the tower. "You people are now involved in a massive rebuilding of their homes and lands. They will most certainly need any and all aid you can give them." She was attempting to help give him a brief new purpose in life. It worked, fire came back into his eyes. He stood up, still a bit weak, but was ready to begin the long walk back to his home, if only someone would show him the general direction. He had no real idea just how far he was from home.

"Before you head out, Able, let's see if she left any of your gear here. Also, let's get some food in you. You must be starving. After you eat, I'll take you there myself," Alison offered. He thanked her for her kind offer and followed her to find his gear. "Darless, you get the last one on the list while I'm helping Able."

Darless, using her staff's stored magical energies, cast the final freedom spell. Shortly, the small body of Jasmine Greenleaf appeared on the floor. She had been imprisoned only ten years. Rufus said, "Oh dear!" and ran to her side, beating even the priest, for she was a gnome just like him. Her eyes had the tell-tale dazed look about them. The priest quickly healed her and as she regained consciousness of her surroundings, he explained that she had just been freed and that she had been imprisoned only ten years. All the while, Rufus kept patting her hand in a comforting manner. And having one of her kind right there with her seemed to greatly relax the small woman. She looked much like Rufus, less the beard of course. She wore gaily colored trousers and similar tunic top. Finally Rufus said, "You are totally safe now. Rufus is here to watch over you until you recover!" She smiled gratefully back at him.

"I am most great full for the rescue. I am Jasmine, Jasmine Greenleaf, Priest-Illusionist Extra-ordinaire." Suddenly, she recalled what had happened to her and exclaimed, "Rufus, we must return to my village in South Desolation. I have found the lair of the great brown dragon! They must be warned!"

"True, true," Rufus agreed with her, but added, "these people have actually seen that dragon and talked with him. I think that their visit is causing the dragon to actually move to somewhere else in the world, hopefully far away from here! First order of business is to get you recovered. Then, I, Rufus Inventor and Illusionist Extraordinaire, will take you home."

"Silly, I can take myself home, if I can find my spell books. She took my stuff from me."

"Ah, then come with me," he said. "We have found a room full of people's things. Your stuff is probably in there. Here, let me help you up." He helped the gnome to her feet and guided her through the tunnel to the other chamber. Once out of the chamber proper, he paused while Darless gave her a welcome drink and a bit to snack upon. It took her nearly an hour to find her things. Small in size, they were buried behind much larger items.

At last, the Canyon Lands native had his equipment as did the gnome. They walked out into the fresh late morning air. "Spring time," said the little gnome with a smile as she walked along, then added, "Yes, I really am quite hungry. So Rufus, where do you live?"

The inventor replied, "Oh very nearby actually. About five years ago, I found this tower and the way inside, before we blasted these doors off, which was through the trap door in the roof. She studied the stars, you see. I also tangled with the two spectral ghosts and barely got away with my hide." He really didn't answer her question.

"You know, Broadleaftown had a Rufus there once. You wouldn't by chance be Rufus Quickenbroadbeam, would you?" she nudged.

The gnome had a choice, he could be defensive — he had actually been run out of his village because of all of his inventions — or he could be himself, a thoroughly happy inventor. He chose the latter, "Ah yes, one and the same. Some of my earlier inventions caused quite a stir in the village. So they ran me out, which turned out to be a very good thing for me. You see, I have found a really terrific place to live and work on any inventions I choose.

I've more possible space than I can ever imagine using. Nice and quiet as well, just what an inventor needs."

"Well, I should like to see this place, it sounds, well, rather nice to me at the moment, especially the quiet part. You don't have a lot of neighbors I hope?" she asked rather shyly.

"Not many, most are quite distant; we all prefer it that way. Except that my two best friends have moved away last winter — they are marrying Alison's twin brother and sister. They were twins too, you see. It's so quiet, especially at night. I can sit and stare at the stars and dream all I want. Suits me, it does. I'd love to show it to you, but first we had better warn your village about the dragon, though." They both continued chatting all the rest of the way into the mansion.

Later that afternoon, while Jasmine and Able napped after eating their first meal in years, the twins took a guided tour of the tower. Alison wanted their opinions on the best way to transport all of the stuff safely back home. It gave her parents time to rest as well, though their strength was returning quickly now. All during this time, everyone purposely avoided the corner where Jon was working his magic on Willow.

At first, he found it tough going with her. She was in an utter hopeless apathy, just waiting for death to take her. His method did work however, she had finally gone completely through the entire set of mental images from the point that she and her husband had arrived at Leeds until her rescue a few hours ago. But it was excruciatingly slow going. All of the others had finished lunch and were off on a guided tour of the tower, when she finished her first complete pass through the images. Jon broke to eat. He quickly fixed a high protein lunch for Willow and himself. She ate it only because Jon told her to eat. She was acting like a robot, doing whatever Jon requested.

"Okay, Willow, let's get back to work. Now I want you to go to the very beginning once more and move through the images and tell me what happens," he said softly once more.

"Doing research — thought an Air Maiden might have been trapped at Leeds — the Count said we should go and see — it's a ruins — not occupied, he said — rode there — took about a week — desolate lands — poking around ruins — heard voices above us — went to see — demons and evil men there — tried to fight — tried to retreat — more demons come — Count surrendered — tried to bargain a way out of there — accused of spying — tied up — teleported someplace — here — led to foul chamber far underground — tortured him — who are we spying for — she beat me — repeated denials — pointless she said — whacked off his head — I screamed — she chanted something — she touched me — all went black — I appear on cold stone floor — priest casts heal spell — here now." Of course, it took over an hour for all this to be said.

"Very good, Willow. Now let's go back to the beginning of it once more. Yes, good. Now go through the situation to its end once more and tell me what happens as you go along." And so she began once more. This time, more vivid details emerged as she started out. She described some of her research She had, in fact, uncovered an old volume that described the fall of Leeds some two hundred years earlier. She had pointed out to her husband that it appeared an Air Maiden had gone missing at that time. It was he who wondered if she could be imprisoned still somewhere in the ruins of Leeds Tower. He had been the one who said it was an abandoned ruins for as long as he could remember. It was the Count who suggested they go explore it for clues. Now she finally began yawning heavily as more details began appearing.

However, when she reached the beheading of her husband, she cried solidly for nearly a half hour before Jon could get her to continue going through her mental pictures of it. When she finally finished, Jon thanked her and asked her to go through it again. Now more vivid details of their capture and torture emerged. Her period of crying shortened to only ten minutes this time.

On the next pass through the events, she became quite angry about nearly everything. The depth of her anger was nearly as great as her apathy had been. Jon was thankful that the others were still out and were not forced to hear the volume and intensity of her wrathful pronunciations. However, she had more periods of heavy yawning interspersed throughout. Two more passes later, she had become exceedingly antagonistic about nearly everything having to do with this whole episode in her life. But the next pass, produced an utter, excruciating boredom; Jon persisted, knowing she was getting close to handling it. He had her go through it one more time. "I cannot, it's just *too* boring. Can't we do something else? I've been through it a dozen times. Nothing is happening to it at all!"

"Humor me, please, once more," he requested. So she started out at the beginning with a most reserved sigh. She had not gotten very far through it before she yawned once more, brightened up, remembering something she had forgotten.

"Say, I communed with Father Ukko about this first. I remember now, he said distinctly in my mind, 'Leave it alone, Willow.' I told him, but he would not listen to me! Oh now I remember, he said we'd be famous if we rescued her. Well, I'll be! You know, he was always after fame! Ever since I first met him, I could tell he was only in it for the fame it brought him and upon his family. Silly me, when I married him, I thought I could change him, get him to start doing things for the right reasons. Ha, ha. What a fool I was!" She started laughing harder and harder. Finally, she laughed so hard that she rolled around on the floor.

"Very, very well done, Willow. Well done indeed. We are done for today," Jon said.

"Done? Ha, ha. He's the one that's gone and done it! Ha, ha. What a stupid thing for me to have done — I'll change him! Ha, ha," and she laughed even harder. Several others came inside to begin fixing dinner. Her laughter was contagious.

Father Johnas came inside, found Willow laughing like mad. She attempted to thank him for healing her wounds, but most of her words were lost in laughter. "Silly fool. Did it for fame! I knew better." She roared even harder. The priest, wide-eyed, looked at the smiling Jon who nodded all was fine. He found it hard to fathom — when he had left her with Jon, he knew here was a total basket case, one who was destined to be insane for the rest of their life. In his priestly duties, he'd seen it countless times before, but now she had put it all behind her somehow. The word "redemption" appeared in his mind unbidden.

Only after eating dinner did Willow finally stop laughing, though she was in a gay mood. "Father Johnas, from your emblems, you and I are at the same grade in the Priesthood, though my specialty has always been the healing arts. I take it that you look after your village's needs? I'm sorry, my emblems of office have been misplaced. I'll look for them tonight."

"I'm honored by your presence. Please accept my sincere apologies for not recognizing your proper place. Yes, I am the village priest, I comfort my flock in the name of Father Ukko. But after these last few days, what I have seen happen — I am truly humbled. I must learn the ways of redemption, that is, if Jon will show me the way it's done."

"Me too," she added. "For in truth, I believe I was lost and now I'm me again. I don't know how else to put it."

"Oh I'm sure you can learn how," broke in Thea. "It's actually very easy to do, I picked it up very quickly."

"Of course you can," Jon finally got the chance to acknowledge them both. "I think the only requirement is a genuine desire to help others, right Darless?"

"Yes, that and perhaps the ability to observe," she added. "Just come to my college in say about six months when its construction is finally finished. You are all most welcome. For it is my intention to spread this technique far and wide."

"Can you imagine a world in which everyone knows how to do this to help others in times of need?" mused Jon. "I sure can. But say, I think Alison is about to continue her story, let's listen." He finally got their attention off of him!

"Okay, mom, dad, now comes this year's part. It all began because of Mandy and Darless. You see, Mandy can sense or see the last traumatic mental images a person leaves upon things. Grim as it was for her, she examined every body that the dwarves recovered from the ruins of the castle as the rubble was cleared away. She viewed each death as it occurred. None were you or my siblings. That meant only one thing; we all got away by using our picture books; there was no other way out of the collapsing castle." She told of their continued search for them and how Lennard had provided some excellent clues. In detail, she described their finding of Christina and Stephen. Their parents seemed pleased to hear that both were happily married and that between them, they now had five grandchildren, one of whom was studying to be a priest like his grandfather. That of course pleased Basil. The finding of Ruben, on the other hand, rather upset both of her parents; he had developed all the wrong attitudes about life.

Jon spoke up, "I think a visit by you two might be the only chance he has of breaking the bonds with which he had fettered himself."

"We'll certainly try our best," declared Basil. Alison then continued describing how, during a careful search of the grounds, Darless found Anna's broach and how Mandy deciphered its message and shown it to them. Next, she told of their journey to the Canyon Lands and what evil they dealt with there. Again, both her parents were aghast at the deeds their daughter had done. If there was any doubts about just how powerful Alison really was or her close friends, the defeat of the demons dispelled them.

Then, she told of their search for the brown dragon and how they had been harried by the Cult of the Black Scorpion. All of which led to their meeting with Threngold in person. Here Jasmine and Able paid close attention. Both were relieved to hear that the dragon alluded to his eminent departure to find a new lair. At last, she told of their adventures with all of the undead in the tower and their final victory over the Archmage Sarah le'Garde, who had been transformed into a lich.

When she finished, everyone was completely silent. That they were impressed would be an understatement. Basil found his voice, "Anna dear, our daughter truly is the Holy Mage of Ukko! I am humbled beyond belief."

"We raised our children well, even if it was only such a very short time we had with them," Anna added. "Now we must do the same with our grandchildren." A new goal had formed in her motherly mind.

"Okay, let's all get some sleep," Jon pronounced. "Tomorrow, you get to go home — well actually to the new castle and meet your other children and grandchildren. No one needed additional encouragement.

Chapter 17 The Weddings

The next day began with a discussion on treasure transportation. All had agreed to let Alison appraise and divide the gems and jewelry up later on when she had more time. All of that had already been taken back home safely in Alison's treasury room. The coin total that Sir Thomas computed was a staggering four hundred-fifty thousand, which he estimated weighed in at a little over twenty-eight thousand pounds! However, Thea, in rummaging through the gear in the magical items storage room, had discovered five more portable holes.

Waving a parchment with her calculations on it, Thea explained, "So you see, I have it all worked out. If we dump out the contents of all the holes we already have, then we ought to be able to get all the coins in them!"

"Well, that settles that problem," grinned Alison, who was about to surprise the others once again. We'll divide the coins up equally and fill the nine holes equally. Then, every one of us can have their own portable hole." It took a few seconds for the significance to sink in to the others.

"Wait, you mean you are giving each of us who does not have one of these portable holes a portable hole?" exclaimed Thea in surprise.

"Yes, you all have more than earned them," she went on, "and it really simplifies everything. On one trip, we can empty out the treasury room. I'm afraid that we will likely need to borrow them back to use to haul out all of the magical item and other personal gear that remains, except the truly evil items which Father Johnas want us to destroy, if we can. After we get it all back to my place and we mages can properly identify each, then we can go about dividing that gear up equally as well. I'd say you all will have a fairly large amount of magical things you may use or dispose of as you see fit. I know that you paladins prefer to only keep sufficient funds for your expenses and donate the rest to the church. That's fine with me, but I insist on each of you getting an equal share. Once we have all the things properly identified, perhaps we can get together one day and have at it."

"And if you also don't mind, we would like to borrow the holes to help cart all of the magical study records and such back as well. We certainly want to study all her records carefully, just in case they point to other atrocities that we may be able to rectify," she added. Of course no one had any objections to that either.

"First, however, we need to teleport Sir Egmont, Francine, Willow, and Able home and make sure they are going to be okay. I assume Rufus will take care of Jasmine. Next, we need to return my parents home. Then, we can move all the other gear. So the next question is how many teleport spells can we each do today, round trips, that is, without using our staffs for energy? Oh yes, one other detail, everyone, I would like to announce that Thea Westfold is no longer my apprentice; she is a full-fledged mage in her own right. In fact, she should now be capable of one round trip each day as well! Congratulations, Thea!"

Everyone clapped while Thea, her face radiant with a broad smile, nodded acknowledgments to her friends. As soon as the applause died down, Thea quickly put in, "This doesn't mean that I don't have just tons to learn from her, though. She's still teaching me lots of new, cool spells and such."

"True, but it really means that she is more than able to stand on her own two feet," Alison explained for the benefit of those who were not magic users. Quickly the teleport tally was noted: Alison and Darless, six each; Thea, one; May, one and a half; Rufus, one.

"Honey, don't forget, I have to stop by and pickup Bessy," Jon interrupted. "My puppy should be ready by now for me to get. I'll stop by on my way on one of the trips. I can do a bunch of trips, just not sure how many. Guess it depends on the weight I have to carry."

"I didn't forget," she teased him, "but I am not letting you go alone, that's for sure. Besides, I have you down for transporting the horses, if that's okay with you?" He nodded, he had actually forgotten about them. "Okay everyone, here comes the plan. Darless and I will make two round trips right away, taking the four back to their towns. While we are doing that, if everyone will help in piling the coins into the portable holes that would really be terrific. Then, we can make one trip to my place and drop off my parents and the treasury. I think that it will be possible to get the treasury moved today and all of the other stuff tomorrow, but you will get a workout man-handling all those coins."

Everyone went to work. The thought that this whole adventure would be completely finished in two more days filled everyone with both relief and happiness. Mandy really wanted to get back to William. Jon wanted to get his puppy, and it went as planned. By noon, Alison and Darless had seen their four safely home to their respective towns. Thea, Rufus and Jasmine used magic spells to load piles of coins into the portable holes relatively quickly, so that by lunch time, the nine were ready for transport.

Thus, after lunch, Rufus teleported Jasmine, his confiscated machine and a huge mound of other stuff he'd collected back to his nearby home. He promised to return tomorrow to help loading the other items. However, Sir Thomas, Sir Lonnie, Mandy, Father Johnas and Thea remained behind to guard the tower until the others returned and to help the priest sort out the items to be destroyed.

While Jon began stepping horses home, Alison, Darless and May teleported their parents, arriving just above the ground where the destroyed castle stood. This gave her parents an overview of the new construction and gently brought the current reality home to them. That is, their home, as they remembered it, along with all of their possessions, were no more. It was still an upsetting experience for both, standing where their living room used to be. Both had to wipe their eyes more than once.

While Alison and Darless headed into the dungeon so that Alison could open up her treasury room, May and Mat pointed out all of the salient features of the new castle and town. Alison dumped the contents of the many portable holes into different locations within her room, placing a parchment with the name of that pile's owner. Then, they all headed back outside.

About this time, having been alerted that their parents had arrived, Stephen and his wife, Mary Ellen and children, Fred and Basil, came walking up, accompanied by Christina and her husband, Helmut along with their children, Ellen, Billie and Annette. Both Stephen and Christina stopped and stared at their parents, they looked just like their childhood memories of their parents. Basil and Anna stared back, trying to grasp how grownup their children were. Then, everyone's emotions flowed unabated. They hugged each other, kissed, hugged, and cried for several minutes. Actually, there was not a dry eye anywhere around.

When their emotions subsided, Christina introduced her husband and children, Basil and Anna's grandchildren. Her mom duly noted Christina had named her only daughter after her. Then, Stephen introduced Mary Ellen and his two sons. His father was exceedingly pleased that one of his grandsons was named after him. All five children were, however, rather shy, never having met these grandparents. Annette, the youngest, spoke up, "How come you don't look old like Grandma Watson?"

Christina tried to hush her, but Anna explained, "We were imprisoned by a very mean and vicious wizard.

It's like no time passed, though we were gone twenty-one years. Magic can do that, Annette, but that is terribly bad, evil magic."

Christina spontaneously hugged Alison, "Oh how can I ever thank you enough? It is just beyond my wildest imaginations! You have my undying gratitude for the rest of my life!"

"That goes for me too, Alison," her brother moved over and hugged them both. "But I expect you already know just how much this means to us, to you. Thank you baby sis! You realize that it is due mainly to you that our family is reunited? If you had not done all that you have, why we'd still be lost! Honestly, we have the best sister in the universe!"

Jon and Darless now joined the group. "Say, things have really progressed really well while we were gone," exclaimed Jon. "The town looks ready for folks to move in, doesn't it?"

Stephen, the steward, replied, "Yes, Saint Jon. Actually, over a hundred folks have already moved into their homes and are helping to get things going. I've told another four hundred that their homes will be ready in about another two weeks. Mom, dad, we've got a brand new home fixed up for you. When Jon told us you had been rescued, why Tina and I went to work fixing up one of the new homes right by where we are temporarily staying. Later on, if you would prefer to live within the castle with the rest of us when it is done, you can move in there along with us all. The Engineer says that it will not be ready for at least another month. Alison had them concentrating their efforts on getting the first four hundred stone homes built. That's way more than we need, Alison. However, while you were away, I've had well over a hundred additional requests for family homes that we had not counted upon in our initial estimations. I do believe word is spreading."

The group next took a guided tour of the new town. Alison pointed out the hot and cold running water system that Jon and Rufus had devised, along with the fancy sewer system. Anna and Basil were flabbergasted with the idea of each home having its own hot water, let alone running water. They kept on saying "Wow!" over and over. Both were extremely impressed with the town Alison had designed and that the dwarves were building.

Finally, Basil had to actually touch the shiny black town walls. "Okay, Alison, I give up. Here is your rock back. I have no idea at all what the silver streaks are. I admit defeat."

She whispered into his ear, "Mithril silver. Its presence in the basalt rock defies magical transmutation of stone to mud, but keep it a secret!" His eyes widened and he ran his hands over the smooth, shiny wall. He realized that these walls must have cost a fortune!

Satisfied that all was going according to her plans, Alison announced, "Well, we have to be getting back to the tower. Tons more to bring home. May, if our folks have any problems, why you just come and get us. We should be making periodic trips back here with stuff tomorrow most likely, if all goes well. I hope that we will be back to stay by tomorrow night." May agreed and Alison quickly teleported the three back to the tower. It was now late afternoon; the rosy sun was approaching the tops of the high western peaks.

The trio found the others in the magical gear room working rapidly. Already a great deal of order had been brought to the immense pile of items. Mandy had taken charge and had them arranging things into piles that would fit into the portable holes. By dinner time, the eight remaining holes had been filled. Father Johnas had made another quite small pile of items out in the hallway, items to be destroyed. These consisted mainly of some dozen evil-aligned weapons and a half dozen books, one of which contained the recipe for the creation of undead beings. He felt confident that all evil items had been identified.

So after dinner, Alison, Darless, Mandy and Sir Thomas set about that task. First, the pile was levitated and then moved outside the tower complex. No one physically touched any of the items. Magical fires consumed all but one of the books. This unholy book required a pair of disintegration spells to destroy it. The blades were placed between boulders and broken by powerful smashes from Sir Thomas and Mandy, who borrowed the priest's mace. Then, the remains were disposed of by Darless. She explained that she had transported the bits into close proximity of the sun. Everyone smiled as they realized that that would vaporize the pieces.

"There, evil destroyed," Father Johnas stated, wholly satisfied with the entire process.

The next day also went according to Alison's plans. First, Jon stepped all of the remaining horses back to her home. Naturally, expending that much energy, Jon was tired and he slept the rest of the morning in the mansion. Meanwhile, Alison and Darless teleported the eight portable holes, along with many larger items that would not fit into the holes, back to her dungeon home. When they returned an hour later, everyone headed into the magical study room to box up the items in there. Rufus had arrived, while Alison was gone. So he was able to lend a helpful hand as well. Here, however, great care was taken to avoid touching many of the books, out of fear of traps and bodily harm. Another trip was made back to Alison's place. After lunch, all of the remaining things were packed and preparations were made for the final trip home.

Rufus said his farewells and added with a twinkle in his eye, "Jasmine really does like my home! Isn't that just something?" Of course, he did not wait for their reply, "And we both want to come to your weddings. Make sure you let us know in time."

"Oh, I'd almost forgotten, Rufus," Alison remembered their plans. "Yes, theoretically we were planning it for the first of May, but that's the day we met the brown dragon. I'll let you know as soon as we all decide on a new date. Thanks. Tell Jasmine thanks for me." He so promised and then left, taking along some minor piles of plates, cups and cooking utensils. The trader in him just could not stand to see them go to waste.

Darless and Thea took everyone back home, while Alison went with Jon to get his new puppy, Bessy. Alison teleported Jon and herself to Michael's homestead, but not before Jon had contacted the dog breeder mentally, not only to let him know they were coming, but also to make sure that it was an okay time. While Jon played with Bessy, who licked him about as frantically as she jumped about him so glad was the puppy to see Jon, Alison briefly told Michael what had happened during their trip to the tower. Awed, he kept saying, "That's incredible. Amazing! Unbelievable!"

When they were ready to go, he quickly told Jon what he needed to do for and with Bessy. She had already begun her training. "As you walk along, she will roam far and wide in front of you and will alert you to any danger. Each day you need to take her for a long walk like that. She'll know instinctively when danger is near, so you don't have to worry about that aspect. Dogs are very smart, as you will see. Feel free to ask me anything at any time, Jon. She should be a really good dog for you." Jon thanked him profusely and proudly held onto the puppy, Alison and a large bag of puppy items, food and toys. He stepped them all home at long last.

They found the others waiting for them. "Ah, so here is the puppy that stole your heart," teased Mandy. "Actually, I had to stick around to see her. She's a cutie,

Jon," she added petting Bessy, who affectionately licked the ranger's hand. For a few minutes, Bessy was the sole object of attention and she loved it.

"Gang, before someone takes me home," Mandy spoke up, "there is one remaining question. We have missed our May Day wedding date. It is now the 14th. So now what?"

Alison thought of the myriad things she needed to handle and was somewhat overwhelmed by all of them. She had wanted to give each a very special wedding present and she guessed that the others probably also had such intentions. "I hate to be a boor, but golly, I've so much to do yet. Could we possibly postpone it until the first of June?" She hoped that no one would feel too upset about the delay, but weddings were one of the most important highlights in a woman's life. "That would give us a couple of weeks to get ready. Will that be enough time for you to get your castle ready for us all?"

"Oh yes! Two weeks is fine with me. The sooner the better!" exclaimed Mandy, the relief she felt was not exaggerated.

"I think giving your parents more time to adjust is an excellent move," Jon added. "I can wait another couple of weeks. Besides, I have not yet had time to get all of my wedding presents for everyone. I could use the extra time, if you don't mind."

"We want to do this right," May put in her thoughts, "I have already done most of the work on our dresses, but you will all have to have a final fitting. So gown-wise, two weeks is fine. Besides, Alison, the rest of us already assumed the date would likely get postponed a bit, but we didn't want to say anything about it. You had enough to worry about."

"Okay, then spread the word about the new date and stay in touch," Mandy declared. "I'll have rooms in my castle ready for as many as want to come. So, who's taking me home? I really want to see William, if you know what I mean," she teased.

"Allow me," Darless offered, "Alison has tons to do and Jon has a new puppy to handle. So it's me and thee. Back in a bit, My Love," she directed that last to Sir Thomas, who smiled and blew her a kiss.

"Come sis, you have to see the arrangements we all have been making while you were gone. We've got one of the new stone houses all fixed up for you and Jon, temporary mind you. When the castle is ready, we will, of course, all move in there," May said, proud of the achievements they had accomplished.

At long last, they all settled into some semblance of orderly life amid the fast, ongoing construction. Jon was taken completely by surprise at just how fast the town was being built and how fast it was being populated. Dwarves are tireless workers, especially when the pay was right. Nearly every day, several new wagons carrying entire families pulled in at the gate, seeking audience with the steward. Usually, Stephen allowed them to become a full-fledged town member. He saw for sure that Christina was checking on their alignment auras and only those who were mostly evil were rejected.

Each day, many wagons bearing huge loads of cut lumber entered the town, usually from the western gate. When he asked, he found out that nearly a hundred workers were being employed to fell trees some forty miles to the west. An old lumber mill had been refurbished to handle the sudden demand. Stephen told Jon that some five hundred craftsmen from all the surrounding towns were temporarily on the payroll. Some made beds, some tables, some cabinets, and on the list went. Jon was truly impressed at just how efficient Stephen was. The steward's job was perhaps one of the most critical ones in the entire operation. It was Stephen's task to make everything run smoothly. Plus, Jon found that he was also planning for the future needs as well. "Nothing has escaped your attention! I'm impressed!" Jon told Stephen. He smiled at the compliment.

"I'll let you in on a little secret," he answered, "this is my love, my passion! It is not work, but play for me! But don't tell Alison," he chuckled.

Now since Alison spent long hours overseeing construction details and the identifying of all of the gear that they had collected from the tower and since Darless was similarly engaged, Jon decided to use his free time wisely. First, he made a list of all those for whom he needed to get a wedding present. It was lengthy. Besides Alison, he wanted to give something to Darless and Sir Thomas, to Mandy and William, to Thea and Sir Lonnie, to May and Jake, and to Jennifer and Mat. His gifts had to be special. However, since he was totally unfamiliar with this land, he had no idea how to go about finding things. He did the only thing he really could, that was, to get them from his world back in Urbana. The problem was what to get. After much thought, he decided to be practical in his choice of gifts.

Jon got the two paladins each a Percheron stud and a pair of mares, all yearlings and of the very best stock he could find. Now they could raise their own high quality, heavy war horses. For Mandy, he got her a trio of Morgan horses, again a stud and two mares. She could now raise the very best trail horses in all the lands. William received a large amount of baking equipment, stainless steel and very expensive. He gave both May and Jennifer a half dozen, hand-made quilts each; they would appreciate the craftsmanship as well as their beauty. Mat received a number of quality locks; Jon got two of each type so that the locksmith could disassemble one and use it as a prototype to produce others of that kind. For Jake, he found a number of excellent live traps of various sizes so that he could continue the way of life he enjoyed, that of a furrier and gardener. He also gave him a wide assortment of garden seed. Since Thea was just starting out, he got her a large amount of kitchenware, including cast iron skillets. All were durable and usable in this world of no electricity.

Finally, he tackled what to get Darless and Alison. For the alu-demon, he got a pair of telescopes; one was a five-inch refractor and the other a reflector whose diameter was more than twice that size. Both came with all the trimmings, as the salesperson professed. For Alison, he got two tall windmill electrical generators with solar cell panel backup; it was a complete electrical generating system. Then, he got a stereo system with tape recorder and a wide variety of music to go with it. He added a pile of electrical lights, a refrigerator and a small stove that could be used for either cooking or for heat. These would seem most magical to citizens of this world.

A week had passed. He enjoyed the surprise each had to their wedding present. Each was impressed and pleased with his gift. Perhaps the least enjoyable thing he endured during this time was the numerous "fittings" that May insisted upon; she wanted his wedding clothes to be just perfect. Indeed, the ladies spent considerable amounts of time getting their gowns just right. Even Mandy popped by twice for fittings.

The second week, Jon felt a bit useless. He dutifully worked on the training and exercising of Bessy. Yet all around him, everyone, including the several hundred townsfolk, who had already moved into their new homes, seemed to have a purpose, a goal, valuable work to be done. Jon had no job as such. Thus, he decided to try to assemble a town band that would play for church services as well as dances and such. It didn't take long to get five others who wanted to make music. So the time passed and the hectic construction continued unabated.

On Wednesday, Raul, now promoted to the captain of the guards, came rushing into the castle looking for the steward, Stephen d'Ambrose. Quickly the two hurried out of the castle to the main town gate. Jon caught a brief bit of their conversation, something about yet another person asking for residency. Something was very different about this request, Jon could sense it. Not more than two minutes later, Stephen came rushing back looking for both Jon and Alison. "I think she is over in the old castle working on magic item identification," Jon replied. "I'll get her; meet you at the main entrance in a minute." Glad for some excitement, Jon stepped himself into the old castle's dungeon into what had been Alison's kitchen. "Alison? You here?"

"Hi Love," her mellow alto voice echoed, "I'm here in the treasury room as usual."

"Stephen says he needs us both at the main gate. Something about someone asking for residency," Jon replied. She joined him momentarily, holding her staff in one hand and a coil of rope in the other.

"Magical rope," her eyes twinkled, "not sure what it does yet. Okay, let's go see what Stephen wants, though I don't know why he needs us." Jon took her hand and stepped them both to the main gate.

Stephen stood on the left, while Raul was on the right. Between them a hooded cloaked figure stood; all were apparently waiting on their appearance. "Ah, Alison, this woman has asked for permission to reside in town, but she claims that she must have both of your permissions, though I do not know why. Name's Glasya, she says."

Both Jon and Alison looked dumbfounded at each other and then at the hooded figure; they though they saw a wry smile on her face. "It's me, but not me," said the familiar voice that both recognized at once. It was Glasya, the Archmage devil, who had helped them in the Canyon Lands. She obviously enjoyed watching their startled looks. "Is there somewhere we can go for a private talk?" she added in a serious tone, still not revealing herself.

Alison thought for a moment, this was a devil; she did not want to give away any information about her castle. She suggested, "Yes, let's use my old dungeon rooms. I was there working on the identification of magical items."

"Take my arms, Ladies," Jon grinned, "Ah yes, one step forward and here we are." He had stepped them into the old underground dining room, which was deserted. Alison quickly uncovered several lights to make the room brighter.

"Forgive the mess, but my old home here is now basically just a workshop, that is, until the new castle is done," she said politely, moving the magical rope off the table. "Can I make you some tea?" she added minding her manners.

"Love some, Love," Jon replied. Glasya agreed. Alison disappeared briefly into the side kitchen area to start water boiling giving her time to think.

When she reappeared with the cups and an assortment of tea, Glasya could contain her excitement no longer. "Okay, have a look," and she flung off her cloak. Jon and Alison stared at her.

"What, what happened to you? Where's your horns and wings?" asked Jon.

"You look lots younger than I remember," Alison added trying to make some sense of this youthful, beautiful woman standing before her. She still had the long black hair, same style. She still wore makeup that made her look more than a bit glamorous. She still had those bright red, very long nails. She still had the old fire in her eyes. But something was different. Perhaps she had concocted a disguise spell that totally hid her horns and wings.

"You are looking at Archmage Glasya *Greenleaf*. How do you like my new body?" she teased them. "No horns or wings this time, Jon. Okay, can you keep a secret?"

Both nodded, but Alison amended, "Unless I have to disclose it for the good of others, that is."

"Agreed," Glasya said with a twinkle in her eyes. "Ah water is hot. Bring the pot and let's sit down and hear my story." In a minute, tea was brewing in the cups and Glasya began. "I could not tell you this earlier, but I have wanted out of Hell for a very long time. However, I owed much to Dispater and I do always follow the Rule of Law, you see, so I could not just up and leave. Besides, where would I go with a devil's body? That's why that spell I learned from the Marquis's spell book was so very important to me — why I risked *everything* to get it. It was a clone spell, a spell that allows the wizard to make a body clone of themselves or anyone else for that matter. Long years have I been planning to make a clone of myself, then leave the clone in Hell fulfilling my duties to Dispater, while I go elsewhere."

"But meeting you, Saint Jon, changed everything, though I suspect you do not know the impact you had on me." Jon looked rather embarrassed. She spoke truthfully, he had no idea at what she was hinting. Neither did Alison. "It was a small point, but a critical one. You showed or reminded me that we are all spiritual beings that inhabit a material body. Plus you demonstrated to me that a being can change, can confront their past traumas and erase its command over you. When I returned to my tower in Hell after our adventures, I thought long and hard about this. Basically, I decided that if you could do it, then there is no reason why I, Archmage Glasya, cannot do it as well. Jon, I now understand why you always do it on another instead of doing your therapy on yourself! Believe me, I really understand that now! But I kept doggedly at it and eventually got to the basic root of why I was being a devil. And you know, once I recalled that dirty deed, why

everything changed for me. I no longer *have* to be evil!"
Both could see the immense relief on her face.

"Go ahead, Jon. Use your Walking Stick of Ukko
and check on me. I insist, see for yourselves, I am no
longer evil-based! You too, Alison, cast one of your
detection spells." She was so insistent that both followed
her orders.

A minute later, Alison gasped, "You are right!
Neutral! Incredible! I've never heard of anyone changing
without coercion perhaps over time and without some
driving influence to do so! This is really amazing!"

"Like I said, Jon, I know just how hard it is to face
what one has done all by one's self! I only got it this far.
One reason that I want to move here is so I can attend
Darless's new college and get more help. Some stuff I just
cannot face as yet; the mental images are all black and
seem to stay that way no matter what I do, but I am
getting ahead of my story. After I realized all this, I then
began to experiment with the clone spell. You see, if I was
no longer totally evil in nature, I sure as heck wanted out
of Hell! With a little tweaking, here you see the cloned
body. Okay, so I took a few years off of it and a tuck here
and there and a bit larger bosom. Men, I find, like larger
bosoms. It turned out perfectly ideal, don't you think?"
She smiled with her success, then continued.

"Once this body was fully formed, I merely moved
out of my devil's body and into this one. Another being
moved into the old devil's body; there is no lack of beings
without bodies in Hell, by the way. Incidentally, Dispater
gave his total approval to my transformation. So it is
really okay that I have left Hell." Both Alison and Jon felt
a weight move off of them. Neither had realized just how
important it had been for her to get the devil's
permission; they might have given sanctuary to a
renegade from Hell and found themselves under attack
by legions of devils!

"Another reason I want to live here is I need a quiet, safe place to pursue my magical studies. I figured the town would be a lot safer if there were two archmages here."

"Ah ha, we have you on that one," Alison smiled, adding, "Three archmages. Darless has become an archmage herself! I think that that is a first for alu-demons."

"That's really terrific!" Glasya exclaimed genuinely glad of the news. "I figured she just might make it. Okay, this is even better, *three* archmages in the same town! Another reason is that I wanted to attend your wedding. It has been so long since I attended a loving wedding. I cannot recall the last time, but it has been at least a hundred years or more ago. So I swore I would not miss this one. I've brought you a wedding present, even if you don't want me to attend. It is something very special, something for your safety. Now that I see the layout of your town, I can offer my services in its extension. Will you allow me to give it to you now?" The glow on her face was almost childlike. She had made something of immense value and was dying to get Alison's reaction to it.

"You are most welcome to attend. I'd, we'd be honored by your presence, under the circumstances, Glasya," Alison replied, genuinely impressed by her.

Glasya removed a portable hole from within her left bra. Jon mused that all women must store their portable holes in the same safe place. His eyes did not miss noting the shape and size of her new endowment. Alison also noticed him noticing and gave him a subtle kick under the table. He winked at her but for once, did not turn red.

"Ah, here it is," she produced a ten inch tall statue of a horse carved from a solid block of jade. The value of the statue alone must have been something close to fifty thousand gold pieces. "It's enchanted, Alison. You put this in your bedroom on a shelf. Then, if at any time anyone ever comes into your room and bears malice of evil intent to harm you or Jon, it sounds an alarm, a loud one, designed to wake even the soundest sleeper, and it then radiates a very bright light. Furthermore, it works even if the assailant is invisible or using some weird body form. And Alison, you can also program it! It will store two spells that are activated when it sounds the alarm. For example, you could program it to cast a volley of magical missiles at the attacker or teleport you two to some preprogrammed location. Use your imagination with this one," she smiled proudly. This was her most powerful creation to-date.

"Wow! Wow!" exclaimed Alison holding it lovingly. "I don't quite know what to say! This is priceless! You know how many assassins seem to be after Jon. I've been somewhat worried about just this very thing. Thank you! Thank you!"

Jon got up and stood beside Glasya. "Here, stand up please." She did not quite knowing what he was intending. "Here, you really deserve this! Thanks, Glasya!" Jon gave her a loving, solid hug, much to her surprise and enjoyment. When they separated, he added, "Thanks again!" Her cheeks actually flushed noticeably. It had been a long, long time since someone had given her a loving hug, spontaneously. It was a moment she treasured.

Though she could feel the heat in her face and the rushing of her heart, she tried to act naturally, "And when I got here today, I found another thing I can do for you, if you allow me to reside here. Due to the design of your walls, I believe that I can, given sufficient time, place similar alarm spells on the entrances and along the wall tops, so that if anyone who is truly evil tries to enter without your expressed permission, an alarm sounds."

Alison's jaw dropped visibly; her eyes widened. "You can? Now that is truly impressive! Of course, I would have to reimburse you for the protection. Golly, that would really make this town protected from assassins and riffraff. Just incredible!" But then she caught herself; let's not be so hasty she thought. "Can you swear that you are not here to spy on us for anyone? That you are not here for some ulterior motive as yet unmentioned? That you do not have some enemies that will swarm down upon us to get at you?"

"Jon, use your Walking Stick to verify," Glasya commanded. "Yes, I swear that I am here of my own freewill, that I have now no connections to any other being, that I have no hidden agendas, save to learn as much knowledge and wisdom as I possibly can, and that I have no enemies. There is still Glasya, the Devil, in Hell, albeit a rather feebleminded Glasya. Thus, if any wanted to get back at Glasya the Devil, she's still there in Hell. I am truly free for the first time and I am so happy too!"

Jon really didn't need his walking stick's magic to know she was telling the truth, he could sense it. "Okay, then you are welcome to live here, Glasya," Alison pronounced. "However, we'd better let the others know what's going on or they will be completely confused! Someone might ask them if this is the Glasya that helped us out?"

She smiled back, "They can say that this is a different Glasya, this is Glasya Greenleaf, not Glasya the devil mage. By the way, it's the name of the last good man I bedded before I went to Hell, such a long time ago."

"At least all of us who were there must be told," Alison considered just whom should be told the complete truth. "And probably also all the rest of my family including my parents," she said thoughtfully, stroking her hair as she often did when pondering a situation.

"I thought they died when your castle here was destroyed?" Glasya interrupted her train of thought.

"Oh my!" Alison suddenly realized, "Yes, we rescued them! They are alive and recovering fairly well I think. Jon, go round up the others, bring them all here, while I tell Glasya the news." Jon nodded and walked outside to begin rounding up those he could find. As he left the dungeon entrance, he heard Glasya gasp in excitement. He smiled to himself, Glasya would be hearing a pretty interesting tale indeed.

It took him a half hour to round everyone up and get them all to the north gate. Mandy was actually here getting a fitting on her wedding gown and was only too happy to get out of it, if only briefly. Just as they were all together at the gate, Sir Thomas rode up. He had taken his new horses back to his castle and arranged for their care and was returning to spend some quiet time with Darless. "Just in time, Sir Thomas, let Raul look after your horse and come with us. We've an interesting surprise for everyone."

He dismounted, grinned, gave Darless a loving kiss and fell in line as they all headed northward to the old dungeon entrance. Everyone was speculating what this was all about, but none were remotely close to the truth. It was just too remarkable an event, Jon mused. Thea, her usual bubbly self, kept asking Jon what this was all about, and, when he refused to answer her to her satisfaction, kept speculating on wilder and wilder things. He only grinned in response, which of course only made her speculations all the wilder.

As they entered the dungeon entrance, Jon said loudly, "Allow me to present to you all the newest resident of our town, Glasya Greenleaf!" Glasya, wearing fur lined trousers and matching silk blouse and black fur lined boots, stepped forward.

Thea, who had taken a fondness for Glasya, the Devil, exclaimed excitedly, "Glasya, is that really you? Wow! You kind of look different. Are you *really* going to live here with us?" And that was the overall tone and ideas that flooded through all the adventurer's minds. Those that had not met the devil found themselves racing through the stories the others had told about the help of the archmage devil.

"Yes, Thea, it is really me, but then not really me," she enjoyed her little tease. "It's the new me. I'd better explain. The body you see before you is a modified clone of my old devil's body. I picked up the clone magical spell from the Marquis's spell book that we found and then modified it to produce this new body. You see, it all rather came together like a flash, when Saint Jon and I were discussing life. He and Darless reaffirmed something for me that I had entirely forgotten about for eons, and that is, that I really am a spiritual being — a being that inhabits a body, much like you inhabit a house or ride a horse. Saint Jon showed me the path. At the top end are spiritual beings that are fully aware of themselves and can cause things to happen directly, such as lifting a stone without the need or presence of a body; we call these beings gods and goddesses or arch-devils, in my former case. Others are aware of themselves, but inhabit and use a body, because they cannot lift a stone without using the body as a via. Others have completely forgotten they are an immortal spirit, and are going around being their bodies — that is, their bodies represent their sole identity."

"Now that is a fascinating viewpoint," interrupted Basil d'Ambrose. "Are you saying that the difference between us mortal folks and our Gods is just a matter of horsepower, so to speak?"

"Yes and no," Glasya frowned trying to figure out a better way of handling this priest. "Mortal folks is the problem here. You are not mortal folks; it is your bodies that are mortal not you; you are immortal. I, for one, have had many bodies over the centuries."

"Ah then, you are talking about or believe in reincarnation?" Basil was growing more confused by the moment, as were several others.

"Whether or not one has lived before or will have other bodies in the future is not the issue, Basil. I leave that up to each one of you to discover for yourselves. Some of you can move out of your bodies and perceive the universe in some manner. You know that you are not your bodies. But, and this is a big but, while separate from your bodies, can you do anything, like lift a stone? I can't. On the other hand, I know that my ex-lord, Arch-devil Dispater certainly can and does, but he often uses a body just for appearance sake, when dealing with others. People can accept his presence and communicate with him better, when they see a physical body standing before them. From what Saint Jon has told me of his visits with Ukko, Father Ukko does not use a physical body as we know it, but more of a tenuous gaseous form."

"Put that way, I can see your concept," said Basil, "but are you implying that we all were once as the gods and have somehow fallen from grace, lost our abilities?" His voice dropped into a definite antagonism.

She laughed, "Ah, now that is a matter of religion. I will not venture to speculate. I believe that is your realm, Basil. I believe Saint Jon will back me up on this one, and that is this: the truth and only the truth sets one free. I have found that to be most definitely the case with me." She adroitly changed the topic here. "Long have I wanted out of Hell, but could find no way. As archmage to Dispater, I could not just leave — obligations. By making a clone of myself, a new identical body, I hoped that I could leave him with this new 'Glasya' clone and take my leave from Hell. At least that was my plan until I ran into Saint Jon. Using his and Darless's mental methods, I erased one particular incident that happened many years ago. When I saw what I really had done and why, I changed. My thirst for evil things evaporated! Actually, Jon, I regained some self-respect. Check me, Basil; I am not evil anymore. Pretty darn amazing. Come on, please check me."

She was so insistent that Basil said a short prayer to Father Ukko and then examined her. "She speaks the truth; no evil, just neutrality. Hum, a devil has changed! Now that is something to ponder."

Smiling, Glasya resumed, "So this is why I altered the clone spell — to make a clone body that was minus some devil characteristics, like the horns and wings. Then, I moved out of my old devil body and into this new one. Dispater has given me permission to leave Hell; he still has the old Glasya body there with all my spells available to it. He yet has his archmage and I have my freedom. I have come here seeking permission to reside in your new town so that I may attend Darless's college and learn more about Saint Jon's therapy. I also wanted to attend your weddings. In return, I offer whatever aid I can provide for the safety of the town. By the way Darless, congratulations on making Archmage status. That's a pretty impressive achievement! So if you grant my request, this town will boast three archmages in it, rather unheard of, if you ask me."

"I gave her my permission," Alison hurriedly added, but her mind was racing on an entirely different matter. The devil that she had freed a few days ago had spoken of a prophesy that Dispater had made on the coming of Saint Jon. What did Glasya know of this? Was there even such a prophesy? If so, what else did it say? Millions of questions flooded her mind, but unfortunately now was not the time to ask them. Jon and Darless also were having similar thoughts.

Basil had one more consideration to voice, "Where are you going to live? I assume that you will be building some kind of tower here? Will it fit into the overall plans that Alison has for the city? We already have a prominent Church of Ukko and Darless's College campus."

She knew she was on delicate grounds with this point. "You are right, Basil, ordinarily, I would build myself a fancy wizard's tower. That would be out of place here. I certainly don't want to compete with Alison or Darless. I want us all to work together as a team." In her mind she saw the images of her adventures with Saint Jon in the Canyon Lands; there, they were a team. It was the first time she was a true team player in eons, and she found she treasured it greatly. "No, I would just like one of these stone homes, but I would like to make an extensive underground laboratory for magical research and such. If that is okay, I'm sure Alison will let me know where I can 'dig' without interfering with any other underground chambers."

"No problem with that," said Alison. "So everyone, from now on, she is to be known as Glasya Greenleaf. If anyone asks, she is just an old friend of us all that we met on our recent journey. She is not a devil anymore."

That settled the matter. Everyone began chatting about where her home should be located, did she have any possessions with which to furnish said home, and so on. Then the others dispersed back to their work. Thea, on her way out, said, "I'm glad you are going to live here, Glasya. I'm really very fond of you. I knew you weren't a bad devil, but no one would listen to me." Glasya smiled and gave her a hug.

"I've got a huge amount of magical items to identify, Glasya, so perhaps Jon here can take you for a tour of the town and help you find a location. When you get settled, I would really appreciate any help in sorting out all these magical things," Alison said. Jon took Glasya for a tour of the town and it also gave him another chance to walk Bessy.

"The town is one big square, a mile on each side," Jon explained, though this was obvious. "Alison's castle complex forms the northwest quadrant." Bessy ran out in front of the pair, circling back toward them and then out again. The gates in the walls are called North, South, East, and West Gate, rather dull if you ask me, but practical, I guess. The main north-south road we are on now is called Main Street. The other main road going from East Gate to West Gate is called Center Street. All of the other east-west streets are numbered starting at First Street which is right up against the north wall. Most private residences are in the north-east quadrant. The cross streets all have letters, the first one against the west wall is A Street. I guess it makes everything very easy to locate." Unimaginative, thought Glasya.

An hour later she decided on her new home. She took the last home on First Street, Number 42. "Alison is in the northwest corner; Darless, in the southeast. So I'll be in the northeast." Jon smiled, all three mages were about as far apart from each other as possible. He wondered if there was any reason for it.

Jon led her back to see Stephen so she could sign the contract. As they walked, Jon asked, "Are you going to need any money to get things for your house and all that? If so, I'm sure I can loan you whatever you may need." He saw that she had nothing but the cloak and clothes she was wearing.

"Thanks, Jon, but you are forgetting that I am an archmage. I've got five portable holes on my person, and all are filled to the brim. What I really need is a safe place to store things. I don't suppose that there is a bank here yet?"

"No, it's under construction still. Maybe Alison would let you store stuff in her treasury room, but it's pretty full at the moment," he offered. "Ah, here's the steward's office. I'll let you talk to Stephen. I guess I had better head over to the church. I'm holding the first rehearsal of the town band in about an hour."

"Say, Jon, I've been meaning to ask you about something. Do you need a drummer for your band or can you use another drummer? I play a mean drum and I really would love to be in a band of some kind."

Jon did a double take. "You play drums? I would never have guessed! Wow. Sure, sure you are more than welcome. I've got five others so far, but no drummer. I hope we can get good enough to play for church services, dances and real concerts — a wide variety of music — that's my initial plan anyway. Come on by when you get done here, if you can. If not, I'll let you know when the group decides to hold rehearsals." Jon walked away smiling, he never would have figured Glasya to be a musician, a percussionist. Amazing. But then, it began to make sense to him. He'd observed a great similarity between music and the wizard's spell casting. Maybe it was not so strange a thing after all.

When she signed her contract with Stephen, Glasya was totally surprised to find that each home had both hot and cold running water, a fancy indoor ceramic toilet and a bathtub facility! Not even Dispater had all three in his palace. When she later found out that this was due to Jon and Rufus, the inventor, it then made sense to her. Next, she visited Mat's new locksmith shop to make an appointment to have him install new locks on her doors. Finally, with a satisfied look on her face and a bounce in her footsteps, she walked home to her new place.

Glasya spent an hour unpacking the relatively few items she had in her portable holes. She had numerous magical items and spell books stored in three of the five. One other was filled to the brim with gems stones of all kinds and sizes. The other held what few treasured personal items she had; there were not many. The largest item was a drum she called Beater that looked like a zarb or dumbec with a flared opening on one end. Beater was magically enchanted. While she was playing it, she could not be attacked by surprise because Beater would always warn her of impending danger. She also had one change of clothing and a few other small items. Carefully, Glasya placed her jade antelope statue on her mantel above the fireplace and smiled back at it. "Glasya, my dear, that's about all of it. No furniture, no clothes, no cooking ware, no food, no safe, no magic study room. My, but you are really going to have to go on a buying spree and soon. Ah, but first, I'd better see if I can help Alison and at the same time find out more about where I can best procure the things I need. I don't want to start digging out my basement tunnel and chamber complex and accidentally run into Alison's tunnels." She smiled at the imagined affront, turned on her heels and left her new house. Once outside, she spoke a command word and a ward of guarding appeared around her door, barring all entry. Carefree for the first time in nearly a hundred years, she strolled down the street to the North Gate and out across the grounds to Alison's underground dungeon.

"Hi, Glasya, all fixed up now?" Alison asked, pausing in her examination of an axe.

"Well I have a new home, Number 42 First Street. However, except for a change of clothes, I need everything else that goes into a house!" Both women laughed. "From all the hectic bustle around here, I suspect you are taxing the local economies to their maximum."

"Yes, you got that right! We're pulling supplies and craftsmen from all the surrounding towns in an attempt to get fully operational before fall. Just about everything you may need, like tables and chairs, are backlogged nearly three months at this point. Probably your best bet would be to try the towns up on the Greenway or perhaps Mennion south of the Durse Woods. I'll take you there later this afternoon, if you like. I need to do some shopping for wedding presents myself. Meantime, want to lend a hand in identifying stuff?"

"You will have to tell me the full details about the tower adventure later when we have more time! I'm all ears, but jeesh this is a huge pile to identify. I'll be glad to lend a hand, or spell rather." Both mages worked for another hour properly identifying another ten items. When they were finishing up and preparing to go shopping in Mennion, Glasya had an idea, "Say, with all this stuff, why don't you open a magic item store, where folks can come and purchase an enchanted short sword or this climbing rope?"

"Well, I had thought of dividing up these things equally with the others. But you may have a better idea. After all how on earth are we going to dispose of two dozen magical daggers? I'll broach the idea with the others tonight over supper. Say care to join us for dinner?" Alison asked, knowing that at this point Glasya had no way to fix a meal, even if she managed somehow to find some food. Further, no inns were yet in operation.

"I'd be very pleased to dine with you and your large family. I have not had such an opportunity for ever so long a time. Lead on to Mennion, then, and let's go shopping. I think I have much to get!" Both laughed at the picture of buying everything needed to fill a new home.

"Don't get too many clothes, though," Alison added, "May's the best seamstress I have ever found anywhere. I'm sure she would enjoy making outfits to your specifications. Sometimes I think that her clothes are of high enough quality to hold a magical enchantment!"

"Ah, I've always wanted a ball gown of flying!" Glasya spoofed, and both women chuckled at the idea. Alison chanted her teleport spell and both appeared at the edge of Mennion. They spent two hours shopping. When they headed home, Glasya had arranged for three wagon loads of her new household goods to be delivered next week.

That evening Mandy and William both joined the greater d'Ambrose family for dinner. They had gotten their next to last fittings on their wedding clothes. Glasya also dined with them; she really had few other options for eating. Of course the first topic of discussion was the upcoming wedding, now just four days away. Jon asked

Alison, "My Love, question for you. I am really unfamiliar with weddings and their traditions around here. Back home, it is traditional that the couple exchange wedding rings, though sometimes only the bride gets a ring. Do we do that here or are there some other things that are done? I don't want to look like a fool come wedding day or embarrass you either."

"Gee, are these wedding rings magical?" she asked, wondering what his tradition was about.

"No, I think it is just a tradition. Sometimes, the rings have a very expensive diamond in them, but really I think it is supposed to be a symbol of marriage. From a guy's view, when meeting a new woman, a glance at her ring finger tells us if she's already married, if you follow me. Is that done here?"

"Kind of like a bondage thing," put in Mandy, "bound together with a ring. No, we don't do that here. When we marry where I come from, it might be different up here, our vows together are what matters. It's our shared pledges that bind us together in a union."

"Same here," Alison concurred. "Sometimes, the woman comes with a dowry, that is, she gives a large financial donation to her new husband. The larger the dowry, the more the man is supposed to appreciate her, but many of us women think that is a bunch of hogwash. It's like Mandy says, our pledges to each other are what binds us together as one. The only thing is that most often the woman changes her last name to the man's last name."

"William and I have come up with a better way to handle the name thing. I'm going to put a dash between names. I'll be Mandy Blackthorn-Conners. This way, everyone will still know me by my current last name. I think that works really well," Mandy explained.

William added shyly, "I really didn't want her to change her name to only Connors. She is the one with all the power and renown, I am just a humble village baker.

Honestly, I am having a devil of a time back at her, or rather our, castle. All the servants and men at arms keep expecting me to give the daily orders. I don't know anything about such. Mandy's compromise is acceptable to me. I was perfectly happy to have her still be Mandy Blackthorn, but she kept insisting."

"Say, I like that idea, Mandy," Alison twisted an errant hair and added thoughtfully, "Alison d'Ambrose-Brown works well too. What do you think of that Jon?"

Before he could comment, Darless interjected, "Names have power, don't forget this detail. As we all know, powerful magic spells permit a caster to summon another being and force them into servitude. But the magic only works if the caster knows the true name of the person to be summoned against their own will." Jon, Alison and Mandy immediately remembered just how serious this had been, when they first met Darless, and how Jon had discovered her true last name and given it to her. Only a few beings knew her true last name, and thus this alu-demon could no longer be summoned into the servitude of others as she had been. "So while I will pretend to be Darless le Bonnaire, I will, in fact, not assume that last name for safety's sake."

"Verily, I insisted," Sir Thomas added strongly, "Anyone would immediately guess my wife would be called Darless le Bonnaire and could thus summon her away. So her true name shall continue to be known only to a very few people."

"Good going, Darless," Jon finally got to insert his thoughts. "That is an excellent way to protect yourself! We'll call you Darless le Bonnaire, but you are really Darless you-know-who. Perfect! Alison, I think your choice works well too, but it is okay with me if you don't change your last name at all. Either way is fine."

"Well, I like the idea of being May Newcastle," May declared, prompting Thea to proclaim she chose to be Thea Smith. But Lonnie pointed out that since he was now Sir Lonnie, she would have to be called Lady Thea Smith. A wide smile told everyone that she fancied the title.

Glasya added, "I think the choices of names are excellent all around. Say, May, I've been meaning to ask you something. Once the weddings are finished, could I hire you to make me a number of dresses and outfits? I've only got one other change of clothes, plus a few items coming in by wagon next week. I've heard that you are the best seamstress around."

"Right on that one! May, the wedding gowns are fabulous!" Mandy interjected. Everyone else seconded her opinion. May blushed visibly. She knew that she would have more orders than she could fill for quite some time in the future. For a brief instant, May glimpsed her future and saw that she would have a very large dressmaking business, one that dwarfed her former establishment back in Freetown.

The five children fidgeted; all this adult talk was boring to them. Grandma Anna interrupted them, "Okay kids. If you all will excuse me and the children, we will go play and leave you to talk." She had found a great satisfaction in her grandchildren. The six left, accompanied by "Tell us another story, Grandma, please." Christina was very pleased indeed that her mom was helping out. Mary Ellen was also happy to be able to spend more time with Stephen, unfettered with her children.

However, the departure of Anna caused Basil to frown. "What's bothering you, Dad?" asked a perceptive Alison, who still worried about her parents adapting to life after their twenty-one years of imprisonment.

"After all you have done for us and our family, I don't have the right to put my burdens on you, Allie," he apologized.

Alison tensed up; Jon's watchful eye caught it as well. Before she could reply, he spoke up, "Mr.

d'Ambrose, Basil Sir, I beg your pardon, but yes you do. You see sir, when we chose to rescue you and Anna, we assumed full responsibility for the outcome of our actions. What kind of a son-in-law would rescue you and then leave you on your own afterwards, to sink or swim? We knew full well what we were letting ourselves in for when we rescued you. Yes, we will be checking up on everyone whom we rescued in a few months' time to see how they are doing and help where we can, including those dozen that suffered being turned into giant scorpions. So you have every right to tell us all about it. We would be affronted if you withheld your feelings and worries from us, right Alison?"

"Right! Dad, I know that you know that with power comes responsibility. I am an archmage and with that immense power comes an even greater responsibility than I can sometimes muster!"

Jon had never seen Basil look so humble, his head hung low. "You are right, Allie," he muttered. "It's just that I've lost everything. I've no castle, no money, no possessions, no nothing anymore. I just can't stand living off of you. Anna has her grandchildren; she loves children, obviously. She's already told me that she'll kill me, if I go off adventuring again. So what am I to do? I'm in my prime and sit here with my hands tied, so to speak."

Alison grieved for her father. Jon spoke up, thankfully for Alison, "I had been wondering how long it would be before this came up with you. Basil, if I may call you by your first name — say, how am I supposed to address you anyway? I cannot call you dad."

"Basil is fine with me. After all, I call you Jon, unless you want me to call you Saint Jon," he answered rather apathetically.

"Please, please just call me Jon!" he answered, bringing smiles to several other's faces. Everyone was listening intently to their conversation. "Okay, Basil. You have a very critical problem here. You are absolutely right in not wanting to live off of Alison's handouts. And I agree with Anna, it is way too soon for you to head off on more adventures for many reasons. Actually, Basil, I've really been thinking a lot about your situation, especially while I am out walking Bessy. When walking her, I have time to think clearly with no interruptions. It all boils down to your goals and purposes in life. It is my opinion that a man is as alive as he has goals and is pursuing them successfully. Only a dead man has no goals and purposes in life. Take myself, for example. I am a musician. I love music — the sheer beauty in music. I want to share that with others everywhere I go. I am not a composer; I've not the talent or ability. I'm a player of what others have created, sharing that beauty with others."

He paused a moment. "In your case, your world, your goals and purposes have all been turned upside down and sideways. I know of no way to undo time, to undo the last twenty-one years for you. We are left with just this: we need to help you establish a new set of goals and purposes for yourself at this point in time. That also brings up another thing I have been wanting to talk to Alison about, but have just never had any chance."

Suddenly, she was all ears. "Alison, you probably haven't even had time to think about this yet, we've all been so busy and all. But just how are you going to rule the Ville? I was assuming that you'd rather be like a benevolent monarch to your townsfolk, am I right?"

"Well, yes, I believe so," she said slowly, not quite grasping his full meaning. "Certainly I've had no time to think much about it. I guess I am the ultimate ruler or authority, since I paid for everything. What's this got to do with dad?"

"Ah, but was not your initial idea for the town that of making a truly 'free' town?" She nodded enthusiastically. "Well, then, if the citizens of the Ville are to be truly free, then every man and woman must be free to have a say in what goes on here, be free to speak to anyone about anything at any time, be free to worship whatever and whomever they choose whenever they want, be free to choose their own goals and livelihoods. Every man and woman must have a say in the governing of the town and know that they have a say in what goes on here. Only then can they be truly free men and women."

"But. . ." said Alison.

"But. . ." Basil broke in.

"But. . ." added Mandy.

"But. . ." exclaimed Stephen.

"You know, we think that," said May.

"You are precisely correct!" Mat finished the sentence.

"Huh?" came from all sides of the twins.

"Honestly, Jon, you think that a blacksmith knows enough about the defense of a castle to have a valid opinion on it?" Alison finally got her "but" into the conversation. "Oops, no offence Helmut." She realized she had just insulted Christina's husband.

Before the blacksmith could respond, Jon quickly said, "Normally, no. But if he is to be a free blacksmith, he must be educated, informed so that he *can* have a valid opinion. Further, who knows better than a blacksmith the strength of iron made items, like your doors? Further, who knows better than a seamstress the quality of clothing. Who knows better than a provisioner how long food stocks can safely be stored and how long said supplies would last in a siege? Poor Stephen, as your steward, is being grossly overworked, if all this falls on his head."

"But it is Alison's money that made the town," Basil interjected his 'but.'

"It certainly is. But, has she not said that she wants to have a free town here?" Jon countered.

"But someone's got to be in control, command the guards, and such or else it is all chaos the likes of which even I don't like," Mandy protested, adding in her 'but.'

"Of course, Mandy, there has to be a leader. That's what leaders are for. But the men and women of the town must be free to elect their own leaders and to replace them if those leaders fail to live up to the town's ideals." Jon found himself becoming more and more animated. "Every man and woman needs to be free to do what vocation they wish, such as me being a musician. Our children should be educated so that they know what vocations are available. They should be free to marry whomever they choose, that is, no prearranged marriages like we had in the Dark Ages where I come from. They should be free to believe what they want about spiritual beings, free to believe and worship freely, free to have their own opinions about anything and to express them, and free to know all about their chosen government and to exercise their rights as a citizen of that group. Yes, given all these, you will then have *free* men and women!" He paused to see if he neglected anything.

"But most of these people are simple villagers," protested Christina getting in her 'but,' "most cannot even read and write. How can one even hope that they can know enough to make a good choice in things?"

"Ah, exactly what you yourself proposed earlier," Jon countered, "we owe it to them to educate, not only the children of the town, but everyone. We must teach and explain and council and deal with their misunderstandings and superstitions. We have a tall order ahead of us. That's where educated, experienced men, like Basil shine. People respect him and would learn from him. You have a golden opportunity to impact all mankind by making the Ville a shining example for the world to see, Basil. It's a tall order indeed!"

"Saint Jon," Basil answered very sternly, "do you realize that what you are proposing is nothing short of a true freedom of which even the gods may be envious?"

"Yes, isn't that what you had in mind, Alison?" Jon replied looking at his fiancé.

"Yes, but. . ." she replied, all this was coming way too fast for her to grasp all the ramifications.

Darless said just as sternly as Basil, "Jon, do you realize that you are proposing nearly a utopia here?"

"It's just that Alison said she wanted a free town and that is what freedom means to me. Anything less is not. That's all," he replied.

"Can *we* finally say something here?" broke in Mat and May in unison. They were slightly annoyed at not yet having had the opportunity to speak their mind. Everyone shut up at once, realizing they had been dominating the conversation.

"Look, we have had some experience with freedom," began May. "Twenty-one years ago, Freetown was anything but free."

"More like the tyranny of bullies and thieves," Mat continued without the slightest pause. "It took us a long time as the secretive 'Twins' to give some of the people there back some small amount of self-dignity, self-pride."

"But look what happened," May picked up without a second's pause. "Their resurgence so far outweighed what little we gave them it's not funny. Six hundred sought their freedom in spite of the overwhelming odds against them."

"And these people were just ordinary townsfolk — nary a fighter among them," Mat carried on. "Merchants, tradesfolk, and children. Please, don't sell these people short just because they cannot read or write or are not privy to all of the worldly information that some of us are, please."

"You will find them eager to learn," May animatedly continued, "if you explain to them what is at stake here, their total freedom in life. They will definitely want to contribute somehow."

"And your biggest challenge is figuring out each can best contribute to the general cause," Mat finished up.

"We would be proud to do anything that we can to help bring this about," concluded May.

Basil opened his mouth to speak, but a sudden realization hit him heavily. No words came out. He became exceedingly animated, eyes bright. Then he burst out into hearty laughter. It was contagious, breaking the solemnity of the discussion thus far. So hard did he laugh, that others could not help but smile as the tensions evaporated. Finally, Alison asked, "Dad? What's going on?"

Between fits of laughter, he managed to blurt out, "Holy Mage of Ukko and Holy Children of Ukko." That's all he could say for the next couple minutes, he kept repeating it over and over, when he could manage it while still laughing.

Ten minutes later, he finally regained some control and explained to everyone, "Please my children, please accept my most humble apologies. I have been an old fool who cannot see!" Everyone looked at him with blank faces. He saw that they had no idea what about what he was talking. So he explained, "When you told me of your titles, biased priest that I am, I assumed that those were just simple titles — that they in fact represented nothing of any real importance, just titles. I am or was biased — that is until just this moment anyway — I considered that Father Ukko's chosen were only his Holy Priests and his Holy Paladins. But in fact, I just realized that you *are* the very embodiment of those titles — that you *are* his Holy Mage and Holy Children!"

As his words sunk into their minds, Alison, May and Mat felt that for the first time their father actually saw them for what they really were and had become, not just as his grown up children. All three felt a strong bond with their father in that instant. But Basil was not finished, "And you know, your ideals for the free town are so, well almost godlike, that I would be honored if you would let me help the men and women achieve that state of freedom. It is as Jon says, as the town priest, I have both their respect and confidence. I know I can help to get them to grasp what they need to know to make intelligent decisions and such. In fact, this is such a worthy goal, I am willing to dedicate the rest of my life to helping you achieve this here!"

"Say, count me in on it too," added Christina, "I've already plans for a school; I only have to expand its scope!" Rapid-fire, all others around the table added theirs as well, even Glasya, who had been silent throughout, while pondering the tremendous significance of this discussion, as well as its ultimate ramifications throughout future time.

When the conversation died down slightly, Glasya spoke up for the first time. "May add a small observation?" she asked.

"Absolutely, we are a free town now!" Alison gaily answered.

"Look, I am beginning to realize the tremendous impact that this can have on this entire world. During the last hundred or so years, I've been to many cities, towns and castles all over. Basically, I have observed that each is run by one strong, domineering person; some are good, some are evil, some are so-so. Yet I can truthfully say that the average person has little freedom in the way that Jon defines freedom. Can you see that, if we bring true freedom to this single town and expand it to all Verbenloc, then it is highly likely to spread throughout the inhabited world, given time? It may take a centuries, but one by one, other towns and cities are going to follow suit. I am truly impressed, Saint Jon, the Redeemer! You bet that I want to play a part in bringing all this about.

You are right, we all have certain skills that we can add to the overall pot, so to speak. To make it work initially is going to require an immense amount of work on our parts. But once every man and woman in the town has been educated and is taking his or her active role as a town citizen, why it will become self-perpetuating!"

She was not finished, "Basil, I suggest that you draw up a document outlining the basic articles or principles of free citizens, including the rights and duties and obligations of said free citizens. Write it in simple terms that everyone can fully grasp."

The priest enthusiastically agreed, "Absolutely, I concur, this should be the first step. I also think that we should form up a governing council, whose purpose is to help organize things so that it all can come about and then disband once the town is operating on its own steam. For starters, we all here should be on the council, but there are plenty of others that probably should be included, like the captain of the guards. Say what's his name?"

"Raul," answered Stephen. "While I can handle stewardship of a castle, without lots of competent help, there is no way I could also do the same for an entire town! This is going to be very interesting indeed. When do we start?"

"We already have," joked Basil.

"Oh yes, dad," added Alison, "as far as money goes, don't forget that as our town priest you are entitled to a salary. Eventually, I expect that the church donations will more than cover it, once it is up and fully running. I was going to give you a year's advance on the salary, but then I realized we don't yet have a bank. I can see we have to really get going on making a safe bank, but I am completely ignorant of banks."

"Say, perhaps I can help out. I disparately need a bank as well," Glasya piped up seeing a chance to be of aid to her newly adopted town. "My specialty is security, both physical and magical. While I don't know either how to run one, I certainly can help get the physical premises in good shape. Don't worry that I'll steal all your money because I'll set it up so that the head banker is the only one with the right combination." She attempted to thwart any possible misgivings any might have about a former devil having access to the entire town's bank. "Basil, can you find the right personnel to run our bank? If so, I'll get on with it as soon as we have a building."

Basil started to protest, but suddenly realized why, "I was about to say I don't hardly know any of these new townspeople, but now I see what you mean — use my priestly abilities to select honest people. Sure that is right in my line of work. I'll get on it tomorrow."

"Well, we actually do have a building set aside to be used for our bank," Alison added. "I believe the shell is done, but the dwarves were waiting for specifics of the internal layout before actually completing it. Something about vaults and such. I'll check on it tomorrow and let you know." Thea noted that Glasya seemed very happy that her assistance was so completely accepted.

"Well, I hate to be the party-pooper, but the big day is only four days away and William and I still have a lot of preparations to finish up," Mandy inserted. She now remembered what she had been meaning to ask everyone. "Say, I nearly forgot, but how about the actual ceremony itself? I'm having my close friend Glenda Appleblossom, a High Priestess of Reylona, bear witness for us. I'm sure she can witness for the rest of you, but perhaps you might like a High Priest of Ukko to do so."

"I know we originally said we didn't mind," Alison answered a bit reservedly, "but now with mom and dad back, perhaps it would be better if we had a priest of Ukko witness for us. What do the rest of you think?"

Various opinions flowed. Thea said it didn't matter to her, but the others agreed with Alison. "Allie, May, Mat — I know that it's tradition that I be the father figure, but considering the circumstances, I would be highly honored it you would permit me to also be your witness in my office as High Priest. It is the very least I can do for you. I'm not sure mother would like it, but I sure would!" His reply was beaming smiles all around!

"Then, that's settled," declared Mandy. "Oh yes, have you all worked out your wedding vows yet? William and I have ours more or less done."

"Huh?" exclaimed Jon. "I think I am missing something. Doesn't the priest just say the words and we repeat them?"

"What kind of a wedding is that?" asked Alison incredulously. Then, she realized that the customs in Jon's world were probably very different from hers. "Here, usually the couple write up the vows that they use to form their union and recite them before the congregation and are witnessed by their priest, who then gives the god's blessing on the union. I'm sorry Jon, I've been so busy with everything else that I forgot about it. We should talk about it tonight."

"Okay, I think that your way will be a far better way to start a marriage!" Jon assented.

"So will someone take us back home now?" Mandy finished up.

"Sure thing," Alison hastily answered. After Mandy and William said their goodbyes, Alison teleported them back to the Blackthorn Castle commons. "Say Mandy, what would you say to us making a permanent gate portal between your place here and the Ville?"

"As much as we come and go, that would be really useful, I think, especially if it were large enough so I could bring horses with me when needed," Mandy replied. "William and I have already talked about such a possibility. His only concern is security and where the location would be. If we had our terminal out here in the common courtyard, then someone might by accident trigger it and come a visiting you. If we make it inside one of my rooms, then that rules out horses, but enemies using it inside my room would be bypassing the defensive castle walls."

"I see your point," Alison replied twisting a strand of hair in thought, "if we set it up like Archmage Sarah did in her tower, anyone can push the activation button. That is completely not acceptable. Maybe it should be activated more like the way the priests had it doing back in Freetown to get into the Artifact Chamber under the central well. You know, say some activation words."

"Cool! But make sure that some ordinary person might not say it by accident," the ranger cautioned. Alison agreed and so did William.

Thus, her mind working on yet another project, the archmage teleported back to her dining room. She found the others had left but Jon was still sitting, sipping another cup of tea awaiting her. "Hi Love," she said and both embraced warmly, certain no one was watching.

"Okay, we best get started on our vows. Here, the basis of marriage are the vows which form the contract by which two people want to join and live their lives. So what do we want to base ours on, my dear?" They began a serious discussion that they should have started long ago. By midnight, they had worked it out to both their satisfactions. They retired for the night to sleep on it and see if they still agreed with it the next day. In fact, they did.

During the hectic next three days, the women became more and more excited about their special day. Each of the women shared with the others their proposed vows, seeking not only moral support, but also confirmation that they didn't forget some detail. Alison found things so distracting that she could not concentrate on her self-appointed task of magic item identification. Indeed, it was all she could do just to keep the high level orders to the dwarven engineers rolling along properly. Finally, the night before the big wedding day, everyone gathered in the new castle courtyard with many packages in tow. So large was the party, that the mages needed to make two round trips to teleport everyone to Blackthorn Castle.

Per Mandy's request, each arriving group, including Thea's family, landed just outside the castle proper on the newly cobblestoned road connecting the village to the castle. Lanterns were hung from the bows of the gnarled oak trees that canopied the road. Ribbons and streamers dangled festively from the branches. Lanterns were placed in all of the castle and keep windows that faced toward the village making the castle more like a light show. Mandy and William stood side by side welcoming all of the visitors personally, while some of their staff led them down the road and into the castle commons.

After the last group arrived, Mandy accompanied them, joining the first group already in her commons area. In one corner, two ancient gnarled oak trees spread their boughs over the castle walls forming a protective green roof. Mandy had gone to great lengths to decorated this location. "Here's where we hold the ceremony tomorrow," she explained to everyone. "I think nearly everyone in the village will be here too. Only this commons is large enough to hold everyone. Do you like our spot?"

"I think it is magnificent," Alison approved. "I like your new cobblestone road. Did you do all the streets in the village?"

"Yes, but some are still under construction. Come on, let me show everyone the keep and where you will be staying tonight." She led the way inside. The brides followed her, while the grooms followed William to their respective quarters. Some of her servants led the other families to rooms that lay between the brides and grooms rooms. Mandy assumed that each family would want their own room for the night.

Once everyone was settled, shown where the restrooms, kitchen area, dining hall and other important spots were located, they all gathered in Mandy's Great Hall for a party. She had spared no expense in decorating the huge room nor in the refreshments. Indeed, William had baked numerous treats, enough to feed a small army. What they didn't eat would be given away tomorrow to all the villagers. In one corner, Mandy had setup a number of games for the children, who gaily made a dash for all the toys. Nearby was a table with rolls and cocoa in vast quantities. Several stopped first to drink a mug or two.

The evening's party began in earnest. "Alison, Jon, come over here, there are two women you just *have* to meet!" In spite of Alison's pleadings, she would not tell them who. She led them to one corner near the main refreshment table. There stood a tall, well-muscled, middle aged woman dressed in priestly robes. Jon recognized her holy symbol immediately.

"Ah, you must be the High Priest Glenda Appleblossom that Mandy has told us all about," Jon bowed.

"Yes, Glenda, this is Archmage Alison d'Ambrose and Saint Jon Brown. You two, this is her Holiness, Priestess Glenda Appleblossom," Mandy happily did the introductions. Jon could tell that Mandy was extremely pleased that her close friends finally met.

Glenda shook both Jon's and Alison's hands firmly. Jon could sense the strength her female form partially disguised. Here was a warrior priestess. "At long last we meet! I've heard so much about you. Somehow, you do not look the imposing figure I had imagined. No offense, Saint Jon," she added hastily. "But I was expecting that you would look more robust, more physical, more godlike. I guess I am a victim of my own stereotyping of priests. Ah, Alison now you look just like I imagined, a mage."

"Why, do all mages look the same?" teased Alison. "Really, we are very pleased to meet you at long last. Mandy is always telling us about you."

"I am a musician," Jon proclaimed. "That's probably why; you should think of me as a musician not a priest or god."

"And here let me present," Mandy interrupted, "one of my very special guests. I and we are all exceedingly honored to have her here. Rolinda, this is Alison and Jon. And this is Rolinda Cetardonion, a powerful grey elf archer. It is very rare indeed when a grey elf attends the weddings of humans." Jon had seen very few elves. Rolinda was barely five feet tall and slender as a flower, but more radiant than a rose. She had long black hair that fell down to her knees. Her face was oval and a pale grey in color. Her ears were pointed at the tops. But her countenance was radiant. When she looked at you, her eyes seemed to pierce you to your soul. She wore a thin silken dress that flowed as she moved.

She spoke very softly, like the maiden that she still was, but commanding was her gentle voice. "It is an honor for me to meet you both personally, Saint Jon and Alison. On behalf of the grey elves, please accept our eternal gratitude for your recent rescue of our imprisoned kin. May the blessings of Ehlona fill your days."

"Very pleased to meet you," Jon kissed her offered hand. "It's hard to imagine that you are an archer."

"Looks are deceiving, Saint Jon, but you already know that," she replied softly. Jon could easily become enchanted with her. Rolinda radiated eternal youth, beauty, and grace.

Mandy just had to compliment her, "I have personally seen Rolinda split an arrow in the center of a target some hundred-fifty feet away. I could not even see the arrow that she aimed at!"

Jon marveled at her accuracy and then had an idea, "Rolinda, by chance do you control the arrow once it leaves your bow?"

"Huh?" said Alison, thinking this was obviously impossible. Once a arrow was loosened, it did its thing. Mandy, likewise. Both were surprised by Rolinda's answer.

"Ah, you are even more observant than I thought from Mandy's description. Yes, you are one of the first people ever to grasp what a master archer can do. If I am concentrating, it hits the intended spot. The nudging forces are very slight. But tell me, how was it that you were able to detect those that were imprisoned at the tower of Archmage Sarah le Garde? I have wondered about that detail ever since I heard the story of the rescue."

"I sensed their minds, though at first I could not tell what I was sensing. It was really weird, not like a normal mind. They were frozen in time, stuck on one thought that never varied," was his reply. "I nudge magic spells too. That's how I guessed you must be doing with your arrows. But I won't tell. Who'd believe me?"

She smiled, "Few that I have met in the last fifteen hundred years would, I am afraid."

"Wow! Just how old are you?" Jon asked incredulously, "You don't have to answer if you don't want to. I keep forgetting women are a bit sensitive about their age." Alison gave him a bump with her hip in a tease.

Gaily she said, "Two thousand and thirty-three of your years is its reckoning. But you have given me something to ponder, Saint Jon, you really move spells?"

"Yes, I've seen him do it," Alison confirmed, "we shot spells wildly and he somehow guided them to their target, the archmage or lich in this case. Pretty darn amazing and unbelievable, if you ask me."

Just then, Mandy spied a new arrival. "Oh my! I am even more honored that I believed!" She waved her hand high, signaling the cloaked person, "Over here! Come on you two, you *have* to meet this elf!" She fairly pulled Jon and Alison with her as she headed toward her new guest.

The person was short, only about five feet tall with a slender build hidden under the gray-green hooded elfin cloak that nearly hid her form. Only her elfin shoes and black pant legs were visible until they drew closer. As they neared, Jon spied the tell-tale pale gray skin of another gray elf. From the dark, long hair barely concealed beneath the hood, Jon assumed it was another elf maiden of some importance.

"I'm so happy you could come!" exclaimed Mandy.

A deep voice, slightly higher than Alison's mellow alto voice, spoke in a hushed, serious tone. "Are these they?" Mandy nodded. "Good. Is there somewhere where we can speak privately, I am combining business with pleasure this trip. I want to get the business handled first."

"Follow me," Mandy said, pulling Alison and Jon along with her. No one spoke further words. It seemed awfully mysterious to Jon and Alison, but they said nothing and followed Mandy. She led them down a long hall and up a flight of stairs to Mandy's personal study, which was deserted. Mandy lit a couple lanterns and only then did her new guest throw back her hood and pull off the cloak. She was indeed a grey elf, though nowhere as pretty as Rolinda. In fact, she was average looking at best. Her face was pot-marked, as if she had contracted some terrible disease. Dressed in clothes that Jon might wear, she did not look like an elf maiden. There was something about this person, Jon thought, something sinister, perhaps.

Before Mandy could say anything, the low voice of the guest said, "For safety, let me cast a spell before we speak." No one objected and she quickly chanted her spell. Alison, of course, recognized it at once and sent mentally to Jon, *Anti-scrying. No one can now hear us talk.*

"Okay, it's safe now. Permit me, Mandy. You are Saint Jon Brown, are you not, and Archmage Alison?" Both nodded. "Let me introduce myself. I am Ra-ell Cirdain. I am a magic user and an assassin, albeit a neutral assassin. You may check my veracity if you desire, I am not and never have been evil in nature, but I have and do kill people. I heard that Mandy here was getting married and so I had to come, if only to see and meet whom she finally chose to marry. Call it female curiosity. I am still single." She spied both looking at her face, "Oh, those are the remnants of mummy rot which I unfortunately contracted a long time ago. I'm afraid this is the best it is going to heal."

"Pleased to meet you," Jon extended his hand. She hesitatingly met his hand, as if unsure if about doing so.

"You shake my hand even though I am an assassin?" she asked slightly confused.

"Sure, why not? You said you are not evil," Jon replied. "Any friend of Mandy's I would trust implicitly." His reply seemed to soften her outlook.

"Glad to meet you too," Alison said formally. She was still not too sure about this assassin, but if she was Mandy's friend, then she would go along with it for now.

Satisfied, Ra-ell continued, "Okay. Down to business. As the world's only Redeemer, I just had to come and warn you, Saint Jon. I come from Greytown, a large city far to the south of here. My outward trade is that of a magic user, though I am a long way from archmage status. But my dark side is that of the 'rectifier of major malevolent wrongs' by the use of thievery and assassinations of evil people. In the course of my dealings, I have come across some critical information that I need to tell you in secret. Are you familiar with the lands south and east of Vyndoc?"

"Not really," Alison answered for Jon, "we've heard that a band of assassins control it. How William passed through their area to get to Freetown last year is a mystery."

"Good. Yes, the band is led by one known only as Hadid. No one knows his last name. Hadid has a contract out for Jon." She paused to let that sink into their minds.

"Well, we kind of figured such," Alison answered her voice full of concern. "We killed one of the assassins who was trying to kill Jon last winter up in the Deadman's Pass."

"Then, perhaps my concerns are not as bad as I feared. The contract comes from Hadid personally, which is a rare event. I hear that he seldom 'gets his hands dirty' these days. So I also did a bit of checking up. 'Why?' I asked myself. After some investigation and from sources I cannot name, I have determined that the demon Lord Jarred is behind the contract. Apparently, you have made some very powerful enemies indeed."

"That's pretty much what we had worked out," Alison replied, a hint of dryness in her voice. She still did not fully trust an self-avowed assassin, even if this cold-blooded killer wasn't actually evil. Jon sensed her aloofness and guessed why Alison felt this way.

Ra-ell, who almost never told anyone of her dark profession, raised an eyebrow. Alison's reaction was actually better than this gray elf had predicted. So she continued, "Yes, my original assumptions have been borne out, Archmage. Any mage of your rank should have figured all this out by now." Ra-ell seldom withheld punches. She grew tired of bandying words with the mage. So she cut to the quick, "But do you know of the assassination attempt tomorrow during your wedding?"

From the shocked look on all three faces, Ra-ell knew they had not. Inwardly, she smiled but outward her thick lips showed only the slightest smirk.

"Zagroot zounds!" exclaimed Mandy suddenly very upset. "Not at my wedding! Of all the low down, dirty tricks! This takes the cake!"

Her face now quite pale, Alison faltered, "How — how do you know this?"

"Like I said, I am a 'rectifier of wrongs.' During my most recent 'recovery' operation, I found this document upon the late perpetrator of evil," the gray elf smiled, confident of her actions thus far. She took a small paper from a concealed pocket in her blouse and handed it to Alison. "You will need to use a spell to translate it. It is in assassin's code, if that helps."

As soon as Alison unfolded the paper, she chanted briefly and read. "Change of orders: take out Ramierez now. Felterwake will take out Saint Jon during the wedding." It was signed in a flowing capital letter, 'H'. She read it aloud for the benefit of the others. "It seems that we are deeply in your debt, Ra-ell. What can we do to repay you for your thoughtfulness?"

Ra-ell did not answer her direct question saying instead, "I thought about the impact of this information for a day and then acted. I am fairly certain that he has already arrived here ahead of me. I've been on his trail, but am a couple days behind his trail of dead bodies and thefts. I have no idea what he looks like, unfortunately."

"I wonder if he's going to try stuff like that one did back in Freetown," Jon said aloud half to himself as he remembered their very close call with that assassin.

Ra-ell turned to Mandy, "Explain, please." So Mandy spent about five minutes outlining their prevention of the assassination of Lord Metrarch last year in Freetown. Jon watched the facial expressions of Ra-ell closely and perceived that she was impressed with their actions. He thought that this was a good sign. So perhaps there was some hope.

"Golly this is going to be a really big problem," Mandy began thinking of preventative measures. "My entire village will be there, several hundred people. He could be in any kind of disguise. This is going to be very tricky. I guess we should postpone the wedding. What do you all think?"

"Well, if we explain it to the rest, I'm sure they would think that is best," Alison answered, still unsure of what the best action to take might be.

Ra-ell deftly changed the subject, perhaps to give them time to think. "Saint Jon, what is this redemption thing anyway? Is it for anyone? Even me?"

Jon, who had concluded that this elf didn't volunteer information easily, detected something about her question. He looked her in the eyes and decided to experiment. "Ra-ell, please have a seat on the bed." She looked perplexed, but did as he asked. To the other two women, he said, "Could you give us a few minutes alone please?" Mandy and Alison, discussing in earnest preventative measures, stepped into a side room, leaving the two of them alone. Jon said, "Okay, anything you say to me will be held in the strictest confidence; it's just between you and me. Something is troubling you. Can you see your mental pictures of it?"

She got very defensive, "Yes, but how do you know? Are you looking into my mind? I have an anti-scrying spell on me."

"Nope, I am not in your mind and have not tried. Now all I want you to do is to go to the beginning of those images and go through them and tell me what is happening as you go along," Jon commanded. He wondered if he would have to explain more or if she would resist him doing this. But to his surprise, she closed her eyes and began telling him. He sensed that she had the idea that telling him all this was of no importance, so why not.

"It was early this morning. I woke up in a cold sweat. The same nightmare I've had all my life had replayed as expected, that's all. I poured cold water on my face and got up," she said rather dryly.

"Thanks for telling me. Now let's go back to the very beginning of it and run through it once more. Tell me what you see," said Jon softly. He thought if she was thousands of years old and if this happened every morning, then he would be in for a very long night of it. He started to wonder if this was such a good idea. She continued and he noticed that she was getting a bit flushed in the face. On the fourth recounting, she looked miserable and he asked, "Do you see an earlier time this happened?" She of course did, it was right there, another morning when it had been particularly bad. Within fifteen minutes, the elf was sweating profusely and slight muscle tremors kept her shaking visibly. Jon pressed on and kept asking if there was an even earlier time she felt this way. Rapidly the early morning nightmares appeared one after the other. Then, suddenly she found a very early one.

"Gods, I'm a very little girl. I see my mother, she is cradling me, she has wonderfully long golden hair. I can smell flowers, jasmine I think. There's dad singing to the stars at night. I think it's our home in the forest. There is a noise, scares us. Great big men come in, swinging giant axes! Mom screams! I see dad's head severed, blood everywhere. They are coming towards us. I see the blade coming at me. Felt mom get hit. Falling. Crash. Hit floor. Cannot breathe. Mom's on top of me. Hear noises, things knocked about. Then all is quiet. Try to push mom up. Can't breathe. All goes black. Relief. Pressure is off of me. Hear voices. Young human saying, 'This one is alive! There, there little one. You are in safe hands now. Oh, it's Father Kellogh. He takes me away. That's all," she said, tears began dripping down her cheeks. She added, "Father Kellogh always said that he found me and raised me. He was my dearest friend, but he passed away, as humans do, so very long ago. I will never forget his kindness."

"Thank you for telling me. Now, let's go back to the very beginning of it once more and go through it telling me what happens as you go along." Jon heard the door open quietly, sensed Mandy and Alison checking on him, but he heard the door shut quietly and knew that they knew what he was doing. He also knew that both of them would stand guard outside the door until he was done. For the time being, they were safe from the assassin.

This time through, the elf woman cried for nearly ten minutes, completely soaking Jon's offered handkerchief. Jon knew that she was getting an enormous amount of suppressed grief released. He kept at it. The next pass, she got violently angry, nearly breaking the bedpost with her fist. This was one strong elf woman, Jon noted, thinking looks can be very deceiving. The next pass through, her anger lightened to antagonism and resentment. Next, a heavy boredom set in and she began yawning heavily wondering why Jon kept her going through it. He persisted. And the next pass through, she smiled and said, "Revenge. I swore revenge as a tiny baby. I decided to rectify all this." She started laughing, "Rectify it. I thought I would get my mom and dad back if I could rectify the evil done by those barbarians!" She continued to laugh. "Now that is really silly! Rectify! Get them back!" She laughed continuously now.

"Thank you very much, Ra-ell. Now I can answer your original question. Yes, it works on elves. It has worked on you. We are done for tonight. If you want more of this, come by Darless' college in a few more months once it is finished. You can get as much of this as you want."

"I feel centuries younger, like a great weight has been lifted from me," she said trying hard to not laugh as she said it. "How can I ever thank you?"

"You already did by coming to warn us and also by looking at your mental pictures for me and being honest about them," Jon explained. Alison and Mandy peeked in, they had heard the laughter and assumed that whatever Jon was doing was now done. "It's okay, come on in, we are now done. Guess what? It works on elves too." He grinned broadly.

"Wow, must of been some therapy session," Mandy exclaimed. "I've never heard Ra-ell laugh before!"

Her friend looked at her and said, "Rectify," and broke into another laugh once more. "Say, I need a bath! Been traveling for days." Mandy took her off to another room to clean up.

"Well, what have you decided?" Jon asked Alison once they were alone.

"Jon, we talked it over. I hope you do not think less of me, but I have decided to carry on with the wedding tomorrow in spite of this threat. In the end, I *refuse* to have my life controlled by a bunch of evil men and demons," she said determinedly.

"Way to go! My sentiments exactly! It's what I would have suggested had I had time to get my two-bits in," Jon said and gave her a long hug and loving kiss.

She interrupted slightly saying, "We are like two peas in the same pod! God do I love you!" A few minutes later, she explained what she and Mandy had already done, while Jon was helping Ra-ell. All of the family members had been notified, along with all of Mandy's guards. Two guards were now posted in front of every guest room. "Since we are the likely targets, Jon, tonight both the women's room and the men's room have now got a magical mansions sitting inside of them. All of us will be safe tonight. Tomorrow, we mages will cover us all with as many protective spells as possible. Glasya promised to assist us during the ceremony. I think she plans to hover above the grounds invisible and watch for and try to detect the coming attack and prevent it if she has time. In spite of appearances, we all will be armed to the teeth. Mandy says she can conceal a nice blade under her gown. The paladins will wear magical protections and hide blades as well. Once the assassin is located, he won't know what all hit him! But come on, we had better get to our rooms and get some sleep. I'm going to need it tonight. First, I am going to make sure you are safely tucked in. Hang on." She cast a brief spell that Jon had not heard her cast before and he found that they were now in the men's quarters. Sir Thomas stood guard by the doors of the mansion waiting for him. "Guard my man well," she teased him. The paladin grinned. Then she disappeared arriving in the women's guest room. Darless stood by the opened mansion doors waiting for her safe arrival.

The wedding day arrived bright and sunny. It was a perfect June morning; the rising sun took the early morning chill from the air. Inside the keep, Mandy's staff bustled with last minute preparations of flowers, while seeing to the breakfast needs of the large group. It is noted here that to avoid the possibility of being poisoned, both high priests, Basil and Glenda, checked all the food before anyone was served. They were being double careful with an assassin on the loose.

The breakfast was delicious and bountiful; Mandy spared no expense. From roast quail to nearly freshly baked breads, from tea to cocoa, all was available. The children particularly went for all the cocoa they could drink. The brides, for the most part, were a bit too nervous to consume much, but the men ate their fill.

Next, came the dressing hour as everyone changed into their new gowns and suits. Here, May had outdone herself, at least everyone kept telling her so. Each gown was white, of course, but all were made from the finest cottons and silk the seamstress could locate and exceedingly well made. None were the traditional wedding dresses that Jon had always seen in pictures and on television back home. No, in these lands, no one seriously considered the luxury of having a very expensive dress handmade to be worn on one occasion only. These could also be worn for dances and other dress up times. All were long and billowing from many petticoats worn underneath.

While all of the gowns were essentially similar, each one had trimmings suited to the wearer. Alison's, for example, had white sable fur trim around the collar, arms and along the bottom hem. (In fact, this trim cost more than the rest of the dress, but ermine and sable were Alison's desires.) Mandy's had white elk leather trim instead, but with the addition of a white leather headband. May's had black silk trim, hinting at all her long years, when she was one of Freetown's black guardian twins. Thea's trim was done in a cherry red silk suggesting her preoccupation with fire-based magical spells. Darless chose a sky blue silk trim matching the colors of priests and paladins of Ukko. Jennifer chose an earthy brown trim in bear fur for obvious reasons. While inherently similar, each dress uniquely and distinctly matched the wearer.

It is noted here, that Mandy made one last minute change in her apparel. Instead of her new matching slippers, she wore her magical boots that enabled her to jump or stride huge distances. Fastened securely to each leg was a pair of magical short swords and daggers. She added her magical bracers of defense to her wrists, but her dress's sleeves effectively hid them. Under her dress, she also wore her newly acquired magical girdle that gave her added strength, that of a stone giant. Try as she might, she could not figure out how to wear her gauntlets of ogre strength and not be totally conspicuous. If she could get to the assassin, she wanted to make sure that just one of her attacks would seriously wound or slay the assailant.

Now the men's outfits tended to match the women's in style. The pants were a heavy white cotton, but their shirts were made of white silk. Each man's jacket, though expensive, was distinctive of that man. Jon's jacket was white linen with white sable fur trim, matching well Alison's dress. William's jacket was linen dyed to a light yellow, reminding one of rising bread. Jake's jacket was trimmed like his sisters in brown bear fur. Sir Lonnie's jacket trim was sky blue silk as was Sir Thomas's jacket. On each, three holy blue crosses were sown, one on each front side and a large one on the back. There would be no mistaking these paladins at the ceremony or at a community dance. Mat's trim was similar to May's, black silk.

Sir Thomas also wore the same borrowed pair of bracers of defense Mandy had lent him when his plate armor had been so badly damaged. No one could talk him out of not wearing his huge two-handed sword strapped upon his back. Sir Lonnie then insisted on wearing his broadsword strapped to his waist. There was no talking these paladins out of doing so. Jon however was ordered by Alison to wear his cloak of displacement over his jacket. She insisted that this would make him appear elsewhere than he was, lessening the chance that a surprise attack would actually hit him. He felt strange wearing it, so May cast an illusion over the cloak making it appear invisible to most eyes. That satisfied Jon's anxiety.

Jon was so impressed with the men's matching clothing, he went to the women's dressing room to compliment May. However, he was greeted at the door by Anna, who explained in no certain terms, "Sorry. You grooms cannot enter or see your brides until the grand procession!" Jon kept insisting, so May stuck her head out the partially opened door.

"Thanks, May. I just wanted to tell you that you did a fabulous job on all our suits! They are really terrific! Very well done indeed!"

She smiled at the compliment, "I know, the women have been telling me that for the last twenty minutes too. Mind you, that is an expensive suit, so don't go getting it dirty."

"Okay, you have me. Just how much would I have to spend to buy one like this?" Jon asked, curiosity getting the better of him.

She thought a moment before answering, "About fifty gold pieces. But the women's are more like a hundred. Now beat it, I have to finish fixing my hair."

Gaping, Jon returned to the men's room. These were really expensive clothes! He resolved to not get his knees dirty. As he returned, the others were discussing strategies for attacking their unknown assailant. Most hinged on when he would strike and how the attack would be carried out. The paladins kept thinking the assassin would make a headlong rushing attack, but Mat kept trying to tell them that would not likely ever happen. Catching the tail end of the conversation, Jon had to agree with Mat. From the little he'd learned about assassins, a direct attack would not occur, unless the assassin was unbelievably stupid and suicidal. Time passed terribly slowly for the men. Jon finally had another cup of tea and several more of William's freshly baked rolls.

Finally, Basil and Glenda came to their door announcing it was time to gather for the processional. Glenda, Jon noted, wore a long green robe, richly made and undoubtedly a badge of her high position in Reylona's church. Still, she looked plump and matronly, Jon observed. Basil wore his newly purchased rich blue robes indicative of his High Priest office within the Church of Ukko. The two led the men to a large antechamber. Shortly the brides arrived and the men gaped at the sight of their magnificently dressed brides! Many compliments filled the room for several minutes.

However, Jon noticed Thea in particular. Her nails were somewhat longer than he had seen yesterday and they were painted bright red as were her lips. A bit of black lined her eyes and a bit of rouge highlighted her cheeks. She looked stunning, and Jon told her so. She grinned shyly and held onto Sir Lonnie, who was nearly speechless with the beauty of his bride. Jon recognized the touch of Glasya and turned to find her. He was very surprised at her appearance as well. She wore an elegant dull red dress and had impeccable makeup highlighting all her features. She wore many pieces of jewelry and six rings, which he assumed were most likely magical. She also wore a golden mini-crown in her hair, holding it back from falling across her face. "Doesn't Thea look grand?" she said catching Jon's glance toward herself. "We couldn't resist, Thea and I. A little magical growth in nails and a little of my red nail paint and she is positively stunning, don't you think?"

"You took the words out of my mouth!" teased Jon. "I see you have really sort of adopted her as a daughter." The archmage blushed, Jon was spot on with his observation. "But you too look terrific, Glasya."

Jon spied Ra-ell and went to check up on his patient. He was quite surprised by her appearance. Instead of the rough, tough looking elf, she had transformed her image. She wore one of her own ball gowns done in many different rich greens. She noticed him noticing her dress and said, "I made it myself. It is actually an enchanted ball gown and has lots of protection in it for me." She seemed quite cheerful this morning.

"You look quite magnificent yourself. I would never have guessed you could look this good after seeing you last night," Jon complimented her.

"Working clothes. That's the way I normally look. But a woman can look just about any way she wants, if you take my meaning," she replied.

"Say, how are you doing this morning? Any more nightmares?" Jon asked his professional question.

"I really don't know how to thank you enough, Saint Jon," she answered professionally. "I slept soundly for the first time in my life, the first time in thousands of years! No, no nightmares. I would never have believed that were possible!" Any further discussion was interrupted by Alison.

"Okay everyone, may I have your attention?" she spoke sternly and commandingly. "It is time that we mages cast our protective spells on everyone. Please gather around us." The next ten minutes were spent with the mages going from person to person casting one or more spells onto each. Jon noticed that Alison, Darless, Glasya, and Thea always used the stored magical energies contained in their staves to power the spells. He knew that this meant that each mage retained their full complement of magical spells. It was reassuring.

Jon in particular was the recipient of numerous spells. Of course, he was given the stone skin spell as were many others. Alison also cast other protective spells onto him. When she was done, he commented, "I feel like a Christmas tree I've so many spells on me."

She chuckled, "I don't want anything bad to happen to my groom. I've big plans for him tonight!" Jon flushed, as he suddenly picked up on her meaning.

Once the casting was done, Basil and Glenda had the couples line up, arm in arm with their partners, readying them for the grand march. Jon noticed Ra-ell and Glasya talking in hushed tones in the back of the group. Presently, both mages disappeared. Jon knew that both would be on guard, protecting Alison and himself from their as yet unseen assassin. It was reassuring.

Suddenly, Mandy's Royal Wind Band began playing and Jon forgot about everything else. Mandy figured that this part of the ceremony would really catch his interest and she was correct. Most were wind instruments. Jon recognized the nasally tones of the different sizes of shawms, crumhorns and something that was reminiscent of a tuba. Various drums accompanied them. The music, Jon thought, was very similar to early Renaissance processionals he'd studied in school. He was totally raptured by the tremendously exciting sounds. He never even heard Alison's whisper to pay attention to the assassin situation. And then the grand processional began.

The two High Priests, arm in arm, were the first to walk out of the door of the keep and onto the large commons. A red carpet ran from the doorway across the wide space and up to the raised platform where the ceremony was to take place. Hundreds of townsfolk stood on either side of the red carpet. Some children occasionally tossed flower pedals onto the couples as they passed by them. Basil and Glenda were followed by Mandy and William. When they stepped out onto the red carpet, the entire village shouted and cheered causing Mandy to flush. It was obvious that the people in her village adored their ranger of Reylona.

Following them came Alison and Jon, then May and Jake, then Jennifer and Mat, then Darless and Sir Thomas, and finally, Thea and Sir Lonnie brought up the rear. The cheering and the loud processional did not diminish until Thea and Sir Lonnie finally stepped up onto the platform and took their places. Anna and Thea's parents were located nearly directly in front of them so they could have a perfect view. However, Mandy's castle guards were positioned between the crowd and the platform giving them about ten feet of breathing space.

Jon looked out on all of the smiling faces, but did not see Glasya nor Ra-ell anywhere around. He assumed that they were still using invisibility spells. When the music ended and the crowd hushed, both priests said a prayer blessing. Jon found out afterwards, that both priests had woven a priestly spell that allows them to detect evil in a wide radius into that seemingly simple wedding blessing. As the proceedings went along, both priests were constantly looking about for anyone or thing that was radiating evil. The platform was three feet above the cobblestone commons. Ten feet above them, several great bows of the gnarled oak trees provided a cool green canopy over their heads.

First, Mandy and William spoke their vows, with Mandy speaking first. "I, Mandy Blackthorn, do declare my total love for William Connors."

"And I, William Connors, do profess my eternal love for Mandy Blackthorn," he inserted on cue. They had rehearsed the vows well.

"Be it known, from this day forward," she continued, "that we have decided to bond together in marriage to form a new family unit that is larger than either of us."

"We pledge our lives to each other, to honor each other, to love each other, to be faithful to each other, to help each other and to grow together and go forth as one," he added. "We promise to honor the individual goals of our mate at all times, as we begin to create new goals for our family unit."

Mandy said, "Be it known that both of us serve Reylona and will continue to help her bring love and happiness to the forest lands. None of that has changed, only now we can assist her even better. Your protective castle is still called Blackthorn Castle. I have chosen to be called Mandy Blackthorn-Connors from this day forward."

William ad-libbed here, inserting slyly, "She wouldn't let me be called William Connors-Blackthorn."

She gave him a playful poke in the ribs, and the crowd roared with laughter.

Going back to the script, he then said solemnly, "I take thee Mandy to be my wife."

She replied, "And I take thee William to be my husband."

And Glenda spoke, "So be it. May the eternal blessings of Reylona be on you both for the rest of your lives. In the eyes of your Goddess, you are now husband and wife." Right on cue, the musicians played a cheerful short song, while the townsfolk cheered and Mandy and William held hands and kissed each other lovingly. Then, the two stepped back and now it was Jon and Alison's turn in the spotlight.

However, just as they stepped forward, Basil cried out, "Look out! Above you coming down from that branch!" Many actions occurred in the next sixty seconds. First, as the couple looked up, they saw a small spider slowly lowering itself down from the tree branch. If left alone, it would land on top of Jon's head. Instinctively Jon and Alison stepped back a bit and Jon began probing for any mind that the spider might have. At that instant, Glasya suddenly became visible to everyone; she was hovering some twenty feet overhead and fifteen from the platform. She let loose a powerful dispel magic spell. At once, everyone saw the spider transform back into a man hanging upside down holding in his right hand a nasty looking crooked dagger that was dripping something oily, while his left hand held some kind of rod or stick with a strange looking feather stuck in its end. A magical rope was slowly lowering him on top of Jon.

Thea knew she could not use a fireball in such close space without burning up half the crowd. Since the purpose was to prevent Jon from being attacked, she had taken an idea from Rufus. She puffed her cheeks and blew a mighty gust of wind at the assassin swinging him on his rope far away from Jon so that any attack of his would initially completely miss, thus giving the other's spells a chance to work.

As the surprised assassin swung far out from Jon, he was hit nearly simultaneously with several things. First, a giant glove, compliments of Darless, smashed into his head like it was a punching bag, stunning him. A huge volley of magical missiles from Alison pierced his head causing him to cry out in pain. From the corner of his eye, Jon saw Mat doing a flying circle kick and saw the assassin's head violently thrown to the left from the sheer force of his martial arts attack. A sickening cracking sound was heard and the assassin involuntarily let go of the dagger and the feather, both of which fell harmlessly to the ground. Jon made contact with his attacker's mind even though the assassin's mind was being overwhelmed with shooting pain. Ra-ell appeared just behind the man, who now was falling and touched him with something in her hand. The body went totally limp. Finally, two great brown bears appeared on either side of the paralyzed falling assassin and each whacked his head but in opposite directions. So strong were the blows of Jennifer and Jake, that the paralyzed assassin's neck broke. It didn't help it any that the next second his head hit the ground squarely. This body slumped motionless, barely alive, on the ground at Jon's feet. Mandy's giant jump, blades in both hands, placed her squarely over the body. She positioned the blades in an X pattern across his neck. If the assassin so much as moved, she would sever his head in one motion. She looked up at Jon to see if he was okay.

Before anyone else could move, Ra-ell darted in front of the assassin placing herself between the party, bears, and the attacker. Carefully, she used a cloth to pick up the rod with the feather, avoiding any contact with that feather. Even more carefully, she inserted it feather first into a bag and tied the bag shut.

For an instant after Ra-ell somehow paralyzed the assassin, Jon felt the massive pain instantly leave his assailant. Now he could concentrate on the man's thoughts and intentions. As he perceived his attacker's mind and being, he saw something weird. There was a tiny, thin black energy line connected to this assassin's mind and led far off into the distance. Suddenly he recognized just what that line actually was. Someone else was monitoring this assassin! *Alison, Mandy, Darless, feed me energy — I don't care how much! Someone is connected to his mind and is watching this. I'm going to keep whomever is watching from breaking the connection.* At once, Jon felt an enormous surge of energy flowing into him, and he grabbed a hold of that black communication energy line and held it tightly.

As he connected up to the line, he suddenly saw who was at the other end watching the proceedings! Jon saw a dark skinned man with handlebar moustache and curly, oily black hair. The man was staring into some kind of crystal ball, only he could now not break the connection. Jon sensed a growing panic in the man's mind. He sent down the line into the man's mind, *Hadid, I assume. Saint Jon here. Your choice: redemption or death. Choose now.*

Jon received angry curses back from the man, who was trying everything he could to break away from his ill-fated crystal ball connection. But Jon had so much energy from the others, it was impossible for him to let go. *You did not answer my question. Redemption now or death. Choose.* Jon sent him once more. He got back a glare and a vicious white teeth attempting to somehow bite into him.

Darless, Mandy, please attack the mind that is at the other end of this black line here. I'll hold the line from disconnecting. He sensed both sending their mental energies crashing into Hadid's mind and he drew on more of Alison's flow of energy to make up for the drop from the other two. Unfortunately, Hadid's crystal ball could not handle this intense energy flow and it shattered or rather just exploded ending the mental connection abruptly. The entire time of the encounter from start to finish was sixty seconds. When the connection was severed, all four jerked violently back, as if they had suddenly lost their footing on an icy pavement. Jon sensed the assassin's body die and spied a blackish energy ball rising up into the sky.

"So much for that assassin," Jon muttered.

"Don't touch anything on or about him!" ordered Ra-ell. "It's a matter of life and death. If possible, Mandy can you have everyone move back another ten feet. I suspect a deadly trap and we don't have much time!" The whole event happened so fast that even Mandy's guards were just staring only now starting to grasp that an assassination had just been foiled. Quickly the ranger ordered her guards to move everyone back, while she motioned for those on the platform and the bears to get as far back as they could, right up against the stone walls. Ra-ell's wizard staff suddenly appeared in her hand and she used it to roll the dead man's body over. He heard Ra-ell curse and then she and the body simply vanished!

Five seconds later, everyone heard a huge explosion overhead and just outside the castle walls! As all eyes involuntarily looked up toward it, they saw Ra-ell flying wildly out of control in a direction that would smash her head into the keep walls. Just before the mage was about to collide, Glasya appeared by her, grabbed her and brought her safely back to the platform. She was still stunned by the concussion of the explosion. Basil chanted a brief prayer to Father Ukko and touched her, sending the blue holy healing energies over the gray elf's entire body. She came around momentarily.

She blinked unsure of just how she managed to be here on the ceremony platform. Glasya spoke up, "You were stunned and heading for a nasty collision with the keep, so I took the liberty of rescuing you. Basil here cured any wounds the blast may have caused."

But at this moment, the crowd had finally had enough time pass for the rapid-fire events to sink in. Many began to scream. Some were terrified, especially after the explosion. Basil and Glenda both knew what could happen next. Basil stood as tall as he could and yelled, "Everything is okay now. All the danger is past. No harm done to anyone. An assassin just tried to kill our Saint Jon. But the attempt failed utterly. Now if the musicians will please play a lively tune, we will shortly get back to the ceremonies. We still have many more vows to hear and then comes the *party*!" He really emphasized that word. The musicians began playing, albeit a bit shakily and the growing fears of the crowd slowly died down as a sense of normalcy resumed. Music soothes the savage beast, thought the priest. In the commotion, no one saw the bears turn back into Jennifer and Jake, who took their positions back on the platform.

"Zagroot zounds belatedly," exclaimed Mandy. "Will someone please tell me what all just happened?"

"When I got Basil's warning, I cancelled his magical transformation into a spider," Glasya began. "That was a brilliant tactic, Thea, to quickly blow his body out away from Jon and the others!" Thea beamed! "Then, you all hit him so hard, he must have been dead before he hit the ground!"

"Not entirely, Glasya," Jon interrupted. "I made contact with his mind. Yes, he was flooded with pain from all the attacks, but the bears broke his neck and that ended the overwhelming pain. I swear he was somehow totally paralyzed or limp before he hit the ground."

"My doing," broke in Ra-ell. "I wanted to make very sure that he would not get another chance to strike at you, Jon, so I got him from behind and paralyzed him. By the way, that was what he was trying to do to you. That feather was a magically enchanted feather — one touch on your skin and you would be completely paralyzed and a sitting duck for his poisoned dagger. I got that devilish thing safely out of the way before anyone could get accidentally hurt by it. But what happened to him after that? Sure was strange."

"I was trying make contact with his mind," Jon tried to explain, but it happened so fast that he was not totally sure of the details as he reflected back upon it. "I intended to attempt to take control of his body like I did back in Freetown so that his body would be under my control. However, I noticed this tiny black energy line connected to him, heading off to who knows where. I guess basically I just latched onto that line in place of the assassin. Suddenly I saw who was at the other end of the line! It was Hadid himself staring into some kind of crystal ball. I thought crystal balls were just a hoax, at least they are where I come from. Anyway at least I now know what our opponent actually looks like."

"Wow! Do you realize the vital significance of that?" interrupted Ra-ell. From the crazy look on Jon's face, she knew that he didn't. "Hadid is the head of a huge and powerful assassin guild. His identity is a closely guarded secret. No one knows what he looks like, so he can pass through any place of his choosing totally anonymously! If he knew that you knew what he looks like, he would have to kill you just to keep that secret!"

"Well in that case, hang on a moment; let me contact all your minds," Jon exclaimed. Without waiting for confirmation, Jon began expanding his awareness out beyond himself. He shut his eyes to block false impressions. This was the largest group of minds he had ever tried to contact at one time and it took him several minutes to get everyone. At last, he placed into all these mind the images he had seen of this master assassin. He let his mental recordings of that brief time play. From Ra-ell's view point, it was as if she were seeing a motion picture in her mind, and she was more than a little fascinated about the experience, and just how Jon could do this to her and the others.

When he finished, Jon commented, "There, now many people know what he looks like. His secret is more broadly known and he will have no way to know to whom I have shown what he looks like."

"Saint Jon, that is amazing! How do you do this? I swear to you that I will use this information wisely," added the gray elf.

"I just do," he sheepishly replied. "As soon as I spied him, I asked Mandy, Darless and Alison to flow me energy. With the effective combined force of four of us holding onto that communication line from his crystal ball, there was just no way he could break off the contact. I was angry with him for trying to kill me and mess up my wedding day, so I sent to him 'Redemption or death — choose now.' At first, I detected swelling fear in him, but then it turned into violent anger the likes of which I haven't seen in a person. I still have not learned how to combat another's mind, so I asked Darless and Mandy, who do, to step in and attack him, while Alison and I held onto the line so he could not break off. Unfortunately, the crystal ball apparently could not take these kinds of forces and it exploded as I showed you."

"Is he dead?" asked Alison. This was the one burning question she desperately wanted to know the answer.

"I can't say," Jon sighed. "It certainly exploded. I imagine glass shards and bits flew in all directions. I suspect a fair number of them hit him squarely in the face. But that's speculation. Sorry, I wish I knew too. But why did the dead assassin explode like a bomb, Ra-ell? And did you know he would explode?"

"My trade," she said quietly. "A contract on as important a person as yourself and for the reputed vast sum of money, any would be assassin would be prepared with many contingency plans. When I got close to him, I heard a slight hissing sound. Rolling him over added the slight smell of burning sulfur. I got his body out of the area as fast as I could, but I was not quite fast enough as it seems. Thanks, Glasya. If you had not intervened, I may have had a very nasty bump and fall."

"Well, you know," put in Basil, "for the first time in quite a while, I do feel particularly useful. My spell and I spotted him, which triggered the whole response."

"Now don't let that go to your head, Basil!" Anna interrupted him sternly. "You know I don't want you going off on any more adventures. I've had more than enough adventures for one lifetime!"

He looked at Alison pleadingly. She only grinned back at him. Sheepishly he answered her, "Yes, dear. I know — think of the grandchildren," but he was still thinking of high adventure.

Glenda brought them all back to the present, "Okay now that that's finished, can we get on with the wedding ceremony? I'm getting hungry." With immense feelings of relief, everyone took their original positions. Basil stood before Jon and Alison, both of which took a deep breath. They suddenly found themselves exceedingly nervous; they were definitely in the spotlight when the musicians finally ended and the silence came once more. The crowd was listening to their every word.

Basil began the ceremony, "Friends we are gathered here today to bear witness to this couple's vows, which create their marriage, their union together as one family unit." He nodded, indicating they should begin.

Alison took a deep breath, wondering why tradition always had the woman speaking first. As she was about to say her first line, Jon, sensing her fears, actually began. "I'm not much for traditions, when I don't understand their purpose. So I will begin by saying that I, Jon Brown, a musician, declare my full and complete love for Alison d'Ambrose, more so than I have ever loved anyone."

Jon had ad-libbed just a bit, so Alison felt free to deviate as well, saying what she felt at this moment. "And I, Alison d'Ambrose, state before all of you that I deeply love Jon Brown and am totally committed to him. In fact, I once gave my life to save his, only Father Ukko undid my sacrifice saying that now was not my time. From this day onward know that we have decided to bond together in marriage, form a new family unit which we both feel is larger and stronger than either of us alone." There, she had somehow gotten them back onto the script.

Jon picked it up, "We both pledge and dedicate our lives to one another, to honor, love and cherish each other, to be faithful to each other at all times, and to help each other to grow spiritually. Further, since we are both different beings, we also promise to honor the individual goals of our partner at all times, even while we begin to create new goals for our family unit. Thus, we go forth from today as a pair united as one."

Alison relaxed a bit; Jon was now following their script. She continued, "Be it known that I serve Father Ukko as his personally proclaimed Holy Mage; this does not change because I marry. Jon, who is not from these lands, does not follow or serve one of our Gods or Goddesses. Instead, he serves all mankind and all spiritual beings, both great and small. In my presence, Father Ukko gave him the title of Saint Jon Brown, the Redeemer. Though we marry, he will still continue to serve all beings in their times of need."

She took a breath and went on, "What about names? We both are already widely known by our current names. Thus, I will follow Mandy's suggestion to avoid confusion. From this day forward, I shall be known as Alison d'Ambrose-Brown."

Jon added an extra line, "However, Archmage Alison threatened to turn me into a toad, if I changed my name to Jon Brown-d'Ambrose or Jon d'Ambrose-Brown." She nudged him in the seat of his pants, but the crowd roared with laughter. "So I guess I am stuck still being called Jon Brown," he added grinning good-naturedly.

He turned to face her, took both her hands in his, and said solemnly, "I take thee Alison to be my wife."

Her eyes glowing radiantly, she replied, "And I take thee Jon to be my husband." She thought that this day would never come! She longed to hold, hug and embrace him.

But once more Jon quickly inserted extra lines, "Alison, I solemnly pledge to never let you go to sleep at night, while we are upset with each other or upset with something else. I promise to tell you fully and completely and in a timely manner about any transgression I should ever do against you or your extended family or against us as a family and to never withhold such information from you." Immediately, many hushed, awed whispers came from those gathered to witness their vows. This, they had never heard before. As Alison grasped the meaning and intention behind them, she too was awed. He added, "Finally, I promise to help create our marriage, our union, every day as long as I live, for a marriage is really something that we create."

"Jon, if you do that, indeed our marriage will last forever! Nothing can break it," she replied. "Yes, I too pledge to never let you sleep on an upset, to never withhold my transgressions from you. And yes, I will help create our marriage each and every day!" Here, whether Jon had intended to say more or not, she could not tell for the townsfolk began cheering and clapping loudly. Many present suddenly realized just how important these actions were, for who among them had not already withheld something from their partner only to have that pull them further apart, not closer together. Now some whistles were added to the general din.

Basil could not help seeing his mental images of heading off to the Abyss to retrieve the Holy Scepter of

Ukko over his wife's strong protests. That action had actually lessened their closeness, their love; he saw that vividly now; before he had ignored it. Raising his hands, Basil spoke, "I do believe that we all have just had a brush with Redemption from Saint Jon, even while he is supposed to be getting married." Many cat calls agreed with him. "As a High Priest of Father Ukko, I bear witness to your vows. May the eternal blessings of Ukko be on you both for the rest of your lives. In the eyes of Father Ukko, you are now husband and wife." The poor musicians had lost track of their cue, so Basil signaled them to play. Soon the cheery sounds of a dance livened the festive mood. Alison and Jon embraced each other and fondly kissed, sealing their union before all. At last, they stepped back and now it was time for May and Jake to share their vows.

The vows of May and Jake, followed by Jennifer and Mat, were essentially similar to those of Mandy and William. All four were very private people. Being a spectacle before an entire village made all four more than a little nervous. They said only what they were expected to say and nothing more. However, each quietly paraphrased Jon's added pledge to Alison for all four could see just how important that could be in a marriage.

Similarly, the paladins, Darless and Thea kept theirs short as well. For the paladins, the ceremony was part of their duty, to set an example and show the way. However, their code also bound them to a simple ceremony just as that same code would only allow them to keep a small portion of any funds they earned, donating the rest to help finance other Churches of Ukko. Darless, an alu-demon, certainly did not want to go around publicizing her body's race. Yet for her, this moment in time was that for which she had been longing all of her adult life. While she treasured every moment of the brief ceremony, she was only too glad for it to be done. However, Sir Thomas did indeed add a short unexpected statement, "I want you all here to know that Darless has taught me an incredibly valuable lesson: judge a person by who they are and what they do, not by their body or it's color or shape." He turned to her and said, "Thank you for helping me discover this truth." And then they embraced.

Of these four, only Thea was excited to be center stage, for she was now sixteen, of age in these lands and full of youthful enthusiasm for life. In truth, she had never been this dressed up ever and never had long red nails or even the small bit of makeup that Glasya had donated. She felt powerful and confident of herself. That other men would perhaps stare a bit at her as she passed by, such as the guards and some of the men from Mandy's village, did not go unnoticed by her. She was very observant. After all, she was now a full-fledged mage and Alison had taught her to be keenly observant. The effect that her appearance had on Sir Lonnie only made her prouder. She swore that he was about to burst from pride in her. Similarly, her parents could not have been happier nor have bigger smiles on their faces. Still, she honored the short, simple vows of Sir Lonnie, it was her first compromise in her new marriage. Sir Lonnie had already made his by agreeing to her request to look so dressed up this special day.

Once Thea and Sir Lonnie had sealed their vows with an embrace, Basil announced loudly, "Unless someone else wants to be married — ah, I see none. Then, let the party begin!" This was the word that most all of the villagers had been waiting to hear. The musicians stuck up a lively dance tune. Mandy's staff bought out more food and wine and the celebration party began in earnest. The first action was the formal wedding dance. The couples stepped down off of the platform and joined the villagers, many of whom had already begun to dance.

Jon noticed that both paladins were excellent dancers. He found out that was because of their training in courtly presence. It was the two sets of twins that stumbled their way through the expected first dance; none of them were particularly practiced in dance movements. Jon and Alison, though better than the awkward twins, found themselves in a distant league from the two paladins and their wives. Only Mandy and William came close to their grace and elegance because they had been practicing for days.

After the traditional first dance, all the couples switched partners, gaily talking about how terrific everything had gone and such. Once this phase was done, they found all sort of others asking for a dance. Jon was asked by Glasya and Ra-ell nearly simultaneously. Laughing, he danced with Ra-ell first, claiming she had beat Glasya's request by one second. "I want to personally thank you for helping to save me from that assassin, Ra-ell. And also, you look really terrific!"

She blushed, "It was the very least I could do after the tremendous gift you gave me last night! I do not often get to dress up fancy like this. My life has been a rather rough one as you partly suspect. But I made this one myself and it is actually magically enchanted, but I won't tell you it's properties for safety's sake."

"Well, congratulations on making such a fine dress. You have more skills than meet the eye. Oh yes, if you want some more of the therapy or to learn how you can do it too, come by Darless' new college this fall. She's getting ready to teach the technique to anyone who wants to learn. We've got our work cut out for us. Have you heard about those poor folks that got turned into half giant scorpions?" She hadn't and Jon spent the rest of the dance telling her about that ghastly transformation.

He'd only finished when Glasya wanted her turn with Jon. As they began moving as one to the stately music, she whispered, "At last. I've been dying to get this close to you and to dance with you. You are fairly good at it I see. I'm a bit rusty."

Jon just gave her a kiss on her cheek. "You are welcome," he whispered back. He thought she blushed.

"You have no idea how much I have missed such a simple thing as this! Say, I do hope we can hold many dances with our new band in the Ville," she said.

"You bet, I'm all for it. I think people need this kind of socializing on a regular basis. Do you suppose that it would be too much to hold a dance every weekend?" he mused.

"That's more than fine by me!" she answered. Glancing at Thea, she added, "And I think Thea would really love that." Glasya turned Jon slightly so he could see the teenager. Both smiled.

When the tune ended, Ellen, Christina's eldest daughter who was turning eleven, came bashfully up to Jon. She wore a newly made dress and had ribbons in her hair. This was obviously the biggest dance she had ever attended. Bashfully, she asked, "May I have this dance, Uncle Jon?"

"Absolutely! My, you look very pretty this afternoon. Is that a new dress?" he graciously replied, taking her hand and leading the way as the band began their next song.

"Yes, Aunt May made it especially for me! I'm so glad that you all got rid of that nasty man who interrupted the wedding. Mom said he was an assassin who was trying to kill you! Why would someone want to kill? I don't understand why someone would want to hurt someone." Jon was on the spot and he knew it. He thought carefully before answering her.

"Ellen, you like to be right, right?" She nodded. "Okay, how do you feel when you have done something very wrong?" She grimaced but did not reply. "Now the next thing that happens after you do something you shouldn't have, say to a friend, is you say that somehow the friend deserved it, he's bad. We make excuses as to why it was right for us to have done that bad thing. We all want to be right. Well, some people do so many bad things that they lose all respect for themselves. When that happens, they lose control. To be right, they just keep on doing the bad things, claiming it is out of their control and that they had nothing to do with it. That bad man that came here today was one of those. He had done so many bad things that he could not trust himself anymore and so he was kind of like a wind up doll running on automatic, doing one bad thing after another because he believed he could not stop himself from doing bad things."

"Well, mommy says we should always try to do good things," she stated.

"And your mommy is right. You try to do good things. But if you do a bad thing, then you should always tell your mommy all about it and not try to hide it from her," Jon suggested.

"That's what you were saying to Aunt Alison, right?" she asked finally grasping the intent behind what Jon had sworn to Alison during their vows.

"You are absolutely right, Ellen!" She beamed, relaxed and enjoyed the rest of the dance.

Of course, Christina asked for the next dance. "Thanks for dancing with Ellen, she was dying to act so grownup. I think she has a crush on you. I saw you talking. I hope she didn't bother you."

"On the contrary, she wanted to know why someone would want to try to kill another. So I explained it to her. You have a very bright young child there. I think she really understands about always telling you about anything she does that she shouldn't have done."

"You're kidding?" she asked. "She asked you that? What on earth did you tell her?" So Jon quickly recounted his explanation. Christina calmed down, gave him a kiss, and said, "What an Uncle you are! Are you sure you are not a priest or a god?"

"I'm a musician," he teased her back. And so the afternoon went by. Even several women from Mandy's village asked to dance with Jon and the others. Occasionally, Jon was even able to get another dance with Alison, who similarly had been asked to dance by many, including her dad.

Finally, as the sun set rosy red through the dense forest, the villagers, having eaten their fill, began to leave. By about seven, only the guests, couples and Mandy's castle staff remained. The staff looked exhausted, but pleased with how well it had all gone. Mandy gave them the rest of the night off, except for a few guards. The happy couples and their family and friends finally sat down, relaxed and ate what was left of the feast, chatting amongst themselves. Mandy received compliment after compliment, and thanks after thanks. Their special day would be long remembered and treasured by all. The attempted assassination was now a distant memory. At last, the couples retired for the night, each to consummate their marriage, something all had wanted to do for a long time.

When the couples finally came down for breakfast the next day, Jon thought that all of the newly wed women were radiant, while the men had a satisfied look about them. He wondered about the difference in viewpoints. However, just as soon as they all ate, it was back to business. After saying farewell and thank you for the umpteenth time, the mages began the teleportation process, taking everyone home. As before, each had to make two round trips.

When he got home, Jon found a message from Rufus waiting for him. The parchment read, "My humblest apologies for missing your wedding. However, I am assisting Jasmine who really needs my help. I will come by for a visit later on." Jon showed it to Alison who teased, "Jon, I wonder if those two will fall for each other? They seem a good match." He smiled back at her.

The new couples began to build their lives together as the Ville neared completion. It was going to be a truly free town with free citizens. Their marriages began most positively. Gazing at the bustling activity of the town from his temporary front porch, Jon had the nagging thought, *Would there be six new babies come spring? Am I going to be a father?*
The End.

Other Books by Vic Broquard

The Trident Series: (fantasy)
Volume 1 The Trident and the Book
Volume 2 The Trident and the Scepter
Volume 3 The Trident and the Resurrection

Without Warning (fantasy)

The Adventures of Elizabeth Stanton Series: (science fiction)
Volume 1 The Evolution of the Path
Volume 2 The Great Messiah
Volume 3 Of Kings and Queens and Troubadours
Volume 4 Chaos in the Aftermath
Volume 5 Power Plays
Volume 6 Age of Exploration
Volume 7 Abducted
Volume 8 The Emperor and Empress
Volume 9 A Job Worth Doing
Volume 10 Degradation
Volume 11 The Second Crusade
Volume 12 When Worlds Collide
Volume 13 Dark Ages

The Lindsey Barron Series: (fantasy)
Volume 1 The Rod of the Apocalypse
Volume 2 The Board of Governors
Volume 3 The Crown of Moses
Volume 4 Dominus for President
Volume 5 The National Health Care Program
Volume 6 States Justice
Volume 7 Cross and Double-cross

Zoran Chronicles Series: (fantasy)
Volume 1 A Dragon in Our Town
Volume 2 Dragons, Power, Courts, and War

Planet of the Orange-red Sun Series: (science fiction)
Volume 1 When Kingdoms Fall
Volume 2 Dark Ages
Volume 3 Age of the Towers
Volume 4 Difficillis Exitus
Volume 5 Age of the Lords
Volume 6 The Renegade Tower
Volume 7 Rebellions
Volume 8 The Aliens Return
Volume 9 Power Struggles
Volume 10 Guilds, Genetics, and Gods
Volume 11 Magi, Witches, Swords, and Superstitions
Volume 12 The Voyage of the Eagle's Seed
Volume 13 Justifications
Volume 14 Responsibilities

The Return of the Wizards: Twelve Companions – The Making of Wizards (fantasy)